READER'S DIGEST
CONDENSED BOOKS

www.readersdigest.co.uk

The Reader's Digest Association
Limited 11 Westferry Circus
Canary Wharf London E14 4HE

For information as to ownership of
copyright in the material of this
book, and acknowledgments, see
last page.

Printed in France
ISBN 0 276 42738 6

READER'S DIGEST
CONDENSED BOOKS

*Selected and edited
by Reader's Digest*

CONDENSED BOOKS DIVISION

THE READER'S DIGEST ASSOCIATION LIMITED, LONDON

CONTENTS

CHASING THE DIME   page 9

Michael Connelly

Henry Pierce, a rising star in the exciting
world of nano-technology, is just settling
into his new apartment when he starts to
get dozens of calls and messages for the
previous tenant. In trying to trace her, to
ask her to change her number, he finds
himself being irrevocably drawn into a
murky, violent world where nothing is quite
what it seems. An irresistible thriller from
an award-winning author.

PUBLISHED BY ORION

UNDER AN
ENGLISH HEAVEN   page 149

Robert Radcliffe

Suffolk, 1943. The skies above the village
of Bedenham are heavy with bombers from
a nearby US air base. While not everyone
welcomes the Americans, their presence
opens up new horizons for evacuee Billy
Street and teacher Heather Garrett, as their
lives become intertwined with those of the
crew of *Misbehavin' Martha*. A vivid evo-
cation of the courage, loyalty and passion
of ordinary people during World War II.

PUBLISHED BY LITTLE, BROWN

CUT THROAT
page 289

Lyndon Stacey

Ross Wakelin, a talented American show-jumper, has come to England hoping for a fresh start after an accident that wrecked his career. But, as soon as he arrives at Oakley Manor stables, the trouble starts. Attacks on horses, petty theft, and an atmosphere of suspicion and hostility abound. Who is out to destroy wealthy horse owner Franklin Richmond—and why? An exhilarating mystery in the tradition of Dick Francis.

PUBLISHED BY HUTCHINSON

DADDY'S LITTLE GIRL
page 423

Mary Higgins Clark

Ellie Cavanaugh was only seven years old when she gave testimony that led to the conviction of the killer of her fifteen-year-old sister, Andrea. Now, after twenty-two years in prison, and still protesting his innocence, Rob Westerfield is out on parole. When Ellie decides to prove his guilt once and for all, she is horrified to find that her own life is in great peril. An utterly compelling portrayal of a young woman's search for justice.

PUBLISHED BY SIMON & SCHUSTER

Michael Connelly

chasing
the dime

Henry Pierce, thirty-four,
is newly single, living in
a new apartment, and
on the verge of a
technological break-
through that could
make his fortune.

But then the calls
begin. Calls for
someone called Lilly.
Messages left day
and night.

Tracing the mysterious
'Lilly' is easy. But as
Henry probes the
dangerous world in
which she once worked,
he finds himself
plunged into
a nightmare.

One

The voice on the phone was a whisper. It had a forceful, almost desperate quality to it.

Henry Pierce told the caller he had the wrong number. But the voice became insistent.

'Where is she?' the man asked.

'I don't know,' Pierce said. 'I don't know anything about her.'

'This is her number. It's on the site.'

'No, you have the wrong number. There is no one named Lilly here. And I don't know anything about any site. OK?'

The caller hung up. Then Pierce hung up, annoyed. He'd plugged in the new phone only fifteen minutes earlier and had already got two calls for someone named Lilly. This was going to be a problem.

He looked around the almost empty apartment. All he had was the couch he sat on, six boxes of clothes and the new phone.

Nicole had kept everything—the furniture, the books, the CDs, and most of all the house on Amalfi Drive. Actually he had given it all to her. The price of his guilt for letting things slip away. The new apartment was high-luxury and high-security, a premier address in Santa Monica called The Sands. But he was going to miss the house on Amalfi. And the woman still living in it.

He reached over to his backpack and pulled out the notepad on which his personal assistant had written down the voicemail instructions. Monica Purl had set up the phone service for him, as he had been too busy in the lab all week preparing for the following week's presentation. Monica had already sent the new number out to his email A list. There were almost eighty people on this list—people he would want to be able to reach him at any time, almost all of them business associates.

Pierce pressed the talk button and called the number for accessing his voicemail program, then followed the instructions. He decided not to record a personal greeting. He would rather hide behind the electronic voice that announced the number and instructed the caller to leave a message.

When he finished setting up the program a new electronic voice told him he had nine messages. Pierce was surprised by the number—his phone had not been put into service until that morning—but only one of the messages was for him: a welcome to the system delivered by the now familiar electronic voice.

The next eight messages were all for Lilly, no last name mentioned. The woman he had already fielded two calls for. All the messages were from men. Most gave hotel names and numbers for calling back. A few gave cellphone numbers or what they said was a private office line. A few mentioned getting her number from the web site.

Pierce erased each message. He then turned the page on his notebook and wrote down the name Lilly. Lilly—whoever she was—had apparently stopped using the number. It had been dropped back into circulation by the phone company and reassigned to him. Judging by the all-male caller list, the number of calls from hotels and the tone of trepidation and anticipation in the voices he had listened to, Pierce guessed that Lilly was a prostitute. He felt a thrill of curiosity and intrigue. Like he knew some secret he wasn't supposed to.

He flipped the page back and looked at the information Monica had written for him. She had included the phone company's customer service number. He should call to get the number changed. But he knew it would be an annoying inconvenience to have to resend email notifications correcting the number.

Something else made him hesitate about changing the number. He was intrigued. Who was Lilly? Where was she? Why did she give up the telephone number but leave it on the web site? There was a flaw in the logic flow there and maybe that was what gripped him. How did she maintain her business if the web site delivered the wrong number to the client base? The answer was she couldn't. Something was wrong and Pierce wanted to know what and why.

It was Friday evening. He decided to let things stand until

Monday. He would make the call about changing the number then.

Pierce got up and walked to the bedroom, where a sleeping-bag was unrolled along one wall. He hadn't used the sleeping-bag in almost three years—since a trip to Yosemite with Nicole. Back when he had time to do things, before the chase began, before his life became about only one thing.

He went out onto the balcony and stared out at the Pacific. He was twelve floors up. The sun was gone and this high up the sea breeze was bracing. He put his hands in his pockets. The fingers of his left hand closed around a coin and he brought it out. A dime. Another reminder of what his life had become.

He flipped the dime into the air and watched it disappear into the darkness. There was a park below, a strip of green between the building and the beach. He had noticed that homeless people sneaked in at night and slept under the trees. Maybe one of them would find the fallen dime.

The phone rang. He went back into the living room and saw the tiny LED caller ID screen glowing in the darkness. He read the display. The call was coming from the Century Plaza Hotel.

He answered without saying hello. 'Are you calling for Lilly?'

The caller hung up. Pierce clicked the phone off. He was returning it to its cradle when it rang again. He hit the talk button without looking at the caller ID display.

'You've got the wrong number,' he said.

'Wait, Einstein, is that you?'

Pierce recognised the voice of Cody Zeller, an A-list recipient of his new number. Zeller often called him Einstein, one of the college nicknames Pierce still endured. Zeller was a friend first and a business associate second. He was a computer security consultant who had designed numerous systems for Pierce over the years as his company grew and moved from larger space to larger space.

'Sorry, Code,' Pierce said. 'I thought you were somebody else. This new number is getting a lot of calls for somebody else.'

'New number, new place, does this mean you're single again?'

'I guess so.'

'Man, what happened with Nicki?'

'I don't know. I don't want to talk about it.'

'I'll tell you what happened,' Zeller said. 'Too much time in the lab and not enough between the sheets. I warned you about that, man.'

Zeller laughed. He'd always had a way of looking at a situation or set of facts and cutting away the bullshit. And his laughter told Pierce he was not overly sympathetic to his plight.

Zeller was unmarried and Pierce could never remember him in a long-term relationship. As far back as college he promised Pierce and their friends he would never practise monogamy in his lifetime. Zeller also knew the woman in question. In his capacity as a security expert he also handled online backgrounding of employment applicants and investors for Pierce. In that role he worked closely at times with Nicole James, the company's intelligence officer. Make that former intelligence officer now.

'Yeah, I know,' Pierce said, though he didn't want to talk about this with Zeller. 'I should've listened.'

'Well, maybe this means you'll be able to take your spoon out of retirement and meet me out at Zuma one of these mornings.'

Zeller lived in Malibu and surfed every morning. It had been nearly ten years since Pierce had been a regular on the waves with him. In fact, he had not even taken his board with him when he moved out of the house on Amalfi. It was still in the garage.

'I don't know, Code. I've still got the project, you know. I don't think my time is going to change much just because she—'

'That's right, she was only your fiancée, not the project.'

'I don't mean it like that. I just don't think I'm—'

'What about tonight? I'll come down. We'll hit the town like the old days.' Zeller laughed in encouragement.

Pierce didn't. There had never been old days like that. Pierce had never been a player. He'd always preferred to spend the night in the lab than pursuing sex with an engine fuelled by alcohol.

'I think I'm going to pass, man. I've got a lot of stuff to do and I need to go back to the lab tonight.'

'Hank, man, you've got to give the molecules a rest. One night out. Come on, it'll shake up your own molecules for once.'

Zeller was the only one on the planet who called him Hank, a name Pierce hated. But Pierce was smart enough to know that telling Zeller to stop was out of the question because that would prompt his friend to use the name at all times.

'Call me next time, all right?'

Zeller reluctantly backed off and Pierce promised to keep the next weekend open for a night out. They hung up and Pierce put the phone in its cradle. He picked up his backpack and headed for the apartment door.

PIERCE USED his scramble card to enter the garage attached to Amedeo Technologies and parked his BMW 540 in his assigned space. The entrance to the building opened as he approached, the approval coming from the night man at the dais behind the double glass doors.

'Thanks, Rudolpho,' Pierce said as he went by. He took the elevator to the third floor, where the administrative offices were located. In the hallway he worked the combination lock on his office door and went in. 'Lights,' he said as he went behind his desk.

The lights came on. He turned his computer on and plugged in the phone line so he could check his emails before going to work. It was 8.00pm. He liked working at night, having the lab to himself.

For security reasons he never left the computer on or attached to a phone line when he wasn't working on it. For the same reason he carried no cellphone or pager. Pierce was paranoid by nature but also a cautious and practical researcher. He knew that every time he plugged an outside line into his computer or opened a cellular transmission it was as dangerous as sticking a needle into his arm. You never knew what you might be bringing into the pipeline.

He had several messages but only three that he decided to read this night. The first was from Nicole. It was short, to the point and so professional it was devoid of any reference to their ill-fated romance. Just a former employee's last sign-off before moving on to bigger and better things.

> Hewlett,
> I'm out of here.
> Everything's in the files. (By the way, the Bronson deal finally hit the media—SJMN got it first.)
> Thanks for everything and good luck.
> Nic

Pierce noted that the message had been sent at 4.55pm, just a few hours earlier. There was no point in replying because Nicole's email address would have been wiped from the system at 5.00pm when she turned in her scramble card.

She had called him Hewlett. In the past she had used the name as an endearment. A secret name only a lover would use. It was based on his initials—HP, as in Hewlett-Packard, the huge computer manufacturer that was a Goliath to Pierce's David. Only she could get away with nicknaming him with a competitor's name. But her using

MICHAEL CONNELLY

it in this final message, what did it mean? Was she changing her mind about them? Was there still a chance, a hope of redemption?

Pierce had never been able to judge the motives of Nicole James. He couldn't now. He saved the message, moving it to a file where he kept all her emails going back the entire three years of their relationship. The history of their time together—moving from coworkers to lovers—could be read in the messages.

He scrolled through the email list in the Nicole James file, reading the captions in the subject lines the way a man might look through photos of an old girlfriend. He smiled at a few of them. Nicole was always the master of the witty or sarcastic subject line. One line caught his eye during the scroll—Where do you live?—and he opened the message. It had been sent four months before and was as good a clue as any as to what would become of them.

I was just wondering where you live because I haven't seen you at Amalfi in four nights.
This is not working, Henry. We need to talk but you're never home. Do I have to come to that lab to talk about us?
That would certainly be sad.

He remembered going home to talk to her after that one and it resulting in a genuine effort on his part. He came home every night by eight for a week before he started to slip and his lab shifts began lasting into the small hours again.

Pierce went back to the current email list and the next message he read was from his partner, Charlie Condon. It was just a reminder about the presentation scheduled for the next week, as if Pierce needed to be reminded. The subject line read RE: Proteus.

It's all set with God. He's coming in Wednesday for a ten o'clock Thursday. The harpoon is sharpened and ready. Be there or be square.
CC

Pierce didn't bother replying. It was a given that he would be there. A lot was riding on it. No, everything was riding on it. The God referred to in the message was Maurice Goddard. He was a New Yorker, an emerging technologies investor Charlie was hoping would be their whale. He was coming in to look at the Proteus project before making his final decision. They were giving him a first look at Proteus, hoping it would be the closer on the deal. The following

14

Monday they would file for patent protection on Proteus and begin seeking other investors if Goddard didn't come on board.

The last message he read was from Clyde Vernon, head of Amedeo security.

Trying to reach you. We need to talk about Nicole James. Please call me ASAP.
Clyde Vernon

Pierce knew that Vernon wanted to know how much Nicole knew and the circumstances of her abrupt departure. Vernon wanted to know what action he would need to take.

Pierce turned off the computer, left the office and went down the hallway to Nicole's office. Her former office.

Pierce had the override combination for all doors. He used it now to open the door to the office. 'Lights,' he said.

But the overhead lights did not respond. The office's audio receptor was still registered to Nicole's voice. That would be changed on Monday. Pierce went to the wall switch and turned on the lights.

He then went to the row of filing cabinets against the wall, opened a drawer and took out a blue file labelled Bronson. He opened the file and glanced through a photocopy of a news clipping from the *San Jose Mercury News*.

Santa Cruz-based Bronson Technologies has agreed to a partnership with Japan's Tagawa Corporation that will provide funding for the firm's molecular electronics project.

Tagawa will provide $12 million in research funds over the next four years and will hold a 20 per cent interest in Bronson.

Elliot Bronson, president of the six-year-old company, said the money will help put his company into the lead in the race to develop the first molecular computer. Bronson and a host of private companies, universities and government agencies are engaged in a race to develop molecular-based random access memory. 'From diagnostic computers that can be dropped into the bloodstream to "smart streets" with microscopic computers in the asphalt, molecular computers will change this world,' Bronson said.

Among Bronson's chief competitors in the private arena are Amedeo Technologies of Los Angeles and Midas Molecular in Raleigh, NC. Several significant advances in the development of molecular computing have occurred in the last five years, with Amedeo seemingly leading the way.

Amedeo is the oldest company in the race. Henry Pierce, 34, the chemist who founded the company a year after leaving Stanford, has registered numerous patents in the areas of molecular circuitry and the creation of molecular memory.

The move to a significant source of financial support—a 'whale' in the parlance of the emerging technologies investment arena—is becoming favoured by the smaller companies. Bronson's move follows Midas Molecular, which secured $10 million in funding from a Canadian investor earlier this year.

'You need the money to be competitive,' Bronson said. 'The basic tools of this science are expensive. To outfit a lab costs more than a million before you even get to the research.'

'Everybody is out hunting whales,' said Daniel F. Daly, a partner in investment firm Daly & Mills. 'Money from the hundred-thousand-dollar investor gets eaten up too quickly, so everybody's into one-stop shopping—finding the one investor who will see a project all the way through.'

THE ELEVATOR OPENED on the basement level and Pierce stepped out. He used his scramble card to enter the first door of the mantrap and then, once inside the small passageway, punched in the October combination on the second door. He opened it and entered the lab.

The lab was actually a suite of several smaller labs clustered round the main room, or day lab as they called it. The suite was windowless. Its inner walls were lined with insulation containing copper shavings that knocked down electronic noise from the outside.

On the right side of the day room was the wire lab, or the furnace room as some called it, and beyond it was the imaging lab, which housed the electron microscope. All the way to the rear of the day lab was the laser lab.

The lab suite appeared empty, the computers off and the probe stations unmanned, but Pierce picked up the familiar smell of cooking carbon. He checked the sign-in log and saw that Grooms had signed in but not out. He walked over to the wire lab and looked through the little glass door. He didn't see anyone. He opened the door and stepped in, immediately being hit with the heat and the smell. The vacuum oven was operating, a new batch of carbon wires was being made. Pierce assumed that Grooms had started the batch and then left the lab to take a break.

Pierce left the wire lab and closed the door. He walked over to the computer next to the probe station and put in his passwords.

Behind him there was a banging sound. Turning round and expecting to see Grooms returning, he saw Clyde Vernon come through the mantrap instead. Vernon was a wide and burly man with just a fringe of hair round the outer edges of his head. He had a ruddy complexion that gave him a look of consternation. In his mid fifties, Vernon was the oldest person working at the company. After him, Charlie Condon was probably the oldest at forty.

This time the look of consternation Vernon carried was real.

'Hey, Clyde,' Pierce said. 'Let me guess, you put out a be-on-the-lookout-for on me and Rudolpho called it in when I came through. And that made you come all the way in from home.'

Vernon ignored Pierce's fine deductive work. 'We need to talk,' he said. 'Did you get my message?'

They were in the early stages of getting to know each other. Vernon might be the oldest person working at Amedeo, but he was also the newest. Pierce had already noticed that Vernon had difficulty calling him by name. Maybe it was an age thing. Pierce was the president of the company but at least twenty years younger than Vernon, who had come to the company a few months earlier after putting in twenty-five years with the FBI.

'I got your email about fifteen minutes ago,' Pierce said. 'I was probably going to call you when I finished here. You want to talk about Nicole?'

'Yes. What happened?'

Pierce shrugged. 'She quit her job and she, uh, quit me. I guess you could say she quit me first.'

'When did this happen?'

'Hard to tell, Clyde. It was happening for a while. But it all sort of hit the fan last week. She agreed to stay until today.'

'Why wasn't I told about this?' Vernon protested.

'Look, I know you should have been told but because there were some personal issues involved . . . I didn't really want to talk about it. And to tell you the truth, I probably wasn't going to call you tonight because I still don't want to.'

'Well, we need to talk about it. She was the intelligence officer of this company. She shouldn't have been allowed to just waltz through the door at the end of the day.'

'All the files are still there. I checked, even though I didn't need to. Nicki would never do anything like you're suggesting.'

'I'm not suggesting any impropriety. I'm just trying to be thorough and cautious. That's all. Did she take another job that you know of?'

'Not as of the last time we spoke. But she signed a no-compete contract when we hired her. We don't have to worry, Clyde.'

'What were the financial arrangements of the separation?'

'Why is that your business?'

'Because a person in need of finances is vulnerable. It's my business to know if an employee with intimate knowledge of the project is vulnerable.'

'Her knowledge of the project was limited. She gathered intelligence on competitors, not on us. She wasn't in a position to know exactly what we're doing or where we are in any of the projects. And I'll answer your next question before you ask it. No, I never told her on a personal level the details of what we were doing. It never came up. In fact, I don't even think she cared. She treated the job like a job and that probably was the main problem with us. I didn't treat it as a job. I treated it like it was my life. Now, anything else, Clyde? I want to get some work done.' He hoped that camouflaging the lie in verbiage and indignation would get it by Vernon.

'Did she receive a severance?' Vernon asked.

'Six months' pay. She's also selling the house and keeping all proceeds. I hardly think she's vulnerable.'

'I am sorry if you don't like the questions,' Vernon said. 'But it's my job to maintain the security of this firm. There are many people and companies whose investments must be safeguarded.'

He was alluding to the reason he was there. Charlie Condon had hired him as a showpiece, to placate potential investors who needed to know that the company's projects—and therefore their investments—were safe and secure. Vernon's pedigree was impressive and more important to the company than the actual security work he performed.

'I understand your concerns, Clyde. But I'm going to get back to work now. After all, all those investors are counting on us, right?'

'Right,' Vernon said. 'Then I'll let you get back to it.'

But after the security man had retreated through the mantrap, Pierce realised he could not get back to it. For the first time in three years he was unencumbered by interests outside the lab and free to do the work. But for the first time in three years he didn't want to.

He shut down the computer and got up. He followed Vernon's wake through the mantrap.

TWO

When he got back to his office Pierce turned the lights on by hand. The voice-recognition switch had been installed simply to impress the potential investors that Charlie Condon walked through the place every few weeks. It was a gimmick. Just like Vernon.

Pierce sat down at his desk, took the notepad out of his backpack and called the number for accessing his home voicemail by remote location. He was told he had one new message. He played it and heard the nervous voice of a man he didn't know.

'Uh, yes, hello, my name is Frank Behmer. And this is for Lilly. I got this number from the web site and I wanted to see if you're available tonight. I'm at the Peninsula so give me a call when you can. Uh, I'm in room four-ten.'

Pierce erased the message but once more felt the weird magic of secretly being inside somebody's hidden world. He thought for a few moments and then called information to get the number for the Peninsula. Behmer hadn't included the call-back number.

He called the hotel and asked for Behmer in room 410.

The call was picked up after five rings. 'Hello?'

'Mr Behmer?'

'Yes?'

'Hi. Did you call for Lilly?'

Behmer hesitated before answering. 'Who is this?'

Pierce was anticipating the question. 'My name is Hank. I handle Lilly's calls. She's kind of busy at the moment but I'm trying to reach her for you. To set it up for you.'

'Yes, I tried the pager number but she didn't call back.'

'The pager number?'

'The one on the site.'

'Oh, I see. You know, she is listed on several sites. Do you mind me asking which one you got her numbers from? We're trying to figure out which one is more effective, if you know what I mean.'

'I saw it on the LA Darlings site.'

'Oh, LA Darlings. Right. Well, I'll get her to call you as soon as I get hold of her. But if you don't hear from Lilly within an hour, then it's not going to happen.'

'Really?' Disappointment tumbled off his voice.

'She's very busy, Mr Behmer. But I'll try my best. Goodbye.'

Pierce hung up. He didn't know what he was doing or why but something was pulling him down a pathway. He rebooted his computer and jacked in the phone line. He then went online and tried a variation of web configurations until he hit on www.la-darlings.com and was connected to a site.

The first page was text. It was a warning/waiver form explaining that there was explicit adult fare on the web site. By clicking the enter button the visitor was acknowledging that he or she was over eighteen and not offended by nudity or adult content. Pierce clicked the enter button and the screen changed to the site's home page. Along the left border was a photo of a naked woman holding a raised finger in front of her lips. The site titling was in a large purple font:

LA DARLINGS
A free directory of adult entertainment and services

Beneath this was a row of red tabs labelled with the available services, ranging from escorts categorised by race and hair colour to masseuses and fetish experts of all genders and sexual orientations. Pierce knew there were countless sites like these all over the Internet, though he had never taken the time to explore one.

He clicked on the blonde escorts tab for no reason other than it being a place to start. The page opened in two halves. On the left side of the page was a scrolling panel of thumbnail photos of the blonde escorts with their first names appearing under each picture. When he clicked on one of the thumbnails the escort's page would open on the right—the photo enlarged for better viewing.

Pierce scrolled down the panel, looking at the names. There were nearly forty different escorts but none was named Lilly. He closed it and went to the brunettes section. Halfway through the thumbnails he came to an escort named Lilly. He clicked her page open and checked the number. It was a match. He had found the Lilly whose phone number he now had.

The photo on the ad was of a woman in her mid twenties. She had dark shoulder-length hair and brown eyes, a deep tan. She was kneeling on a bed with brass railings and was naked beneath a black fishnet negligee. Her eyes looked directly into the camera. Her full lips formed what Pierce thought was meant to be an inviting pout.

If the photo had not been altered, and if it really was Lilly then she was beautiful. Pierce understood why his phone had been ringing constantly since he had plugged it in.

His eyes moved to the ad copy below the photo:

Hello Gentlemen. My name is Lilly, I'm 23 yoa, 34-25-34 (all natural), 5-foot-1 and 105lbs.

I'm part Spanish and part Italian and All American! So if you're looking for the time of your life, then give me a call and come visit me at my town house near the beach. I never rush and satisfaction is guaranteed! And if you want to double your pleasure, visit my girlfriend Robin's page in the blonde escorts section. We work together as a team. So call me!

Below the ad was the phone number now assigned to Pierce's apartment as well as a number for a voice pager.

Pierce picked up the phone and called the pager number. There were three beeps and then her voice came on.

'Hi, it's Lilly. Leave your name and number and I'll call you right back. If you're in a hotel, remember to leave your full name or they won't put my call through. Thanks. I hope to see you soon. Bye.'

Pierce had made the call before he was sure what he wanted to say. The beep sounded and he started talking. 'Uh, yes, Lilly my name is Henry. I have a problem because I have your old phone number. What I mean is the phone company gave it to me—it's in my apartment and I'd like to talk to you about it.'

He hung up, went back to the keyboard and returned to the home page. He opened the blonde escorts panel again and scrolled down until he found a thumbnail photo with the name Robin beneath it.

He opened the page. The woman named Robin was blonde as advertised. She lay naked on her back on a bed. Red rose petals were piled on her stomach and strategically used to partially cover her breasts and crotch. He scanned down to the ad copy:

Hello Gentlemen. My name is Robin. I'm a true blonde and blue-eyed All American girl. I'm 24 yoa, 38-30-36 and almost six feet tall. I can come to you or you can come to me. It doesn't matter because I never rush you. And if you want to double your pleasure, visit my girlfriend Lilly's page in the brunettes section. We work as a team. So give me a call!

There was a phone number and a pager number at the bottom of the ad. Pierce wrote them down on his notepad, then moved back up to the photo. Robin was attractive but not in the aching sort of way that Lilly was. Robin had sharp lines to her mouth and eyes and a colder look. She was more in line with what Pierce had always thought he would find on one of these sites. Lilly wasn't.

Pierce noticed as he looked at the photo that the same brass bed was in both photos. He pulled down his Internet directory and quickly switched back to Lilly's web page to confirm. The bed was the same. He didn't know what this meant other than perhaps another confirmation that the two women worked together.

He looked at his watch. It was almost eleven. Abruptly he leaned forward and picked up the phone. Checking his notes, he called the number from Robin's page. He lost his nerve and was about to hang up after four rings when a woman answered in a sleepy, smoky voice.

'Uh, Robin?'

'Yes.'

'I'm sorry, did I wake you?'

'No, I'm awake. Who's this?'

'Um, my name's Hank. I, uh, saw your page on LA Darlings. Am I calling too late?'

'No, you're fine. What's Amedeo Techno?'

He realised she had caller ID. A shock of fear went through him. Fear of scandal, of people like Vernon knowing something secret about him.

'Actually, it's Amedeo Technologies. Your read-out must not show the whole name.'

'Is that where you work?'

'Yes.'

'Are you Mr Amedeo?'

Pierce smiled. 'No, there is no Mr Amedeo. Not any more.'

'What happened to him?'

'Amedeo was Amedeo Avogadro. He was a chemist who about two hundred years ago was the first to tell the difference between molecules and atoms. But he wasn't taken seriously until after he was dead. He was a man ahead of his time. The company was named after him.'

'What do you do there? Play around with atoms and molecules?'

'Sort of. We're building a computer out of molecules.'

'Really? Cool.' He heard her yawn.

'Anyway, the reason I'm calling is that I see that you work with Lilly. The brunette escort?'

'I did. Not any more.'

'What happened? I've been trying to call her and—'

'I'm not talking about Lilly with you. I don't even know you.'

Her voice had changed. It had taken on a sharper edge. Pierce knew he could lose her if he didn't play it right.

'OK, sorry. I was just asking because I liked her.'

'You'd been with her?'

'Yeah. A couple times. She seemed like a nice girl and I was wondering where she went. That's all. She suggested the last time that maybe all three of us could get together next time. Do you think you could get a message to her?'

'No. She's long gone and whatever happened to her . . . just happened. That's all.'

'What do you mean? What exactly happened?'

'You know, Mister, you're really creeping me out asking all these questions and the thing is I don't have to talk to you. So why don't you just spend the night with your own molecules.' She hung up.

Pierce hung up too and looked at the photo of Lilly still on his computer screen. He thought about Robin's cryptic comment.

'What happened to you?'

He moved the screen back to the home page and clicked on a tab marked ADVERTISE WITH US. It led to a page with instructions for placing ads on the site. It could be done through the Net. But the site's brick and mortar location was on Sunset Boulevard in Hollywood. The page listed its hours as Monday to Saturday, nine to five during the week and ten to three on Saturdays.

Pierce wrote the address down on his notepad. He was about to disconnect from the site when he decided to call up Lilly's page once again. He printed out a colour copy of her photo, then shut down the computer. A voice from inside told him he had gone as far with this as he could go. As he should go. It was time to change his phone number and forget it.

But another voice—a louder voice from the past—told him something else.

THE STAIRWAY WAS DARK and the boy was scared. He looked back to the street and saw the waiting car. His stepfather saw the hesitation and put his hand out of the car window. He waved the boy forward. The boy turned back to the darkness and switched on the flashlight.

He kept the light on the steps, not wanting to announce he was coming up by lighting the room at the top. Halfway there one of the stairs creaked under his foot. He froze. He could hear his heartbeat banging in his chest. He thought about Isabelle and the fear she probably carried in her own chest every day and night after night. He drew his resolve from this and started up again.

Three steps from the top he cut the light off and waited for his eyes to adjust. In a few moments he thought he could see a dim light from the room up ahead of him. It was candlelight. He took the last three steps.

The room was large and crowded. He could see makeshift beds lined against the two long walls. Still figures, like heaps of rummage-sale clothes, slept on each. At the end of the room a single candle burned and a girl, a few years older than he, heated a bottle cap over the flame. The boy could see it wasn't Isabelle.

He started moving down the centre of the room, between the sleeping-bags and the newspaper pallets. From side to side he looked, searching for the familiar face. He got to the end, by the girl with the bottle cap. And Isabelle wasn't there.

'Who are you looking for?' asked the girl. She was drawing back the plunger on the hypodermic, sucking the brown liquid through a cigarette butt filter from the bottle cap.

'Just somebody,' he said.

She looked up. 'You're a young one,' she said. 'You better get out of here before the houseman comes back.'

The boy knew what she meant. All the squats in Hollywood had somebody in charge. The houseman. He exacted a fee in money or drugs or flesh.

'He finds you, he'll bust your cherry ass and put you out on—'

She suddenly stopped and blew the candle out. He turned back to the door and all his fears seized up in him like a fist crushing a flower. A silhouette stood at the top of the steps. A big man. Wild hair. The houseman. The boy took a step back and tripped over someone's leg. He fell, the flashlight clattering on the floor next to him and going out.

The man in the doorway moved and started coming at him.

'Hanky boy!' the man yelled. 'Come here, Hank!'

PIERCE WOKE AT DAWN, the sun rescuing him from the dream of running from a man whose face he could not see. He had no curtains in the apartment yet and the light streamed through the windows. He crawled out of the sleeping-bag and went into the shower. When he had finished he had to dry off with two T-shirts he'd dug out of one of the clothing boxes. He'd forgotten to buy towels.

He walked over to Main Street to get coffee, a citrus smoothie and the Saturday newspaper. He read and drank slowly, almost feeling guilty about it. Most Saturdays he was in the lab by dawn.

When he was finished with the paper it was almost nine. He walked back to The Sands and got into his car, but he didn't go to the lab.

Pierce got to the Hollywood address he had written down for LA Darlings fifteen minutes before ten o'clock. The location was a multi-level office complex. LA Darlings was located in Suite 310. On the glass door the largest lettering read Entrepreneurial Concepts Unlimited. Beneath this was a listing in smaller letters of ten different web sites, including LA Darlings, that apparently fell under the Entrepreneurial Concepts umbrella. Pierce could tell by the site addresses that they were all sexually oriented.

Pierce turned as a woman approached the door with a key. She was about twenty five and had crazy blonde hair that seemed to point in all directions. She wore cut-off jeans and sandals and a short shirt that exposed her pierced navel.

'You're early,' she said.

'I know,' Pierce said. 'I came from the Westside and I thought there'd be more traffic.'

He followed her in. There was a waiting area with a reception counter that guarded an entrance to a rear hallway. To the right and unguarded was a closed door with the word PRIVATE on it. Pierce watched as the woman walked behind the counter.

'You'll have to wait a couple minutes until I get set up. I'm the only one here today.'

'Who's watching the machines if you're the only one here?'

'Oh, well, there's always somebody back there. I just meant I'm by myself up front today.' She slid into a chair behind the counter.

The silver ring protruding from her stomach caught Pierce's eye and reminded him of Nicole. She had worked at Amedeo for two years before he happened upon her in a coffee shop on Main Street on a Sunday afternoon. She had just come from a workout and was dressed in grey sweatpants and a sports bra exposing a gold ring piercing her navel. It was like discovering a secret about someone of long-time acquaintance. She had always been a beautiful woman in his eyes but everything changed after that. Nicole became erotic to him and he went after her, wanting to know all her secrets.

Pierce wandered round the confines of the waiting room while the woman behind the counter did whatever it was she had to do to get set up. He heard a computer booting and some drawers opening and closing. He glanced back at the woman and saw she was preoccupied with something on her computer screen. He tried the door marked PRIVATE. It was unlocked and he opened it. It led to a hallway with three sets of double doors.

'Um, excuse me,' the woman said. 'You can't go in there.'

Signs hanging on thin chains from the ceiling in front of the doors marked them as Studio A, Studio B and Studio C.

Pierce closed the door. He turned and went back to the counter. He saw that she was now wearing a pin with her name on it.

'I thought it was the rest rooms. What is that back there?'

'Those are the photo studios. We don't have public facilities here. What can I do for you?'

'I've got a problem, Wendy. One of the advertisers with a page on LA Darlings dot com has my phone number. Calls that should be going to her are going to me instead.' He told his story of getting a new phone number only to learn it was the same line on the web page ad for the woman named Lilly.

'Why don't you just get another number?'

'Because I've already had change-of-address cards with the number on it printed and mailed out. It would be very expensive to do that again with a new number.'

'All right, let me see something.' Wendy turned to the computer and went to the LA Darlings site and into the brunette escorts list. She clicked on the picture of Lilly and then scrolled down to the phone number. 'You're saying this is your number, not hers, but it used to be hers.'

'Exactly.'

'If she changed her number why didn't she change it with us, too?'

'I don't know. Can you see if there is another contact number and then call her and tell her about this problem?'

'What about this pager number?'

'I tried it. It takes voicemail. I've left three messages for her but she hasn't called. I don't think she's getting the pages.'

Wendy pushed her chair back and stood up. 'I'm going to check something. I'll be right back.' She went round the partition behind the counter and disappeared into the back hallway, the slapping sound of her sandals receding as she went. When she came back she was holding a thin file. 'Well, I figured out one part of the problem,' she said, sitting down. 'This girl stopped paying her bill.'

'When was that?'

'In June she paid up to August. Then she didn't pay for September.'

'Then why's her page still on the site?'

'Because sometimes it takes a while to clean out the deadbeats. Especially when they look like this chick. I wouldn't be surprised if Mr Wentz wanted to keep her on there even though she didn't pay. A guy sees girls like that on the site and they'll keep coming back.'

Pierce nodded. 'Is Mr Wentz here today? I'd like to speak to him.'

'No, it's Saturday. You'd be lucky to even catch him here during the week, but I've never seen him on a Saturday.'

'What can be done about this? My phone's ringing off the wall.'

'Well, I can take notes and maybe on Monday somebody could—'

'Look, Wendy, I don't want to wait until Monday, I have a problem now. If Mr Wentz isn't here, then get the guy baby-sitting the servers to take her page down.'

'I don't think he's authorised to do anything. Besides, he was sort of asleep when I looked in there.'

Pierce leaned over the counter and put a forceful tone into his voice. 'Wendy, listen to me. I insist that you wake him up. You have to understand something here. You are in a legally precarious position. I have informed you that your web site has my phone number on it. Because of this error I am receiving phone calls of what I consider to be an offensive and embarrassing nature. So much so that I was here at your place of business this morning before you even opened. I want this fixed. If you put it off until Monday then I am going to sue you, this company and Mr Wentz. Do you understand?'

'You can't sue me. I just work here.'

'Wendy, you can sue anybody you want to in this world.'

She stood up, an angry look in her eyes, and pirouetted round the partition without a word. Pierce didn't care if she was angry. What he cared about was that she had left the file on the counter. As soon as the sound of her sandals was gone he bent over and flipped open the file. There was a photo of Lilly along with her ad copy and an advertiser's information form.

Her name was Lilly Quinlan. Her contact numbers were the same phone and pager she had put on her web page. On the address line she had put a Santa Monica address and apartment number. Pierce quickly read it and then put everything back in the file, just as he heard the sandals and another pair of shoes approaching from the other side of the partition.

PIERCE STARTED THE CAR and headed back towards Santa Monica. The address of Lilly's apartment was on Wilshire Boulevard. When he finally pulled up in front of the building with the matching address on the door, he saw it was a private mail drop, a business called All American Mail. The apartment number 333 Lilly Quinlan had written on the info sheet was actually a box number.

Pierce parked at the kerb, got out and walked into the building. Behind the counter a young man with a swath of pimples on each cheek and a name tag that said Curt asked how he could help him.

'I need a mailbox,' Pierce said, 'but I want a specific number. It goes with the name of my business—Three Cubed Productions.'

The kid seemed confused. 'So what number do you want?'

'Three, three, three. Is it available?'

Curt reached under the counter and came back up with a blue binder, which he opened to pages listing boxes by numbers and availability. His finger drew down a column of numbers and stopped. 'Well, it's occupied at the moment but it might not be for long.'

'What's that mean?'

'It means there's a person in that box, but she didn't pay this month's rent. So she's in the grace period. If she shows up and pays, she keeps the box. If she doesn't show up by the end of the month then she's out and you're in.'

Pierce put a concerned look on his face. 'That's kind of long. I wanted to get this set up. Do you know if there's a number or an address for this person? You know, to contact her and ask if she still wants the box.'

'I've sent out two late notices and put one in the box.'

Pierce became excited but didn't show it. What Curt had said meant that there was another address for Lilly Quinlan.

'Is there a number? If you could call this woman right now and find out I'd rent the box right now. And pay for a year up front.'

'Well, I'll have to look it up. It will take me a minute.'

'Take your time. I'd rather get it done now than have to come back.'

Curt went to a desk that was against the wall behind the counter and took out a thick file. He ran his finger down one page and then held it on a spot. With his other hand he picked up the phone on the desk and punched in a number. Pierce tried to watch his finger and get the number but it was too fast. Curt waited a long time before speaking into the phone.

'This is a message for Lilly Quinlan. Could you please call us at All American Mail. Rent on your box is overdue and we'll be re-renting it if we do not hear from you. My name is Curt. Thank you.' He hung up, then came towards Pierce at the counter and shook his head. 'I got her machine. There's nothing I can do until I either hear from her or the end of the month comes.'

'I understand. Thanks for trying.'

'Want to leave a number where I can reach you if I hear from her?'

'I'll just check with you tomorrow.' Pierce took a business card off a plastic rack on the counter and headed for the door.

Curt called after him. 'What about twenty-seven? I've got that box open. Isn't that what three cubed is?'

Pierce nodded. Curt was smarter than he looked. 'I'll think about it,' he said, and turned back to the door.

In the car he checked his watch. It was almost noon. He had to get back to his apartment to meet Monica Purl, his assistant. She had agreed to wait at his apartment for the furniture he had ordered. The delivery window was noon until four and Pierce had decided that he'd rather pay someone to wait while he used the time in the lab preparing the next week's presentation for Goddard. Now he doubted he was going to go to the lab but he would still use Monica to wait for the delivery. He now had another plan for her as well.

When he got to The Sands he found her in the lobby. The security officer on the door would not let her go up to the twelfth floor without the approval of the resident she was going to visit.

'Sorry about that,' Pierce said. 'Were you waiting long?'

Monica was carrying a stack of magazines for reading while she waited for the delivery. 'Just a few minutes,' she said.

Monica Purl was a tall, thin blonde with skin so pale that just touching it might leave a mark. She was about twenty-five and had been with the company since she was twenty. She had been Pierce's personal assistant for only six months.

They took the elevator to the twelfth floor and walked down the hall to his apartment.

'Where am I going to tell them to put everything?' Monica asked.

'Just tell them to put stuff where you think it will look good. I also need you to do me a favour before I leave.' He opened the door.

'What kind of favour?' Monica asked suspiciously.

'Just a phone call.' He went into the living room and picked up the phone, then pulled the business card out of his pocket. 'I want you to call this number and say you are Lilly Quinlan. Ask for Curt and tell him you got his message. Tell him his call was the first you'd heard about your payment being overdue and ask him why they didn't send you a notice in the mail.'

'Why—what is this for?'

'I can't explain it all to you but it's important.'

'I don't know if I want to impersonate somebody. It's not—'

'What you are doing is totally harmless. Curt is going to tell you he did send a notice. Then you say, "Oh, really? What address did you send it to?" When he gives you the address write it down. That's what I need. The address. As soon as you get it you can hang up.'

'Dr Pierce, this doesn't seem—'

'Don't call me Dr Pierce. You never call me Dr Pierce.'

'Then Henry. I don't want to do this. Not without knowing what I'm doing.'

'All right then, I'll tell you. You know the new phone number you got me? Well, it belonged previously to a woman who has disappeared or something has happened to her. I'm getting her calls and I'm trying to figure out what happened. And this call I want you to make might get me an address where she lived. I want to go there and see if she's OK. Nothing else. Now will you make the call?'

She shook her head. 'This is crazy. How did you get caught up in this? Do you know this woman? How do you know she disappeared?'

'No, I don't know her. It was purely random. Because I got the wrong number. But now I know I have to find out what happened or make sure she's OK. Will you please do this for me, Monica?'

'Why don't you just change your number?'

'I will. First thing Monday I want you to change it.'

'And meantime, just call the police.'

'I don't have enough information yet to call the police. What would I tell them? They'll think I'm a nut.'

'And they might be right.'

'Look, will you do this or not?'

She nodded in resignation. 'If it will make you happy and it will keep me my job.'

'Whoa. Wait a minute. I'm not threatening you about your job. If you don't want to do it, fine, I'll get somebody else. It's got nothing to do with your job. Are we clear on that?'

'Yes, clear. But don't worry, I'll do it. Let's just get it over with.'

He dialled the number of All American Mail and handed the phone to Monica. She asked for Curt and then pulled off the call as planned with only a few moments of bad acting and confusion. Pierce watched as she wrote an address down on the notepad. When she hung up she handed him the pad and the phone.

Pierce checked the address—it was in Venice—then tore the page off the pad, folded it and put it in his pocket.

The phone rang and he answered it. But the caller hung up. Pierce looked at the caller ID directory. The call had come from the Ritz Carlton in the marina.

'Look,' he said, 'you need to leave the phone plugged in so when the furniture comes security can call up here for approval to let them up. But meantime you're probably going to get a lot of calls for Lilly. So you might want to say something right off like, "This isn't Lilly, you've got the wrong number." Otherwise—'

'Maybe I should pretend I'm her so I can get more information for you.'

'No, you don't want to do that.' He opened his backpack and pulled out the print-out of the photo from Lilly's web page. 'That's Lilly.'

'Oh my God!' Monica exclaimed. 'Is she a prostitute or something?'

'I think so.'

'Then what are you doing trying to find this prostitute when you should be—?' She stopped abruptly.

Pierce looked at her and waited for her to finish. She didn't.

'What?' he said. 'I should be what?'

'Nothing. It's not my business.'

'Did you talk with Nicki about her and me?'

'No. I just think it's strange that you're running around trying to find out if this prostitute is all right. It's weird.'

Pierce knew she was lying about Nicole. He also knew that she was right about what he was doing. But his life and career had been built around following his curiosity. In his last year at Stanford he sat in on a lecture about the next generation of microchips. The professor spoke of nanochips so small that the supercomputers of the day would be built to the size of a dime. Pierce was hooked and had been pursuing his curiosity—chasing the dime—ever since.

'I'm going to go over to Venice,' he told Monica. 'I'm just going to check things out and leave it at that.' He slung his backpack over his shoulder. 'If you talk to Nicki, don't mention this, OK?'

'Sure, Henry. I won't.'

Pierce knew he couldn't count on that but it would have to do. He headed to the apartment's door and left.

THREE

There was something wrong about the address, but Pierce couldn't place it. He worried over it as he drove into Venice.

The address Lilly Quinlan had given to All American Mail was a small white bungalow on Altair Avenue. There was a fat royal palm squatting in the front yard. Pierce parked across the street and studied the house for signs of recent life. The yard and ornamentation were neatly trimmed. But if it was a rental that could have been taken care of by a landlord. There was no car in the driveway and no newspapers piling up near the kerb. Nothing seemed outwardly amiss.

Pierce got out of the BMW, crossed the street and followed the path to the front door. He rang the doorbell and waited. Nothing.

He pushed the bell again, then knocked on the door. He waited. And nothing.

He looked around. The venetian blinds behind the front windows were closed. He turned and walked over to the driveway, which went down the left side of the house to a garage in the rear yard.

The garage door was open. It was made of wood that had been bowed by time and its own weight. It looked like it was permanently fixed in the open position. It showed the garage empty except for a collection of paint cans lined against the rear wall.

To the right of the garage was a postage-stamp yard with a tall hedge round it. Two lounge chairs sat in the grass. Pierce went to the rear door and knocked again. The door had a window cut into its upper half. He cupped his hands against the glass and looked in.

It was the kitchen. It appeared neat and clean. There was nothing on the small table pushed against the wall to the left. A newspaper was neatly folded on one of the two chairs.

On the counter next to the toaster was a large bowl filled with dark shapes that Pierce realised were rotten pieces of fruit.

Now he had something. Something that showed something wasn't right. As he turned to look around the yard for something to break the window with, he instinctively grabbed the knob and twisted it.

The door was unlocked.

Pierce wheeled back round. The knob still in his hand, he pushed the door open six inches. He waited for an alarm to sound but his intrusion was greeted only with silence and the sickly sweet stench of the rotten fruit. He pushed the door open wider, leaned in and yelled. 'Lilly? It's me, Henry.'

He didn't know if he was doing it for the neighbours or himself but he yelled her name two more times, expecting and getting no results. Then he turned round and sat down on the stoop, considering whether to go in. He thought about Monica's reaction earlier to what he was doing and what she had said: just call the cops.

Now was the moment to do that. Something was wrong here and he certainly had something to call about. But he wasn't ready to give this away. Whatever it was, it was his still and he wanted to pursue it. His motivations, he knew, were not only about Lilly Quinlan. They reached further and were entwined in the past. He knew he was trying to do now what he hadn't been able to do back then.

Pierce got up from the back step and opened the door fully. He stepped into the kitchen and closed the door behind him.

He opened the refrigerator and saw a carton of orange juice and a plastic bottle of low-fat milk. The milk had an August 18 use-by date. The juice's was August 16. It had been much more than a month since the contents of each had expired.

Pierce went to the table and slid back the chair. On it was the *Los Angeles Times* from August 1.

Pierce moved into the hallway running from the kitchen to the front of the house, where he could see the pile of mail building below the slot in the front door. He explored the rooms on either side of the hallway. In the bathroom, he found every horizontal surface crowded with perfumes and beauty aids. In the master bedroom, both closets were open and jammed with clothing on wooden hangers. The third room appeared to be used as a workout location. There was a step machine and a rowing machine. Pierce opened the only closet and found more clothes. But these were different. Almost two feet of hanger space was devoted to small things—negligees and leotards. He saw something familiar and reached in for the hanger. It was the black fishnet negligee she had posed in for the web-site photo.

This reminded him of something. He put the hanger in its place and went back into the bedroom. It was the wrong bed. Not the brass railings of the photo. In that moment he realised what was wrong, what had bothered him about the Venice address. Her ad copy. Lilly had said she met clients at a town house on the Westside. This was no town house and that was the wrong bed. There was another address connected to Lilly Quinlan that he still had to find.

Pierce stepped back into the hallway and made his way to the front of the house. There was a living room on the left and a dining room on the right. The living room was filled with Craftsman style furniture that was in keeping with the house. What wasn't was the double rack of high-end electronics below the plasma television hanging on the wall. Lilly Quinlan had a home-entertainment station that had probably cost her twenty-five grand.

Pierce stepped over to the front door and started looking through the mail. Most of it was junk. There were two envelopes from All American Mail—the late notices. There were credit card bills and bank statements. There was a large envelope from the University of Southern California. He looked for bills from the phone company and found none. He thought this was odd but assumed her phone bills might have been sent to the box at All American Mail. As he stood up, he put one of the bank statements and a Visa bill into the back pocket of his jeans without a second thought—the first being that he was compounding the crime of breaking and entering with a federal mail theft rap.

In the dining room he found a roll-top desk against the wall. He pulled a chair over, opened the desk and sat down. He quickly went through the drawers and determined that this was her bill-paying station. There were chequebooks, stamps and pens in the centre drawer. The drawers going down either side of the desk were filled with envelopes from credit card companies, utilities and other bills. Again, noticeably missing was a stack of old phone bills.

Pierce went back to the centre drawer and went through the registers of the chequebooks. There had been no activity in either account since the end of July. Going back through one of the books he found record of payment to the telephone company in June. So she did pay the phone bill with the account he held in his hand and very likely at the desk where he sat. But he could find no other record of the billing in the drawers.

He gave up on the contradiction and closed the drawer. He

reached to the handle to pull the roll top down when he saw a small book pushed far into one of the storage slots at the top of the desk. He reached in for it and found it to be a small address book. He used his thumb to buzz through the pages and saw it was filled with hand-written entries. He shoved the book into his back pocket with the mail he had decided to take.

He rolled the top down, stood up and took a last survey of the two front rooms. Almost immediately he saw a shadow move behind the closed blinds of the living-room window. Someone was going to the front door.

A blade of panic sliced through Pierce. He didn't know whether to hide or run down the hallway and out of the back door. Instead, he couldn't do anything. He stood there unable to move his feet as he heard a footstep on the tiled stoop outside the front door.

A metallic clack made him jump. Then a small stack of mail was pushed through the slot in the door and fell to the floor on top of the other mail. Pierce closed his eyes.

'Jesus!' he whispered as he let out his breath and tried to relax.

The shadow crossed the living-room blinds again going the other way. And then it was gone.

Pierce stepped over and looked at the latest influx of mail. A few more bills but mostly junk. He used his foot to push the envelopes around to make sure and then saw a small envelope addressed by hand. He picked it up. In the upper left corner of the envelope it said '*V. Quinlan*' but there was no return address. The postmark was par-tially smeared and he could only make out the letters 'pa, Fla'.

Something about opening this obviously personal piece of mail seemed more intrusive and criminal to him than anything else he had done so far. But his hesitation didn't last long. He used a fingernail to prise open the envelope and pulled out a small piece of folded paper. It was a letter dated four days earlier:

Lilly,

I am worried sick about you. If you get this please just call me to let me know you are OK. Please, honey? Since you stopped calling I have been very worried about you and that job of yours. Things around here were never really the best and I know I didn't do everything right. But I don't think that you shouldn't tell me if you are all right.

Please call me if and when you get this.

Love, Mom

Pierce refolded the page and returned it to the envelope. He closed the envelope as best as he could and buried it in the pile of mail on the floor. Then he turned and headed back down the hallway to the kitchen, went through the back door and closed it.

As nonchalant as an amateur criminal can be, he walked round the corner and down the driveway towards the street.

'LIGHTS.'

Pierce swung round behind his desk and sat down. From his backpack he pulled out the things he had taken from Lilly Quinlan's house. He had a Visa bill, a bank statement and the address book.

He started leafing through the address book first. There were several entries for men by first name or first name with only a following initial. The phone numbers ran the gamut of area codes. Many were local but still more were from outside Los Angeles. There were also several listings for hotels and restaurants. He saw an entry for Robin and another for ECU, which he knew was Entrepreneurial Concepts Unlimited.

He found a listing for Vivian Quinlan with a phone number and address in Tampa, Florida. Near the end of the book he found an entry for someone listed as Wainwright, which included a phone number and an address in Venice that Pierce knew was not far from the home on Altair.

He used his desk phone to call the number for Vivian Quinlan.

A woman answered the phone in two rings. Her voice sounded like a broom sweeping a sidewalk. 'Hello?'

'Mrs Quinlan?'

'Yes?'

'Hi, I'm calling from Los Angeles. My name's Henry Pierce and—'

'Is this about Lilly?' Her voice had a desperate tone to it.

'Yes. I'm trying to locate her and I was wondering if you can help.'

'Oh, thank God! Are you police?'

'Uh, no ma'am, I'm not.'

'I don't care. Someone finally cares.'

'Well, I'm just trying to find her, Mrs Quinlan. Have you heard from her lately?'

'Not in more than seven weeks and that just isn't like her. She always checked in. I'm very worried.'

'Have you contacted the police?'

'Yes, I called and talked to the missing persons people. They weren't interested because she's an adult and because of what she does for a living.'

'What does she do for a living, Mrs Quinlan?'

There was a hesitation. 'I thought you said you knew her.'

'I'm just an acquaintance.'

'She works as a gentleman's escort.'

'I see.'

'No sex or anything. She told me she goes to dinner with men in tuxedos mostly.'

Pierce let that go as a mother's denial of the obvious. It was something he had seen before in his own family. 'What did the police say?'

'Just that she probably went off with one of these fellows and that I'd probably hear from her soon.'

'When was that?'

'A month ago. You see, Lilly calls me every Saturday. When two weeks went by with no phone calls I called the police. They didn't call me back. After the third week I called again and talked to missing persons. They didn't even take a report or anything, just told me to keep waiting. They don't care.'

A vision bled into his mind and distracted him. It was the night he had come home from Stanford. His mother was waiting for him in the kitchen, the lights off. Just waiting there in the dark to tell him the news about his sister Isabelle.

When Lilly Quinlan's mother spoke it was his own mother.

'I called in a private detective but he can't find her neither.'

The content of what she was saying finally brought him out of it. 'Mrs Quinlan, is Lilly's father there? Can I talk to him?'

'No, he's long gone. He hasn't been here in about twelve years— ever since the day I caught him with her.'

'Where did you hire a private detective, in Tampa or here in LA?'

'Out there. The policeman in missing persons sent me a list. I picked from there.'

'Did you come out here to look for her, Mrs Quinlan?'

'I'm not in good health. I've got emphysema and I've got my oxygen that I'm hooked up to. There wasn't much I could do comin' out there.'

'Lilly told me she was sending you money.' It was a guess. It seemed to go with the whole mother–daughter relationship.

'Yes, and if you find her tell her I'm getting real short about now. I'm real low. I had to give a lot of what I had to Mr Glass.'

'Who is Mr Glass?'

'He's the private detective I hired. But I don't hear from him any more. Now that I can't pay him any more.'

'Can you give me a number for him?'

'I have to look it up.' She put down the phone and it was two minutes before she came back and gave him the number for the private investigator.

'Mrs Quinlan, are there any other contacts you have for Lilly out here? Any friends or anything like that?'

'No, she never gave me any numbers or told me about any friends. Except she once mentioned this girl Robin who she worked with sometimes. They had stuff in common, she told me.'

'Did she say what?'

'I think they both had the same kind of trouble with men in their family when they were young. That's what I expect she meant.'

'OK, Mrs Quinlan, I'm going to keep trying to find her and I'll tell her to call you when I do.'

'I'd appreciate that and make sure you tell her about the money, that I'm getting real low.'

'Right. I will.' He hung up and thought for a few moments about what he knew. Probably too much about Lilly. It made him feel depressed and sad. He hoped one of her clients had taken her away with a promise of riches and luxury. But he doubted it. 'Guys in tuxedoes,' he said out loud.

'What?'

He looked up. Charlie Condon was standing in the door. Pierce had left it open.

'Oh, nothing. Just talking to myself. What are you doing here?' He realised that Lilly Quinlan's address book and mail were spread in front of him. He nonchalantly picked up the daily planner he kept on the desk, looked at it as if he was checking a date and then put it down on top of the envelopes with her name on them.

'I called your new number and got Monica. She said you were supposed to be here while she waited for furniture to be delivered. But nobody answered in the lab or in your office so I came by.'

He leaned against the door frame. Charlie was a handsome man with what seemed like a perpetual tan. He had worked as a model in New York for a few years before going back to school for a masters in finance. They had been introduced by an investment banker who knew that Condon was skilled at taking underfinanced emerging technology firms and matching them with investors. Pierce had joined with him because he'd promised to do it with Amedeo Technologies without Pierce having to sacrifice his controlling interest to investors. In return, Charlie would hold ten per cent of the company.

'I missed your calls,' Pierce said.

Charlie nodded. 'I thought you'd be in the lab.'

Meaning, why aren't you in the lab? There is work to be done. We're in a race. We've got a presentation to a whale to make.

'Yeah, don't worry. I'll get there. I just have some mail to go through. You came all the way in to check on me?'

'Not really. But we only have until Thursday to get our shit together for Goddard. I wanted to make sure everything was all right.'

'Don't worry, we'll be ready. Is Jacob coming in for it?'

'He'll be here.'

Jacob Kaz was the company's patent attorney. They had fifty-eight patents already registered or applied for and Kaz was going to file nine more the Monday after the presentation to Goddard.

'Did you look at the patents yet?' Condon asked.

Pierce had to check off on the patent drafts before they were filed.

'I'm planning to get to them today or come back in tomorrow.'

'Great. So, everything else OK? You doin' all right?'

'You mean with Nicki and everything?'

Charlie nodded.

'Yeah, I'm cool. I'm trying to keep my mind on other things.'

'Like the lab, I hope.'

Pierce leaned back in his chair, spread his hands and smiled. He wondered how much Monica had told him when he had called the apartment. 'I'm here.'

'Well, good.'

'By the way, Nicole left a new clip in the Bronson file on the Tagawa deal. It's hit the media.'

'Anything?'

'Nothing we didn't know already. Elliot said something about biologicals. Very general, but you never know. Maybe he's gotten wind of Proteus.'

As he said it Pierce looked past Condon at the framed poster on his office wall next to the door. It was the poster from the 1966 movie *Fantastic Voyage*. It showed the white submarine *Proteus* descending through a multicolour sea of bodily fluids. He had got the poster from Cody Zeller who had obtained it through an online Hollywood memorabilia auction.

'Elliot just likes to talk,' Condon said. 'I don't know how he could know anything about Proteus. Anyway, let me know if you need anything and I'll get it done.'

'Thanks, Charlie. You going back home now?'

'Probably. Melissa and I are going to Jar tonight. You want to go? I could call and make it for three.'

'Nah, that's OK. But thanks. I've got the furniture coming in today and I'll probably work on getting my place set up.'

Charlie nodded and then hesitated for a moment before asking the next question. 'You going to change your phone number?'

'Yeah, I have to. First thing Monday. Monica told you, huh?'

'A little bit. She said you got some prostitute's old number and guys are calling all the time.'

'Yeah, well, when I see you Monday I'll probably give you a new number, OK?'

'OK, man, I'll see you Monday.'

Condon left, and after Pierce was sure he was down the hall he got up and closed his door. He wondered how much more Monica had told him, whether she was spreading alarm about his activities.

He went back to Lilly's address book, leafing through it once again. Almost at the end he came across an entry he hadn't noticed before. It simply said USC. Pierce thought about the envelope he had seen in her house. He picked up the phone and called the number. He got a recording for the admissions office of the University of Southern California. The office was closed on weekends.

Pierce hung up. He wondered if Lilly had been in the process of applying to USC when she had disappeared. Maybe she had been trying to get out of the escort business. Maybe it was the reason she had disappeared.

He put the address book aside and opened the Visa statement. It showed zero purchases on the card for the month of August and notice of an overdue payment on a $354.26 balance. The payment had been due by August 15.

The bank statement from Washington Savings & Loan was next. It was a combined statement showing balances in current and savings accounts. Lilly Quinlan had not made a deposit in the month of August but had not been short of funds. She had $9,240 in current and $54,542 in savings. It wasn't enough for four years at USC but it would have been a start if Lilly was changing direction.

Pierce looked through the statement and the collection of posted cheques the bank had returned to her. He noticed one to Vivian Quinlan for $2,000 and assumed that was the monthly instalment on maternal upkeep. Another cheque, this one for $4,000, was made out to James Wainwright and on the memo line Lilly had written '*Rent*'. It seemed to him that $4,000 was exceedingly high for monthly rent of the bungalow on Altair.

The copy room was a short walk down the hall from Pierce's office. Along with a copier, the room contained a shredder. Pierce entered the room, opened his backpack and fed Lilly Quinlan's mail into the shredder. When he had finished he opened one of the cabinets where packages containing copy paper were stored. He took Lilly Quinlan's address book from his backpack and reached into the cabinet with it, dropping it behind one of the stacks of paper. He believed it could go as long as a month there without being discovered.

Pierce took the elevator down to the basement and passed through the mantrap into the lab suite. At the computer console he entered the three passwords in correct order for a Saturday and logged in. He called up the testing protocols for the Proteus project. He started to read the summary of the most recent testing of cellular energy conversion rates.

But then he stopped. Once again he could not do it. He could not concentrate on the work. He was consumed by other thoughts, and he knew from past experience—the Proteus project being an example—that he must run out the clock on the thing that consumed him if he was ever to return to the work.

He shut down the computer and left the lab. Back in his office he took his notepad out of his backpack and called the number he had for the private investigator, Glass. He got a machine and left a message.

'Mr Glass, my name is Henry Pierce. I would like to talk to you as soon as possible about Lilly Quinlan. I got your name and number from her mother. You can call me back at any time.' He left both his apartment number and the direct line to his office and hung up.

Pierce drummed his fingers on the edge of his desk, trying to figure out the next step. He decided he was going up the coast to see Cody Zeller. He put his notepad back in his backpack.

'Lights,' he said.

FOUR

When Pierce got into the first stretch of Malibu and his view of the ocean was stolen by the houses crowding the ocean's edge, he slowed down and watched for Cody Zeller's house. He didn't have the address to hand and he hadn't seen the house in more than a year. The houses on this stretch were jammed side to side and all looked the same. No lawns, built right to the kerb. Flat as shoe boxes.

He was saved by the sight of Zeller's black Jaguar XKR, which was parked in front of his closed garage. Zeller had long ago illegally converted his garage into a workroom and had to pay garage rent to a neighbour to protect his $90,000 car. The car being outside meant Zeller had either just got home or was about to head out. Pierce was just in time. He pulled a U-turn and parked carefully behind the Jag.

The front door of the house was opened before he reached it, either because Zeller had seen him on one of the cameras mounted under the eaves or because Pierce had tripped a motion sensor. Zeller was the only person Pierce knew who rivalled himself in paranoia. It was probably what had bonded them at Stanford.

'Dr Strangelove, I presume,' Zeller said.

'Mein Führer, I can walk,' Pierce replied.

It was their standard greeting since Stanford, when they had seen the movie together at a Kubrick retrospective up in San Francisco.

They gave each other a handshake invented by the loose group of friends they belonged to in college. They called themselves the Doomsters, after the Ross Macdonald novel about disaffected youths who surfed California's coastline. The handshake consisted of fingers hooked together like train car couplings and then three quick squeezes like gripping a rubber ball at a blood bank—the Doomsters had sold blood on a regular basis while in college in order to buy beer, marijuana and computer software.

Pierce hadn't seen Zeller in a few months and his hair hadn't been cut since. Sun-bleached and unkempt, it was loosely tied at the back of his neck. He wore a Zuma Jay T-shirt, baggies and leather sandals. His skin was the copper colour of smoggy sunsets. Of all the Doomsters he always had the look that the others had aspired to. Now it was wearing a little thin. At thirty-five he was beginning to

look like an ageing surfer who couldn't let it go, and that made him all the more endearing to Pierce. In many ways Pierce felt like a sellout. He admired Zeller for the path he had cut through life.

'Check him out, Dr Strange himself out in the Big Bad 'Bu. Man, you don't have your wets with you and I don't see any board, so to what do I owe this unexpected pleasure?'

He beckoned Pierce inside and they walked into a large loft-style home that was divided in half with living quarters to the right and working quarters to the left. Beyond these areas was a wall of glass that opened to the deck and the ocean beyond. The steady pounding of the ocean's waves was the heartbeat of the house.

'Just thought I'd take a ride out and check on things out here.'

They moved across the beech-wood flooring towards the view. In a house like this it was an automatic reflex. You gravitated to the view, to the blue-black water of the Pacific. As they got close to the glass, Pierce could look down through the deck railing and see the swells rolling in. A small company of surfers in multicolour wet suits sat on their boards and waited for the right moment.

Pierce felt an interior tug. 'I keep forgetting how nice you got it out here, Code.'

'For a college dropout, I can't complain. Beer, dude?'

'Yeah, sure. Either one.'

While Zeller went to the kitchen, Pierce moved towards the work area. A large floor-to-ceiling rack of electronics acted to knock down the exterior light and partition off the area where Zeller made his living. There were two desks and a bank of shelves containing code books and manuals. He stepped through the plastic curtain that used to be where the door to the garage was, took a step down and was in a climate-controlled computer room. There were two computer bays on either side of the room, each equipped with multiple screens. Each system seemed to be at work. Slowly unspooling data trails moved across each screen—digital inchworms crawling through whatever was Zeller's project of the moment.

The walls of the room were covered in black foam padding to knock down exterior noise. Affixed to the padding of the rear wall was a procession of stickers depicting company logos and trademark names, most of them household words. Pierce knew that Zeller put up a logo every time he conducted a successful intrusion into that company's computer system. They were the notches on his gun.

Zeller earned $500 an hour as a white-hat hacker. He was the best of the best. He worked as an independent, usually hired by one of the big accounting firms to conduct penetration tests on their clients. In a way it was a racket. The system that Zeller could not defeat was rare. And after each successful penetration his employer usually turned round and got a fat digital security contract from the client, with a nice bonus going to Zeller. He constantly fielded high-price offers from big firms to come on board full time, but he always demurred, saying he liked working for himself.

Zeller came into the room with two bottles of San Miguel. They clicked bottles before drinking. Pierce indicated the screens with his bottle. 'You working on something right now? It looks busy.'

'No, not really. I'm just doing a little trolling. Looking for somebody I know is out there hiding.'

'Who?'

Zeller smiled. 'If I told you that I'd have to kill you.'

It was business. They were friends who went back to good times and one seriously bad time—at least for Pierce—in college. But business was business, and part of what Zeller sold was discretion.

'I understand,' Pierce said. 'And I don't want to intrude so let me get to it. Are you too busy to take on something else?'

'When would I need to start?'

'Uh, yesterday would be nice.'

'A quickie. I like quickies. And I like working for Amedeo Tech.'

'Not for the company. For me. But I'll pay you.'

'I like that better. What do you need?'

'I need to run some people and businesses, see what comes up.'

Zeller nodded thoughtfully. 'Heavy people?'

'I don't really know but I'd use all precautions. It involves the adult entertainment field, you could say.'

Now Zeller smiled broadly, his burned skin crinkling round the eyes. 'Oh, baby, don't tell me you bumped your dick into something.'

'No, nothing like that.'

'Then what?'

'Let's sit down. And bring something to make notes with.'

In the living room, Pierce gave him all the information he had on Lilly Quinlan without explaining where it was coming from. He also asked Zeller to find what he could on Entrepreneurial Concepts Unlimited and Wentz, the man who operated it.

'You got a first name?'

'No. Just Wentz. Can't be too many in the field.'

'Stay inside the lines?'

Pierce hesitated. Zeller was asking if Pierce wanted him to stay within the law. Pierce knew from experience that there was much more out there to be found if Zeller crossed the lines and went into systems he was not authorised to enter. And he knew Zeller was an expert at crossing them. The Doomsters were formed when they were college sophomores. Computer hacking was just coming into vogue for their generation and the members of the group, largely under Zeller's direction, did more than hold their own. They mostly committed pranks, their best being the one where they hacked into the local telephone company's 411 information bank and changing the number for the local Domino's Pizza to the home number of the dean of the computer sciences department.

But their best moment was also their worst. The Doomsters were busted by the police and later suspended. On the criminal side everybody got probation, with the charges to be expunged after six months without further trouble. On the school side they were all suspended one semester. Pierce went back after serving both the suspension and the probation. Under the magnifying glass of police and school administrators, he switched from computer sciences to a chemistry curriculum and never looked back.

Zeller never looked back either. He didn't return to Stanford. He was scooped up by a computer security firm and given a nice salary.

'Get whatever you can get,' Pierce finally answered.

'When do you need this?'

'Like I said, yesterday will be fine.' Pierce finished his beer. He didn't want to hang around because he wanted Zeller to get to work on the assignment he was giving him.

But Zeller seemed in no hurry. 'Want another beer, Commander?'

'Nah, I'm gonna pass. I've gotta get back to my apartment. I have my assistant baby-sitting the furniture movers. Besides, you're going to get on this thing, aren't you?'

'Oh, yeah, man. Right away.' Zeller gestured towards his work area. 'Right now all my machines are booked. But I'll get on it tonight. I'll call you soon.'

'All right, Code. Thanks.'

BY THE TIME Pierce got to his apartment the movers were gone but Monica was still there. She'd had them arrange the furnishings in a way that was acceptable. It didn't take much advantage of the view from the floor-to-ceiling windows that ran along one side of the living room and dining room, but Pierce didn't care that much. He knew he'd be spending little time in the apartment anyway.

'It looks nice,' he said. 'Thanks.'

'You're welcome. I was just about to leave.'

'Why did you stay?'

She held up her stack of magazines in two hands. 'I wanted to finish a magazine I was reading.'

Pierce wasn't sure why that necessitated her staying at the apartment but let it go. 'Listen, there's one thing I want to ask you before you leave. What is your job title at Amedeo Technologies?'

'What do you mean? You know what it is.'

'I want to see if you know what it is.'

'Personal assistant to the president, why?'

'Because I wanted to make sure you remembered that it is *personal* assistant, not just assistant.'

She blinked and looked at his face for a long moment before responding. 'All right, Henry, what's wrong?'

'What's wrong is that I don't appreciate you telling Charlie Condon all about my phone number problems and what I'm trying to do about it.'

'All I told him was that you'd gotten this prostitute's old number and you were getting all kinds of calls. I had to tell him something because when he called I didn't recognise his voice and he didn't recognise mine and he said, "Who's this?" and I kind of snapped at him because I thought he was, you know, calling for Lilly.'

'You didn't tell him about how you got her address for me and I went to her house?'

'No, I didn't. What's the big deal anyway? You guys are partners.'

'The big deal is that loose lips sink ships, you understand that?'

She shrugged her shoulders and wouldn't look at him.

'My actions reflect on the company,' Pierce said. 'Especially right now and even what I do in private. If what I do is misrepresented or blown out of proportion it could seriously hurt the company. Right now our company makes zero money, Monica, and we rely on investors to support the research, to pay the rent and the salaries, everything. If investors think we're shaky, then we've got a big problem. If things about me—true or false—get to the wrong people, we could have trouble.'

'I didn't know Charlie was the wrong people.'

'He's not. He's the right people. That's why I don't mind what you said to him. But what I will mind is if you tell anybody else about what I am doing or what's going on with me. Anyone, Monica. Inside or outside the company.' He hoped she understood he was talking about Nicole and anybody else she encountered in her daily life.

'I won't. I won't tell a soul. And please don't ask me to get involved in your personal life again. I don't want to baby-sit deliveries or do anything outside of the company again.'

'Fine. I won't ask you to. It was my mistake. I didn't think it would be a problem and you told me you could use the overtime.'

'I can use the overtime but I don't like all these complications.'

Pierce waited a moment, watching her the whole time. 'Monica, do you even know what we do at Amedeo? I mean, do you know what the project is all about?'

'Sort of. I know it's about molecular computing. I've read some of the stories in the press, but they're very scientific and everything's so secret I never wanted to ask questions. I just try to do my job.'

'The project isn't secret. The processes we're inventing are. There's a difference.' He leaned forward and tried to think of the best way to explain it to her. 'Right now, everywhere in the world, microprocessing chips are made of silicon. What we are trying to do at Amedeo is create a new generation of computer chips made of molecules. Build an entire computer with only organic molecules. A computer that will one day come out of a vat of chemicals, that will assemble itself from the right recipe being in that vat. We're talking about a computer without silicon or magnetic particles. Tremendously less expensive to build and astronomically more powerful—in which just a teaspoon of molecules could hold more memory than the biggest computer going today.'

'Wow,' she said in an unconvincing tone.

Pierce smiled. 'Believe me, Monica, whoever gets there first, they're going to change this world. This will affect almost all technology on the planet. It is conceivable with this technology that we could build a whole computer that is smaller than a silicon chip. Take a computer that fills a room now and make it the size of a dime. That's our goal. That's why in the lab we call it chasing the dime. I'm sure you've heard the saying around the office.'

She shook her head. 'But why would someone want a computer the size of a dime?'

'That's just an example. But what if your computer was in the button of your shirt or the frame of your glasses? What if in your office your desktop wasn't on your desk but in the paint on the walls of your office? What if you talked to the walls and they talked back?'

Monica shrugged. 'That would be cool, I guess.'

He could tell he still wasn't making a dent. He decided to stop trying to impress her and get to the point. 'Monica, the thing is, it's highly competitive out there. There are a lot of private companies like Amedeo. A lot of them are bigger. Most of them are well funded and dug in. We're not. So to keep going we need the funding stream to keep flowing. We can't do anything that stops that flow or we drop out of the race and there is no Amedeo Technologies. OK?'

'OK. But if all this is so important maybe you ought to think about what you're doing. I just talked about it. You're the one who is out there going to her house and doing things underhanded.'

'Look, I was curious about this and just wanted to make sure the woman was all right. But now I'm done with it. On Monday I want you to get my number changed. Hopefully that will be the end of it.'

'Good. Can I go now?'

Pierce nodded. He gave up. 'Yes, you can go. Thanks for waiting for the furniture. Have a good weekend and I'll see you on Monday.'

He decided that once things blew over he would get another personal assistant and Monica could go back to the general pool of assistants at the company.

After a while Pierce picked up the phone and called information in Venice for the number of James Wainwright. A man answered his next call.

'I'm looking for Lilly Quinlan's landlord,' Pierce said. 'For the house over on Altair in Venice.'

'That would be me.'

'My name's Pierce. I'm trying to locate Lilly and want to know if you've had any contact with her in the last month or so?'

'I don't answer questions about my tenants with strangers unless they state their business and convince me I should.'

'Fair enough, Mr Wainwright. I'd be happy to come to see you in person if you'd prefer. I'm a friend of the family. Lilly's mother, Vivian, is worried because she hasn't heard from her daughter in seven weeks. She asked me to do some checking around. I can give you Vivian's number in Tampa if you want to call and check on me.'

It was a risk but Pierce thought it was worth taking in convincing

Wainwright to talk. It wasn't too far from the truth, anyway.

'I have her mother's number on her application. I don't need to call because I don't have anything that will help you. Lilly Quinlan's paid up through the end of the month. I don't have occasion to see or talk to her unless she has a problem. I have not spoken to or seen her in a couple of months, at least.'

'The end of the month? Are you sure?' Pierce knew that that didn't jibe with the cheque records he had examined.

'That's right.'

'How did she pay her last rent, cheque or cash?'

'That's none of your business.'

'Mr Wainwright, it is my business. Lilly is missing and her mother has asked me to look for her.'

'So you say.'

'Call her.'

'I don't have time to call her. I maintain thirty-two apartments and houses. You think I have—?'

'Is there somebody who takes care of the lawn I could talk to?'

'You're already talking to him.'

'So you haven't seen her when you've been over there?'

'She hasn't been there the last few times I've been there. I didn't think anything of it. People have lives, you know.' He hung up.

Pierce opened his backpack and got out the notepad in which he had written down the number for Robin, Lilly's escort partner.

This time when she answered he tried to deepen his voice. His hope was that she would not recognise him from the night before.

'I was wondering if we could get together tonight.'

'Well, I'm open, baby. Have we ever dated? You sound familiar.'

'Uh, no. Not before.'

'Whatcha got in mind?'

'Um, maybe dinner and then go to your place. I don't know.'

'Well, honey, I get four hundred an hour. Most guys want to skip the dinner and just come see me. Or I come see them.'

'Then I can just come to you.'

'OK, fine. What's your name?'

He knew she had caller ID so he couldn't lie. 'Henry Pierce.'

'And what time were you thinking about?'

He looked at his watch. It was six o'clock.

'How about seven?' It would give him time to get to a cash machine. He had a card that could get him $400 maximum on a withdrawal.

'That's fine with me,' she said.

'Where do I go?'

She gave him an address of a Smooth Moves shop on Lincoln in Marina del Rey. She told him to go into the shop and get a straw-berry blitz and then call her from the payphone out front at five min-utes before seven. When he asked her why she did it this way she said, 'Precautions. I wanna get a look at you before I bring you on up. And I like those little strawberry thingies anyway.'

Pierce said he would get the smoothie and make the call and thanked her and that was it. As he cradled the phone, a wave of trep-idation swept through him. He thought about the speech he had given Monica and how she had correctly turned it right back at him.

'You idiot,' he said to himself.

AT THE APPOINTED TIME Pierce picked up a payphone outside Smooth Moves and called Robin's number. Turning his back to the phone he saw that across Lincoln was a large apartment complex called the Marina Executive Towers. Only the building didn't really qualify as a tower or towers. It was short and wide—three storeys of apartments over a garage. A banner hanging from the roof announced short-term executive rentals and free maid service. Pierce realised it was a perfect place for a prostitute to carry out her busi-ness. The place was probably so large and the turnover of renters so high that a steady procession of different men coming in and out would not be noticeable to other residents.

Robin picked up after three rings.

'It's Henry. I called—'

'Hey, baby. Let me get a look at you here.'

He scanned the windows of the apartment building across the street, looking for someone looking back at him. He didn't see any-body or any curtain movement but he noticed that the windows of several of the apartments had mirrored glass.

'OK,' she said. 'You look all right to me. Go across the street to the building and at the main door push apartment two-oh-three.'

'OK.' He hung up and followed her instructions.

When he pushed the button marked 203, the door lock was buzzed. Inside, he couldn't find the stairs so he took the elevator the one flight up. Robin's apartment was two doors from the elevator.

She opened the door before he got a chance to knock on it. There was a peephole and she had apparently been watching. She took the smoothie from his hand and invited him in.

The place was sparsely furnished and devoid of personal objects. There was just a couch, a chair, a coffee table and a standard lamp.

As Pierce stepped in he could see the glass doors to the balcony had the mirrored film on them. They looked almost directly across at the Smooth Moves shop.

'Come sit down,' Robin said.

She moved to the couch and gestured for Pierce to sit next to her. He did. He tried to look around. The place reminded him of a hotel room but he guessed atmosphere wasn't important for the business conducted within the apartment. He felt her hand take his jaw and turn his face to hers.

'You like what you see?' she asked.

She was barefoot and wore a light blue tank top T-shirt and a pair of red corduroy shorts cut so high that a bathing suit might have been more modest. She was braless and her breasts were huge, most likely the result of implants. Her blonde hair was parted in the middle and cascaded down the sides of her face in ringlets.

'Yes, I do,' he answered.

'People tell me I have a Meg Ryan thing going.'

Pierce nodded, although he didn't see it. The movie star was older but a lot softer on the eyes.

'Did you bring me something?'

At first he thought she was talking about the smoothie but then he remembered the money. 'Yeah, I've got it here.' He leaned back on the couch to reach into his pocket. He had the four hundred ready in its own thick fold of twenties fresh out of the cash machine.

This was the part he had rehearsed. He didn't mind losing the four hundred but he didn't want to give it to her and then be kicked out when he revealed the true reason he was there. He pulled the money out so she could see it and know it was close and hers for the taking.

'Thank you.'

She reached for the money but Pierce pulled his hand back.

'Before I give you this, I have to tell you I don't want to have sex with you. You're very attractive but all I want is some information.'

'What the fuck are you talking about?'

'I have to find Lilly Quinlan. You can help me.'

'Who is Lilly Quinlan?'

'Come on, you name her on your web page. Double your pleasure? You know who I'm talking about.'

'You're the guy from last night. You called last night.'

He nodded.

'Then get the hell out of here.' She stood up and walked towards the door.

'Robin, don't open that door. If you don't talk to me then you'll talk to the cops. That's my next move.'

She turned around. 'The cops don't give a shit.' But she didn't open the door. She just stood there, angry and waiting, one hand on the knob.

'Maybe not now but they'll care if I go to them.'

'Why, who are you?'

'I have some juice,' he lied. 'If I go to them, they'll come to you. They won't be as nice as me . . . and they won't pay you four hundred dollars for your time.' He put the money down on the couch where she had been sitting. He watched her eyes go to it. 'Just information, that's all I want. It goes no further than me.'

He waited and after a long moment of silence she came back over to the couch and grabbed the money. She somehow found space for it in her tiny shorts. She folded her arms and remained standing.

'What information? I hardly knew her.'

'You know something. You talk about her in the past tense.'

'I don't know anything. All I know is she just . . . disappeared.'

'When was that?'

'More than a month ago. Suddenly she was just gone.'

'How do you know it was so sudden? Maybe she just packed up and left.'

'I know because one minute we were talking on the phone and the next minute she didn't show up, that's why.'

'Show up for what?'

'We had a gig. A double. She set it up and called me. She told me the time and then she didn't show up. I was there and then the client showed up and he wasn't happy. First of all there was no place to park and then she wasn't there and I had to scramble around to get another girl to come back over here to my place—and there are no other girls like Lilly and he really wanted Lilly. It was a fiasco.'

'Where was this?'

'She had a gig pad. She didn't work anywhere else. No outcall. Not even to here. I always had to go to her. Even if they were my clients wanting the double, we had to go to her pad or it didn't happen.'

'Did you have a key to her place?'

'No. Look, you've gotten your four hundred worth. That's it.'

Pierce reached into his pocket and pulled out the rest of his cash. It was $230. He'd counted it in the car. 'Take this because I'm not done. Something happened to her and I'm going to find out what.'

She grabbed the money and it disappeared. 'Why do you care?'

'Because. Maybe because nobody else does. Now if you didn't have a key to her place, how do you know she didn't show up that night?'

'Because I knocked for fifteen minutes and then me and the guy waited for another twenty. I'm telling you, she wasn't in there.'

'Did she have something set up before the gig with you?'

Robin thought for a bit before answering. 'She said she had something to do but I don't know if she was with a client. Because I wanted to do it earlier but she said she was busy then. So we set the time she wanted and so she should have been there but wasn't.'

'So when you got there and knocked on the door, she could've been inside with another client but just not answering.'

'I guess so but she should've been done by then and she would have answered. It was all set up. So maybe it wasn't a client.'

'Or maybe she was not allowed to answer. Maybe she couldn't.'

This seemed to give Robin pause, as though she realised how close she might have come to whatever fate befell Lilly.

'Where is this place? Her apartment.'

'It's over in Venice. Off Speedway.'

'What's the exact address?'

'I don't remember. I just know how to get there.'

Pierce nodded. 'How'd you two meet in the first place?'

'We met at a shoot and sort of hit it off. It went from there.'

'A shoot? You mean, for a magazine?'

'No, a web site.'

'Was it for one of the sites Entrepreneurial Concepts operates?'

'Look, what does it matter?'

'Where was the shoot, at Entrepreneurial Concepts?'

'Yeah. At the studios.'

'So you got the job through LA Darlings and Mr Wentz, right?'

Her eyes flared at the mention of the name but she didn't respond.

'What's his first name?'

'I'm not talking to you about him. You can't tell him you got any information from me, you understand?'

'I told you, everything you tell me here is private.'

'Look, he's got connections and people who work for him who are very mean. *He's* mean. I don't want to talk about him.'

'Just tell me his name and I'll leave it at that, OK?'

'It's Billy. Billy Wentz. Most people call him Billy Wince because he hurts people, OK?'

'Thank you.' He stood up and looked round the apartment. He walked over to the corner of the living room and looked into a hallway that he guessed led to the bedroom. 'You don't live here, do you?'

'No. I work here.'

'You keep any clothes here?'

'What do you mean?'

'You have any clothes besides those? And where are your shoes?' He gestured to what she was wearing.

'Yes, I changed when I got here. I don't go out like this.'

'Good. Change back and let's go.'

'What are you talking about? Where?'

'I want you to show me where Lilly's place is. Or was.'

'Uh, uh, man. You got your information, that's it.'

Pierce looked at his watch. 'Look, you said four hundred an hour. I've been here twenty minutes. That means I get forty more minutes or you give me two-thirds of my cash back.'

'That's not how it works.'

'That's how it works today.'

She stared angrily at him for a long moment and then walked silently past him towards the bedroom to change. Pierce stepped over to the balcony doors and looked out across Lincoln.

He saw a man standing at the payphone in front of Smooth Moves, holding a smoothie and looking up at the windows of the building Pierce was in. Another smoothie, another client. He wondered how many women were working in the building.

Robin came out of the bedroom in faded blue jeans and a white T-shirt. She slipped her feet into a pair of sandals she pulled from under the coffee table, then walked past him into the kitchenette, opened a cabinet over the sink and took out a small black bag. 'Let's go. You've got thirty-five minutes.' She went to the front door, opened it and stepped out into the hallway.

He followed. 'You want your smoothie?'

It was sitting untouched on the breakfast bar.

'No, I hate smoothies. Too fattening. My vice is pizza. Next time bring me a pizza.'

'Then why'd you ask for it?'

'It was just a way of checking you out.'

Pierce stepped into the hallway and closed the door, then followed Robin to the elevator.

FIVE

Pierce drove and Robin directed. It was a short trip from the Marina over to Speedway in Venice. He tried to make the best use of his time on the way over. But he knew Robin was reluctant to talk.

'So you're not an independent, are you?'

'What are you talking about?'

'You work for Wentz—the guy who runs the web site. He's what I guess you'd call a digital pimp. He sets you girls up in that place, runs your web page. How much does he get? I saw on the site he charges four hundred a month to run your picture but I have a feeling he gets a lot more than that. He gets a share of that first four hundred I gave you, doesn't he?'

'Look, I'm not talking to you about him. You'll get me killed, too. When we get to her place, that's it. We're done. I'll take a cab.'

'Too? What do you know about what happened to Lilly?'

'Nothing.'

'Then why did you say "too"?'

'Look, man, if you knew what was smart for you you'd leave this thing alone *too*. You don't know these people or what they can do.'

'I have an idea.'

'Yeah? How would you have any fucking idea?'

'I had a sister once . . .'

'And?'

'And you could say she was in your line of work.'

He looked at Robin. She kept her eyes straight ahead.

'One morning a school bus driver up on Mulholland spotted her body down past the guard rail. I was away in my second year up at Stanford at the time.' He looked back at the road.

'It's a funny thing about this city,' he continued after a while. 'She was lying out in the open, naked . . . and the cops said they could tell by the . . . evidence that she'd been there at least a couple days. And I always wondered how many people saw her and didn't do anything about it. Didn't call anybody. This city can be pretty cold sometimes.' He glanced back at Robin. He could see the distress in her eyes.

'Did they ever catch the guy?' she asked.

'Eventually. But not until after he killed four more.'

She shook her head. 'What are you doing here, Henry? That was a long time ago. It's got nothing to do with any of this.'

'I don't know what I'm doing. I'm just . . . following something.'

'Turn left up here and go down to the end. There's only one parking space for her unit. She used to leave it open for the client.'

He turned off Speedway as instructed and was in an alley behind rows of small apartments on either side.

When he got to the last building, Robin said, 'Somebody took it.' She pointed to a car parking in a spot below a stairway to an apartment door. 'That's the place up there.'

'Is that her car?'

'No, she had a Lexus.'

The car in the space was a Volvo station wagon. Pierce backed up and squeezed his BMW between two rows of trash cans. It wasn't a legal space but cars could still get past in the alley and he wasn't expecting to be there long.

They got out. As soon as Robin was out she started heading back down the alley towards Speedway.

'Look,' Pierce said. 'Thanks for your help. If I find her I'll let you know.'

'Who, Lilly or your sister?'

That gave him pause for a moment. From those you least expect it comes insight. 'You going to be all right?' he called after her.

She suddenly stopped, turned and strode back to him, the anger flaring in her eyes again. 'Look, don't pretend you care about me, OK? That phoney shit is disgusting.' She turned and walked off again down the alley.

Pierce walked round the Volvo and noticed that blankets in the back were being used to cover the tops of two cardboard boxes and other bulky items he couldn't see. He climbed the stairs to Lilly's apartment. When he got there he saw that the door was slightly ajar. With one finger he pushed the door, remaining on the porch as it swung inwards. As it opened he could see a sparsely furnished living room with a stairway going up the far wall to a loft. Under the loft was a small kitchen with a hatch to the living room. Pierce leaned forward and looked in without actually entering the apartment. He saw three cardboard boxes on the floor of the living room. Through the hatch he could see the torso of a man who was moving about and putting liquor bottles into a box on the counter.

Pierce reached over and knocked on the door and called, 'Lilly?'

Startled, the man in the kitchen almost dropped a bottle of gin. 'She's not here any more,' he called. 'She's moved.'

'Then who are you?'

'I'm the landlord and I'm busy.'

Pierce stepped into the apartment and moved towards the kitchen. When he got to the doorway he saw that the man had long grey hair pulled back into a ponytail. He wore a dirty white T-shirt and dirtier white shorts. He was deeply tanned.

'You can't come in here. She's gone.'

'You're Wainwright, aren't you?'

The man looked up at Pierce. 'Who are you?'

'I'm Pierce. I talked to you today. I told you she was gone.'

'Oh. Well, you were right, she's long gone.'

'The money she paid you was for both places. The four grand. You didn't tell me that.'

'You didn't ask.'

'Do you own this building, Mr Wainwright?'

'I'm not answering your questions, thank you.'

'Or does Billy Wentz own it and you just manage it for him?'

Acknowledgment flickered in his eyes and then went out. 'OK, leave now. Get out of here.'

Pierce shook his head. 'I'm not leaving yet. If you want to call the cops go ahead. See what they think about you clearing her stuff out even though you told me she was paid up through the month. Maybe we look under the blankets in the back of your car, too. I'm betting we'd find a plasma TV that used to hang on the wall of the house she rented on Altair. You probably went by there first, right?'

'She abandoned the place,' Wainwright said testily. 'You should have seen the refrigerator in there.'

'I'm sure it must've been just awful. So awful I guess you decided to clear the place out and maybe even double dip on the rent, huh? Housing in Venice is tight. You already got a new tenant lined up?'

'What do you want?'

'To look around.'

'Then hurry up because as soon as I'm done in here I'm leaving.'

Pierce moved up the staircase and headed up to the loft. A king-size brass bed took up most of the available space.

He went to a small closet and slid the door open. It was empty, the contents now in one of the boxes below.

Pierce looked at the bed. It looked like it had been carefully made, the bedspread tucked tightly under the mattress. But there were no pillows, which he thought was strange. He got down on the carpet and looked underneath the bed base. There was nothing but dust.

But then he saw a dark spot in the beige carpeting. Curious, he straightened up and pushed the bed back to uncover the spot.

Whatever had spilled or dripped on the carpet was dry. It was a brownish-black colour and Pierce didn't want to touch it because he thought it might be blood. He pulled the bed back over the spot.

'What the hell are you doing up there?' Wainwright called up.

Pierce didn't answer. He took hold of one corner of the bedspread and lifted it up, revealing the mattress below. No mattress cover or top sheet. No blanket.

He started pulling off the bedspread. He wanted to see the mattress. Sheets and blankets could easily be taken from an apartment and thrown away. Even pillows could be discarded. But a king-size mattress was another matter.

As the bedspread slipped off the mattress, Pierce felt as though his intestines had collapsed inside. The centre of the mattress was black with something that had congealed and dried and was the colour of death. It could only be blood.

'Jesus Christ!' Wainwright said. He had come up the steps to see what the dragging sounds were all about. 'Is that what I think it is?'

'Is there a phone here?' Pierce asked.

'No, not that I know of.'

'You have a cellphone?'

'In the car.'

'Go get it.'

PIERCE LOOKED UP when Detective Renner walked in. He tried to keep his anger in check, knowing that the cooler he played this the faster he would get out and get home. Still, two hours in an eight by eight room had left him with little patience. He had already given a statement twice. Once to the patrol cops who responded to Wainwright's call and then to Renner and his partner when they had arrived on the scene. One of the patrol cops had then taken him to the Pacific Division station and locked him in the interview room.

Renner had a file in his hand. He sat down at the table across from Pierce and opened it. Pierce could see some sort of police form on it with handwriting in all of the boxes. Renner looked like a cop who'd been around more crime scenes than most. Early fifties and still solid, he reminded Pierce of Clyde Vernon.

'You're thirty-four years old?'

'Yes.'

'Your address is twenty-eight hundred Ocean Way, apartment twelve-oh-one.'

'Yes.' This time exasperation crept into his voice.

Renner's eyes came up momentarily to his and then went back to the form. 'But that is not the address on your driver's licence.'

'No, I just moved. Ocean is where I live now. Amalfi Drive is where I used to live. Look, it's after midnight. Did you really keep me sitting in here for two hours so you could ask me these obvious questions? I already gave you my statement. What else do you want?'

Renner leaned back. 'No, Mr Pierce, I kept you here because we needed to conduct a thorough investigation of what appears to be a crime scene. I am sure you don't begrudge us that.'

'I don't begrudge that. I do begrudge being kept in here like a suspect. I tried that door. It was locked. I knocked and nobody came.'

'I'm sorry about that. There was no one in the detective bureau. It's the middle of the night. But the patrol officer should not have locked the door because you are not under arrest. If you want to make a complaint I'll get you the necessary forms.'

'I don't want to make a complaint, OK? Can we just get on with this so I can get out of here? Is it her blood?'

'What blood?'

'On the bed.'

'How do you know it is blood?'

'I'm assuming. What else could it be?'

'You tell me.'

'What? What is that supposed to mean?'

'It was a question.'

'Wait a minute, you just said I was not a suspect.'

'I said you are not under arrest.'

'So you're saying I am not under arrest but I *am* a suspect in this?'

'I am not saying anything, Mr Pierce. I am simply trying to figure out what happened in that apartment.' Renner went back to his form. 'Now in the statement you gave earlier, you say that your new telephone number on Ocean Way belonged at one time to the woman whose apartment you went to this evening.'

'Exactly. That's why I was there. To find out if something happened to her.'

'Do you know this woman, Lilly Quinlan?'

'No, never met her.'

'Then why did you go to her apartment? Why didn't you just change your number?'

'For the last two hours I've been asking myself the same thing. I mean, you try to check on somebody and maybe do some good and what do you get? Locked in a room for two hours by the cops.'

'Tell me again how you knew about the apartment.'

Pierce's earlier statement had been replete with shadings of the truth designed to cover any illegalities he had committed. But the story he had told about finding the apartment had been a lie designed to keep Robin out of the investigation. He had kept his promise not to reveal her as a source of information. Of everything he had said over the last four hours, it was the only thing he felt good about.

'As soon as I plugged in my phone I started getting calls from men who wanted Lilly. A few of them were former clients who wanted to see her again. I tried to engage these men in conversation, to see what I could find out about her. One man told me about the apartment and where it was. So I came over.'

'I see, and what was this former client's name?'

'I don't know. He didn't give it.'

'You have caller ID on your new phone?'

'Yes, but he was calling from a hotel. All it said was that it was coming from the Ritz Carlton.'

Renner nodded. 'And Mr Wainwright said you called him earlier today to ask about Miss Quinlan and another property she rented from him.'

'Yes. A house on Altair. She lived there.'

'Have you ever been to the house on Altair?'

Pierce chose his words like he was choosing steps through a minefield. 'I went there and nobody answered the door. That's why I called Wainwright.'

'I'm trying to get the chain of events correct,' Renner said. 'You told us you went to this place Entrepreneurial Concepts in Hollywood first. You get the name Lilly Quinlan and an address for a mail drop in Santa Monica. You go there and get the address to the house out of the guy at the mail drop, right? You go to the house first, then you call Wainright, then you run into him at the apartment. Do I have all this straight?'

'Yes.'

'You have said in both your statements so far tonight that you knocked and no one answered and then you left. That true?'

'Yes, true.'

'Between the time you knocked and got no answer and when you left the premises, did you go into the house on Altair, Mr Pierce?'

There it was. The question. It required a yes or no, a true answer or a lie that could easily be found out. He had to assume he had left fingerprints in the house. He remembered specifically the knobs on the roll-top desk. He had given them the Altair address more than two hours ago. For all he knew they had already been there and already had his fingerprints.

'The door was unlocked,' Pierce said. 'I went in to make sure she wasn't in there. Needing help or something.'

Renner was leaning forward across the table. His eyes held Pierce's. 'You were inside that house? Why didn't you tell us that before?'

'I don't know. I didn't think it was necessary.'

'What did you find in that house?'

'Not a lot. Spoiled food, a giant pile of mail. I could tell she hadn't been there in a long while.'

'Did you take anything?'

'No.' He said it without hesitation, without blinking.

'What did you touch?'

Pierce shrugged. 'I don't know. Some of the mail. There's a desk. I opened some drawers.'

'Were you expecting to find Miss Quinlan in a desk drawer?'

'No. I just . . .' He didn't finish. He reminded himself that he was walking on a ledge. He had to keep his answers as short as possible.

Renner leaned back in his seat. 'Tell me something. How did you know to call Wainwright?'

'Because he's the landlord.'

'Yes, but how did you know that?'

Pierce froze. He knew he could not give an answer that referred to the address book or mail he had taken. 'Um, I think . . . no, yeah, it was written down somewhere on the desk in her house. Like a note.'

'You mean like a note that was out in the open.'

'Yeah, I think so I . . .' Again he stopped himself before he gave Renner something else to club him with. Pierce lowered his eyes.

'Mr Pierce, I just came from that house over on Altair and I looked all through that desk. I didn't see any note.'

Pierce nodded. 'You know what it was, it was my own note I was picturing. I wrote it after I talked to Vivian. She was the one who told me about Wainwright.'

'Vivian? Who is Vivian?'

'Lilly's mother. In Tampa, Florida. She asked me to look for Lilly and gave me some contacts. That's where I got Wainwright's name.'

'This is all new information, Mr Pierce. You are now saying that Lilly Quinlan's mother asked you to look for her daughter?'

'Yes. She said the cops weren't doing anything. She asked me to do what I could.'

'And the mother had the name of her daughter's landlord?'

'Well, I think she got a bunch of names from a private detective she had previously hired to look for Lilly.'

'A private detective. Do you have his name?'

'Glass.'

'What about Vivian in Tampa? How did you know to contact her there?'

Pierce coughed. Renner had trapped him again. He now saw only one way out. He had to give her name. He told himself that Renner would eventually get to her on his own anyway. Lilly Quinlan's site was linked to hers. The connection was inevitable. At least by giving it now he might be able to control it. Tell them just enough to get out of there, then call her and warn her. 'A girl named Robin,' he said.

'Well, well, another new name,' Renner said. 'Tell me, Mr Pierce, who is Robin?'

'On Lilly Quinlan's web page she mentions another girl she works with called Robin. There's a link from Lilly's page to Robin's. I went to the page and called Robin's number. I was able to convince her that I wanted to make sure everything was all right. She couldn't help me much. She said she thought Lilly might have gone home to Tampa where her mother lived. So I called information in Tampa and got phone numbers for people named Quinlan. That led me to Vivian.'

Renner nodded. 'OK, thank you. Almost there, Mr Pierce.' Renner's eyes dropped to the statement again.

'I don't understand. What else is there to talk about?'

Renner's eyes came to Pierce's without any movement of his head or face. 'Well, your name came up a couple of times on the computer. I thought maybe we'd talk about that.'

Pierce felt his face flush with heat. And anger. The long-ago arrest was supposed to have been erased from his record. *Expunged* was the legal term. He had completed the probation and did the forty hours of public service. That was a long time ago. How did Renner know?

'You're talking about the thing up in Palo Alto?' he asked. 'I was never officially charged. It was diverted. I was suspended from school a semester. I did public service. That was it.'

'Arrested on suspicion of impersonating a police officer.'

'It was almost fifteen years ago. I was in college. I was on the phone, trying to get some information. I acted like I was a campus cop so I could get a phone number. That was it.'

'A phone number for who?'

'A professor. I wanted his home number and it was unlisted.'

'The report says you and your friends used the number to persecute the professor. To pull an elaborate prank on him.'

'It was harmless but they had to make an example of us. We were all suspended and got community service but what we had done was minor.'

After a moment Renner continued. 'That arrest came a year after your name came up on a crime report here. It's on the computer.'

Pierce started to shake his head. 'No. I've never been arrested for anything down here. Just that time up at Stanford.'

'I didn't say you were arrested. I said your name's on a crime report. Everything's on computer now. You're a hacker, you know that. You throw in a name and sometimes it's amazing what comes out.'

'I am not a hacker. It must be a different Henry Pierce.'

'I don't think so. Did you have a sister named Isabelle Pierce?'

Pierce froze. He was amazed that Renner had made the connection.

'The victim of a homicide. May nineteen-eighty-eight.'

All Pierce could do was nod. It was like a bandage being ripped off an open wound. Then he came out of his thoughts and looked at Renner. 'Yes, my sister. What about it? What's it got to do with this?'

'She was older than you, wasn't she?'

'A few years.'

'She was a runaway. You used to go look for her, didn't you? Says so on the computer. At night. With your dad. He'd—'

'Stepfather.'

'Stepfather, then. He'd send you into the abandoned buildings to look because you were a kid and the kids in those squats didn't run from another kid. That's what the report says. Says you never found her. Nobody did, until it was too late.'

Pierce folded his arms and leaned across the table. 'Look, is there a point to this? Because I would really like to get out of here.'

'The point is you went searching for a lost girl once before, Mr Pierce. Makes me wonder if you're not trying to make up for something with this girl Lilly. You know what I mean?'

'No,' Pierce said in a voice that sounded small, even to himself.

Renner nodded. 'OK, Mr Pierce, you can go.'

Pierce stood up and walked to the door. He thought of something before leaving. 'Where's my car?'

'Your car? I guess it's wherever you left it. Go to the front desk. They'll call a cab for you.'

As he walked through the deserted squad room to the exit, Pierce checked his watch. It was twelve thirty. He knew he had to get to Robin before Renner did but her number was in the backpack in his car. And as he approached the front counter he realised he had no money for a cab. He had given every dollar he had on him to Robin. He turned and walked out of the police station. On Venice Boulevard he started jogging west towards the beach.

As PIERCE CAME down the alley to his car he saw that Lilly Quinlan's apartment was still a hive of police activity. Several cars were clogging the alley and a mobile light had been set up to spray the front of the apartment with illumination.

He noticed Renner standing out front, conversing with his partner. It meant Renner had probably driven right by Pierce on his way back to the crime scene and had not noticed him or had decided not to offer him a ride, probably the latter. A cop on the street, even at night, would notice a man jogging in full dress.

When Renner and his partner went back inside the apartment, Pierce unlocked his BMW and slipped in. As he gently closed the door he realised the ceiling light was off. He thought it must have burned out because it was set to come on when the door was open. He reached up and tapped the button anyway and nothing happened. He tapped it again and the light came on.

He sat for a long moment, considering this. The light had a three-setting cycle controlled by pushing the button. The first position engaged the light when the door was open. The light would fade out about fifteen seconds after the door was closed or with the ignition of the car, whichever came first. The second position turned the light on full time, and the third turned it off full time.

Pierce knew he always kept the light set on the first position, so the interior would be lit when he opened the door. That had not occurred when he got into the car. The light had to have been in the third position of the cycle. Someone must have been in his car and changed the setting.

Suddenly panicked by this realisation, he reached between the front seats to the rear foot space. His hand found his backpack. He pulled it forward and made a quick check of its contents. His notepads were still there. Nothing seemed missing. He knew that the leather backpack was probably the most expensive thing in the car, yet it had not been taken. He concluded that the car had been searched not burglarised. That explained why it had been relocked. A car burglar wouldn't have bothered to disguise what had happened.

He looked up at the lighted doorway of the apartment and knew what had happened. The police had searched his car.

The searcher would have opened the door, probably with a professional window-channel device, entered the car and closed the door, the overhead light going out on its timer delay. The searcher would have pushed the overhead button to turn the light back on. When the search was completed he would have pushed the button again to turn the light off, leaving it in the third cycle position.

He knew then why Renner had not given him a ride. He had wanted to beat Pierce back to the scene and search his car.

The search would have been illegal without his permission but Pierce wasn't angry. He knew there was nothing in the car that incriminated him. He started the car and headed home.

At his apartment ten minutes later he lifted the phone and got the broken dial tone indicating he had messages. Before checking them he hit the redial button because he knew the last call he had made had been to Robin. The call went to voicemail without a ring, indicating she had turned the phone off or was on a call.

'Listen, Robin, it's me, Henry Pierce. After you left I found the door to Lilly's apartment open. The landlord was in there clearing the place out. We found what looked like blood on the bed and had to call the cops. I pretty much kept you—'

The beep sounded and he was cut off. He hit redial again, wondering why she had set such a short message window on her phone service. After one ring the phone was picked up by the real Robin. Her voice was sleepy.

'Robin?'

'Yeah, Henry?'

'Yes, don't hang up. I was just leaving you a message. I—'

'Did you get mine?'

'No. I just got home. I've been with the cops all night. Listen, like I was trying to say on the message, the cops are going to be calling you. I didn't say you brought me there or anything else. But when they asked me how I knew Lilly's mother was in Tampa, I told them you told me. It was the only way out. For me, I admit, but I didn't think it would be a problem for you. I mean, your pages are linked. They would have got around to talking to you anyway.'

'It's OK.'

He was silent for a moment, surprised by her reaction. 'I told them I convinced you I wanted to find Lilly to make sure she was OK and that you believed me and that's why you told me things about her.'

'You know, you did convince me. That's why I called and left a message. Good thing I have caller ID and had your number. I wanted to tell you I was sorry about what I said in that alley.'

'Don't worry about it.'

'Thanks.'

'Look,' Pierce said. 'The mattress in that place . . . There was a lot of blood. I don't know what happened to Lilly but if she was trying to get out of the business . . . I know you're afraid of Billy Wentz but you should be more than that, Robin. Whatever you do, be careful.'

She didn't say anything.

'You have to get away from him and that business. But, listen, when you do, don't tell a soul about it. Just disappear without them knowing. I think that might have been the mistake Lilly made. She might've told him or told somebody that took it back to him.'

'And you think he did this? She made him money. Why would he—?'

'I don't know what to think. It could've been the person she was with before she was supposed to meet you. It could've been a lot of things. All I'm saying is that it's a dangerous world you work in, Robin. You should get out of it and be careful when you do.'

'It's not so easy, you know. Quitting. I make a lot of money doing this. What should I do, work at McDonald's?'

'Robin? I don't even know your last name.'

'LaPorte. And my name isn't Robin, either.'

'What is it?'

'Lucy.'

'Well . . . Lucy, if I can call you that. When you're ready to walk away from that life, you call me and I'll do everything I can to help you do it. Money, job, an apartment, whatever you need, just call me and you've got it. I'll do what I can.'

'It's because of your sister that you'd do it, isn't it?'

'I don't know. Probably.'

'I don't care. Thank you, Henry.'

'OK, Lucy. I think I'm going to crash now. It's been a long day and I'm tired. I'm sorry I woke you up.'

'Don't worry about it. And don't worry about the cops. I'll handle them.'

'Thanks. Good night.' He hung up and then picked up the phone again to listen to the message from Lucy LaPorte.

'Hey, it's Robin. Look, I just wanted to say I'm sorry about what I said to you at the end. I can tell you care about Lilly and want to make sure she's OK. Maybe I acted the way I did because I wish there was somebody in the world that cared that way about me. So anyway, that's it. Give me a call sometime if you want. We can just hang out. And next time I won't make you buy a smoothie. Bye.'

For some reason he saved the message.

SIX

At exactly noon on Sunday the phone woke Pierce up. A man said, 'Is it too early to speak to Lilly?'

Pierce said, 'No, actually it's too late.' He hung up and groaned as the memory of the night before poked into his thoughts. He climbed out of the sleeping-bag and off the bed to take a long, hot shower.

By the time he was dressed his stomach was loudly demanding food but there was nothing in the kitchen, he had no money and his ATM card was tapped out until Monday. He knew he could go to a restaurant or a grocery store and use a credit card but that would take too long. He had come out of the baptism of the shower with a desire to put the Lilly Quinlan episode behind him and let the police handle it. He had to get back to work. And he knew that any delay in getting to Amedeo might undermine his resolve.

By one o'clock he was entering the offices. On his desk he kept a coffee mug full of spare change. Before beginning work he dropped his backpack on the desk, grabbed the mug and took the stairs down to the second floor where snack and soda machines were located. He almost emptied the mug buying two Cokes, two bags of potato crisps and a pack of cookies.

One bag of crisps was empty by the time he got back to the office. Pierce opened the other and popped one of the Cokes open after sliding behind the desk. He removed the new batch of patent applications from the safe below his desk. Jacob Kaz was an excellent patent attorney but he always needed the scientists to back-read the introductions and summaries of the legal applications. Pierce always had the final sign-off on the patents.

Pierce ate two of the cookies, hoping the sugar charge would help him to focus. He began reviewing the applications. This batch was for protection of a formula for cellular energy conversion. In layman's terms, Amedeo was seeking patent protection for a power supply system for the biological robots that would one day patrol the bloodstreams of human beings and destroy pathogens.

They called the formula Proteus in a nod to the movie *Fantastic Voyage*. In the 1966 film a medical team is placed in a submarine called the *Proteus*, then miniaturised with a shrink ray and injected into a man's body to search for and destroy an inoperable blood clot in the brain.

The film was science fiction. But the idea of attacking pathogens within the body with biological or cellular robots not too distant in imagination from the Proteus was on the far horizon of science fact.

Since the inception of nanotechnology the potential medical applications were always the sexiest side of the science. More intriguing than a quantum leap in computing power was the potential of curing cancer, AIDS, all diseases. The possibility of patrolling devices in the body that could identify and eliminate pathogens through chemical reaction was the Holy Grail of the science.

The bottleneck, however—the thing that kept this side of the science on the theoretical side—was the question of a power supply. How to move these molecular submarines through the blood with a power source that was compatible with the body's immune system.

Pierce along with Larraby, his immunology researcher, had discovered a rudimentary yet reliable formula. Using the host's own cells—

in this case Pierce's were harvested and replicated for research in an incubator—the two researchers developed a combination of proteins that would bind with the cell and draw an electrical stimulus from it. That meant power to drive the nanodevice could come from within and therefore be compatible with the body's immune system.

The application package was ready to go in Pierce's opinion. He was excited. He knew that floating a patent application package like this into the nano-world would bring a raft of publicity and a subsequent rise in investor interest. The plan was to show the discovery to Maurice Goddard first and lock down his investment, then submit to the application process. If all went well, Goddard would realise he had a short lead and a short window of opportunity and would act accordingly, signing up as the company's main funding source.

Pierce wrote a congratulatory note to Jacob Kaz on a yellow Post-It and attached it to the cover sheet of the Proteus application package. He then locked it back in the safe. He'd have it sent by secure transport to Kaz's office in Century City in the morning.

The phone rang. Pierce picked up the receiver.

'Mr Pierce?'

'Yes?'

'It's Philip Glass. You called me yesterday?'

The private investigator. Pierce had forgotten.

'Oh. Yes, yes. Thanks for calling back.'

'I didn't get the message until today. What can I do for you?'

'I want to talk to you about Lilly Quinlan. She's missing. Her mother hired you a few weeks ago. From Florida.'

'Yes, but I am no longer employed on that one.'

'I understand that. But I was wondering if I could talk to you about it. I have Vivian Quinlan's permission. You can check with her if you want. You still have her number?'

'Yes, but can you tell me what your interest is in all this?'

'Well, I want to find her.'

This was met with silence and Pierce decided to press his case.

'I'm a friend of the family,' he lied. 'Vivian asked me to see what I could find out.'

'Have you talked to the LAPD?'

Pierce knew that Glass's cooperation might be riding on his answer. He thought about the events of the night before and wondered if they could already be known by Glass. He decided it was too soon. 'No,' he lied again. 'My understanding was that the LAPD wasn't interested.'

'Who do you work for, Mr Pierce?'

'No one. Myself, actually.'

'You're a private investigator?'

'No, I'm a research chemist. I don't see what this has to do with—'

'I can see you today. But not at my office.'

'OK, then where? When?'

'One hour from now. Do you know a place in Santa Monica called Cathode Ray's?'

'On 18th, right? I'll be there. How will be know each other?'

'Do you have a hat or something distinctive to wear?'

Pierce opened a desk drawer. He pulled out a baseball cap. 'I'll be wearing a grey baseball cap. It says "Moles" in blue above the brim.'

'Moles? As in the small burrowing animal?'

'As in molecules. The Fighting Moles was the name of the company's softball team. When we had one. It was a long time ago.'

'I'll see you at Cathode Ray's, Mr Pierce. Please come alone. If I feel you are not alone or it looks like a set-up, you won't see me.'

'A set-up? What are you—?'

Glass hung up and Pierce was listening to dead space.

He put the phone down and put the hat on. He thought about what the private detective had said and how he had said it. Pierce realised it was almost as if he had been scared of something.

CATHODE RAY'S was a hangout for the tech generation—usually everybody in the place had a laptop or a personal organiser on the table next to their double latte. The place was open twenty-four hours and provided power and phone and high-speed jacks at every table. Pierce thought it was an odd choice for a meeting. Glass sounded like an older man over the telephone, his voice gravelly and tired. He would stand out.

At three o'clock Pierce entered Cathode Ray's and took a quick scan around the place. No one stood out. No one looked at him. He got in line for coffee. Before leaving the office he had dumped what change remained in his desk mug into his pocket. He had just enough for a basic coffee, medium size.

After hitting the cup with cream and sugar he moved out to the patio area and selected an empty table in the corner. He sipped his coffee slowly but it was twenty minutes before he was approached by a short man in black jeans and a black T-shirt. He had dark, deep-set eyes and was younger than Pierce had guessed, late thirties at the most. He had no coffee; he had come straight to the table.

'Mr Pierce?'

Pierce offered his hand. 'Mr Glass, I presume. Do you want to get a coffee before we start to talk?'

'No, I don't use caffeine.'

'Then I guess we should get to it. What's with the "make sure you're alone" stuff? It seems a little strange.'

Glass nodded. 'What do you know about Lilly Quinlan?'

'I know she was an escort. She advertised through the Internet. I'm pretty sure she worked for a guy named Billy Wentz. He's sort of a digital pimp.'

'Have you spoken to Mr Wentz yourself?'

Pierce shook his head. 'I went to Entrepreneurial Concepts yesterday—that's his umbrella company—but he wasn't there. Why do I feel like I am telling you things you already know? Look, I want to ask questions here, not answer them.'

'There is little I can tell you. I specialise in missing persons investigations. I was recommended to Vivian Quinlan by someone I know in the LAPD's missing persons unit. She paid me for a week's work. I didn't find Lilly or much else about her disappearance.'

Pierce considered this. He was an amateur and had found out quite a bit in less than forty-eight hours. He doubted Glass was as inept as he was presenting himself to be. 'Did you talk to Lucy LaPorte?'

'Who?'

'She uses the name Robin. Her web page is linked to Lilly's.'

'Oh, yes, Robin. I spoke to her on the phone. She wasn't cooperative.'

Pierce was suspicious of whether Glass had really called. It seemed to him Lucy would have mentioned to him that an investigator had already inquired about Lilly. He planned to check with her about the supposed call.

'How long ago was that? The call to Robin.'

Glass shrugged. 'Three weeks. It was at the beginning of my week of work.'

'Did you go see her?'

'No, other things came up. And at the end of the week Mrs Quinlan was not willing to pay me for further work on the case. That was it for me.'

'You talked to Wentz, didn't you?'

Glass looked down at his folded arms but didn't reply.

'What did he tell you?'

Glass cleared his throat. 'Listen to me very carefully, Mr Pierce. You want to stay clear of Billy Wentz.'

'Why?'

'Because he is a dangerous man. You could get very seriously hurt if you are not careful.'

'Is that what happened to you. Did you get hurt? Did he threaten you?'

Glass shook his head. 'Forget about me. I came here today to try to help you. To warn you about how close you are to the fire. Stay away from Wentz. I can't stress that enough. *Stay away.*'

Pierce could see in his eyes the sincerity of the warning. And the fear.

'OK,' he said. 'I'll keep clear.'

PIERCE TOYED with the idea of going back to the lab after his coffee with Glass but ultimately admitted to himself that the conversation with the private detective had stunted the motivation he had felt only an hour before. Instead he went to the Lucky Market on Ocean Park Boulevard and filled a shopping cart with food and other basics he would need in the new apartment. He paid with a credit card and loaded the numerous bags into the trunk of his BMW. It wasn't until he was in his parking space in the garage at The Sands that he realised he would have to make at least three trips up and down the elevator to get all his purchases into the apartment.

On the first trip he took the new plastic laundry basket he had bought and filled it with six bags of groceries, including all the cold products he wanted to get into the refrigerator first.

As he came into the elevator alcove two men were standing by the door to the storage area. At the elevator one of the men pushed the call button. Pierce exchanged nods with them and guessed that they might be a gay couple. One man was in his forties with a small build and a spreading waist. He wore pointed-toe boots that gave him two extra inches in the heel. The other man was much younger, taller and harder, yet he seemed to defer in body language to his older partner.

When the elevator door opened they allowed Pierce to step on first and then the smaller man asked him what floor he wanted.

After the door closed Pierce noticed that the man did not push another button after pressing 12 for him. 'You guys live on twelve?' he asked. 'I just moved in a few days ago.'

'Visitors,' said the smaller one.

Pierce nodded. He turned his attention to the flashing numbers above the door. Maybe it was being so close in time to the warning from Glass or the way the smaller man kept stealing glances at Pierce in the reflection in the chrome trim on the door, but as the elevator rose so did his anxiety. He remembered how they had been standing near the storage room door and only approached the elevator when he did. As if they had been waiting there for a reason. Or for some person.

The elevator finally reached twelve and the door slid open. The men stepped to the side to allow Pierce to get out first. Both hands holding the laundry basket, Pierce nodded forward.

'You guys go ahead,' he said. 'Can you punch the first floor for me? I forgot to get the mail.'

Nobody moved. The three of them stood there looking at each other until the door started to close and the big man reached out and hit the bumper with a hard forearm. The door shuddered and slowly reopened. And finally the smaller one spoke.

'Fuck the mail, Henry. You're getting off here. Am I right, Six-Eight?'

Without answering, the man obviously named because of his height grabbed Pierce and hurled him into the twelfth-floor hallway. Pierce's momentum took him across the hall and crashing into a closed door marked ELECTRICAL. He felt his breath blast out of his lungs and the laundry basket slipped from his grasp.

'Easy, now, easy. Keys, Six-Eight.'

Pierce's breath had still not returned. The one called Six-Eight moved towards him and with one hand pressed him back against the door. He slapped his pants pockets with the other. When he felt the keys his hand dived into the pocket and pulled out the key ring. He handed it to the other man.

With the smaller man leading the way—and knowing the way— Pierce was pushed down the hall towards his apartment. When he got his breath back he started to say something but the bigger man's hand came around from behind and covered his face and his words.

The small one held up a finger. 'Not yet. Let's get inside so we don't disturb the neighbours more than we have to.'

They got to the door and the smaller man opened it with the key. Six-Eight pushed Pierce into the apartment and shoved him down on the couch. He then stepped away and the other man took a position in front of Pierce. He noticed the phone on the arm of the couch and picked it up. Pierce watched him play with the buttons and go through the caller ID directory.

'Been busy, Henry,' he said as he scrolled the list. 'Philip Glass . . .' He looked back at Six-Eight, who was standing near the apartment's front hallway, his massive arms folded across his chest. 'Isn't that the guy we had a discussion with a couple weeks back?'

Six-Eight nodded. Pierce realised that Glass must have called the apartment number before reaching him at Amedeo.

The small man went back to the phone read-out and soon his eyes lit on another familiar listing. 'Oh, so now Robin's calling *you*. That's wonderful.'

But Pierce could tell by the man's voice that it wasn't wonderful, that it was going to be anything but wonderful for Lucy LaPorte. 'It's nothing,' he said. 'She just left a message. I can play it for you if you want. I kept it.'

'You falling in love with her, are you?'

'No.'

The smaller guy turned and gave a false smile to Six-Eight. Then suddenly he hit Pierce with the phone on the bridge of his nose, delivering a blow with the full power of the sweeping arc.

Pierce saw a flash of red and black cross his vision and a searing pain screamed through his head. He fell back onto the couch. He couldn't tell if his eyes were closed or he'd gone blind. Then strong, large hands clamped around his arms and he was pulled upright.

He could feel himself being hoisted over Six-Eight's shoulders and carried. He felt his mouth filling with blood and he struggled to open his eyes but still couldn't do it. He heard the rolling sound of the balcony's sliding door, then felt the cool air from the ocean touching his skin.

Suddenly the hard shoulder that had been in his gut was gone and he started a head-first free fall. His muscles tightened and his mouth opened to emit the final furious sound of his life. Then, at last, he felt the huge hands grab his ankles and hold. His head and shoulders slammed hard against the rough concrete of the textured exterior of the building. But at least he was no longer falling.

Pierce brought his hands to his face and touched his nose and eyes. His nose was split vertically and horizontally and was bleeding profusely. He managed to wipe his eyes and open them partially. Twelve storeys below he could see the green lawn of the beachside park. There were people on blankets down there, most of them homeless.

He saw his blood falling in thick drops into the trees directly below.

Then the hands that held his ankles shook violently, bouncing him off the outside wall again.

'Do I have your attention?'

Pierce spat out a mouthful of blood and said, 'Yes.'

'Good. I suppose by now you know who I am.'

'I think so. What do you want?'

'What do I want? Well, first I wanted to get a look at you. And then I wanted to give you a message. Six-Eight.'

Pierce was suddenly hoisted up. Still upside-down, his face had come up to the open bars of the balcony railing. Through the bars he saw that the talker had squatted down so they were face to face.

'What I wanted to say was that not only did you get the wrong number, you got the wrong world. And you've got thirty seconds to decide whether you want to go back to where you came from or go on to the next world. You understand what I'm saying to you?'

Pierce started to cough. 'I . . . unnerstan . . . I'm done.'

'You're damn right you're done. I ought to have my man drop your stupid ass right here and now but I don't need the heat so I'm not going to do that. But if I catch you sneaking and sniffing around again, you're gonna get dropped. OK?'

Pierce nodded. The man Pierce was pretty sure was Billy Wentz then reached a hand between the bars and patted Pierce's cheek.

'Be good now.' He stood up and gave a signal to Six-Eight.

Pierce was pulled back over the railing and dropped onto the balcony's floor. He broke the fall with his hands and then pushed his way into the corner. Straddling the edge of consciousness, he tried to shake off the encroaching clouds. It occurred to him that, the threat to himself aside, it was important to try to protect Lucy LaPorte.

'What about Lucy? What are you going to do?'

'Lucy? Who the fuck is Lucy?'

'I mean, Robin.'

'Oh, our little Robin. You know, that's a good question, Henry. Cause Robin's a good earner. I have to be prudent. Rest assured that whatever we do to her, we won't leave marks and she'll be back, good as new, in two, three weeks at the most.'

'Leave her alone,' Pierce said as forcefully as he could. 'I used her and she didn't even know it.'

The small man looked at Six-Eight and smiled, then shook his head. 'Do you believe this? Telling me like that?'

He turned back towards Pierce, took one step towards him and then swiftly brought his other foot up into a vicious kick. The pointed toe of the boot struck Pierce on the right side of the rib cage. Burning pain spread across his chest.

Wentz leaned down over him. 'Don't you dare tell me how to run my business.' He straightened up. 'And one other thing. You tell anybody about our little discussion here today and there will be consequences. Dire consequences. For you. For Robin. For the people you love. Do you understand?'

Pierce weakly nodded.

'Good. Then let's go, Six-Eight.'

And Pierce was left alone, gulping for breath and clarity, trying to stay in the light when he sensed darkness closing in all around.

PIERCE GRABBED A T-SHIRT out of a box in the bedroom to hold to his face to try to stop the bleeding. He went into the bathroom and saw himself in the mirror. His face was already ballooning and changing colour. The swelling of his nose was crowding his vision and widening the wounds on his nose and around his left eye. Most of the bleeding seemed to be internal, a steady stream of thick blood going down the back of his throat. He knew he had to get to a hospital but he had to warn Lucy LaPorte first.

He found the phone on the living-room floor. He tried to go to the caller ID directory but the screen remained blank. He tried the on button but couldn't get a dial tone. The phone was broken.

Holding the shirt to his face, involuntary tears streaming out of his eyes, Pierce looked about the apartment for the box holding the earthquake kit he had ordered for delivery with the furniture. He knew it contained a basic phone that did not use electric current. It simply needed to be jacked into the wall and it would work.

He found the box in the bedroom closet and found the phone and took it to the bedroom wall jack next to the bed. He got a dial tone. Now all he needed was Robin's number.

He had it in a notebook in his backpack in his car. He didn't think he could make it down there without passing out.

So he called information for Venice and tried the name Lucy LaPorte, asking the operator to check under various spellings. But there was no number, unlisted or otherwise.

He thought of something and tried Charlie Condon's office and home but got machines at both numbers. He thought about Cody

Zeller but knew he never answered his phone. The only way to reach him was by page and then he would be at the mercy of waiting for a call back.

He knew what he had to do. He punched in the number and waited. After four rings Nicole answered.

'It's me. I need your help. Can you go to—?'

'Who is this?'

'Me, Henry.'

'It doesn't sound like you. What are you—?'

'Nicki!' he shouted. 'Listen to me. This is an emergency and I need your help. I can explain after.'

'OK,' she said in a tone that indicated she wasn't convinced. 'What is the emergency?'

'Go to your computer. Hurry go!'

When she got to the computer she switched to a headset she kept at the desk.

'OK, I need you to go to a web site. It's LA dash darlings dot com.'

'Are you kidding me? Is this some—?'

'Just do it! Or somebody might die!'

'OK, OK. LA dash darlings . . . OK, I'm there.'

He tried to visualise the web site on her screen. 'OK, double click the escorts folder and go to blondes.' He waited. 'You got it?'

'I'm going as fast as—OK, now what?'

'Scroll through the thumbnails. Click on the one named Robin.' Again he waited. He realised his breathing was loud, a low whistle coming out of his throat.

'OK, I've got Robin. Those tits have gotta be fake.'

'Just give me the number.'

She read off the number and Pierce recognised it.

'I'll call you back.'

He disconnected the call and got a new dial tone. He called the number for Robin. He was getting lightheaded. What was left of his vision was starting to blur round the edges. After five rings his call went to voicemail. He didn't know what to do. He couldn't send police to her. He didn't even know where her real home was. The message signal beeped after her greeting. As he spoke his tongue started to feel like it was too big for his mouth.

'Lucy, it's Henry. Wentz came here. He messed me up and I think he's going to see you next. If you get this message get out of there. Right now! Just get the hell out of there and call me when you get somewhere safe.' He added his number to the message and hung up.

He held the bloody shirt back up to his face and leaned back against the wall. The deep throb of pain was penetrating his whole body. It seemed as though every muscle and joint was aching. His face felt like a neon sign pulsing with rhythmic bursts of searing fire.

The phone rang and he raised it back to his ear.

'Lo?'

'It's Nicki. Can you talk? Is everything all right?'

'No, ehry'ing's nah all ri.'

'What's wrong? Why are you talking funny? Why did you need the number of *that* woman?'

'Lohn story and I gah . . . I . . .' He felt himself fading out but as he started to roll off the wall to the floor the angle of his body sent jabbing pain through his chest and he groaned.

'Henry! Are you hurt? Henry! Can you hear me?'

Pierce slid his hips down along the rug until he could lie flat. The phone was on the carpet next to his head. He could hear the tinny sound of a far-off voice calling his name. Then the voice drifted off and there was only darkness. And he liked the darkness.

WHEN HE REGAINED consciousness, Pierce was lying in an ambulance and Nicole was sitting next to him. He tried to speak and his voice sounded like a muffled echo.

A paramedic leaned into his field of vision, looking down at him. 'Don't speak,' she said. 'You've got a mask on.'

He tried again, this time speaking as loudly as he could. Again it was muffled.

The paramedic leaned in again and lifted the breathing mask. 'Hurry, what is it? You can't take this off.'

He looked past her arm at Nicole. 'Gaw Lucy. Geh er ow a dare.'

Nicole leaned close to him and spoke. 'Lucy? Who's Lucy, Henry?'

'I me . . . Robin. Gaw er.'

Nicole nodded. She got it. The mask was put back over his mouth and nose.

Clarity came and went over the next two hours as he was taken into the ER, examined by a doctor, treated and then admitted into the hospital. His head finally cleared and he woke in a private hospital room. He looked round and saw Nicole sitting on a chair.

'Ni'i,' he said in a hoarse voice. 'Thas . . .' It was still hard to make the K sound without pain. 'Where am I?'

She stood up and came to his side. 'St John's. Henry, what happened? The police got there before I did. They said these people on the beach called on their cellphones and said two guys were hanging somebody over the balcony. You, Henry. There's blood on the outside wall.'

Pierce looked at her through swollen eyes. The swelling of the bridge of his nose and the gauze on the wound split his vision in half. He remembered what Wentz said right before he left. 'I dohn remember. Wha else di dey say?'

'They started knocking on doors in the building and when they got to yours it was wide open. You were in the bedroom. I got there when they were taking you out. A detective was here. He wants to talk to you.'

'I don't remember anything.' He said it with as much force as he could. It was getting easier to talk. All he had to do was practise.

'Henry, what kind of trouble are you in?'

'I don't know.'

'Who is Robin? And Lucy? Who are they?'

He suddenly remembered he needed to warn her. 'How long have I been here?'

'A couple hours.'

'Gi' me your phone. I've got to phone her.'

'I've been calling that number every ten minutes. I keep getting voicemail.'

A man in a doctor's coat came through the door. He had a clipboard. He was in his late fifties with silver hair and matching beard.

'This is Doctor Hansen,' Nicole said.

'How are you feeling?' the doctor asked.

'Only hurts when I breathe. Or talk.'

'Well, you've got some pretty substantial injuries here. You have a grade two concussion, two fractured ribs and of course the broken nose. The lacerations on your nose and surrounding your eye are going to require plastic surgery to close properly without permanent scarring. I can get somebody in here to do that tonight. Try to stay as horizontal as possible.' The doctor nodded and left the room.

Pierce looked at Nicole. 'Looks like I'm going to be here a while. You don't have to stay.'

'I don't mind.'

He smiled and it hurt but he smiled anyway. He was very happy with her response.

SEVEN

Pierce came out of a murky dream about freefalling while blind-folded and not knowing how far he was falling. When he finally hit the ground he opened his eyes and Detective Renner was there.

'You.'

'Yeah, me again. How are you feeling, Mr Pierce?'

'I'm fine. Why are you here? I don't remember what happened. I have a concussion, you know.'

Renner nodded. 'Oh, I know all about your injuries. The nurse told me the plastic surgeon put a hundred and sixty micro stitches across your nose and round that eye yesterday morning.'

Pierce raised his hand and gently touched the bridge of his nose. There was no gauze. He could feel the zipper of stitches and the puffi-ness. He tried to remember things. The last thing he could clearly recall was the plastic surgeon hovering over him with a bright light. After that he had been in and out, floating through the darkness.

'What time is it?'

'Three fifteen.'

There was bright light coming through the window shades. He knew it wasn't the middle of the night.

'It's Monday? No, it's Tuesday?'

'That's what it said in the paper today.'

Pierce felt physically strong—he had probably been asleep for more than fifteen straight hours. 'What do you want?'

'Well, first of all, let me read you your rights.' The detective pulled the sliding food tray over the bed and placed a minirecorder down on it. 'Now I'm going to record everything from here on out.' He pressed a button on the recorder and a red light came on. He announced his name, the time and date and the location of the inter-view. He identified Pierce and read him his constitutionally guaran-teed rights from a little card he took from his wallet. 'Now, do you understand these rights as I have read them to you?'

'Yes, I understand my rights.'

'Good. Now is it all right if I ask you a few questions?'

'Am I a suspect?'

'A suspect in what?'

'I don't know. You tell me.'

'Well, that's the thing, isn't it? Hard to tell what we've got here.'

'Have you found Lilly Quinlan?'

'We're working on it. You don't know where she is, do you?'

Pierce shook his head and the movement made his head feel a little sloshy. He waited for it to subside before speaking. 'No. I wish I did. Was it her blood on the bed?'

'We're still working on it. Preliminary tests showed it was human blood. But we have no sample from Lilly Quinlan to compare it to. I think I've got a line on her doctor. We'll see what records and possible samples he has. Now, what about this girl Robin that you mentioned before? Have you talked to her?'

'No. Have you?'

'No, we haven't been able to locate her. We got her number off the web site like you said. But all we get is a message.'

Pierce felt the bottom drop out of his stomach. Nicole had tried to reach Lucy repeatedly and was also unsuccessful. Wentz might have got to her—or maybe even still had her.

He realised he had to make a decision. He could dance around with Renner and continue to hold up a veil of lies in order to protect himself. Or he could try to help Lucy. 'Did you trace the number?'

'It's a cellphone.'

'What about the billing address?'

'The phone's registered to one of her regular clients. He takes care of the phone for her and the lease on her gig pad and she gives him a free pop every Sunday afternoon while his wife does the shopping. Anyway, she didn't show up yesterday at the pad. We were there. We went with this guy but she didn't show.'

'And he doesn't know where she lives?'

'Nope. She never told him.'

'Shit.' He envisioned Lucy in the hands of Wentz and Six-Eight. He reached up and ran his fingers along the seams in his own face. He hoped she got away. He hoped she was just hiding somewhere.

'Yeah, that's what we said. And the thing is, we don't even have her full name—we got her picture from the web site, if it is her picture, and the name Robin. And I get the feeling neither one is legit.'

'What about going to the web-site office in Hollywood?'

'We did and we caught a lawyer. No cooperation. We need a court order before they'll share client information. And as far as Robin goes, we don't have enough to go talk to a judge about court orders.'

One more time Pierce thought about his choices. Protect himself or help Renner and possibly help Lucy. If it wasn't already too late.

'Turn that off.'

'What, this tape? I can't. This is a formal interview. I'm taping it.'

'Then it's over. But if you turn it off, I think I can tell you some things that will help you.'

Renner clicked a button on the tape recorder and the red record light went off. 'OK, whadaya got?'

'Her name isn't Robin. She told me her name is Lucy LaPorte. You've got to find her. She's in danger. It might already be too late.'

'In danger from who?'

Pierce thought about Wentz's threat. He thought about the warnings from the private investigator, Glass. 'Billy Wentz,' he finally said.

'Wentz again. He's the boogie man in all of this, huh?'

'Look, man, you can believe what I say or not. But just find Robin—I mean, Lucy—and make sure she's OK.'

'That's it? That's all you've got for me?'

'Her web-site picture is legitimate. I saw her.'

Renner nodded. 'When did you see her?'

'Saturday night. She took me to Lilly's apartment but left before I went in. She didn't see anything so I tried to keep her out of it.'

'And if the statement you made before about Wentz being this big bad digital pimp is right, then her showing you the way to Lilly's apartment sort of puts her in harm's way, doesn't it?'

Pierce nodded.

'So you want to talk about what happened on that balcony yesterday? Was it Wentz?'

'I don't remember what happened. I remember I was carrying groceries up to my apartment and then I woke up in the ambulance.'

'Look, if he threatened you, we can protect you.'

'I told you, I don't remember what happened.'

Renner nodded. 'Sure, sure. OK, forget the balcony. Let me ask you something else then. Where did you hide Lilly's body?'

Pierce's eyes widened. 'What? Are you—?'

'Where is it, Pierce? What did you do with her? And what did you do with Lucy LaPorte?'

A cold feeling of fear began to rise in Pierce's chest. He looked at Renner and knew the detective was deadly serious. And he knew suddenly that he wasn't a suspect. He was *the* suspect.

'Are you kidding? You wouldn't even know about this if I hadn't called you people. I was the only one who cared about it.'

'Yeah, and maybe by calling us and traipsing all over that scene and the house you were setting up a nice defence. And maybe the job you had Wentz or one of your other pals do to your face was part of the defence. Poor guy gets his nose smashed for sticking it in the wrong place. It doesn't get my sympathy vote, Mr Pierce.'

'You're wrong,' Pierce said, his voice shaking. 'I didn't do it.'

'Yeah? Am I wrong? Well, let me tell you what I've got. I've got a missing woman and blood on the bed. I've got a bunch of your lies and a bunch of your fingerprints all over the woman's house.'

Pierce closed his eyes. He thought about the house on Altair. He knew he had touched everything. Her closets, her clothes, her mail.

'No . . .' It was all he could think to say.

'No what?'

'This is all a mistake. All I did . . . I mean . . . I got her number. I tried to help her because . . . it was my fault . . . I thought if I . . .'

He didn't finish. The past and present were too close together, one confusing the other, moving in front of the other like an eclipse. He opened his eyes and looked at Renner.

'You thought what?' the detective asked.

'I don't know. I don't want to talk about it.'

'Come on, kid. It's good to unburden. Good for the soul. It's your fault Lilly's dead. What did you mean by that? It was an accident? Tell me how it happened. Maybe I can live with that and we can go to the DA together, work something out.'

Pierce felt fear and danger flooding his mind. 'What are you talking about? Lilly? It's not my fault. I didn't even know her.'

'You said it was your fault.'

'No, you're putting words in my mouth. It's not my fault. I had nothing to do with it.'

He opened his eyes to see Renner reach into his coat pocket and pull out another tape recorder. The red light was on. The detective had taped the whole conversation.

Renner clicked the reverse button for a few seconds and then jockeyed around with the recording until he found what he wanted. He replayed what Pierce had said moments before.

'This is all a mistake. All I did . . . I mean . . . I got her number. I tried to help her because . . . it was my fault . . . I thought if I . . .'

The detective looked at Pierce with a smug smile on his face.

'No,' Pierce said. 'I wasn't talking about her. About Lilly Quinlan.

I was talking about my sister. I was—'

'We were talking about Lilly Quinlan and you said it was your fault. That is an admission, my friend.' Renner leaned over the bed until his face was only inches from Pierce's. 'Where is she, Pierce? You know this is inevitable, so let's get it over with now. Tell me what you did with her.'

'Get out. I want a lawyer.'

Renner straightened up and smiled in a knowing way. 'Of course you want a lawyer. And you're going to need one. I'm going to the DA, Pierce. I've already got you on obstruction and breaking and entering for starters. Got you there cold. But I want the big one. As soon as that body turns up, it's game over.'

'I'm not talking to you any more. I want you to leave. I want a lawyer.'

Renner nodded and left the room without another word.

Pierce looked around to see if the room had a phone. There was nothing on the side table, but the bed had side railings with electronic buttons for positioning the mattress and controlling the television. He found a phone that snapped out of the right railing.

He made a call to Jacob Kaz, the company's patent lawyer. His call was put through to the attorney immediately.

'Henry, are you OK? I heard you were attacked—'

'It's a long story, Jacob. I'll have to tell you later. What I need from you right now is a criminal defence attorney. Somebody good but who doesn't like getting his face on TV or his name in the papers.'

Pierce knew that containing the situation was going to be as important as possibly defending himself against a murder charge. It had to be handled quickly and discreetly.

Kaz cleared his throat. He gave no indication that Pierce's request was anything other than normal in their professional relationship. 'I think I have a name for you,' he said. 'You'll like her.'

ON WEDNESDAY MORNING Pierce was on the phone to Charlie Condon when a woman in a grey suit walked into his hospital room. She handed him a card that said *Janis Langwiser, Attorney at Law*. He cupped his hand over the phone and told her he was wrapping up the call.

'Charlie, I've got to go. My doctor just came in.'

Pierce clipped the phone back into the bed's side guard. Langwiser put out her hand and he shook it.

'Janis Langwiser. Pleased to meet you.'

'Henry Pierce. I can't say the circumstances make it a pleasure to meet you.'

'That's usually the way it is with this work.'

He had already got her pedigree from Jacob Kaz. Langwiser handled the criminal defence work for a small but influential downtown firm so exclusive, according to Kaz, that it wasn't listed in any phone book. Their clients were A-list, but even people on that list still needed criminal defence from time to time. That's where Langwiser came in. She'd been hired away from the district attorney's office a year earlier. Kaz told Pierce that the firm was taking him as a client as a means of establishing a relationship with him, a relationship that would be mutually beneficial as Amedeo Technologies moved towards going public. Pierce didn't tell Kaz that there would be no eventual public offering or even an Amedeo Technologies if this situation wasn't handled properly.

After polite inquiries about Pierce's injuries and prognosis, Langwiser asked him why he needed a criminal defence attorney.

'Because there is a police detective out there who believes I'm a murderer. He told me he was going to the DA's office to try to charge me with a number of crimes.'

'An LA cop? What's his name?'

'Renner. I don't think he ever told me his first name.'

'Robert. I know him. He works out of Pacific Division.'

'You know him from a case?'

'Early in my career at the DA I filed cases. I filed a few that he brought in. He seemed like a good cop. I think *thorough* is the word I would use. He's going to the DA for a murder charge?'

'He said he was going to charge me with other stuff. Breaking and entering. Obstruction of justice. He'll try to make a case for the murder after that. I don't know how much is bullshit threats and how much he can do. But I didn't kill anybody so I need a lawyer.'

She gestured to his face. 'Is this related to your injuries?'

Pierce nodded.

'Why don't we start at the beginning?'

'Do we have an attorney–client relationship at this point?'

'Yes, we do. You can speak freely.'

Pierce nodded. He spent the next thirty minutes telling her the story in as much detail as he could remember. He told her about everything he had done, including the crimes he had committed.

As he talked, Langwiser took notes on a yellow legal pad. When Pierce had finished telling the story, she went back to the part about what Renner had called an admission from him. She asked several questions about what medications Pierce was on at the time and what ill-effects from the attack and surgery he was feeling. She then asked what he had meant by saying it was his fault.

'I meant my sister Isabelle. She died. A long time ago.'

'Come on, Henry, don't make me guess about this. I want to know.'

He shrugged. 'She ran away from home when we were kids. Then she got killed . . . by some guy. Then he got killed by the police and that . . . was it.'

'OK. So how did that get confused with Lilly Quinlan in your conversation with Detective Renner?'

'Well, I've been thinking about my sister a lot lately. Since this thing with Lilly came up. I think it's the reason I did what I did.'

'You mean you think you're responsible for what happened to your sister? How can that be, Henry?'

'My stepfather and I, we'd go down to Hollywood and look for her. Mostly at night. I would dress up in old clothes so I would look like them—one of the street kids. My stepfather would send me into the places where the kids hid and slept, where they would have sex for money or do drugs . . .'

'Why you? Why didn't your stepfather go in?'

'At the time, he told me that it was because I was a kid and I could fit in and be allowed in. If a man walked into one of those places by himself everybody might run. Then we'd lose her.'

Langwiser waited but then had to prompt him. 'You said at the time he told you that was the reason. What did he tell you later?'

Pierce shook his head. 'Nothing. It's just that . . . I think . . . I mean, she ran away for a reason. The police said she was on drugs but I think that came after. After she was on the street.'

'You think your stepfather was the reason she ran away.'

She said it as a statement and he gave an almost imperceptible nod. He thought about what Vivian Quinlan had said about what her daughter and the woman she knew of as Robin had in common.

'What did he do to her?'

'I don't know and it doesn't matter now.'

'Then why would you say to Renner that it was your fault?'

'Because I didn't find her. All those nights looking for her and I never found her. If only . . .' He said it without any conviction or emphasis. It was a lie. He couldn't tell the truth to this woman he had known for only an hour.

Langwiser looked like she wanted to go further with it but also seemed to know she was already stretching a personal boundary with him. 'OK, Henry. I think it helps to explain things—both your actions in regard to Lilly Quinlan's disappearance and your statement to Renner. I am sorry about your sister. Are your parents alive?'

'My stepfather is, last I heard. I don't talk to him, haven't in a long time. My mother isn't with him any more. She still lives in the Valley. I haven't talked to her in a long time either.'

She nodded. She studied her notes, flipping back the pages on the pad as she reviewed everything he had said from the start of the conversation. Then she finally looked up at him.

'Well, I think it's all bullshit.'

Pierce shook his head. 'No, I'm telling you exactly how it hap—'

'No, I mean Renner. I think he's bullshitting. There's nothing there. He'd get laughed out of the DA's office on the breaking and entering. What was your intent? To steal? No, it was to make sure she was OK. As far as the obstruction goes, people lie and hold back with the police all the time. I can't even remember the last obstruction case that went to court.'

'What about the tape? He said what I said was an admission.'

'He was trying to rattle you and see how you'd react, maybe get a damaging admission out of you. Your explanation in regard to your sister is certainly legitimate, and I'm sure you were under the influence of a variety of medications. Besides, with no body it is very difficult to make a case against anyone—especially in this case when you consider the victim's source of income. She could be anywhere. And if she is dead then the suspect list is going to be very long. I think that unless things change in a big way, you'll be OK, Henry.'

'What big way?'

'Like they find the body and somehow link it to you.'

Pierce shook his head. 'Nothing will link it to me. I never met her.'

'Then good. You should be in the clear.'

'Should be?'

'Nothing is ever a hundred per cent. Especially in the law. We'll still have to wait and see.'

Langwiser reviewed her notes for a few more moments before speaking again. 'OK,' she finally said. 'Let's call Detective Renner.'

'Call him?' Pierce said. 'Why?'

'To put him on notice that you have representation and to see what he has to say for himself.'

She took a cellphone out of her case and opened it. Her call to the Pacific Division was answered quickly and she asked for Renner. It took a few minutes but she finally got him on the line. While she waited she turned the volume up on the phone and angled it from her ear so Pierce could hear both ends of the conversation.

'Hey, Bob, Janis Langwiser. Remember me?'

'Sure,' Renner said. 'I heard you went over to the dark side, though.'

'Very funny. Listen, I'm at St John's. I visited Henry Pierce.'

'Henry Pierce, the Good Samaritan. Long time rescuer of missing whores and lost pets.'

'You're just full of good humour today, Bob,' she said drily.

'Henry Pierce is the joker, the stories he tells.'

'Well, that's why I'm calling. No more stories from Henry, Bob. I am representing him and he's no longer talking to you. You blew the chance you had.'

'I didn't blow anything,' Renner protested. 'Anytime he wants to start telling me the complete and true story, I'm here. Otherwise—'

'Look, Detective, you're more interested in busting my guy's chops than figuring out what really happened. That's got to stop. Henry Pierce is now out of your loop. And you try to take this to court and I'm going to shove that two-tape-recorders trick up your ass.'

'I told him I was recording,' Renner protested. 'I read him his rights and he said he understood them. I did nothing illegal.'

'Maybe not per se, Bob. But judges and juries don't like the cops tricking people. They like a clean game.'

'You really did cross over, didn't you?' Renner said. 'I hope you'll be happy over there. I gotta go now. Goodbye.'

Renner hung up and Langwiser closed her phone.

'You're not out of the woods on this yet, Henry. I think you're in the clear but other things could still happen. Stay away from it.'

'OK, I will.'

'Do you know when you are getting out of here yet?'

'Supposed to be any time now.' He looked at his watch.

'Well, I need to go. I have an arraignment downtown.'

'OK. Thanks for coming to see me here.'

'I'll make some calls and let you know what I hear. But meantime, you really need to stay away from this. OK? Go back to work.'

Pierce held his hands up in surrender. 'I'm done with it.'

She smiled professionally and left the room.

Pierce detached the phone from the bed's side guard and was punching in Cody Zeller's number when Nicole James stepped into the room. He put the phone back in its place.

Nicole had agreed to come by to drive Pierce home after he was checked out by Dr Hansen and released. Her face silently registered pain as she studied Pierce's damaged face. She had visited him often during his hospital stay but it seemed as though she could not get used to seeing the stitch zippers on his face.

Pierce had taken her frowns and sympathetic murmurings as a good sign. He would consider it all to have been worth the trouble if it got them back together.

'Poor baby,' she said, lightly patting his cheek. 'How do you feel?'

'Pretty good,' he told her. 'But I'm still waiting on the doctor to sign me out. Almost two hours now.'

'I'll go and check on things.' She went to the door but looked back at Pierce. 'Who was that woman who just left your room?'

'Oh, she's my lawyer. Kaz got her for me.'

'Why do you need her if you have Kaz?'

'She's a criminal defence lawyer.'

She stepped away from the door and came closer to the bed. 'Criminal defence lawyer? Henry, what is going on?'

Pierce shrugged his shoulders. 'I don't really know any more. I got into something and now I'm just trying to get out in one piece. Let me ask you something.'

'What?'

'When we leave here, where are you taking me?'

'Henry, I told you. I'm taking you home. Your home.' She turned and went through the door to look for the doctor.

Pierce lay back on the bed and tried to remember the time when everything seemed so perfect in the world.

THE BLOOD WAS EVERYWHERE. A trail of it across the rug, on the brand-new bed, on two of the walls and all over the telephone. Pierce stood in the doorway of his bedroom and looked at the mess and could remember almost none of what had happened after Wentz and his sidekick monster had left.

He stepped into the room and stooped down next to the phone. He gingerly lifted the receiver to hear the tone and determine if he had any messages. There were none.

He thought it unusual. He had not been home for nearly seventy-two hours yet there were no messages. Then he remembered something. He punched in his number at Amedeo and waited for the call to ring through to Monica Purl's desk. 'Monica, it's me, Henry. Did you change the phone number at my apartment?'

'Yes, you told me to. It was supposed to start yesterday.'

'I think it did. What's my new number?'

She gave him the number and he grabbed a pen off the bedside table and wrote it on his wrist.

'Thank you, Monica. I'll see you later.'

He hung up, got a fresh dial tone and called Lucy LaPorte's number, knowing it now by heart. Once again he got her voicemail but the greeting was now different. It was her voice but the message was that she was taking a vacation and would not be accepting clients until mid November.

More than a month, Pierce thought. He felt his insides constrict as he thought about what Renner had intimated and about Wentz and his goon and what they could have done to her. He left a message regardless of what she had said in her greeting. 'Lucy, it's Henry Pierce. I don't know what happened or what they did to you, but call me. I can help you. I've got a new number now.' He read the number off his wrist and then hung up.

In the refrigerator Pierce found all the cold items he had been carrying when he first encountered Wentz and Six-Eight. He remembered that he had dropped the laundry basket outside the elevator. Now everything was here in the refrigerator and the empty laundry basket was on the counter. He wondered who had done this. Nicole?

Pierce remembered that he still had several bags of groceries in the trunk of his BMW. He decided to go and get them.

After he got back to the apartment with the basketful he checked the phone again and learned he had missed a call. He had a message.

Pierce went through the process of setting up a voicemail access code again. Soon he was listening to the message.

'Help me? You helped me enough, Henry. They hurt me. I'm all black and blue and nobody can see me like this. I'm not talking to you again. Stop calling here, you understand?'

The message clicked off. Pierce hung up and closed his eyes.

The phone rang while he was still holding it. It was Monica.

'I forgot to tell you, between Monday and Tuesday Cody Zeller left three messages for you. I guess he really wants you to call him.'

'Thank you, Monica.'

Pierce could not call Zeller back directly. His friend accepted no direct calls. To contact him Pierce had to call his pager and put in a return number. He settled in to wait for the call back but his page was promptly returned. Unusual for Zeller.

'Jesus, man, when are you going to get a cellphone? I've been trying to reach you for three days.'

'I don't like cellphones. What's up?'

'What's up is that on Saturday you wanted this stuff in a damn hurry. Then you don't call me back for three days—'

'Code, I've been in hospital. I just got out.'

'The hospital? They take out your solid gold gallstones?'

'Not quite. I had a little trouble with some guys.'

'Not guys from Entrepreneurial Concepts?'

'I don't know. Did you find out about them?'

'Full scan as requested. These are bad dudes, Hank.'

'I'm getting that idea. You want to tell me about them now?'

'Actually, I'm in the middle of something right now and don't like doing this by phone anyway. But I did drop it all in a FedEx yesterday—when I didn't hear from you. Should've gotten there by this morning. You didn't get it?'

Pierce checked his watch. It was two o'clock. The FedEx run came at about ten every morning. He didn't like the idea of the envelope from Zeller sitting on his desk all this time.

'I haven't been to the office. But I'll go get it now. Thanks, Code.'

THE FEDEX ENVELOPE was on his desk when Pierce walked into his office. Almost every step of the way he'd had to fend off enquiries about his face. By the time he got to the third floor he was giving one-word answers to all questions—'Accident.'

'Lights,' he said as he swung round behind his desk.

But the lights didn't come on and Pierce realised his voice was different because of the swelling of his nasal passages. He got up and turned on the lights manually and then went back to the desk.

The envelope said HENRY PIERCE, PERSONAL AND CONFIDENTIAL. He opened it and pulled out the sheaf of print-outs from Zeller.

Zeller's report on Lilly Quinlan was short. He had traced her from Tampa to Dallas to Vegas and then LA. She had a record of two arrests for solicitation in Dallas and one arrest in Vegas. After each arrest she spent a few days in jail and was released for time served.

She had come to LA three years earlier, according to utilities records. She had avoided arrest and notice of the police until now.

There was a knock on his door and it opened before he could react. Charlie Condon stuck his head in. He was smiling, until he saw Pierce's face.

Pierce casually turned over the print-outs from the Zeller package.

Condon came in and closed the door. 'Man, how do you feel? Are you all right?'

'I'll live.'

'You want to talk about it?'

'No.'

'Henry, I am really sorry I didn't get over to the hospital. But it's been busy around here getting ready for Maurice.'

'So I take it we're still presenting tomorrow.'

Condon nodded. 'He's already in town and waiting on us. No delays. We go tomorrow or he goes—and takes his money with him. I talked to Larraby and Grooms and they said we're—'

'—ready to go. I know. I called them from the hospital. It's not Proteus that's the problem. It's my face. I look like Frankenstein's cousin. And I'm not going to look much better tomorrow.'

'I told him you had a car accident. It's not going to matter what you look like. What matters is Proteus. He wants to see the project and we promised him a first look. Before we send in the patents. Look, Goddard's the type of guy who can write the cheque on the spot. We need to do this, Henry. Let's get it over with.'

Pierce raised his hands in surrender. Money was always the trump card. 'He's still going to ask a lot of questions when he sees my face.'

'Look,' Condon said. 'It's a dog and pony show. No big deal. You'll be done with him by lunch. If he asks questions just tell him you went through the windshield and leave it at that. I mean, you haven't even told me what happened. Why should he be any different?'

Pierce saw the momentary look of hurt in his partner's eyes. 'Charlie, I'll tell you when the time is right. I just can't right now.'

'Sure, Henry, whatever you want. What are you working on now?'

'Nothing. Just some bullshit deskwork.'

'Then you're ready for tomorrow?'

'I'm ready.'

Condon nodded. 'Either way we win,' he said. 'We either take his money or we put in the patents, go to the press with Proteus and come January there will be a line like *Star Wars* at ETS to talk to us.'

Pierce nodded. But he hated going to Las Vegas for the annual Emerging Technologies Symposium. 'If we last until January. We need money now.'

'Don't worry about that. My job's finding the money. I think I can come up with a few fish to hold us until we land a whale.'

Pierce nodded. With the situation he was in, thinking forward even a month seemed ridiculous. 'OK, Charlie.'

'Good. Then I'll let you get back to work. Tomorrow at nine?'

Pierce leaned back in his chair and groaned. His last protest on the timing. 'I'll be here.'

Charlie left. Pierce waited a moment and then got up and locked the door. He wanted no more interruptions.

He went back to the print-outs. After the short report on Lilly Quinlan came a detailed report on William Wentz, owner-operator of Entrepreneurial Concepts Unlimited. The report stated that Wentz sat at the top of a burgeoning empire of Internet sleaze, from escort services to porn sites.

Zeller had also uncovered Wentz's criminal past in the states of Florida and New York. Contained in the print-out package were several mug shots of Wentz. Pierce read Zeller's opening summary:

Wentz arrived from Florida six years ago. This was after multiple arrests in Orlando made things tough for him there. According to intelligence files with the Florida Department of Law Enforcement (FDLE), he operated a chain of strip joints on the Orange Blossom trail in Orlando.

IMPORTANT NOTE: The FDLE box connects this guy to one Dominic Silva, 71 Winter Park, Fl, who in turn is connected to traditional organised crime in New York.

BE CAREFUL.

Wentz's pedigree as a mobster didn't surprise Pierce. What he did find odd was the idea that the man who could calmly wield a phone as a weapon and wore pointed boots for better bone crunching would be the man in charge.

Pierce had seen Wentz in action. His first and lasting impression was that Wentz was muscle first and brains second. His guess was that somewhere there was a man behind the man. He thought of the mobster mentioned in Zeller's report. Was Dominic Silva the man?

He went to the next page and found a summary listing of Wentz's criminal record. Over a five-year period in Florida he had a variety of arrests for pimping and two arrests for assault. There was also an arrest for manslaughter.

The summaries did not include final disposition of these cases. But reading them—arrest after arrest in five years—Pierce was puzzled as to why Wentz was not in prison.

EIGHT

Pierce never made it home Wednesday night. Instead, he spent the night in the basement at Amedeo Tech, reviewing the work conducted in his absence. But fatigue finally overcame him in the pre-dawn hours and he went into the laser lab to sleep.

The laser lab, where the most delicate measurements were taken, had one-foot thick concrete walls and was sheathed in copper on the outside and thick foam padding on the inside to eliminate the intrusion of outside vibrations and radio waves that could skew nano-readings. The bed-sized pieces of padding were attached to the walls with Velcro straps. It was a common occurrence for an overworked lab rat to go to the laser lab, pull down a pad and sleep on the floor, as long as the lab wasn't being used.

Pierce slept for two hours and woke up refreshed and ready for Maurice Goddard. The second-floor men's locker room had shower facilities and Pierce always kept spare clothes in his locker. He dressed in blue jeans and a beige shirt with small drawings of sailfish on it. He knew Goddard and Condon and everyone else would be dressed to impress at the presentation but he didn't care. It was the scientist's option to avoid the trappings of the world outside the lab.

In the mirror he noticed that the stitch trails on his face were redder and more pronounced than the day before. He had rubbed his face repeatedly through the night as the wounds itched. Doctor Hansen had told him that they would itch as the skin mended. Hansen had given him a tube of cream to rub on them, but Pierce had left that behind at the apartment. He leaned closer to the mirror and checked his eyes. The blood had almost completely cleared from the cornea of his right eye. The purple haemorrhage markings beneath each eye were giving way to yellow.

By 9.00am he was back in the lab. Larraby and Grooms were there and the other techs were trickling in. Brandon Larraby was tall and thin and a few years older than Pierce. An immunologist, he had come over from the pharmaceutical industry eighteen months before. He was the only researcher at Amedeo who liked to wear a white lab coat.

Sterling Grooms had been with Amedeo Technologies the longest of any full-time employee. He had signed on after completing his post-doc at UCLA, and had been Pierce's lab manager through three separate moves, starting at the old warehouse near the airport where Amedeo was born. Grooms and Pierce were the same age.

At 9.20 word came from Charlie Condon's assistant: Maurice Goddard had arrived. The show was about to begin. Pierce went through the mantrap and took the elevator up to the administration level. They were in the board room. Condon, Goddard and Goddard's second, a woman named Justine Bechy. She was a lawyer who protected the gates to Goddard's investment riches. Jacob Kaz, the patent attorney, was also seated at the table and Clyde Vernon stood off to the side, an apparent show of security at the ready if needed.

Goddard was saying something about the patent applications when Pierce walked in, announcing his presence with a loud hello, which ended conversation and drew their eyes and then their reactions to his damaged face.

'Oh, my Gosh,' exclaimed Bechy. 'Oh, Henry!'

Goddard said nothing. He just stared and had what Pierce thought was a small, bemused smile on his face.

'Henry Pierce,' Condon said. 'The man who knows how to make an entrance.'

Pierce shook hands with Bechy, Goddard and Kaz and pulled out a chair across the table from the visitors. He touched Charlie on the expensively suited arm and looked over at Vernon and nodded.

'Thank you so much for seeing us today, Henry,' Bechy said in a tone that suggested he had volunteered to keep the meeting set as scheduled. 'We had no idea your injuries were so serious.'

'Well, it's no problem. And it looks worse than it is. I've been back in the lab and working since yesterday.'

'It was a car accident, we were told,' Goddard said.

Goddard was in his early fifties with all of his hair and the sharp eyes of a bird that had amassed a quarter billion worms in his day. He wore a cream-coloured suit, white shirt and yellow tie.

'Yes,' Pierce said. 'I hit a wall.'

'When did this happen? Where?'

'Sunday afternoon. Here in Santa Monica.'

'Had you been drinking?' Goddard asked bluntly.

'No. I wasn't even driving. But I don't drink and drive anyway, Maurice, if that's what you mean.'

'Well, I am glad you are OK. If you get a chance, could you get me a copy of the accident report? For our records, you understand.'

There was a short silence.

'I'm not sure I do. It had nothing to do with Amedeo and what we do here.'

'I understand that. But let's be frank here, Henry. You are Amedeo Technologies. It is your creative genius that makes this company. I've met a lot of creative geniuses in my time. Some I would put my last dollar behind. Some I wouldn't give a buck to if I had a hundred.'

Bechy took over. She was twenty years younger than Goddard, had short dark hair, fair skin and a manner that exuded confidence and one-upmanship. 'What Maurice is saying is that he is considering a sizeable investment in Amedeo. To be comfortable doing that he needs to be comfortable with you. He doesn't want to invest in someone who might be reckless with his investment.'

'I thought it was about the science. The project.'

'It is, Henry,' she said. 'But they go hand in hand. The science is no good without the scientist. We want you to be dedicated and obsessed with the science and your project. But not reckless with your life outside the lab.'

Pierce held her eyes for a long moment. He suddenly wondered if she knew the truth about what happened and about his obsessive investigation of Lilly Quinlan's disappearance.

Condon cleared his throat and cut in, trying to move the meeting forward.

'Justine, Maurice, I am sure that Henry would be happy to cooperate with any kind of personal investigation you would like to conduct. I've known him for a long time and I've worked in the ET field for even longer. He is one of the most level-headed and focused researchers I've ever come across. That is why I am here. I like the science, I like the project and I'm very comfortable with the man.'

Bechy broke away from Pierce to look at Condon and nod her approval. 'We may take you up on that offer,' she said.

The exchange did little to erode the tension that had quickly enveloped the room. Pierce waited for somebody to say something but there was only silence.

'Um, there's something I should probably tell you then,' he finally said. 'Because you'll find out anyway.'

'Then tell us,' Bechy said. 'And save us all the time.'

Pierce could sense Charlie Condon's muscles seize up under his thousand-dollar suit as he waited for the revelation.

'Well, the thing is . . . I used to have a ponytail. Is that going to be a problem?'

At first the silence prevailed again but then Goddard's stone face cracked into a smile and then laughter came from his mouth. It was followed by Bechy's smile and then everybody was laughing, including Pierce, even though it hurt to do so. The tension was broken.

'OK, then,' Condon said. 'You people came to see a show. How about we go down to the lab and see the project that is going to win this comedian here a Nobel prize?'

'One thing before we go downstairs,' Pierce said. 'Jacob, did you bring the nondisclosure forms?'

'Oh, yes, right here,' the lawyer said. 'I almost forgot.' He pulled his briefcase up from the floor and opened it on the table.

'Is this really necessary?' Condon asked.

It was all part of the choreography. Pierce had insisted that Goddard and Bechy sign nondisclosure forms before entering the lab and viewing the presentation. Condon had disagreed, concerned that it might be insulting to an investor of Goddard's calibre. But Pierce didn't care and would not step back. His lab, his rules. So they settled on a plan in which it would appear to be an annoying routine.

'It's lab policy,' Pierce said. 'I don't think we should deviate. Justine was just saying how important it is to avoid risks. If we don't—'

'I think it is a perfectly good idea,' Goddard said, interrupting. 'In fact, I would have been concerned if you had not taken such a step.'

Kaz slid two copies of the two-page document across the table to Goddard and Bechy. He took a pen out of his inside suit pocket and placed it on the table in front of them. 'It's a pretty standard form. Basically, any and all proprietary processes, procedures and formulas in the lab are protected. Anything you see during your visit must be held in strict confidence.'

Goddard didn't bother reading the document. He left that to Bechy, who took a good five minutes to read it twice. At the end of her review she picked up the pen and signed it. She then gave the pen to Goddard, who signed the form in front of him.

Kaz collected the documents and put them in his briefcase. They all got up from the table and headed towards the door.

THEY STOOD IN THE CENTRAL LAB in a tight semicircle in front of Pierce and Larraby. It was crowded with the five visitors plus the usual lab crew trying to work. Introductions had been made and the tour of the individual labs given. It was time now for the show.

'On your first visit we talked about the main emphasis of the lab work here for the last several years,' Pierce said. 'Today we want to talk about an offshoot of that work—the Proteus project.' He described his long-running fascination with the potential medical applications of nanotechnology and his decision almost two years earlier to bring Brandon Larraby on board to be Amedeo's point man on the biological issues of this pursuit.

'Every article you read in every magazine and science journal talks about the biological side of this. It's the hot topic. From the elimination of chemical imbalances to possible cures for blood-carried diseases. Well, Proteus doesn't actually do any of these things. They're still a long way off. What Proteus is is a delivery system—the battery pack that will allow those future devices to work inside the body. We've created a formula that will allow cells in the bloodstream to produce electric impulses that will drive those future inventions.'

He stopped and Condon jumped in, as he had been choreographed to do. 'What you are saying is that this formula, this energy source, is the platform on which all of this other research and invention will rely. Correct?'

'Correct,' Pierce said. 'Once this is established in the science journals and through symposiums and so forth it will also act to foster that research and invention. It will excite the research field. Scientists will now be more attracted to this field because this problem has been solved. We are going to show the way. By Monday morning we will be seeking patent protection for this formula. We will publish our findings. And we will then license it to those who are pursuing this branch of research.'

'To the people who invent and build these bloodstream devices.'

It was Goddard and he had said it as a statement, not a question. It was a good sign. He was joining in. He was getting excited.

'Exactly,' Pierce said. 'If you can supply the power you can do a lot of things. A car without an engine is going nowhere. Well, this is the engine. And it will take a researcher in this field anywhere he wants to go.'

'For example,' Larraby said. 'In this country alone more than one million people rely on self-administered insulin injections to control diabetes. In fact, I am one of them. It is conceivable in the not too distant future that a cellular device could be built, programmed and placed in the bloodstream that would measure insulin levels and manufacture and release the amount needed.'

'Tell them about anthrax,' Condon said.

'Anthrax,' Pierce said. 'We all know from events of the last year how deadly a form of bacteria this is and how difficult it can be to detect. What this research field is heading towards is a day when, say, all postal employees or maybe members of our armed forces or maybe just all of us will have an implanted bio-chip that can detect and attack something like anthrax before it is allowed to cultivate and spread in the body.'

'You see,' Larraby said, 'the possibilities are limitless. The science will be there soon. But how do you power these devices in the body? That's the bottleneck to the research.'

'And we think the answer is our recipe,' Pierce said. 'Our formula.'

He looked at Goddard and knew he had him. Goddard had probably been in the right place at the right time and got in on a lot of good things over the years. But nothing like this. Nothing that could make him money—plenty of it—and also make him a hero.

'Can we see the demonstration now?' Bechy asked.

'Absolutely,' Pierce said. 'We have set up on the SEM.'

He led the group to the imaging lab. It contained a computerised microscope that was built to the dimensions of an office desk with a twenty-inch viewing monitor on top.

'This is a scanning electron microscope,' Pierce said. 'The experiments we deal with are too small to be seen with most microscopes. So we put the experiment in the SEM's vault and the results are viewed on the screen.' He opened a door to the boxlike structure located on a pedestal next to the monitor and removed a tray on which a silicon wafer was displayed. 'What we have on the wafer are human cells and to them we add a combination of proteins, which bind with the cells. That binding process creates the energy conversion we are talking about. A release of energy. To test this we place the whole experiment in a chemical solution that is sensitive to this electric impulse and responds to it by glowing. Emitting light.'

He put the experiment tray back in the vault and closed it. He then nodded to Larraby, who took the seat in front of the monitor and began working the keyboard. 'Brandon is now putting the elements together,' Pierce said. He stepped back and ushered Goddard and Bechy forward so they would be able to look over Larraby's shoulders at the monitor. He moved to the back of the room. 'Lights.'

The overheads went off, leaving Pierce happy that his voice had returned enough to normal to fall within the audio receptor's parameters. The blackness was complete in the windowless lab save for a dull glow from the grey-black screen of the monitor—not enough light for Pierce to watch the other faces in the room. He put his hand on the wall and traced it to the hook on which hung a set of heat-resonance goggles. He unhooked them and pulled them over his head. He reached to the battery pack on the left side and turned the device on, but flipped the lenses up, not ready to use them. He had put the goggles on the hook that morning. They were used in the laser lab but he had wanted them here in imaging because it would allow him to watch Goddard and Bechy secretly and gauge their reactions.

'OK, here we go,' Larraby said. 'Watch the monitor.'

The screen remained grey-black for almost thirty seconds and then a few pinpoints of light appeared like stars through a cloudy night sky. Then more, and then more, and then the screen looked like the Milky Way.

'Go to thermal, Brandon,' Pierce said.

Larraby worked the keyboard, so adept he did not need any light to see the commands he was typing. 'Going thermal means we'll see colours,' he said. 'Gradations in impulse intensity, from blue on the low end to green, yellow, red and then purple on the high end.'

The screen came alive with waves of colour. Yellows and reds mostly but enough purple to be impressive. The colour rippled in chain reaction across the screen. It undulated like the surface of the ocean at night. It was the Las Vegas strip from thirty thousand feet.

'Aurora borealis,' someone whispered.

Pierce thought it might have been Goddard. He flipped down the lenses and now he was seeing colours, too. Everyone in the room glowed red and yellow in the vision field of the goggles. He focused on Goddard's face. The gradations of colour allowed him to see in the dark. Goddard was intently focused on the computer screen. His mouth was open. His forehead and cheeks were deep red—maroon going to purple—as his face heated with excitement.

The goggles allowed him to see what people thought they were hiding. He saw Goddard's face break into a wide smile as he viewed the monitor. And in that moment Pierce knew the deal was done.

THEY RAN TWO MORE experiments on the SEM using new wafers. Both lit up the screen like Christmas and Goddard was satisfied. Pierce then had Grooms go over the other lab projects with him once more just to finish things off. After all, Goddard would be investing in the whole programme, not just Proteus. At 12.30 the presentation ended and they broke for lunch in the board room.

The conversation was convivial; even Bechy seemed to be enjoying herself. There was a lot of talk about the possibilities of the science. No talk about the money that could be made from it. During a dessert of key lime pie, Goddard brought up Nicole.

'You know who I miss?' he said. 'Nicole James. Where is she today? I'd like to at least say hello.'

Pierce and Condon looked at each other. It had been agreed earlier that Charlie would handle any explanations in regard to Nicole.

'She is no longer with us,' Condon said. 'In fact last Friday was her last day at Amedeo.'

'Really now? Where did she go?'

'Nowhere at the moment. I think she's taking time to think about her next move. She signed a no-compete contract with us so we don't have to worry about her showing up at a competitor.'

Goddard frowned and nodded. 'A very sensitive position,' he said.

'It is but it isn't,' Condon replied. 'She was focused outward not inward. She knew just enough about our projects to know what to look for in our competitors. For example, she did not have lab access and she never saw the demonstration you saw this morning.'

That was a lie, only Charlie Condon didn't know it. Just like the lie Pierce had fed Clyde Vernon about how much Nicole knew and had seen. The truth was she had seen it all. Pierce had brought her into the lab on a Sunday night to show her, to light up the SEM screen like the aurora borealis. It was when things were falling apart and he was desperately grasping for a way to keep it together, to hold on to her. He had broken his own rules and taken her to the lab to show her what it was that had drawn him away from her so often. But even showing her the discovery had not worked to stop the momentum of destruction that had enveloped them. Less than a month later Nicole ended the relationship.

Coffee was served and then it was time to get back to business.

'Tell us about the patent,' Bechy said.

Pierce nodded to Kaz and he took the question.

'It's a stepped patent. In nine parts, covering all processes related to what you saw today. We think we have covered everything. We think it will hold up to any kind of challenge, now or in the future.'

'And when do you go with it?'

'I'll be flying out to Washington Saturday. The plan is to deliver the application personally to the US Office of Patents at nine o'clock Monday morning.'

'We want to make sure we get our formula on the books first,' Pierce said. 'Brandon and I have also completed a paper on this and will be submitting it tomorrow.' He checked his watch. It was almost two. 'In fact,' he said, 'I need to leave you and get back to work now. If anything further comes up that Charlie can't answer, you can reach me in my office or in the lab.'

He pushed back his chair and was getting up when Goddard raised his hand and grabbed his arm to stop him.

'One moment, Henry, if you don't mind.'

Pierce sat back down. Goddard looked at him and then deliberately cast his glance into every face at the table. Pierce knew what was coming. He could feel it in the tightness of his chest.

'I just want to tell you while we're all here together that I want to invest in your company, to be part of this great thing you are doing.'

There was a raucous cheer and a round of clapping. Pierce put out his hand and Goddard shook it vigorously, then took Condon's hand that was stretched across the table.

'Nobody move,' Condon said. He got up and went to a corner of the room where there was a phone on a small table. He punched in three numbers and murmured something into the receiver.

He then returned to his seat and a minute later Monica Purl and Condon's personal assistant came into the board room carrying two bottles of Dom Perignon and a tray of champagne glasses. Condon popped the bottles and poured. The assistants were allowed to stay and take a glass.

Condon made the first toast. 'To Maurice Goddard. We're happy to have you with us on this magical ride.'

Then it was Goddard's turn. He raised his glass and simply said, 'To the future!'

Pierce began moving about the room, shaking hands and sharing words of thanks and encouragement. When he came to Monica she lost her smile and seemed to treat him coldly.

'There are some messages for you on your desk,' she told him. 'The lawyer said it was important but I told her I couldn't interrupt your presentation.'

'OK, thanks.' As calmly as he could Pierce went back to Goddard and told him he was being left in Condon's hands to work out the investment deal. He shook his hand again and then backed out of the board room and headed down the hallway to his office.

PIERCE SLID IN behind his desk and picked up the message slips Monica had left for him. They were from Janis Langwiser. The message on both was simply. 'Please call ASAP.'

Pierce punched the number in on the phone. A secretary answered and his call was put right through.

'Where have you been?' she began. 'I told your assistant to get the message to you right away.'

'She did what she's supposed to do. I don't like to be interrupted in the lab. What's going on?'

'Well, I have my sources in the police department. And what I am telling you is highly confidential. It's information I shouldn't have. If it got out there would be an investigation just on this alone.'

'OK. What is it?'

'A source told me that Renner spent a good part of today at his desk. He was working on a search warrant application. He then took it to a judge.'

Pierce was underwhelmed. 'OK. What does that mean?'

'It means he wants to search your property. Your apartment, your car, probably the home where you lived before moving because that was likely to be your domicile when the crime occurred.'

'You mean the supposed murder of Lilly Quinlan.'

'Exactly. But the application was rejected. The judge told him he hadn't presented enough evidence to justify the warrant.'

'Does that mean it's over?'

'No, he can go back any time he gets more. Or he might take the application to a different judge, someone more accommodating.'

Pierce suddenly thought of something. 'You know, they already searched my car. I could tell when I got into it that night outside Lilly's place.'

There was a moment of silence before Langwiser spoke. 'If they did then it was illegal. We'll never be able to prove it without a witness. Anyway, now they'll do it legally and they'll do more than a quick once-over. They'll go for hair and fibre evidence, things like that. Things too small to have been seen during a flashlight search that night.'

'Let them do it,' Pierce said, a note of defiance in his voice. 'Maybe they'll start looking at the real guy once I come up clean.'

'You mean Billy Wentz?'

'Yes.'

'Well, for now you should worry about yourself. You don't seem to understand the gravity of this situation. Renner is a patient man and he will continue to work this thing until he finds what he wants to get that search warrant signed.'

Pierce felt his body heat riding. He didn't know what else to say. A long silence went by before Langwiser broke it.

'There's something else. On Saturday night you told them about Lilly Quinlan's home and gave them the address. Well, they went over there and checked it out but they did not formally search the place until Sunday afternoon after Renner got a search warrant. It wasn't clear whether she was dead or alive and it was obvious she was or had been engaged in a profession that involved prostitution and other illegalities.'

Pierce was beginning to understand how Renner thought. 'So to protect himself he went and got a warrant,' he said. 'In case they came across something in regard to these other illegal activities. Or if she turned up alive and said, "What the hell are you doing?"'

'Exactly. And under the law he had to file what is called a search warrant return within forty-eight hours. It basically is a receipt for anything that was taken by police in the search. I got a copy of it. Anyway, it lists personal property that was taken, things like a hairbrush for DNA sampling, and many items for fingerprint analysis.'

'How long before they do the fingerprint stuff?'

'Probably a few days. Without a body this case is probably not a priority to anyone but Renner. I heard his own partner is working on other things, that they aren't seeing eye to eye on this and Renner's going it alone. But I'll call you back if anything else comes up.'

Pierce said goodbye and hung up. He thought about the information he had just been given. Renner was making his move. Even without a body.

Pierce knew he had to call Nicole and somehow explain that the police believed he was a murderer and would be coming to search the home they had shared. 'Jesus,' he said out loud.

He decided to analyse his situation in the same way he would analyse an experiment in the lab. From the bottom up. Believe nothing about it at the start.

He got out his notepad and wrote down the key elements of his conversation with Langwiser on a fresh page:

> Search: apartment
> Amalfi
> Car—second time—material evidence
> Search warrant return: fingerprints everywhere

He stared at the page but no answers came to him. Finally, he tore the page out, crumpled it and threw it towards the trash can in the corner of the room. He missed. He knew he had to call Nicole to prepare her for the inevitable. The police would come and search through everything: hers, his, it didn't matter. Nicole was a very private person. The invasion would be hugely damaging to her and the explanation for it catastrophic to his hopes of reunification.

'Oh man,' he said as he got up. He came round the desk and picked up the crumpled ball of paper. Rather than drop it in the trash can he took it back with him to his seat. He opened the paper and tried to smooth it out on the desk. 'Believe nothing,' he said.

The words on the wrinkled page defied him. They meant nothing. In a sweeping move of his arm he grabbed the page and balled it in his hand again. He cocked his elbow, ready to make the basket on the retry when he realised something. He brought his hand down and unwrapped the page again. He looked at one line he had written:

> Car—second time—material evidence

Believe nothing. That meant not believing the police had searched the car the first time. A spark of energy exploded inside. He thought he might have something. What if the police had not searched his car? Then who had?

The next jump became obvious. How did he know the car had been searched at all? The truth was he didn't. He only knew one thing; someone had been inside his car while it had been parked in the alley. The overhead-light setting had been changed. But had the car actually been searched?

He realised that he had jumped the gun in assuming that the

police—in the form of Renner—had searched his car. He actually had no proof or even indication of this. He knew only that someone had been in the car. This conclusion could support a variety of secondary assumptions. Police search was only one of them. A search by a second party was another. The idea that someone had entered the car to take something was also another.

And the idea that someone had entered the car to put something in it was yet another.

Pierce got up and left his office. In the hallway he punched the elevator button but immediately decided not to wait. He charged into the stairwell and went quickly down four flights to the first floor. He went through the lobby and into the adjoining parking garage.

He started with the trunk of the BMW. He pulled up the lining, looked under the spare, opened the tool pouch. He noticed nothing added, nothing taken. He moved to the passenger compartment, spending nearly ten minutes conducting the same kind of search and inventory. Nothing added, nothing taken. The engine compartment was last and quickest. Nothing added, nothing taken.

That left his backpack. He relocked the car and returned to the Amedeo building, taking the stairs again. As he passed by Monica's desk on his way back to his office he noticed her looking at him.

'What?'

'Nothing. You're just acting . . . weird.'

'It's not an act. I am weird.'

He closed and locked his office door. The backpack was on his desk. He started unzipping and looking through its many compartments. It had a cushioned section for a laptop computer, a divided section for paperwork and files, and three different zippered compartments for carrying smaller items like pens and chewing gum.

Pierce found nothing out of order until he reached the front section, which contained a compartment within a compartment. It was a small zippered pouch big enough to hold a passport and possibly a fold of currency. It wasn't a secret compartment but it could easily be hidden behind a book or a folded newspaper while travelling. He opened the zipper and reached his hand in.

His fingers touched on what felt like a credit card. Maybe he'd put it in his pack and forgotten about it. But when he pulled it out he was looking at a black plastic scramble card. There was a magnetic strip on one side. On the other side it had a company logo that said U-Store-It. Pierce was sure he had never seen it before. Whoever had been in his car Saturday night had planted the scramble card.

U-Store-It was a nationwide company that rented storage rooms in warehouses. Pierce reached down to the cabinet beneath the computer monitor and pulled up the yellow pages. He quickly found the listings for self-storage facilities. U-Store-It had a half-page ad that listed eight different facilities in the Los Angeles area. Pierce started with the location closest to Santa Monica. He picked up the phone and called the U-Store-It franchise in Culver City. The call was answered by a young man's voice.

'This is going to sound strange,' Pierce said. 'But I think I rented a storage room there but I can't remember. I know it was U-Store. It but now I can't remember which place it was.'

'Name?' The kid acted like it was a routine request.

'Henry Pierce.' He heard the information tapped onto a keyboard.

'Nope, not here.'

Pierce thanked the voice, hung up and called the next closest franchise listed in the yellow pages.

He got a computer hit on his third call. The U-Store-It franchise in Van Nuys. The woman who answered his call told him he had rented a storage room at the Victory Boulevard facility six weeks earlier. She had him on her records under the Amalfi Drive address. She told him the room was climate-controlled, had electric power and was alarm-protected. He had twenty-four-hour access to it.

'What is the room number?' he asked.

'I can only give you that if I see a photo ID, sir. Come in and show me your driver's licence and I can remind you what space you have. The office is only open nine till six.'

'OK.' He thanked the woman and hung up. He put his hand on the phone again but didn't lift it. He could call Langwiser but he didn't need her cool and calm professional manner, and he didn't want to hear her tell him to leave it alone. He could call Nicole but that would only lead to raised voices and an argument. He knew he would get that anyway when he told her about the police search. He could call Cody Zeller but didn't think he could take the sarcasm.

For a fleeting moment the thought of calling Lucy LaPorte entered his mind. He quickly dismissed the idea but not the thought of what it said about him. Here he was, in the most desperate situation of his life, and who could he call for help and advice?

The answer was no one. And the answer made him feel cold from the inside out.

NINE

With his sunglasses and hat on, Pierce entered the office at the U-Store-It in Van Nuys and went to the counter, his driver's licence in his hand. A young woman was sitting there reading a book. It seemed to be a struggle for her to take her eyes from it and bring them up to Pierce. When she did her chin dropped as she was startled by the ugly zipper of stitches that wandered down Pierce's nose. She tried to cover up like she hadn't noticed anything unusual.

'That's OK,' Pierce said. 'I'm getting that a lot.' He slid his licence across the counter. 'I called a little while ago about the storage space I rented. I can't remember the number.'

She picked up the licence and looked at it and then back up at his face, studying it. Pierce took off his hat but not the sunglasses.

'It's me.'

'Sorry, I just had to be sure.'

She turned to a computer and Pierce watched her type in his name. In a few moments a data screen appeared and she started checking information from his driver's licence against the screen. Satisfied, she scrolled down and read something.

'Three three one,' she said, slapping the driver's licence down.

He nodded his thanks and started to turn from the counter. He looked back at her. 'Do I owe you any money?'

'Excuse me?'

'I can't remember how I paid. I was wondering if I have a bill coming.'

'Oh.' His information was still on the computer screen. She scrolled down and said, 'No, you're fine. You paid six months up front in cash. You still have a while.'

'OK. Great. Thank you.'

He stepped out of the office and rode the elevator up to the third floor. He stepped out into a deserted hallway with roll-down doors running along both sides. He walked down the hall until he came to a door marked 331.

To the right of the door was a scramble card reader with a glowing red light next to it. But at the bottom of the door was a hasp with a padlock holding the door secure. Pierce realised that the scramble card he had found in his backpack was only an alarm card. It would not open the door.

He pulled the card from his pocket and slid it through the reader. The light turned green; the alarm was off. He squatted down and pulled the lock but it was secure. He couldn't open the door.

After weighing his next move, he stood up and headed back towards the elevator. He decided he would go to the car and check the backpack again. The key to the padlock must be there.

In the parking lot, Pierce raised his electronic key and unlocked his car. The moment he heard the snap of the locks disengaging he stopped in his tracks and looked down at his raised hand. A memory vision played through his mind. Wentz walking in front of him, outside his apartment door, the keys in his hands.

One by one Pierce turned the keys on the ring, identifying them and the locks they corresponded to: apartment, garage, gym, Amalfi Drive front and back, office back-up, desk, lab back-up, computer room. He identified all keys on the ring but two. The strangers were stainless steel and small, not door locks. One was slightly larger than the other. Wentz must have slipped the keys on the ring as they had moved down the hall. Or maybe afterwards, while he had been dangled off the balcony. When he had returned from hospital he had to be let into his apartment by building security. He had found his keys on the living-room floor.

Pierce turned and headed back to the elevators. Three minutes later he slid the larger of the two keys into the padlock at the bottom of the door to storage unit 331. He turned it and the lock snapped open. He pulled it out of the hasp and dropped it on the floor, then gripped the door handle and raised it with a loud metallic screech. The door banged loudly when it reached the top.

The space was ten by ten and dark. But the corridor threw light in over his shoulder. Standing at the centre of the room was a large white box. There was a low humming sound coming from the room. Pierce stepped in and his eyes registered the white pull cord for the overhead light. He pulled it and the room filled with light.

The white box was a freezer. A chest freezer with a top door that was held closed with a small padlock that Pierce knew he would be able to open with the second key.

He didn't have to open the freezer to know what was in it but he opened it anyway. He felt compelled, possibly by a dream that it might be empty and that this was all part of an elaborate hoax.

More likely it was simply because he knew he had to see with his own eyes, so that there would be no doubts.

He raised the smaller key and opened the padlock. He removed it and flipped up the latch. Then he lifted the top of the freezer, the air lock breaking and the rubber seal making a *snik* sound. He felt cold air puff out of the box and a damp, fetid smell invaded his nose.

With one arm he held the lid open. He looked down through the mist that was rising up out of the box like a ghost. And he saw the form of a body at the bottom of the freezer. A woman naked and crumpled in the fetal position, her neck a terrible mess of blood and damage. She lay on her right side. Blood was pooled and frozen black at the bottom of the freezer. White frost had crusted on her dark hair and upturned hip. Hair had fallen across her face but did not totally obscure it. He recognised the face. It was Lilly Quinlan.

He let go of the lid and it slammed closed with a heavy thump that was louder than he had expected. It scared him but not enough to obscure the sense of dread that had engulfed him. He turned and slid down the front of the freezer until he was sitting on the floor, elbows on his knees, hands gathering the hair at the back of his head.

He closed his eyes and heard a rising pounding sound like someone running towards him. He then realised it was internal, blood pounding in his ears as he grew light-headed. He thought he might pass out but realised he had to hold on and stay alert.

Pierce reached to the top of the freezer and pulled himself up. He fought for his balance and to hold back the nausea creeping into his stomach. He pulled himself across the freezer and hugged it, putting his cheek down on the cold white surface. He breathed in deeply and after a few moments it all passed and his mind was clear. He stood up straight and stepped back from the freezer, listening to its quiet hum. He knew it was time to analyse and evaluate.

Pierce was looking at a freezer sitting in the middle of a storage room that he—according to the office records—had rented. The freezer contained the body of a woman he had never met but for whose death he would certainly now be blamed. What Pierce knew was that he had been carefully and convincingly set up. Wentz was behind it or at least part of it. The scramble card and the padlock keys had been hidden or at least camouflaged. Had it been meant for him to find them? He decided no. So he concluded that he had an edge. He knew what he was not supposed to know. He knew the location of the trap before it had been sprung.

Next question. What if he had not found the scramble card and had not been led to the body? Langwiser had warned him of an impending police search. Surely, Renner and his fellow searchers would have found the card and the padlock keys and would have been led to the body. He felt his scalp grow warm as he realised how narrowly he had escaped—if only for the time being. And in the same moment he felt a full understanding of how careful the set-up had been. It was reliant on Renner making the moves he was making.

It also relied on Pierce. And as he came to understand this he felt the sweat start to bead in his hair. The set-up had counted on his moves. Every one of them. It was reliant on his own history.

Pierce quickly relocked this freezer, as if that would stop its contents from coming out and haunting him. He then pulled his shirt out of his pants and used the tail to wipe every surface on the freezer that he could have conceivably touched. Then he backed out of the space and pulled the door down. He locked it with the padlock, slid the scramble card through the reader to set the alarm and then wiped the lock and door with his shirttail.

As he moved away from the unit and towards the elevator, a terrible fear swept over him. He knew he was far from harm's way. It was possible that Renner would find the storage unit even without the clues of keys and scramble card. He could count on nothing. If Renner found the freezer then everything ended. Amedeo Tech, Proteus, his life, everything. He needed to know what was happening to him. He needed to come up with a plan that would save his life.

THE IMMEDIATE URGE was to curl up on the floor in the same position as the body in the freezer, but Pierce knew that to collapse under the pressure of the moment would be to ensure his demise. He unlocked the door and came into his apartment shaking with fear and anger and the knowledge that he was the only one he could rely on to find his way out of this dark tunnel.

He sat down on the couch then immediately stood up. He had just found a body—a murder victim. Sitting down seemed like the least wise thing to do. Yet he knew he had to. He had to sit down and look at this. He had to approach this the way he had approached and solved the question of the car search. From the bottom.

The first object of his scrutiny was Wentz. A man that in initial view was the lynchpin of the frame. The question was: why would Wentz choose Pierce to hang a murder on?

After a few minutes of turning it and grinding it and looking at it from opposite angles, Pierce came to some basic case logic.

Conclusion 1: Wentz had not chosen Pierce. There was no connection that would allow for this. The two men had never met before the set-up was already in play. And this conclusion led to the supposition that Pierce had to have been chosen for Wentz by someone else.

Conclusion 2: There was a third party in the set-up. Wentz and the muscle he called Six-Eight were only tools, cogs in the wheels. Someone else's hand was behind this.

Now Pierce considered this. What did the third party need to build the frame? The set-up was complex and relied on Pierce's predictable movements in a fluid environment. He came to a basic realisation about himself and the third party.

Conclusion 3: Isabelle. The set-up was orchestrated by a third party with knowledge of his personal history that led to an understanding of how he would react under certain circumstances. The customer phone calls to Lilly were the inciting element of the experiment. The third party understood that Pierce would investigate. That he would chase his sister's ghost.

Conclusion 4: The wrong number was the right number. He had not been randomly assigned Lilly Quinlan's old number. It was intentional. It was part of the set-up.

Conclusion 5: Monica Purl. She was part of it. She had set up his phone service. She had requested the phone number that would trip the chase.

Pierce got up and started pacing. If the set-up was tied to Monica then it was tied to Amedeo. It meant that the frame was part of a conspiracy of a higher order. It wasn't about hanging a murder on Pierce. It was about something else. In this respect Lilly Quinlan was like Wentz. A tool in the set-up, a cog in the wheel. Her murder was simply a way to get to Pierce.

Why was Pierce the target of the frame? What did they want?

He looked at it from another angle. What would happen if the set-up succeeded? In the long run he would be arrested, tried and convicted. He would be imprisoned, possibly even put to death. In the short run there would be media focus and scandal, disgrace. Maurice Goddard and his money would go away. Amedeo Technologies would crash and burn.

He turned it again and the question became one of means to an end. Why go to the trouble? Why the elaborate plot? Why kill Lilly

Quinlan and set up a vast scheme that could fall apart at any step along the way? Why not simply kill Pierce instead of Lilly to achieve the same end? He would be out of the picture again, Goddard still walks and Amedeo still crashes and burns.

Conclusion 6: The target is different. It is not Pierce and it is not Amedeo. It is something else.

'Proteus,' he whispered. They wanted Proteus.

Conclusion 7: The set-up was designed to push Pierce so hard into a corner that he would have no choice but to give up what they wanted. The Proteus project. He would trade Proteus for his freedom, for the return of his life.

Pierce ran his fingers through his hair. He felt sick to his stomach. Not because of concluding that Proteus was the ultimate target. But because he had jumped quickly ahead of that. He had put it together. He had the big picture and in the middle of it stood the third party. She was smiling at him, her eyes bright and beautiful.

Conclusion 8: Nicole. She was the link. She was the one who connected all the dots. She had secret knowledge of the Proteus project because he had given it to her. And she knew his most secret history, the true story about Isabelle he had never told to anyone but her.

Pierce figured she had gone to Elliot Bronson or maybe Midas Molecular. It didn't matter. What was clear was that she had told of the project, agreed to steal it or delay it enough until it could be replicated and taken by a competitor to the patent office first.

He folded his arms tightly across his chest. He knew he needed a plan. He needed to test his conclusions somehow. There was only one way to do that, he decided. He would go and see her, confront her, get the truth. But first he called Jacob Kaz's office.

The patent lawyer picked up the transfer quickly. 'Henry, you were fantastic today,' he said by way of greeting.

'You were pretty good yourself, Jacob.'

'Thank you. What can I do for you?'

'Is the package ready to go?'

'Yep. I finished with it last night. I'm going to fly out Saturday, visit my brother in Maryland, and then be there first thing Monday morning to file. Like I told Maurice today.'

Pierce cleared his throat. 'Jacob, I want you to take a red-eye tonight. I want you to file it first thing tomorrow morning. As soon as they open.'

'Henry, I . . . that's going to be a bit expensive to get a flight tonight on such short notice. I usually fly business class and that's—'

'I don't care what it costs. I don't care where you sit. I want you on a plane tonight. In the morning, call me as soon as it's filed.'

'Is something wrong, Henry? You seem a bit—'

'Yes, something's wrong, Jacob, that's why I'm sending you tonight.'

'Well, do you want to talk about it? Maybe I can help.'

'You can help by getting on that plane and getting it filed first thing. Other than that, I can't talk about it yet. But just get over there and get the thing filed and then call me. I don't care how early it is out here. Call me.'

'OK, Henry, I will. I'll make the arrangements right now.'

'When does the filing office open?'

'Nine.'

'OK, then I will talk to you shortly after six my time. And Jacob?'

'Yes, Henry?'

'Don't tell anyone other than your wife that you're going tonight.'

'Uh . . . what about Charlie? He said today that he might call me tonight to go over last-minute—'

'If Charlie calls you, don't tell him you're going tonight. If he calls after you leave, tell your wife to tell him you had to go out with another client. An emergency or something.'

Kaz was silent for a long moment.

'Are you all right with this, Jacob? I'm not saying anything about Charlie. It's just that at the moment I can't trust anybody. You understand?'

'Yes, I understand.'

'OK. Thank you, Jacob. Call me from DC.'

Pierce clicked off. He felt bad about impugning Charlie Condon in Kaz's eyes. But Pierce knew he could take no chances. He opened a fresh line and called Charlie Condon's direct line. He was still there.

'It's Henry.'

'I just went down to your office to look for you.'

'I'm at home. What's up?'

'I thought maybe you'd want to say goodbye to Maurice. But you missed him. He just left. He heads back to New York tomorrow but said he wants to talk to you before he leaves. He'll call in the morning.'

'Fine. Did you make the deal?'

'We came to an agreement in principle. We'll have contracts the end of next week.'

'How did it come out?'

'Thirteen million over three years. He becomes chairman of the board and gets ten per cent. Are you happy?'

'It's a good deal, Charlie. For us and him.' Pierce knew that Condon was looking for excitement over the deal but he couldn't give it. He wondered if he'd even be around at the end of the next week.

'So where did you disappear to?' Condon asked.

'I had things to do. Listen, did Maurice or Justine ask anything more about the accident?'

'No. I thought they might bring up that thing about wanting the accident report again but they didn't. I think they were so blown away by what they saw in the lab that they don't care any more what happened to your face.'

'I hope so.'

'You ever going to tell me what happened to you?'

Pierce hesitated. He was feeling guilty about hiding things from Condon. But he had to remain cautious.

'Not right now, Charlie. The time's not right.'

This put a pause in Condon's reply and in the silence Pierce could feel the injury he was inflicting on their relationship.

'Well,' Condon said. 'I'm going to go. Congratulations, Henry. Today was a good day.'

'Congratulations, Charlie.'

After hanging up, Pierce pulled out his key ring to check for something. Not the padlock keys. He had left them behind at the storage facility, hidden with the scramble card on the top of an exit sign on the third floor. He checked the ring to make sure he still had the key to the house on Amalfi Drive. If Nicole wasn't home, he was going to go in anyway. And he would wait for her.

AS PIERCE DROVE past his old home he glanced down the driveway and saw Nicole's Speedster in the carport. It appeared she was home. He yanked the wheel and came to a stop next to the kerb. He sat still for a moment, pulling his courage together. Ahead of him he saw a Volkswagen idling in a driveway, blue smoke pumping out of the twin exhaust pipes, a Domino's Pizza sign on the roof. It reminded him he was hungry. He had only picked at his catered lunch because he had been too keyed up from the presentation and the anticipation of making a deal with Goddard.

But food had to wait. He got out of the car.

Pierce stepped into the entry alcove and knocked on the door. It was a single-light French door, so Nicole would know it was him the moment she stepped into the hallway. But the glass worked both ways. He saw her the moment she saw him. She hesitated but knew she couldn't get away with acting like she wasn't home. She stepped forward and unlocked and opened the door.

But then she stood in the opening, not giving him passage. She was wearing washed-out jeans and a lightweight navy blue sweater. The sweater was cut to show off her flat and tanned stomach and the gold ring that pierced her navel. She was barefoot.

'Henry. What are you doing here?'

'I need to talk to you. Can I come in?'

'Well, I'm expecting some calls. Can you—?'

'From who, Billy Wentz?'

This gave her pause. A puzzled look entered her eyes. 'Who?'

'You know who. How about Elliot Bronson?'

She shook her head like she felt sorry for him. 'Look, Henry, if this is some kind of jealous ex-boyfriend scene you can save it. I don't know any Billy Wentz and I am not trying to get a job with Elliot Bronson. I signed a no-compete, remember?'

That put a chink in his armour. She had deflected his first attack so smoothly and naturally that Pierce felt a tremor in his resolve.

'Look, can I come in or not? I don't want to do this out here.'

She hesitated again but then moved back and motioned him in. They walked into the living room. It was a large room with cherry-wood floors. One wall was a vast floor-to-ceiling book case. Most of the shelves were filled with her books.

'Are you feeling all right?' she said, trying for a level of cordiality. 'You look a lot better.'

'I'm fine.'

'How did it go with Maurice Goddard today?'

'It went fine. How did you know about it?'

Her face adopted a put-out expression. 'Because I was working there until Friday and the presentation was already scheduled. Remember?'

He nodded. 'I forgot.'

'Is he coming on board?'

'It looks like it.'

She didn't sit down. She stood in the middle of the living room and faced him. 'OK, Henry, you're here. I'm here. What is it?'

He nodded. 'Well, it probably doesn't matter any more in the scheme of things but I want to know for myself so maybe I can live with it a little easier. Just tell me, Nicki, did somebody get to you, did they pressure you, threaten you? Or did you just flat out sell me out?'

Her mouth formed a perfect circle. Pierce had lived with her for three years and believed he knew all her facial expressions. He doubted she could put a look on her face he hadn't seen before. That perfect circle of a mouth he had seen before. But it was not the shock of being found out. It was confusion.

'Henry, what are you talking about?'

It was too late. He had to go with it.

'You know what I'm talking about. You set me up. And I want to know why and I want to know for who. And did you know they were going to kill her, Nicole? Don't tell me you knew that.'

Her eyes started to get the violet sparks that he knew signalled her anger. Or her tears. Or both. 'I have no idea what you are talking about. Set you up for what? Kill who?'

'Come on, Nicole. Are they here? Hey, is Elliot hiding in the house? When do I get the presentation from them? When do they make the trade? My life back for Proteus.'

'Henry, I think something's happened to you. When they held you over the balcony and you hit the wall. I think—'

'Bullshit! You were the only one who knew the story about Isabelle. You were the only one I ever told. And then you used it to do this. How could you do that? For money? Or was it just to get me back for messing things up between us?'

He could see her starting to tremble, to weaken. Maybe he was cracking through. She raised her hands and backed away.

'Get out of here, Henry. You're crazy. If it wasn't the wall then it was too many hours in the lab. It finally made you snap.'

'What I'd like to know is who killed her? Was it you or did you have Wentz do it for you? He took care of all the dirty work, didn't he?'

That stopped her. She turned and almost shrieked at him. '*What? What are you saying? Killed who?*'

He paused, hoping she would calm down. This wasn't going the way he had thought or hoped it would. He needed an admission from her. Instead, she was starting to cry.

'Nicole, I loved you. I don't know what's wrong with me because I still do.'

She composed herself, wiped her cheeks and folded her arms across her chest. 'Will you do me one favour, Henry?' she asked quietly. 'Would you please sit down on that chair there and I'll sit over here.' She directed him to the chair, then moved behind the one where she would sit. 'Just sit down and tell me what has happened. Tell me as though I didn't know anything about it. I know you don't believe that but I want you to tell me like you do. Tell me it like a story. You can say whatever you want to say about me in the story, any bad thing, but just tell it. From the start. OK, Henry?'

Pierce slowly sat down on the chair she had pointed him to. He stared at her the whole time, watched her eyes. When she had sat down across from him he began to tell the story. 'I guess you could say this started twenty years ago. On the night I found my sister in Hollywood. And I didn't tell my stepfather about it.'

TEN

An hour later Pierce stood in the bedroom and saw that nothing had changed. Right down to the stack of books on the floor next to her side of the bed. He stepped over to look at the book that was open and left on the pillow where he used to sleep. It was called *Iguana Love* and he wondered what it was about.

She came up behind him and lightly touched his shoulders. He turned into her and she brought her hands to his face to hold it while she studied the scars running across his nose to his eye.

'I'm sorry, baby,' she said.

'I'm sorry for that downstairs. That I doubted you. I'm sorry for everything about this past year. I thought I could keep you and still work like—'

Her hands went behind his neck and she pulled him down into a kiss. He turned her and gently pushed her down onto the edge of the bed and they kissed again. Soon he felt one of her hands working the buttons of his shirt. They struggled with each other's clothing until finally they broke apart to work on their own clothes. Both knew without saying it that it would be faster.

When he pulled his shirt off she grimaced at the sight of the bruising on his chest and side. But then she leaned forward and kissed him there.

And when they were finally naked they moved onto the bed and pulled each other together in an embrace that was fuelled by equal parts carnal lust and tender longing.

Her eyes were closed. He opened his to look down on her face. She stopped and opened her own eyes. She let go of him.

'What?' he said.

'Henry, I am so sorry but I can't do this.' She brought both her hands up to his chest and pushed him off.

He rolled onto his side, next to her. She sat up on the edge of the bed, her back to him.

Pierce reached up and lightly touched her neck and then ran his thumb down her spine. 'What is it, Nicki? What's the matter?'

'I thought after what we talked about downstairs that this would be good. That it was something we needed. But it's not. We can't do this, Henry. We're not together any more and if we do this—I don't know. I just can't. I'm sorry.'

Pierce smiled. He reached over and touched the tattoo on her right hip. It was *Fu*, the Chinese character pictogram that meant happiness. She had told him it was a reminder that happiness came from within, not material things.

She turned and looked at him. 'Why are you smiling? I would think you'd be upset. Any other man would be.'

He shrugged. 'I don't know. I guess I understand.'

But slowly it dawned on her. What he had done. She stood up from the bed and turned to him. She reached over for a pillow and held it in front of her. The message was clear. She no longer wanted to be naked with him.

'What?' he asked.

'You bastard.'

'What are you talking about?'

He saw the sparks in her eyes but this time she wasn't crying.

'This was a test wasn't it? Some sort of perverted test. You knew if I fucked you then everything downstairs was a lie.'

'Nicki, I don't think—'

'Get out.'

'Nicole . . .'

'You and your goddamned tests and experiments. I said get out!'

Embarrassed now by what he had done he stood up and started putting on his clothes. 'Can I say something?'

'No. I don't want to hear.' She turned and walked to the bathroom.

'I'm sorry, Nicole. I thought that—'

She closed the bathroom door without looking back at him. 'Go,' he heard her say from within.

Then he heard the shower come on and he knew she was washing away his touch for the final time.

Pierce finished dressing and went downstairs. He wondered how he could have been so desperately wrong about her.

Before leaving he went back into the living room and stood before her bookcase. He found a book he knew was there and pulled it out. It was about Chinese pictograms. He turned the pages until he found *Fu* and read the copy. It quoted Confucius.

'With coarse rice to eat, with only water to drink, and my bended arm for a pillow, I am happy.'

He should have known. Pierce knew he should have known it wasn't her. The logic was wrong. The science was wrong. It had led him to doubt the one thing he should have been sure of.

He turned the pages of the book until he came to *Shu*, the symbol of forgiveness. 'Forgiveness is the action of the heart,' he read out loud. He took the book to the coffee table and placed it down still open to the page displaying *Shu*. He knew she would find it.

Closing the door, he locked it behind him and then walked to his car. He sat behind the wheel, slid the key in and turned the engine over. His mind produced the image of the pizza delivery car he had seen earlier. A reminder that he was hungry.

And in that moment atoms smashed together to create a new element. He had an idea. He turned the car off and got back out.

Nicole was either still in the shower or not answering the door. But he didn't care because he still had a key. He unlocked the door and walked down the hallway towards the kitchen.

'Nicole,' he called. 'It's me. I just need to use the phone.'

There was no response.

On the kitchen phone he dialled information for Venice and asked for the number for Domino's Pizza. There were two locations and he took both numbers, writing them down on a pad Nicole kept by the phone. He dialled the first number and while he waited he opened the cabinet above the phone and pulled out the yellow pages. He knew if Domino's didn't work he would have to call every pizza delivery in Venice to run out the idea.

'Domino's Pizza, can I help you?'

'I want to order a pizza.'

'Phone number?'

From memory Pierce gave Lucy LaPorte's cellphone number. He heard it being typed into a computer. He waited and then the man on the other end said, 'What is your address?'

'You mean I'm not on there?'

'No, sir.'

'Sorry, I called the wrong one.' He hung up and called the second Domino's and went through the same routine, giving Lucy's number to the woman on the other end of the line.

'Is your address nine-oh-nine Breeze? Name LaPorte?'

'Uh, yeah, that's it.'

'What would you like?'

'Um, does your computer say what we got last time?'

'Regular size, onion, peppers and mushrooms.'

'That's good. Same thing.'

'OK, thirty minutes.' She hung up without saying goodbye.

Pierce hung up and turned to head to the door.

Nicole was standing there. Her hair was wet and she wore a white terrycloth robe. She glanced down at the yellow pages, open to the ads for pizza delivery. 'I can't believe you, Henry. After what you did, you just come on down and order a pizza like it's nothing.'

'It's not what you think, Nicole. I'm trying to find somebody and this is the only way.'

'I asked you to leave,' she said.

'All right, I'm leaving.' He made a move to squeeze between her and the kitchen's centre island. But suddenly he changed course and moved into her. He grabbed her by the shoulders and pulled her towards him. He kissed her on the mouth.

She quickly pushed him back.

'Goodbye,' he said before she could speak. 'I still love you.'

As he walked towards the door he slid the key to the house off his key ring. He dropped it on the small table by the door. He turned and looked back at her as he opened the door. And she turned away.

BREEZE WAS ONE of the Venice walk streets, which meant Pierce would have to get out of his car to get close to it. In several neighbourhoods near the beach the small bungalows were built facing each other with only a sidewalk between them.

Pierce found a parking space on Ocean and walked down to Breeze. It was near seven o'clock and the sky was beginning to turn a burnt-orange colour. The address he had got from Domino's was halfway down the block. Pierce strolled down the sidewalk like he was on his way to the beach for the sunset. As he passed 909 he nonchalantly took a look. It was a yellow bungalow with a wide front porch and a white picket fence out front with a gate. The curtains behind the front windows were drawn closed.

He continued his walk to where Breeze ended at Speedway and there was a beach parking lot. He loitered in the lot and watched the sun drop towards the horizon for another ten minutes. He then started back down Breeze. He passed 909 again and saw no indication that the tiny house was currently inhabited.

As he got to the end of Breeze a pick-up truck pulled up at the mouth of the sidewalk. It had the Domino's sign on top. A small man of Mexican descent jumped out with a red insulated pizza carrier and quickly headed down the sidewalk. Pierce let him get a lead and then followed. When the man walked across the porch to the front door of 909, Pierce slowed to a stop and used a red bougainvillea tree in the next-door neighbour's yard as a blind.

The pizza man knocked twice and looked like he was about to give up when the door was opened. Pierce heard a voice.

'I didn't order that.' It was Lucy LaPorte.

'Are you sure? I have nine-oh-nine Breeze.' The pizza man opened the side of his carrier and pulled out a flat box. He read something off the side. 'LaPorte, regular with onion, pepper and mushroom.'

She giggled. 'Well, that's me and that's what I usually get but I didn't order one tonight. Maybe it was a computer glitch or something and the order came in again.'

The man looked down at the pizza and sadly shook his head. 'Well, OK then. I'll tell them.'

He shoved the box back into the carrier and turned from the door. As he came down off the porch the door was closed behind him.

Pierce was waiting for him by the bougainvillea tree with a twenty-dollar bill. 'Hey, if she doesn't want it, I'll take it.'

The pizza man's face brightened. 'OK, fine with me.'

Pierce exchanged the twenty for the pizza. 'Keep the change.'

The pizza man's face brightened further. He had turned a delivery disaster into a large tip. 'Thank you! Have a good night.'

'I'll try.'

Without hesitation, Pierce carried the pizza to 909 and knocked on the door. He was thankful there was no peephole.

It only took a few seconds for her to answer the door this time.

When she saw Pierce and registered the damage to his face the shock contorted her own unbruised, undamaged face.

'Hey, Lucy. You said next time bring you pizza. Remember?'

'What are you doing here? I told you not to bother me.'

'You told me not to call you. I didn't.'

She tried to close the door but he was expecting it. He shot his hand out and stiff-armed the door. He held it open while she tried to push it closed. But the pressure was weak. She either wasn't really trying or she just didn't have the juice.

'We have to talk,' he said.

'Not now. You have to go.'

'Now.'

She relented and stopped what little pressure she was putting on the door. 'OK, what do you want?'

'First of all, I want to come in. I don't like standing out here.'

She back away from the door and he stepped in. The living room was small, with barely enough room for a couch, an armchair and a coffee table. Pierce closed the door. He stepped farther into the room and put the pizza box down on the coffee table.

'Why don't you sit down, have a piece of pizza?'

'I don't want pizza. If I wanted it I would have bought it from that guy. Is that how you found me?' She was wearing cut-off blue jeans and a green sleeveless T-shirt. No shoes. She looked very tired.

'Yeah, they had your address.'

'I ought to sue them.'

'Forget them, Lucy, and talk to me. You lied to me. You said they hurt you, that you were too black and blue to be seen.'

'I didn't lie.' She pulled her shirt up, exposing her stomach and chest. She had deep purple bruising on the left side along the line where her ribs crested beneath her skin. Her right breast was mis-shapen. There were small and distinctly separate bruises on it that Pierce knew came from fingers.

'Jesus,' he whispered.

She dropped her shirt. 'I wasn't lying. I'm hurt. He wrecked my implant, too. It might even be leaking but I can't get to the doctor until tomorrow.'

Pierce studied her face. It was clear she was in pain and that she was scared and alone. He slowly sat down on the couch.

'Lucy, I'm sorry.'

'So am I. I am sorry I ever got involved with you. That's why you have to leave. If they know you came here they'll come back and it will be a lot worse for me.'

'Yeah, OK. I'll leave.' But he made no move to get up. 'I don't know. I'm batting zero tonight. I came here because I thought you were part of it. I came to find out who was setting me up.'

'Setting you up for what?'

'For Lilly Quinlan. Her murder.'

Lucy slowly lowered herself into the armchair. 'She's dead for sure?' He nodded. 'The police think I did it. They're trying to make a case.'

'The detective who I talked to?'

'Yeah, Renner.'

'I'll tell him you were trying to find her to make sure she was OK.'

'Thank you. But it won't matter. He says that was part of my plan. To cover that I did it.'

She didn't speak for a long while. Pierce studied the headlines of an old issue of the *National Enquirer* that was on the table.

'I could tell him that I was told to lead you to her place,' Lucy said. Pierce looked up at her. 'Is that true?'

She nodded. 'I swear I didn't know he was setting you up, Henry.'

'Who is "he"?'

'Billy.'

'What did he tell you to do?'

'He just told me that I would be getting a call from you, Henry Pierce, and that I should set up a date and lead you to Lilly's place. He said to make it seem like it was your idea to go there. That was all I was to do and that's all I knew. I didn't know, Henry.'

He nodded. 'That's OK. I understand. I am not mad at you, Lucy. You had to do what he told you.'

'I could tell the detective that,' Lucy said. 'Then he would know it was part of a plan.'

Pierce shook his head. 'No, that would put you in danger from Wentz. Besides . . .' He almost said that a prostitute's word would not count for much with the police. 'I don't think it would be enough to change the way Renner's looking at this.' He thought of something and changed tracks. 'Lucy, if that's all he told you to do with me, and then you did it, why did he hurt you?'

'To scare me. He knew the cops wanted to talk to me. He told me exactly what to say. It was a script I had to follow. Then he just wanted me to drop out of sight for a while. He said in a couple of weeks everything will be normal again.'

'So everything you told me about Lilly was part of the script.'

'No. There was no script for that. What stuff?'

'Like about the day you went to her apartment but she didn't show up. That was just made up so I'd want to go there, right?'

'No, that part was the truth. Actually, all of it was true. I didn't lie to you, Henry. I just led you. I used the truth to lead you where they wanted you to go. And you wanted to go. The client, the car, all that trouble, it was all true.'

'What do you mean, the car?'

'I told you before. The parking space was taken and that was supposed to be left open for the client. My client. It was a pain in the ass because we had to go park and then walk back and he was getting all sweaty. I hate sweaty guys. Then we get there and there's no answer.'

It all came back to Pierce. He had missed it the first go round because he didn't know what to ask. Lilly Quinlan didn't answer the door that day because she was dead inside the apartment. But she might not have been alone. There was a car.

'Was it her car in the space?'

'No, like I said she always left it for the client.'

'Do you remember the car that was there?'

'Yeah, I remember because they left the top down and I wouldn't leave a car like that in that neighbourhood. Too close to all the dregs that hang out at the beach.'

'What kind of car was it?'

'It was a black Jag.'

For a moment Pierce felt light-headed. Everything came rushing into his mind at once. He saw it all, lit up and shining, and everything seemed to fit. 'Aurora borealis,' he whispered.

'What?' Lucy asked.

Pierce pulled himself up from the couch. 'I have to go now.'

'Are you all right?'

'I am now.'

'Do you want to take your pizza?'

Pierce shook his head. 'I don't think I could eat it.'

IT WAS TWO HOURS before Cody Zeller showed up at Amedeo Technologies. Because Pierce needed time to prepare things, he hadn't even made the call to his friend until midnight. He then told Zeller he had to come in, that there had been a breach in the computer system. Zeller had protested that he was with someone and

125

couldn't get away until morning. Pierce said the morning would be too late. He said he would accept no excuse, that it was an emergency. Pierce made it clear without saying so that attendance was required if Zeller wanted to keep the Amedeo account and their friendship intact. It was hard to keep his voice under control because at that moment the friendship was already irreversibly sundered.

Two hours after that call Pierce was in the lab, waiting and watching the security cameras on the computer station monitor. It was a multiplex system that allowed him to track Zeller as he parked his black Jaguar in the garage and came through the main entrance doors to the security dais, where the lone security man on duty gave him a scramble card and instructions to meet Pierce in the lab.

Pierce watched Zeller ride the elevator down and move into the mantrap. At that point he switched off the security cams and started the computer's dictation program. He adjusted the microphone on the top of the monitor and then killed the screen. 'All right,' he said. 'Here we go.'

Zeller could only get into the mantrap with the scramble card. The second door had a keypad lock. When he came through the trap to the interior stop he pounded on the copper-sheathed door.

Pierce got up and let him in. Zeller entered the lab with the demeanor of a man who was seriously put out.

'All right, Hank, I'm here. What's the big crisis? You know, I was right in the middle of knocking off a piece when you called.'

Pierce went back to his seat at the computer station and sat down. He swivelled the seat around so he was looking at Zeller. 'Well, it took you long enough to get here. So don't tell me you stopped because of me.'

'How wrong you are, my friend. I only took so long because being the perfect gentleman I had to get her back to the Valley. I got here as fast as I could. What's that smell anyway?'

Zeller was speaking very fast. Pierce thought he might be drunk or high or both. He didn't know how this would affect the experiment. It was adding a new element to the settings.

'Carbon,' he said. 'I figured I'd bake a batch of wires while I waited for you.'

Zeller snapped his fingers repeatedly as he attempted to draw something from memory. 'That smell . . . it reminds me of when I was a kid . . . and I'd set my little plastic cars on fire.'

'That's a nice memory. Go in the lab there. It's worse. Take a deep breath and maybe you'll have the whole flashback.'

'No thanks, I'll pass on that. OK. So I'm here. What's the rumpus?'

Pierce identified the question as a line from the Coen brothers' film, *Miller's Crossing*, a Zeller favourite and dialogue bank from which he often made a withdrawal. But Pierce didn't acknowledge knowing the line. He wasn't going to play that game with Zeller this night. He was concentrating on the experiment he was conducting. 'I told you, we've been breached. Your supposedly impregnable security system is for shit, Code. Somebody's been stealing our secrets.'

The accusation made Zeller agitated. His hands came together in front of his chest, the fingers seemingly fighting with one another. 'Whoa, first of all, how do you know somebody's stealing secrets?'

'I just know.'

'All right, you just know. I guess I am supposed to accept that. OK, then how do you know it's through the data system and not somebody's big mouth leaking it or selling it? What about Charlie Condon? I've had a few drinks with him. He likes to talk, that guy.'

'It's his job to talk. But I'm talking about secrets Charlie didn't know. That only I and a few others know. People in the lab. And I'm talking about this.' He opened a drawer in the computer station and pulled out a small device that looked like a relay switch box. It had an AC/DC plug and a small antenna attached. From one end of it stretched a six-inch cable attached to a computer slot card. He put it down on the desk. 'I looked at the hardware on the mainframe and found this little attachment. It's got a wireless modem. I believe it's what you guys call a sniffer.'

Zeller stepped closer to the desk and picked up the device. 'Us guys? Do you mean corporate computer security specialists?'

He turned the device in his hands. It was a data catcher. Attached to a mainframe, it would intercept all email traffic in the computer system and ship it out over the modem to a predetermined location. Zeller's face showed deep concern. It was a good act, Pierce thought.

'Homemade,' Zeller said.

'Aren't they all?' Pierce asked. 'It's not like you can bop into a Radio Shack and pick up a sniffer.'

Zeller ignored the comment. 'How the hell did that get on there and why didn't your system maintenance guy see it?'

Pierce leaned back and tried to play it as cool as he could. 'Why don't you quit bullshitting and tell me, Cody?'

Zeller looked from the device to Pierce. He looked surprised and hurt. 'How would I know? I built your system but I didn't build this.'

'Yeah, you built the system. And this was built into the mainframe. Maintenance didn't see it because they were either bought off by you or it was too well hidden. I only found it because I was looking for it.'

'Look, anybody with a scramble card has access to that computer room and could've put this on there. I told you when we designed the place you should've put it down here in the lab. For the security.'

Pierce shook his head. 'Too much interference from the mainframe. You know that. But that's beside the point. That's your sniffer. I may have diverted from computer science to chemistry at Stanford but I still know a thing or two. I put the modem card in my laptop and used it as my dial-up. It's programmed. It connected with a data dump site registered as DoomstersInk.' He waited for the reaction and got a barely noticeable eye movement from Zeller. 'One word, ink like the stuff in a pen. But you know that. My guess is that you installed the sniffer when we moved here. For three years you've been watching, listening, stealing. Whatever you want to call it.'

Zeller shook his head and placed the device back down on the desk. He kept his eyes down as Pierce continued.

'A year or so ago—after I'd hired Larraby—you started seeing email back and forth between us about a project called Proteus. Then there was email back and forth with Charlie and then my patent lawyer. You could've put together what was happening from the email. Not the formula itself, we weren't that stupid. But enough for you to know we had it and what we were going to do with it.'

'All right, so what if I did? So I listened in, big deal.'

'The big deal is you sold us out. You used what you got to cut a deal with somebody.'

Zeller shook his head sadly. 'Tell you what, Henry, I'm gonna go. I think you've been spending too much time in here. You know, when I used to melt those plastic cars I'd get a really bad headache from that smell. I mean it can't be good for you. And here you are . . .' He gestured towards the wire lab door.

Pierce stood up. His anger felt like a rock the size of a fist stuck in his throat. 'You set me up. I don't know why, but you set me up.'

'I don't know anything about a set-up, man. Yeah, sure I've been sniffing your shorts. It was the hacker instinct in me. Once in the blood, you know about that. Yes, I put it on there when I set up the system. Tell you the truth I mostly forgot about it, the stuff I was seeing was so boring. I quit checking that site a couple years ago at least. So that's it, man. I don't know anything about a set-up.'

Pierce was undaunted. 'I can guess the connection to Wentz and his pet monster. You probably set up the security on his systems. I mean, I doubt the subject matter would have bothered you. Business is business, right?'

Zeller didn't answer and Pierce wasn't expecting him to. He forged ahead.

'And the phone number. The number was the key. At first I thought it had to be my assistant, that she had to have requested the number for the scheme to begin. But then I realised it was the other way round. You got my number in the email I sent to my A list. You then put it on the site. On Lilly's web page. And then it all began. And that was why I found no phone records at her house. Because they would have shown that I never *had* her number.'

Again he waited for a response and got none.

'But the part I'm having trouble with is my sister. You had to know about her, about the time I found her and let her go. You had to know that this time I wouldn't let it go. That I would look for Lilly and walk right into the set-up.'

Zeller didn't respond. He turned and moved to the door. He turned the knob but the door wouldn't open. The combination had to be entered to go in or out. 'Open the door, Henry. I want to leave.'

'You're not leaving until I know what the play is. Who are you doing this for? How much are they paying you?'

'All right, fine. I'll do it myself.' Zeller punched in the combination and sprang the door lock. He pulled the door open and looked back at Pierce. '*Vaya con Dios*, dude.'

'How'd you know the combination?'

That put a pause in Zeller's step and Pierce almost smiled. His knowing and using the combination was an admission. Not a big one, but it counted.

'Come on. How'd you know the combo? We change it every month—your idea, in fact. We put it out on email to all the lab rats but you said you haven't checked the sniffer in two years. So how'd you know the combo?'

Pierce turned and gestured to the sniffer. Zeller's eyes followed and landed on the device. Then the focus of his eyes moved slightly and Pierce saw him register something. He stepped back into the lab and let the mantrap door close behind him with a loud *fump*.

'Henry, why do you have the monitor off? I see you've got the tower on but the monitor's off.' Zeller stepped over to the computer station and reached down and pushed the monitor's on/off button.

The screen activated and on it was the transcription of their conversation, the last line reading: 'I see you've got the tower on but the monitor's off.'

It was a good program, a third-generation voice-recognition system. The researchers in the lab used it routinely to dictate notes from experiments or to describe tests as they were conducted.

Pierce watched as Zeller pulled out the keyboard drawer and typed in commands to kill the program. He then erased the file.

'It will still be recoverable,' Pierce said. 'You know that.'

'That's why I'm taking the drive.' He slid the computer tower round so he could get to the screws that held the shell in place. He took a folding knife out of his pocket and snapped open a Phillips bit. He pulled out the power cord and began with the top screw on the shell. But then he stopped. He had noticed the phone line jacked into the back of the computer. He unplugged it and held the line in his hand. 'Now Henry that's unlike you. A paranoid like you. Why would you have the computer jacked?'

'Because I was online. Because I wanted that file you just killed to be sent out as you said the words. It's a SacredSoft program. You recommended it, remember? Each voice receives a recognition code. I set up a file for you. It's as good as a tape recording. If I have to I'll be able to match your voice to those words.'

Zeller stood up, going into one of his pockets again. He turned round, opening a silver cellphone. 'Well, I know you don't have a computer at home, Henry,' he said. 'Too paranoid. So I'm guessing Nicki. I'm going to have somebody go by and pick up her drive too, if you don't mind.'

A moment of fear seized Pierce but he calmed himself. The threat to Nicole wasn't counted on but it wasn't totally unexpected either. But the truth was the phone jack was just part of the play. The dictation file had not been sent anywhere.

Zeller waited for his call to go through, but it didn't. He took his phone away from his ear and looked at it as if it had betrayed him. 'Goddamn phone.'

'There's copper in the walls. Remember? Nothing gets in but nothing gets out either.'

'Fine, then I'll be right with you.' Zeller punched in the door combination again and moved into the mantrap.

As soon as the door closed Pierce went over to the computer station. He picked up Zeller's tool and unfolded a blade. He knelt down by the computer tower and picked up the phone line, looped it in his hand and then sliced through it with the knife.

He stood up and put the tool back on the desk along with the cut piece of phone line just as Zeller came back through the mantrap, holding the scramble card in one hand and his phone in the other.

'Sorry about that,' Pierce said. 'I had them give you a card that would let you in but not out. You can program them that way.'

Zeller nodded his head and saw the cut phone line on the desk.

'And that was the only line into the lab,' he said.

'That's right.'

Zeller flicked the scramble card at Pierce. It bounced off Pierce's chest and fell to the floor.

'Where's your card?'

'I left it in my car. I had the guard take me down here. We're stuck, Code. No phones, no cameras, nobody coming down here to let us out for at least six hours, until the lab rats start rolling in. So you might as well make yourself comfortable and tell me the story.'

ELEVEN

Zeller looked around the lab, at the ceiling, at the desks, anywhere but at Pierce. He caught an idea and abruptly started pacing through the lab with renewed vigour, head swivelling as he began a search for a specific target.

Pierce knew what he was doing. 'There is a fire alarm. But it's a direct system. You pull it and fire and police come. You want them coming? You want to explain it to them?'

'I don't care. You can explain it.' Zeller saw the red emergency pull on the wall next to the door to the wire lab. He walked over and pulled it. He turned back to Pierce with a smile on his face.

But then nothing happened. Zeller's smile broke. His eyes turned into question marks and Pierce nodded as if to say, yes, he had disconnected the system.

Dejected by the failure of his efforts, Zeller walked over to a probe station farthest from Pierce in the lab, pulled out the desk seat and dropped heavily into it. He closed his eyes, folded his arms and put his feet up on the table, just inches from a $250,000 scanning tunnelling microscope.

Pierce waited. He had all night if he needed it. Zeller had masterfully played him. Now it was time to reverse the field. Pierce would play him. Fifteen years before, when the campus police had rounded up the Doomsters, they had separated them and waited them out. The cops had nothing. Zeller was the one who broke, who told everything. Not out of fear, not out of being worn down. Out of wanting to talk, out of a need to share his genius. Pierce was counting on that need now.

Almost five minutes went by. When Zeller finally spoke it was while in the same posture, his eyes still closed.

'It was when you came back after the funeral.'

A long moment went by. Pierce waited, unsure how to dislodge the rest. Finally, he went with the direct approach.

'What are you talking about? Whose funeral?'

'Your sister's. When you came back up to Palo Alto you wouldn't talk about it. You kept it in. Then one night it all came out. We got drunk watching a game and then afterwards I had some good stuff left over from a Christmas break in Maui. We smoked that up and, man, then you couldn't stop talking about it.'

Pierce didn't remember this. He did remember drinking heavily and ingesting a variety of drugs in the months after Isabelle's death. He just didn't remember talking about it with Zeller or anyone else.

'You said that one time when you were out cruising round with your stepfather that you did actually find her. She was sleeping in this abandoned hotel where runaways had taken over the rooms. You found her and you were going to rescue her and bring her back home. But she convinced you not to do it and not to tell your stepdad. She told you he had done things to her, raped her or whatever, and that's why she ran away. You said she convinced you she was better off on the street than at home with him.'

Now Pierce closed his eyes. Remembering the moment of the story if not the drunken confession of it to a college room mate.

'So you left her and lied to the old man. Said she wasn't there.'

Pierce remembered his plan. To get older, get out and then come back for her, to find and rescue her then. But she was dead before he got the chance. And all his life since then he knew she would be alive if he had not listened and believed her.

'You never mentioned it again after that night,' Zeller said. 'But I remembered it.'

Pierce was seeing the eventual confrontation with his stepfather. It was years later. He had been handcuffed, unable to tell his mother what he knew because to reveal it would be to reveal his own complicity in Isabelle's death, that one night he had found her but then let her go and lied about it. But, finally, the burden grew until it outweighed the damage the revelation could cause him. The confrontation was in the kitchen. Denials, threats, recriminations. His mother didn't believe him and in not believing him she was denying her lost daughter as well. Pierce had not spoken to her since.

Pierce opened his eyes, relieved to leave the haunting memory for the present nightmare. 'You remembered,' he said to Zeller, 'and you held it tight and you kept it for the right time. This time.'

'It wasn't like that. Something just came up and what I knew fitted in. It helped.'

'Nice penetration. You have a picture of me up on the wall with all the logos now?'

'It's not like that, Hank.'

'Don't call me that. That's what my stepfather called me. Don't ever call me that again.'

'Whatever you want, Henry.' Zeller pulled his folded arms tighter against his body.

'So what's the set-up?' Pierce asked. 'My guess is you have to deliver the formula to keep your end of the deal. Who gets it?'

Zeller turned his head and looked at him, challenge or defiance in his eyes, Pierce wasn't sure which. 'I don't know why we're playing this game. The walls are about to come down on you, man.'

'What walls? Are you talking about Lilly Quinlan?'

'You know I am. There are people who will be contacting you. Soon. You make the deal with them and everything else goes away. You don't make the deal, then God help you.'

'What is the deal?'

'Simple. You give up Proteus. You hand over the patent. You go back to building your molecular memory and computers and make lots of money that way. Stay away from the biologicals.'

Pierce nodded. Now he understood. The pharmaceutical industry. One of Zeller's other clients was threatened by Proteus.

'You can't be serious,' he said. 'Proteus is just a start—we're at least ten years away from any kind of practical application.'

'But that's ten, fifteen years closer than it was before Proteus. The formula will kick start the research. Maybe you're ten years away and maybe you're five. Doesn't matter. You're a threat, man. To a major industrial complex.' Zeller shook his head in disgust. 'You scientists think the world is your oyster and you can make your discoveries and change what you want and everybody will be happy. Well, there's a world order and if you think the giants of industry are going to let a little worker ant like you cut them down at the knees, then you're living in a dream. I'm *helping* you by doing this, Einstein. You understand? This is your dose of reality. Because don't expect the semiconductor people to sit around while you cut them down either.'

'And what do you get for this grand gesture?'

'Me? I get money. Lots of it.'

'So what happens? I make the deal and they bury Proteus. It will never see the light of day.'

'The pharmaceutical industry invents and studies and tests hundreds of new drugs for every one that eventually comes to market after the FDA is through with it. Do you understand the costs involved? It's a huge machine, Henry, and it's got energy and momentum and you can't stop it. They won't let you.'

'They're going to come to me and take away Proteus.'

'They're going to pay you for it. Pay you well. The offer's actually already on the table.'

Pierce sprang forward in his seat, the pose of calm completely disappearing. 'Are you telling me Goddard is behind this?'

'Goddard is only the emissary. The front. He calls you tomorrow and you make the deal with him. You give him Proteus. You don't need to know who is behind him.'

'He takes Proteus from me, then holds ten per cent of the company and sits as chairman of my fucking board.'

'They want to make sure you steer clear of internal medicine. They also know a good investment when they see it. They know you're the leader in the field.' Zeller smiled, as if he was throwing in a bonus.

'What if I don't do it? What if I go ahead and file the patent?'

'You won't get the chance to file it.'

'What are they going to do, kill me?'

'If they have to, but they don't have to. Come on, man, you know what's going on. The cops are this close behind you.' Zeller held up his right hand, his thumb and forefinger an inch apart.

'Lilly Quinlan,' Pierce said.

Zeller nodded. 'Darling Lilly. They're only missing one thing. They find it and you're history. You do as you're told here and that will all go away. I guarantee it will be taken care of.'

'I didn't do it and you know it.'

'Doesn't matter. They find the body and it points to you, then it doesn't matter.'

'So Lilly is dead.'

Zeller nodded. 'Oh, yeah. She's dead.' If not on his face, there was a smile in his voice when he said it.

Pierce looked down. He put his elbows on his knees and his face in his hands. 'All because of me. Because of Proteus.' He didn't move for a long moment. He knew if Zeller was to make the ultimate mistake, he would do it now.

'Actually . . .'

Nothing. That was it. Pierce looked up from his hands.

'Actually what?'

'I was going to say don't beat yourself up about that. Lilly . . . you could say circumstances dictated she be folded into the plan.'

'I don't—what do you mean?'

'I mean, look at it this way. Lilly would be dead whether you were involved in this or not. But she's dead. And we used all available resources to make this deal happen.'

Pierce stood up and walked to the back of the lab where Zeller sat. 'You son of a bitch. You know all about it. You killed her, didn't you? You killed her and set the frame round me.'

Zeller didn't move an inch. But his eyes rose to Pierce's and then a strange look came over his face. The change was subtle but Pierce could see it. It was the incongruous mixture of pride and embarrassment and self-loathing.

'I had known Lilly since she first came to LA. You could say she was part of my compensation package for LA Darlings. And by the way, don't insult me with that thing about me doing the work for Wentz. Wentz works for me, you understand? They all do.'

Pierce nodded to himself. He should have expected as much.

Zeller continued. 'Man, she was a choice piece. Darling Lilly. But she got to know too much about me. You don't want anyone to know all your secrets. At least not those kind of secrets. So I worked her into the assignment I had. The Proteus Plan I called it.' His eyes were far off now. He was watching a movie inside and liking it. He and Lilly, maybe the final meeting in the town house off Speedway.

'You killed her didn't you?' Pierce said quietly. 'You did it and then you were ready, if necessary, to put it on me.'

Zeller didn't answer at first. Pierce studied his face and could tell he wanted to talk, wanted to tell him every detail of his ingenious plan. It was in his nature to tell it. But common sense told him not to, told him to be safe.

'Put it this way, Lilly served her purpose for me. And then she served her purpose for me again. I'll never admit more than that.'

'It's all right. You just did.'

Pierce hadn't said it. It was a new voice. Both men turned at the sound and saw Detective Robert Renner standing in the open doorway of the wire lab. He held a gun loosely down at his side.

'Who the fuck are you?' Zeller asked as he dropped his feet to the floor and came up out of the chair.

'LAPD,' Renner said. He moved from the lab doorway towards Zeller, reaching behind his back as he came. 'You're under arrest for murder. That's for starters. We'll worry about the rest later.' His hand came back round his body holding a pair of handcuffs. He moved in on Zeller, twirled him around and bent him over the probe station. He holstered his weapon, pulled Zeller's arms behind his back and started cuffing them. He worked with the professionalism of a man who had done it a thousand times or more. In the process he pushed Zeller's face into the hard steel cowling of the microscope.

'Careful,' Pierce said. 'That microscope is very sensitive—and expensive. You might damage it.'

'Wouldn't want to do that,' Renner said. 'Not with all these important discoveries you're making in here.' He glanced over at Pierce with what probably passed for him as a full-fledged smile.

ZELLER DIDN'T SAY anything as he was being cuffed. He just turned and stared at Pierce, who threw it right back at him. Once he was secured, Renner started searching him. When the detective patted down the right leg he came up with something. He lifted the cuff of Zeller's pants and pulled a small pistol out of an ankle holster. He displayed it to Pierce, then put it down on the table.

'That's for protection,' Zeller protested. 'This whole thing is bullshit. It will never stand up.'

'Is that right?' Renner asked good-naturedly. He pulled Zeller up off the table and roughly sat him back down in the seat. 'Stay there.' He stepped over to Pierce and nodded towards his chest. 'Open up.'

Pierce started to unbutton his shirt, revealing the battery pack and transmitter taped across his ribs. 'How did it come through?' he asked.

'Perfect. Got every word.'

'You motherfucker,' Zeller said with a steel hiss in his voice.

Pierce looked at him. 'Oh, so I'm the motherfucker for wearing a wire. You set me up for a murder and *you* get upset that I'm wired. Cody, you can go—'

'All right, all right, break it up,' Renner said. 'Both of you shut it.'

As if to accent the point, he tore the tape securing the audio surveillance equipment off Pierce's body with a hard tug. Pierce almost let out a scream but was able to reduce it to 'Goddamn that hurt!'

'Good. Sit down over there, Mr Righteous. It will feel better in a minute.' He turned back to Zeller. 'Before I take you out of here, I'm going to read you your rights. So shut up and listen.' He reached into one of the inside pockets of his bomber jacket and pulled out a stack of cards. He shuffled through them, finding the scramble card Pierce had given him earlier. He reached over and handed it to Pierce. 'You lead the way. Open the door.'

Pierce took the card but didn't get up. His side was still burning.

Renner found the rights card he was looking for and started reading it to Zeller. 'You have the right to '

There was a loud metallic clack as the mantrap door's lock was sprung. The door swung open and Pierce saw Rudolpho Gonsalves, the security guard from the front dais, standing there. His eyes looked dulled and he had one hand behind his back. In his peripheral vision Pierce saw Renner tense. He dropped the card he was reading from and his hand started inside his jacket for his holster.

'It's my security guy,' Pierce blurted out.

In the same moment he said it he saw the security man suddenly propelled into the lab by an unseen force from behind. The guard crashed into the computer station and went over the top of it, the monitor then falling onto his chest on the floor. Then the familiar figure of Six-Eight followed through the door.

Billy Wentz stepped in behind him. He held a large black gun in his right hand and his eyes sharpened when he saw the three men on the other side of the lab. 'What's taking so—?'

'Cops!' Zeller yelled. 'He's a cop!'

Renner was already pulling his gun from his holster but Wentz had the advantage. With the utmost economy of movement the little gangster pointed his weapon across the lab and started firing. He stepped forward as he fired, moving the barrel of the gun in a two-inch-wide back and forth arc. The sound was deafening.

Pierce didn't see it but he knew Renner had started returning fire. He heard the sound of gunfire to his right and instinctively dived to his left. He rolled and turned to see the detective going down, a spray of fat drops of blood hitting the wall behind him. He turned the other way to see Wentz still advancing. He was trapped. Wentz was squarely between him and the mantrap door.

'Lights!'

The lab dropped into darkness. Two flashes of light accompanied the last two shots from Wentz and then blackness set in. Pierce rolled to his right so he would not be in the position Wentz remembered him to be. On his hands and knees he held perfectly still, trying to control his breathing, listening for any sound that was not his own.

There was a low guttural sound to his right and behind him. It was either Renner or Zeller. Hurt. Pierce knew he could not call out to Renner because it would help Wentz focus his next shot.

'Lights!'

It was Wentz but the voice reader was set to receive and identify only the top tier of the lab team. Wentz's voice would not do it.

'Six-Eight? There's gotta be a switch. Find the light switch.'

There was no reply or sound of movement.

'Six-Eight, goddammit!'

Again no reply. Then Pierce heard a banging sound ahead of him and to the right. Wentz had walked into something. He judged by the sound that it was at least twenty feet away. Wentz was probably near the mantrap, searching for his back-up man or the light switch.

Pierce turned and crawled silently back towards the probe station. He remembered the gun Renner had found on Zeller.

When he got to the table he reached up and ran his hand along the top surface. His fingers dragged through something thick and wet and then touched what he clearly identified as someone's nose and lips. He let his fingers follow the face up, over the crown of the head until they found the knot of hair at the back. It was Zeller. And it appeared that he was dead.

After a moment's pause he continued the search, his hand finally clasping round the small pistol. He turned back in the direction of the mantrap. As he made the manoeuvre his ankle clipped a steel trash can that was under the table and it went over in a loud clatter.

Pierce ducked and rolled as two more shots echoed through the lab and he saw two microsecond flashes of Wentz's face in the darkness. Pierce did not return fire; he was too busy moving out of Wentz's aim. He heard the distinct *thwap thwap* sound of the bullets hitting the copper sheeting of the laser lab at the end of the room.

Pierce tucked the gun into the pocket of his jeans, calmed his breathing and started crawling forward and to his left. He reached out one hand until he touched the wall and gathered his bearings, then crawled forward again, using the wall as a guide. He passed the threshold to the wire room—he could tell by the concentrated smell of burned carbon—and moved to the next room down, the imaging lab. Then he slowly stood up.

'Hey, Bright Boy,' Wentz called out. 'It's just you and me now. I'm coming for you. And I'm gonna do more than make you put the lights back on.' He cackled loudly in the darkness.

Pierce slowly turned the handle on the imaging-lab door and opened it without a sound. He stepped in and closed the door. Working from memory, he took two steps towards the back of the room and three to his right. He put his hand out and in another step touched the wall. With fingers spread wide on each hand he swept the wall until his left hand hit the hook on which hung the heat -resonance goggles he had used during the morning's presentation.

Pierce turned on the goggles, pulled the top piece over his head and adjusted the eyepieces. The room came up blue-black except for the yellow and red glow of the electron microscope's computer terminal and monitor. He reached into his pocket and pulled out the gun. He looked down at it. It too showed blue in the vision field. He put a red finger through the stirrup and pulled it in close to the trigger.

As he quietly opened the lab door, Pierce saw a variety of colours in the general lab. To his left he saw the large body of Six-Eight sprawled near the mantrap, his torso a collage of reds and yellows tapering in his extremities to blue. He was dead and turning cold.

There was a bright red and yellow image of a man huddled against the wall to the right of the main computer station. Pierce raised the gun and aimed but then stopped himself when he remembered Rudolpho Gonsalves. The huddled man was the security guard Wentz had used to gain entrance to the lab.

He swept right and saw two more still figures, one slumped over the probe station and turning blue in the extremities. Cody Zeller. The other body was on the floor. It was red and yellow in the vision field. Renner. Alive. It looked like he had turtled backwards into the leg space of a desk. Pierce noted a high-heat demarcation of the detective's left shoulder. It was a drip pattern. The purple was warm blood leaking from a wound. He swept left and then right. There were no other readings, save for yellow reactions off the screens of the monitors in the room and the overhead lights. Wentz was gone.

But that was impossible. Pierce realised that Wentz must have moved into one of the side labs. He took one step through the door-way when suddenly hands were upon him, grabbing his throat. He was slammed back into the wall. The vision field filled with the blaring red forehead and otherwordly eyes of Billy Wentz. The barrel of a gun was pressed harshly into the softness under Pierce's chin.

'OK, Bright Boy, this is it.'

Pierce closed his eyes and prepared for the bullet the best he could. But it didn't come.

'Turn the fucking lights on and open the door.'

Pierce didn't move. He realised Wentz needed his help before he could kill him. In that moment he also realised that the little gangster probably wasn't expecting that he would have a gun in his hand.

The hand that gripped his shirt and throat shook him violently.

'The lights, I said.'

'OK, OK. Lights.'

As he said the words he brought the gun up to Wentz's temple and pulled the trigger. There was no other way. The blast came at the same instant that the lights in the lab suite came on. The vision field went black and Pierce reached his other hand up and shoved the goggles off. They fell to the ground ahead of Wentz, who fell back onto the floor and lay dead still.

Pierce looked down at him for ten seconds before taking his first breath. He then collected himself and looked around. Gonsalves was getting up slowly, using the far wall to hold himself steady.

'Rudolpho, OK?'

'Yes, sir.'

Pierce swung his view to the desk beneath which Renner had crawled. He could see the cop's eyes, open and alert. He was breathing heavily, the left shoulder and chest of his shirt soaked in blood.

'Rudolpho, get upstairs to a phone. Call paramedics and tell them we have a cop down. Gunshot wound.'

'Yes, sir.'

'Then call the police and tell them the same thing. Then call Clyde Vernon and get him in here.'

The guard hustled to the mantrap door. He had to lean over Six-Eight's body to reach the combo lock. He then had to step over the big man's body to go through the door. Pierce saw a bullet hole in the centre of the monster's throat. Renner had hit him squarely and he had gone down right in his tracks.

Pierce moved to Renner and helped the injured detective to crawl out from beneath the desk. 'Where are you hit?'

'Shoulder.' He groaned with the movement.

'Don't move. Just wait. Help is coming.'

'Hit my shooting arm. And I'm useless at distance with a gun in my right hand. I figured the best I could do was hide.' He pulled himself into a seated position and leaned back against the desk. He gestured with his right hand towards Cody Zeller, handcuffed and slumped over the probe table. 'That's not going to look good.'

Pierce studied his former friend's body for a long moment. He then broke away and looked back at Renner.

'Don't worry. Ballistics will show it came from Wentz.'

'Hope so. Help me up. I want to walk.'

'No, man, you shouldn't. You're hurt.'

'Help me up.'

Pierce did as he was instructed. As he lifted Renner by the right arm he could smell the carbon that had permeated the man's clothes.

'What are you smiling at?' Renner asked.

'I think our plan ruined your clothes, even before the bullet. I didn't think you'd be stuck in there with the furnace so long.'

'I'm not worried about it. Zeller was right, though. It does give you a headache.'

'I know.'

Renner pushed him away with his right hand and then walked over to Wentz's body. 'Doesn't look so tough now, does he?'

'No,' Pierce said.

'You did good, Pierce. Real good. Nice trick with the lights.'

'I'll have to thank my partner, Charlie. The lights were his idea.' Pierce silently promised never to complain about the gadgetry again. It reminded him that he had held things back from Charlie, been suspicious. He knew he would have to make up for it in some way.

'Speaking of partners, mine's going to kick himself when he finds out what he missed,' Renner said. 'And I guess I'll be in trouble for doing this on my own.' He looked glumly at the bodies.

'Look,' Pierce said. 'Nobody could have seen all this coming.'

Renner lowered himself into a chair, his face screwed up from the pain. 'You know that stuff Zeller was talking about?' he said. 'About when you were a kid and found your sister but didn't tell anybody?'

Pierce nodded.

'Don't beat yourself up on that any more. People make their own choices. They decide what path to take. You understand?'

Pierce nodded again. 'OK.'

The door to the mantrap snapped. Gonsalves came through. 'They're on the way. ETA on the ambulance about four minutes.'

Renner nodded and looked up at Pierce. 'I'll make it.'

'I'm glad.'

'You know, I guess the shame of it is they're all dead. Now we may never find Lilly Quinlan. Her body, I mean.'

Pierce leaned back against a desk. 'I know where it is.'

Renner looked at him for a long moment and then nodded. 'I should have known. How long?'

'Not long. Just today.'

Renner shook his head in annoyance.

'This better be good. Start talking.'

PIERCE WAS SITTING in his office on the third floor, waiting to face the detectives again. It was six thirty Friday morning. The investigators from the county coroner's officer were still down in the lab. The detectives were waiting for the all-clear signal to come down and were spending their time grilling him.

After an hour of that Pierce had said he needed a break. He retreated from the board room, where the interviews were being conducted, to his office. He got no more than five minutes by himself before Charlie Condon stuck his head through the door. He had been roused from sleep by Clyde Vernon, who had been roused from sleep by Rudolpho Gonsalves.

'Henry, can I come in?'

'Sure. Close the door.'

Condon came in and looked at him with a slight shake of his head, almost like a tremor. 'Wow!'

'Yeah. It's wow all right.'

'Anybody told you what's going on with Goddard?'

'Not really. They wanted to know where he and Bechy were staying and I told them. I think they were going to go over there and arrest them as co-conspirators or something.'

'You still don't know who they worked for?'

'No. Cody didn't say. One of his clients, I assume.'

Condon sat down on the couch to the side of Pierce's desk.

'We have to start over,' Pierce said. 'Find a new investor.'

Condon looked incredulous. 'Are you kidding? After this? Who would—?'

'We're still in business, Charlie. The science is still the thing. The patent. There will be investors out there who will know this. You have to go out and find another whale.'

'Easier said than done.'

'Everything in this world is easier said than done. What happened to me last night and in the last week is easier said than done. But it's done. I made it through and it's given me a stronger fire than ever.'

Condon nodded. 'Nobody stops us now,' he said.

'That's right. We're going to take a media firestorm today and over the next few weeks. But we have to figure out how to turn it to our advantage, to pull investors in, not scare them away. I'm not talking about the daily news. I'm talking about the journals, the industry.'

'I'll get on it. But you know where we're going to be totally screwed?'

'Where?'

'Nicki. She was our spokesperson. We need her. She knew these people, the reporters. Who is going to handle the media on this? They'll be all over this for the next few days, at least, or until the next big thing happens to draw them away.'

Pierce considered this for a few moments. He looked up at the framed poster showing the *Proteus* submarine moving through a sea of many different colours. The human sea.

'Call her up and hire her back. She can keep the severance. All she has to do is come back.'

Condon paused before replying. 'Henry, how is that going to work with you two? I doubt she'll consider it.'

Pierce suddenly got excited about the idea. He would tell her that the rehire was strictly professional, that they would have no other relationship outside of work. He would then show her how he had changed. How the dime chased him now, not the other way around.

He thought of the book of Chinese characters he had left open on the coffee table. Forgiveness. He decided he could make it work. He would win her back and he would make it work. 'If you want, I'll call her—'

His direct line rang and he immediately answered it.

'Henry, it's Jacob. It's so early there. I thought I was going to get your voicemail.'

'No, I've been here all night. Did you file it?'

'I filed it twenty minutes ago. Proteus is fully protected, Henry.'

'Thank you, Jacob. I'm glad you went last night.'

'Is everything OK back there?'

'Everything except we lost Goddard.'

'Oh my gosh! What happened?'

'It's a long story. When are you coming back?'

'I'm going to go visit my brother in Owings, Maryland. I'll fly back Sunday.'

'Do they have cable down in Owings?'

'Yes. I'm pretty sure they do.'

'Keep your eye on CNN. I have a feeling we're going to light it up.'

'Is there—?'

'Jacob, I'm in the middle of something. I have to go. Go see your brother and get some sleep. I hate red-eye flights.'

Kaz agreed and then they hung up. Pierce looked at Condon.

'We're in. He filed the package.'

Condon's face lit up. 'How?'

'I sent him last night. They can't touch us now, Charlie.'

Condon thought about this for a few moments and then nodded his head. 'Why didn't you tell me?' Pierce could see the realisation in his face, that Pierce had not trusted him.

'I didn't know, Charlie. I couldn't talk to anybody until I knew.'

Condon nodded but the hurt remained on his face. 'Must be hard. Living with all that suspicion. Must be hard to be so alone.'

Now it was Pierce's turn just to nod. Condon said he was going to get some coffee and left him alone in the office.

For a few moments Pierce didn't move. He thought about what Condon had said. The words were cutting but true. It was time to change all of that.

It was still early in the day but he didn't want to wait to begin. He picked up the phone and called the house on Amalfi Drive.

MICHAEL CONNELLY

Michael Connelly was midway through one of his acclaimed Harry Bosch novels, and had just moved from Los Angeles to Florida, when the inspiration for *Chasing the Dime* came to him completely out of the blue.

In order to escape the building work he was having done on the new house, he rented an apartment as temporary accommodation for his family. 'But,' he explains, 'I have a five-year-old daughter who made it difficult to get any writing done at the apartment, so I started going to the empty house to work. When I had the phone connected I discovered fourteen messages waiting for me. They turned out to be for a woman who had previously had the same number as mine, and they were from her mother and friends who were worried because she hadn't been in touch for several months. When I rang the mother to explain that the number was now mine, she told me her daughter hadn't been answering calls because she wanted to be by herself for a while. There was no suggestion of foul play, but it served as a springboard for my imagination. I put aside the novel I'd been working on and started writing *Chasing the Dime*. I knew from experience that I wouldn't be able to concentrate on my existing project while my mind was gripped by another idea.'

At the heart of the novel is the science of molecular technology, a subject that has interested Connelly for years. 'My brother has a similar job to that of Charlie Condon in the book, helping to put scientists and financiers together. I've met some of the scientists he works with and find the almost obsessive drive that many of them have quite fascinating.'

Such was the complexity of the subject matter, that Michael Connelly hired a researcher for the first time. 'He put me in touch with one of the leading scientists in this field, Professor Heath at UCLA. I spent a day with him in his lab and that really helped me to flesh out the novel. In general, the things that the scientists do and talk about in *Chasing the Dime* are true. That's the way we are going with technology.'

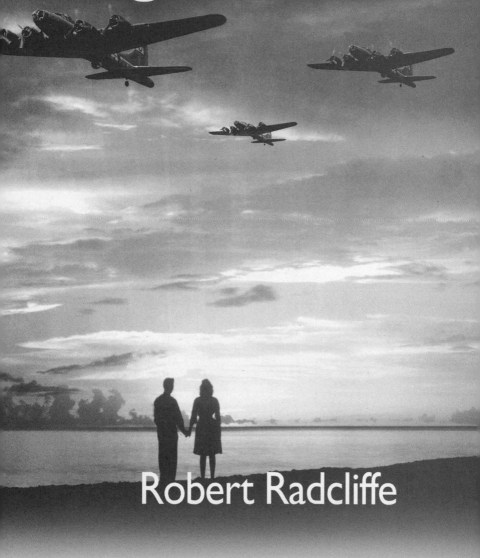

Under an
English Heaven

Robert Radcliffe

As each day dawns, from dozens of
American air bases in East Anglia,
thousands of B-17 bombers take off to
strike against Germany's mighty war
machine. As dusk falls, hundreds fail
to return.

Lt John Hooper is determined to bring
his men, the crew of *Misbehavin' Martha*,
safely through their twenty-five
missions. But the odds, he knows, are
stacked heavily against him.

CHAPTER ONE

'July second 1943. From milk-run to bloodbath in half a second.' Major Finginger, nodding, quickly copied the words into his Intelligence report folder. It was pure poetry. A guileless, unpremeditated nine-word grouping that effortlessly encapsulated the totality of the air war they waged. In the weeks and months that followed, the words would return to him endlessly. From milk-run to bloodbath in half a second. They should drill it into the new crews in basic training back home. They should paint it on signboards suspended above the entrance gate of every air base in East Anglia. It said it all.

It was just such a damn shame he never recorded which of the seven ashen-faced young men slumped around the table in his office that sultry July afternoon had actually said it.

LOREN SPITZER SAID IT.

It happened at 18,000 feet. The formation was on its way home, duty done. The worst was over, behind them, and they were somewhere over the Pas de Calais, heading out across the Channel for home. The mission, Spitzer's first, his whole crew's first, bombing the railway marshalling yards at Rouen, had gone like a dream. Accomplished without a hitch and without loss. A milk run. No fighters showed up, or if they did Spitzer never saw them. Some light 88mm antiaircraft flak sprang up, as predicted, on the run-in to the target, but it never came near. A couple of aircraft in the high formation took flak hits, but both ships were still flying, still maintaining speed and tight in formation.

Spitzer could see them now as he peered up through the convex plastic astrodome set into the roof of his B-17's nose compartment. The high formation, forty bombers, winging its way steadily homewards 1,000 feet above him. Forty silhouetted cruciforms glinting against a flawless milky blue. It was a beautiful, heart-stirring sight.

A thousand feet below him flew the low formation, another flat layer of forty aircraft. And, sandwiched protectively between the two layers, the middle formation. Their formation. It was the perfect defensive box, and *Misbehavin' Martha*, their ship, was tucked right in the middle of it. The safest place of all.

Spitzer tugged at the oxygen mask sucking at his face. His cheeks felt numb and chafed, his mouth was dry and tasted of rubber. Seven hours. Not long, not short; average. To the front, he could see the heads of his pilot, Rudy Stoller, and copilot, Irv Underwood, moving behind the flight-deck windscreen. Spitzer reached for his intercom switch. 'Navigator to pilot.'

Rudy's head came up. 'What is it, Spitz?'

'Just wondered if I could go aft and say hello to the guys back there.'

A chorus of groans and catcalls broke out over the intercom.

'Watch out, fellas, officer prowling.'

'Someone wake up tail gun. He still asleep back there?'

'Be my guest.' Rudy's voice crackled over the headphones. Relaxed, amused. One mission down, twenty-four to go.

Spitzer began clipping his oxygen hose onto a portable walk-around cylinder. At the front of the cramped nose compartment, the bombardier, Dan Broman, shifted on his seat.

'I'm going aft, OK, Dan?' Spitzer called, shuffling awkwardly into the crawlway beneath the flight deck. Broman said nothing, his eyes riveted to the surface of the English Channel almost four miles below. But as Spitzer exited the nose compartment, something caught Broman's eye. A tiny black speck had appeared on the Plexiglas. A squashed bug? An oil spot? But then it moved. A speck that moved?

'That isn't right,' he muttered to himself.

AT LAST THE TRUCK APPEARED. Drab olive green, with a faded white star on its bonnet, it pulled up outside the school gate in a haze of blue exhaust, a grinding of gears and raucous honking of its horn.

'This is it!' Billy announced needlessly. 'Right, now then, everyone follow behind me.'

In an instant, a score of cheering fourteen-year-olds surged past him, sprinting across the playground towards the waiting truck. Billy, his round cheeks red with indignation, stared after them in disbelief. 'Hey! I fixed this, you've bloody well got to wait for me!'

He stamped across the playground towards the truck where his classmates were already swarming over the tailgate. Billy ignored them, stepping up ostentatiously into the driver's cab. His teacher, Heather Garrett, looked on, then rose from the playground bench, lowered sunglasses to her eyes and followed.

They rode, high and riotous, through the village, intoxicated with excitement, cheering and singing, waving and shouting at the bemused passers-by. Heather, limp with heat and languor, quickly relinquished any pretence at control. Instead, she just watched them, young people with no cares other than how to fill both the daily hollowness of their stomachs and the gaping void of the approaching summer holidays. A Yank tea on the base would deliver them, gloriously sick with sugary surfeit, from the first; the second yawned deliciously ahead, ripe with infinite possibility.

Quickly through the village, the truck ground on, accelerating along winding lanes into open countryside. They passed high above tangled hedgerows littered with poppies, busy with sparrows, then sank into the brief cool of the woods, until, all at once, the truck rounded a bend and pulled up before a barrier. Beside the road a wooden signboard: 520TH BOMBARDMENT GROUP, 8TH US ARMY AIR FORCE, BEDENHAM. Two military policemen stood at the barrier. They glanced cursorily at the truck, threw a lazy winking salute in Heather's direction, and waved them through.

WITH A CLOSING SPEED of more than 500 miles an hour, the single-seat Messerschmitt fighter flashed head-on through *Misbehavin' Martha*'s middle formation of bombers in the twinkling of an eye. A momentary glimpse of mottled grey paintwork, a sparkling of cannon fire from a yellow-painted nose, and it was gone, scything through the formation virtually before anyone realised it had ever been there.

Loren Spitzer had just entered *Martha*'s rear fuselage area. It had taken him nearly five minutes to get there. Clutching his portable oxygen cylinder awkwardly to his chest, he had scrambled out of the nose compartment, squeezed along the eight-inch walkway that ran the length of the empty bomb bay, and on through a bulkhead door into the radio operator's cabin. The radio operator, Gerry Via, was busy, headphones clamped to his head, a radio manual open on his desk. The two men exchanged a thumbs up before Spitzer opened a second bulkhead door at the rear of the radio room. Ahead stretched the tapering tubular rear section of the aircraft, *Martha*'s two waist gunners standing at their guns on either side, towards the back. On the floor immediately in front of him, the four-foot spherical ball turret hung in its socket in the floor. Squeezed into it and suspended in space beneath the aircraft, Eldon Ringwald, the youngest and smallest member of the crew, sat hunched over his gun sights, idly watching the French coast unravel behind them. Spitzer began to step awkwardly round the turret.

At that moment there was a muffled but audible clunk, as if someone had rapped on the outside of the fuselage with a spanner. Simultaneously, the right-hand waist gunner, Dave Greenbaum, jerked, then doubled over sideways to the floor. At the same time there was a single long burst of machine-gun fire from the aircraft's tail gunner and the sensation that the bomber was tilting over slightly onto its side.

Spitzer and the other waist gunner, Marion Beans, stared down at Greenbaum's inert form. As they looked, a dark stain seeped from beneath him, quickly spreading across the floor of the fuselage.

'Dave? Greener?' Beans dropped to a crouch beside his friend.

Spitzer moved down the walkway. 'No. It's, ah, OK, Beans, stay at your gun, there may be more fighters. I'll see to him.' Beans hesitated, his round face wide with confusion and disbelief. A gasp of pain escaped from behind the gunner's oxygen mask. 'It's all right,' Spitzer went on, arriving beside Greenbaum's body. 'It's all right, he's alive. Man your gun,' Spitzer repeated. Beans swallowed, then turned back to the machine gun at his window.

'Greenbaum?' Spitzer plugged his intercom lead into a socket. Instantly his head was filled with confused shouts from all over the aircraft. Spitzer slipped off his glove, easing a hand under Greenbaum's chest. The gunner's heavy flying jacket was soaked through already, the leather slick with blood. Spitzer probed gently with his fingers, but could find no tear, no sign of a hole. 'Greenbaum!' he hissed. 'Can you hear me, Dave? Where are you hurt?'

The aircraft was still tilting, banked over ten or fifteen degrees to starboard, and it felt as though it was sliding downwards. They were dropping out of formation, Spitzer realised, his mind numb suddenly with panic. He tried breaking in over the shouts on the intercom. 'Navigator to pilot.' Nothing. He tried again. 'Copilot, this is Spitzer. I'm in the waist with an injured gunner, do you copy that?' Still nothing. Blood was everywhere. Yet still he couldn't see where it was all coming from. Gritting his teeth, he heaved the gunner over onto his back. Greenbaum gasped, his eyes fluttering open. Blood spurted from a gaping rent in his flying suit, down between his legs, bubbling like a geyser. Wrenching at his neck, Spitzer unwrapped the scarf his mother had sent from Boise only a week before, bundled it into a ball and pressed it onto the gunner's groin.

'Ah, listen up, everyone. This is navigator to crew. For God's—' Spitzer struggled to keep his voice calm. 'Gerry? Can you get back here, fast, with the big medical kit?'

The balled scarf in Spitzer's fist was already soaked through. Gingerly he lifted it, peering forward over Greenbaum's body. Instantly blood welled once more, thick and dark, from the torn flesh of the gunner's inner thigh. The wound was shocking. Obscene. But it didn't look fatal. It was just the bleeding—they had to stop it. Greenbaum's eyes stared up into Spitzer's, more in disbelief than in pain. Spitzer pressed down again hard with the sodden scarf. The gunner groaned.

Gerry Via appeared at the radio-room door and began to move awkwardly towards him. He was carrying a medical box under one arm, bracing himself with the other against the increasingly pronounced tilting of the aeroplane. It was up to twenty degrees now. They were in a steepening descending turn. Dropping down and away from the protection of the formation. Easy meat.

The noise of the slipstream was rising, climbing steadily to a shriek as the aircraft accelerated into a diving spiral. Via lost his footing, skidding on blood. As he fell, his hands wrenched open the medical box. Morphine vials, sulphur packs, splints, bandages spilled out onto the floor. 'Jesus.' He scrabbled around on all fours, gathering the contents into his arms, his eyes, shocked, on the pulpy mess at Greenbaum's groin. 'Look at it. What the hell do we do?'

'I don't know.' Spitzer grabbed a compress and tore it open. 'I don't know. We have to stop the bleeding somehow. I think an artery got severed. Or something. In his thigh.' He glanced at Via. 'I thought you were the expert.'

Via stared down at Greenbaum. He had no idea, had only half listened as he daydreamed his way through a two-day course in basic first aid back at Riverdale. It all seemed so remote then. His hands were shaking as he ripped open a sulphur pack, emptying it like a bag of icing sugar over Greenbaum's groin. He and Spitzer grabbed a compress each and covered the wound, pressing down together. He felt the compresses sinking, their hands sinking, into the flesh, the blood warm between his fingers.

SOMEWHAT TO HEATHER GARRETT's surprise, Billy Street, up until that moment supremely cocksure, suddenly suffered an attack of stage fright. With his classmates arranged, at last, in a semi-respectful circle before him, the parked bomber at his back, he now stood in uneasy silence shifting his weight from one foot to the other.

'Take your time, William,' she coaxed. One of the girls standing next to her stifled a giggle.

Movement caught Heather's eye. Nearby, a sergeant mechanic in oil-stained overalls was trying to attract Billy's attention. Nodding minutely, he was touching a finger to the cap on his head. Billy reached behind him and pulled an identical green army cap from his back pocket. After a second's hesitation, he tugged it onto his head, tipped up the brim, American style, and launched into his speech.

Heather inclined her head attentively, glancing at the same time at the mechanic. The name Knyper was stencilled onto his overalls.

Billy's confidence returned as he warmed to his theme, and he was soon conducting the group on a guided tour of the bomber, under the watchful eye of Sergeant Knyper. Heather followed behind, shepherding wayward classmates, nodding encouragingly as Billy paused to point out another important technical feature. She started. The ringing clang of a spanner dropped onto concrete. It really was unusually quiet; there were practically no aircraft to be seen anywhere. She looked at Knyper. He was gazing towards the eastern horizon. 'You've got aeroplanes out on a mission,' she said quietly to him. The children were clustered beneath one of the propellers, Billy holding sway in their midst. Knyper's eyes met hers.

'Yes, ma'am. Due back any time.'

'It must be awful. This waiting.'

'Worst part, no doubt about it.'

'Thank you, Sergeant, for organising all this, for Billy. It's wonderful to see how enthusiastic he is.'

'No problem. Bill's a good kid; practically part of the fixtures.'

'In any case, it really is very kind of you to give up so much of your time for the children. I'm quite sure you must have a thousand more important things to attend to.'

'No,' the sergeant said simply. 'If not for them, then who the hell is it all for?'

FROM THEN ON, from the perspective of Lieutenant Loren Spitzer, everything happened in extreme slow motion.

'Do what you can for him,' his voice said, low and slurred, to Gerry Via's blankly nodding face. He hauled himself wearily to his feet and squeezed through the door to the forward cabin.

There was a loud, piercing whistling coming from up in the cockpit. He stooped round the side of the upper gun turret, then hoisted himself onto the step-up to the flight deck. As he did so, his boot trod on something soft and slippery. He hauled himself up.

The first thing he saw was the horizon; sea and sky, shining wide, flat and blue through what was left of the windscreen. The horizon was canted over at twenty degrees and looked as if it was about 5,000 feet below them. They were still turning, and descending. But not, evidently, as badly as they had been before. This, he guessed, was mostly due to the fact that the twenty-year-old upper turret gunner, Emmett Lajowski, was leaning across the erectly inert form of the copilot, Irv Underwood, and, despite the fact that Underwood's hands were gripping it too, was hauling back for all he was worth on the half-wheel of the copilot's control column.

In fact there were three pairs of hands on the flying controls. In the left-hand seat, pilot Rudy Stoller also gripped his half-wheel, firmly, one fist on either side of it. Spitzer added his two hands to the fray.

For about a minute they laboured with the aircraft's flight controls. Nobody spoke. Then, after what seemed like an aeon, Spitzer saw that *Martha*'s wings were slowly beginning to roll level, and her nose was creeping back up the horizon. Finally, his limited flight experience told him that the bomber was more or less back on an even keel, flying straight and level once more. But he waited until he was quite sure, holding the bomber tightly in his hands, until both the grim nodding of Lajowski's sweat-stained face and the needles on the blood-splattered flight instruments told him it was safe to let go.

Only then did he begin the difficult task of prising away the vice-like grip Rudy Stoller's fingers had on the control column.

'HERE THEY COME,' Knyper said. Heather followed the direction of his pointing arm, and saw a small flat cross climb from the horizon, then another, and another. Gradually they grew larger, shape and detail emerging, crawling across the sky. Then came the noise. A whispered low murmur at first, then a rumble like distant thunder. Finally the noise grew to the familiar pulsating roar of a hundred throbbing engines, until the whole sky seemed filled with it.

The leading bombers were right overhead now. Dozens more followed. One or two of the girls had their hands clamped over their ears. The boys, feigning nonchalance, jumped up and down, punched each other on the arm, pointing excitedly.

One of the bombers banked steeply out from the formation and began to descend for landing. A burst of incandescence appeared at its cockpit window and a red flare flew out, spinning smoke.

'What's that?' Heather shouted above the din.

'It's the wounded-on-board signal. It'll come in to land first. Must have taken a hit.'

The aeroplane was descending too quickly to the runway, Heather could see that. She heard Knyper's sharp intake of breath as tyres struck concrete with an audible squeal of protest and twin puffs of smoke. The aeroplane bounced, rearing into the air again before settling unceremoniously to the ground once more, this time for good.

'He's coming past,' Knyper said. 'Better get the kids to stand back.'

Heather quickly gathered Billy's classmates together as the aeroplane taxied ponderously round the perimeter track towards them, slowing as it came. Behind it, others were lining up to land.

Suddenly the aeroplane stopped. Without warning, right there on the perimeter track next to the clustered children.

A girl screamed. One hand on her mouth, she pointed with the other up at the aircraft's flight-deck window. Another joined in, pointing and screaming. 'Get 'em away!' Knyper was yelling suddenly. 'For God's sake, get 'em away!'

Heather looked up to the window. Red smears.

The screaming went on and on. One of the boys was vomiting onto the concrete at his feet. The aeroplane was called *Misbehavin' Martha*. The inside of the flight-deck window was smeared red. Almost completely obliterated, as though painted out. But not quite. A figure was slumped against it. Heather could clearly see its shoulder pressing against the glass, and, above it, a purple pulpy stump where its head should be.

'WILLIAM STREET, if you are not dressed and downstairs in less than one minute I'm donating your breakfast to the chickens!' There was the usual pause, then the usual follow-up. 'Did you hear me, Billy? And the same goes for you, Claire. Downstairs in the kitchen helping me, right now, young lady. At the double!'

He stirred, the warm constancy of the voice banishing into flight, as always, the pursuing chaos of the night. Fire. The usual dream. That and the running, and not knowing where to run.

He breathed deeply. Another sunny day with lots to do. A bit of foraging first; business is business. Then perhaps a spot of fishing by the river with the lads. A visit up the air base, of course. Maybe even a stroll in the woods, later, with Ruby Moody, if he could persuade her. Saturday. Holidays. Perfection.

Five minutes later his boots were clumping down the narrow stairway and onto the flagstoned floor of the kitchen. The back door was open. A cat, its tail flicking lazily, blinked up at him from a rectangle of sunlight flooding in from the yard.

'Oh, Billy. Good morning, dear. Did you sleep well?' Maggie Howden, a middle-aged woman in a striped butcher's apron, turned to him from the cooking range. She was short and round with red cheeks and newly home-permed hair dyed the colour of polished conkers. She was smiling at him. Kindly. Almost anxiously. There was an egg at his place on the table. A boiled egg. And toast and dripping. And no ticking-off. Something was wrong.

'Yes, thanks, Mrs H. Pretty good.'

'Thank goodness,' said Maggie. 'No more bad dreams then?'

Dreams? He thought back, confused. The bomber! She meant the bomber. Three days ago. He'd completely forgotten. *Misbehavin' Martha*. Blood dripping into puddles on the concrete, a dead gunner in the waist, and a pilot with his head blown off. Puking boys and hysterical, screaming girls. The whole village had heard about it within hours. Those poor children, what a dreadful thing to have to witness. Dr Chillaman had been round to visit everyone. And the vicar. Be nice to them, they'd said to all the grown-ups. Go easy on the kids.

'No. No dreams.' Billy sighed, his eyes falling to the scrubbed pine breakfast table. 'Well, a bit p'raps. You know, there was a lot of blood. And gore and that. Turned the stomach, it did.'

'Yes, quite. Do you think you might be able to manage an egg today? I know it's not Sunday, but the hens seem to be laying a little, and, well, I thought you could probably do with it.'

'I could try my best, Mrs H.' He sat at the table, closed his eyes, sank teeth into warm, greasy toast.

After breakfast, Maggie made him carry a mug of tea out to her husband. Ray Howden's blacksmith's shop was next door to the cottage. Inside it was dim, shadowy and hot. To Billy it was a hellhole, a humourless, airless place of fire and fear and darkness. In the far corner an ancient foot-operated bellows fed wheezing lungfuls of air into a wide, brick forge that shimmered menacingly, white-hot, beneath a charred chimney. A man was bent over it, hammering rhythmically at an anvil. One big tap, followed by a small one.

'Mrs H said to bring you this.'

The tapping stopped. Ray Howden emerged from the shadows at the rear of the shop, accepted the tea with a nod, blew and sipped.

'I'd better be off then,' Billy said, turning to go.

'Just a minute.' Ray's Suffolk accent was softer than Maggie's, his voice measured and quiet. He was a slightly built man, in his late forties, but tough and strong, with sinewy arms and a thick neck. His hair was short, greying, the colour of his eyes. 'Room tidied?'

'Yes, Mr Howden.'

'Breakfast all cleared and washed up? Yard swept?'

'Yes, Mr Howden,' Billy repeated, adding: 'Managed the egg Mrs Howden kindly cooked me all right, too.'

Ray's eyes above the mug were fastened on his. 'You can spare me any of your claptrap, boy. You and I both know there's nothing wrong with your appetite.'

'Can I go now, Mr Howden? Got errands to run for Mrs Howden.'

'Mind you get straight to them, and straight back again. Know what I mean?'

Billy turned on his heel. 'Fair enough. I'll be on my—'

'One more thing.'

He was halfway to the light, the urge to run almost irresistible.

'I don't want you going up the air base today. In fact, I don't want you going up there nearly so much from now on. You're getting far too pally with the Yanks. Do you hear me?'

'Righto then.' He began to edge forward once more. Out of the flames, into the light.

'They've got a job to do and so have we. Far better that we all leave one another alone and just get on with it.'

'Got you, Mr H. Better get going though. Errands and that.'

'HELLO, DEAR. No news, I take it?'

'No. No news.' Heather Garrett leaned forward dutifully for a powdery kiss on the cheek, then held the door wide for her mother-in-law to pass. As usual, she felt a familiar twinge of unease at the arrival. Rosamund Garrett's eyes missed nothing. 'Inspection, surveillance and Intelligence-gathering raids,' David used to call them. 'Comes of being married to a brigadier.'

Heather made tea and carried the tray through from the kitchen. Her mother-in-law was arranged on the slightly threadbare striped armchair Heather kept by the window for reading.

'Well, I have some news,' Rosamund said. 'Gerald's been pulling strings like mad and he's been assured that the Foreign Office is putting terrific pressure on the Japanese authorities, who have promised to look into the whole matter of our missing men and the prisoners of war. Now, what do you think of that?'

Seventeen months of silence. That's what she thought. Seventeen months since a husband of barely six months had held her in his arms, kissed her, marched cheerfully through the door, boarded a troopship for Singapore and vanished into thin air. Seventeen months. She had been separated almost three times as long as she had been married. She had been separated for longer than they had even known each other. For all anyone knew she might be a widow. Might have been for a year or more. Writing pointless weekly letters to a ghost. Nobody knew. Nobody knew anything. Her eyes drifted to the photograph on the table by the fireplace. David, in uniform, his humour-filled eyes beaming proudly from beneath the glossy peak of his cap. So certain, so assured, so visibly, tangibly alive.

A peal of thunder broke on the stairs and a moment later the door opened and Billy appeared, a large cardboard box in his arms.

'I say, miss, couldn't 'ave these, could I?'

'Oh, er, William, this is Mrs Garrett, my husband's mother, Brigadier Garrett's wife? At the Grange?'

'Bill, missus.'

'I beg your pardon, young man?'

'Folks call me Bill. Pleased to meet you, missus.'

'Rosamund, this is William Street, from my class at school. He's helping me clear up the spare bedroom. He lives at the Howdens'. You know, the blacksmith's cottage at the end of Bridge Lane?'

'Good heavens, yes. You're the evacuee, aren't you? From London. Tilbury, wasn't it?'

'Yes, ma'am.'

'And how do you like living here in Bedenham?'

'I love it,' he said simply. 'I love it best in the world.'

'Well, that's good. But you must miss your parents.'

'Um, dunno, missus.' Billy glanced towards Heather, hefting the box in his arms. 'S'pose.'

'Your father. Is he in the Forces?'

'He works on secret stuff, missus. 'Ush-'ush and that. Bank of England.'

'Goodness, how intriguing. And your mother?'

'Dead, missus. Blitz. Direct hit in the Balls Pond Road.'

'But how simply dreadful.' Rosamund looked in astonishment from Billy to Heather and back. Heather stifled a smile. 'And what is that you have there in the box, young man?'

'Just a, er, couple of old jigsaw puzzles and games, and stuff. And this old bashed-up clock.'

'But those are some of David's old things from school. Aren't they, Heather?'

'The games and puzzles all have pieces missing and the clock doesn't work. I'm sure David would have been pleased to know they were going to an East London evacuee with barely a possession to his name.' She hadn't meant to sound so hard. And had she slipped in a conditional perfect? *He would have been pleased.* The past tense?

Rosamund hadn't noticed. 'Well, I don't know.' She shook her head fretfully.

'PSSST. LEN. LENNIE! Can I come in? Where's your dad?'

'Down the Fleece. Get on in here quick.'

Billy slid through the door of his friend's garden shed, pulling it quickly to behind him. Len Savidge, a scrawny thirteen-year-old with a permanently running nose, was emptying out the contents of a box onto a workbench. 'What did you get?' Billy asked immediately. A couple of metal coat hangers, a rusting toy car and a badly dog-eared pack of playing cards fell onto the bench. 'What the hell is all that bloody old junk?' he asked, poking a finger into the pile.

'That's not junk, you idiot, that's all good stuff. Anyway, where's yours then, if you're so clever?'

'Stashed down the mill, of course. What about the bike?'

'I got this,' Lennie announced proudly, pulling a circular mud-guard reflector from his pocket. 'What did you get?'

'Brakes, and the metal holders they go in.' Billy tossed them casually onto the bench.

'Blimey. Where did you get them from?'

'Off the verger's bike, queuing outside the greengrocer's. And I know where we can get a back wheel complete with sprocket, and all.'

They walked back through the village, along a narrow, twisting street that meandered for more than a mile through the fields and woods of the flat Suffolk countryside. At the crossroads they turned left and crossed a narrow humped bridge over a dried-up stream. Next to the stream stood the mill, long since fallen into disuse. Inside, it was damp, gloomy. A corner of floor had been roughly cleared, and in the centre of it a shed door laid over bricks served as a makeshift table, upended beer crates as stools. Three bicycle frames in various stages of dismemberment stood in a corner next to piles of scrap and Billy's boxes of salvage. Two boys were poking through them.

'You're late,' the taller of the two said, without looking up.

'Bollocks. Got the goods then?' Billy replied a little breathlessly.

'Yep.' The second boy produced a small sack and held it up. Something wriggled inside it. 'Got yours?'

Billy handed him a packet of cigarettes. 'Navy Cut, like you said.'

'Right. We're off. See you later. Coming, Len?'

'Wait,' Billy said. 'Aren't you coming up the base?'

'What for? It's miles of bloody walking, and when you get there the MPs just turf you off again. We're going up the riverbank, meet some of the girls. Shirley's coming, Dolly Makepeace said she might too. And Ruby Moody. Stan Bolsover's got a bottle of cider, so we'll have a wet and a smoke.'

'Ruby's coming?' Billy looked from one to the other.

'Too right. You?'

'No . . .' He hesitated. 'No, got business. Anyway, what about the bikes? We said we was going to work on them today.'

'You work on them. We're off.' The three turned as one for the door.

'They sell for four quid apiece up the base!' Billy called after them. 'I ain't giving you any of it if you don't help fix them up.'

'Keep it.' A voice from outside. Muffled laughter. 'You want to get out more, Bill Street! She fancies you, Ruby does. She said so.'

IT WAS EARLY EVENING when Billy slipped behind the big number two hangar and back into the woods beyond the base. Without pausing, he hurried along the familiar path until the sounds of the airfield had fallen well behind. Only then did he stop.

He still couldn't believe it. The best day ever. He'd sold the lot. Everything. But better than that, most important of all in fact, was Hal Knyper's present. Billy took the bundle from under his arm and unrolled it. They were army green, of course, and secondhand, and slightly too big. But no matter, they were the real thing, real mechanic's overalls and, best of all, Hal had got his name stencilled on the chest. 'Street B. Pfc.' Bill Street, Private first class.

For what seemed like ages he just stared down at the overalls in amazed silence. Then, with a deep sigh, he rolled them up once more and began emptying his pockets.

Apart from the sticks of gum and candy bars, there was a total of eighteen shillings and threepence halfpenny in cash. He'd managed to get eight bob for the kitten he'd traded with Len's mate for the Players. One of Hal's trainee mechanics bought it. Next, he got a confirmed order for one of the bikes from a rookie gunner in hut six. Billy told him that demand for bicycles was high, which it was, and that the gunner had to put down a deposit of five bob. He paid up without a murmur, which meant that Bill could put the money towards buying tyres which were the most expensive part.

The rest of the stuff he sold piecemeal, wandering unchallenged from one hut to the next, his box tucked under his arm. The 'lucky' horseshoes he pinched from Ray's forge always went well, and he got a florin for Mrs Garrett's husband's alarm clock.

The only tricky bit had been the business in hut twelve. It wasn't until after he'd actually banged on the door and got in there, after he'd begun his sales pitch in fact, that he realised that the men in the hut, lying unusually quietly on their bunks, or sitting at a little table playing poker, were the ones from *Misbehavin' Martha*.

'Good luck charms?' one of them interrupted incredulously halfway through Billy's spiel. He was sitting on his bed, smoking a cigarette, rocking backwards and forwards. 'Did he say good luck charms?'

'Scram, kid,' another of them added. 'We don't want any of it, and you shouldn't be in here anyways, so beat it before I call the MPs.'

'Take it easy,' a third said. 'He ain't doing any harm.'

'Shove it up your ass, Tork. We don't want it, it's kids' junk.'

'Good luck charms. Now, I sure would like to see that,' the first man kept saying. His cigarette had finished, burned right up to his fingers. He immediately lit another. 'Do they work?'

Something about his voice, a calm, a chill, was not right. Billy turned to go. 'Listen, I'd better be off. Next time, see, I can bring more, um, goods and stuff.'

'No, wait!' The man sprang from his bed. 'Wait. I really want to take a look at the good luck charms.' The man, Lajowski, tall, with a heavy jaw covered in thick black stubble, began to rummage through the box. 'Oh, well now, looky here. A little toy car, no wheels. That's lucky. Should work well against 88-millimetre flak, wouldn't you say? Oh, and here's a little kiddie's christening spoon. Stephen, it says on it. Lucky as hell that, Focke-Wulf one-nineties just hate those little baby spoons. What's your name?' he said, his voice deathly quiet.

'Bill, um, Billy, Street.'

'You see the thing is, Billy Street, I don't think it's very nice you coming in here, trying to sell us your garbage. That's profiteering. We're up there busting our asses, just to save yours, and all you want to do, all any of you want to do, in fact, is see just how much you can screw out of us before we go and get killed.'

'Emmett. It's enough now, let him go.' Gerry Via had got up from the card table, was resting his hand lightly on Lajowski's shoulder.

'Take your hands off of me, Via.'

'Let the kid go,' Via soothed. 'Emmett, it's OK.' He took Billy's arm, pulling him away from Lajowski and round behind him. 'Go, now, Billy, it's OK, the guys are just a little tired right now. Go.' A moment later Billy found himself back in the open air, heart thudding, the door to hut twelve closing quietly in his face. He looked round uncertainly, then, hefting his box under his arm once more, he set off back along the perimeter towards Hal Knyper's hangar.

IKEN WAS MORE than an hour away from Bedenham by bicycle, but for Heather, setting off from the cottage into the early-evening balm, her pencil and notebook lying in the handlebar basket together with a sandwich and an apple, it was a much longed-for hour, brimming with rare and unexpected happiness.

At first she pedalled quickly, her head bent to the task of putting distance between her and the village. In no time at all she found herself gliding clear of the last cottages and on, unnoticed, into open countryside. She cycled generally eastwards, bypassing the busy town of Framlingham.

Iken was a village, little more than a hamlet, nestling amid a belt of marshy farmland three miles from the coast. Its church was legendary.

It stood alone on a little wooded hill, above the broad sweep of a wide river that curved back sharply beneath it to steep sandy cliffs thick with bracken and overhanging trees. Its origins, Heather knew, were Saxon at least, but almost certainly older. It was a place of pilgrimage, a place people felt compelled to return to.

Heather leaned the bicycle against a gate, plucked her notebook from the basket and wandered across the empty churchyard. The sun was setting over to her left, the air above her hung still and soft. She would never get back to Bedenham before dark, but she didn't care. She pulled the pencil from her notebook and pushed the door open.

A man was sitting, his back to her, in a pew near the front. She hesitated, momentarily uncertain, mildly irritated. He wasn't praying, evidently, just sitting. Perhaps she should wait outside until he was finished; perhaps she should carry on and ignore him.

But then he stirred, as though from sleep, turned, saw her and stood up quickly. He was an American. A flier, a lieutenant in uniform, his cap in his hand. He had dark hair and eyes, and a sort of sad, apologetic smile.

'It's kind of difficult to make sense of man's apparently unending need to create war against his fellow man,' he said, 'when he is also able to create a place like this.'

FOR JOHN HOOPER, sitting in the cool evening quiet of that church, the journey there begins, and ends, four weeks earlier, with the dawn rap of knuckles on door.

A click. Harsh light rudely severs the night's warm embrace. The Ops orderly's hand rocks his shoulder. 'Good morning, Lieutenant, it is four o'clock. You are flying today.' Another mission, the same routine. It is takeoff minus three hours.

He struggles from the warmth of his blankets, showers, shaves and dresses. Thermal underclothes first, then his uniform. Olive-green wool trousers and shirt, low-cut brown Oxford shoes, black wool tie. He likes to wear the short Eisenhower uniform jacket for flying. It is smart, comfortable, rides easily beneath the heavy flying suit, and if he gets shot down and has to spend the rest of the war in a POW camp, it's the one he wants with him.

A truck pulls up. He goes outside, climbs up in the back with the others, shivers. Low, murmured exchanges only; the day is too young, and they are too pensive, for anything more. The short ride to the mess hall. The two American Red Cross girls standing at the entrance smile beatifically. It is practically the middle of the night, yet there they are again, their hair fixed, their faces made up, uniforms clean-pressed, mission after mission, fresh and perfect. It does a man's heart good. 'Good morning, Lieutenant. Coffee?' Mission breakfast: better coffee than usual, crisp Canadian bacon, pancakes, real eggs. He eats sparingly, but savours the coffee. Not too much; it is a cold trek from the cockpit to the relief tube in the bomb bay. The hollowness fills out a little and people start to talk.

Takeoff minus two hours. He walks with the others to the briefing room, a large Quonset hut. Smack on time, the doors swing open at the back and the station adjutant's voice barks the hall to attention. Talking stops, everyone stands and pops raggedly to. The Group CO marches down the centre aisle together with Group Intelligence and a couple of senior brass hats from HQ.

Everyone sits again, then the Group Intelligence major steps up to the stage, pauses for effect, then peels the drape off the wall map.

'Gentlemen, today we go to Kiel,' he announces portentously.

Around the room 250 men draw breath. A long line of blood-red ribbon is pinned across the wall map behind the major's pointing arm. It is their route to the target: Kiel.

There is a second's stunned silence in the hall, then a low groan, and instantly the buzz starts up. Muttered incredulities, low whistles, a few feeble wisecracks. It's insane. The distance. It's the deepest penetration of Germany ever attempted. They will be over enemy territory, in broad daylight, for hours and hours. There's worse. It's too far for their fighters, the little Mustangs and Thunderbolts, to escort them. For a large part of the distance, the most dangerous part, they will be on their own. And Kiel. Germany's precious shipyards. Kiel will be defended to the teeth. Then the major shushes everyone down again and the briefing proper gets under way.

Takeoff minus one. The truck drops them at the plane. On the way they stop at Equipment to collect the leather flying suits with electrically heated elements woven inside them, fur-lined overboots, Mae West life jackets, parachutes and harnesses. Out at the hardstanding the B-17 sits heavy on its tyres, visibly overloaded.

While the others board, Hooper makes his walk-around inspection, Altman, his crew chief, at his side. It's a needless formality, the walk-around, Altman's the best, but it's time-honoured, a ritual handing over of the ship from engineer to pilot. He checks that the control locks are out and that the wheel chocks are in. He inspects damage repairs, runs a finger under a tightened oil line, kicks a tyre. On board the others are settling in.

On the far side of the field an engine shatters the peace, sputtering noisily to life. Then another. It is time. 'Good work, chief. Ship looks swell.' He signs Altman's clipboard, and shakes his hand, his own little ritual, swings up through the hatch and locks it behind him.

LIEUTENANT JOHN HOOPER was wrenched to wakefulness upon the perspiration-drenched sheets of his hospital bed by the agonised cries of his dead tail gunner. He heard them constantly, in his waking dreams, in the long, still watches of the night, in the echoing cries of the other patients around the hospital. But this time was different. Now, for the first time, he could remember why he heard them. And who they belonged to. And how they got there. His eyes had been wet when he'd woken. Maybe it was a good sign.

'It's a good sign, John,' Brent Wallis said, shining a torch into Hooper's left eye an hour later. Hooper recoiled, his body rigid on the bed. At last the probing heat was withdrawn. Wallis sat back, apparently satisfied. 'What else do you remember?'

'Not much,' Hooper replied selectively. Terror. The overwhelming need to escape. Sorrow beyond bearing. Guilt. 'Running. Soft ground, gasoline fumes, a big bang. Then nothing, until waking up in the base hospital two days later.'

'Five days, as it happens. The mission? The crash?'

Hooper exhaled, shaking his head. 'Sorry, Major, not a thing.'

'No matter, it'll come, it's already starting to.' Wallis gathered his instruments together. 'I'd like to talk to you again later, in my office. Feel like getting up?'

It took Hooper the best part of an hour and the patient assistance of two nurses. They hauled him upright where at last he stood, swaying, a nurse on each arm, like a drunk at a party. Finally, after a couple of experimental laps of the room, they gave him a wheelchair and a stick, and left him to get on with it.

'THIS IS A NEUROLOGICAL unit, officially,' Wallis explained later in his office. 'You know, nervous systems, their disorders, all that hokum. Unofficially, it's just where they send all the head cases.'

Hooper shifted on his chair, unnerved by the doctor's apparent indifference. Is that why I'm here? he wondered. Across from him, Wallis sat at a mahogany desk. His eyes were locked on Hooper's.

He leaned forward. He wore a white coat over his uniform. He clasped his hands together on the desk before him. A buff document file lay beneath them.

'So, we get the whole bag here, anything and everything, in other words, that can't be fixed with a sticking plaster. The confused, the unstable, the delusional and the suicidal. The amnesiac, of course—that's you, John.' He was counting off on his fingers. 'The insomniac, the euphoric and the catatonic. Those that don't sleep, don't eat, don't talk. Those that don't even move, sometimes.'

'Don't or won't?' Hooper broke in quietly.

'Same difference in my view. Do you know what the Brits call combat fatigue, John?' Hooper shook his head. 'Get this, they call it "lack of moral fibre". Can you believe that?'

'I don't have combat fatigue, Major. I want to get back into it.'

'Yes, I believe that.' Wallis picked up the file at last. 'Trouble is, John, you don't remember what or where the hell "it" is.'

THEY TALKED FOR OVER AN HOUR. After a hesitant start, Hooper found that he could recall with comparative ease details of his early life in Pennsylvania and his decision to join the Air Corps following Pearl Harbor. Wallis dropped the file to his desk. 'And after training you were assigned to the 95th Bombardment Group, based firstly at Alconbury, where you arrived with your crew in the delivery aircraft in March of this year, then on to the 95th's permanent home up the road at Horham. Which way did you fly the Atlantic crossing, by the way? North about, was it? Gander, then Greenland, Iceland, Scotland?'

'Yes, uh, yes it was, north about, that's correct.'

'What else? Can you remember anything else?'

But there was nothing. After arriving in England the fog was a wall. He fumbled in vain for the slenderest finger-hold, a fragment of memory, any slight detail. There was none. Except one.

'There was an explosion. A huge one. At Alconbury. One afternoon, shortly after we arrived. I remember that. A B-17 blew up on the ground.' It was fully laden, armed, bombed and fuelled to the gills. Its ground crew were still working on it when without warning it simply vanished, taking them all with it.

'Yes, I heard about that.' Wallis was jotting on a notepad. 'You were there?'

'Yes. I . . . well, I believe so. It sort of stuck in my memory.'

'Uh-huh. Anything else?'

'No. Sorry. That's it.'

There was a long pause while Wallis resumed his note-taking. At last he looked up. 'Do you know what sodium pentothal is, John?'

'No.' Hooper swallowed.

'It's a drug. Sometimes known as the truth drug. We find it quite effective, in certain cases, in trying to help people who are suffering from amnesia. It can be very helpful in that respect.'

'I don't want it.'

'It's nothing to be afraid of, John. It can help break down a log jam, and the side effects are negligible.'

'I don't want it. Major, the amnesia is getting better, you said so yourself. I just need a little time.'

Wallis tore the page off the pad and slid it across the desk. 'I'm sending you to the 101st RCD, John. A flak-shack, in other words. It's a quiet little country house not far from here that the 8th Air Force uses for officers in need of a break. I want you to go there, get some R and R, get strong and then come back here and we'll talk again.'

Hooper took the note and rose from the chair. 'Thank you, Major.' He turned for the door.

'One more thing you should know, Lieutenant. Two, in fact. Firstly, you did not fly your aircraft across the Atlantic north about, you came south about: West Palm Beach, Natal, Dakar, Morocco then St Eval, Cornwall. And that explosion you mentioned at Alconbury. On that date, according to your records, you were on a precision-flying course in Catterick. Hundreds of miles away.'

AFTER HIS FIFTH NIGHT at the 'flak-shack', Hooper placed a call to Brent Wallis. 'Something happened. On the Kiel mission. Something bad. Didn't it?'

'Lieutenant, I trust you are not expecting me to discuss mission details over an open telephone line,' Wallis replied formally. Yet there was no mistaking the flicker of interest in his voice.

'I . . . no. Sorry.' Eyes squeezed shut, Hooper pressed fingers, pincerlike, into his temples. 'Major,' he pleaded, his voice little more than a whisper. 'Please, can't you tell me anything?'

It had woken him in the night. Kiel. One moment he had been resting in comparative peace between the clean sheets and warm blankets of his private bedroom, the next, the night was split by a man's scream and instantly he was sitting upright, a trembling arm reaching for the bedside light. The shout, unearthly, blood-chilling, echoed through his head. Was it his? One of the other guests? Or Bowling, yet again? Young Danny Bowling, his baby-faced dead tail gunner. And he *was* dead. That much was certain.

Kiel. Hooper had hoisted himself up in the bed, his chest damp with perspiration. He reached for his water tumbler, drank greedily. He definitely remembered Kiel. Some of it. Being woken, the dawn, the briefing, taking off, forming up. Then the nightmare, the fighters, the flak, Fortresses falling all about him like flaming leaves. Then a bang. Then the fog. They'd been hit. An 88mm flak hit, right over the target. But what then? Had they crashed? Bailed out? Ditched in the ocean? No, he was home. Concussed but alive, back in England. They'd got back, they must have. Wallis was talking.

'John. Don't you see? That's why we need you to tell us.'

'You mean you don't know?'

Fractional hesitation. 'No. I mean, if I tell you, anything, then it defeats the whole damn object of the exercise. My job is to help you recover your memory yourself. Listen. You've still got my Jeep, right? Why don't you come over this afternoon and we can discuss it here? The sooner we get your memory back, the sooner we can get this whole thing cleared up. There's nothing to be fearful of.'

Hooper put the telephone down.

He left the flak-shack thirty minutes later. He dropped his bag into the back of the Jeep, climbed behind the wheel and thumbed the starter. There was a map in a side pocket; Wallis had given it to him together with directions. He found the base on it, Horham, home of the 95th; it could only be forty minutes' drive. He'd go there, find the guys, get to the bottom of this once and for all.

Halfway there, he wrenched the Jeep onto a grass verge and braked to a stop. Maybe not the base. His thoughts were coming in wild batches; a mad rush, a pause, a regroup. The base, maybe not such a good idea. Technically he was still hospitalised. Under Wallis's guardianship. Or custody? He needed to speak to someone, anyone, who might know something.

He drove on, mind in turmoil. After a while he came to a small town and stopped at a post office.

'Yes, Lieutenant?' The woman behind the counter beamed, her eyes brazenly on his.

'Yes, uh, I need to use a telephone, if possible.'

'There's a queue.' The woman gestured towards a booth at the back of the post office.

It took twenty minutes. Finally his turn came, and he gave the operator the number and waited. Eventually, a series of clicks and she put him through.

'Ninety-fifth Bomb Group, station adjutant speaking,' an American voice said.

Suddenly Hooper didn't know what to do.

HOOPER AND HIS CREW had taken off, together with twenty-four other aircraft of the 95th Bomb Group, a little after 7.00am and headed out over the North Sea. They were flying in a new formation devised by Brigadier General Nathan Forrest. Somehow, he had persuaded the 8th US Army Air Force to abandon the defensive three-layered box formations so beloved of the crews that flew them. Instead, he argued, a flat formation, with the aircraft spread out in groups of six across a horizontal plane, would provide a more effective field of fire. Despite problems in training, the new formation, together with a new oil that had been developed for the B-17's machine guns, would be tried out on the mission to Kiel. Forrest was leading the mission. Personally. From the front.

The first German fighters appeared before they'd even reached the enemy coast. Until that day, the pilots that flew the tiny Focke-Wulf and Messerschmitt fighters against the formidable defensive box formations had but one main tactic at their disposal. Try to dive straight down through the middle of the box in the hope of breaking it up; a courageous but dangerous and often futile manoeuvre. Now, to their surprise, they found that there was no box and began to attack head-on, with lethal effect. Within minutes Fortresses were falling. And as the formations droned steadily deeper into their airspace, the German pilots, emboldened by their success, began calling up their friends, summoning more and more fighters up to the fray.

'Jesus. They're like gnats around a camel's ass,' a lone voice broke in soberly over the radio. Hooper and his copilot stared out in awe. The air above and ahead of them was thick with fast-moving specks. Many more, they knew, circled to the rear.

'Keep it quiet, keep it tight, cover your backs.' That was the lead aircraft, General Forrest's, breaking radio silence to steady nerves and bring formations in tighter. Tighter? Hooper, perspiring within his heavy flying suit, wrestled with the controls in the turbulent air. They were too close already.

'Here they come!' Hooper's copilot, Pete Kosters, pointed ahead through the windscreen. In silence they watched four fighters peel down from above and slice through the formation at enormous speed. Hooper could do nothing but hold position and duck. Instantly, a Fortress to their left reared slowly upwards, rolled over onto its back, flames pouring from its belly, and dropped away towards the sea.

Still the disintegrating formations kept on towards the target. As they drew nearer to it, flak, ground-based antiaircraft shells, began to explode in the sky around them. Bursts of dirty orange amid puffs of black smoke, sporadic and inaccurate at first, then growing in intensity and accuracy as the gunners on the ground found range and distance. All around them was carnage, but nobody turned and fled. They just went on and on into a waking nightmare of exploding skies and falling planes.

Then, almost without realising it, they were at the IP, the Initial Point, and turning in at last for the bomb run. Somehow, impossibly, it got worse. Hooper switched on the autopilot, handing over control of the plane to the bombardier lying prone in the glass nose dome beneath his feet. Now there was nothing to do except sit in numb helplessness, and wait and pray. The air was thick with flak, an intense, furious barrage flung up at them by hundreds of antiaircraft guns, completely filling the sky with exploding clouds of white-hot hail that tore through the flimsy skins of the bombers like paper.

Forrest's aircraft got hit. Hooper saw it, far out in front, set upon by two fighters simultaneously. Flying one down each side, they raked it with fire from end to end. Straight away it flopped over and dropped away. 'Is that the lead airplane going down?' a voice asked over the headphones. A hand grabbed suddenly at Hooper's shoulder, and he jumped, turned in alarm. The hand was a bloody mess, the fingernails torn and bleeding. It was Joey Galba, his soft-voiced upper turret gunner from Iowa.

'Joey, Jesus, are you hit?' Hooper shouted. Galba shook his head. There were tears in his eyes from the pain and cold. His guns had frozen up. The charging handles, seizing solid, had snapped off in his hands. He'd torn off his gloves and been trying to charge them with his bare fingers. He hadn't been able to fire a single round. The new oil.

And then there was an almighty thump from behind, like a two-fisted punch to the back. The aircraft bucked, then it staggered. Thick, acrid smoke filled the cockpit; someone was shouting over the intercom. But Hooper just sat in stunned silence, watching in detached fascination while the ground, a kaleidoscopic spiral of fields and buildings and shipyards and trees, swirled nearer and nearer. He eventually regained control of the plummeting aircraft at 3,000 feet, banking steeply away from the smoke-enshrouded target and turning roughly west. Then he took stock. One propeller, the port outer, was windmilling uselessly. Quickly he feathered it. There were flak holes along the wings and fuselage, a large section of rudder was missing, two of the fuel tanks had been holed. The controls were shaking in his hands as he called up the crew one at a time over the intercom. And one at a time, they reported back to him. All nine. All alive. It was scarcely believable. No one killed, not one.

Fortune favoured them a while longer, their escape from enemy airspace, by a miracle, going undetected as Hooper turned on to the heading for home. But then the tide changed against them. The number three engine, the starboard inner, began to overheat, boiling oil streaming back over the wing. The temperature gauge needle slid off the dial and the seizing engine began to shudder violently in its mountings. Hooper shut it down before it tore the wing off. From that moment on, heading out over the wide North Sea on just the two remaining engines, they began to lose height.

And so they jettisoned everything, but still they fell and soon there was nothing left to ditch. Almost nothing. Lodged at a slight angle in its rack nestled a single bomb. When the bombardier had toggled the bomb release switches over the target, all except one had dropped from the racks. This one. The biggest. It was fully armed, ready to go. The two waist gunners offered to try to kick it free, but Hooper forbade anyone to go near it.

And now, finally, the fog. Hooper's plan—overfly the English coast, order the crew to bail out, turn the deserted airplane to face back out to sea, then follow the crew over the side—was now seriously compromised. Firstly the coast, together with the sea, the land, everything below them in fact, had vanished. Secondly, with every passing minute they sank lower and lower. Within just a few minutes, the doomed aircraft would be too low for anyone to bail out. They would be crash-landing into the sea, or onto the land. In zero visibility. With a live 500-pound bomb on board.

HOOPER ASKED TO BE put through to the maintenance section. Ground crews know everything there is to know. So it was Altman who told him. His trusted crew chief. Marooned in the telephone booth in the crowded post office, a steady flow of people eddying by, he listened in silence and let the words fall like tears.

'They're gone, Hoop, buddy,' Altman said simply, towards the end. 'Didn't they tell you that in the hospital?'

'Gone? All of them? But it isn't possible.'

'One of the coastal batteries near Orford, I think it was. They reported hearing a lone B-17 coming in very low over the coast at around three that afternoon. A while later a couple of local people heard a crash landing on farmland somewhere in the neighbourhood. Then a confirmed report of an explosion, some time later.'

He felt sure he'd watched them jump clear, one by one, watched as their parachutes streamed then blossomed, watched them, alone in his cockpit, drifting down towards the fog layer. A flooding sense of relief, tinged with an acute loneliness.

'You were found a hundred yards from the wreck.' Altman was still talking. 'Unconscious. Severe concussion, we were told later. There was the remains of one body found in the debris. Danny Bowling, tail gunner. The rest turned up over the next few days.'

'Turned up?' A flicker of confused hope.

'On the beach. It took a week or so, but their bodies all washed up in the end. Much better that way, wouldn't you say, buddy? At least we got them back and they got to be sent home to their families.'

He left the post office and wandered back to the Jeep. After a while he started the motor and began to drive, following Altman's directions, to the crash location in Orford. By the time he found the site it was early evening. The salvage crews had done their usual thorough job. There was nothing left except a wide circle of scorched crops, a slight depression in the ground, and a few missed fragments. He stood in the centre of the crash site, stooped to pick up a twisted shard of fuselage. He'd killed them all.

He began to walk. Slowly, away from the site, skirting fields. Following tracks, crossing ditches, the river on his right. He climbed a steep bank and saw it flowing brown and slow, with wide mud flats that glistened in the setting sun like burnished copper. He kept walking, following the bank. In the distance a low, tree-covered hill jutted into the river, a small church tower peeking through above.

He'd killed them all. It was what Wallis wanted to know. How? How on earth could it possibly happen that nine members of a ten-man crew perished, yet one, their leader, escaped with a bump on the head? Even though the details were still not clear to him, even though, in truth, he could not recall the exact final events, and perhaps never would, he didn't need to. He knew enough. He'd ordered them to bail out before they crossed the coast and thus dumped them into the freezing waves miles from shore where they all drowned. All but Danny Bowling who, for reasons unknown, crash-landed with him. Then he'd abandoned him too, left him, trapped and injured. With Danny's anguished cries ringing in his head, he'd scrambled through the cockpit window, dropped to the ground and fled into the mist. Then the bomb went off.

The church was small, still and cool. It was deserted. He went in and sat on a pew at the front. He was alone. It was as it should be.

After a while, ten minutes, an hour, he had no idea, he stirred in his pew. It was getting late. He stood and turned to leave, and then he heard a movement. A young woman was standing in the arched door-way, the last of the evening light throwing her body into silhouette.

CHAPTER TWO

'Spam casserole?' seventeen-year-old Claire Howden poked at the watery lumps on her plate, wrinkling her nose distastefully. 'I can't possibly eat this.'

'I can!' Billy's arm reached over. Instantly, Maggie's hand shot out, slapping his wrist.

'You keep your thieving hands off, William Street, and as for you, young lady, you'll eat what you're given and jolly lucky to have it.' She sat down at the kitchen table, eyeing her own plate forlornly.

'It's fine, Mags, love,' Ray soothed, patting her hand. Four heads lowered as one. 'Billy? Mind you do it proper now.'

'What about recede truly thankful amen.'

They began to eat. A moment later a tiny tinkle of shaking cutlery was followed by the deafening thunder of passing engines. Instinctively they all ducked. 'That's a bit bloody low, isn't it?' Ray scowled.

'Got an ME tomorrow, they have,' Billy sputtered through bulging cheeks. 'Got to get everything up.'

'What's an ME then, Billy?' Maggie asked.

'Maximum Effort. It means that all the bombers from all the bases will be joining in and everyone's got to pull out all the stops to get all the ships flying.'

'This is that dreadful powdered mash potato muck, isn't it?' Claire interjected, gesturing accusingly at her plate. 'Why can't we have real mash like the old days? This tastes like Lux flakes.'

'Oi, that's enough, you.' Ray shot his daughter a warning glance. 'You know well enough there are no potatoes now, they won't come in until the autumn. Just eat your lunch and stop your complaining.'

'I can get real spuds,' Billy offered. Nobody spoke. 'Tinned fruit and veg and stuff too. I can, you know, if you want it.'

Maggie stole a sidelong look at her husband. He was shaking his head. 'We don't,' he said doggedly. 'I told you before. We don't need Yank charity.'

'Ray. Love. Billy says the boys up there on the base will pay five bob a week, each, just for a bit of laundry. What's the harm in him bringing a couple of loads of it back here and me adding it to the Monday wash? You know we could do with the money, what with the forge being a bit quiet right now.'

'That's right, Mr H. And guess what else? Bikes! They're totally desperate for 'em. I've been thinking, perhaps we could turn over a bit of the forge, like. To a cycle repair place. Do 'em up and flog 'em.'

'We don't need it!' With a crack like a gunshot, the flat of Ray's hand struck the table. They all jumped. In the sudden silence that followed there was a knock at the window. Claire leapt to her feet.

'Postman. I'll get it.' A moment later she returned, dropping the pile onto the table.

'We do not need handouts, not from the Yanks, not from anyone.' Ray's voice was very quiet. 'As for bicycles, I am a blacksmith. I shoe horses, I fix farm machinery, I don't—'

'It's another one, look,' Maggie said softly. She was holding a letter. 'Like the last one. Isn't it? From the Ministry—'

'So you can forget all about bicycles and taking in Yank laundry—'

'Yes, look. Something about a census of unregistered evacuee placements. They're missing one, an Albert Harold Crossley. Writing to registered evacuee placements in the area asking if we have any information on his whereabouts. I'm sure we had a letter about him a while back.' She looked around the table. 'Didn't we?'

'COME IN, JOHN.' Papers in hand, Colonel LeBrock, Hooper's Group Officer Commanding, ushered him into his cluttered office. 'Sorry about the delay at the gate when you arrived. Got an ME on tomorrow, huge one. Between you and me, though, there's a good chance the mission will get scrubbed. Lot of thunderstorm activity expected in the target area, apparently.'

It was a confidence, a big one, telling him about the ME. Fewer than half a dozen out of the 3,000 people on the base would know there was a possibility of weather cancelling the mission. Instead of putting him at his ease, however, somehow the knowledge just made him feel more tense. Something bad was coming. Hooper sat across the desk from his colonel, damp palms pressed between his knees.

'I see here you had the full third degree from Brent Wallis,' LeBrock said, flicking through the file. 'Quite a guy, huh? Folks here call him Dr Frankenstein the way he screws around inside your head.' Another confidence. 'So, John, how do you feel?'

'Good, Colonel. Some residual symptoms from the concussion, odd headaches and so on, but Major Wallis said they're normal and will wear off in time.'

'Excellent.' LeBrock hesitated, unsure, momentarily, how to proceed. 'I guess Brent told you about your crew,' he said clumsily.

'No, sir, I kind of figured it out for myself.' That was a test. Hooper had the line well rehearsed.

'Bad business, John. I was real sorry to hear about it. About them. About all of them. That whole day.' His gaze wandered to the window. 'Kiel.'

'Yes, sir.'

'What do you want to do, John?'

'I want to get back in the war, sir. Finish my tour of duty.'

'Are you sure you feel up to it? Wallis says there're still some neurological problems, some amnesia. There's nothing dishonourable about a medical discharge, you know.'

'Sir, I came into this thing, we, my crew and me, came into this thing, to fly our twenty-five combat missions. It's all I want to do. It's something I need to do. For me, and for my crew. Otherwise, what was it all for?'

LeBrock nodded, studying the file. 'Things have . . . kind of changed around here in the weeks since Kiel, you know. We took a bad beating on that mission, lost a lot of men and a lot of aircraft. We're back up to strength now, almost, which is good. But it's not the same. We've changed. Grown up, moved on. Different people, different ways of doing things.'

'Yes, sir.' He doesn't want me here.

'I've got a proposition for you, John.'

HOOPER WALKED across the wide apron towards his old hut. To his relief it was deserted. There were four beds in his room. All had new owners, he noted, his included. Kiel had cleaned it out. His bags and possessions had been brought out from stores, left in a tidy heap behind the door. It was a small gesture of humanity. When a crew was overdue, they were generally only permitted a few hours before all their belongings were removed and stored. Dead men's personal effects lying about a barracks were bad for morale.

The door burst open and a youthful face appeared. 'Oh, hi. Sorry, ah, I didn't know anyone—'

'It's OK, come on in. I was just dropping by.'

'Oh, right. Moving in?' the young man replied, confused at Hooper's baggage. He held out his hand. 'Jack Meeley, pleased to meet you.'

'John Hooper. And no, not moving in, moving out.'

'Oh, right,' he said again. Calculating. Hooper could see the boy was putting it together, adding it up. Hooper? Wasn't there a Lieutenant Hooper managed to get back from Kiel, then dumped his entire crew in the ocean or something, ended up over at Frankenstein's place on some kind of a breakdown? 'Shipping home?' Meeley asked.

'No. Got a transfer to the 520th over at Bedenham. Rookie crew there lost a pilot, I'm his replacement.'

'But you were based here, isn't that right?'

It was time to go. 'Once I was. A while back. Good luck, Jack.'

He picked up his bags and walked outside.

'How many, sir?' he'd asked Colonel LeBrock at the end of their interview. He needed to know. 'If you don't mind me asking, how many did we lose at Kiel?'

LeBrock studied him. Maybe it was one confidence too far, but Hooper had the right; he'd earned it. 'A hundred and two killed or missing from Horham alone.'

'OK, THAT'S IT, I've had it, I'm getting out of here.' Marion Beans clumped towards the hut door. 'Any of you guys coming?'

'Too right, Beaner, count me in.' Emmett Lajowski ground his cigarette underfoot and made to follow.

Gerry Via looked up. 'Now, just wait a minute, fellas, the whole place is on full alert, there's an ME tomorrow, and no one but no one is allowed off base.'

'Wrong.' Beans leaned over the table. Around it Gerry Via, Eldon Ringwald and the three other hut members from a different crew instinctively held their cards to their chests. 'You are wrong in one detail. Everyone else may be on alert to fly, but *Misbehavin' Martha*'s crew, good old Crew 19, are not. We haven't been since Rudy Stoller got his head blown off, Dave Greenbaum bled to death'—he paused fractionally—'and since Lieutenant Broman went AWOL. We are stood down, remember? We don't exist. Nobody gives a damn, nobody knows, nobody wants to know. And I just can't be doing with it any more, so I'm going to Ipswich, tonight, to get drunk. Now, are you with me or not?'

There was a brief stand-off. Eldon Ringwald, the youngest, turned from one to the other, awaiting a cue. Via checked his card-hand. The other hut members looked embarrassed. Then Al Tork, Crew 19's softly spoken tail gunner, rose quietly from his bunk in the corner. He picked up his jacket, heading for the door.

'Let's go.'

THEY TOOK THE BUS. They had to walk the first three miles to the bus stop, five solitary figures tramping wordlessly along the quiet lanes in the gathering dusk.

Ipswich was crowded, as always. The pavements thick with wandering servicemen, strolling couples, giggling girls and cruising streetwalkers. There were uniforms everywhere.

Misbehavin Martha's five surviving enlisted crewmen drifted, rudderless, through the throng for a while, before eventually elbowing their way into a pub near the bus terminal. It was hot and steamy, dimly lit, inadequately blacked out, and packed to the rafters.

'So, how's Cheryl?' Lajowski blew a plume of smoke, his voice raised against the din.

Beans was leaning heavily over the bar. 'She's lonesome, same as a million other wives back home. She hates living on her own, doesn't understand about the war, just keeps writing and writing, asking when I'm ever going to get home.'

Lajowski shook his head. Further along the bar, Tork, Via and Ringwald were chatting to three English girls. Gerry Via, brown eyes glinting, was murmuring in the tallest girl's ear, one hand resting on her arm. Beans continued, picking sodden shreds from a beer mat. 'I miss the farm. I miss Cheryl. Lousy way to run a marriage.'

'You said it.' Lajowski drained his glass. Gerry Via was leading his group over towards them, his girl in hand. Three English sailors in ratings' uniforms followed unseen in their wake. Over on the far side of the room a commotion was starting up.

'Lajowski? Beaner? I'd like to introduce you to some friends of mine. This beautiful young lady here is Dot, this is her friend Vi, she's had a little to drink, and young Kid Ringwald here is standing next to the lovely Claire. Ladies, this here is Technical Sergeants Marion Beans and Emmett Lajowski.'

'Excuse me, Yank. These three was with us.' One of the sailors was tapping on Via's shoulder, the two others crowding in behind. Via froze, his back to the sailors, his eyes on Lajowski's. Lajowski shook his head minutely. Beans straightened from the bar.

'OK, Navy, let's just take it easy, OK?' Al Tork said quietly to the leading sailor. 'MPs are everywhere, nobody wants any trouble now, do they? Come on, buddy, why don't we all get a drink and—'

'I am not your buddy!' The sailor shrugged Tork's hand away.

'Eldon.' Claire was tugging at Ringwald's sleeve.

Beans began to push forward. Lajowski and Via were still watching each other.

'Eldon, come on!' Claire dragged at Ringwald's arm. 'Come on, let's go!'

'You bloody Yanks. You come over here all flash, with your free candy bars and your free cigarettes and your free nylons. You ponce about in your fancy uniforms and your fancy aeroplanes, helping yourselves to our beer and our rations, and our women. But when it comes down to the real fighting—'

He got no further. Beans's fist landed squarely between his eyes. He staggered backwards, disbelief on his face, one hand to his streaming nose. The sailors lunged forward as one, Lajowski, head down, barrelled forward. Then all the lights went out.

THE NIGHT'S HEAVY TORPOR dragged Heather from a troubled sleep long before dawn. The air about the room lay thick and oppressive, and her mind began, inevitably, to ponder the uncertainties of her situation. A missing brother, domineering in-laws, an unwell mother, an absent husband. David.

She threw back the sheet and padded barefoot to the kitchen to boil water for tea. As she waited for the kettle's asthmatic wheeze, she detected another sound: a far-off low murmur, like the rumble of distant thunder. It was a sound she recognised. The warming up of aero engines. A hundred or more. After only momentary hesitation, she flicked off the gas beneath the kettle and ran upstairs.

Three-quarters of a mile away Billy Street was lobbing gravel at a window. Stones struck glass with a noise that to him sounded like machine-gun fire. Nothing happened. He threw more. The blackout curtain beyond the glass twitched and a face appeared.

'Billy? Billy Street? Is that you?'

'Ruby,' he hissed. 'Ruby, it's me. Get dressed and come down. There's something I've got to show you. Please. It's dead important.'

After an age he heard the click of a gate latch, the soft fall of her foot on gravel.

'What?' she hissed in his ear, her anger tinged with excitement. He could smell her hair, the warmth of her body from bed. She was wearing someone else's too-large jacket over a simple floral dress, her school gym shoes on her feet. 'What is it, Billy?'

'Come on.' He grasped her hand and pulled. They began to run, slowly at first, then faster and faster. And as they ran, the noise of engines grew louder.

Finally she dragged him to a breathless halt. 'Where are we going?' she gasped. 'We're not going on the base, are we? It's not allowed.'

'Don't be scared, Rube. It's all right, we're not on the base. Look, here's the fence, we're on the perimeter.' The terrain ahead of them stretched flat and treeless in every direction. The light was coming. 'It's all right, see? Look, there's the end of the runway just over there. They'll all be along it in a minute.'

'Who will? What's going on?'

A mile away at the far end of the dark stripe of the runway, a single green flare popped like a distant firework.

'It's the most fantastic thing in the world, Rube, and I wanted to show it you. It's an ME. Right this very instant, all the bombers on all the bases all over Suffolk are getting ready. Hundreds of 'em. They're going to take off and form up into one huge formation in the sky. And our base, Rube, the 520th, is joining in with it.' Suddenly at the far end of the runway a hum detached itself from the background rumble, and rose quickly to a roar. It grew louder and louder until it was deafening, a high-pitched throbbing snarl. 'Here they come!' His yell was exultant.

Twenty yards away Heather stood in the shadows by the trees and watched the bombers lifting off. She could see the two figures silhouetted against the pale dawn sky ahead. It took her a while to identify them, Billy Street's roundly gesticulating profile first, the slighter, donkey-jacketed outline of Ruby Moody rather later. She smiled, left them in peace and, as the last bomber clawed its way into the sky above her, turned and started back for the cottage.

A quarter of a mile away, Crew 19 lay sprawled on the dew-soaked grass. The five of them were lying in a row, like corpses at a battle site. Al Tork, despite the noise, had fallen asleep. Above and behind them the rumble of the departing bombers had receded to a hum.

On the far side of the airfield, a single empty bomber, theirs, stood alone on its hardstanding.

'Do you think that we're ever going to get back into this war?' Beans asked.

Lt J A Hooper 520th BG

> *Dear Mother and Father,*
>
> *A great many thanks for all your mail. I can't tell you how much of a boon it is to hear that life continues as normal back home. Thank you also, Mother, for the little book of the Psalms. It is a real treasure.*
>
> *I'm sorry for my slowness in replying, but a great deal has happened in the past few weeks. I suppose the most important news from my perspective is a switch of groups. For operational reasons, I have transferred to a new group (the 520th) on a base near a little village called Bedenham. I moved in here a few days ago.*
>
> *I have also transferred crews. My job is to train up a new crew here that lost its pilot. I hope to meet them all tomorrow. I hear they are a fine bunch of guys.*
>
> *I forgot to mention that I suffered a slight injury on my last mission with the old crew. It is nothing to be concerned about, the injury was superficial, I passed a week or so in the hospital and am now completely recovered. But as a whole, the mission was only partially successful. My crew, the one I trained with back in Rapid City,*

. . . is gone. All dead. Hooper stared down at the page, then tore it from the pad, screwed it into a ball and dropped it onto the growing heap on the floor beside him. Hooper sank his face into his hands, elbows propped on the little table. It was very late, the hut in almost total darkness. Hopeless. There was nothing to say, and no form of words in which to say it.

'BILLY! BILLY, LOVE. For goodness' sake, what on earth is it?'

He fights, struggles, drowning, suffocating. And all the while the flames crackle nearer, and louder. He can feel their heat. He begins to try to scream.

Someone is shaking him. 'Billy, stop struggling, wake up now!'

The fire dream. The disused warehouse down by the river at Southwark. Night-time, the whole site deserted, just he, Ron and Jimmy. Freezing cold, February, jet-black sky. Slip through the corrugated-iron fencing, NO TRESPASSING, dash across the piles of brick rubble to the smashed door, duck inside. Then running, up and up, thumping up stairwells, panting to an exhausted halt at the top. Breathless giggles. 'Christ, it's cold!' Their shivering laughter fogs the crisp night air. 'I know,' says Ron. 'Let's get a little fire going.'

Maggie is shaking him, but still he can't breathe. A fire is going all right. The flames rush nearer, cracking and snapping all around him. Hungry, angry. Everywhere. 'Ron? Jimmy! Where are you?' But he is alone, and they are gone. For ever.

His chest bursts at last like a dam, a gasping sob racks him and he opens his eyes. Mrs H. She pulls him close, holding him tight. Like a mother. His face is hot and flushed, his eyes wet.

'Steady. Steady does it. A bit better now, love?'

'Yes.' He gasps, hugging her to him. 'Yes.'

Maggie's eyes were wandering the darkened attic. 'That asthma again, I'll be bound. And I suppose it is a bit musty up here.'

'It's all right.' He wheezed. 'I feel better now.'

Her fingers combed hair from his forehead. 'Hmm. Your poor mum, what would she have said? You must miss her so. And your dad. Perhaps we could organise a visit. Up to London. Go and see him, your dad. Would you like that?' In the eight months since Billy had arrived in the village, together with the others, he had not received a single word. Not a letter, not a card. Nothing.

'It's all right, Mrs H. I feel a bit better now.'

Maggie said nothing, patting his leg through the blankets.

He'd arrived, one rainy afternoon the previous November, with two other evacuees. Little girls, twin sisters. And a bossy local coordinator from the Ministry ticking off names on a clipboard. Ray had been dead against the idea of an evacuee, of course. 'What the hell do we need with another mouth to feed. And where's the little so-and-so going to sleep?' The two girls went off to the Bolsovers' farm near Dennington. Billy stayed with the Howdens. It was his third billeting. Somewhere near Felixstowe had been first, she thought. Something had gone wrong there, Billy said. They didn't like him, accused him of pilfering, locked him in the cellar, fed him dog scraps out of a bowl. So he was moved to another family, an elderly couple, on the coast. That was all right, he said, he liked it there. But then the Ministry decreed it was too dangerous billeting evacuees near the coast, what with the beaches being mined, and the air attacks on the shore batteries. All evacuees were to be billeted at least ten miles inland. So he came to Bedenham to be billeted bang next door to the huge American bomber base being built there. It made no sense at all, Ray said. The Yanks were a prime target. The Ministry must be off its head.

But Ray had come round in the end. War effort, Maggie had reminded him. It always worked; he was very conscientious about doing their bit. Anyway, she had continued, as an evacuee Billy came with a ration card, a few shillings a week from the Ministry and an extra pair of hands to help about the house. Maybe Ray could even train him up to help out in the forge. And he could sleep in the attic. She'd hoped it might even be good for Ray. Bring him out of himself a bit. And what with Billy being a boy, too.

'You mustn't mind him, you know, Billy, love,' she murmured. 'Ray. He comes over all gruff sometimes, but deep down he has a golden heart.' She turned her face to the blacked-out window, the light from Billy's night candle soft yellow on her cheek. His breathing was steadying and he was beginning to feel sleepy again. He liked it when she called him 'love'.

'We had a little boy before, once, you see,' she was saying very softly. 'Long time ago, about four years before Claire was born. Stephen, we called him. He died when he was very little. In that fearful winter of '23. Pneumonia, the doctor said.'

'Hi. Crew 19 in here?' A square-jawed face had appeared round the door of hut twelve. Fifteen pairs of eyes looked up.

'That's us. Among others,' Gerry Via murmured, the draught from the door fluttering the cards at his table. 'Who wants to know?'

The door opened wide and a tall, gangly youth of about twenty entered. He held out a hand to Via. 'Herman Keissling. I'm your replacement waist gunner.'

Lajowski's head came up. Via and Keissling shook hands. 'Gerry Via. Radio operator. Well, er, Herman, good to have you aboard.'

Tork, hitching his trousers, rose from a writing table. 'I'm Al Tork, tail gun. Over there is Lajowski, we call him Polecat, he's upper turret. Kid Ringwald, ball turret, is outside somewhere. That lard-arse, lying over there, is Beans.' It felt good, introducing Crew 19 to a replacement. That meant they weren't going to break it up.

The door flew wide suddenly, banging against its stop. Cards fluttered like leaves to the floor. Via cursed. 'Hell, Ringwald, will you just shut the goddamn door!'

The distant burble of engines was drifting into the hut. 'It's *Martha*!' Eldon Ringwald was pointing outside. 'Quick! Knyper and the ground crew're prepping her. Someone's going to fly her!'

Half a mile away, Hooper's Jeep, driven by his new squadron commander, Gene Englehardt, raced round the perimeter towards the distant bomber.

'Get out the way, dummy!' Englehardt roared as a sergeant wobbled past on a bicycle. He winked at Hooper. 'So now, John, here's the score. We got the four squadrons here on base that make up the 520th. Each squadron flies with an average of six ships apiece. That means the 520th generally puts up between twenty and thirty ships a time. You got that?'

'Got it, Major.' Hooper had to raise his voice over the clatter of the Jeep's engine.

'Call me Gene. We don't stand for any boot-camp chicken-crap in my squadron, John.'

'Hoop.'

'Hoop, right. Mighty glad to have you with us!' To Hooper's horror, Englehardt, grinning widely, took his hand off the wheel and reached across to shake. He was the classic dashing bomber-jockey. Early thirties, non-regulation haircut, pencil-thin Errol Flynn moustache. Bright-eyed, tough, contagiously confident. Englehardt's enthusiasm was irrepressible. And invigorating, like a blast of fresh air up an airless mineshaft. 'Mighty glad, I don't mind telling you. We've been hurting, sometimes just three or four serviceable ships in the squadron. Pitiful.'

'I see.' They passed two B-17s, parked, empty, on their hardstandings. Then a third hove into view. Hooper could see ground crew and refuelling vehicles clustered round it.

'There's *Martha*! She's a part of my squadron. Or was. Thing is, she hasn't flown since Rudy Stoller got killed.'

'Oh, yes. How so?'

Englehardt was slowing as they drew nearer to the bomber. 'Two reasons. First, Operations stood the crew down while the pen-pushers decided what the hell to do with them.' He glanced at Hooper. 'They're basically good kids, Hoop, but their morale's shot, they never had a chance to settle into the job. And there's been some . . . trouble among the enlisted guys.'

'Trouble?'

'Yeah, well, you know, bickering, infighting, that kind of thing. There was a minor incident last week with some Brit sailors in a bar in Ipswich. MPs picked them up. It's nothing serious, Hoop, we've been trying to cut them some slack. They just need to get back on the job. Tough break losing three members of the crew on their first mission like that.'

'Three? I thought it was the pilot and one waist gunner?'

'The bombardier, Broman. He walked off the ship and went AWOL. Colonel Lassiter, our Group CO, finally gave up on him and assigned a new one. A Lieutenant Holland, you'll meet him later. Regular guy.'

'I see. And the other officers?'

'Spitzer's pure gold, straight, positive and reliable, although as a navigating officer he's completely green, of course. Irv Underwood, he's your copilot. He, well, he was in the cockpit when Stoller got hit. He, uh, he's been calling in sick most days since.'

'What's the second reason?' he asked.

'What's that, buddy?'

'You said there were two reasons *Martha* hasn't flown again.'

'Oh, yeah.' Englehardt nodded towards the waiting bomber. 'Well, the clear-up crews, they all did the best they could cleaning up the ship. But it was one hell of a mess on the flight deck. As you can imagine. Twenty-millimetre cannon shell straight to the head like that. One evening last week, a mechanic went on board, just to run engine checks. Came running straight off again, yelling there was, like, pieces of . . . tissue, human remains, on the throttle quadrant. Once a ship gets a reputation, jinxed, like that . . . Well, it's all horseshit, we both know that. That's partly the reason we're out here now. To fly this mother and blow away all the horseshit jinx crap.'

The Jeep slewed to a halt. An unlucky pilot, a screwed-up crew, now a jinxed ship. It was hardly auspicious. The ground crew were standing to one side now, waiting. 'Partly?' Hooper asked, although he already knew.

'Yep, Hoop. Partly.' Englehardt turned to him in the Jeep, his voice quiet suddenly. 'I heard all the stories. About what happened to you, and to your crew. After Kiel. Frankly, it don't interest me one jot. Or Colonel Lassiter. He just told me to check out your flying, and that's all I care about. If you can fly this ship OK, then we can sure use you. If you can't, then Lassiter will have you off this base and on your way home with an honourable medical discharge by nightfall. Do we have an understanding?'

Hooper nodded, his eyes on the waiting bomber. There was still a choice, even now. A line of retreat, a last way out. It couldn't get any worse. A tiny spark flickered. Like rebellion. He found he was smiling, at himself.

'Let's get to it, Gene.'

IT WAS ALL RIGHT. Better than all right. They park up and walk over to the ship. Immediately Englehardt swings himself up through the nose hatch and disappears on to the flight deck, shouting to come up and join him when he's ready. He begins a walk-around. It feels good, everything looks familiar, exactly as it should, he can remember it all. The crew chief is watching, from a distance. Hoop beckons him over. His name is Hal Knyper. They shake. I like to do the walk-around with my crew chief, if that's OK with you, Hal. No problem, Knyper shrugs. There's nothing wrong with this ship, Lieutenant, he says at the end of the walk-around, his china-blue eyes on Hoop's. She just needs to get back in the war, that's all. Like her crew.

He signs Knyper's clipboard, swings up through the hatch, and clambers up to the flight deck. In the right-hand seat, Englehardt's face is expressionless, his head down, scribbling on a notepad. Hoop settles into his seat and they begin start-up checks.

Fifteen minutes later he's taxiing the big aeroplane slowly round the perimeter track towards the runway. From the corner of his eye, Hoop sees binoculars glinting from the control tower. There's a crowd on the balcony there. Elsewhere, airmen are trickling from their huts, mechanics wander out, drivers pull up their vehicles. The buzz has gone round. Is that *Martha* taxiing out? Say, isn't that Englehardt? I hear he's checking out *Martha*'s new pilot.

'Looks like you've got yourself an audience, Hoop.' Gene chuckles over the headphones.

'Here's hoping I don't give them anything to see.'

'Hmm. Maybe.' Englehardt grunts. 'Then again, maybe not. There's your green.'

Cleared to go. Sweet and steady. Ahead the runway stretches to infinity, wide and grey, tapering to a point more than a mile away in the far-off distant trees. He's ready. Now.

'Say, Hoop,' Englehardt pipes up. 'Tell me, did you ever slow-roll a B-17?'

SOMETHING WAS WRONG with Heather's bicycle. It felt distinctly wobbly. She braked to a halt and dismounted.

The back wheel was loose. In fact the frame was broken, one fork completely sheared from the weld under the rear mudguard. It was a miracle the whole thing hadn't collapsed beneath her. As she began to push, a Jeep pulled up beside her.

'May I help you, ma'am?' It was Finginger. A moment later he was lifting the bicycle into the back of the Jeep. Brushing the dirt from his hands he clambered in beside her. 'We're all set,' he chirped, pressing the starter.

'This really is too kind of you, um, Major,' Heather replied. 'But hardly necessary; I was practically home.'

'I know,' Finginger winked. He sped off in the direction of her cottage, one or two heads turning, she noted resignedly, as they passed. The word would spread quicker than flu in school.

'You do?'

'Yep. You're Heather Garrett, schoolteacher, of Walnut Tree Cottage, Dennington Road.'

'That's very impressive, Major, but, well, I'm afraid you have me at a disadvantage.'

'Scott, ma'am. Scott Finginger. And it's my job to find out things. I work in Intelligence. I was on my way to visit you.'

Heather glanced across at the major. He was slender, about thirty-five, thinning grey hair above a cheerful, angular face.

'You see, there's a dance, next Saturday week. On base. We're inviting several local dignitaries. I wondered whether you might like to come. As a guest of the 520th. And as my guest.'

Heather laughed. 'Well, Major, I'm obviously very honoured, but—'

She broke off. Gerald Garrett's car was sitting outside her cottage. She could see Gerald at the wheel. Rosamund was standing by the front gate, looking up at the empty house. As the Jeep drew up the hill she turned towards them.

'You're married. I know that too. To Brigadier Garrett's son, an officer in the infantry. He's missing in action, isn't he? Pacific

Theatre. You have my sincerest condolences and best wishes for his safe return. And you also have my complete assurance that you have nothing to fear, Mrs Garrett. I am an honourable man.'

'I believe that, Major, um, Scott.' The Jeep lurched to a halt outside the cottage. Finginger leapt out and began unloading the bicycle. The drone of some approaching engines was growing louder.

'Well, ah, good afternoon, then, dear,' Rosamund blustered, standing to one side. Finginger wheeled the bicycle past her.

'My bicycle has broken and Major Finginger here kindly gave me a lift home. He has invited me to a dance next Saturday week. On the base. Isn't that a kind thought?'

'A dance? Well, yes, but, Heather—'

At that instant *Misbehavin' Martha* rocketed over their heads, so fast that they felt the ground shake beneath their feet, and so low even Finginger ducked. Rosamund screeched inaudibly, her face contorted with terror. Gerald's mustachioed face, puce, strained at the window of his car. As they all stared, *Martha*, tail on to them, rose slightly, paused, then, with agonising yet majestic slowness, began to roll, impossibly, right over onto its back, then still on, without stopping, in one smooth, slow rotation until it was upright again. A second later it vanished behind a clump of trees.

'What the bloody hell does that lunatic think he is doing?' Gerald was hauling himself from his car.

'Didn't know a B-17 could do that.' Finginger whistled.

'Who was that, Scott?'

'That was Major Eugene Englehardt. He's checking out the new pilot for Crew 19 today. I guess he passed.'

'GOT YOU THIS.' Billy produced the small paper-wrapped package from his pocket and placed it quietly on the kitchen table.

'What's that then, dear?' Maggie turned from the sink. The package was stained with blood. She wiped her hands on her apron and began to unwrap it. Outside the light was failing, a chill breeze stirred last year's leaves in the corner of the yard, the chickens fretted halfheartedly in their hutch.

'Pork! Good heavens, pork chops? But, Billy, where on earth did you get them? We've had the meat this week. It's not Friday, is it?' Maggie stared down at the two pale cuts lying in her hand, her face a mix of suspicion and wonderment. 'All right. Where did you get them then? Please tell me you didn't pinch these, Billy.'

'No, Mrs H. Honest I didn't. They're a present, like. For you and Mr H. For your tea.' His voice was unusually subdued, eyes down. 'I got them off the ration.'

'The ration? But how?'

He looked up at last, the ghost of a glimmer in his eyes. 'Easy, Mrs H. Old Mr Day at the butcher's, his eyesight's dodgy, and 'e never looks that close at the ration book anyhow. Also, he uses pencil when he cancels the coupons. You can rub it out, then go back again a few days after, and use the same coupon again.'

'But, Billy, that's dishonest. You shouldn't be doing it.'

'Why not? Lennie's mum does it, and the Frys. Fisks too, I'll bet.'

'The Frys? Doris Fry fiddles her coupons? Are you sure?'

Heavy footsteps were crossing the yard. A moment later two figures appeared at the back door: Americans, in uniform, shirts and ties, polished shoes. Billy, with a start, recognised them. Two of the crew from *Misbehavin' Martha*, from hut twelve: the tall one with the Polish name who picked on him, and the little blond ball turret gunner, Ringwald.

'Good evening, ma'am,' said Lajowski, bowing towards Maggie. 'We're real sorry to disturb you, we were looking for Mr and Mrs Howden's place. Would this be it?'

'Oh, er, well, yes it would be,' Maggie stammered, still clutching the chops. 'It is, yes.'

'What's up, lads?' Ray Howden squeezed past them into the kitchen.

'Well, sir, my name is Emmett Lajowski, and this here is Kid, I mean Eldon, Ringwald. We're here to see Lucky Charm, ah, that is, young Billy.'

'Are you indeed,' Ray said flatly.

Heather appeared, following Billy into the kitchen. 'Oh goodness, please excuse me. I'm so sorry to trouble you.'

'Mrs Garrett! This is a nice surprise. I'll put the kettle on.'

'No, Mrs Howden, that's terribly kind, but you have visitors. I just popped by to ask Mr Howden whether he could possibly take a look at my bicycle. Billy here said that your husband does cycle repairs, so I thought I'd drop it in. I'm so sorry, did I say something . . .'

Heather, confused, looked from one face to another as the room went quiet. They were all, Billy and the Howdens, staring at the taller of the two Americans standing in the doorway. Looking at his hand. He was holding a child's silver spoon.

'Tracked it down for you, kid. Kind of a peace offering.'

There was a crash at the front door and Claire burst in. 'Old Vic's frying!' she cried, then her hand flew to her mouth. 'Eldon!'

'Eldon?' said Ray.

'Vic?' said Maggie. 'Opening the chip shop? Are you sure, love? I mean, how?'

'His son, Bobby,' Claire sputtered. 'He's on the boats at Lowestoft, dropped a load of cod and skate in this afternoon, on the quiet. Plaice too, Deirdre says. She said Vic's been hoarding stocks of old lard for months, greengrocer managed to get hold of half a sack of spuds off the base, so Vic's opening the shop, just for tonight. Well, come on then! What are we waiting for? Fish and chips!'

T/SGT ELDON RINGWALD 520TH BG

Dear Mom and Pop,

Well what a day! First off, we got assigned a new pilot at last, Lt John A. Hooper, to replace poor old Rudy. We didn't get to meet Lt Hooper yet but our Squadron Commander checked him out good in the ship and so tomorrow we all get to go back on ops training together. Can't tell you how good THAT feels at last, though you can imagine, me and the guys are raring to go!

Tonight, me and Polecat Lajowski had a truly amazing time. Get this, we ate REAL English fish and chips. No kidding. We had to go into the village to see some of the village folk about some things, anyway their daughter, who is a real respectable girl name of Claire, comes in hollering about fish and chips and so we all hurry like crazy down to the fish and chips place together. It was all done in secret like, what with the rationing and so on, but when we got there, the entire damn village was out on the street, all talking and laughing together. Everyone, even the village policeman, and the pastor, mothers with babies, everyone. The fish and chips place was just this old guy's back door and we had to bring our own newspapers to carry it in which is what they do with fish and chips. I tell you, I NEVER ate anything quite like it. The chips were what we call fries only bigger but I swear they were practically the best things I ever ate in my whole life. The best thing I ever ate over here, that's for sure.

It was truly magical, all the village people just standing out in the road eating their fish and chips in the moonlight together, smiling and laughing, even singing some, in hushed voices. It was like there was no war, no hardship, no rationing, like they had no cares in the whole world. Just for a few minutes. I felt real privileged to be invited along. Emmett too. A little home-sick as well I don't mind admitting tho' I'm not sure why. Claire's a fine girl, you'd like her.

Well that's all for now. Write me. Your loving son, Eldon

CHAPTER THREE

'**N**avigator to pilot.'

'Go ahead, navigator.'

'Turn left, heading two three zero degrees.'

'Two three zero? Are you quite sure about that?'

'Ah, yes, pilot, pretty sure.'

'OK. Turning left on to two three zero.' Raising eyebrows at his copilot, Irv Underwood, Hooper hauled the bomber over into a steep left turn, rolling her nose level exactly on the new course.

Silence descended once more, for about a minute. Hooper waited.

'Navigator to pilot.'

'Yes, Spitz, go ahead.'

'I, ah, when I said two three zero, I might have meant three two zero.'

'You might have meant.'

'Yes. No, well I guess I did mean three two zero. I must have made a mistake reading the heading off the plot. Sorry about that.'

A chorus of groans floated over the intercom. Somebody unidentifiable blew a raspberry.

'Right, now you can all just cut it out back there!' Hooper snapped. 'Any more spurious intercom chatter and there's going to be serious trouble, OK? Now then, pilot to navigator. It's OK. Take your time, go back, double-check your position, then verify it with a beacon fix from Sergeant Via in radio. Then I want you to plot a fresh course for the Moray gunnery range. Now have you got that?'

'Got it. Thanks, pilot.'

'Radio here. Did somebody call me?'

'No, Via, you idiot, pilot was talking to navigator. Don't you ever listen?'

'Why don't you just mind your goddamn business, Tork! I thought the lieutenant was calling me on the intercom.'

'No, ah, radio, it's OK, pilot here. Navigator will be calling you in a while for a beacon fix, that's all.'

'OK, got it, pilot. See, Tork? He was calling me.'

'That's enough, everybody! Quiet down now.'

Another silence. Another minute.

'Upper turret to pilot.'

Hooper sighed. 'What is it now, Lajowski?'

'Sir, what does spurious mean?'

And so it went on. After another hour, nearly four into the training mission, Crew 19's third within a week, *Martha*, descending cautiously, broke through a thin undercast. To Loren Spitzer's audible relief, 2,000 feet below them lay the slate-grey waters of the Moray Firth. With it came the plaudits.

'Way to go, Spitz, baby, right on the money!' Tork.

'Well it's about time, if you don't mind me saying so.' Via.

Hooper waited until silence settled once more. 'Right then. There it is. Good work, navigator, we got here in the end. Now listen up everyone, here's the drill. The drogue target will be coming by in a few minutes. The drogue is a large oblong canvas banner, painted white. It is towed through the air on a wire a thousand yards behind the towing aircraft. You can't miss it. Do *not* shoot until the towing aircraft is safely past us. Remember to keep your bursts short and controlled. OK, now, does anyone have any—'

'There it is! Jesus, right over there, look, look, three o'clock!' Immediately, the road-drill rattle of machine-gun fire hammered over the open intercom. Long, wild bursts from at least three of *Martha*'s eight firing positions. Simultaneously, everyone began shouting. Hooper, completely unable to break in over the mayhem, waited for the frenzy to subside. But it never did. Finally, gesturing to Underwood to take over the controls, he tore off his headphones and clambered from his seat.

Emmett Lajowski, standing in his upper turret directly behind and above the pilots, was still shooting. Hooper punched him hard in the thigh as he passed. There was a muffled yelp and the shooting stopped. Hooper continued aft without pause, on through the bulkhead door and into the aircraft's waist. Ringwald, sealed into his ball turret under the bomber, was still shooting. Hooper snatched a fire-axe from the bulkhead, and brought the wooden handle down hard on the turret's curved lid. The shooting stopped.

That just left Beans. He was at the left-hand waist window, leaning right through it, wrenching at the charging handle of his machine gun, which appeared to be jammed. Behind him, the new right-hand waist gunner, Keissling watched, arms folded, as Beans, cursing furiously, attacked his lifeless weapon. Keissling looked up as Hooper entered. He stepped forward, tapping Beans on the shoulder.

Beans turned and caught sight of Hooper's expression. 'Uh, the gun, sir. You see. It's jammed. Sir.'

'Correction, Sergeant. The gun is empty. You have managed to expend your entire ammunition allowance, that is enough rounds of fifty calibre, I would remind you, to last an eight-hour mission over enemy territory, in a little over five minutes. As a consequence, the gun has suffered severe heat damage, is probably beyond repair, and will almost certainly have to be scrapped.'

There was less talking over the intercom on the way home. Hooper stayed in the nose for much of the flight, crouched next to Loren Spitzer as the navigator plotted a fresh route back from Scotland. Then he stood at the shoulder of Crew 19's new bombardier, John Holland, while Holland guided the bomber towards their practice target. Suddenly, seconds before bomb-release, he pulled a paper sack from his pocket and vomited into it. To Hooper's astonishment, he then resumed his position, smiling sheepishly, and toggled the electrical switches to release their dummy bombs. Nothing happened. *Martha* flew on, her bombs firmly locked in their racks above her gaping bomb bay doors. Seconds ticked by.

'Master release?' Hooper prompted at last.

'Master release! Forgot the damn master release.' Immediately the bombardier threw the switch and toggled the release buttons once more, watching through the viewfinder with a satisfied 'There they go!' as the four bombs tumbled earthwards, to impact at least two miles beyond the practice target marked out on the Essex mud flats 8,000 feet below.

Hooper clambered back onto the flight deck. Irv Underwood, his face pale and perspiring, seemed relieved to see him.

'Everything OK, Irv?' Hooper asked, strapping himself into his seat.

'Uh, fine, fine, thanks. Would you like to take the controls now?'

'No. I think I'd like you to bring us in today.'

'I, uh, if it's OK with you, Captain, I'd rather not bring her in. Not today. I . . . well, I don't . . . feel so good.' Hooper, adjusting his seat straps, regarded his copilot. In their three flights together so far, Underwood had yet to perform a takeoff, or a landing. It occurred to Hooper that he probably hadn't done so since *Martha*'s ill-fated first mission when he'd had to be forcibly coaxed from the flight deck and into the waiting ambulance.

A navigator who couldn't navigate. An airsick bombardier who could barely bomb. Undisciplined, wildly trigger-happy gunners who couldn't hit fish in a barrel. Now a copilot who couldn't fly. It was hopeless. It was never going to work. He should have taken the medical discharge. He reached for the control column. 'OK, Irv,' he said quietly. 'I'll bring her in today. We can talk about this later.' Underwood's hands fell from the controls without a word.

A moment later a voice came over the intercom.

'Radio to pilot.'

Hooper drew a long breath. 'Yes, Via, this is pilot. What is it?'

'Well, uh, fighting, sir. In the waist.'

'What's that? Via? What are you talking about?'

'Something must have happened between Tork and Beans. And now, well, sir, they're fighting. Sir. On the floor. In the waist.'

'RAY, RAYMOND? I brought your tea, love.' Maggie peered into the gaping maw of the shop. Ray was right at the back, sweeping up. She looked around. It was unusually quiet inside, and tidy, and empty. And something smelt different. Fire, she realised. There was no fire in the forge. It was the first time she could remember it like that in months. 'Having a clear out, then?' she enquired lightly.

Ray took the mug, parking his broom against a wall. 'Yes, well, what with business not being so bright just now, thought I'd take the chance to clean up a bit before the autumn rush sets in.'

Maggie nodded, hugging a thin cotton cardigan closer to her shoulders. 'Ray, love. Billy—'

'He's got to go, Mag. I can't be doing with it. He's thieving, lying, deceiving. He skips school, swindles the ration, runs black-market fiddles up the base. He's a bad lot and he's got to go back.'

'Back? But back where?'

'Back home, of course. To his rich dad, the big house and that hush-hush job at the Bank of England he keeps telling us about.'

'But you don't really believe any of that, do you?'

'Course not! That's the whole point. He can't be trusted. That's why he's got to go.'

'It's just, like, his way of coping. He just wants to be someone. He desperately needs to belong.'

'Not to us, he doesn't. And that's just it. He's not ours, so he's not our problem. Sorry, Mag, but he's had every chance and my mind's made up. I've already been onto that blasted local evacuee coordinator woman; she can sort him out. He's not staying here.'

Anger flashed in her brown eyes. 'All right then! Do it! Send him away, if that's what you want, and I hope it makes you happy. But don't blame me if your life is all the emptier for it. And don't blame him neither. It's not his fault, don't you see? Not his fault there's a bloody war on. Not his fault that we lost little Stephen. It's not Billy's fault your business is going under, though God knows if only you'd listen to him sometimes, he's got more of a nose for it than the rest of us put together.' She was crying now, big rolling tears spilling on to her cheeks. 'You had it once, Ray. A fire like his in your belly. Ambition. You were going to take on the world. That's why I loved you. Why I married you. There wasn't nothing we couldn't do, you said. Nothing. And I believed you.'

'THIS ONE.'

'Um, let's see. It's signed—I can't read it properly, the writing's terrible—Betty? It says dear Maggie, hope you are keeping well. Bob and me are doing fine—'

Billy snatched the letter away, returning it carefully to its envelope. 'It's all right. Betty is Mrs H's sister. What about this one?' He handed her another letter. Ruby took it, eyeing him doubtfully. They were in the old mill, sitting side by side on upended beer crates. 'What do you want to know for anyway, Billy?'

'Never mind that. It's, um, to do with Intelligence, that's what. Military Intelligence. Go on, Rube, read it.'

'It's just from the Electric. Why don't you read them yourself, if it's all so bloomin' 'ush-'ush?'

'I told you, Rube. Eyesight, remember? I've got dodgy eyesight for the reading, like. We couldn't afford the specs, back home.'

'I thought you said you was rich.'

'We are! Was. That is, we were, before.'

'Before your mum and dad got killed by them bombs, you mean.'

She watched him nod, his eyes falling to the Howdens' letters on the table. Billy'd been quiet the last few days, Ruby reflected. 'Bill? Shall we go up the woods for a bit? Would you like that?'

He walked along the lane beside her in pensive silence. Passing the Howdens' cottage, and checking briefly that the coast was clear, he stuffed their mail back through the letterbox. A little further on, Ruby slipped her hand into his. It felt limp and lifeless.

'What about that Claire then?' she asked cheerfully.

'What about her?'

'Is she having it off with that Yank then? That little blond tail gunner from your plane, what's it called, *Misbehaving Mary*?'

His hand pulled away. 'It's *Martha*, Rube. And it's Technical Sergeant Ringwald, and he's not the tail gunner, he's the ball turret gunner. And as for Claire bloomin' Howden, how the hell should I know what she gets up to? She don't tell me nothing.'

'Sorry. Only asking.' They walked on. After half a mile the field on their right ended abruptly at a wall of trees. A narrow track beside the lane led into the woods. As they turned onto it, the ceaseless rumbling of the airfield in the distance grew nearer.

'I got to pop on base,' he said. 'Little bit of business to tend to. It's all right, you can come too, there won't be any trouble.'

'As you please.' He seemed to have forgotten their woodland tryst. They trudged deeper into the woods, the air dank and still.

Ten minutes later, they emerged behind a hangar and stepped onto the base. Ruby was amazed at the transformation in him. He seemed to grow taller, and older, stand straighter, his head higher. She hurried to keep up with him as he marched round the perimeter track towards a row of huts. Americans spoke to him, said hello as they passed, as though he belonged there.

'Wait here,' he said, pausing outside one of the huts. He disappeared behind it. A moment later he was back, striding purposefully towards the next. 'Dogs. They all want dogs. God knows why, when they just run away again. But then that's the good part.'

'It is?'

'Yeah, dogs are a doddle. You see, they're not supposed to keep pets in the huts, although they do, there's hundreds of 'em. I'm forever finding the buggers wandering in the woods. I just keep rounding them up and selling them to the next bloke.'

'But don't they know?'

'Rube, look at the size of this place.' He gestured around at the airfield. 'It's huge. Hal Knyper says there's more than three thousand people living here. There's bars and shops and canteens and things. A hospital, libraries and stuff. Nobody gives a toss about a few mangy mongrels.' He broke off. They'd arrived at a hut, number six. A scruffy-looking bicycle was parked outside. Billy fingered it. 'That's a bit peculiar.'

The hut was long and narrow, like all the others, a dozen beds down both sides. Men lounged on a few of them. Reading, playing cards, writing letters, but towards the far end, one row of six beds stood empty, freshly made, the walls behind them bare.

'Where's Sergeant Boonebose?' Billy asked.

'Hanover,' one of the men murmured.

'What? All of them? Everyone from *Goin' South*?'

'Crashed and burned. No 'chutes.'

He didn't even look up. None of the men in the hut did, their carefully composed expressions of casual indifference inadequately concealing their shock, grief and fear.

Billy, too, was disbelieving. 'But, well, that's my bike. Outside. Sergeant Boonebose hasn't finished paying me for it.'

'Take it.'

Billy was staring at the floor six feet in front of him, jaw set, eyebrows fixed in a frown. Ruby, bewildered, standing at his side, could see that his fists were clenched. She plucked at his sleeve. 'Billy?'

'No,' he said, turning for the door. 'You take it. I don't want it.'

ON SATURDAY EVENING, a week later, Scott Finginger was outside Heather's cottage precisely at eight. Through the door, he heard the muffled thump of feet on stairs.

Heather hurried down into the hall. She stopped by the hall table to collect her handbag, her eye catching her face in the mirror.

Her hair was curling about her shoulders but fastened at the side with a tortoiseshell clip. She'd applied a little make-up to her eyes and lips, and a dab of scent to her throat. She wore a yellow summer dress with matching shoes, a white cardigan with a silver butterfly brooch David had given her pinned to it. Her legs were bare, her only pair of stockings holed beyond salvation, but it would just have to do. 'Local dignitary,' she muttered, reaching for the door.

She needn't have worried. The venue, a large wooden hall on the base, gaily decorated with paper streamers, posters and flags, was packed to the seams. A band on a stage at the far end of the hall was already in full swing, couples gyrating energetically on the floor in front of it. Long trestle tables had been set up down the full length of one wall. They bowed visibly beneath crates of beer, vast tureens of raspberry-red punch and platters of food. Heather gaped. It was almost beyond comprehension.

With his hand at her elbow, Scott Finginger steered her back and forth through the growing throng. She met his boss, a bespectacled lieutenant called Stracey. Then she met a succession of majors whom Finginger introduced as Joe, Operations, Deke, Meteorology, Conrad, Maps, and finally Gene Englehardt, squadron commander.

'Dance?' Finginger shouted suddenly above the growing din. 'Day-ance', it sounded like.

'No, I, well, Scott, really I don't think . . .'

He took her hand and led her to the front of the hall. They found a spot close by the stage, and there she danced, for hours, it seemed. She felt unburdened and renewed. For the first time in as long as she could remember, she felt alive.

Finally, breathless and perspiring, she stopped. The band had fallen still. It was at that moment that she caught sight of John Hooper. He was standing across the room, side on to her, his head bent towards one of the majors that Finginger had introduced her to earlier. Englehardt. Englehardt was doing the talking while Hooper listened, nodding. It took her a second or two to place him as the man she'd seen in Iken church. He seemed taller, fuller, less gaunt than the brief shadowy figure of her memory. But the eyes were the same, unmistakable, deep and dark, and as she watched he smiled briefly at Englehardt, the same modest, gentle smile he'd given her, so apologetically, weeks ago in the church.

'Who's that?' she found herself asking.

'That? With Gene Englehardt? That's Hooper. Crew 19's new pilot. The one who nearly took your roof off barrel-rolling *Misbehavin' Martha* last week. Why, do you want to meet him?'

Englehardt, laughing, still talking, was punching Hooper lightly on the shoulder. Slowly, Hooper's smile spread out into a shy grin. Then he looked up and their eyes met.

'No,' Heather said at last. She tore her gaze from his, began moving towards the food tables. 'I already have.'

THAT THEY SHOULD MEET, Heather sensed, that they should touch, was as inevitable as the coming dawn. It was late; suddenly tired, feeling deflated after too much food and excitement, she was ready for Scott to take her home. He set off to find her cardigan and arrange a Jeep. 'Here,' he said, grabbing an arm from the crowd as he went. 'This is John Hooper. Talk to him while I'm gone, he doesn't know too many people here either.'

Then there he was. Standing before her, that shy smile on his lips, his eyes searching hers, as though struggling to recall something.

'Hello. Again,' she said, taking his proffered hand. It was absurd. She could actually feel her heart moving the collar of her dress.

'Again?'

'The church? At Iken. One evening a few weeks ago?'

'Ah. Sorry.'

'You don't remember?'

'Not exactly. Kind of a murky time.' He smiled, looking away, embarrassed. On the stage the band were playing a final number. Jerome Kern. 'The Way You Look Tonight'. She said yes almost without realising it. His hand soft yet firm in hers as they walked across to the dance floor. They began to move, together. Time stood still, the other couples melting from awareness. She inhaled deeply, lifting her chin, her eyes, until they were directly on his. They were waiting for her. Their bodies were close, barely moving. The music was winding to a climax, the saxophonist, eyes closed, soaring to a finish. *Because I love you. Just the way you look tonight.*

Scattered applause broke out, the spell broke. Gently, he lifted her hand from his shoulder, held it, then brought it to his lips and, his eyes still on hers, lightly kissed the slender gold band on her finger.

'This has to be goodbye,' he said and led her from the floor.

'GOOD MORNING, LIEUTENANT HOLLAND, it is five o'clock. You are flying today.'

Dutch had risen from his bed the second the orderly's hand left his shoulder. He was already wide awake, yet dizzy with sleeplessness. He laced on his shoes, then reached for his uniform jacket.

The occupants of the seven other beds in his hut were up now, donning their flying gear in sleepy silence. Irv Underwood was sitting on the edge of his bed, hair awry, pulling on his kit slowly, clumsily, like a young kid trying to dress himself for school. Irv was the only other one of *Martha*'s four officers who lived in Dutch's hut. Spitzer and Hooper bunked next door.

Dutch fished under his bed for his bombardier's flight bag, began rummaging through. He glanced round the room then dug into a side pocket. Four little brown-paper grocery sacks. Checked and counted. Nobody outside Crew 19 knew about them, or the hours aloft he spent vomiting into them. He snapped the flight bag shut and rose for the door.

He and Irv met Spitz and Hooper at breakfast. He still couldn't say he knew any of them very well. Irv, the oldest of the four, was silent and withdrawn. Little Loren Spitzer, 'Thumbs-up', the gunners called him, ever the optimist, raring to go. Hoop was good, the ideal commander, a joshing joke or two, a reassuring smile, a kind word. Today was the day, their first mission, but don't sweat it, he seemed to be saying. We got a good team and a good ship. They all walked to the briefing room together. The real thing at last.

AT MARTHA'S HARDSTANDING, Hooper and Underwood, arms laden, clumsy in their heavy flying suits, jumped down from their truck's tailgate and picked up their parachutes and bags. Martha, the morning dew still wet on her wings, stood ready before them. 'Go ahead, Irv.' Hooper patted his copilot's back. 'Get aboard and make yourself at home.' Underwood was visibly nervous, Hooper could see. But then so was every one of the airmen arriving at the twenty-four aircraft parked, fuelled, armed and ready around the field.

Martha was in Englehardt's squadron, the high layer, one of three squadrons of seven, plus the usual three reserves, or supernumeraries, who would follow only as far as the RP, the Rendezvous Point. The other two squadrons would fly the middle and bottom layers, the whole making up the classic three-layered defensive box.

Knyper came over, wiping oily hands on a rag. Hooper dumped his bag and parachute by the nose hatch. 'OK, chief?' Knyper nodded and they began a walk-around together. Inside Martha all was business, the gunners completely immersed, for once, in the job at hand, double-checking everything. Another truck pulled up: Dutch Holland and Thumbs-up Spitzer clambered out.

Then it was time for Hooper to board and start up. He swung up through the nose hatch, locked it shut, clambered awkwardly up onto the flight deck, stowed his parachute in the rack behind his seat. Underwood turned to him, his face a fearful, sickly mask.

'OK, Irv,' Hoop said. 'Let's have those pre-start-up checks.'

Then everything went blank. Everything. Just like that. He couldn't do it. It wasn't fear, it wasn't nerves. It was erasure, as if he had never sat in a plane before in his life. Underwood, his voice perplexed, the checklist trembling in his hand, kept calling the start checks. Hoop, head shaking in disbelief, kept trying to go through the motions. But each time he got to hitting the start and mesh buttons, the number one engine just turned over and over, stubbornly refusing to start.

All the other bombers, their engines running, were starting to taxi away round the perimeter track towards the runway. But not *Martha*. Nothing. Lifeless. No engine start. Not so much as a cough. Farther aft, Gerry Via swung open the radio-room door. Ringwald, legs dangling, was sitting on the floor, ready to drop down into his ball turret as soon as they were airborne. Beans and Keissling stood waiting beside their guns.

'What the hell's going on?' Dutch whispered, down in the nose, to Spitzer. But Spitzer just shrugged, eyes wide with confusion. Behind the flight deck Lajowski, perched on his upper turret platform, ducked down to peer into the cockpit. At that moment the intercom crackled to life in their headphones. Hooper came on.

'OK, uh, crew, this is pilot. Sorry about this, but I seem to be having a problem starting the engines. Turret, could you get the nose hatch open and ask Sergeant Knyper to come on board, please.'

Tork's hiss floated up from the tail. 'Hey, guys. Did I get that right?'

'I just knew the guy was a dead-beat no-hoper. I just knew it,' fumed Beans. Scowling in disgust, he slumped, arms folded, over his gun. From the floor, Eldon Ringwald's boylike face swung questioningly from Keissling to Via, to Beans, then back to Keissling.

'Maybe not.' Keissling shrugged. 'Maybe there's just some kinda technical problem up there.' Ringwald nodded in agreement.

'Technical problem! The technical problem is in Hooper's goddamn head. Keissling, I tell you, the guy's a total screwball.'

There was another crackle on the headphones. Hooper's intercom was still on. Knyper was aboard, Hooper was talking to him. Nine pairs of ears strained to listen.

'Sergeant. Thanks for coming up. Listen. As you know, ah, this is our first combat mission together. And I know that I'm feeling a little spiky. Clearly I am doing something wrong during the engine-start procedures. I wonder if we could just run through them together, see if we can't get these damn fires lit.'

Fifteen minutes later, with all four engines burbling contentedly, *Martha*, lurching inelegantly on her wheels, was hurrying round the airfield perimeter towards the runway. She was alone, the airfield empty. All the others had gone, exactly on schedule.

Holland and Spitzer braced themselves against the rocking, the questions hanging unanswered between them. Had Hooper left

Martha's intercom open deliberately? Was his public admission that he was so damn nervous he couldn't remember what to do accidental or calculated? Yet he was man enough to admit it to the whole crew. That took guts. Somehow it made Dutch feel a little less anxious. You had to admire the man. He swivelled on his seat, managed a half-grin at Spitzer, who returned it with a hesitant thumbs up.

And the intercom was still on. Above them, in the cockpit, Irv Underwood was clearing his throat. 'Um, what are we doing, Hoop?'

'We're going after them.'

'But they're long gone, we'll never catch them. Anyway, the supernumerary will be in our slot by now.'

'Supers don't get to take the slots until the rendezvous point. We'll head them off, beat them to it.' Hooper swung the bomber onto the runway and pushed the throttles to the stops.

'You're not cleared! Hooper, the control tower, look! They're firing a red! Jesus, you're not cleared to go!'

'We're already gone.' *Martha* strained forwards, accelerating swiftly down the runway. Hooper pushed forward slightly on the control column, lifting the tail, and suddenly *Martha* was ready, skipping, the wheels off, then on, then off again, lifting clear, pointing her glass-domed nose towards the waiting clouds.

'Pilot to navigator.'

Below, Spitzer fumbled for his intercom switch. 'Er, yes, yes, pilot, this is navigator here.'

'Spitz, where's the RP today?'

'The rendezvous point today is off Harwich.'

'Correct. But the formation is currently climbing up to height over the Splasher Six beacon at Diss, isn't that right?'

'Yes, sir, that's right.' He was going to leave them. Leave them all there at the radio beacon circling laboriously up through the clouds. Cut across country direct to Harwich, get to the RP before them.

'We'll stay low for the moment. I'll need headings and position information soon as you can get them to me. Have you got that?'

'Yes. Yes, I have. Ah, give me thirty seconds, I'll get you there.'

Thirty minutes later, *Misbehavin' Martha* intercepted Gene Englehardt's formation as it was approaching Harwich at 14,000 feet. Hooper drew up alongside the seven tightly bunched aircraft. The supernumerary ship *Looky Looky* was already slotted in next to Englehardt's. Hooper edged *Martha* closer to it, right alongside, wing tip to wing tip. Looking across, he could see the pilot,

Lieutenant Dickinson's masked face at the controls. His ungloved fist was at the window, middle finger extended upwards.

'That's not very polite,' Underwood said. 'I guess we're too late.'

'We'll see about that.'

Back in the waist, Keissling, Beans and Ringwald were crowded round Keissling's window. Their opposite numbers in *Looky Looky* were similarly positioned, gesturing rudely, waving them away.

There was a click in their headphones.

'Dickinson. This is Hooper. Listen to me.'

Everyone froze. He was on the radio. Not the intercom, but the high-frequency radio. Hooper was breaking radio silence. Against every rule in the book. Everybody could hear: the whole squadron. The whole group. Everyone back at Bedenham.

'Here it is. You know as well as I do that supers don't get the slot until the RP. So either you move out of my way right now, or I'm coming down over the top and will not hesitate to knock the living shit out of you.'

Dickinson, his body erect with disbelief at his window, stared out at Hooper, then turned to look over at Englehardt flying on his right. Then, after what seemed like an eternity, he slowly pulled *Looky Looky* up and out of the formation and banked steeply for home.

Hooper slid *Martha* into position next to Englehardt's ship. For several minutes the formation flew on, exactly as if nothing had happened. Then at last Englehardt turned towards *Martha*. He was shaking his head. He was laughing.

'Tail to pilot.'

'Yes, Tork, what is it?'

'Well. Sir. Well, hot damn. That's all.'

CHAPTER FOUR

Hooper was waiting for Heather. Sitting there, arms folded, on the rough wall outside her cottage when the Garretts dropped her off on the way back from a trip to Ipswich.

Dumbfounded, Heather stepped from the car. She seemed constantly to be introducing her parents-in-law to Americans. 'Ah, well, um, Rosamund, Gerald, this is Lieutenant, um, Hooper. He's a pilot, up at the base here. I'm sorry, Lieutenant, I don't know your first name. These are my parents-in-law, Gerald and Rosamund Garrett.'

'John. It's John.' Hooper ducked to the window. 'Ma'am, sir.' Gerald reached across to shake, Rosamund, tightlipped, nodded minutely. A moment later they drove off.

'I'm sorry,' he said, watching them go. 'Last thing I wanted was to cause you any embarrassment.'

Heather sighed. 'It's all right. You weren't to know. It's, well, it is rather a difficult time just at the moment. Um, do you want to come in? Have some tea or something?'

He smiled, shook his head. 'No. Thanks.'

They walked along a footpath that ran beside the field. After a while they reached the stream, following it until they came to a grassy bank. They sat down. Hooper split grass stems as he spoke, the soft cadences of his voice mingling with the trickle of water.

She heard it all. Every detail. All about not being able to get the plane's motors running, then being left behind by the others, rushing frantically to get to the, what did he call it, the rendezvous point. Breaking radio silence. Everything.

His eyes clamped onto hers and stayed there, insisting, almost imploring her to understand.

They were practically home, more than halfway across the North Sea, coast in sight, and mission accomplished. It had gone well. Englehardt's high squadron hadn't been touched, the bomb run carried off without a hitch. All things considered, it had been a textbook mission for them. And no fighters. They had been very lucky.

Understandably, perhaps, the crew were in high spirits. But not Hooper. He was shattered. Utterly exhausted. He felt as if he was forcing *Martha* to function by will power alone. And the effort needed to sustain it, the strain of it over the past few weeks, and the lost months before, was crushing him. And so he had snapped.

'Tail to pilot.'

'Yes, um, Tork. What is it?' Hooper pulled himself straighter in his seat. His neck and shoulders ached, white sparks of incandescence danced before his eyes, his head hurt like the end of the world.

'Well, sir, me and Beans have this little bet going, about which one of us gets to shoot down an enemy fighter first. I was wondering if you'd care to put a twenty in the pot. In my pot, that is, naturally.'

'Ah, no. No I wouldn't.'

'I'm in.' Via came on. 'Twenty on Torky.'

'Geraldo, my man!'

Ringwald piped up. 'What do you want to bet on him for? I bet it'll be me.'

'Kid! Little Kid Ringwald? Those square-head Focke-Wulf jockeys will eat you for breakfast. You leave them to me, I'll—'

'Stop!' Hooper roared suddenly, then gasped. Pain lanced down the back of his neck, the white orbs danced higher, filling his vision. He felt himself teetering on the edge of a faint. 'All of you, for God's sake, what the hell do you think you're doing? This isn't a game. Men have died today. And you're betting on it like it was all just some big joke.'

'Navigator to pilot—'

'No!' He should stop, he wanted to stop. But his voice, taut and tinny through his headphones, kept raging on and on. 'OK, I'll take you on if that's what you want. Count me in. I bet a hundred bucks on the German fighter pilot. And why? Because he's better than you, better than any of you. He's a fighter pilot of the German Air Force, highly trained, professional and dedicated, and if you want to stay alive you'll show him some respect—'

'Hoop, Hoop, it's OK.' Spitzer was gripping his arm. 'It's OK, take it easy.'

He slumped back into his seat, spent. His hands flopped to his sides; he closed his eyes, crushing a tear onto his cheek which seeped hotly beneath the black rubber of his oxygen mask. After a while, much later, he felt the mask being removed, hands loosening the neck of his flying suit. 'Sorry,' he wanted to say, to them all, but the intercom was off. 'Sorry.' But it was too late. He had to get away. Walk in honey-coloured fields. Feel the earth against his skin.

Fifteen minutes later, his copilot, Irv Underwood, teeth gritted in determination, landed *Martha*, a little untidily, but safely, on the main runway at Bedenham.

T/SGT MARION BEANS 520TH BG

Dear Cheryl,

I hope you are well, I got your last letters, thanks for the latest photo, you look real cute, I put it straight in my wallet.

Me and the boys are doing fine. We just completed mission number seven and tho' I say so myself, I say we're shaking down pretty good. seven down eighteen to go—be home before you know it! The missions are going fine, Cher, you must stop worrying about that. The other day Lieutenant Hooper came down to see us in the waist during one mission, and he says Beans old buddy I want to swap you and Herm Keissling over, left and right, because we were always getting in each other's ways and our aims was off and so forth. So now Herm shoots left waist and I shoot right waist. Guess what? It's a whole deal better! I don't know why he didn't think of it before.

Anyway the good news is that after the seventh mission we get a two-day pass so me and the guys are off to London to see the sites! All except Lieutenant Hooper of course, and Kid Ringwald who's got a girl in the village. I'll write tell you all about our London siteseeing tour on our return.

Take care, Cher honey.

Yours for always, Marion

'NO, LOOK, BILLY, not like that, you're over-tightening it, for God's sake, you'll strip the thread. Slacken it off, lad, go on, that's it, a little more.' Ray watched as Billy, his face a frown of concentration, slotted the spanner onto the wheel nut and began turning. 'Good, that's better. See, there's no need to tighten it so much, is there?'

'Sorry, Mr H. It's the Wright Cyclones, see.'

'The what?' Ray squinted along the bicycle's upturned wheel, spinning it with the flat of his hand. Somehow, since Maggie's outburst on the subject, the matter of Billy's leaving the forge hadn't been mentioned again.

'The engines on the B-17s. Sergeant Knyper showed me. You have to torque the nuts right down as hard as you can, and even then it takes two mechanics to do the last bit together.'

'Ah, yes, well, that's as may be. But this isn't any thundering great aeroplane engine, is it? This is Mrs Garrett's bicycle. Put two of your Sergeant Knightly's hairy great mechanics onto fixing this and they'd break it in half.'

'Knyper, Mr H. His name's Hal Knyper. Um, he wondered if you wanted to, like, stop in. One day. Have like a little tour round his workshop. Only if you wanted to, like. It's massive, Mr H. And he's very interested in your metalwork and smithing and that.'

'Is he?'

'Dead keen. So, like, I could take you up there, 'e could show you about the place, then we could bring him back here for a look at the forge. And tea.'

'Tea?'

Billy nodded, scratching an oily finger on his cheek. Ray began gathering tools into a tray. 'Well, we'll have to see. Now then, what about this other bicycle, who does it belong to?'

'Polecat. Um, Sergeant Lajowski, from *Misbehavin' Martha*. He says the brakes don't work and the handlebars are loose.'

Ray examined the machine. 'Won't take five minutes.'

'That's good, then, 'cos I already charged him a crown.'

'Five shillings! In advance?'

A shadow fell across the doorway. 'Mr Howden? I'm sorry to trouble you. It's Mrs Blackstone. Area evacuee coordinator.'

Ray led her into the lounge, a small, neatly furnished room at the end of the house. It was the room for best and special occasions only, and therefore rarely used. Billy had only looked inside it once or twice in passing. He saw little more of it now. Mrs Blackstone stopped him in the doorway.

'Oh, Mr Howden, I do think it would be best if we went through things on our own without, er, William present.'

Billy clumped slowly up the stairs to the attic. That's it, he reflected, curling into a ball on his bed. The end of the only good thing that had ever happened. Finish.

An hour later Ray called him down to the lounge. The woman had gone. Maggie looked pale and drawn.

'Well, lad,' Ray began. 'I'd say you've got some explaining to do.'

BILLY STREET, SO IT APPEARED, was not Billy Street at all. He was Albert Crossley. Mrs Blackstone, the area evacuee coordinator, had sat with the Howdens and produced a thick sheaf of documents from an envelope. Ray and Maggie listened, pale-faced, from the sofa.

'Well, now, born on or about the 18th of September, 1928, the boy was registered, probably by his maternal grandparents, as Albert Harold Crossley in October that year. He was put up for adoption.'

'But what about his parents?' Maggie interrupted straight away. 'What about his mother?'

Mrs Blackstone, a tall, grey-haired woman of about fifty, arched her eyebrows. 'According to what little information we have on her, Billy's—Albert's—mother was only sixteen or seventeen at the time, and unmarried. She lived with her parents who ran a public house down near the docks in Tilbury. I would hazard to suppose that Albert was most likely the unfortunate product of a brief, um, liaison between a passing sailor and this Crossley girl. Wouldn't you?'

Maggie cleared her throat. 'Billy. He may have been born Albert, but as far as he's concerned and we're concerned, his name is Billy.'

'As you prefer,' Mrs Blackstone said stiffly. 'Albert—Billy—was fostered many times over the years, and spent a great deal of time in various children's homes and orphanages. Sadly, however, as with so many of his kind, he was never found an adoptive family.'

'His kind?'

'I beg your pardon?'

'You said his kind.'

Mrs Blackstone stiffened. 'Mrs Howden, these are just the facts. I am simply relaying them to you as they came down to me. They are not my doing. It is an unfortunate fact that hundreds of babies are born in the poorer parts of London to impoverished and unmarried girls every year. Few of them are fortunate enough to find families to adopt them. Billy was not one of those, so he was raised by the state. At least he was until he was twelve.'

'Then what happened?'

Mrs Blackstone looked up at them. 'He went to prison. Well, a correctional institution for young offenders. In Kent.'

'But what for?'

'For arson.'

CREW 19, WITH THE EXCEPTION of Hooper and Ringwald, who had decided to stay behind, left Bedenham in the early evening, catching a base bus to Ipswich station then a slow train to London Liverpool Street. Emerging uncertainly onto the cavernous station concourse, the party split into two by unspoken agreement. The three officers, Spitzer, Holland and Underwood, took a taxi straight to the West End and their private rooms at the Grosvenor Hotel.

'Lord above!' Holland exclaimed. The three, clean-shaven, showered and changed, had regrouped downstairs in the officers' mess. The bar was packed, mostly with Americans, including many women. 'All this and breakfast too, for twelve bucks?'

'Too steep for you, Dutch?' Spitzer joked. 'We could be in the Dorchester for fifteen.'

Meanwhile Beans, Via, Tork, Lajowski and Keissling, anxious not to miss a minute's sightseeing, made their way by cab to Piccadilly Circus. They paid the driver off and spilled out onto the street, looking around in bemused wonderment. The pavements were packed, London awash with homegoing office and shop staff, tourists, shoppers, showgoers, street vendors and milling uniforms of every colour and description. And the emerging night shift. Within seconds, as if by magic, three girls had materialised before them.

'Oi, Yanks!' they giggled. They were dressed in tight dresses hemmed above the knee, their cheeks rouged, their lips ruby red. 'Looking for a good time, are ya? We can show you round, get you in all the posh places. Show you some sights.' They nudged one another. 'What d'ya say?'

After a brief, hissed conference, Lajowski, Tork and Beans were led off in the direction of Leicester Square, arm in arm with the girls. Gerry Via remained at the kerb, Herman Keissling at his side.

'You married, Herm?' Via asked, sniffing up at the sky. Occasional fine droplets of rain fell like mist.

'You bet,' Keissling was saying. 'Four years. Blanche. Want to see a picture? We got a kid too. Elvin, see, there, he's gonna be two. Looks just like me, wouldn't you say?'

'Cute.' Via handed back the photograph.

'What about you, Gerry, you married?'

'Nope.' He glanced in the direction of the others. 'Not even close. But I never paid for the company of a lady yet, and I have no intention of starting now. Shall we walk a ways?'

In gathering darkness they set off, at random, downhill. At Pall Mall they turned east into Trafalgar Square where they paused on the steps of the National Gallery to admire Nelson's Column. Off St Martin's they stopped at a Lyons Corner House for some shepherd's pie. Drifting along the Strand they stopped outside a rowdily noisy pub. A sign in the window said: WE WELCOME US ENLISTED. It boasted real Kentucky bourbon under the bar, and it was stiff with shouting GIs. They fought their way to a table, once again propositioned en route by English girls.

'Well, now I know why they call them Piccadilly commandos!' Keissling grinned sheepishly. 'Nothing seems to stop them.'

'Two quid, mate,' one said, leaning over the table towards Via. 'Mite', she pronounced it. Despite the lines of her face and the dullness in her eyes, she looked barely eighteen. 'Two quid. 'Ow about it?'

'What's your name?' Via asked.

'Kate.' Kite. 'What's yours?'

'Gerry. Gerry Via. How old are you, Kate?'

'Twenty-one, so are you comin' or what?'

'Not just now. Take a seat for a few minutes, Kate. Let me buy you a drink.'

'Say, listen, Gerry, buddy, it's getting late.' Keissling, glancing towards the girl, was rising from the table. 'I gotta tell you I am just completely tuckered. I think I'll head along to the United Services Organisation's quarters and hit the sack. I could sleep for a week.'

Half an hour later, Via left the bar, alone, and began to walk. Aimlessly at first, then more briskly, and with purpose. He found his way to the river, then, hunched into the turned-up collar of his uniform jacket, he followed the blacked-out Embankment east. Towards the City. An hour after that the air-raid warning sounded.

JOHN HOOPER CAME round once or twice a week, usually, Heather soon divined, after he had flown a mission. He never announced his visits, he simply arrived at her door, cap in hand, asking in his quiet way if it was any trouble to her that he was there. Sometimes she was out when he visited, and she found herself briefing him on her movements, her working hours, shopping habits and so on, telling him when she was most likely to be at home.

She would make him tea, or if it was later, pour him a glass of sherry from her meagre stock. Usually both, although gratefully accepted, would remain untouched at his side until he departed. Together they would sit on a pair of David's rickety deck chairs outside the back door, overlooking her vegetable garden. Or opposite one another in her sitting room. Or, if the evening was fine, beside the stream at the bottom of the field across from her cottage.

And talk. His appetite for it was insatiable. It was as though conversation provided his only release from the demons that drove him through his war. That very afternoon he had sat, hunched forward on the armchair in her front room, his hands pressed between his knees, talking nonstop for an hour about his home, his childhood, his sister, growing up in Pennsylvania. Then, just as suddenly, he had switched tack and begun quizzing Heather about hers.

'You said your father was a doctor,' he began. 'What kind of medicine did he practise?'

'He's a general practitioner. Or was. Retired now.'

'Oh, right, yes. And your parents live in Lincoln, where you grew up. Tell me about that. You have a younger brother too, no?'

'Yes, Richard. He's missing, of course. As well.'

'Yes, yes, like David, I know. A year and a half. Your brother, and your husband. I thought it would be impossible to imagine loss like that.' His eyes lifted to hers. 'But you know, I find that I can.'

Sometimes, without warning a distance might come over them, a cloud of concentration. As though in his head he was somewhere else, or trying to be. Then he would be back, the cloud would vanish and his gaze would soften and crinkle into a smile.

And so it went on. Long, fervent bursts of monologue followed by brief spells of reflective silence. Usually, after a couple of hours, he began to slow as fatigue finally overcame him. He rarely slept the night before a mission, she'd learned. His silences would become protracted, so much so that she thought he might be asleep. But then suddenly he would stiffen, rise, and with formal correctness thank her, apologise and leave.

Afterwards she would feel like a wrung-out dishcloth. She was sharing his burden, that's what she was doing. Helping him, providing a means to ease his pain, his fear, his suffering. She was able to help this man as surely as she was unable to help her husband. It felt wrong, yet it felt so right. And deep down the core questions heaved and stewed inside her like a witch's cauldron. What were her real feelings, and how much longer could she go on denying them?

'RAY? RAY, LOVE? Is that you?'

Ray pushed the door quietly to and tiptoed into their darkened bedroom. 'Yes, Mags, only me. Didn't want to disturb you.' He sat down on the edge of the bed and began unbuttoning his shirt.

'Did you speak to Billy again? Did you talk to him?'

Ray nodded in the darkness. 'Tried to.'

'What did he say?'

He'd broken down. Completely. Pleading, begging tearfully for forgiveness. No, not forgiveness. For help. Hunched, shaking, into a ball on his bed, sobbing silently. The fervour, the fear, had been shocking. Ray drew a breath, shutting the image from his mind.

'Ray?'

'He didn't say much. The arson thing, the fire at the warehouse, he said that was an accident. A prank gone wrong. He got trapped inside, turned out he was probably lucky to escape with his life, which explains why he doesn't like the forge much, scared to death of fire. Anyway, both the other kids involved died, and since Billy already had some previous form—you know, a bit of shoplifting, petty thievery and that—he got sent down to this boys' correctional institute place near Maidstone.'

'But it's so unfair. It was an accident, and he could only have been, what, eleven? Twelve? And those places, they're so awful. Did he say anything about it?'

'Nothing.' Ray hesitated. 'Wouldn't say.' I'd die first, Mr H, he'd vowed tearfully through gritted teeth. Before going back there. I'd rather be dead. Precious little else, but Ray had guessed the rest. Systematic bullying and victimisation from the other boys, regular and vicious beatings from the custodians, living conditions no better than those of a caged animal. He'd lasted barely a month.

'What happened to him?'

'Well, from what that Blackstone woman said, and what little else Billy himself had to say about it, turns out he absconded from the place. Then he spent three weeks living rough, scrounging food and sleeping in sheds and that, until eventually he found his way back to London and one of the orphanages he'd stayed at earlier.'

'And they let him stay?'

'No, not officially. But he had a friend there, one of the matrons, an Irish girl apparently, who had a soft spot for him and took him under her wing.' And then he'd had a piece of luck. Bombs began to fall on the capital. It was the end of 1939, the evacuee programme was getting under way. All London's children, including those in homes and orphanages, were to be sent to the country for safety. Billy's Irish nurse friend had simply added his name to the orphanage's list. A day or two later, he found himself on a train full of children bound for Suffolk.

'That children's home,' Ray went on. 'The London one where the Irish girl worked. Guess where it is.'

'London.'

'No, what address?'

'Go on.'

'King William Street. Do you see? That's where he got the name.'

'What are we going to do about him, Ray? What are we going to do about our Billy?'

Ray exhaled. 'I don't know. It's out of our hands now. Mrs Blackstone is going to get in touch soon as she hears from the authorities. He'll probably have to go back and serve out his sentence.'

'He can't. You know that. He just can't. It'll kill him.'

THE AIR-RAID SHELTER was little more than a pedestrian underpass, a wide, low-ceilinged corridor running under the street. It was unlit, although a roving ARP warden in a black tin hat shone a masked torch here and there. The shelter held about seventy people, mostly stray audience members from the cinemas and shows nearby. People seemed bored, resigned, but unmoved. Near the steps at one end, Spitzer, Holland and Underwood waited for the all clear.

'How long we been down here?' Holland asked.

'Lord knows.' Spitzer checked his watch. 'Forty-five minutes maybe.' They'd heard the muffled crump of explosions, about twenty minutes earlier, felt the vibration of impact beneath their feet.

'Terrific way to spend your hard-earned weekend pass,' Holland grumbled good-naturedly. 'Holed up in the ground like rats in a trap, while the enemy drops high explosives on your head.'

'Does have a certain irony about it, though, wouldn't you say, Dutch? Now we know a little of what it feels like to be on the receiving end. Though I don't think we've had any hits closer than a mile.'

'Close enough for me, thank you, Lieutenant.'

'Hmm. Makes you think, though, doesn't it?' Spitzer squatted down beside Irv Underwood who was now sitting on the bottom step, staring at his feet, his head hunched into his shoulders. 'Irv? How you doing there, old buddy?'

Underwood nodded but made no response. Then he felt Spitzer's hand on his shoulder. A wave of emotion swept over him. 'I'm sorry,' he whispered. Spitzer's hand gripped his shoulder in response.

On the steps, Dutch was unfolding a tourist map of London. 'Where the hell are we anyway?'

They were off Regent Street. They had stayed rather longer in the bar at the Grosvenor Hotel than they intended, unwilling to relinquish the warm splendour, the cheap Manhattans and the rowdily cheerful company of their own kind, yet at the same time anxious to step out into the mysteries of the Mayfair night. They drank rather too much, found it hard to tear themselves away. Eventually they had reeled down the steps and into the night.

Outside, the sky was clearing. They went to a cinema, off Golden Square, bought tickets and were fortunate to squeeze their way into a trio of seats right at the front of the dress circle. Before the main attraction, a James Stewart movie, there was a Pathé newsreel. Much of it featured war news from the different theatres of operation, and footage from the fronts. It was an unerringly optimistic review devoid of a single negative item. Even when describing the ongoing hardships, dangers and deprivations British civilians faced day after day, the newsreader, his English voice plummy and strident, managed to sound unnervingly enthusiastic.

'. . . no time now for the little woman to worry about life's little shortages! She has home fires to keep burning, and a hubby in Tunis, busy pushing back Rommel's mighty Panzers!'

Spitzer nudged Underwood in the darkness. Irv seemed to be nodding off. 'Hey, Irv, will you get a load of this guy!'

'. . . meanwhile, the Yanks are here! And gosh-darn, aren't we pleased to see them! These bomber boys know what's what . . .'

It happened very quickly. One second the film, clearly from an airborne camera, grainy, jerky, black and white, showed a stick of bombs tumbling earthwards towards a smoke-covered target. The next, it cut to a formation of B-17s flying through puffs of dirty grey flak. Then the camera swung forward before fastening on a small, fast-moving cross turning in towards the bombers. A second later it captured the Messerschmitt fighter as it attacked the camera-carrying plane. Then it was gone and the camera was inside the bomber, aimed at the two waist gunners firing after it.

'No!' Irv Underwood jerked suddenly in his seat, yelping loudly, like a panicked child pursued by wasps. Heads turned in surprise. He was totally oblivious, his eyes fastened to the screen, his arms scrabbling at his head.

'Irv!' Holland leaned away from the wildly thrashing copilot. 'Irv! Spitzer, what the hell is wrong with him?'

'Get it away!' Underwood pleaded, his eyes wild with terror. All around them spectators gaped in astonishment. Holland and Spitzer shushed and struggled to control him. The newsreel moved on to a different story. 'For God's sake,' he kept begging, again and again, 'for God's sake. Please get it away!'

GERRY VIA WAS MILES from them, off the Southwark Bridge Road, lost, but until that moment largely unconcerned about it, when the first bombs began to fall. It was a residential area, as far as he could tell, row upon row of blacked-out houses.

He had just stopped in the middle of a road, searching in vain for a street sign, when the eerie drone of air-raid sirens began to swell in the gloom around him. Within seconds there was a series of dull crumps, some distance away, and a brief flicker of orange far beyond some rooftops. Then came the irregular unsynchronised thrumming of approaching German bombers. Fascinated, he watched fingers of harsh white light spring skywards, as searchlights began raking the night. Then, from somewhere down near the river, the steady boom of an antiaircraft battery opened up. Then another, then a third.

The noise was incredible, the roaring thrum of hundreds of bombers' engines, interspersed with the pounding flash and crack of antiaircraft guns, with their glowing tracer shells arcing thousands of feet into the night. Searchlights, more and more by the minute, criss-crossed the sky, hunting their targets. And then there were the bombs, falling everywhere now, a continuous unrhythmic tattoo of heavy, concussive thuds that you heard inside your head, and felt deep in your guts. What was it the Londoners called it? The Blitz. Short for *Blitzkrieg*, German for lightning-war.

He watched in detached fascination as a stick of bombs fell nearby, erupting not three blocks away. He recoiled, gasping at the flash, an image, a church, lit from behind, seared on to his eyes. A second later, the blast from the explosion reached him, rocking him on his heels.

It was only then that the danger of his own situation struck him. He was in the open. Nowhere to go, nowhere to hide. Paralysed into inaction. He forced himself to look round, forced himself to move, stumbling backwards, away from the bombs. More were falling, all around him; the noise was deafening, numbing. Terror welled in him. Soon, his arms and legs pumping, he was in full flight, sprinting, as though from ravenous wolves, desperate and directionless. He heard the harsh ringing of feet on asphalt, the hoarse gasps of his own panicked breathing. Then there was a long, whistling shriek from somewhere behind him, and an instant of silence. Then a blinding flash lit the whole street, a blast of heat and shock followed, and a monstrous explosion lifted him, bodily, arms and legs flailing, high into the air. Then everything went black.

'DID YOU EVER SEE anything the like of it in all your born days?' Marion Beans, hands on hips, stepped gingerly onto the station platform, Lajowski and Tork on either side. The platform, an east-bound Central Line station on London's Underground, was packed. Spread out before them, covering every available yard from the curving tiled wall right to the platform's gaping edge, was a sea of people. Old and young, large and small, sound and infirm. Mothers with babies, snoring old men and gossiping crones. Sailors and shopgirls, soldiers and students, sweethearts and schoolchildren. And they were on the ground, almost all of them, sitting, reclining or lying.

Nearby, a dozen youths played cards in a circle. Another, older group, further along the platform, sang pub songs. Some had brought baggage with them, keepsakes and valuables, as if going on a journey. They read newspapers, held huddled conversations, told jokes or just slept. They ate sandwiches, drank beer from bottles and soup from flasks. Running in and out of it all, streamed curling lines of children screaming with excitement, their arms spread wide like wings.

'It's like—well, it's like something out of the Bible.' Lajowski stared around incredulously.

Al Tork nodded. He knew what Lajowski meant. Even the noise that rose from the gathered host sounded biblical, like a sort of rapidly spoken Mass prayer. It reminded him of the noise inside the rearing shed on his parents' goose farm. He shook his head. 'I had absolutely no idea. It's like those refugee camp films we get on the newsreel, in Holland and Belgium and places. Kind of pitiful to see. But then again, it's kind of cheery, don't you think? Nobody seems to give much of a damn.' He leaned towards an old man sitting on a bench nearby. 'Excuse me, sir. But how long do you have to stay down here in the subway like this?'

'We don't 'ave to stay at all, mate.' The old man grinned.

Tork looked confused. 'Then why—'

'Listen, son. When you're copping two or three raids a night, you soon get brassed off tramping up and down them bloody escalators. Damn sight less bother to stay put.'

Beans, his head turning this way and that, was moving slowly up the platform. Lajowski set off in the opposite direction, threading his way carefully among the litter of bodies, until he came to the circle of card players. They looked about fifteen or sixteen years old. 'So, what's the game, fellas?'

'Beggar's bluff, mate. Want to play? Cost you a tanner in.'

'Sure, ah, beggar's bluff. Can't say I know it, but what the hell. Tanner in, did you say?'

WHEN VIA AWOKE it was dark, and cold, and deathly quiet. His cheeks were wet. He lay still for a moment, blinking. Was he wounded? His head hurt and he felt dizzy, a little nauseous, but nothing else. He struggled slowly to a half-sitting position, checking himself for injuries. The street was completely silent, empty. The raid was over. No injuries, he concluded, pulling himself more upright. Damn miracle. There was a needle-sharp pain, high on his forehead. He reached up, fingering it carefully. It was a big bruise with a small gash on it, sticky with blood. And his cheeks had been wet; he hadn't imagined it. So he had been crying. Fear? He remembered the raw rush of panic, his screaming, terrified flight as the bombs, falling nearer and nearer, pursued him down the street.

But no, they weren't tears of fear.

It was big, smiling Dave Greenbaum. Lying in his arms, his bright eyes dulling, while his blood, his life, flowed from him like a river. And all the while he, Gerry Via, ship's nominated medic, did nothing.

It was the femoral artery, he'd learned later. The base paramedics told him, after they'd lifted Dave's lifeless body from the ship and carried it to the hospital for post-mortem. He'd waited outside until they came and told him. Severed femoral, they said. Dave had bled to death. They acted kind, but their faces told him all he had to know. The death had been needless.

He rose unsteadily to his feet, brushed the dirt from his uniform and began to walk, retracing his steps back along the street. It looked the same. Yet not. It was pocked with holes and craters, bricks and rubble were strewn everywhere, broken glass crunched beneath his feet. Reaching the end of the road, he paused for breath. The little traffic island, the one he had been standing on when the bombs began falling, was gone. In its place a twenty-foot crater yawned. Peering in, he could see water spewing into it from a fractured main.

'Oi! You! Get the bloody hell away from there, right now!' A shout echoed from the corner. Two men, tin hats and dark boiler suits, were standing against a van. Via approached them.

'Are you hurt?' the second one said, glancing at Via's forehead.

'What? Ah, no, no. It's nothing. A scratch. What's going on?'

'Well, as a wild guess, I'd say the street got bombed.' The first man nudged his mate. 'Wouldn't you, Reg?'

'We're waiting for back-up, before going in for survivors,' the second man added.

'Survivors? There are people in there? Alive? But why wait? Shouldn't we be trying to get them out?'

'Yanks.' The first man rolled his eyes, then began counting off, on his fingers. 'In case you hadn't noticed, chummy, there's a mighty strong pong of gas around here. The Gas Board boys need to get it turned off, up the road there at the main. Next, you can bet your boots there's bombs in the middle of that lot that didn't go off so we need a bomb-disposal crew to take a shufti before we can go in and start poking around. Next, we can count ourselves bloody lucky that there's no fire. Yet. But there could be, any minute, so we need fire cover, plus the fire boys' masonry shifting gear. Finally, there's injured, and there's dead. So a couple of ambulances and some medics might be handy for that, wouldn't you say?'

'But where the hell are they all? When will they be here?'

'Soon as they can,' the second man, Reg, said gently.

He stayed for the rest of the night, helping. Digging, fetching, carrying. He worked tirelessly, as though driven, and without a break. He spoke little, except when spoken to, or to acknowledge instructions. OK, laddie, we're done in here, you can move through to the next room, now. Or the next house. And the next.

Everywhere there was an air of calm urgency. Everyone worked steadily, and hard, but without wasteful desperation. And there was a kind of stoic cheerfulness about it, a togetherness. Then, from time to time, a shout would go up as someone shifted rubble to find a human limb lying amid the debris. Sometimes the limb was attached to a dead body. Sometimes it wasn't attached to anything. Three times during the night it turned out to be attached to a living person.

'Who's the Yank?' a young nurse in overalls asked Reg, at one point. Via had joined a line of firemen, straining with them to pull down a teetering wall with ropes and grappling poles.

'No idea, love. Walked out of this mess shortly after we got here, hasn't stopped since.'

A while later, around the time a thin grey dawn was breaking over the scene, she tapped him on the arm and thrust a tin mug into his hand. 'Here, have this. You look as though you could do with it.' Panting, he stopped, as though ordered, grasped the mug, nodding gratefully. His face was grey with fatigue and brick dust, his uniform torn and filthy. 'Look at the state of you,' she scolded, gently brushing plaster from his shoulder. He smiled, faintly, just for a second. The tea, tepid and sweet, tasted wonderful. He stood at the shattered roadside, just for a few minutes, while it purged the dust from his throat, and warmed his empty stomach. Then he went back to work.

Suddenly, at around seven in the morning, more vans and trucks pulled up at the roadside. The men and women in Via's group, about thirty in all, began to pack up.

'What's happening?' he asked.

'Day shift, laddie. We're all done here, for now, anyway.'

'But can't I stay?'

The man, it was the one who'd shouted at him the night before, shook tobacco onto a paper, rolling it deftly between stubby fingers. 'No, son, you cannot. You're done, exhausted. That's when mistakes happen, see? Accidents.' He licked the paper. 'But you did well, really you did. You can be proud of yourself.'

'Proud?'

The man punched him lightly on the shoulder, then stepped up into the cab of his truck. 'Certainly. You did a fine job. What's your name and outfit, by the way? You'll get a mention in the report.'

'Excuse me.' It was the nurse who'd brought him the mug of tea. She was standing beside him. 'I'm off duty now, too. Do you fancy some breakfast?' She had brown hair, brown eyes. She was smiling.

'I'm sorry, what did you say?'

'Breakfast? I could clean up that bruise for you, too.'

The truck's engine barked to life. 'Name, laddie!'

Via turned to look back down the street. It felt like he was abandoning a kind of home. 'Technical Sergeant David O. Greenbaum, sir. Five-twentieth Bomb Group, USAAF. Bedenham, Suffolk.'

KEISSLING DAMN NEAR missed the train. Liverpool Street Station was seething, as usual, the destination board incomprehensible. He gave up, elbowing his way across the concourse to the nearest barrier.

'Ipswich!' he sputtered at a ticket collector. 'Which track is it?'

'Eight. But you'd better get your skates on, it's just pulling out.'

Five minutes later, breathless and sweating, he was squeezing his way along the gently rocking corridor of the train when he spotted a familiar face beside a window.

'Gerry! Hey, it's me, Keissling!'

'Oh.' Via started, as if from a dream. 'Right. Herm. You made it.'

'Only just, bud. Went to that National Gallery art place, you know it? Amazing pictures, Gerry, just amazing, you should see it. Anyway, I completely lost track of the damn time and had to make a run for it. Say, what happened to your head?'

Via fingered the bandage that the nurse, Joanna Morrison, had taped to his forehead that morning. A lifetime ago. 'This? Oh, nothing. Fell down in the street. Hit my head, that's all. Damn stupid.'

'Yeah. After I left you and that Kate broad in the bar last night, I'll bet.' Keissling nudged Via in the ribs. 'Where are the rest of the guys? Did you find them yet? Did they make the train?'

'I, uh, I'm not sure. I haven't caught up with them.'

'Well, let's get going, bud! Maybe they got a compartment.'

They found the rest of *Martha*'s crew. The train was packed, practically every seat occupied. Keissling and Via worked their way along corridors lined with cursing recumbent bodies, carriage after carriage filled to overflowing with sleeping airmen. Eventually, they forced themselves into yet another compartment. Its blinds were drawn, its sliding door appeared to be jammed. Peering round it, they caught sight of Emmett Lajowski's booted foot wedged on the other side.

'What's the damn password, assholes?' He grinned.

'Let us in or we'll break your neck?'

'That oughta do it.'

Everyone was there. They slammed the door, dumped their bags in the overhead nets and squeezed onto the bench seats, Keissling next to Lajowski, Tork and Spitzer, Via on the facing seat between Marion Beans and Dutch Holland. Irv Underwood, jammed against the window beside Holland, had his face to the glass as the train laboured slowly through London's eastern outskirts.

They swapped air-raid stories. Tork and Lajowski related their exploits in the Underground station. Beans talked little, just turning from Tork to Lajowski as they spoke, nodding his agreement.

'And what about our 'lustrious officer corps?' Lajowski prompted. 'Get stuck under anything interesting, so to speak?'

Spitzer glanced towards Underwood. His eyes were still focused sightlessly through the window. After the raid, Irv had returned to the bar at the hotel, remaining there for most of the night. He hadn't shown up again until it was time to leave for the station. 'Nope. Sorry to disappoint, fellas. Quiet time. Cleaned up, had a meal, walked the sights a little. Went to the movies. Spent an hour in a shelter near the movie house but didn't see or hear much.' He shrugged. 'Dutch and I went walking in the park today. Saw that Speaker's Corner thing.'

'Say, I wanted to see that!' Keissling interjected. 'But I damn overslept. Left Gerry in that bar last night, went straight back to the hostel, hit the sack and slept right through.'

The compartment fell quiet, its eight occupants submerged in thought. The train rocked slowly on, rattling through a station and across a bridge over a wide brown river. To the west, a soft orange sun was dipping towards the horizon.

'You know . . . our bombing? Our missions?' Beans began hesitantly. Some of the others looked up. Discussing operational matters in public places was an instant court-martial offence.

'What of them?'

'Well, they are, you know, strictly, like, strategic, aren't they? You know, ball-bearing plants, ammunition factories, railheads and so on? Isn't that right? Strategic. We don't, like, we don't bomb civilians. Ordinary folks, that is. Do we?'

'Relax, Beaner. The day we start bombing civilians is the day I step down from my turret and walk away from this war.' Lajowski leaned forward, patting Beans's knee.

''S what I figured. Just making sure.'

'I wonder how Kid Ringwald made out,' Spitzer murmured. 'With that new girl of his. What's her name?'

'Claire Howden. The blacksmith's daughter. Lives up that little lane, to the left of the pub.'

'Oh, yeah, that's right. Nice girl.'

Via stirred, wincing uncomfortably in his seat.

'What happened to your head, Gerry?' Tork asked. He had been studying Via curiously. 'And your uniform, for God's sakes. Looks like you been dragged through a hedge backwards.'

She'd led him to her rooms. Somewhere near Waterloo, so she said. They walked in silence through empty Sunday morning streets, stopped to buy provisions from a kiosk, walked on once more until they came to a door next to a hardware shop. Joanna produced a key. 'It's not much, I'm afraid. I share it with a room-mate, Bridget. She's a nurse too, at St Thomas's. She won't be here, she's on days.'

'Right.' He'd followed her up the stairs to her flat, exhaustion dragging at his heels like lead. She opened the door and stood aside for him. It was three rooms: a bedroom with two single beds, a sitting and eating room with a little curtained-off kitchen, and a poky little bathroom with mildewed walls and a rust-streaked tub.

'Could I use that?' he asked, gesturing at the bath.

'Of course. I'll make tea. Give me your uniform, I'll see if I can sponge some life back into it.'

Five minutes later the bathroom door opened. He was already sinking into oblivion, the water, warm and soft, caressing his bruised and aching limbs. Barely conscious, he heard the door click shut again, heard shoes being kicked off, buttons popping undone, the whisper of falling underclothes. Then her hands were at his shoulders, easing him forwards. She was stepping into the water behind him, sliding her feet down beside his legs, pulling him down, deeper and deeper against her, his head sinking to the softness of her breasts, her arms closing over him, folding about his shoulders and chest.

Later, they made love in her cramped single bed. She cupped his cheeks in her hands, crossed her legs over his back, and with a frown of concentration furrowing her brow surrendered herself, eyes closed, to her desire.

Then they'd slept. When they'd woken, he'd told her everything. About *Martha* and that first disastrous mission. Stoller, Broman, Spitzer, Irv. Dave Greenbaum. He couldn't stop himself. He wanted no pity, no forgiveness, no exorcism. He just wanted it out. 'I could have saved him.' He wept. 'I could have, and I should have.'

'No. You couldn't. You didn't know how.'

'I should have known how! It was my job to know how.'

She'd turned to him then on the bed, run her fingers through his thick black hair, still damp from the bath. 'I could teach you.'

The train lurched into darkness, entering a tunnel. Beyond the compartment, grunts of protest, scuffing of feet, the sound of passengers gathering themselves together. They were drawing into Ipswich. Via looked round the compartment.

'It's good to see you guys,' he said.

CHAPTER FIVE

In the last two weeks of September, the 520th Bomb Group, including *Misbehavin' Martha*, racked up four more mission credits, bringing her crew's total to eleven. All four missions went to German-occupied France, and losses, although serious, were not as high as those suffered on missions to Germany. Nevertheless, they were high enough. The bunk next to Al Tork's changed hands four times in a month. He began to believe it was cursed.

On September 23rd, the 520th bombed a German aircraft factory outside Paris, and on the 27th another aircraft works, all the way down in Bordeaux-Mérignac. It was a long flight, ten hours, much too far for their fighter escort. So for most of the way they were unprotected from harrying attacks by the Messerschmitts and Focke-Wulfs. The fighters stood off above and to the side, paralleling the formation, taking their time. Then, upon a given signal, they peeled off, often from opposing directions, and hurtled down onto the bombers at phenomenal speed, three or four at a time, wing and nose guns blinking. In an instant *Martha* and the other Fortresses were shuddering from the collective firing of their own weaponry, the air filled with tracer. Then the fighters were through and gone, circling, climbing, re-forming. For the next attack. And the next.

After each pass, the casualties. A Fortress, its engines streaming smoke, unable to maintain speed, began to slip helplessly back from the formation, there to be picked off by the waiting fighters like wolves at a crippled pack-mule. Another simply blew up, leaving little evidence of its passing save an ugly brown stain on the sky and a litter of falling bodies and debris. By the time the formation was nearing Bordeaux-Mérignac, a quarter of its force had gone.

'Here they come again!' Tork's voice, tense and urgent over the intercom. 'Stern attack, left side! Eight o'clock, three of them, coming in now! There! Keiss, Ringwald? Do you see them?'

'I see them!' the two choruses simultaneously. Keissling swung his waist gun rearwards, wrenched back the charging handle and squinted out along the barrel. The leading fighter, a Focke-Wulf 190, grew rapidly in his sights. 'Come on in, big fella.' He forced himself to wait, his singsong catchall on his lips. 'Short bursts, short bursts, come on come on come on.'

Beneath his feet, eighteen-year-old Eldon Ringwald, his head bent to his sights, depressed the pedal to swing the ball turret towards the oncoming fighter, then on, past it, right through it, in a single steady sweep, until his guns were ahead of it, leading it, by 100 yards or more. *This time*, he breathed. *This time.* He waited a second longer, held his breath and squeezed the triggers. At the same moment Keissling and Tork opened up from the waist and tail positions. Instantly something—a section of cowling, a piece of canopy—flew off the fighter, spinning into its slipstream, and a second later a thin plume of white smoke appeared from its engine. It broke off, veered away, rolling over to expose its oil-streaked underside. As it passed abeam, Lajowski opened up from the top turret; three, four, high-speed bursts of half a second each, his tracer shells arcing across and into the fighter's belly. A second later it exploded into a ball of orange flame. He lifted his head from the sights, gaping in astonishment. In the nose, Holland and Spitzer, their boots skidding, ankle deep, on hundreds of spent shell cases from their own guns, followed the flaming wreck as it fell.

'They got it.' Spitzer could scarcely believe his eyes. 'Good God, they got it.'

Three days later, on September 30th, *Martha* flew her eleventh mission, attacking the airfield at Vannes on the Atlantic coast of the Brest peninsula. The flak was intense over the target but their fighters were able to provide escort cover for 80 per cent of the route. Apart from an instant of disquiet for Gerry Via, when a florin-sized piece of flak shrapnel burst up through the floor of the radio room, passed between his knees and punched on out through the roof, by the crew's own standards the trip was a milk run.

Slowly, imperceptibly, they were beginning to think, and act, as a single unit. They were also, instinctively, drawing closer to one another, and at the same time further apart from everyone else. When they landed after missions, Hal Knyper often had to wait twenty minutes or more before he could board *Martha* to begin working on repairs or snags.

'What the hell is it you do in there?' he asked Underwood one day.

Irv shrugged. 'We talk.'

Scott Finginger, too, noticed the changes. Debriefing them, he noted that the earlier mistrust and bickering was giving way to a sense of common purpose. That the fact a German fighter had been shot down was more important to them, collectively, than which one of them had actually hit it. That their aggression was being directed more at the enemy than at each other. That the false bravado was gone, the feistiness, the infighting. Almost.

'Say, Cap, right waist here.'

'What is it, Beans?' They were on the way back, descending through tiny islands of cottonball cumulus towards a Sussex coast glinting in late-afternoon sunshine.

'Well, sir, I was reading *Stars and Stripes* the other day when I come across this piece about the German Air Force and one of the big-shot Luft-waff generals who's in charge of it.'

'What about him?'

'Well, sir, his name, get this, is General Herman Keissling. Exactly the same name as our very own Herm Keiss here. Now, don't you think that's kind of suspicious?'

Hooper sighed. 'Sergeant. I think you'll find that the Luftwaffe general's name is Kesselring, not Keissling.'

'Oh. Right. Got you. Thank you, sir.'

A pause.

'Left waist to pilot.'

'Yes, Keissling, what now?'

'Sir, did you know that when Sergeant Beans was an itty baby, his mom and pop wanted to call him Marlon? But when they got to filling out the forms, they couldn't spell, being simple country folk and all. And so they spelled it Marion by mistake.'

'OK, everyone, now that's quite enough of that. Let's just cut out the backchat on the intercom.'

Another pause.

'Radio to pilot.'

'Via. Yes. Now what is it?'

'Fighting in the waist.'

'BILLY STREET?'

'Not here, miss.'

'What? Again? But where is he?'

'Len said Rube said he's being carted off to a Borstal place in Maidstone.'

'What? Is this true, Ruby?' Heather searched out Ruby Moody's head, shrouded in brown curls, off to one side of the classroom. 'What's this about a Borstal?'

'Don't know. He don't tell me much of anything any more. Spends all his time up on the base or doing the cycles with Mr Howden.' Ruby looked close to tears.

Heather hadn't heard from Hooper for days and days. As though he was trying to avoid her, a prospect that consumed her with dread whenever she dared consider it. As though she could only deal with it, with what they were, only manage it, as long as it went on. If it stopped, God only knew what might happen. Apart from the teaching, it was the only piece of sanity in her life. Now, nothing. Days. It was worse than she would ever have imagined possible.

They'd attended a choral evensong together the previous Sunday. That was the last time she'd seen him. Hoop had managed to borrow Scott Fininger's Jeep for a few hours and they'd driven north through misty drizzle. After half an hour they topped a low crest above a valley not far from the sea. A river was spread out before them and on a heathy knoll beside its banks, towered a huge church. Hooper lurched the Jeep to a stop. 'Good God, look at that!'

'Blythburgh,' Heather explained, watching him. 'One of the largest churches, and many say the most beautiful, in Suffolk. People know it locally as the cathedral of the marshes. Wonderful, isn't it?'

'Magnificent.' He shook his head, standing at the roadside beside the Jeep. A bus laboured noisily up the hill behind them. The minutes ticked by, yet still he remained, gazing down at the church's solitary grandeur. Finally Heather nudged him from his reverie.

'"It's difficult to make sense of man's unending need to create war when he is also able to create a place like this." Who said that?'

'Hmm? Sorry, I have no idea. Sounds pretentious.'

'You did. The evening we first met. The little church at Iken, remember?'

'Not really. But it figures.'

'John. We'll miss the service.'

'I shouldn't be doing this. I don't have the right. It's wrong. And completely unfair on you.'

'Shouldn't be doing what? You're not doing anything. We're not.'

'No?' He turned to her then, stared right in at her, his dark eyes hunting across her face.

AFTER THE SERVICE they drove to a nearby pub. It was large, low ceilinged, empty, he noted thankfully, of American servicemen. They sat in a corner by the window drinking halves of bitter. Outside, a hazy dusk was descending over the river.

'Is this wrong, John? Do you really believe what you said earlier, that what we are doing is wrong?'

He sighed. 'Heather. If I feel secretly relieved that you've received no news from a husband who is lost out there, maybe fighting for his very life, I guess it might count as wrong. Wouldn't you say?'

'God, why do you have to be so honest all the time!'

'Because if we can't be honest with each other, then we shouldn't be doing this at all.'

'We're not *doing* anything! That's the whole point. And anyway, all this "we". It's not fair you telling us what we should and shouldn't be doing, you're not the one with the entire village watching your every move! You don't have to go home to your missing husband's house every night, sleep in his bed, have his mother breathing down your neck twenty-four hours a day.' A trio at the bar had turned to listen. She broke off in exasperation, pushing back her chair. 'You don't even have a bloody mother-in-law!' There was a catch in her throat. She picked up her bag, hurrying for the Ladies.

'I've got a bloody mother-in-law, missus,' she heard one of the men at the bar call after her. 'He can 'ave her with pleasure.'

Hooper waited by the Jeep, face raised to the sky. It was madness, putting her through all this. And she was right, the risk was all hers, the pressure, the strain. It must be stopped, one way or another. The certainty clutched, like a cold hand, at his heart. Heather was all he had. All that mattered. Then the pub door was opening and she was coming towards him, hurrying, running, one hand to her face, her eyes round and fearful. In a second she was in his arms, falling against him. 'I'm so sorry!' she sobbed. 'I'm so sorry.'

He held her like that, his cheek to her head, one hand on her hair, not moving, not speaking. Until the crying stopped and she grew still and calm, and until the dusk gave way to darkness.

'FUEL BOOSTER PUMP PRESSURE?'

'Booster . . . Hold on, over here somewhere. Yeah, it's good.'

'Carburettor coolers open?'

'Carburettor cool—Damn, where the hell . . . OK, I got it, I think they're open.'

'Lajowski.' Hal Knyper, standing behind the pilot's seat, lowered the checklist. Billy, in his green mechanic's overalls and cap, looked on from the copilot's seat. 'Listen, bud, when I call out one of the checks, it's no damn use going "ah" and "um" and "maybe over here somewhere", you got to know exactly where everything is and come back straight away with the correct response. OK?'

'Yeah, Hal, got it. Sorry about that.'

'I'm going outside to help fix the supercharger on number two engine. In a couple of minutes we'll need to start it up for a ground check. Do you think you can manage that?' He dropped the checklist on Billy's lap. 'Get Private Street here to practise it with you.'

A moment later they heard the crunch of Knyper's boots on the tarmac beneath the nose hatch. Lajowski sighed. 'OK, lucky charm kid, I guess we'd better take it from the top.'

Billy stared at the checklist. 'Um, Polecat, look, I don't have my glasses . . .'

'You wear glasses? I never seen them.'

'Yes. No, well I would've, but my dad couldn't afford—'

'You don't read. You don't. Do you?'

'Yes, I do. But not very well. Checklists and things. Sorry.'

Lajowski's hand clapped him on the knee. 'And I can't tell a carburettor supercharger from the air intake regulator, so what the hell!'

'Indicator. It's the carburettor air intake indicator. And that's the supercharger regulator. There, look, in front of the throttles.'

'It is? Damn, you're right. How d'you know that?'

'I watched Hal. Doing engine runs on the ground. Loads of times.' He leaned forward, peering through the sidescreen. 'Why's he making you do this?'

'He's not. It's Hooper's idea. He said we should all get to know each other's jobs on the ship, so if one of us gets injured, there's others can take his place. Like a back-up. Makes a lot of sense. So he's got us running around all over. I get to be flight engineer, which is the most important back-up of all.'

'How come you got that?'

'First off, I'm the smartest. Second, I'm the nearest, what with my turret being situated right here behind the flight deck. Third, my dad runs an auto repair shop back home in Brooklyn. Fourth—' He broke off, gazing round the cockpit.

'Fourth, what?'

'Fourth, well. That day, that first mission, when poor Rudy, our original pilot, got his head blown—Well, when Lieutenant Stoller got killed, that is.'

'I know. I was here.'

'You were? Oh, yes. You were, too. Well, when it happened, I was up there in my turret. I heard the bang, ducked down here onto the flight deck. It was the worst sight imaginable. Rudy, he . . . well, he was gone and the whole place was just covered in his blood and his brains and that. Lieutenant Underwood, he was covered in it too, head to toe. He was kind of in shock, he couldn't move, couldn't speak. The ship was all leaned over on its side and going into a dive, so I just grabbed the controls and hung on, best I could, until Spitzer got here. Probably just a few minutes, but it seemed like for ever. I decided then and there that if I ever had to do something like that again, I oughta find out first how the hell I was supposed to do it.'

'Polecat?'

'Huh? What is it, kid?'

'Do you want to come to tea?'

There was a shrill whistle from outside. They looked up. Hal Knyper was standing back from the engine making rotating movements with his hand. 'Do you think there's any chance you ladies could get the number two engine started now?' he called. 'Only if it's convenient, of course.'

Later, after the engine run, Billy joined Hal on the scaffold, helping him replace the cowlings. A fitter on a ladder was painting an eleventh bomb stencil on *Martha*'s nose, just below the cockpit window. After a while two bicycles rolled up and Beans and Via boarded. 'I'm radio back-up,' Beans said importantly. 'Geraldo's showing me round the equipment.' A few minutes later, an open-backed truck came grinding by. Hooper, Underwood and Tork jumped out.

'How's it going, Hal?' Hooper asked. Underwood and Tork were hoisting themselves through *Martha*'s nose hatch.

'It would be going a hell of a lot better if folks left us in peace to get on with the damn job.'

'Sorry. We need to run some procedures, we'll try and stay out of your hair.'

'What the hell is all this about, Hoop?'

'It's about staying alive, Hal, that's all. Beating the odds.' He took his cap off, running fingers through his dark hair. 'The other day, remember, when we got back from Vannes. That was *Gotcha*'s twenty-fifth mission, you know. Done, finished, they can all go home.'

'So? They made it. I was at the party. *Martha*'s going to make it too.'

Hooper was shaking his head. 'I did some checking. *Gotcha*'s crew were among the first to be deployed here with the 520th. They are also the first to get through a complete tour of twenty-five missions. There will be no more. Not from that group. Of the original thirty ships deployed here last year, she's the only one left. Sure, some have gone elsewhere, some have been scrapped and replaced, some of the crews have been redeployed, some have been shot down and are in captivity, but when all is said and done, it's one in thirty, Hal. Loss rates on missions were averaging six per cent the last few months. Now it's higher. Six per cent per mission. Doesn't sound a lot. But multiply twenty-five missions by a six per cent loss rate?'

'A hundred and fifty per cent,' Billy said quickly.

'You've got it. Rate of losses for a full tour of twenty-five missions is one hundred and fifty per cent. And climbing. Shitty odds. I have to shorten them. Last week, a ship from the 95th got hit just before the IP and had to turn back for home, its pilot injured and the navigator killed. That left the copilot to fly the ship and no one to navigate. They lost their way over the sea, flew round in big circles for three hours, ran out of gas and crashed into the ocean. No survivors, just because nobody knew how to plot a course for home.'

'Hoop. You're going to survive. Don't ask me how, but I just know you will.'

Hooper looked up at him in surprise. 'This isn't about me, Hal.'

He pointed towards *Martha*. 'This is about them.'

Ten minutes later a Jeep came speeding round the perimeter. 'Now what?' Knyper muttered irritably. The Jeep braked to a halt.

'Billy Street! Thought I'd track you down here.' It was Major Finginger. 'I found these two ladies at the front gate. Looking for you.'

'Hello, Billy.' Ruby squinted coyly up at him. Beside her sat Heather Garrett.

'Oh, hello, Rube. Mrs G. Um, would you like to come to tea later?'

'How kind.' Heather stepped from the Jeep. 'Scott, thank you for the lift. Sergeant Knyper, could you possibly spare Billy for a few minutes? Just for a chat.'

FINGINGER DROPPED the four of them at the main gate. Billy and Ruby hurried on ahead, Hooper and Heather strolling behind.

'Do you think Mrs Howden knows Billy's invited my entire crew for tea?' he asked.

'Heaven knows. I doubt it. Their daughter's involved too, or something. Either way, it won't be easy, feeding everyone.'

A chill October wind stirred fallen leaves at their feet. Hooper turned up his collar. 'Is Billy in some kind of trouble? Was that why you came on base?'

'Yes, he is. And, well, yes it was. Partly.' She hesitated. 'John, why have you stopped coming to visit? Is it that you would prefer not to see me? I do understand if that's the case.'

'Of course it isn't the case! My God, Heather, I want to see you more than you can imagine.' He swung round, walking backwards in front of her. 'Our evenings, our talks together, they're more important to me than you'll ever know. Coming to see you, after a mission, say, well it's a wonderful oasis of reality in an unreal world.'

'Then what's the problem?'

'The problem is that it is completely one-sided. The gain is all mine, there's nothing in it for you. Nothing but trouble, that is. I hadn't thought about just how difficult a position you were in. I can't allow that to go on. It's unbelievably selfish. I gain, you lose.'

'I gain too.' she said quietly. 'For better or for worse, I made vows to someone who, seventeen months ago, and through no fault of his own, completely, and perhaps permanently, removed himself from my life. If David ever does comes back, then, well, I'm his, no matter what happens. But in the meantime, I'm nothing, neither wife nor widow, a sort of half-person. Being friends with you isn't going to change that, but believe me, it makes the whole mad situation much, much easier to bear. If that's wrong, then so be it. I don't care.'

'OK.' His face was clouded with uncertainty. 'I see.'

They resumed walking. 'John, I've got a suggestion. Why don't we just take it one day at a time. If either of us begins to feel, you know, pressured or uncomfortable or it all gets too much, we'll simply put a stop to it. Just like that. What do you say?'

'One day at a time, and just like that. Think it'll work?'

She nudged his arm. 'I'm willing to give it a try if you are.'

By the time they reached the Howdens' house, Billy's party was already in full swing. A heap of bicycles lay outside the gate, and Scott Finginger's Jeep was parked outside the forge. Maggie opened the door to them, looking slightly flustered. 'Mrs Garrett! What a wonderful surprise. And you must be Lieutenant Cooper. Do, please, come in. I've heard so much about you from Billy and Hal.' She ushered them into a little hall. 'Ray! Love? Two more chairs! Claire, quickly, more cups and saucers!' Obediently, like newlyweds visiting relatives, they followed her into the living room.

HOOPER SURVEYED THE ROOM. It was getting late, they should be going soon. He was sitting on the Howdens' piano stool, holding a plate with a homemade jam tart on it. It was his third. The room was filled with animated chatter and peals of laughter. His crew, most of them, were sitting or reclining on the floor, Billy and his friend Ruby in their midst. Every so often one of the crew would spring to his feet, to fetch another dish from the kitchen, gather up empty plates or relieve Mrs Howden of her huge brown teapot. Each time she came in, those on chairs would rise, insisting she sit and rest and join in. Giggling like a schoolgirl, she would comply for a minute, before jumping up again to fill someone's cup or go and make more sandwiches.

Mr Howden, Ray, was talking to Hal Knyper. Hal seemed to know the Howdens well. From their hand gestures, he guessed they were discussing matters mechanical. Beside them Spitzer, Underwood and Finginger were talking to Heather.

Irv Underwood. Each mission, at briefing, he looked like death. White-faced, trembling and sweating, he hauled himself through mission preparation and then up into the copilot's seat. His fear was so great that you could smell it. Yet he never complained, he never cried off. Never gave in to his terror. As far as Hooper was concerned he was the bravest man in the squadron.

Lajowski came reversing in through the door, a plate in each hand. He seemed to be a part of the household, too. 'Emmett, dear,' Mrs Howden called to him. 'Why don't you put that one on the piano, near Lieutenant Cooper, sorry, Hooper! And give the other one to the boys on the floor. Eldon. Eldon? Where is that boy?'

He was in the kitchen, Hooper had learned from a winking Marion Beans. Washing up. With the daughter, Claire. He'd had no idea, not the first inkling, but the moment he saw them together, he realised something profound was passing between them. It was a surprise and a worry. Ringwald. Kid, the rest of the crew called him. The youngest, yet with a maturity far surpassing his years. He never riled anyone up, never caused trouble. On the contrary, he was quick to intervene, expert at defusing disputes before they blew up. All at eighteen. It was barely comprehensible.

There was more. The door opened once again and Claire came in, bearing a cake on a tray. A picture had been iced onto it, a Flying Fortress, complete with wheels and propellers. There were exclamations of appreciation, scattered applause, wisecracks.

'I have something to say.' Ringwald was standing by the door, Claire, still holding the cake, at his side. The room fell quiet. 'Everyone was invited here today because, well, with Mr and Mrs Howden's permission, of course, Claire and me would like to become engaged. To get married. After the war.'

Just like that. A fractional silence. Maggie's hand went to her mouth, then there was an explosion of cheers, catcalls and whistles. The crew got to their feet as one, crowding round Ringwald, clapping him on the back.

Hooper, swallowing, joined in; it seemed appropriate. The odds, he kept thinking, the odds. Maggie was shaking her head, her cheeks between her hands; her husband, eyebrows arched, seemed in shock. Hoop sought Heather's eyes, found them, held them. They were waiting for him. She smiled, and his heart lurched. One day at a time. Simple. Absurd. Finginger was standing beside her. Poor faithful Finginger, waiting patiently on the sidelines. He too was looking at Hooper, gesturing pointedly at his watch. 'We have to get going,' Finginger said, reaching to shake Ray Howden's hand. 'Many congratulations on your happy news.' Maggie, tearful, pushing past the boys to embrace her daughter, and to take Ringwald's bemused face in her hands. We have to go. To blood and bombs and thunder and death beyond description.

BREMEN. IT BEGAN in the usual way. The flicker of overhead lights, the rough shake of the shoulder, 'Good morning, fellas, oh-five-thirty, you are flying today.' Everything normal, everything standard issue. Until the briefing.

Hoop and the other officers, Irv, Spitz and Dutch, sit up front for the briefings. It's not that they don't want to sit back with the crew, they all know that. It's just that he doesn't want them to miss the slightest little detail. He's right. The other day, a ship takes off for a mission. It's cloudy, a heavy overcast all the way up to 12,000 feet. Climbing up and up through soup so thick you couldn't see your wing tips, this ship takes off, then makes the wrong heading for the RP. Blind as a bat, it flies into a bomber stream coming the other way, and collides head-on with one of them. Full fuel, full bomb load, it's a massive explosion. Two crews killed. Twenty guys. All for not copying the details down correctly at the briefing.

It's Bremen. The mission. The biggest ME to date, Intelligence says, standing up front on the dais. Seven hundred bombers, plus their escorts, flying in three waves. It's an armada.

Finally they get airborne. It's a cold, clear day. Forts and Liberators in every direction as far as the eye can see, while above them the little fighter escorts scurry to and fro like dogs herding sheep. The 520th forms up into the division with all the other groups, then the whole shooting match splits into three separate wings, and their wing, 200 ships, heads straight out across the North Sea towards Germany.

The first fighters appear soon after they cross the enemy coast, and keep coming all the way to the IP, the run-in to the target, the turn for home, the rally point, and all the way back out to the coast and beyond. There are so many attacks that Tork, back in *Martha*'s tail, stops counting, stops praying, stops thinking. He's an automaton, a machine. The 520th, with Englehardt's squadron on top, is flying almost at the back of the entire formation. Most of the attacks are coming from the rear. He's the busiest man in the 8th.

The fighters hang back, and a little above, just out of range. Minutes at a time, trying to sucker you into wasting ammunition. Then, when they're ready, the Luftwaffe boys suddenly stop weaving, fall into single line astern and come slicing in. All hell breaks loose. He watches them come, picks one out, leads, waits, shoots, picks another. Then another, then the sky is full of them and the world goes mad. It's total chaos, a free-for-all. Everyone's shouting. Everyone's firing. Seconds later, a Fort from the middle formation starts dropping back, pouring flames. To his left, next to him, a sudden flash as *Toledo Toots* takes a hit; he watches, mesmerised, as it staggers in the air, like a little stumble. Then there's another flash and the midsection just explodes, bursts right open. Hanging there in the sky, the ship breaks clean in two. He sees the ball turret fall clear, plummeting earthwards like a dropped stone, its gunner still trapped inside. As the two halves of the ship separate, he sees bodies falling from the gaping rear section, arms and legs flailing, tumbling over and over.

It goes on and on. After a while time ceases to have meaning, and the world contracts into a single seamless interval of shuddering guns, thunder, smoke and shouting. At some point Tork hears over the intercom that they've reached IP and are commencing the bomb run. It is meaningless to him, signifying only that, apart from the fighters, the sky is now also thickly pocked with thousands of exploding flak shells. He thinks of nothing, keeps his head down and the charging handles cocked. Stretching out for miles behind, unrolling before his eyes like a bizarre aerial tapestry, a smoke-covered industrial landscape, the grey glint of a river, burning buildings, impact craters. Crawling across the tapestry, an overlay of limping, crippled bombers, smoking wrecks, falling debris, drifting parachutes.

'DID YOU HEAR the ME this morning? I never heard anything like it in my life. There must have been hundreds of them up there.'

'You should try getting up a bit earlier, young lady,' said Ray. 'Of course we heard it, you couldn't miss it, the whole house was shaking from about five thirty onwards.'

Maggie turned from the cooking range, depositing breakfast plates on the table. Stale bread beneath an off-white blob of powdered egg. Billy, knife and fork at the ready, set to with his customary zeal.

Ray tipped the cat off his chair and sat down. 'Could do with some help out there in the forge today, Billy,' he said quietly.

'No!' Maggie turned from the range. 'Billy promised Mrs Garrett he'd be in school every day this week, didn't you, love?'

'Well, I—'

'Mag, I've got two horses to shoe this morning, two more this afternoon, everywhere you turn there's heaps of broken bicycles waiting to be fixed, and to top it all Harold Knyper says he's sending one of his boys over with yet another truckload this afternoon.'

'Well, perhaps you should think about hiring an assistant.'

'I've got an assistant!'

'Not while he's supposed to be at school, you haven't.' She began pinning on her WRVS hat. 'Now then, I'm up the old folks' home this morning, then I've got a wool-drive meeting in the village hall this afternoon. I'll be home teatime.'

'Do you remember bacon?' Claire said, staring wistfully at her plate. 'That real, crispy bacon, and real fried eggs, with them brown crunchy bits at the edges. And real sausages, and ketchup.'

'And you can just stop right there with your complaining, madam,' Maggie went on. 'The entire family gave over their egg ration for a month, I would remind you, and most of their butter, to make cakes and pastries for your engagement party.'

'I wasn't complaining, just remembering. What's wrong with that?'

'It was not an engagement party.'

'What?' Everyone turned to Ray.

'Ray, love, couldn't this wait—'

'You're not getting engaged. Not now.'

'But, Dad, you can't do this. We *are* engaged!'

'No you're not and yes I can. You're too young, the pair of you.'

'Dad! Mum, say something!'

Maggie opened her mouth, but Ray cut her off. 'Your mother agrees with me, Claire,' he said. 'Eldon, well, he's a good boy, we can see, and we do like him. But he's eighteen years old for heaven's sake, and you're seventeen. You're too young and there's an end to it.'

'Mr and Mrs Howden?'

The hall door opened. It was Mrs Blackstone, the evacuee coordinator. 'I'm so sorry, we did knock.' Instantly, Billy's face went slack, his eyes, his whole body, slumping in defeat. Following immediately behind her was a uniformed policeman.

'Albert Harold Crossley?' The policeman cleared his throat in the silence, began reading from a folded paper. 'This warrant authorises me to take you into custody for absenting yourself without permission from the Sir Reginald Haslam Young Men's Correctional Institution, Deal Road, Maidstone, Kent. You are required therefore to come with me to Framlingham police station, where arrangements have been made for your return to the aforementioned correctional institution forthwith.' He looked round uncertainly. 'Well, get a move on, lad. I haven't got all day.'

HEATHER HAD SEEN Hooper just once in the last four days. He'd slipped out to the cottage the evening after the ME. The Bremen raid. The day Billy was arrested. He'd listened in unaffected astonishment as she'd recounted the story, promised to relay the news to Hal Knyper and the rest of the crew, asked if there was anything they could do. He was genuinely concerned for Billy, she could tell, but at the same time understandably distracted. Tense and agitated, constantly moving about the cottage, picking things up, replacing them. Bremen had been a big one, apparently. That was all he said about it. Big and bad.

'I can't stay long,' he said then, standing before her. He seemed to be studying her, every detail. 'I'm not supposed to be off base at all. We're on ops again tomorrow. Oh-four-thirty takeoff. One of those days when you have to get up before you go to bed.' He forced a smile.

'You needn't have come. Not on my account.'

'I needed to.'

That was three days ago. Late the next day she finally got word that *Martha* had returned, overdue but safe, from somewhere called Marienberg. Then they'd had to fly yet again, making it three days in succession. Another ME. To Münster, this time. Something had gone badly wrong, the 8th had suffered terrible losses, but once again *Martha* had come through. The waiting, the tension, was becoming unbearable. She didn't know how much more she could endure, and still be there for him, calm and smiling, when he visited.

THEN, FINALLY, CAME SCHWEINFURT. A huge and complex double-strike mission to attack, among other targets, the biggest ball-bearing factory in Europe.

There was a delay at takeoff. They had boarded as normal, Hooper and Knyper making their walk-around in milky predawn half-light, while the gunners unhooked their guns, checked them, replaced them and checked them again. Spitzer and Holland busied themselves in the nose, poring over their navigation tables and bombing charts, while Gerry Via, alone in his radio room, ran through the signal codes for the day. Up on the flight deck, Irv Underwood completed a weight and balance sheet, totting up how changing fuel, armament and bomb loads would affect the aircraft's weight and centre of gravity. After a while, though, the crew ran out of things to do and surrendered to their thoughts and anxieties. Hooper clambered aboard and locked the nose hatch closed.

'So,' he said, slumping into his seat. 'I guess we wait.'

Irv Underwood turned to him and forced a sickly grin. 'Don't laugh but I have a very bad feeling about this one.'

He was right.

'Fighters! Eleven o'clock, three of them! Jesus! Polecat! D'you see them? Do you see them for Christ's sake!'

'Yes! Yes I see them!'

'There's two more! Watch out, they're going straight underneath! One-oh-nines. Left to right. There! Right below us!'

'OK, I got it. I got it!'

A massive flash. 'What was that, for God's sakes?'

'A Focke-Wulf. Christ. It just flew straight into *Alleycat*.'

'Ringwald! Two more, right under you, right to left, d'you see 'em?'

'No, no wait yes! I got them now. Watch out, they're veering off!'

'Oh my God. Look. Englehardt's hit.'

A flak shell burst directly beneath *Shack Time*. She reared, twisting in the air beside them like a lanced bull. For a moment it looked as though Englehardt had lost all control, the bomber rolling drunkenly, gouts of black smoke belching from one engine. Hooper veered away to give him room; the other two aircraft in the high formation did the same. Six had taken off that morning. One had turned back halfway with a failed oxygen system. A second, *Split Shift*, had been seen falling from the squadron, trailing smoke, soon after the fighters appeared. Four were left.

Englehardt's voice crackled over the command radio. 'Hoop, can you see where the bastards hit us?'

'Stand by.' Hooper peered upwards at the blackened belly of Englehardt's B-17. 'Ah, Gene, looks like the shell burst right below the floor of the radio room.' His radio operator and ball turret gunner couldn't have stood a chance. 'And you're losing gasoline. Left side tank. It's just pouring out.'

'Right.' Gene hesitated. 'Listen, Hoop, she's handling like a plucked turkey, my navigator's hit, and I believe there's badly injured further aft. We'll have to drop out. You take over squadron lead, keep it in tight as you can, the three of you, and just make damn sure I see you all back at the ranch in a couple of hours, OK?'

'Got it.' *Martha*'s crew, together with those of the two remaining high-squadron aircraft, *Danny Boy* and *Patches*, watched wordlessly as Englehardt pulled his stricken Fortress down and away for home.

Hooper's new command lasted bare minutes.

Patches was raked, mercilessly, from tail to nose by diving fighters. Slowly, almost gracefully, *Patches* slipped over onto her back and fell from view. An instant later there was a deafening explosion and *Martha* bucked violently from a shell burst.

'What was that!'

'Shit, are we hit?'

'Quiet, everybody.' Irv Underwood's voice. Something felt odd with the controls, a big dragging yaw to the right. Hooper, frozen, stared at the column in his hands, images popping like flashbulbs in his head.

'Fire! Number three engine! John? Hoop! Don't do this, Hooper.'

'What?' Singing. He maketh me to lie down in green pastures.

'John! We have a fire in number three!'

'Englehardt! This is Baker Group leader.' It was Group Commander, way out at the head of the formation, calling over the command radio. 'Englehardt, for God's sake pull your squadron together, man!'

Underwood looked over at *Danny Boy*. 'We are together, sir,' he replied calmly. 'Englehardt's gone. There's only two of us left.'

'*What?*'

'Irv, hit the fire button, number three engine.' Hooper was back, his free hand racing around the cockpit, shutting the burning engine down. 'Get it feathered, quick as you can, the drag is killing us.'

Irv palmed the button. 'Prop's feathered, but she's still burning.'

'Right. We'll have to dive.' Hooper had heard about it. Nothing more than that. Rumours. You stuff the airplane into a near-vertical dive, the air speed snuffs out the fire. Like blowing out a candle. He peered past Irv's window. Ten feet away the number three engine was an inferno. His eye flicked to the bail-out button on the pilot's console. Jump? Or burn? Nine men floating, vanishing through soft white mist. For ever. Not this time. He pushed forward on the column.

Martha's nose sagged groundwards. 'Hooper to *Danny Boy*. Jack, we're going down. You peel off and join up with middle formation.'

'OK, Hoop. Good luck, buddy.' *Danny Boy*'s crew looked on forlornly. Not *Martha*. Not Hooper and the boys. They were legendary.

'Hooper to crew, we're diving to try to kill the fire in number three.' *Martha*, steeply angled, was accelerating fast. He glanced at the indicator: 200mph and rising. The control column was shaking violently. Then, barely 1,000 feet above the ground, and at 300 miles an hour, *Martha* pulled out of the dive. The fire was out. The dead engine still trailed a plume of grey smoke, the wing behind it was scorched and blackened, but the flames were gone.

They took stock. Apart from the dead engine and some minor collateral damage from shell fragments, *Martha* was intact. But the mission was over. On reduced power and with the added drag from the dead engine, she could never regain the formation. Hooper dropped down even lower. They were flying over open farmland, board-flat and crisscrossed with dykes and water-filled ditches.

'Spitz, where the heck are we?'

'North of Osnabrück. Near the Dutch border.'

They dumped their unarmed bombs into a waterlogged field. Then, still flying barely above treetop level, they raced northwards towards the coast. They almost made it unnoticed.

It was a lone Messerschmitt 109, sleek, fast and heavily armed. And its pilot was out to prove something. For ten minutes he ducked and weaved, probing their defences, assessing, waiting.

Hooper inched *Martha* yet lower. The terrain was flat. Sand dunes began to appear. Ahead gleamed a wide strip of blue-grey sea. 'I can't allow this,' he was saying, over and over. 'I can't. I won't.'

Thundering out over slate-grey waves, he reached out to the throttle quadrant, pulling back power to the engines. *Martha* began to slow. At the same time he began moving the mixture lever to the number two engine, pushing it in and out. Instantly it began misfiring loudly, black smoke exploding from the exhaust.

'What the hell are you doing?' Underwood stared in astonishment.

'Irv, I can't allow this to happen. We've come too far. He'll think we're losing another engine. Go ahead now and shut it down.'

'But what—'

'Just do it, Irv.' He reached for his intercom switch. 'Listen up, everyone. I want you to let go your guns, just let them go and leave them hanging down.'

'Ah, waist to pilot, I—'

'DO IT! All of you! Right now. Except Lajowski. Bring the upper turret round until your guns are at nine o'clock. Then wait.'

The number two propeller sputtered to a stop. Now *Martha* was flying on the two outer engines alone. 'Lower the undercarriage, Irv.'

'Hooper, that's the surrender signal . . .'

'I know that! Just do as I say and put the goddamn wheels down!'

It worked. After a minute or two, Tork reported that the fighter was approaching for a closer look. Hooper, nursing *Martha* along at minimum flying speed, flaps and wheels lowered as though for landing, rocked the wings from side to side, for further encouragement.

The Messerschmitt drew right alongside, to Hooper's left. It was barely twenty yards away. The pilot pulled off his mask. They could see his face. He had fair hair and a wide grin. He looked very young.

He waved at them cheerily, made circular motions with one finger, then pointed back the way they'd come.

'He wants us to follow him back to his base,' Underwood said, watching the little fighter. It was mesmerising, so small, like a toy. Yet so deadly. The enemy. 'Thinks he's bagged a whole B-17.'

Hooper nodded, slowly, at the young face. It was still smiling. Then he closed his eyes. And gave the word.

'Lajowski.'

HOOPER WALKED FOR HOURS. In the darkness. In the rain. It soaked right through the shoulders of his coat, to his skin. His shoes became wet through, his feet numb with cold. He didn't care, he didn't notice. It was a turning point, a crossing over, a point of no return. There was no health in him, no life in the world to come, and no redemption. It didn't matter. It had gone beyond mattering.

But it did hurt. Deep inside, like grief, like loss. Whatever had been left, whatever small, battered shreds of his former self remained, were finally gone. The transformation was complete. Now there was nothing to do but see it through to its logical conclusion. It was a pang of sadness, nothing more. Like losing a distant friend.

He stood outside her door, the rain gurgling down the gleaming black lane behind him, drumming on the sodden cloth of his cap. Five minutes? An hour? Then he began to knock.

'I killed a man today,' he said, when she opened. 'He was just a boy.'

Heather reached out to him. 'Please, come inside.'

'I'm so afraid.'

'I know.' She folded the soft fingers of her hands about his, like closing lily petals, and drew him into the hall.

CHAPTER SIX

'Well then, Billy. So, how are you keeping, lad?'

'Crossley. You have to call me Crossley. Nobody uses first names, it's not allowed. Anyway, my name's not Billy, it's Albert.'

Ray shrugged. 'It's Billy to us.' He looked round the room, shivering involuntarily. It was small, grey-painted brick, with a concrete floor and a single barred window high in one wall. They sat at a plain wooden table. 'How's the food? Are you getting enough? I brought you a bag of things, not much, I'm afraid. Something, though.'

'Thanks.' Billy's head was down. 'But I won't prob'ly never see 'em. We're not allowed food presents.'

'Ah. Yes.' Ray had been relieved of the package, carefully wrapped by Maggie, by the duty officer inside the main entrance. 'Well. Never mind, eh? Maybe later on.'

Billy said nothing, just stared down at his hands lying on the table. His knuckles were skinned. When the guard had brought him in, Ray had immediately noticed a fading yellow bruise on one cheek. Billy's eyes, round and wary, had met his momentarily, then moved away.

He shouldn't have come. It was hopeless, clearly a mistake, and upsetting for Billy. For them both.

And all for ten minutes.

The detention centre was awful, like a prison. Worse. Bars on everything, uniformed guards, jangling keys, young boys' echoing shouts. Filthy language, obscene, high-pitched screams. It made the hairs stand up on Ray's neck. And the stench. Boiled cabbage, stale tobacco, urine. It made you want to gag.

Billy. He looked completely different. Ray tried not to appear shocked when they led him in, but he was scarcely recognisable. Physically the same, of course; a little thinner perhaps, and sort of holding himself in more. But inside, it was as though a light had gone out. The spirit. The heart. It was gone, like a snuffed candle. In its place a wall had arisen, a barrier. The cheerful, mischief-loving Billy Street of old, with the wicked grin and a hundred bright ideas a day, was no more. Maggie was right. It was killing him.

'Hal Knyper came round. He sends his best.'

'Oh. Right.'

'He says—what was it?—he says you've got to hang in. Keep your head down and hang in. Says he'll write again soon as he can.'

'All right.' People wrote him letters. He kept them stuffed beneath his mattress. Took them out to stare at, when he could bear to. Sitting alone on his bed, his mouth working, his round face crunched into a frown, while the loops and squiggles writhed and twisted, his head felt like bursting, and the pages blurred with frustration in his hands.

'They're very busy up there on the base. Had a rough time of it lately, so the word goes in the village. Some shocking losses. Oh, but Hal says the boys from your plane are all A-OK. In fact, come to think of it, tomorrow evening we've got Eldon coming round for supper. And Beryl Moody's girl stopped in. Ruby? Said for me to say hello. Asked especially.' *Say something, Billy. Speak to me.*

'Maybe it would be better if you was to go now, Mr H.'

'Is that what you want, lad?'

He looked up at last, his face crumpling. 'No!'

A thump on the door. 'Time's up, Crossley. Out you come, the both of you.'

'Christ!' Suddenly Ray was on his feet. He flung open the door. 'Listen! I haven't spent the entire day travelling halfway across the bloody country to be ordered about by the likes of you! Now, you'll bugger off and give me another couple of minutes with my boy here, or else your governor is going to be getting a letter from my MP about your bloody manners. Do I make myself clear?'

The guard took a step back, blinking at Ray in astonishment. 'Right. All right then. Two minutes.'

'Thank you!' Ray slammed the door. Turning, he saw the tears starting in Billy's eyes.

'I can't, Mr H, I can't . . .' It was all he managed. In a moment Billy was hugging him, burying his face in Ray's jacket. Clutching at him as though drowning. 'I can't do it! I know I can't!'

'Yes. Yes, you can. You must.' Shushing softly, Ray held on to him, lightly at first, then more strongly, one hand rubbing at his back. Slowly the spasms subsided. 'Listen, Billy, listen to me now. Maggie and Mrs Garrett went to see Brigadier Garrett and his wife up the Grange. They've got influence. They're going to look into all this and see what's what. I've also talked to Ted Bolsover's brother-in-law. He's a solicitor, retired now, but he knows his oats. He thinks possibly you weren't represented properly at your court case.'

'It's no use, Mr H. I'm stuck here.'

'No, you're not, we'll find a way. But for now you've got to do like Hal says. Keep your head down and hang on. You've just got to.'

They parted in the corridor outside. Ray, fists clenched, watched Billy being led away, dwarfed by the key-jangling warder. 'You'll be all right, lad!' Ray called suddenly, but Billy didn't look back.

'DO YOU REALLY think he'll be all right, miss?'

Heather dropped the pile of exercise books into her bicycle basket. 'Yes, Ruby, I'm sure of it. He's a strong boy, and very resourceful. Try not to worry.'

With a furtive glance round the empty playground, Ruby produced an envelope. 'I wrote him this. It's a letter. But I don't know where to send it.' She stared down at the letter forlornly. 'All them stories he made up. About his rich dad. And his mum getting blown up and that. I knew they was just stories, I knew it. He'd never really lie to me. Would he, miss?'

'No he wouldn't, and I believe he knew that you knew it, too, Ruby. I believe he only made those things up to try to draw a line over his past, and because he was afraid we might—you might—be disappointed in him if we found out.'

'Disappointed? But how could I be disappointed, miss? I love him. I really love him.' She looked up at Heather, her freckled face wide with anguish. 'What on earth am I going to do?'

Heather pulled her bicycle from the rack. 'Write, Ruby. Write to him as often as you can. I'll get the address for you.'

'But he don't read too good. Does he?'

'He is much more able than he believes, Ruby. You must make him read. Make him understand. Tell him how you feel. Tell him you love him and he has nothing to be ashamed of.'

Heather pedalled slowly through the village. The previous night's rain had all but dried, but a dank autumn mist hung like a veil over the roofs and gardens.

He wasn't at the cottage, but his cap and overcoat were on the hook where she'd hung them the night before. She called softly, checking upstairs and out in the back yard. Then, donning Wellington boots, she walked across the lane and into the fields.

He was right at the bottom, down by the stream, sitting on a tree stump staring into the little river. He turned as she neared, rose, smiled, reached out his hands towards hers. Kissed her. 'It's very good to see you,' he said.

That evening they stayed in the cottage. Hoop lit a fire in the little grate in the sitting room, while Heather made a sort of kedgeree. She'd had the haddock a week, it was a little dry but the egg was real, and, sitting face to face on the floor by the fire to eat, it didn't matter.

'Tell me about your day. School. The children.' Normal things. Not war and bombs and killing.

She told him, a soft smile playing across her face as she recalled an amusing detail.

'What about Billy?' he asked, resting his chin on one knee. She'd reached the part about Ruby, and her letter, in the playground.

'It's very sad. The classroom just isn't the same without him. Not that he was there all of the time, I have to admit, but our lives are definitely poorer without him. Did you know he used to slip me all the news, about *Martha*, and your missions? When you'd got home safely.'

Hooper nodded. Beyond the window, from far out in the darkness, across the fields, drifted the plaintive calling of cattle. 'I reported back this morning. We've been stood down. Three days.'

'Good. You've all earned it.'

'The boys are out on a weekend pass. Most of them have gone to London.'

'I expect they'll manage to find ways to have a good time.'

'I expect they will.' Hooper smiled reflectively. 'Gene's alive. My squadron commander, Gene Englehardt, remember?'

'I remember. From the dance. Thank goodness.'

'Yes. He lost his ship, and two crew members, but he got back in one piece, thank God. He's kind of a linchpin at the 520th. If he breaks, we all break. Sure, he's loud and cocky and fearless, and he drinks too much and swears too much. But the kids, the new guys especially, they all look up to him. As though, if they can be like him, just a little, then nothing can touch them. Do you know what I mean?'

'You must be very fond of him.'

'We're completely different.' Hoop gazed into the flames. 'But, when I arrived here, from my old base, he made me believe I could do this. As though there was never any doubt in his mind.'

'And in your mind?'

'Then? God knows!' He smiled, turning to look into her eyes. 'But I do remember you. At that dance. You were the most beautiful thing I had ever seen in my life. I just knew I had to hold you, then and there, in my arms. Just once.'

'Yes. It was a strange evening for me too. Poor Scott Finginger, I doubt I was very good company for him. Do you think he knows?'

'He's an Intelligence officer. It's his job to know.' He leaned forward. She closed her eyes. Their lips met.

'COFFEE.' JOANNA MORRISON placed the cup on the bedside table. Via stirred from sleep.

'What time is it?'

'A little after seven o'clock. I have to go to work.'

'Wait.' Via hauled himself to a sitting position. 'Give me a minute and I'll walk with you.'

He dressed quickly; five minutes later they were on the streets of

Waterloo. It was Saturday, still early. A stiff breeze spiralled litter high into the air. Joanna, a nurse's cape about her shoulders, slipped an arm through Via's.

'Now then. Have you been studying your books like a good boy?'

'I have. As it happens.'

'We'll make a medic of you yet.' She hesitated. 'Would you like to come up to the ward? You could meet some of the patients.'

She'd told him about it. A mixed general ward. Toothless ancients waiting to die, bank clerks with burst appendixes, a sailor with terminal cancer, youngsters with bomb-shattered limbs. He felt a shiver of apprehension. Reading about it was one thing, meeting it face to face quite another. 'Sure. I'd like that.'

Her arm squeezed tighter. 'It was lovely to see you again.'

'You make it sound like it's over already.'

'Well, I suppose it is, isn't it? Oh, I know you're staying tonight. But tomorrow you go back to Suffolk. You probably won't get another pass for ages. In a few weeks you'll have finished your tour of duty, and then you'll be on your way home. Isn't that how it works?'

'Well, yes. I guess.' Something nagged at his subconscious. 'But I have to tell you, somehow I don't feel that good about it.'

'What do you mean?'

'It's like, well, it feels like a drop-in war. Drop in on good old England for a few months, fly your twenty-five, then drop the hell out again. Back to the States, pick up your life where you left off. As if the whole war was just a far-off dream. It don't feel quite right, somehow.' He pulled her closer. They were nearing the entrance to St Thomas's. 'Don't feel quite right leaving you, neither.'

'Oh, I wouldn't worry. I knew it would have to be like this. Relationships. In wartime, they're temporary things. Like your drop-in war. We're both grown up enough to understand that, aren't we?'

'Yeah, I guess. But is that how you'd want it to be? Between us?'

She considered. 'No, but it's the nature of war. Nothing lasts.'

THIRTY MILES AWAY to the southeast, Herman Keissling and Marion Beans were standing outside Maidstone railway station.

'Now what?' They looked around uncertainly. Beans approached a taxicab and tapped on the window. He pulled a scrap of paper from his pocket. 'The Haslam kids' detention place, sir. Do you know it?'

They rode in silence for a while. 'You heard from Cheryl?' Keissling asked.

'Sure. Every week. Regular as clockwork.'

'How's she doing?'

'Hates it. Never stops bitching. She's at her mom's. But at least she keeps writing, though, and there's something . . .'

'What?'

'Her letters. Over the months, it's like we're really talking at last. Listening and talking. Like I never really knew her before. Doesn't make any sense, does it?'

'Yes, it does.' Keissling was staring down at an object in his lap. It was a large and ornate doll, with long blonde locks and pink cheeks. 'Blanche is suing for divorce.'

'You're kidding! Why?'

'I got this to send her. She loves dolls. Thought it might make things better.' He paused. 'Do you remember the last time we had a pass for London? I kept going on and on about art galleries?'

'Uh-huh.'

'Well, I never went to no art galleries. I did a stupid thing.'

'You went whoring, and then you wrote and told your wife.'

'No! Well, yes. But nothing happened. Nothing like that. I wanted it to, if I'm honest. But when it came down to it I couldn't go through with it. I picked up this girl, one of those Piccadilly commandos. She took me back to her place, and then we just talked. I paid her to. All night.'

'*Then* you wrote and told your wife all about it. Herm, don't you get it? We're in a different world from them. There's things we'll never be able to tell them, things they could never understand. What it feels like to see your buddies crash and burn up, right in front of your eyes. Or what it feels like to shoot a man dead. Or, come to that, why you might just feel the need to sit up all night talking to a ten-dollar hooker.'

Fifteen minutes later they were at the door of the detention centre.

'Visiting's Thursday,' said a face at the hatch. 'Buzz off.'

'Couldn't we just have five minutes, sir? We've come a long way.'

'No. I'd lose my job. Who d'you want to see, anyway?'

'Billy Street. No, hold on, where's that damn paper. Crossley, is it?'

'Him again? Christ, he's more popular than the bloody Pope.' The face eyed the two Americans warily. Beans held up a grocery bag.

'We brought him some things. Gum, candy. Magazines.'

'No parcels allowed, neither.'

'There's a couple of packs of Lucky Strikes in it for you.'

'Don't smoke neither.' Yet the face was still waiting. Somewhere in the compound behind him a fire-bell was ringing. He didn't move, his eyes on Keissling's doll.

THE NEXT DAY, Hooper and Heather went to the Suffolk coast. They checked into a hotel in a seaside town and were shown to a fourth-floor room with a large sash window overlooking the sea. Hooper threw it open and for a while they sat beside it, just listening to the waves, inhaling the fresh salt air and watching wooden fishing boats ply the waters below them. After a while she reached out, taking his hand.

'I know this is against the rules.' She smiled. 'But supposing there was no war, no David, no complications. Nothing but the two of us.'

'I'd ask you to marry me,' he said straight away. 'I'd want us to be together. For ever.'

'Good. I accept, of course. Where do we live, in America?'

'No. Here, England. Or maybe Europe. France, Italy, perhaps.'

'Sounds wonderful. What would we do?'

'I have no idea. Live together in a small house deep in the country. I get to stay at home and grow vegetables, while you go out to work, teaching kids.' Heather laughed, squeezing his hand. His face held a rare look of briefly imagined contentment.

They ate lunch in a pub, then walked arm in arm along the seafront. Despite the chill wind and threatening grey clouds, the esplanade was busy.

'It doesn't change anything, Hoop, and it has absolutely nothing to do with us. But I should never have married David. I've known that for a long time. Even before he went to Malaysia.'

'What is he like?'

'Irrepressible. Very dashing. Funny. Rather headstrong. Wonderfully exciting. But wrong, for me. I know that now. We were wrong for each other. In more normal circumstances we'd have probably discovered that long before we ever contemplated marriage. But the circumstances weren't normal, I was silly and weak. And young. And what with all the excitement of the outbreak of war, well, it was rather like getting caught up in a whirlwind.'

He put his arm about her, drawing her close. She rested her head on his shoulder. 'I wish things could be different, Heather, you know that. But the irony is, if they were different, if there was no war, no killing, no David, we wouldn't have found each other. And I'm just so thankful that we did. Even if it's just for a short while.'

'Shush, now. That's enough.'

Hands clasped, they fell into contemplative silence, stranded upon a tiny island of timelessness. Seagulls wheeled overhead. Passers-by ebbed and flowed around them like tide water.

'I just have to see these guys safely through to the finish of their tour of duty, Heather. Nothing else matters. Not the war, not defeating the Germans, nothing. With my first crew, it didn't happen. I let them down, something just went wrong. I've got to get it right this time. Get them through to the end. That's all there is to it.'

'BY THE WAY. I've put my name down for the ATS.'

'What did you say?' Maggie turned at the sink. Ray looked up, his accounts books spread over the kitchen table before him.

'The ATS. The Auxiliary Territorial Service. At the recruiting office in Fram.' Claire, her face a carefully composed study in nonchalance, flicked through the pages of her magazine. 'Apparently the Royal Artillery are putting together women's antiaircraft batteries. I'm going to be eighteen in a few weeks, so I've signed up.'

There was a moment's silence. 'You? An antiaircraft gunner? But, Claire, love, you don't know anything about guns.'

'That's the whole point, Mum. I'll learn. They'll train me. Gunlaying, ballistics, that new radio tracking thing. All that.'

Maggie, appalled, wiped her hands on her apron, lowering herself to a chair. Ray was staring at his books.

'Well, say something, you two!'

'But what about Eldon? Have you discussed it with him?'

'Of course, Mum. He thinks it's a terrific idea. We'll both be out there, in uniform, doing our bit for the war effort together.'

'But antiaircraft batteries. I mean, won't you be in terrible danger? You're only a child, for goodness' sake. A young slip of a girl.'

'I'm old enough to join up and do my bit. It's what you and Dad have been going on and on about for years. People pulling together, facing up to their responsibilities. Doing their bit.'

'I agree with Eldon,' Ray said quietly. 'Just as long as you are doing it for the right reasons.'

'What do you mean?'

He pushed his books to one side and began laying forks for supper. 'Well, love. So long as this isn't just some crackpot scheme to get back at us somehow. You know, old enough to fight in a war, but not old enough to get engaged . . .'

'Dad, listen. I understand what you're saying, but it's not that. It's just, well, for so long now, years really, I never thought about the war, not properly. But then I met Eldon and we talked, really talked, about it. And I started reading the papers and paying more attention to the news on the wireless. Suddenly, it sort of dawned on me that sooner or later everyone has to face up to it. Deal with it, as quick as we can. To stop it dragging on and on. Like the last one.'

Ray was studying his daughter. 'Chances are you'll get posted somewhere else. You and Eldon do both realise that?'

'Yes. We've talked about that too. It'll be hard. But we're strong. We'll manage.'

Maggie was sniffing into a corner of her apron. 'This bloomin' family. Billy gone, and now Claire leaving home to join up. It's falling apart. I don't think I can bear much more of it.'

'No, it's not falling apart, Mag. It's growing up, that's all. This is a family you can be proud of. Our daughter is joining the Royal Artillery. And we're going to get Billy back somehow. Wait for him to serve out his time if necessary, but we'll get him back.'

CHAPTER SEVEN

In November the weather turned abruptly, revealing, like a malevolent twin brother, the other face of an English autumn. The rain was incessant and all-pervading, whipped across the unprotected flatlands by treacherous, gusty winds. Missions were cancelled. Time after time crews were roused before dawn and trucked, tense and bleary, through the oil-black rain to their waiting aircraft, only to have the mission scrubbed at the last minute on account of the weather.

When they did fly, inevitably the accident rate shot up. Aircraft failed to attain flying speed on water-laden runways, and crashed off the end. Others, landing too fast or too long, found that wet brakes and tyres wouldn't stop them. Midair collisions between bombers assembling in cloud became commonplace, the debris and the bodies falling from the clouds like the rain.

Martha and the rest of the 520th returned to operations, completing five missions in the first half of the month. Wilhelmshaven on the

Friesland coast, Gelsenkirchen near Essen, twice to Düren to the west of Bonn. And Bremen again. Another four missions were scrubbed before takeoff, or aborted en route, usually because of weather problems at base or over the target. To the crew, cancelled missions brought no relief. You still had to endure the dawn hand on your shoulder, the wordless breakfasts, the kitting up, the boarding. The waiting. 'All the misery, without the mission credit', as Irv Underwood put it, handing in his parachute after yet another cancellation.

Then, for more than a week in the middle of November, the weather closed right in. *Martha*'s mission tally, stencilled beneath the pilot's side window, remained stubbornly on twenty. Yet, despite the inactivity, the base was held on a state of maximum alert. Security was tightened and all leave was cancelled for days on end.

Then, suddenly, the waiting was over.

It was Berlin. The big 'B'.

And then it wasn't.

In the morning the weather looked promising. They were roused even earlier than usual, a sure sign of a longer mission, deeper penetration. Breakfast was better too, another bad sign. Waffles, pancakes and real Vermont maple syrup, to go with the fresh eggs and Canadian bacon. Rookies, food trays in hand, queued in salivating amazement, but seasoned crewmen, their mouths drier, knew better, exchanging knowing glances. Briefing was packed with senior brass, the tension was palpable. When everyone finally saw the ribbon stretching on and on, all the way, piercing right into Germany's heart, even those who understood the full implications felt a visceral thrill of excitement and joined with the rookies' cheers.

Berlin at last.

But it would be like flying into the very teeth of the dragon.

Then, as if that wasn't enough, there was a delay at start-up.

Hooper, head back in his seat, closed his eyes. Beside him, as always, Underwood stared out through the side window. To the west, stars still twinkled feebly in the blue-black firmament, while low on the eastern horizon tendrils of orange tinged the fields and hedgerows with the first pale light. A breath of wind rolled across the airfield, gently rocking *Martha* on her wheels. In the next field, an early-rising farmer, oblivious of the hundreds of airmen cooped aboard the nearby aeroplanes, strolled among his beet crop.

'I heard the flak over Berlin ain't nothing special.'

'You heard wrong.'

Ten minutes later the Berlin mission was cancelled.

'Waste of a fine breakfast,' Holland muttered, lowering himself to the concrete.

But the next morning the 520th returned to action with a vengeance.

'This is a short one, so it's a double run,' the Intelligence officer announced at briefing. On the map behind him, a short length of ribbon stretched just across the English Channel to northern France and back. Crewmen glanced at each other, an expectant buzz washing over the hall like a warm breeze. 'Milk run.'

They were wrong. 'OK, listen up now. The Germans have been developing a new secret weapon, a V-1. It's a kind of bomb that flies. With wings, and a motor. They've started launching these things from sites hidden along the French coast here. Reconnaissance have located two of them and today the 8th is going to blow them off the map.'

The group was split into two halves. Englehardt's squadron, including *Martha*, flew in the first wave. They reached the target in less than an hour from the RP. The flak was light, but accurate and highly concentrated, and the sky was thick with fighters. There was a mix-up on the run-in to the target. Bombers from the middle squadron released their bombs while they were directly above the low squadron. Two B-17s in the low squadron were hit. Then a flak shell punched right through a brand-new G-Fortress in *Martha*'s squadron. They watched in horror as its gleaming silver fuselage crumpled, like tinfoil, before tumbling from the sky. Seconds later a Focke-Wulf appeared out of nowhere, barrelling in, straight at them. At the last moment Hooper hauled *Martha* from its path. As it flashed by he glimpsed its pilot, slumped dead over his controls.

'Pilot, this is radio. I'm picking up a Boston signal.'

Boston. The code word for mission aborted. Hooper looked around. Some aircraft were already breaking off the attack. Something was wrong.

'What do you make of it, Via?'

'I, uh, I'm not sure. It's not right, the letter groupings, the way the Morse is being keyed. It doesn't feel right.'

In a moment Gene's voice came over the radio. 'All aircraft, this is Charlie leader, belay that Boston, d'you hear me? It's bogus enemy horseshit. Hold station, close up and continue the damn attack.'

The first wave returned to Bedenham three aircraft down. Chastened, *Martha*'s crew disembarked to the hardstanding, blinking in rare morning sunshine. It was still only ten thirty.

'Man, am I glad that one's over. That was scary.'

'Too right. Give me Bremen any day.'

'Point me at the hut, someone. I am going to sleep for a week.'

Seconds later Englehardt's Jeep pulled up.

'Second wave's four ships short, Hoop. I'm going back out there with them. There's a slot for you too, if you want it.'

Hooper didn't hesitate. 'We'll do it.' He turned back to the bomber.

'Hey, now, Lieutenant, wait there just one moment.'

'I said we're doing it, Lajowski! Get on board.'

'Hoop, listen.' Underwood rested an arm on Hooper's. 'You're bone-tired. We all are. Are you sure this is the smartest idea?'

'Irv, I know.' It had started again, the pounding in his head, and the lights popping before his eyes like flashbulbs. 'We're running out of time, I can feel it. This will give us another mission credit. Two in one day. Twenty-two. It just leaves three.'

An hour later, refuelled and rebombed, they took off for Calais once more. Three hours after that they were back in Finginger's office.

'I'm sorry, guys,' he said, shrugging at them helplessly. 'There's only one mission credit.'

'What—did—you—say?' Keissling stared in disbelief.

'You don't get two mission credits. I'm sorry, I thought that had been made clear to everyone.'

'Well, it was not.' Accusatory eyes were directed towards Hooper.

'It isn't fair.' Spitzer was shaking his head. 'It isn't fair, it isn't right.'

'Major.' Lajowski leaned forward. 'Do you mean to tell me we flew back there to that target today, got blasted about the sky by some of the meanest flak I ever saw, all for nothing?'

'Take it easy, Sergeant. I understand how you feel—'

'No, you don't! One of our ships got blown clean out of the sky, for God's sakes! Ten men died. Do you understand how that feels?'

An uneasy silence descended. Finginger, pencil wiggling, studied his debriefing form.

'Maybe you should have checked, John,' Underwood said quietly. Hooper said nothing, staring as though mesmerised at his hands.

Finginger cleared his throat. 'Look, guys, I'm sorry, but I don't make the rules. Why don't I look into it, speak to Colonel Lassiter. Maybe he could take it up with HQ, talk to some of the brass—'

'Fuck it.' Lajowski pushed back his chair, striding for the door. 'This is your doing, Hooper, you son of a bitch! You damn near got us all killed for nothing.'

'AH, MRS GARRETT, there you are. Please, come in, pull up a chair.'

'Thank you.' Heather closed the headmaster's door. Needham had called her Mrs Garrett, she noted. Not a good sign.

'Now then,' he began pleasantly. 'Tell me, is there any news on the Billy Street front?'

He was stalling, she knew it. 'I believe the Howdens have retained a solicitor to look into his case. It appears to be quite complicated and might take a while to sort out.'

'Good. And, er, Captain Garrett? Your husband? Any word?'

'Not as yet.'

'Ah. Well, you have everyone's best wishes, of course, and prayers for his safe and early return to the village.'

'Thank you.'

'Which sort of brings me to the point of this meeting, as it were. You see, the reason I asked you to come here this afternoon . . . Oh dear me, this is so very difficult—'

'I am having a relationship with an American officer from the air base. This places you in a very difficult position, as you feel it sets a bad example to the children and brings the school into disrepute.'

Needham raised his eyebrows. 'Well, perhaps I wouldn't have put it in those exact terms, but that is the general gist of it, yes.'

'I quite understand. Would you like me to resign my position now, to save you and the school any further embarrassment?'

'Heather, for heaven's sake, couldn't we just talk about it first?'

She lowered her head. 'Of course. I'm sorry.'

Needham pushed back his chair. 'Please let me say straight away that nobody wants you to resign, that's the first thing. At least I don't, and the children certainly don't. However, Bedenham is a small village, and whether we like it or not, the parents of our pupils look to us to imbue their children with a simple sense of right and wrong . . .'

But she wasn't listening. Right and wrong. That's what it boiled down to. What was right and what was wrong. The job she loved, everything she had worked so hard for was finished. One or two parents, that's all it had taken, just one or two. She'd seen them in the greengrocer's, outside the post office, at the school gate. Averted eyes, dark glances of disapproval. She'd known how it must end. She was ready, yet despite her best intentions, her careful composure, she felt the prickling of her eyes. Overcome suddenly, profoundly fearful, she excused herself and fled to her empty classroom.

Later, she walked home, her bicycle at her side. 'Think about it,'

Needham had pleaded, towards the end. 'If you could just, you know, put a stop to this . . . unfortunate situation. Quickly. I am sure this would then all blow over and you could stay on.' Finish it, in other words. Finish it now. Or leave. But she would not. It had gone too far.

Rosamund's car was outside the cottage. Heather leaned her bicycle against the wall with a sigh and pushed the door open. It was the last straw. She was at the sitting-room window. In Heather's chair, in Heather's cottage. It didn't matter any more. Those things, the chair, the bed, even the cottage, everything, none of it belonged to her. It related to someone else. Someone who had once existed as a minor player in a brief, silly drama, but now was gone. 'I'm making some tea,' she said, moving towards the kitchen. 'Would you like some?'

'No, thank you. I came to pass on some information about the Crossley boy.'

'No, you didn't!' Suddenly she turned, colour rising in her cheeks. 'You did not! You came to pour out your contempt at the shame I have brought upon the good name of Garrett. You came to be prim and judgmental and play the grievously wounded mother of the poor wronged son. You came to gloat over the fact that I've ostracised myself from the community, the fact that nobody talks to me any more. You came to gloat over the fact that I've lost my job.'

'You've lost your job?'

'Yes!' She was crying now, her cheeks flushed pink. 'It was the most important thing in my life and now it's gone. And do you know what? I don't care. Because what I am doing means more than any job. Means more than a marriage that hasn't existed in years. What I am doing is trying to save someone's life.'

'I know.'

But she didn't hear. Racked with sobs, she sank, spent, into a chair. 'I'm so sorry!' she wailed. 'I never meant to hurt you.'

'I know that too.' Rosamund rose and left the room. A moment later she was back, glass of water in hand. 'Here, drink this.'

Slowly, Heather grew calmer. 'I'm sorry,' she whispered again. 'I failed you. I lost faith. Let you down.'

'No. No, you didn't.' Rosamund's back was to her, her voice quiet, resigned. 'You came to terms with the hopelessness of the situation, when I stubbornly refused to. You did what you felt you had to. I don't approve, of course. And I cannot condone. But blaming, being prim and judgmental, as you put it, was wrong. I see that now and apologise for it.' She turned, a faint, faraway smile on her lips. 'He is my son, you see, Heather. Being parted like this, for so long, even permanently perhaps, doesn't change that. Do you understand what I mean?'

'I think so.'

'You two were together such a short time. And so young. You are right to begin to consider your own life, your own future. You must. This . . . thing, with this pilot. I cannot pretend that it doesn't shock me. And pain me. But I know it is not something you would ever have entered into lightly. I know you're not that sort of person.' The light had gone, leaving the room cold, deep in shadow. She stood, silhouetted against the window, erect, white-haired, solitary. 'I was afraid, you see. I was frightened that if you gave up, then I might too.'

'Well, you mustn't. You mustn't be afraid, and you mustn't give up. You must remain hopeful.'

'Yes, perhaps. But perhaps it is also time to be realistic.'

A FEW DAYS LATER, *Martha* flew to Rjukan in Norway, a long, cold, 1,500-mile trek. The target was another secret enemy test site, but at the briefing crews learned even less about it than they had about the V-1 launch sites the week before. 'All you boys need to know,' the briefing officer told them with unusual solemnity, 'is that what those Germans are cooking up there don't bear thinking about, and so we have got to take it out, and good.'

'What the hell is heavy water, anyways?' Beans queried over the intercom three hours later. The group had climbed, circling up and up, through layer after layer of dense cloud, all the way to 27,000 feet, before breaking out into the clear. The sight that greeted them was almost biblical. Everywhere around them, bombers rose like magic, emerging from beneath the smooth white carpet, like mayflies hatching from a lake.

'It's what you get when you swallow too much of that limey beer.'

'Jeez, I hate that stuff. How the hell does anyone drink it?'

'I believe it has something to do with a new kind of bomb,' Holland said.

'A bomb full of water? Well, that ain't nothing new. I was making those things back in fifth grade.'

'All right, quieten down, now. We've got a long day ahead of us. Go on and test your weapons.' After the stresses and strains of the last few days, it seemed to Hooper that everyone was in unusually good humour. He flicked the button once more. 'Pilot to navigator.'

'Yeah, Hoop, this is ol' Thumbs-up here, come on.'

Hooper, eyebrows raised, glanced at Underwood. But his copilot just shrugged, grinning. At the same time *Martha*'s guns sprang to life as each gunner test-fired his weapon. Some of the bursts went on much longer than necessary. Or normal.

'Yeah! All right, this is Kid in the ball! Everything down here is working just fine and dandy. We are locked, loaded and ready to roll!'

'Quiet! Everyone!' Hooper rubbed at the back of his neck. What the hell was going on? 'Pilot to navigator, have you got an e.t.a. for the Norwegian coast yet?'

'Not as yet, Hoop old buddy, but it's a-coming right up.'

Something wasn't right. Hooper tore off his headphones. 'Take it, Irv, I'm going down in the nose.'

Underwood, reaching casually for the controls, held up a gloved thumb and finger in a perfect circle. 'Gotcha.'

Hooper unclipped his oxygen hose, attached it to a walk-around bottle and ducked down from the flight deck. Forward in the nose compartment, Spitzer was leaning, slouching almost, across his little navigation table, his face resting in one hand. Beyond him, Holland was staring through *Martha*'s Plexiglas nose dome.

Hooper plugged in his intercom. 'Spitz. Spitzer. The e.t.a.?'

Spitzer slowly raised his head. 'Oh. Yeah. I'm on it. Right on it . . .'

'Ball to pilot.'

'Yes, Ringwald, go ahead.' He glanced forward again. Holland's head was down. And *Martha*. Was she beginning to turn?

'Lieuten'n', I have to repor . . . I'm sorry to say, hate to . . . I don't feel so good.'

At that moment there was a muffled thump from behind him. Hooper turned. Lajowski's inert body had slumped to the base of his turret. At the same time he felt *Martha* sliding over onto her side.

'Jesus!' He leapt back, struggling past Lajowski's body. It took barely thirty seconds to regain the flight deck but by then *Martha* was practically inverted, rolling onto her back like a dying whale. He struggled into his seat and seized the controls. Beside him, Underwood was limp, slumped forward against his seat straps.

Within ten minutes the situation was restored. Having quickly rolled *Martha* upright once more, he forced the bomber's nose down into a near-vertical dive towards the waiting cloud carpet. *Martha* dropped like a rock. He continued to dive, flying blind, watching the altimeter spin. At 10,000 feet he began to haul back and levelled off, finally, 15,000 feet above the freezing waves.

One by one the crew revived.

'What the hell happened?' Underwood moaned, rubbing his temples. 'Feels like the worst hangover in history.'

'Oxygen starvation. The O2 supply to the whole ship failed. We all got hit. It was just lucky I was on a walk-around bottle.' Very lucky. Oxygen failure at 27,000 feet. Light-headedness, euphoria, insensibility, unconsciousness, death, in just a few minutes.

The mission was over, yet again. With no oxygen they were unable to climb above 10,000 feet, so could not regain the bomber stream. Hooper held *Martha* low and turned for home.

They hardly spoke the entire return trip. And after landing, the mood turned even blacker.

'Yet another goddamn no-credit mission,' Lajowski complained, lowering himself gingerly to the concrete. He was nursing a bad bruise to his forehead from his fall. 'This is getting to be tedious.'

'Can your bitching just for one minute, can't you, Polecat? I'd say we're pretty damn lucky to be alive.'

'Who the hell rattled your cage, Keissling? I'm just saying that I'm getting tired of busting my ass for no-credit missions every day.'

'And we're getting pretty sick and tired of your bitching every day!'

'All I'm saying is, now that we're this close to finishing our tour, people should just be damn careful about checking important things like oxygen, or accepting half-assed no-credit missions to France.'

'Sergeant, do you have a problem with the way I command this crew?' Hooper, hands on hips, was staring at the ground at Lajowski's feet. 'It's OK, you can say what's on your mind.'

'I heard you dumped your entire last crew in the ocean and they all drowned except you. You didn't even get your feet wet.'

Underwood stepped forward. 'Sergeant, you are way out of line.'

'It's OK, Irv, let him be, it's OK. You're right, Emmett. It happened. Just as you say. As far as I know. I can't tell you much about it, but it did happen, and I blame myself for it. Is there anything else you want to know? Anybody?'

'Did they kick you out the 95th for it?' It was Al Tork, squatting, pulling weeds from cracks in the concrete.

'I suppose the answer to that is kind of. They offered me a medical discharge or a transfer here. I chose the transfer.'

'Why?'

'Good question. I guess I have Major Englehardt to thank for that. He told me about a rookie crew that Operations wanted to disband. He told me that despite a few problems, he had complete faith in this crew's ability to pull through. For what it's worth, so do I.'

'Yeah, but medical discharge. You could have been home free.'

'I didn't want to be home free. That would mean my crew had died for nothing. I wanted to finish my tour. Do my duty. I still do.'

'For them,' Underwood said quietly.

Hooper smiled. 'Yes, Irv. For quite a while, I suppose it was for them. But then, over time, well, it's the present that counts, isn't it? You all taught me that. Now, all that matters to me is to get us all safely through these last four missions, and home. Nothing else.'

'Um. Five.'

'What?' Everyone turned to Keissling. He was smiling sheepishly.

'I came here straight from training, remember. When I joined the crew, you guys had already flown one mission. So I'm one down on the rest of you. I've got five to go.'

'So have I.' Holland shrugged. 'Same thing.'

TEN MINUTES LATER the door to Scott Finginger's office burst open. Gerry Via, still in full flying kit, strode in.

'How many missions has he got?'

'I beg your pardon?'

'Hooper. How many missions?'

'Well, I have to say, Sergeant, it's not normally approved policy to discuss a flier's combat record with someone other than—'

Via leaned over Finginger's desk. 'His last crew. At the 95th. They all died. How many missions did Hooper fly with them?'

'Eleven.'

'Jesus!' His fist hit the desk. 'I knew it, I just damn knew it!' He began pacing Finginger's floor. 'So, that crazy son of a bitch has flown, what, thirty-two missions?'

'If you say so.'

'But why? He's finished his tour. He could be home. He should be. Weeks ago. With survival odds like ours. Who in their right mind would do a thing like that?'

'Do I really have to spell it out for you, Sergeant? Hooper could be a lead pilot by now, his own squadron even. Englehardt already put him up for it. But he keeps turning it down.'

'To stay with us? And *Martha*?'

'It's his way, I believe, of making sense of it all. And dealing with what happened before. Start all over again. From the beginning. From zero. Well, from one, that is. Like the rest of you.'

Via sank into a chair. 'No, Major. Zero is right.'

It had been Kid Ringwald's idea. Who else? Back there on the tarmac when Keissling and Holland made their little confession about mission totals. I vote we stay together, Ringwald had said, holding his hand in the air like a little schoolkid. I vote we fly one extra mission, and all finish this thing together. To Via's astonishment, to everyone's, one by one, the hands went up. All of them.

THEY GATHERED ROUND the Howdens' kitchen table. The newly convened Friends of Billy Street Committee. Rosamund Garrett was there at the head of the table. Ray and Maggie sat to either side of her, Heather and Claire beside them. Hal Knyper was at the far end.

Rosamund drew up the minutes, the Howdens read out submissions on behalf of Mrs Blackstone, and their solicitor. Heather handed in a petition signed by Billy's class. Hal produced a huge bar of Billy's favourite chocolate while Maggie fretted and made tea.

'Hopeless!' Rosamund scolded disparagingly, when everyone had finished speaking. 'Thank goodness someone here is able to coordinate things properly. Now then, here's what I propose we should do.'

An hour later an action plan had been drawn up and agreed. The Howdens' solicitor was fired, to be replaced by the Garretts' Lincoln's Inn barrister—at Gerald's expense. The Garretts would also speak to the local Member of Parliament. 'He comes to dinner once a month anyway.' Maggie and Claire were put in charge of parcels. 'Make sure they go direct to Billy, care of the prison governor, mind you. And Recorded Delivery. We don't want those thieving guards getting their hands on them again.'

Hal offered to produce a letter of support from the USAAF.

'Can you really do that?' Rosamund asked.

'Sure. Get Finginger to do it. He owes me. Let's see, the kid Crossley was always a, uh, cheerful, positive, and helpful presence at the 520th. Always willing to lend a hand, run errands, pitch in, that kind of thing. What d'you say, think it might help?'

Ray was to contact Billy's old orphanage, and begin tracking down his past. His records, his birth certificate. Even his mother.

'You do want to adopt him, don't you?' Rosamund asked at one point.

Maggie and Ray looked at each other. 'If he'll have us.'

Eventually the meeting broke up. Heather slipped away into the night as soon as she could. The cottage was in darkness when she arrived, breathless, ten minutes later. Heart pounding, she let herself inside. He was lying on the sitting-room floor, by the dying embers of the fire. She knelt, leaned over him, kissed him lightly. Immediately he stirred, his arms reaching for her, pulling her down beside him.

They lay there, their bodies entwined. Not speaking, not moving, until their breathing became slow and deep. Until the fire grew cold, and the moon rose over the fields across the lane.

IT WORKED. The Billy Street relief offensive. Within three weeks, Rosamund Garrett's meticulously drawn-up and militarily executed strategy, brought about a swift and sympathetic reappraisal of his case.

Billy was allowed out. Temporarily. On probation. On the strict understanding that he remain under the supervised guardianship of the Howdens, that he report to the local police station weekly, and that he eventually be retried for the warehouse fire incident.

It was good enough. One cold, clear December afternoon shortly afterwards, a perceptibly thinner and taller, older-looking Billy stepped from the train to the platform at Ipswich Station. He looked around in unhurried bemusement. Then, before he knew it, he was enveloped by well-wishers.

Ray and Maggie were there. Ray stood back, looking Billy up and down. 'Hello, lad.' He smiled, and ruffled his hair briefly. Maggie was less reserved, peppering him with kisses. She cried, then laughed, then cried again. Claire, too, had come.

There was a small if noisy American contingent. Eldon Ringwald, of course, arm in arm with Claire. Polecat Lajowski and Hal Knyper. They cracked jokes, poked him in the ribs, punched his shoulder.

'How's *Martha*?' he asked Hal, straight away.

'Holding together. No thanks to the flight crew here.'

'The tally?'

Lajowski held up two fingers. 'Just two to go now, old buddy.'

'Hello, Billy.' Ruby was there too. Standing shyly, a little apart from the others.

'Rube. 'S good to see you. Thanks for coming. And for your letters.'

Rosamund had sent Gerald's car. It was parked outside.

'She says hello and sorry she can't be here,' Maggie explained. 'She's been such a tower, what with all the organising and letter-writing and everything. And the other Mrs Garrett, too, your teacher. They've both done so much. They wanted to be here, but couldn't. Something come up.'

Ray drove Rosamund's car back to Bedenham. On the way Billy said little, Ruby at his side. After a while his hand closed on hers. Back at Forge Cottage he went straight to his room, then to each room in turn, as though checking that all was as he'd left it.

He went outside. Ray was in the workshop, standing beside the glowing forge. Billy nodded. 'How's the repairs?'

'Booming. As you can see.' Bicycles filled every available space. 'There's dozens more waiting outside. I had to take on one of your mates, that sniffing Lennie Savidge boy. Couldn't cope on my own.'

'Oh.'

'And you needn't be looking so sorry for yourself, neither. You're going to have your hands well and truly full dealing with the customers. You know, handling the business end and all that.'

Billy stared around the forge. 'Am I staying, Mr H? You know, after the court case, and all that. After the war, even. After everything. Is this where I'm stopping? Like, home?'

'Would you like to?'

'Very much.'

HOOPER ARRIVED at Heather's later in the evening. She met him at the door, kissed him warmly, took his overcoat and cap. He turned to her then, studying her, as always, as though for the first time. Or the last. And in that moment he knew. Before her eyes, his back seemed to sag, as though finally acknowledging the full weight of the load upon it. As though there was no need to pretend any more.

'He's alive, isn't he? David. You've heard something.'

'Yes. Yes, he is. I heard today.'

'Heather, that is wonderful, wonderful news. And Richard?'

'Still no word. But they were in the same battalion. There are grounds for hope.'

'Of course there are. But David, what a relief. How did you hear?'

'The War Office received another list of prisoners of war from the Japanese authorities, via the Red Cross. David's name was on it. He's in a POW camp in southern Burma somewhere.'

Rosamund had received the news first, of course. One of her contacts at the Ministry had telephoned her. The moment Heather saw her hurrying towards the garden gate, she knew something had happened. 'Bless you, Rosamund,' she'd said, over and over, while they'd embraced. It was all she could think of. Yet she meant it.

'Strangely,' Rosamund had replied tearfully, 'just now, I find that all my thoughts are with you.'

Heather and Hooper ate their dinner at the table by the fire. Her hand stole across the table, into his. Immediately their fingers slid tightly between one another.

'John, I'm afraid. Of things changing between us.'

'You mustn't be afraid.'

'Will you still come?'

'Of course,' he lied. 'Whenever you want me to.'

Things had already changed. And it had to be that way; he'd known it all along. It made no difference that David's situation was exactly the same as it had always been. Or that it would remain the same for years more, until the war ended and he was released. He was alive, and that changed everything. It was the single unspoken condition of their union. The sense of loss was worse than he would ever have imagined it could be. It was like losing his closest friend. It *was* losing his closest friend. Arriving back on base, he went straight to the officers' bar, took a table in the corner and began ordering up doubles.

'Mind if I join you?'

It was Gene Englehardt. He pulled out a chair, signalling to a passing waiter. Within seconds their drinks were replenished. They touched glasses in wordless salute. Gene drank deeply.

'Old buddy of mine from the 490th called me tonight,' he said eventually. 'Sam Banning, did you ever meet him?' Hooper shook his head. 'We went through basic together, Rapid City, Kearney, the whole shebang.'

Hooper waited. Younger faces were stealing glances at them from the bar. That's Englehardt there, talking to Hooper. The two oldest hounds in the pack.

'He's three-quarters of the way into his second tour of missions. Group lead pilot, more decorations than a goddamn Christmas tree, just heard he's up for promotion to lieutenant colonel, the works.'

'Impressive. Not too many still on operations with that kind of record.'

'He's quitting, throwing it in. That's why he phoned me. He says he just woke up this morning, and for no particular reason a voice in his head said he'd done enough and it was time to go home. So he is.'

'My God.' Hooper stared at his glass. 'Just like that?'

'Just like that.'

Underwood, Spitzer and Holland entered the bar. Spitzer caught Hooper's eye and gave a discreet thumbs up. They'd changed, he realised. Completely. Older, of course; ageing in double time. But worse, all the youthful callowness was gone, all the innocence. Erased. In five months. They too had done enough.

'Good people,' Englehardt mused. 'You did them proud.'

'They did it themselves.'

'See that they get through, Hoop. See that you all get through.'

'I'll do my best. Gene? What is it?'

Englehardt was tilting drunkenly across the table towards him.

'They're going to screw us over, old buddy,' he murmured in Hooper's ear. 'They're going to screw us over and good.'

'What? Gene, what the hell are you talking about?'

'You didn't get this from me. But, hand on heart, Hoop, it's the truth. They're raising the mission total.'

'What?' Hooper froze. 'What did you say?'

'It's not official, but they're upping the number of missions in a tour to thirty-five.' He held Hooper's eye for a moment. 'So I guess maybe Sam was trying to tell me something today. Maybe, in fact, he was trying to tell us both.'

TWO DAYS LATER they flew to Kiel.

When Hooper saw the line of red, and where it ended, he felt his heart falter. He stared at the map, his mind blank.

'What is it?' Irv hissed from beside him. 'Hoop?'

'Nothing. It's nothing.'

It was Kiel. Once again. But it was to be different. No foul-ups. And no sea mist over the English coast when they came back, too, the met officer assured them.

The form-up was fuss-free, the 520th was towards the rear, *Martha* in her customary slot to the left of and slightly behind Englehardt's *Shack Time II*.

'Happy twenty-fifth mission, everyone.' A wistful voice came over the intercom. 'I mean, those of us who are on their twenty-fifth, that is. Those of you on your twenty-fourth, well, have a nice day and thanks for nothing.'

A pause. 'Say, Polecat, by any chance are you trying to make me and Dutch feel bad about you guys flying an extra mission?'

'Herm. Would I do such a thing?'

'You bet. But you can forget it. We'd do the same for you.'

'Would you? Really, Keiss, would you?'

'Not a chance!'

Down in the nose compartment, Loren Spitzer patted Holland's back. 'They're just kidding around, Dutch!' he called.

The bombardier turned and grinned. 'I know.' His face was pink with cold above his mask. But not sickly. In fact, he rarely vomited any more, Spitzer realised. Fought his way past his sickness, somehow. Sheer will power.

'Navigator to pilot. Enemy coast in sight.'

Ten minutes later, right on schedule, the first fighters appeared.

It was ferocious and dogged and bloody, but no worse than usual. The Germans split themselves into small hunting packs of two or three and careered through the formation from all directions, dividing their fire and confusing their escorts. Soon the sky was alive with dogfighting Mustangs and Messerschmitts, falling bombers and billowing parachutes. Inside *Martha*, the acrid tang of cordite, and voices, clipped, urgent, but calm, filled the air.

'OK, we got one coming in, a one-one-oh, right to left, high. Polecat?'

'Got it.'

'There's another, low and slow. He's hit. Rolling clear.'

'Navigator to pilot, two minutes to the IP.'

'Roger, nav. Bomb doors coming down. Bombardier, you set?'

'Set.'

'Fort dropping out from low squadron. Flamer. Two 'chutes.'

'Tail here. Fighter, six o'clock, level, I'm on him. Wait. Wait! He's rolling right. He's out of control!'

A monstrous flash lit the sky outside Underwood's side window. *Martha* bucked, rolling violently to the left, shock from the blast tossing her onto her side, like a wave hitting a boat. Hooper wrenched at the controls, struggling to right her, then a shadow passed over his head. He looked up. And froze.

Directly above them, barely feet away, rolling, upside-down, right over the top of them, was *Shack Time II*. It was like looking up at a mirror image. They were so close Hooper could see into her cockpit, see Englehardt's face, his eyes staring, unblinking, into his own. Another split second and the bomber was over the top and dropping, still inverted, down past *Martha*'s left wing tip. As it went they saw the whole rear half of the aeroplane was gone, exploded into nothing but jagged shards. An instant later the right wing became detached.

Immediately, the Fortress flipped into a tight spin, huge at first, then growing smaller as it fell, spinning, towards the ground.

Horrified, they watched it go. There would be no getting out, they all knew that. Everyone from the radio room back was already dead. The five that remained were trapped, pinned by centrifugal force to the walls and floor of the spinning nose section. *Martha*'s crew watched, transfixed with shock. *Shack Time II* spun on and on, receding, smaller and smaller, with mind-numbing slowness, like a dropped sycamore seed. Until at last the doomed men's misery came to an end in a soundless burst of red, and *Shack Time II* exploded into the ground.

CHAPTER EIGHT

'**W**ell, well! John, as I live and breathe. How the hell are you, Lieutenant?' Brent Wallis rose from behind his mahogany desk, striding, one hand extended, across the floor. 'It's damn good to see you.'

'You too, Doctor.'

'Are you quite sure about this, John?' Wallis, shrugging on a white laboratory coat, gestured to a couch by the wall. Hooper sat, testing the springs, as though trying a bed in a furniture store.

'Quite sure, Major.'

'I mean, you were pretty damn certain you didn't want anything to do with this the last time you were here.'

'I realise that. But that was then. Things are different now. I want to know what happened. I have to know.'

'What for?'

'I guess it's a matter of getting everything in order. You know, tidying loose ends. Putting out the trash.'

'Why?' Wallis asked. 'Thinking of going somewhere?'

'No, sir. Nowhere in particular.'

'Sodium pentothal is not something to be messed around with lightly, John. I can't promise you anything. You may remember good things, you may remember bad. You may remember nothing at all. You might, I have to warn you, remember things you wished had stayed buried for ever. Do you understand me?'

'Shall we just get on with it, Major?'

AFTERWARDS, HE LAY, dozing groggily for a while. Time passed. Then a nurse came, brought him hot soup and sandwiches on a tray. Wallis came and they talked while he ate. He slept a little more. When he awoke the light was just beginning to fail. But he felt refreshed and ready to get up. He dressed, then Wallis walked him to the Jeep.

'Sure you feel up to driving?'

'I'm fine. Thanks, Brent.'

'Take good care of yourself, Lieutenant.'

He drove straight to Orford. The field was changed, winter greens poking through a blanket of dirty sleet, but the view was the same. Just as he'd seen it as his stricken plane had broken out of the bottom of the sea mist. And the sea. He could smell it, it was so close behind him. They had been so close, but not close enough; his navigator had been wrong. 'It's safe now, Hooper!' he'd yelled over the intercom. 'We're over land, I'm sure of it!' A small mistake. Five minutes more, that's all it would have taken to save them. But there was no five minutes, they were at 700 feet, and the navigator was sure. So Hooper hit the button and let them go, drifting into the mist and the freezing waters beneath.

Then, within seconds, he too was in the fog, sinking blindly down and down. There was no time to prepare, no time to do anything but cut the last of the power and hold on. The impact was shocking, a sickening metallic crump as the plane flopped lifelessly into the field, bounced, smashed down again and slithered, shuddering, through the waist-high corn.

Teeth gritted, he held on uselessly to the controls, bouncing in his seat, waiting for the bomb to go off. The 500-pounder sitting, wedged in its track in the bomb bay. But the bomb didn't go off and at last the wrecked Fortress, curling, slid to a halt. He sat there, for just a second, stunned by the silence. Then his harness was off and he was struggling aft. Bowling. Baby-face Danny Bowling was waiting for him in the tail.

'I can't move, Hoop!' he cried. His legs were gone, a shattered mess of steel and bone and blood-soaked leather from the flak hit. He was delirious with pain and shock.

'For the love of Jesus, don't leave me!' Danny screamed. Hooper, fumbling, found the first-aid box, tore it open. The metal morphine phials, like little toothpaste tubes with needles on the end. He reached out, grabbed a wildly thrashing arm, plunged.

'I'm going to get you out of here,' he repeated, over and over, until Danny began to grow calm once more. But he needed help. The gunner was trapped, his lower half completely pinned beneath the wreckage of his turret.

'Don't go, Hoop,' he pleaded softly. 'Don't leave. Stay. Just for a minute.' And so he'd stayed. Lying, full stretch in the cramped tunnel, his arm reached forward over the gunner's shoulder, tightly gripping his hand. They'd talked. And then they'd prayed. Calmly. Quietly. The twenty-third psalm. 'The Lord is my shepherd . . .'

At last Danny nodded into unconsciousness. Hooper slipped his hand from the young gunner's, shuffled back up the tunnel. Reaching the waist, he kicked open the exit. He began to run, awkwardly, stumbling in his heavy flying suit through the rustling corn.

Then the bomb went off.

HE WENT ON, to the little church on the sandy bluff by the river, near the farm. The church where he had sat, so long ago, unable to think, unable to grieve. Where he had first met Heather.

And there, as the last of the day's winter light died in the coloured glass windows around him, he hung his head and wept for the souls of his lost comrades.

After a while he grew still. Then he became aware of a presence, standing beside him. A hand touched his shoulder.

'We've been looking for you everywhere, John.' Finginger's voice echoed softly. 'Heather said I might find you here.' The hand shook his shoulder a little. 'We have to go.'

Hooper nodded and began to rise. 'It's OK. I'm ready.'

FINGINGER MET THEM outside the front gate at five. It was still dark, and very cold. They clambered aboard his Jeep while he went into the hut to square it with the sleepy-looking MP on the barrier. 'Are we too late?' Heather shivered anxiously. All across the blacked-out airfield came the whine and splutter of starting engines.

'No, miss. Don't worry,' Billy said from the back seat. He was wearing his overalls and cap. Over them a crisp new leather bomber jacket, '*Misbehavin' Martha*' hand-painted across the back.

Finginger returned. 'We're in.' He grinned. 'Amazing what you can achieve with two bottles of Kentucky's finest and a persuasive tone. Here, for God's sake put this on, you'll freeze.' He passed her one of the bulky, fleece-lined flying jackets.

'Thank you, Scott. I greatly appreciate it.'

'No problem.' He let out the clutch and set off.

It took nearly fifteen minutes. The base roads were thick with last-minute to-ing and fro-ing. Gradually the traffic thinned, then they were on the perimeter and moving out towards the flight line. Shadowy outlines of aircraft began to appear from the gloom, their flight and ground crews clustered beside them. They passed five, six, then Billy leaned forward, tapping her on the shoulder. 'There she is.'

They were all there, just preparing to board. Knyper's boys too. They came up to Billy first, pulling his cap, spinning him round to admire his new jacket, kidding about. He smiled shyly, then excused himself for a moment, and went over to the flight crew. They were pleased to see him, too. But quieter, more inwardly focused. Instinctively sensing this, he shook their hands formally, wished each of them good luck, and went back to the mechanics.

Hooper was round *Martha*'s far side, crouching beside an under-carriage leg with Knyper. When he saw Heather he hesitated, fractionally, as though not able to believe his eyes, before straightening, coming to her. He took both her hands, kissed her.

'I had to come,' she said. 'Today of all days.'

'I'm so glad you did.' He smiled. He walked her across the concrete, hand in hand, to the fence by the beet field.

'I wish I was coming with you.' Thirty yards away *Martha* stood waiting. The others were already boarding.

'You are.'

'Are we allowed to hold each other? Just for a moment.'

They clung on, a single, motionless, tightly wrapped shadow in the last of the darkness. 'I love you,' she whispered. 'God speed.'

Then it was over and he was leading her back to the Jeep. He squeezed her hand once more, and turned away.

On board, all was quiet preparation. He reached the flight deck in time to see the Jeep disappearing along the perimeter track.

Hooper pulled on his headphones. One by one the crew called in, confirming in turn that their electrically heated suits, headsets, oxygen and weapons systems were all functional.

'Listen. While you're all on,' Hooper began, when they were done. 'I had wanted to say something, to you all. About what these past months have taught me. About the real meaning of loyalty and honour. Courage. Friendship. But I think that maybe now is not the time.'

'Thank the Lord for that.'

'Amen.'

'Thank you, Sergeants. Anyway, I would, however, just like to say it has been a privilege to fly with you gentlemen, and to wish us all good fortune today.'

'Irv,' he said, a few minutes later. They were preparing to start engines. 'I've been meaning to ask. Why is this ship called *Martha*? I mean, who is she?'

'Rudy Stoller's daughter. She's three years old. Always getting into mischief. His wife used to write him all the time, with the latest news of all the jams she'd got herself into. How's Martha? we used to kid. Misbehaving again, he'd say.'

'Well.' Hooper reached for the generator button. 'This one's for her.'

FINGINGER DROVE HER HOME. 'Are you sure I'm not putting you to too much trouble?' she said, as they sped through the main gate. It was light; they'd stayed to watch the takeoff. Finginger spread his hands. 'I'm off duty. There's nothing more to be done.'

'Except wait.'

'That's right.'

They drove slowly back through the waking village. Thin plumes of smoke were appearing at chimneys. Blackouts were coming down from windows. He followed her into the cottage. It was cold and lifeless.

'I expect you'd like coffee, but I'm afraid I haven't any.'

'Tea's fine.'

They talked. Heather seemed tense, but resigned.

'He isn't coming back, Scott.'

'What?'

She was leaning against the kitchen sink, waiting for the kettle to boil. Her overcoat was still on, she was hugging herself. 'I can't explain it. But I just know. He knows. It's as if he's already decided.'

Finginger left her a while later, drove back to the base. He was exhausted, dog-tired, more than ever before. He collected coffee and doughnuts from the canteen, went back to his office and began to work. It was half an hour before he came to it. A message slip. Nothing more. It had been received during the night. Dropped, along with everything else, into his overflowing in-tray. He stared at it uncomprehendingly, an icy chill settling in his stomach. Then he leapt from his chair and ran for the door.

Skidding his Jeep to an untidy halt beneath the control tower, he sprang for the door, doubling up the stairs. Colonel Lassiter was there, arms folded, talking to the waiting controllers.

'Sorry, Major,' Lassiter shrugged, a minute or two later. He reread the note. 'But I don't get it.'

'Crew 19, sir.' Finginger struggled for calm. He was out of breath, could feel his heart banging beneath his jacket. 'Hooper and the boys, in *Martha*. They flew a double mission a few weeks back. To the Pas de Calais. Attacking those V-1 flying-bomb sites, remember?'

'I remember the mission, Scott. What of it?'

'They flew twice that day. Yet at the time, they were only credited with one mission. They were pretty unhappy about that. So I said I'd make a few enquiries, put a request through to HQ for clarification.'

'And you didn't hear anything.'

'No, sir. Nothing. I forgot the whole thing. Until now.'

'Now they've been credited with the second mission.'

'Yes, sir. This piece of paper. It means they've finished. It means they completed their tour of duty the day before yesterday, when they flew to Kiel. It means they should not be up there today.'

'I know what it means, Major!' Lassiter glared at him, then began pacing the wooden floor of the control room. Finginger waited.

'You are right, Scott, they should not be up there today. But there's not a damn thing I can do about it.'

'Sir, we can recall them.'

'No, we cannot!'

'But why?'

'Why? I'll tell you why. First, they're over two hours into the mission. The supers came back an hour ago, so there's no one to take their slot if they drop out. Second, Hooper's commanding the high squadron. If I pull him out, who the hell is going to take over? Third, what do you think the rest of the group is going to think when they hear a radio signal recalling just one of their number? Fourth . . .' His voice fell. 'Fourth, I believe, if they had the choice, they'd want it to be this way.'

MUNICH WAS A LONG HAUL, practically into the foothills of the Alps and the border with Austria, at the farthest extremes of their protective escorts' range.

Martha flew at the head of a spread-finger formation of five, with two more tucked in behind. As predicted by the weather forecasters, small tears began to appear in the undercast. Snow-covered hills could be glimpsed. Meandering strips of black road. An arrow-straight section of railway, vanishing into a hillside.

A short while after that the fighters came in.

'My God,' Holland murmured, peering at the circling swarms. 'Look at them. There must be a hundred or more.'

Seconds later *Martha*'s airframe was shuddering from the collective firing of her guns. Hooper forced himself to ignore them, carefully leading his formation through a twenty-degree turn onto the bomb run. As their wings levelled once more the familiar black islands of flak began exploding directly ahead of them.

'Pilot to bombardier, she's all yours, Dutch.'

'Roger. I have it.'

Martha lurched slightly as the automatic pilot took over. Hooper released the controls. The bomb-bay doors came down, further slowing their progress. It was the worst moment. Four or five minutes flying dead straight and dead slow from the IP to the target. Behind Holland, Spitzer ducked instinctively as a fighter flashed past. Without thinking, he swung his machine gun through the arc of its trajectory, jabbing repeatedly at the firing button. In an instant the fighter exploded into a ball of flame.

'Way to go, Spitz!'

Martha bucked suddenly, then there was a gut-wrenching lurch and splintering crash.

'Holland's hit!' Spitzer's voice crackled over the intercom. 'He's hit in the head. Christ, there's blood everywhere!'

'Get down there, Irv!' But Underwood was already moving. It was what they'd practised. What they'd trained for.

Martha bucked again, another near miss. Engine dials were jumping. A shadow flashed past Hooper's head; he looked up, a fighter, rolling through onto its back, guns blinking. He sensed hits, then a section of instrument panel in front of him jumped and exploded, dissolving into shattered fragments. He felt a thump, a stinging blow to his right hand. He yelped, glimpsed torn flesh through a smoking rent in his glove. There was shouting in his head.

'We're hit!'

'Two more coming by under! Yours, ball, do you see them?'

'Jesus did you see that, get him! Torky yours yours yours!'

They were still flying on automatic. Straight and slow. Bomb doors gaping, 6,000 pounds of high explosives hanging in the daylight. Down in the nose a freezing gale tore through the shattered glass of the nose dome. Maps and papers flew in a storm. Underwood and Spitzer were hauling Holland back from the bombardier's seat. His arms flailed weakly. He coughed, his face a mask of blood.

Via arrived. 'I've got him!' he yelled above the shrieking slipstream. 'It's OK. Irv, go!' Spitzer helped drag Holland back out of the nose compartment. 'Dutch! Dutch, can you hear me?' Via ripped open his medical kit. From the corner of his eye he saw smoke pouring from the starboard outer engine. He ignored it, bringing a compress to Holland's forehead. 'Dutch? Speak to me!'

'Waist to pilot. Hooper, this is Beans. We're hit back here.'

'Where, Beans? What damage? Can you track it down?'

Suddenly *Martha* surged upwards, released from the dead weight of her bombs tumbling from their racks.

'Bombs gone!' Irv's voice. 'Doors coming up. Manual flight control, Hoop.'

'Got it!' Hooper, right glove sodden, rammed open the throttles, hauling the bomber away from the target. 'Waist! Beans, this is pilot. What about ball turret?'

'Christ.' Beans's voice again. 'Pilot. This is waist. Ringwald's hit.'

FROM TWENTY MILES and 11,000 feet, the Alps were an unbroken jumble of gigantic, cloud-covered ice blocks. Above, the sky stood hazy blue. And empty. For more than fifteen minutes there had been no flak, no enemy fighters. No aircraft at all, in fact, neither friend nor foe. They were alone. They were leaving.

Hooper, his right hand hanging limply at his side, flew *Martha* with his left. She was down to three engines. Half the instrument panel was shattered. She was losing fuel from a ruptured wing tank. And an arctic blast whistled through her fuselage from the smashed nose, but she was still flying. Holding steady and level. The fire in number four was out. Hooper was taking them southwest.

'You called me, Lieutenant?' Lajowski appeared breathlessly beside him. His parachute, like Hooper's, was clipped to his chest.

'What?' Hooper stirred. 'Oh, yes, I did, Emmett. How's it going back there?'

'Well, we got everybody together down in the waist. Dutch is OK. Piece of Plexiglas from the nose dome must have caught him on the head. There was a lot of blood, but Gerry got it stopped. Ringwald took one in the thigh and another in the upper chest. Gerry's working on him now.' He looked down at Hooper's hanging arm. A dark puddle was collecting on the flight-deck floor below it. 'Are you going to get that seen to?'

'In a minute.' Hooper kept checking his watch, staring down at a map strapped to his knee. 'Is everyone wearing their parachute?'

'Yep. We got the waist door hanging open too, just in case, like you said.' He looked around the cockpit. 'Why? Is she going down?'

'Not yet. Listen, Emmett, step up into the copilot's seat here. All you have to do is hold her level, and steady. That's all. See that distant ridge of mountains poking up through the clouds there? Keep them where they are, ahead and to your left. Nothing more.' He began to climb from his seat. 'I'll be right back.'

Lajowski's hands closed uncertainly over the control column.

'Uh. Are those, like, the German Alps?'

'No.' Hooper dropped to the floor, clambering aft. 'Not any more.'

The waist looked like a battle field-station. The injured crew were sitting, propped along the walls. The others sat or crouched at their sides. They all looked up as Hooper entered.

'It's time to go,' he called. 'The ship's had it. Fuel's going. We can't risk a crash landing, not through low cloud over this kind of terrain. We'll jump, it's safest.' His right arm was completely numb, his head spinning. He must hurry. 'We'll secure Ringwald's ripcord to the ship when he jumps, and send Gerry Via straight out after him. The rest of you follow on his heels. Keep it tight. Lajowski and me will jump from the nose hatch. We'll be right behind you.'

He helped them prepare, organising them into a line beside the gaping waist door. Gerry Via stood, one arm round Ringwald, who, pale but conscious, managed to grin weakly at Hooper. Next came Holland and Tork, followed by Keissling, Underwood and Spitzer. Marion Beans was at the back. Right at the last moment, barely seconds to go, he turned to Hooper, eyes wide with fear.

'What? Sergeant, what is it?'

Wordlessly, lips trembling, Beans lifted the parachute pack on his chest. There were tears in his eyes.

'What?' Hooper looked. 'What is it?' Then he saw. A hole. A rough tear. The size of a finger. It went in through the bottom corner of the pack and out of the side.

Hooper hesitated, his eyes on Beans's. The parachute was useless. A deathtrap. Despair washed over him, just for a second. How much more? The others were ready. In the cockpit Lajowski still waited.

Then his face broke into a smile. He clapped Beans on the shoulder. 'No problem, Sergeant, it's probably nothing.' He began quickly unclipping his own pack. 'But best not to risk it. Here, take mine. I'll go with the spare.'

'Spare? Uh, I didn't know—'

'In the nose, under the pilot's seat. Didn't think we'd be flying about the place without spare parachutes, did you? Via! Are you ready? Irv! Get everybody together, head south, hand yourselves in at the first place you come to. See to the injured.'

'But what about the Germans?' Underwood's voice rose above the howling slipstream. 'What about evade and escape?'

'There aren't any Germans. This is Switzerland.'

IT IS BETTER THIS WAY. Far better. The relief, the peace, the release, is beyond beauty. Like a warm mountain breeze. Like weightlessness. It is over. Complete. He sits, relaxed and comfortable in his seat at the top of his empty airplane. They are both spent, both finished. Spiritually, mechanically, it is the same thing. But they have accomplished with dignity that which has been asked of them, and are now free to travel the last few miles together. In peace.

He pulls the headphones from his head. Then struggles to his feet, planting them wide so that he is standing, straddled between the two pilots' seats, his good hand on Martha's *control column. She is easy to fly like this. Like a ship, a sailboat. She is a joy. A friend.*

He reaches into the neck of his shirt, grasps his identity tags. He removes them, drops them into the well at his feet. He is clean again. Untainted. Martha *coughs, shakes a little in his hand. He checks the gauges; the fuel is all but gone, the number one propeller already spinning to a stop. It is time. He is ready. He stands at the helm of his ship, feet braced, and slips down with it into the waiting clouds.*

CHAPTER NINE

The man parked the Range Rover by the gate. 'Are you two coming or what?' he asked, collecting his camel's-hair overcoat from the back.

'No, Dad. We'll wait in the car, shall we?' said the girl in the back seat. She was in her early twenties, dressed in duffle coat and scarf. She glanced at the young man sitting beside her. 'Geoff's not feeling too good, and, well, it does look sort of cold, and muddy out there.'

'Suit yourself.' He slammed the boot and set out across the field.

The young man watched him go. 'Could somebody please tell me what the bloody hell we're doing here? What are we looking at? Oh yes. Holes in the ground, that's it. Forty-year-old holes in the ground.'

The girl sighed. 'Humour him, Geoff, couldn't you? Just for a bit. We are staying with him, after all. Anyway, it's one hole in the ground, and it wouldn't do you any harm to show a little interest. You are supposed to be a history graduate, you know.'

'But I mean, what's it for? What on earth is he doing?'

Alice watched the squat outline of her father receding across the field. 'He's looking for something.'

The man went carefully. At last he reached the hole, roughly circular, about twenty feet wide and six deep. Three youths were at the bottom of the hole, operating a small mechanical digger. As he approached, one of them looked up.

'Oh, Mr Howden, you made it. Great. Thought you'd want to see this.' He handed up a tubular shard of metal. 'I believe it's a piece of bomb-door actuator.'

Billy stood at the edge of the hole, turning the metal over and over in his hands. He was in his late fifties, squat, powerfully built, accustomed to getting his way. He wiped a finger back and forth across the manufacturer's plate. Then he handed the shard back down to the youth. 'Keep digging,' he said, turning from view.

ALICE HOWDEN SPOKE to Scott Finginger the day after her excursion to the Essex crash site in her father's Range Rover.

'Oh, er, hello there,' an American voice said, when she picked up the telephone. 'Would that be Mrs Howden I'm talking to?'

'No. I, er, well, no, this is one of her daughters. Alice. Who's speaking, please?'

'My name is Finginger. I'm calling from Seattle. Your father wrote me a few weeks back, wanting some information about an old wartime bomber base.'

'Oh, yes! He mentioned you. You're the one who kept all the records and things from when he was at Bedenham with Granny and Granddad Howden.'

A faint chuckle floated down the line. 'That's right, kind of. Ah, is he there, by any chance? Or your mother?'

'My mother died four months ago. Sorry, I should have said.'

'Please don't apologise. I'm real sorry to hear that. Your dad didn't mention it in his letter.'

'No. He doesn't talk about it much. He's at church, by the way. He likes to go to evensong most Sundays. He'll be back in a while.'

'Oh, fine. I can call back a little later. Tell me . . . Alice, isn't it? Your mother, was her name Ruby?'

'Ruby, yes. How did you know that?'

'I met her a few times when I was stationed at Bedenham. Your dad and she were just kids then. But I always had a hunch those two would end up together. When were they married, do you know?'

Alice was forming the impression Finginger was taking notes. 'Um, let me see. Helen was born in '54. Mum and Dad got married four years earlier, in 1950. No, it was the year after that. 1951.'

'And Helen, you say she was born in '54? She's your sister?'

'That's right. There's three of us. Helen is thirty-one, Rose twenty-nine, then I'm the youngest at twenty-two.'

They talked a while longer, then Geoff began to make annoyed faces. 'News is on!' he hissed. She hung up. 'What on earth was that about?' he added, without interest.

'Nothing much. Old war stuff, from when Daddy was an evacuee.'

Alice knew very little of her parents' time together as adolescents, even less of her father's earlier childhood. 'Nope, can't recall it, girl,' he'd quip, in his faded cockney. 'Proper life begun for me when your grandparents took me on, God bless 'em. It was in 1943. Same year as your mother started giving me the eye!'

And now, suddenly, he wanted to dredge it all up again. Or at least parts of it. A buff folder lay on the desk, its cover bearing the same year, 1943. It was already thick with newspaper clippings, letters, photocopied pages from books. It was a therapy, she knew. A way of trying to come to terms with the death of the woman he'd loved above all else.

HOWDEN'S CYCLES opened in Framlingham in 1946, one year after the 520th Bombardment Group had been officially stood down. The business was an instant success. Within a few years, Billy, by then an adopted member of the family, persuaded Ray to branch out into motorbikes. When Ray and Maggie retired in the mid fifties, Ray passed the business on to the son who had made it all possible. Billy, his instincts sharper than ever, took it to new heights, and it went on to become the biggest motorcycle dealership in eastern England. He and Ruby moved their young family into a modern home on the outskirts of Ipswich. They joined the ranks of the new wealthy; became well known and respected. Ray and Maggie were regular visitors.

So too, although less frequently, was Claire. She fulfilled her wartime ambitions and became a member of an artillery battery, but she and Eldon Ringwald never married. They both knew it wasn't to be, and called it off without fuss. After the war she moved to Norwich, married a typesetter in a printing works and had two children.

She was Alice's godmother. Hopelessly forgetful of birthdays, frequently absent from Alice's life, she nevertheless remained in contact as best she could. Alice was very fond of her.

Ray died in 1970, Maggie a decade later. Alice, being only seven at the time of Ray's death, did not go to her grandfather's funeral. But at seventeen she returned with her family to Bedenham for Maggie's. It was the first and only time that she saw her father incapacitated with emotion. He stood at the graveside openly weeping, Ruby, her arms round him, at his side. 'She gave me everything,' he kept saying. 'She gave me everything.'

'IS THERE ANYTHING I CAN DO?' Alice asked Billy, a couple of weeks after Finginger had called.

'I don't know, girl. Is there?'

'Dad!' She jabbed him on the arm. 'I meant, to help you. You know, typing, or filing or something.'

'Hmm. Got your passport handy?'

'What?'

'I'm going to France tomorrow. You can come too, if you like.' He picked up a large package with an American postmark from the table. 'But first off, assuming you really do want to help, that is, you've got some reading to do.'

She spent the rest of the day in his study. Apart from the buff 1943 file, which was in some semblance of order, there were several old boxfiles, stuffed to overflowing, which most certainly were not.

Then there were the photographs. She found one of her father, aged about thirteen. She stared at it for a long time. There were others. A big propeller-driven aeroplane with four engines and American markings. A man in wartime uniform, an officer, wearing a cap and a parachute harness. A posed group of nine more men. They were outside, in a field somewhere: four of them standing, four kneeling, one sitting cross-legged in front. They were wearing thick, fleece-lined leather flying suits, boots and gloves. They looked very young, smiled shyly into the camera. Her age, she guessed, some even younger. Names were written against each one: Underwood, Beans, Spitzer . . .

Billy appeared at her side, picking up the photograph.

'Who are they? Is that them? Is that Crew 19?'

He raised eyebrows in mock surprise. 'You do learn fast. That expensive education wasn't a complete bloody waste of time, then.'

She read on. They'd all survived, she learned during the afternoon. The nine members of Crew 19 in the photograph. They'd all survived the war, several of them keeping in touch with Billy and Ruby over the years. Letters, Christmas cards, family photos, all told their stories. But Mr Finginger's dossier, the fat packet that had arrived that morning, revealed everything. It was a remarkable document, part archive, part memoir. 'From milk-run to bloodbath in half a second,' he'd typed on the first page. He said it summed up the nature of the war these young men had fought in. Reading on, Alice at last began to see why. Before she knew it, the light was going. She reached to turn on the desk lamp. By the time she finished the manuscript, it was gone midnight.

They'd landed in a snow-filled field near St Gallen, Crew 19, after they'd parachuted from the stricken bomber. Shedding their parachutes, they began gathering themselves into a group. After a while Lajowski appeared, struggling over a low ridge, plastered in snow.

'Where's Hooper?' Al Tork, evidently, had asked the question. Down on the ground, Gerry Via was tending to Eldon Ringwald. Although seriously injured and in considerable pain, the ball turret gunner was still able to manage a weak smile.

'He wouldn't want us to wait.' Irv Underwood was the one to voice it. Without fuss he took charge. He saw that they buried their parachutes in the snow, then he gathered everybody together, arranged for the two biggest crewmen, Beans and Lajowski, to carry Ringwald between them, and then struck out southwards. At last, hungry and exhausted, long after dark, they stumbled upon a road. Soon after that they came to a village.

That was the last day of their war. Switzerland was neutral but under obligation to intern combatants found on its soil. The Swiss knew how to take care of visitors, and they were particularly fond of Americans. The crew spent the first night in a *Gasthaus* in the village where they were fed royally and plied with schnapps. They slept between clean sheets in their own private rooms. Ringwald was taken to hospital in Zurich where a bullet was removed from his lung. Gerry Via's careful ministrations had without doubt saved his life.

Within a few days they were moved to an internment camp at Adelboden, in the very shadow of the Alps, not far from Gstaad. It was simple but comfortable, and they passed the winter going for walks, playing cards with the other inmates and reading.

Under the terms of a prisoner exchange agreement for airmen, they were repatriated the following spring, arriving back in the US, in time to read of the D-Day landings in June. They demobilised and went their separate ways.

Irv Underwood went back to his bank teller's job in Indianapolis. He married his girlfriend Linda in 1948 and they had two children. Similarly, Loren Spitzer resumed his accountancy training in Boise. He eventually joined a large insurance group where he rose to become a vice-president in charge of finance. He never married.

After a brief spell as a civilian, John Holland, the fourth of *Martha*'s commissioned officers, resumed a career in the air force. He qualified as a navigator, distinguished himself in the Korean War, finally rising to the rank of lieutenant colonel. In 1959 he married a Filipino girl called Tasmin, and they had two children.

Marion Beans went straight back to his home and to Cheryl. Within two months she was pregnant. They moved into a small house on his father's farm where the baby, a boy whom he insisted they call Herman, was born. They went on to have three more, all sons. In time he took over management of the farm from his father.

Early on, his close friend Herman Keissling became a regular visitor. True to her word, Herm's wife Blanche divorced him in 1945. He too re-enlisted in the air force and served in Korea, but upon his return he was rudderless. He spent much of the sixties wandering aimlessly from job to job. He got married again but it didn't last. He ran out of money and got into trouble with the law over trying to sell his ex-wife's car. Finally, broken and penniless, he turned up on the Beanses' doorstep once more. They took him in without a murmur, their boys immediately adopting him as honorary uncle. He began working on the farm and found a house nearby.

Gerry Via fulfilled his destiny and became a doctor. There was some parental difficulty, because his Italian father wanted him to join the family business back in Atlantic City. But a changed Geraldo was adamant and he qualified in 1950, going on to specialise in cardiothoracic surgery. He lost touch with Joanna Morrison, but did marry a nurse, Sandy, in 1952. They had two daughters.

Emmett Lajowski went back to Brooklyn where he resumed work as an auto engineer in his father's workshop. In time the business expanded enough for him to run his own. He also bought and sold used cars, trading under the name Polecat Autos. He married his secretary, Donna, in 1957. Every few years they would drive south for a get-together with the Beanses and Herm Keissling.

Al Tork also kept in touch. In 1947 he was accepted into a seminary in Raleigh, and was ordained five years later. Thereafter, he stayed in the South, taking over a difficult ministry in a run-down sector of Charleston, South Carolina. When local kids asked about his war service, he always said that God found him hunched over his sights at 25,000 feet over Bremen, on that interminable October day in '43.

Kid Ringwald, fully recovered from his injuries, returned to his South Dakota farming roots. But he too found that his priorities had changed and he was unable to settle. At twenty he enrolled in college, majoring in social sciences and was accepted into law school. From there he joined a San Francisco firm specialising in corporate law. Always an admirer of John Kennedy, he joined the Democratic Party and in his mid forties he was elected to the Senate. He married Pat in 1950, with whom he had two sons.

CHAPTER TEN

Alice awoke with her father nudging her. The car was trundling up a ramp on the ferry.

'Dad, listen, where are we going?' she asked, unable to contain her curiosity further. 'Is it *Martha*? Is it looking at more holes in the ground? Has someone found a crash site in France, or something?'

'No, it's not that. We're going to see someone. I don't know if you remember, but at your mum's funeral there was a woman standing on her own. Your sort of height, grey hair, mid to late sixties.'

Alice shook her head. The bleak misery of that grey November day was etched for ever in her memory. Yet the details, who was there, who was not, were a misty blur.

'That was Heather Garrett, my old teacher. We didn't get to speak much, what with—well, what with everything. But she wrote a very nice letter a month or so later. Told me she lived down in the South of France and to come and visit any time.'

'Oh.' Alice pondered. 'So you've spoken to her, then?'

'Spoken? No. That's what we're going for.'

'But she does know we're coming. She is expecting us, isn't she?'

'Well, not exactly, but she did say come any time. So, like, we are.'

Alice shook her head in exasperation. 'Dad. Your trouble, you know, is that you expect everyone to just be there, ready for you. Like one of your showroom managers. You've always been that way.'

'I know. Your mum told me often enough, God rest her soul. It's time to change all that. That's why I'm selling up and retiring.'

'You're *what?*'

'The company, the showrooms. I'm selling the lot.'

'Selling it?' Alice could scarcely believe her ears. 'You can't sell it. You and Granddad got it started, from nothing. It's your life. I don't believe I'm hearing this.' Alice's head was in her hands. 'And this is all part of it, isn't it? Paying anoraks to dig up aeroplane wrecks, making two-hour telephone calls to retired airmen halfway round the world. Driving five hundred miles to drop in on an old schoolteacher. This is part of that, right?'

'Kind of. The retirement, well, that's for me. But this is for them. So as people won't forget.'

THEY ARRIVED AT LUNCHTIME the next day. The house was brick, old and rambling, but in good repair, with outhouses and once-formal gardens. A woman was outside the front door, training a wisteria along one wall. It was Heather. She led them out onto a sheltered verandah overlooking a terraced garden, an ancient labrador panting at her heels. 'Perhaps we won't embarrass each other by calculating how many years it has been, shall we, Billy?' she said.

'Forty-two, now you mention it. Since you upped and left, that is.'

'Dad!'

Heather laughed. 'It's all right, Alice, your father was always quick at figures. Not quite so strong with his letters, as I recall.'

'Nothing much changed there, then.'

Heather told them what they wanted to know. Unhurriedly, pausing frequently, her voice quiet and mellifluous.

After *Martha*'s loss she had left Bedenham quickly, she confirmed. There was nothing more for her there, except pain and humiliation, although the headmaster begged her to reconsider her resignation. She left the village, moved to Lincoln, and never went back.

David was repatriated in 1946. She travelled to Southampton to meet him. When she did, he was beyond recognition. The war, the horror and brutality of his experiences at the hands of his Japanese captors, had broken him, as surely as it had killed her brother Richard, who had died in David's arms a year earlier.

He was still very ill, stick-thin, incontinent, convulsed with fevers, plagued by nightmares. She ministered to his needs as best she could. Fed him, bathed him, calmed his night demons. Slowly, he told her what he could bear to of his war. In time, when she felt he was strong enough, she told him of hers; her growing despair at David's wordless absence, her descent into hopelessness. Hooper. And Molly.

She was born at the end of August 1944. 'Yes, Billy, and you needn't look so shocked,' she chided, seeing his expression. Food was beginning to appear on the verandah table, brought by a plump, elderly woman in a grey apron. 'It is a little chilly, but I thought we might all eat lunch out here.'

'All?' Billy queried.

'That would be lovely, Heather,' Alice said. 'Please go on. What about Molly? Does she live here too?'

'No. She lives in Epsom, married with two teenage children. They come out for the summer holidays.'

She, David and Molly settled together in Lincoln. She talked at length with David about it. She would stay with him, be the best wife she could, as she had always promised. But in return, she asked only that he treat her daughter as their own. David, instantly taken with the dark-eyed two-year-old, gratefully accepted.

But the fire had gone from him, the irrepressibility, the drive. He was plagued by chest complaints and recurrent bouts of malaria. Finally, five years after his return from the jungles of Burma, he took to his bed. He never rose from it, dying of pneumonia six weeks later.

'So after that, you upped sticks and moved out here to France?'

'Not quite. That came a little later.'

The first word came from Finginger. He wrote to her in 1952 saying he was compiling notes for a memoir of his time at Bedenham, and would be eternally grateful for anything she could provide in the way of background material. He concluded his letter by saying that it was his goal to locate as many 520th aircrew as possible, including those listed as missing or killed in action. As a result he was following up literally hundreds of leads, including one story about a man reportedly living in a monastic community near Interlaken, in Switzerland.

She thought nothing more of the matter until a year later, when she received a second letter from him thanking her profusely for the material she had sent, and updating her on the news of Spitzer, Underwood and the others. *Sadly, Hal Knyper died last year*, he reported. *Cancer of the bone. It is a terrible loss; he was a mainstay of the 520th. He leaves a wife, Mary, and two fine boys.* There was a PS. *I have received permission to pass you this.* It was an address. Poste Restante, care of a post office in Grenoble.

A man appeared round the side of the house, wiping his hands on a cloth. There was a faded scar along the back of one of them.

'Well. This must be the man I once knew as Billy Street.'

Alice gasped. 'Is this . . .'

'My God, yes, it bloody well is!' Billy stepped forward, gripping Hooper's hand. 'Hello, Lieutenant, it's damn good to see you.'

Hooper smiled. 'Billy, you too. Although it's a very long time since anyone called me that.'

After a typically Gallic lunch, leisurely and informal, Heather led Alice on a tour of the gardens while Hooper walked with Billy back along the track towards the vine field.

'I'm setting up a memorial,' Billy explained to Hooper. 'On the old base. Stan Bolsover owns the land now. He said he'd be happy to go along with the idea.'

'It's a fine one, Bill.'

'I'm putting up the cash, so there's no fundraising needed, but I do want people's ideas, and involvement. I want to build something fitting, and lasting, like. So's people can come and visit.'

'I see. What did you have in mind?'

'Well, a little museum ideally. Where the control tower used to be. I've been trying to find an old B-17. Not a flying one, but one in good enough nick to put in a little hangar we could build. Been paying a gang of hairy student archaeology types to go round digging up wrecks. But all they find is bits and pieces.'

'Ah.' Hooper said. 'I believe I know where we might find one.'

Six months later, pouring mud, rust-streaked, corroded, but intact, *Misbehavin' Martha*, was hoisted to the surface of Lake Brienz, thirty miles to the southeast of Bern, in Switzerland. Billy was there to witness the moment, as were Hooper and Heather. Scott Finginger, too, was unable to resist the sense of occasion. Silver-haired, portly, red-faced, he had flown over at the last minute. Together they stood on the dockside and watched *Martha*'s return to dry land. Despite her age and battle damage, the still, ice-cold and fresh waters of the lake had protected her from the worst ravages of time.

'What happened, John?' Finginger, ever the Intelligence officer, had waited forty years to close the file on *Martha*'s final mission.

'I took them away from it,' Hooper said simply. 'It's all very hazy, and not something I care to think about too much. But I just felt they'd done enough. So I flew them out of the war.'

'I can understand that. And you were right, they had done enough. You all had.'

Hooper was thoughtful. 'Quite a while after they jumped clear, *Martha* was going down. There was a thick cloud layer. We just kept drifting down and down. It was incredibly peaceful. Then suddenly, the lake was sitting there, dead ahead. We just glided straight down onto it. Or so I believe. There are, you know, a lot of gaps, and so much of it all seems so dreamlike now.'

Finginger nodded. There were gaps. But Heather had filled them, speaking quietly to him at the lakeside that afternoon.

The monastery was on the far side of the lake. Hooper had been found the next morning on the shore nearby. He was half-dead from exposure, his head and hand were injured, and he was without any kind of identification. They took him in. 'He stayed nearly four years,' she said. 'It was twelve months before he even spoke.'

Later that summer, just in time for the fortieth anniversary of the end of the war, a jumbo jet landed at Stansted carrying 200 veterans of the 520th. They spent four days being bussed all over the Suffolk countryside, revisiting old friends, haunts and memories. On the Sunday, they gathered beneath blustery but sunny skies outside the new hangar. A simple stone cross had been erected before it, and a brass plaque read:

To the memory of the men of the 520th Bombardment Group, 8th US Army Air Force, Bedenham, England, who gave their lives in the name of freedom, 1942–1945. Their names liveth for evermore.

A few minutes later, ten men, aged in their sixties and seventies, assembled themselves, a little shyly, but proudly, into a group in front of their old aeroplane, *Misbehavin' Martha*. Shutters clicked by the hundred, eyes grew moist. In the fields around them, clouds of seagulls wheeled overhead, while a tractor clawed fresh furrows into the rich earth.

ROBERT RADCLIFFE

'*Under An English Heaven* has been a very personal and special project for me,' says author Robert Radcliffe. 'It's something I've always wanted to have a crack at. I live smack in the middle of a part of Suffolk that was home to hundreds of thousands of US servicemen during World War II. It is an area full of memories and tangible reminders of that period. I wanted to try to tell the story of the 8th Air Force's time here and to look at the impact they had on the area.'

Radcliffe carried out extensive historical research, as well as being inspired by the personal anecdotes of local inhabitants and some of the wartime pilots. Many of the incidents and missions described in the book are based on real-life experiences, and although the village of Bedenham and the air base are fictional, they are amalgamations of real places near to Radcliffe's home. Still, today, there is clear evidence all around of the wartime presence of the American air crews. 'Nearly all the US air bases are commemorated in some way,' Radcliffe says. 'At Framlingham there is a farmer who owns the land where a B-17 base used to be. He was here during the war and has now turned the old control tower into a museum. Former servicemen still come for reunions and to revisit their old haunts, so there is a living link between the past and the present.'

The author's lifelong fascination with aviation adds another dimension to *Under an English Heaven*, creating an outstandingly vivid and realistic atmosphere. 'I trained as a pilot and I flew commercially for ten years,' he explains. 'I wanted to show what it was actually like to be up there.'

The name Robert Radcliffe is a pseudonym adopted by the author especially for *Under an English Heaven*. He usually writes contemporary fiction under his own name, which he prefers not to reveal. Now he plans to write a further two novels as Robert Radcliffe, which will develop into a loosely based trilogy set in 1943.

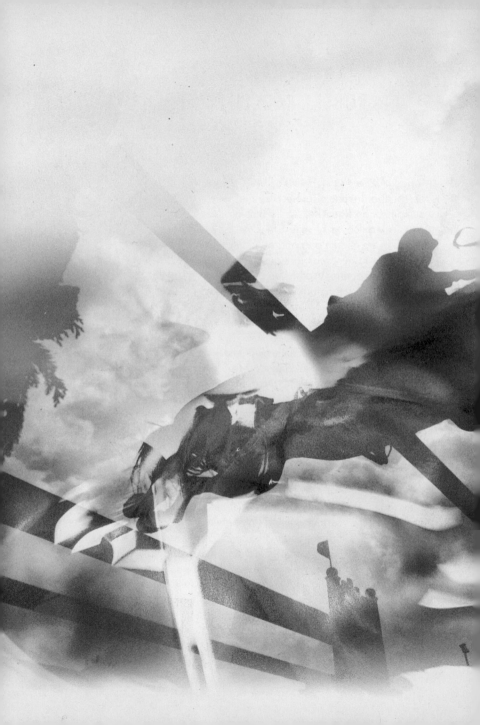

Lyndon Stacey
CUT THROAT

American showjumper Ross Wakelin always suspected that starting a new job in a new country wouldn't be easy, but when he arrives at Oakley Manor stables he is surprised by the hostility of his workmates.

And when malicious gossip and a series of petty attacks start to damage his reputation, Ross knows it's time to fight back. Time to find out exactly who is trying to destroy him.

ONE

Twelve hundred pounds of charging horseflesh hit the wooden railings chest high and somersaulted into the north stands. Faces, frozen with horror, moved in desperate slow motion to get out of the path of the crazed beast, and their screams were all that its helpless rider could hear. The slamming, sickening impact, the smell of horse sweat and newly painted wood and the taste of blood were all crowded out by those piercing, hysterical cries.

He couldn't move, couldn't breathe. Pain filled his chest. Panic rose, constricting his throat, and the animal's flailing hooves threatened to decapitate him at any moment. Still they screamed. Why couldn't they stop? The noise filled his mind, tore at his senses, on and on and on . . .

'No!' Ross cried out, kicking at the bed covers that had twisted round his legs, and sat up gasping for breath. Sweat glistened on his face and arms, and his hair clung damply to his scalp.

He swung his legs over the side of the bed and sat, waiting for the pounding of his heart to steady. His head throbbed heavily and his mouth tasted bad. The jeans he still wore bore testimony to his nocturnal ramble along the beach. Sand grated between his toes and he felt unwashed and very sick. Considering the amount of alcohol he had consumed, he was surprised he hadn't fallen into the sea.

The delicate state of his health was not improved by the loud buzz of the doorbell, a moment later.

Ross groaned, head in hands.

It buzzed again, the sound reverberating inside his head. Muttering darkly, he pushed himself to his feet.

Stumbling across the room, he stubbed his toe on a chair leg and swore, as yet unfamiliar with the layout of his mother's Florida beach house. Needing a peaceful refuge and knowing the house to be empty, he had flown down from Georgia the previous day, finally forced to admit to himself what the rest of the world had long ago decided: that his career as a professional rider was over.

The slight, blonde female who stood on the doorstep surveyed him from head to toe with wide-spaced blue-grey eyes. She tilted her shoulder-length bob to one side and pursed her lips. 'My, you have had a bad night,' she observed in aristocratic English tones.

'I've been out jogging,' Ross lied blandly. Lindsay Cresswell, friend and fellow rider, was someone he would normally have been pleased to see, but not today, and especially not in the condition he was in.

'Yes, of course.' She sounded unconvinced. 'It's half past twelve. That must have been some run!'

Ross looked at his watch and grudgingly conceded the point. He stood back, allowing her to step past him and into the dim interior.

'You'll have to wait while I freshen up,' he mumbled. All he really wanted was to be left alone.

Lindsay threw open the curtains to admit the sunlight and righted an empty wine bottle that was lying on the coffee table.

'Fine,' she said brightly, sitting on the luxurious cream leather sofa.

Ten minutes later he emerged, having showered and changed, his dark brown hair towelled dry and combed back.

'That's better, you look almost human,' Lindsay said, coming through from the kitchen and handing him a cup of steaming coffee.

His temper in some part restored, Ross surveyed her with affection. Her thick blonde hair framed a face with almost classical bone structure and flawless, lightly tanned skin. They had met on the show circuit some eight months before and had quickly struck up an easy companionship. She was in America for a year as nanny-cum-groom for a friend with a young family, and the knowledge that when she returned to England she was expected to become officially engaged to James, her childhood sweetheart, had provided the relaxed atmosphere in which their friendship had grown.

At first the existence of this distant relationship hadn't worried Ross; lately it had begun to prey on his mind.

'I guess you didn't come all this way just for coffee,' he said, collapsing onto the immaculate upholstery.

'No, I have a proposition for you.' She sat opposite him. 'You remember I told you my uncle has a small showjumping yard back in England? Well, two weeks ago he lost his rider. The young lad he had wasn't up to the job. So now they're stuck, and I suggested you.'

'Oh, yeah?' Ross laughed mirthlessly. 'And they're so short of riders in England that he'll jump at the chance of taking on an unknown from the States with a reputation for unreliability.'

Lindsay ignored the sarcasm. 'It's midseason. Most of the riders worth their salt already have enough on their plates. If he doesn't find someone soon, the other owners will take their horses elsewhere. Uncle John trusts me and is willing to give you a try.'

Ross was silent for a moment. 'I'm through with that game,' he said then, avoiding her hopeful eyes. 'I'm sorry.'

'What do you mean? You can't just give up—it's your life! Horses are in your blood. That's what you told me, remember?'

'Well, I was wrong. I've changed my mind, and now I've quit. Finished. OK?' Ross stood up, his lithe six-foot-two frame towering over her briefly before he walked away towards the window.

'No, it's not OK!' Lindsay exclaimed incredulously. 'You can't let them win. It's like admitting they're right to doubt your nerve!'

'Maybe they are.' Ross watched the waves lazily lapping the sand.

'You *are* feeling sorry for yourself, aren't you?' She rose to her feet. 'All washed up at twenty-seven. Well, don't let me interrupt your self-pity.' She picked up her bag and whisked out of the room.

Ross sighed as he heard the door slam. He was disgusted with himself, but most of all he was conscious of having lost Lindsay's respect, and that hurt. She, of all people, deserved better treatment. Throughout his long hospitalisation and convalescence following the accident, she had been one of his most frequent visitors, and one of the few to continue to support him as his comeback fell apart. He ran his fingers through his hair and groaned.

The doorbell buzzed again. Crossing to the door, he opened it.

'My car keys,' Lindsay said huffily.

Ross obligingly fetched them but kept them enclosed in his hand.

'Stay and eat?' he suggested sheepishly.

'I shouldn't have thought you'd feel like food,' she remarked, avoiding his gaze.

'Guess you're right,' Ross agreed, holding the keys out obediently.

Suddenly, Lindsay smiled. 'Thanks, I'd love to stay.'

HE COULD NEVER SAY for sure just how the decision was made, but the following week found Ross alighting onto the tarmac at Heathrow after a flight from Miami that had been delayed by a bomb hoax.

Lindsay had painted a very tempting picture of life in her uncle's small Wiltshire yard. When Ross's alcohol-induced depression wore off, the challenge of a completely new start began to exercise a strong attraction. No small part of the allure lay in the knowledge that Lindsay stabled her own horse in the yard and would sooner or later return from the stalls to her home just three miles away.

He phoned Colonel Preston—Lindsay's Uncle John—before taking a bus to Woking, then a train to Salisbury. There he was met by a neatly dressed man of fifty or so by the name of Masters, who announced that he had been sent to collect Ross and led the way to a gleaming dove-grey Jaguar.

It was nearly dark when Masters turned the Jaguar off the road and onto a gravel drive set between two huge limes, the car's headlights picking out a sign that announced Oakley Manor.

'I'll take you straight to the yard,' he told Ross. 'The Colonel won't be able to see you at the moment. He's had to go out.'

The car swept into a well-lit yard. No sooner had they rolled to a halt than a stocky young female burst out of a nearby doorway.

'Oh, I thought you were the vet!' she wailed as Ross climbed out.

'What's the problem?' Ross asked.

The girl stared at him. 'You're the new rider—of course. It's Sailor—one of the two-year-olds. When I went down to check on him after dinner, he was thrashing about on the ground, covered in sweat and drooling at the mouth.'

'Is anyone with the horse now?'

'Yes, Leo, but *he* can't get him up either. Oh, thank God!' she exclaimed as a Range Rover decelerated into the yard. 'Here's Roger.'

The occupant of the Range Rover, a youngish man with a friendly face and a shock of curly hair, leaned across and opened the passenger door. 'Where's the patient?' he asked without preamble.

'Bottom field,' the stocky girl told him.

'OK, Sarah, jump in.'

As the girl climbed in next to the vet, Ross slipped, uninvited, into the back seat. Nobody queried his right to be there.

They bumped 200 yards down a grassy track. At a metal field gate, the three of them scrambled out. A few strides took them to where the stricken horse lay, convulsing weakly.

A lean, wiry figure rose at their approach and Ross could just make out the aquiline features of a young man with close-cropped dark hair and a glint of gold in one ear. Leo, he presumed.

'Hi,' Roger said. 'How is he now?'

'Quieter. He's stopped thrashing about.'

'Hmm, that's not necessarily a good sign,' the vet said as he knelt at the horse's head. 'How long has he been like this?'

'I found him about forty minutes ago,' Sarah told him, her voice shaking. 'What d'you think's wrong with him?'

'Can't say for sure,' Roger said, shining a pocket torch into the horse's accessible eye and then moving to listen to his heart, lungs and gut through a stethoscope. 'His pupils are dilated and his pulse is rapid and very weak. It could be colic. But I think there's something else. I'm worried about the salivation. It's not usual.'

'Poisoning?' Ross suggested.

The vet looked up, noting his presence with a momentary frown. 'It's a possibility,' he admitted. 'All I can do at the moment is try and make him more comfortable.' He straightened up and headed for the Range Rover.

Sailor shuddered and kicked all four legs as a spasm took him. Sarah made a small despairing sound.

'Diazepam,' Roger said, coming back, syringe in hand. 'An anticonvulsant. It'll help relax his muscles.' He knelt to inject the horse.

Seconds later, Sailor heaved a huge, rattling sigh and relaxed.

'Ah,' the vet said regretfully, patting the still neck. 'That's not the drug. I'm sorry, I'm afraid he's gone. Is he one of the Colonel's?'

'No. Mr Richmond's,' Sarah told him, and Ross recalled from Lindsay's briefing that Franklin Richmond was a wealthy businessman and one of two owners besides John Preston himself who kept horses in training at the Oakley Manor yard.

'It would be, wouldn't it?' Roger said heavily.

Sarah stifled a sob. 'I can't believe it! He was so full of life this morning. We had a digger down here, clearing ditches, and the youngsters were all racing round together. How could it have happened?'

'This field's quite marshy, isn't it?' the vet commented thoughtfully. 'Are there any other horses still in here?'

'Yes. Why?'

'Right. Well, I think we should get them back to the yard where we can keep an eye on them. Just as a precaution.'

Catching the remaining four two-year-olds took nearly a quarter of an hour. Halfway back to the yard the vet received another call-out on his mobile phone, handed his charge to Leo, and departed.

The remaining group were met in the yard by a wiry, taciturn little man who introduced himself to Ross as Bill Scott, stable manager, and suggested that the youngsters be put in the schooling area for the night. It seemed that Roger had given him the bad news on his way through the yard.

Ross let his two-year-old loose in the school along with the others, and turned back to the yard where Scott stood waiting.

'So, you're Ross Wakelin. You're late,' Scott observed.

'The flight was delayed,' Ross said.

'I know.' Scott's tone implied this was no excuse. 'I'll show you your room. The Colonel said to tell you he'd see you in the morning.'

Scott led the way across the yard to a door set between two stables. Automatic security floodlights came on at their approach and horses peered out at them, wisps of hay trailing from their muzzles.

'This used to be a coach house,' Scott told him, opening the door to reveal a flight of wooden steps. 'Now it's two bedsits. Your room is on the left; the other belongs to Leo. Bathroom's straight ahead. You'll eat with me and the missus in the cottage. Dinner's normally at seven thirty but she'll have saved you something, so come over when you're ready.'

Without further ado he turned and ambled away with that rolling, slightly bow-legged gait peculiar to seasoned horsemen.

Long and low, Ross's room had cream-painted walls and masses of dark beams. The floor was scattered with bright rugs, and against one wall sagged a huge sofa that had seen better days but was preserving its dignity under a striped horse blanket. Seated smugly on top of a portable TV was a polished mahogany Buddha, a souvenir of some far-off land. At the far end of the room, underneath the sharply sloping ceiling, was the bed.

Ross dumped his bags, and went in search of Bill Scott's 'missus'.

The door of the Scotts' cottage stood open. Ross found himself in a large room that obviously served as kitchen, dining room and lounge. Directly in front of him was a scrubbed pine table and beyond it, sprawled in an armchair and watching television, was Bill Scott. He didn't look up as his wife bustled forward to greet Ross.

In the mellow light inside the cottage, the couple appeared to be in their mid-forties: he tanned, with receding salt-and-pepper hair and a deeply lined face, she a comfortably rounded, attractive brunette.

'Sit down, Ross,' Mrs Scott said, pulling a chair out for him. 'Your dinner's ready.'

A pie with melt-in-the-mouth pastry appeared before him, followed shortly by a large wedge of something she called Dundee cake.

Bill came to sit at the table but his attention was clearly still on the television and it was left to his wife to initiate conversation.

'Poison!' she said, shaking her head in disbelief at the fate of poor Sailor. 'Whatever next? Poor Mr Richmond is *so* unlucky.'

'In what way?' Ross asked.

'Oh, don't let's go raking all that up,' Bill said wearily.

His wife ignored him. 'His best horse was killed in a knife attack last year,' she told Ross. 'It was horrible.'

'Oh yeah. I remember now,' Ross said. 'Lindsay told me about it when it happened. Didn't he win the Hickstead Derby?'

'Yes, and it's history now, so just let it be,' Bill cut in.

Ross would have liked to have questioned Bill Scott about the horses and other staff, but as soon as the meal was over, the stable manager retired to his armchair and the flickering screen once more.

'Do the others eat here?' he finally asked Mrs Scott, as she wiped the table.

'During the day,' she replied. 'Then Sarah usually goes home for her dinner and Leo goes out, as often as not. They stayed on this evening because Bill was out. Are you sure you've eaten enough?'

'Yes, thank you, ma'am. That was lovely.'

Mrs Scott laughed. 'The only person we call ma'am in this country is the Queen. You call me Maggie, like everyone else does.'

Ross smiled, liking her a lot more than he did her husband.

Soon, pleading exhaustion, he excused himself and made for bed.

APART FROM LEO banging the bathroom door when he came in at some ungodly hour, nothing disturbed Ross's sleep that night. He rose early from habit and spent ten minutes going through the exercises his physiotherapist had set him.

On a table opposite his bed he had found a kettle, two mugs, and instant coffee, tea and dried milk. He made himself coffee, drinking it black while standing at the window overlooking the yard.

The buildings surrounding it were of red brick, old but immaculately maintained. All the paintwork gleamed and no stray buckets or abandoned tools were to be seen. It seemed that the Colonel liked his yard run with military precision.

To his left was a row of loose boxes that opened directly onto the yard; opposite was a long wall with two archways, which he guessed led into a corridor with more stables. To his right were a barn, the driveway to the main house and, out of sight, the Scotts' cottage and the gravel drive leading to the road. In the far right-hand corner of the yard, the grassy track they had followed the night before led to a wooden five-bar gate and a field bounded by woodland. From a second window at the other end of his room he had a view of the large sand arena where they had put the two-year-olds, and a steeply rising field. Thankfully, the youngsters all looked fit and well.

It was a glorious May morning and a second chance beckoned. Whistling softly, Ross began to dress.

When he made his appearance in the yard, feeding had been completed and mucking out was well under way. Bill, Leo and Sarah, bustling about with muck-sacks and buckets of water, greeted him.

Unsure what was expected of him and anxious not to get in the way, Ross drifted into the tack room. There, neat rows of gleaming saddles and bridles hung above wooden blanket chests, each bearing a different name: Simone, Clown, Ginger, Bishop . . .

'Time for breakfast.' Bill Scott spoke from the doorway. 'The Colonel wants to see you ride after you've eaten.'

As they crossed the yard towards the cottage, Scott gave Ross a sidelong glance. 'You're lame.' His tone was faintly accusing.

'A little,' Ross agreed. 'It doesn't affect my riding.' Considering that after his accident he had been told he would be lucky if he ever walked without a stick again, he had always felt it would be churlish to resent the slight limp he'd been left with.

Scott grunted. 'I hope not.'

Breakfast would have been a solemn affair without Maggie's chatter. Bill Scott was clearly not disposed to talk and Leo Jackson proved to be reserved to the point of surliness. He acknowledged the newcomer with only a brief nod and then returned his attention to his eggs and bacon. Wearing black jeans and a khaki T-shirt, he looked in daylight to be something over thirty, with dark hair and eyes, and a faintly olive complexion. Sarah Owen appeared to be little more than a teenager and was painfully shy. She turned pink whenever Ross spoke to her and never once met his gaze.

Breakfast was barely over when the vet arrived, collected Bill and drove on down to the scene of the previous night's tragedy. They had been gone some twenty minutes when a white Mercedes pulled into the yard, and Sarah, who had at Ross's request been putting names to the horses' faces, said unhappily, 'That's Mr Richmond.'

Going across to meet the expensively dressed, middle-aged man who was climbing out of the car, Ross found him to be slightly over-weight but good-looking, with dark hair going grey at the temples and brown eyes that clearly reflected his sadness at his horse's death.

'Mr Richmond? I'm Ross Wakelin. Bill's with the vet. I shouldn't think they'd be much longer,' he said as they shook hands.

'Have they said how it happened?' Richmond was plainly agitated.

'I gather some kind of poison is a possibility,' Ross told him.

'Bastards!' Richmond said bitterly. He pulled himself together. 'I'm sorry. What a way to welcome you!' He turned as they heard the Range Rover returning. 'Ah, here's Roger.'

The vehicle drew up beside them and the vet erupted from it in his typically energetic way. 'Franklin, what a bloody shame.'

'Was it poison?' Richmond demanded.

'It was,' Roger confirmed. 'Hemlock water dropwort, to be precise. I had my suspicions when Sarah told me there'd been a digger in, clear-ing the ditches. You see, the whole plant is poisonous but the root is the worst part. The digger must have exposed some of the roots and Sailor must have helped himself.' Roger held up a polythene bag that contained several creamy-white, elongated roots, three to four inches long. '*Oenanthe crocata*'. He stepped back towards the Range Rover. 'Look, I must go. I'll do a gut sample and let you know for sure.'

Colonel Preston arrived in the yard five minutes later. The epitome of the retired army officer, from the tips of his carefully tended mous-tache to the toes of his gleaming brown shoes, he wore a tweed suit and had greying hair under a flat cap and blue-grey eyes that missed nothing. He greeted his new employee politely with a handshake and a brief smile, subjecting him to a long searching look.

'I've heard a lot about you, young man,' he said. 'Lindsay would have it that you're a hot property. I shall expect great things.'

'I'll do my best, sir,' Ross promised, returning the smile.

Behind them, Leo led a big brown gelding out of the stables.

'Ah, King,' the Colonel said. 'King's Defender. Let's see what you make of him.'

'Sure.' Ross nodded. He greeted the animal with a pat and a Polo mint and then tightened the girth. Leo gave him an efficient leg-up into the saddle, and he rode into the school.

Richmond and the Colonel leaned on the fence. Bill Scott stood beside his employer and Leo and Sarah stood at the gate. The two-year-olds had been moved to another field, and half a dozen show-jumps of varying sizes had been erected for Ross's use. Nobody had told him anything about any of the horses yet and he knew this was a test of his ability to read and adapt to his equine partners.

King felt mature, calm and confident. After ten minutes or so of suppling exercises—circles, serpentines and changes of speed—Ross put him at one of the easy fences. The horse flicked his ears back and forth as he approached, waiting for Ross's command. Sensing what the horse wanted, he drove him hard at the jump. King responded and the coloured poles flashed safely by beneath his neatly folded legs.

Ridden decisively, the horse didn't put a foot wrong and Ross relaxed and began to enjoy himself. The satisfaction of settling into a smooth partnership was immense.

Leo led a second horse through the gate as Ross slowed up. Without stopping to speak to the Colonel, he changed horses.

This mare, Flowergirl, was smaller, much younger and bubbling with nervous energy. Ross rode her with gentle hands, playing with the bit in her mouth, asking her to listen. Gradually she settled. He turned her towards a small jump and she exploded into action. Caught momentarily off guard, Ross had to use much skill and not a little strength to bring her under control again. Rebelling, she threw her head up, legs ramrod stiff, and stopped with her nose touching the poles. He circled a time or two, then put her at it again.

This time he kept her on a short bouncy stride and urged her on from three strides out. She bounced over the fences like a rubber ball. As he slowed the mare down, Ross caught sight of the Colonel and Richmond smiling, and knew he had passed the first test.

As Ross dismounted in the yard, the Colonel came over. 'Not bad,' he commented. 'She's not the easiest ride. Come up to the house tonight and we'll have a chat, all right?'

'Sure.'

Franklin Richmond lingered a little longer.

Ross said impulsively, 'I didn't realise Bellboy was yours until yesterday. He was found dead with his throat cut, wasn't he?'

Richmond nodded. 'I thought it was happening all over again.'

'But didn't they ever find out who killed him?'

'No.' Richmond sighed. 'The general consensus was that I had it done for the insurance. After all, he *was* seventeen—a fair age for a competition horse—and we *were* thinking of retiring him at the end of the year. The value of the current Hickstead champion, still in training, would be far greater than that of a retired one.'

'But that's not how it was.' Ross watched the businessman's face.

'I loved that horse, Ross,' Richmond said simply, and the remembered anguish showed clearly in his eyes.

THE DAY PASSED quickly. There were ten horses to exercise, to rub down, and to feed. Then tack to clean, and finally the yard to be washed down and swept. At six thirty in the evening, contented horses munched hay, knee-deep in dry straw beds, and the four weary workers were free for the evening.

Ross was exhausted. It was the hardest day's work he'd done since leaving hospital four months previously and a dull ache in his left knee reminded him of that.

Sarah had climbed onto her bicycle and departed for her home in the village. As Ross lay where he had collapsed on the sofa in his room, he heard Leo go down the wooden stairs and, a few moments later, the roar of his motorbike as he left the yard.

After the evening meal, Ross made his way to the main house.

The large grey-stone building looked centuries old as it sat basking in the last of the evening sunshine. Masters opened the impressive, stone-arched, oak front door and showed Ross into the study.

Colonel John Preston turned away from the darkening window as Ross entered. His gaze travelled up over cowboy boots, faded Levis and blue cotton shirt to Ross's face.

'So,' the Colonel said, after offering his visitor a leather-upholstered chair and a glass of sherry, 'you're a Yank.'

Ross didn't rise to the bait, merely inclining his head. He sipped the sherry, which was horribly sweet.

'I don't like Yanks,' his employer stated uncompromisingly. 'We could have won the war without them and we don't need them now.'

'Then why hire me?' Ross asked evenly.

The Colonel snorted. 'I didn't have much choice. Robbie Fergusson, who owns King's Defender, was threatening to take his horses away if I didn't find someone soon.' He paused, observing Ross thoughtfully. 'Lindsay says you're good. Are you?'

'Yes,' Ross said, returning his gaze steadily.

The Colonel harrumphed. 'I've made enquiries about you,' he said after a moment. 'Rumour has it you've lost your nerve.'

'But you don't listen to rumour.'

'You think not?'

'I'm here, aren't I?' Ross observed with indisputable logic.

The Colonel chuckled suddenly. 'You don't beat about the bush, do you, Mr Wakelin?'

'You're not exactly pussyfooting around yourself,' Ross said, deciding the gloves were off.

'No, it's not my way.' The Colonel regarded him thoughtfully. 'Tell me, how do you like the place? Do you think you'll fit in?'

Ross relaxed a little, sensing another hurdle safely negotiated. 'I like it. You've got some promising young horses, I'd say.'

The Colonel nodded, pleased. 'Yes, I'd agree there's a fair bit of talent there. All they need is the right jockey.'

They sat in silence for a moment, sipping sherry.

'I think you'll find the grooms are good workers,' the Colonel continued. 'Leo's new, of course, barely a month here, but he's worked in racing stables in Ireland and he's a competent rider. He had good references. Sarah's a local girl, young but immensely dedicated. Bill's a real gem. He's been around stables all his life. He was a very good steeplechase jockey in his day, until injury put him out of the game.'

Ross nodded. 'Who's in charge in the yard?'

The Colonel looked at him keenly. 'You are, if you want to be. But I had hoped you would work as a team.'

'Sure. *I* hope we will, too, but I like to know where I stand.'

Colonel Preston grunted and poured himself another sherry, offering Ross a top-up that was politely declined.

Ross looked around appreciatively at the Colonel's comfortable study. Worn leather armchairs, an untidy desk, book shelves, and family photographs everywhere. One caught his eye particularly.

'My late wife,' the Colonel said, seeing the American's interest. 'Lindsay's aunt. There is quite a family resemblance, isn't there? I see Caroline every time Lindsay smiles.'

'I see what you mean.' Ross leaned forward to look more closely. 'She's very beautiful. You must miss her.'

'Her car was forced off the road by a drunk driver. Our twelve-year-old daughter was in the passenger seat. Both killed instantly.'

'I'm sorry.' There didn't seem to be anything else to say.

The Colonel looked bleak for a moment then pulled himself together. 'Tell me about yourself. How long have you been riding?'

'About fifteen years. I started when I was twelve, when I went away to school and spent the holidays with my uncle who was a dealer with a small spread in Indiana. It wasn't—ah—convenient for me to go home at that time.' No need to mention his overworked lawyer father, and his flighty socialite mother. 'Gradually it got so I'd be the one who sorted out the awkward horses, and as I grew older I got a name for it. People would send my uncle their problem horses for retraining, and then one or two of them wanted me to continue riding for them. I went to law school—Dad wanted me to join him in partnership—but I couldn't settle to it. I took a year out, started riding for a yard near my uncle's, and never went back.'

'So you're quite well known in the States?' the Colonel enquired.

'In Indiana, maybe.' Ross laughed. 'A couple of years ago, I went to ride for a trainer-cum-dealer with some really promising horses and began to have some success. The trouble was that every time I got a horse up to top level he would sell it on and I'd be back to square one again. Last year I toured the circuit with a string of horses, including one permanent ride, Vixen. A mare with a great deal of talent and, unfortunately, a brain tumour.'

'Hence the accident,' the Colonel observed.

'That's right.' Ross had no wish to talk about that day.

'You were out of action for . . . how long?'

'Nearly six months. While I was laid up I decided I was through with building somebody else's career. I wanted to become a full-time showjumper. I told my boss I quit and struck out on my own.'

'And?'

'I couldn't get the rides. I found I was on a kind of unofficial blacklist. Somehow word had gotten round that I'd lost my nerve.' The American looked bleak.

'Sour grapes?'

Ross nodded. 'I guess so. He took it pretty bad when I left.'

'I've done a little checking up on you—newspapers and such. You were pretty smashed up, by all accounts,' the Colonel stated bluntly. 'It must have affected you to some degree. How do I know you *won't* let me down when the going gets tough?'

'You don't. But I'm confident I can make a go of it,' Ross said, meeting the Colonel's gaze steadily. 'If at any time I think I can't, I promise you'll be the first to know. All I ask is that you give me the same assurance. I've had enough of backstabbers.'

The Colonel nodded. 'That's fair enough. Is there anything you want to ask me?'

'Uh . . . What happened to your last rider?'

'Ah, that was unfortunate,' the Colonel said. 'Stephen Douglas was a young lad with an ambitious father. He wasn't really experienced enough for a responsibility of this magnitude and eventually Robbie Fergusson became so unhappy with the way his horses were going he wouldn't let Stephen ride them any more. The situation was untenable so he had to go.' He sighed. 'But it's all in the past now and we have to move on. And so, to that end, it seems we have a Yank.'

A slow smile curved the American's lips. 'I've never worked for a Limey before, either,' he said, then added, after a carefully judged pause, 'sir.'

The Colonel smiled in return. '*Touché*,' he said.

TWO

The days took on a certain pattern as Ross settled into the rhythm of the yard. They made a good working team, each pulling their weight, but where there should have been a growing camaraderie they remained just four separate people. Sarah reddened and became tongue-tied if Ross spoke to her. Leo ignored him. He did as he was told but Ross often had the feeling that offensive gestures were being made—even if only metaphorically—behind his back. Bill Scott was always civil but not disposed to be friendly.

Towards the end of his first week, Ross was in the arena working a big grey called Woodsmoke, a ponderous old warrior of sixteen, when he noticed that Franklin Richmond had come to watch with Bill. He completed his intended workout and then reined in.

'He's working well, Ross.' Franklin patted the horse as Ross dismounted, clearly pleased. 'I'd say things are looking up, wouldn't you, Bill?' he asked, turning to the stable manager.

'Maybe,' Bill replied without enthusiasm. 'But schooling's one thing, competing's quite another.' He took the horse's reins.

'That was a double-edged remark, if ever I heard one,' Ross said with amusement, as Bill led Woody away towards the stables. 'What is it with that guy? He's been acting like that from day one.'

'At your age, Bill was a top steeplechase jockey,' Franklin said. 'Then, just as he was having the best season of his career and on the way to becoming Champion Jockey, he had a fall. No different from many others he'd had, by all accounts, but something in him changed and he never rode the same way again. He's convinced history is about to repeat itself. Thinks you're him all over again. But he'll come round. He only wants what's best for the yard.'

ROSS WAS EATING a solitary meal that evening when the telephone rang in the cottage. Bill had taken Maggie to a nearby village for a bingo night. After a moment's hesitation Ross answered it.

'Ross, it's Franklin. Are you free to come and see a couple of horses with me tonight? An old dealer friend rang me and said he had a couple I might like to look at.'

'Sure, but the thing is, I'm not sure Bill can make it.'

'Well, it's just a preliminary look. We won't be making any decisions tonight. You can borrow the Land-Rover, I imagine?'

'Yeah, I guess so. Where do I have to get to?'

'It's not easy to find. Best thing would be if I met you on the way and we went on together. Go to Salisbury, take the Blandford road, and I'll meet you at the Dog and Crook—it's a pub about fifteen miles along on the right-hand side. Eight thirty all right?'

'Sure.' Ross looked at his watch. 'I'll be there.'

As ROSS HAD THOUGHT, Bill was committed to picking Maggie up at half past ten, and when told of Franklin's call he agreed, with rather bad grace, that Ross had better go on his own.

There was no sign of Franklin's Mercedes when Ross pulled up at the Dog and Crook, so he switched off the Land-Rover's engine and sat watching the activity behind the lighted windows of the pub.

'Ross Wakelin?' A cultured voice spoke through the open window of the Land-Rover, right next to Ross's ear.

He turned his head and came face to face with a complete stranger. In the fading light, Ross could see exquisite tailoring, a fiftyish fine-boned face and neatly cut, steel-grey hair.

'My name is Edward McKinnon.' The man offered him a business card. 'Franklin Richmond asked me to meet you here.'

'Where *is* Franklin?' Ross asked, bewildered. 'We were supposed to be looking at some horses.'

'Ah, yes. The horses. A little subterfuge, I'm afraid. I'm sorry about that. I run a company that specialises in industrial security. Also, on a small scale, and mostly for existing clients, a private investigative service. I work for Franklin Richmond.'

'Why would you want to talk to me?' Ross asked.

'Look, why don't we go inside?' McKinnon said.

Ross hesitated and McKinnon held out a tiny, flip-top mobile phone. 'Would you be happier if you checked with Franklin?'

'No, it's all right. I've come all this way.'

Five minutes later, at a quiet corner table, the American faced McKinnon over a half-pint of beer.

'My company is investigating the killing of a horse called Bellboy. What I'm about to tell you is in the strictest confidence.' He paused and looked calculatingly at Ross, as if trying to assess the risk. 'Franklin was keen that you should know. You seem to have made quite an impression on him.'

'But how can *I* help? Hasn't the trail gone a little cold?'

'It might have, if that was all there was to it,' McKinnon agreed. 'Look, I need to fill you in on a little background information.'

'OK.' Ross was interested in spite of himself. 'Shoot.'

'Franklin Richmond is a successful and extremely wealthy businessman. He has built up his financial consultancy to international proportions. In common with many other wealthy men, he indulges a passion for horses. In fact, he devotes every spare minute that he has to his showjumpers. You can imagine how he felt when one Sunday evening last October he received an anonymous phone call telling him that Bellboy, his internationally successful jumper and personal favourite, was lying in the straw with his throat cut.'

'That's really sick! Did you trace the call?'

'Yes. A phone box on a lonely stretch of road near Blandford. Not a chance of anyone having seen anything at that time of night, and the telephone had been wiped clean. Not a single print.'

'Sick but clever,' Ross observed. 'You're absolutely sure Richmond didn't do it himself for the insurance?'

'I'd stake my life on it,' McKinnon stated firmly, then added a little sheepishly, 'besides we checked. His alibi was watertight. Admittedly he could have employed a third party, but in reality the sums involved would be chicken feed to a man like Franklin.'

Ross smiled at this flawed avowal of trust. He supposed a lack of faith came with the job. 'Obviously he didn't recognise the voice?'

'He said it sounded Irish. But no, he didn't recognise it.'

'He has no obvious enemies?'

'No, we don't think so. In general, Franklin Richmond is honest and fair. He seems to be almost universally well liked.'

'So,' Ross said slowly, 'I guess that makes it extortion. A demand for money. Pay up or we'll do worse.'

McKinnon inclined his head, a faint smile playing about his lips. 'Impressive, Mr Wakelin. Yes, a message was left exactly a week later, again from a remote telephone kiosk. Richmond was to make regular, specified payments into a numbered account in the Cayman Islands or another of his horses would meet with a sticky end. The police were not to be involved.'

No wonder Franklin was edgy when he was told Sailor had been poisoned, Ross thought. He swallowed the last of his beer. 'And now, I guess, we get to the reason why you're telling me all this.'

'Well, Franklin thinks it might be worth asking you to keep your eyes and ears open for anything that might seem unusual.'

'But what about the police? And the insurance company? What did they make of it?'

'They investigated, of course. The insurance company had Franklin bring in a security firm to guard his remaining horses day and night. But after a couple of months they were convinced that it was a one-off. We obviously couldn't tell them what was really going on. For one thing they would probably have withdrawn their cover in a flash.'

Ross was thoughtful. 'If I agreed to report anything unusual, that's all I would do—no snooping around or asking questions.'

'Just keep your eyes and ears open,' McKinnon agreed. He handed Ross a slip of paper. 'If you need to contact me, you can ring that number,' he said. 'It's my private line. So you will help?'

Ross sighed. 'I guess so,' he said at last. 'Just eyes and ears, though. Nothing more.'

ROSS HAD LITTLE OPPORTUNITY to think over what McKinnon had told him, for that weekend saw his first show in England. It was a big agricultural show not far from Basingstoke.

Ross drove the Oakley Manor horsebox, glad of the distraction. He was nervous. So many people were going to be watching him closely, assessing his ability not only to ride but also to compete. A supportive team would have been a great plus, but Ross had the uneasy feeling that Leo, who sat beside him in unfriendly silence, would not be too devastated if he made a fool of himself.

'What's the time?' Ross asked as they began to gain speed on the main road.

'Haven't you got a watch?' Leo returned cockily.

'Sure, but I can't find it . . .' Ross's voice tailed off and he glanced sideways at Leo, who wore what could only be described as a smirk. 'Have *you* got it?' he demanded.

'What would I want with your watch, Yank? I've got my own.'

Ross wasn't sure what to think. He could have sworn he'd put the watch on the shelf above the sink in the tack room while he groomed King, but it wasn't there when he went back. It hadn't occurred to him before that anyone might have taken it, but now . . .

When they reached the showground Leo became a model of efficiency. He unloaded and tacked up the horses as they were needed, and warmed up King while Ross walked the course.

Once in the saddle, Ross's nerves evaporated. This was his job. He knew what had to be done and he would do it. Lifted by Ross's confidence, King's Defender took his first class easily and added a fourth place later in the day. Simone, an excitable mare whose speciality was speed classes, rounded the day off with a first and a third.

Colonel Preston had arrived shortly after ten o'clock, and watched the proceedings with every appearance of satisfaction. Even Bill Scott looked a little less sour as the day wore on.

The Colonel appeared in the horsebox park as the horses were being loaded for the return journey. 'All well?' he asked.

'Sure.' Ross heaved up the spring-loaded ramp and secured it in place. 'I'm pleased with them—they all did well.'

'You didn't do so badly yourself,' the Colonel said. 'For a Yank.'

'Thank you, sir.' Ross smiled, well satisfied.

THE NEXT DAY was Monday, officially the yard's day off. Leo and Sarah were free and Bill looked after the horses with help from a local farmer's daughter. Bill's rest day was supposed to be Tuesday, but according to Sarah he seldom took it.

Ross rose later than normal, but out of habit went down to the yard to help, unable to remain idle. Over breakfast he voiced his intention to ride some of the horses that had missed out on exercise the day before.

After working Bishop in the arena, Ross saddled Red Queen, a chestnut mare nicknamed Ginger, and set off to explore the countryside. Like Black Bishop and King's Defender, Red Queen belonged to Robbie Fergusson, who, Ross had discovered, was an international chess player of standing, which explained the names.

Ross rode down the lane behind the Manor and past some farm

cottages where a German shepherd came leaping to the end of its chain. As he made his way down a narrow bridleway and into the shelter of a valley the sun became quite hot and flies began to buzz round both horse and rider. Ross broke a whippy branch from a willow tree and used it to fan his face. Ginger swished her tail and shook her head.

'The flies bothering you too, girl?' he asked, and leaned forward to flick the leafy branch round her ears.

She stopped dead, her body taut and quivering.

Ross laughed. 'Come on, girl. Stop messing me about.'

In spite of his urging her, the chestnut mare refused to budge. Exasperated, he stung her with the twig in his hand.

With a high-pitched squeal, Ginger ripped the reins through his fingers and bolted, heading at top speed for a copse halfway up the valley side. Ross searched desperately for a gap in the trees large enough to admit a horse and rider at speed, and found none. He abandoned attempts to slow the mare, throwing all his weight onto one rein in an effort to turn her. Gradually she came round, and tore downhill into the boggy stream that ran through the valley.

As her forefeet sank into the mud, her momentum carried her body up and over to land heavily on her back. Ross was catapulted clear, hitting the soft ground with his shoulder and rolling to his feet, the reins, from long practice, still gripped firmly in his left hand.

Ginger regained her feet swiftly and lunged clear of the marshy ground, dragging Ross with her for a few feet before stopping. Her ears were flicking back and forth and her whole body shook.

'Steady, girl. Easy does it.' Ross kept his voice low and steady, trying to convey a calmness he was far from feeling.

Ginger stared past him with white-rimmed eyes, her attention apparently focused on some terror he could not comprehend. Then, suddenly, she heaved a shuddering sigh and was quiet.

Ross stepped closer and patted her. She seemed relaxed now. He straightened the saddle and leaned weakly against her neck with his eyes closed and began to shake uncontrollably.

TUESDAY DAWNED clear and sunny. Ross trudged out into the yard feeling as though he hadn't slept for a week. The nightmares had returned with a vengeance. He did not mention the Ginger incident.

After breakfast he rode Flowergirl, the bouncy mare he had ridden on his first morning, out in the fields with the others and survived a spirited attempt to buck him off. He rode back to the yard half-believing he had imagined his fears of the day before. If only he could get the picture of Ginger's wild, unfocused stare out of his mind . . .

When he returned, Bill was leading Ginger out into the sunshine. The mare was due for a schooling session with Ross as she was entered in an evening show the following day.

Once aboard, any apprehension he may have had vanished. Ginger did all that was asked of her. She was no more or less dangerous than any other horse. It was just an unfortunate coincidence that she was a chestnut mare, as Vixen had been. Vixen had had a brain tumour—a once-in-a-lifetime chance. Ginger was just a little moody, as redheads often are.

Bill seemed pleased, which was unusual for him. 'Stephen Douglas didn't like that mare, but she seems to go well for you.'

'She can certainly jump when she feels like it,' Ross agreed. 'Let's hope she feels like it tomorrow.'

Bill nodded. 'Mr Richmond has just arrived. He's brought Peter with him. I think Peter's hoping to see you ride Clown.'

Peter, Ross had learned, was Franklin Richmond's twelve-year-old son, whose developing passion for horses had been rewarded by the birthday gift, some months before, of Clown, an exuberant young skewbald who, at six, was just being introduced to serious training.

Leo had brought Clown out and Ross could see Franklin running his hands over the horse, watched by a slim, fair-haired boy.

'Morning, Ross.' Franklin turned to meet him with a smile. 'This is my son Peter, who's got a day off school,' Richmond said, putting his hand on the boy's head. 'Peter owns Clown.'

The boy glowed with pleasure and held out his hand to Ross, a touch of shyness in his serious grey eyes.

'Hi, Peter. That's a fine animal you have there.' Ross shook the small hand solemnly.

'He's out of a Grade-A jumping mare, by the son of a Grand National winner, so he should jump.' Pride echoed in every syllable of Peter's voice.

'Oh, he will,' Ross assured him. 'Once we get his mind on the job.'

The schooling session went well, on the whole. Clown put on a rodeo act, to the delight of his youthful owner, but eventually worked off his high spirits and began to work quite sensibly. It was clear, as Ross rode up to the gate at the end of the session, that Clown's exhibition had done Ross no harm in Richmond Junior's eyes.

AT THE LEA FARM indoor show the next evening, the Oakley Manor horses were in sparkling form. Ross pulled off a marvellous win on Butterworth in the Open class, the biggest of the show. But his contentment was short-lived, for as Sarah led Butterworth from his stable the next morning, it was clear that something was very wrong. The big gelding walked stiffly into the yard with his back hunched and head held low.

With a cold, sinking feeling, Ross signalled to Sarah to stop and walked over to inspect the horse. He ran his hands along Butterworth's spine and down his hind legs and was rewarded by a distinct flinch and a flattening of chestnut ears.

Bill came up behind the American. 'Back?' he asked.

'Yeah. He's in a fair amount of pain.' Ross sighed, motioning Sarah to put Butterworth back in the box.

'I'll call Annie,' Bill said.

'Who's Annie?' Ross wanted to know.

'A kind of equine chiropractor,' Bill told him.

ANNIE HAYWARD ARRIVED at noon in a Land-Rover that looked as though it had seen service in both World Wars. Somewhere between thirty and fifty, she was a huge woman with a weather-beaten face and a voice that would have put a foghorn to shame. Although she dressed like a farmer, in jeans and a checked shirt, her long, honey-gold hair was plaited and secured with an incongruous pink ribbon.

Annie pushed, pulled and prodded, and finally slammed the heel of her palm into the side of Butterworth's spine with a force that made him stagger. 'Now lead him out,' she boomed.

Bill led the chestnut into the yard. The horse moved gingerly at first, as though waiting for the pain, but then gradually relaxed.

Ross was impressed.

Annie nodded. 'No more jumping for a bit for this one, I'm afraid. Turn him out to grass for six weeks or so then I'll come again.' She mopped her brow with something that looked suspiciously like a dishcloth. 'Any beer in the fridge?' she enquired.

'Sure.' Ross smiled and went to the stable office next to the tack room to fetch some.

As he stepped inside there was a slithering crash to his right. Leo was standing by the refrigerator. Behind him on the floor lay a jumble of pens and papers and an upturned tray.

'What in hell are you doing?' Ross demanded.

'Just getting a beer, Yank. What are you doing?' Leo returned.

'You don't need to turn the office upside-down to find the fridge.'

'I knocked it. It slipped,' Leo said dismissively.

'OK. Bring a four-pack while you're there.' Ross swallowed his irritation. To rise to the bait would only give Leo satisfaction.

WITH BUTTERWORTH out of action, Ross had to concentrate on bringing the others up to his standard. He had high hopes of King's Defender, who was a definite prospect for the international shows at Hickstead or Birmingham. At fourteen, however, King could not have many more seasons in him. Of the younger horses, Ross's greatest expectations lay with the big, German-bred Black Bishop.

In the copse behind the home meadow, somebody had at some time built a small cross-country course of rustic jumps, and on the day following Annie Hayward's visit, Ross saddled Bishop and took him out into the copse for a training session. The value of the low rustic fences was in their rigid construction, which encouraged the horses to pick their feet up, and the undulating terrain, which promoted sure-footedness and good balance.

Bishop worked like a dream. He skimmed through the wood, giving all the jumps at least a foot's clearance, enjoyment evident in every stride. Ross walked him back, dreaming of the places he could go with this exceptional young horse.

A sudden rustling in the hedge caused Bishop to shy and Ross turned to see a long black snout and forepaws pushing through the quickthorn. The newcomer scrambled out and proved to be the German shepherd from the local farm.

'You're trespassing,' Ross told it with mock severity.

The dog watched him warily but when he rode on it followed, and when he reached the yard it flopped down in the shade of the overhang and appeared happy to stay there.

Ross fed the dog on scraps from the cottage kitchen before setting out to exercise Clown on the roads. It trotted at a discreet distance from Clown's heels as if it had been doing so all its life.

Ross called in at the farm on his way past and discovered the farmer mending a fence in his back garden.

'Brought the bugger back, have yer?' the farmer grunted. 'Thought it might have got run under this time. More trouble than it's worth.'

'I'll take him off your hands if you don't want him,' Ross offered. 'I'll give you fifty pounds for him.'

The farmer rubbed his chin. 'Well now, he's worth a lot more . . .'

'Not to me, he's not.' Ross turned away.

'Cash?' the farmer said hurriedly.

'Cash,' Ross agreed, taking his wallet from his back pocket.

AFTER LUNCH, Ross took Flowergirl into the arena for a schooling session. There was a big show on Sunday, and the exuberant little mare had been having trouble with spread fences so he wanted to get her sorted out if he could.

At the end of an hour both horse and rider were damp with sweat. Flo was a rewarding pupil, though, and Ross was well content with her progress as he turned her loose.

'Nice work.'

Ross turned to see Franklin Richmond leaning on the gate.

'Are you mad at me for last Thursday?' Franklin asked.

'No, not really. McKinnon explained your reasons.' Ross paused, hunting for a way to say what he wanted to. 'Look, I appreciate the difficulty you're in, but I don't see what good I can possibly do.'

'Well—I thought it couldn't do any harm, your knowing. We've come to a dead end and you might just stumble onto something.'

'You seem very cool about this blackmail thing, I'd be tearing my hair out.'

'I did at first,' Richmond told him with a resigned smile. 'But it's been nearly eight months now. You can only live in fear so long. Then the threat becomes part of your life. Until something like the other night happens, and then you start jumping at shadows again.'

Or in my case, something like Ginger, Ross thought, wryly.

'Isn't this ruining you?' he asked.

'No, but I've had to tighten my belt quite a few holes. Whoever it is has gauged it about right.'

'But surely this guy doesn't imagine you're going to go on paying him for ever? He must know you'll try to catch him.'

'Oh, yes, he knows. He likes to show off what he's learned about my actions. This guy is playing with me and he's enjoying watching me wriggle. He's left several messages on my answerphone. "Good to see Woodsmoke going so well"; "Had a puncture today, did you, Richmond?" That sort of thing. I feel like nothing I do is private.'

'You think it's someone you know personally, then?'

'I suppose so. It smacks of personal spite. But I can't conceive who would do such a thing.'

'Your marriage . . . ?' Ross let the question tail off, wondering if it would be considered impertinent.

'Over,' Richmond said, shortly but without rancour. 'Divorce.'

'Does she hold a grudge?'

'Marsha? She wouldn't even know how to spell it. She certainly couldn't put together anything like this. Besides, the courts made sure she'd never lack for money.'

'Does she have a boyfriend?' Ross asked.

'Dozens.' Richmond shook his head at Ross's enquiring glance. 'No, nothing there, I wouldn't have thought. All lightweights, flotsam and jetsam. Pretty boys attracted by her face and her money.'

'And there was no trouble over custody of Peter or anything?'

'No, Marsha's mercenary instincts are far stronger than her maternal ones. Peter visits her about once a month and she never gives me the impression that parting from him is any great wrench. A small boy would cramp her style pretty much, I imagine.' Richmond changed track as Bill appeared in the tack-room doorway. 'Well, I have to be going. I'll see you at the show on Sunday. I'm bringing Peter along to see Clown's debut. He's very excited.'

WHEN ROSS AND LEO set off for the South Midlands show that Sunday morning, they took with them an extra pair of hands in the person of Danny Scott, Bill's fifteen-year-old son. Ross had met him fleetingly the previous weekend, but during the week the boy lived with his aunt to be nearer his school in Salisbury. Danny was a slim youth, with dark hair and a thin, intense face. When they arrived at the showground, he proved to be every bit as capable as Leo.

Clown came out of the horsebox looking like a kid at Disneyland: bright, eager eyes darting every which way. Ross tacked the horse up, sprang into the saddle and rode him off to a quiet corner of the field.

By the time he was called for his first class, Clown had settled a little, but his round was patchy. While he concentrated, he jumped well, but a fair few poles adorned the turf when they left the ring. There was as yet no sign of Franklin Richmond and his son, for which Ross was grateful.

The Colonel arrived midmorning, in time to see Flowergirl win her novice class. Afterwards, as Ross rode Clown round the showground, hoping to familiarise him with all the sights and sounds, he watched Stephen Douglas, the Colonel's previous rider, jump a lucky clear round on an impetuous grey gelding. He knew Douglas would recognise the skewbald from the Colonel's yard, and so smiled in a friendly fashion as the boy came out of the ring. Douglas deliberately turned away and Ross was mildly disappointed.

Around midday, the bigger classes began in the main ring, and Ross jumped an immaculate round on King's Defender. When he returned to the ring on King for the jump-off against the clock, two horses had already gone clear and the time to beat was fairly tight.

As Ross circled the ring to settle his mount, the public address system crackled into life. 'Next to jump we have number three five six, Ross Wakelin on Mr R. Fergusson's King's Defender. Ross has recently come over from America, where he had a particularly disastrous last season, and has taken over the ride on this horse from one of our own young riders.'

Ross was surprised to listen to this rather unflattering description of his recent history.

He rode King on a fluent, time-efficient line, turning tightly, but not so tightly as to interrupt his rhythm. As they turned to the last line of fences, Ross pushed King for every ounce of effort, lifting him with hands and heels at each jump. They flew the triple bar, King's toes just clicking on the top pole as they went over, and steadied for the upright to finish. The crowd cheered and clapped as horse and rider shot between the timing beacons.

'Mr Wakelin goes into the lead with a time of forty-two-point-eight-five seconds,' the commentator announced over the loudspeaker.

Colonel Preston was waiting outside the collecting ring, accompanied by a tall wiry man with a shock of red hair and piercing blue eyes that were almost hidden by low bushy brows. Ross jumped down.

'Ross, this is Robbie Fergusson,' the Colonel announced.

Ross had guessed as much. He held out his hand with a smile. 'Hi. How d'you do? This is one hell of a horse, you know.'

Fergusson's clasp was strong and brief. 'It's the first time he's been ridden properly for months,' he said, somehow making the compliment sound more like a complaint. The Scotsman fixed Ross with a bright blue gaze. 'I'll expect significant improvement from all my horses this summer,' he told him. 'I pay a fortune to keep them with the Colonel and lately I've seen sod-all in return.'

'I'll do my best,' Ross promised. He caught sight of Leo approaching, riding Clown and flanked by Franklin and Peter Richmond.

'They're calling you for your other class,' Leo told Ross as he jumped off the skewbald and exchanged reins with the American.

Ross vaulted onto Clown's back and turned towards the novice ring.

'How's he going, Ross?' Peter asked excitedly.

'Oh, fine,' Ross lied cheerfully. 'But you must remember it's all very new to him and not expect too much.'

Clown's class was testing and Ross didn't hold out much hope of completing the course, but the skewbald surprised them all. After an experimental buck as he began to canter, he settled down and actually started to concentrate on the job in hand. They left the ring with eight faults and a feeling of satisfaction on Ross's part.

Peter was thrilled with Clown's progress. Together with Franklin, they made their way back to the main ring.

'How many more to go?' Ross asked one of the other riders.

'This is the last and you're still the fastest clear.' Then as a pole dropped to the turf, 'That's it! You've done it! Well done!'

Ross mounted King and rode into the ring to receive his rosette and prize. He was aware of Stephen Douglas scowling at him from lower down the line but didn't let it bother him. Peter's face was radiant.

Ross's last classes of the day were for Black Bishop. The horse proved to have the perfect competitive temperament. Completely unruffled by the occasion, he jumped everything high and wide with intense concentration, never hitting anything.

'Come up in the world, haven't we?' a husky female voice commented from slightly behind Ross, before their second class.

He turned. 'Danielle!' he exclaimed delightedly. A petite, pretty brunette, Danielle Moreaux was a successful international rider from Belgium and a girl he had dated a time or two.

'Ross, it's nice to see you again,' she said warmly. 'Back on the winning track I see, too. I was told in America you had given up.'

'I had.' Ross grinned. 'One last try.'

'You have some nice horses this time, I think,' she said.

Ross nodded. 'This fella's one of the best I've ever ridden,' he agreed. 'But he's young yet. I don't want to rush him.'

'You deserve some luck. Oh, number thirty-five, that's me!'

Ross watched appreciatively as she rode away, a neat figure in black jacket and cream breeches astride a grey thoroughbred.

In due course, Bishop jumped an immaculate clear and followed it with another in the jump-off. Ross didn't push him for a fast time, unwilling to do anything to upset the young horse's wonderful rhythm and balance at this early stage.

'A clear round,' the commentator confirmed. 'But a slow time of fifty-eight seconds. You'll have to try a bit harder than that, Ross.'

Ross was furious. 'What's with that guy?' he demanded of Danielle as they passed in the collecting ring.

'Well, I suppose you can't expect him to be your biggest fan,' she said matter-of-factly. 'That's Harry Douglas. He does the commentary on TV and at all the big shows over here.'

The light dawned. 'Douglas, as in *Stephen* Douglas?'

'Exactly.' Danielle nodded. 'In his eyes you're riding the horses his son should be riding. The fact that Stephen made a mess of the job is presumably beside the point to daddy's way of thinking.'

Her number was called and she rode away, leaving Ross to reflect that with opposition in such influential places, gaining recognition in England could prove to be just as hard as it had been in the States.

THE NEXT MORNING, Ross was busy schooling Simone in the arena when the Colonel appeared. Ross did another ten minutes or so and then rode over to the gate where the Colonel waited, watching.

'Ross, I'm afraid Fergusson has decided to sell King. He had a good offer yesterday and sees it as a way to cover some expenses.'

Ross's face hardened against the familiar disappointment. 'I see.'

'I'm sorry.' The Colonel sounded genuinely so. 'The thing is, King is in good health and the form of his life but at fourteen, as you know, his value can realistically only go down.'

'Sure, I understand,' Ross said with resignation. 'You know he qualified for Birmingham yesterday?'

'Yes, I know,' the Colonel said quietly. 'That clinched the deal.'

JUST BEFORE NOON the following day, a red MG Roadster drew up in the yard and Lindsay climbed out, looking slim and tanned in cotton hipsters and a cropped top. Ross had just finished hosing Bishop down after a hard session in the school. He turned the tap off and went towards her, smiling widely. 'Hi! When did you get back? And why didn't you tell me?' He gave her a welcoming kiss on the cheek.

'Yesterday. It was a spur-of-the-moment decision. I've been longing to see how you're getting on and suddenly I couldn't wait any longer, so I rang the airport and they had a cancellation. I was going to ring but then I thought I'd surprise you all.'

'You're just in time for coffee,' Ross told her. 'Let me put Bishop away and we'll go and find Maggie.'

'Do you know, that's one of the things I've missed most about England. Maggie's baking.' Lindsay laughed. 'That and Gypsy. I'm longing to ride her again.'

The Colonel's yard was barely three miles from the sizeable Georgian manor where Lindsay's family lived and which was managed as a venue for conferences and up-market functions. She had told Ross that throughout her childhood her ponies and horses had been stabled at Oakley Manor to prevent her becoming, as her mother put it, 'one of those abominable little horsy girls who always smell of stables'. As the only child of the Cresswells of Cresswell Hall, she was expected to make a suitable marriage and in due course take over the running of the Hall.

Seated at the table in the Scotts' cottage, Lindsay demanded to hear, in detail, about all Ross's successes to date. Eventually Ross remembered that he had another horse to ride before lunch.

'Come on, back to work,' he said, standing up.

Lindsay finished her coffee and cake. 'Thanks, Maggie, that was lovely. I want to see my darling Gypsy. Is she here or out in the field?'

'She's in the paddock behind the barn. I'll come with you,' Ross suggested.

As they walked, Lindsay glanced appraisingly at him. 'So how're things, really?'

'Good,' he stated. 'I'm glad I came. Thanks.'

'Oh, don't be silly! I must say you look a lot better than last time I saw you. You had me worried for a bit.'

They had reached Gypsy's field and she called the mare over.

'Yeah, well, I'm not especially proud of that little episode,' he admitted, uncomfortably.

'You had good reason.' Lindsay reached out to pat her horse. 'Anyway, it's all in the past. Now you can show them what you're really made of!'

Shortly after that, Lindsay departed to visit 'Uncle John' and Ross was left with mixed emotions. Seeing her again had lifted his spirits, but his pleasure was tempered by the knowledge that somewhere in the wings lurked the man she was to marry.

'James? Oh, he's still in Hong Kong at the moment,' she had said in answer to his casual query. 'I spoke to him two days ago but he wasn't sure how soon he'd be back.'

Ross banished the absent James to the dim recesses of his mind, along with Ginger. He was getting quite good at it.

THREE

Lindsay's return acted like a breath of fresh air blowing through the yard at Oakley Manor. She spent at least part of most days at the yard, exercising Gypsy and sometimes one of the other horses. She seemed unaware of the growing strength of feeling Ross had for her and he took care to keep it that way.

A few days after her return Ross bought a battered Jeep. Although he had been told he could borrow the yard's Land-Rover, he didn't like to use it on anything other than yard business. Besides, it was in his nature to be independent. He also equipped himself with a mobile phone. His dog took to the Jeep at once, jumping into the back as soon as Ross started the engine and travelling with his black muzzle resting on his master's shoulder. He had settled in well, lying around in shady corners while Ross was in the yard or the school, and following him into his room at night.

The horses travelled to a couple more shows and were beginning to accumulate the placings that would move them up the grades and qualify them for the bigger shows at Hickstead, Birmingham and Olympia. Franklin's problem began to fade into the back of Ross's mind. Then the spell was broken.

It was a Tuesday. Lindsay's MG swept into the yard as usual, just after breakfast, but in place of the habitual jeans and jodhpur boots, she wore a smart skirt and blouse, with pearls gleaming at her throat.

'Sorry, folks,' she said with a rueful smile. 'James is coming home at the end of the week and I've got to go shopping in London for something to wear at our engagement do.'

Ross promised to exercise Gypsy and with a cheery wave she was gone, leaving him feeling more depressed than he cared to admit.

Bill and Sarah had gone out to do road work on Flowergirl and Woodsmoke, and Leo was in the jump store repairing broken wings, when Ross rode Ginger into the school.

Moodily wondering what kind of a man Lindsay's fiancé was, Ross didn't notice the signs at first. Ginger's ears began to flick to and fro nervously and she tossed her head. Her back hunched and stiffened, and her stride became choppy and uncomfortable.

Now fully alert, Ross guessed that the hammering noises emanating from the jump store were probably at the root of her unease and he called out to Leo to stop working for the moment. At first he thought Leo had not heard, but then the door opened and, with a reverberating crash, several planks were tossed out onto the concrete.

Ginger exploded.

She whipped round and tore across the arena, heading blindly for the rails. Ross put all his weight onto one rein and pulled her head round until her muzzle was almost touching his knee and then, when a collision with the fence seemed inevitable, she lost her footing in the soft sand and fell heavily onto her side. Ross rolled off and tried to hang on to the reins as she scrambled furiously to her feet, but she ripped them through his fingers and whirled away. The mare circled the arena five times at top speed before she started to slow up.

He could see by the look in her eyes that she would run him down if he got in her way, so he waited for her to calm down in her own time. Eventually she stopped by the gate, flanks heaving. Ross steeled himself to walk quietly up and take hold of her broken rein.

She didn't move; didn't even seem to notice him. Then she shuddered and her body drooped with released tension.

Ross patted her sweaty neck and then looked round.

Leo was leaning on the fence, watching with evident enjoyment. 'Did I frighten her?' he asked innocently. 'I'm so sorry.'

Ross didn't trust himself to answer. He put the broken ends of the rein together over Ginger's neck, raised his foot to the stirrup and swung aboard once more. Ginger didn't move a muscle.

Ross knew that he hadn't remounted only to show the mare that she couldn't get away with such behaviour. He had done it to prove his nerve, and it bothered him that he should have needed to.

THE NIGHT WAS WARM and humid. Just before midnight, Ross heard Leo come in; an hour later he was still awake, tossing and turning in the too-warm darkness, aware of his throbbing leg. The knee that he had fractured when he fell from Vixen had today borne the brunt of his fall from Ginger.

At some point he must have slept, for the dreams came again: the familiar nightmare of the chestnut mare crashing through the rails, the screaming crowd, the struggling horse . . . With a gasp he awoke.

He sat up, reluctant to sleep again lest the nightmare return. His thoughts turned involuntarily to an unopened bottle of Scotch that nestled in his suitcase under the bed. He had used whisky in the past to dull the pain in his leg and help him sleep, but not for months. Now, just as he had begun to feel that things were going right at last, Ginger had reawakened the old self-doubt.

Whisky. Temptation. So easy to give in.

Ross gave himself a mental shaking. He swung out of bed, and pulled on his jeans. If he couldn't sleep, he would go for a walk.

The dog seemed pleased to be out, running round him, wagging its tail. The moon was about three-quarters full and gave just enough light through the high cloud for the American to see when he moved out into the home field. The tranquillity of the night restored some sense of perspective and after ten minutes he headed back towards his room in a much better frame of mind. Then the dog growled.

Ross stopped, eyes searching the shadows. Just as he was convinced that the dog had heard a cat or a fox, he saw a pool of light moving along the ground behind the horsebox. His heart thumping heavily, he moved forward quietly.

The torchlight flashed higher once or twice, as if searching at the stable doors for a particular head, then disappeared. It occurred to Ross that the prowler might be making for the covered corridor where the other horses were housed. Throwing caution to the winds Ross sprinted round the back of the horsebox. The dog shot past him and into the darkness of the doorway before he could stop it. Ross cursed and made to follow. Then a flicker of movement at the edge of his field of vision halted him. The prowler was still outside. He shrank into the shadows and watched.

He could hear the dog barking. He had obviously come out of the other doorway at the far end of the corridor and was now running aimlessly round the home field.

After a minute or two, a shadow detached itself from the cover of the building. Ross stepped out after it.

'Stop right there!' he said sharply.

To Ross's surprise, the shadowy figure obeyed. The prowler was of similar height and build to Ross himself and as such presumably male. His face was in darkness. He raised his hands in apparent surrender. Ross took a step closer, trying to see the man's features.

Suddenly the intruder moved. Before Ross could react, his wrist was grasped, a hand hooked under his armpit and he found himself sprawling on the gravel, gasping for air. The intruder sprinted away and as Ross regained his feet he could hear footsteps receding on the gravel drive.

Ross leant against the stable wall, deeply winded, as the dog returned and swept past him growling, apparently on the trail of the intruder at last. Seconds later Ross heard a car pull away. He waited for his breathing to become less painful, and after a moment a cold wet nose pushed itself into his hand.

'Stupid mutt,' Ross chided the dog, ruffling its coat affectionately. 'Where were you when I needed you?'

He made his way round the stables. Everything seemed in order. Most of the horses were wide awake, alerted by the commotion. None lay with its throat slit. Calling softly to the dog, he returned to his room. He knew he should have woken Bill, but Bill would probably feel it his duty to inform the police. He decided, as he lowered himself thankfully into bed, that his best course of action was to contact Franklin Richmond as soon as he could.

THE NEXT MORNING, Lindsay arrived while the exercise rota was being set, and the day settled into a familiar routine. Ross rode out with Leo and the two girls. When they clattered back into the yard an hour later, the Colonel was waiting, talking to Bill and a younger man whom Ross didn't know.

'Roland!' Lindsay cried delightedly, slipping off Gypsy and running forward to meet him.

Roland was her cousin, Ross remembered, the Colonel's son, and from the way she had spoken of him Ross knew she adored him. He jumped off Woody and followed, observing the newcomer.

Roland Preston was straight out of a fashion plate, a vision in a pale cream 1930s-style suit. His sandy hair was short and brushed back from an aristocratic brow. A pair of tinted spectacles hid his eyes and, despite the heat, a silk paisley scarf was knotted loosely about his neck. The whole effect was very P.G. Wodehouse.

He received Lindsay with open arms and swept her off her feet, swinging her round in a full circle before putting her down.

Lindsay hugged him. 'When did you get back? It's been so long,' she said, her eyes shining. 'How long has it been? A year?'

'Surely not?' Roland said in mock dismay. 'I've got a few days off and drove up from London last night.'

'Ross,' Lindsay said, drawing away from Roland, 'meet my absurd cousin Roland. Roland, this is Ross.'

The fashion plate held out a lean, tanned and perfectly manicured hand. 'Delighted, dear boy,' he drawled, smiling amiably.

'Delighted. Lindsay's told me so much about you.'

'Don't believe a word of it.'

'No?' Roland queried thoughtfully, one eyebrow raised. 'A shame. I was quite impressed.'

'Don't listen to him, Ross,' Lindsay advised.

FRANKLIN RICHMOND, when Ross telephoned him later on his mobile, seemed philosophical about the night-time intruder.

'Thanks for doing what you did,' he said, 'but be careful. I don't want anybody getting hurt over this. If it *was* our man, I can't imagine what he was up to. I mean, I'm paying up as it is. It doesn't make sense. It's almost as though he wants to keep me on edge.'

Ross had immense admiration for Richmond's strength of character. He supposed a man who daily thought and dealt in millions became used to pressure.

SLEEP WAS TENACIOUS in its grip on him that night and Ross was just emerging from under the duvet when he heard the chorus of whinnies that habitually greeted Sarah's arrival in the yard. He pulled his jeans on and padded on bare feet out into the bathroom. He was on his way back to his room when he heard the scream.

He was down the stairs and across the yard before its echoes had died away, Leo right behind him. Bill appeared from the cottage as Ross burst through the doorway into the covered corridor and collided with Sarah on her way out at top speed.

'It's Clown!' she sobbed. 'Oh, God, it's happened again!'

Ross pushed her away. 'No. Please, no,' he begged under his breath as he raced along the corridor to Clown's stable.

The skewbald stood in the corner of his box, eyes rolling wildly, his whole body trembling with violent muscular spasms. What stopped Ross in his tracks, however, was the blood. Clown's white throat was drenched with it and in places it had splashed and run down the whitewashed brick walls of his stable. It seemed inconceivable that a horse could have lost so much blood and still be standing.

'Jesus!' Leo had caught up and was peering over Ross's shoulder.

'Go and call the vet,' Ross urged. 'Quickly!'

For once Leo obeyed instantly and without question, collecting the office key from Bill as he passed him in the corridor.

Ross unhooked Clown's head collar from its place outside the door and advanced slowly into the stable, murmuring soothing nonsense to the distressed animal. Clown backed further into his corner.

'Steady, little fella,' Ross told him. 'Easy now. Nobody's gonna hurt you. You'll be all right now. Steady, fella.'

Slowly, very slowly, Ross slid the head-collar rope over Clown's neck and after a minute was able to slip the head collar on.

'West is coming straight away,' Leo reported, appearing abruptly behind Bill in the doorway.

'What do you think, Ross?' Bill asked softly. 'How bad is he?'

'I may be wrong,' Ross said, looking the horse over, 'but at the moment I can't see any major wounds.'

Bill looked puzzled. 'There must be. There's so much blood.'

Ross nodded. 'But I don't think it's his.'

'What?' Bill struggled to take in Ross's words. 'I don't understand.'

'Me neither.' Ross shivered. 'Best make up another box for him.'

When Roger West arrived fifteen minutes later, Clown had been washed down, covered with a blanket and moved to a different stable. The vet examined him, eventually pronouncing him free from injury but deeply traumatised. He gave him a sedative injection and left after taking samples of the blood from the walls of his stable.

'What now?' Ross asked, as he and Bill watched West's Range Rover depart. 'Shouldn't we call the police?'

Bill shook his head. 'I rang the Colonel. He said no, he'll speak to Mr Richmond first. He wants us both up at the house at ten.'

ROSS AND THE STABLE manager walked up to the house. As the two men approached the door, Bill looked at his watch. 'It's about ten, isn't it? This old watch is slow and I've lost my other one.'

'What, your gold one?' the American exclaimed. 'I thought that was on a chain.'

'It was. Bloody thing broke,' Bill said disgustedly.

'That's a shame! Well, you might find it yet, though I never found mine. Maybe Leo will turn it up while he's raking the school.'

The Colonel and Richmond were awaiting them in the Colonel's study. The four men rearranged chairs and other articles of furniture until they could all be seated comfortably.

'Franklin and I have been discussing this deplorable business,' the Colonel began. 'And we feel we should take steps towards better security, at night at least. Having said that, we have decided that intensive and complicated security measures are undesirable and impractical. We wouldn't wish to turn Oakley Manor into a Fort Knox.'

A light tap at the door heralded the arrival of Masters bearing a coffee tray. He was followed closely by Roland, immaculately attired in the kind of expensive country casuals that might grace the models in *Country Life*, and by Lindsay, in jeans and jodhpur boots as usual. Ross's spirits lifted instantly.

'Oh, I say! Are we interrupting something?' Roland exclaimed, in a manner that suggested he had no intention of letting the possibility deter him. He greeted Franklin and nodded to Ross and Bill.

'Franklin, I'm so sorry about Clown,' Lindsay said. 'What a horrible thing to have happened!'

Coffee was served and conversation became general.

Roland, Ross discovered, had a positive genius for making sudden changes of conversation, quite often in response to some remark which he appeared to have misheard. Ross watched him carefully, but try as he might could not decide whether the Colonel's son was really as flaky as he appeared or whether he was privately amusing himself. If he was trying to annoy his father he was certainly doing a good job of it.

'Dangerous sport, showjumping,' Roland observed, apparently to his coffee cup. 'Don't fancy it, myself.'

'You wouldn't fancy anything that might soil your hands or spoil your favourite suit,' the Colonel said with undisguised contempt.

'No, I shouldn't think I would,' his son agreed. 'I'll leave that sort of thing to our all-American action boy.' He observed Ross with a fleeting glint of amusement in his grey eyes.

'Don't let him fool you,' Lindsay said to Ross, laughing. 'You are looking at the hardest rider to hounds Wiltshire has ever seen. Roland was tipped to become Master a few years ago.'

'So, what happened?' Ross enquired.

'He went to Sandhurst,' Lindsay informed him.

'Sandhurst?' Ross was lost.

'Army officer training,' the Colonel supplied. 'Like West Point. They were wasting their time, though.'

Roland made a face. 'Up at dawn, square-bashing, assault courses, mud, bossy sergeant majors . . . and guns! I never could get used to those guns.' He shuddered dramatically.

'Oh, shut up,' Lindsay said, exasperated. 'He was in the army for eight years, Ross. He was very good at it.'

The Colonel stood up, heading for his desk. 'He threw away a promising career,' he grunted. 'Works in a bloody china shop now.'

'Antiques,' Roland said, mildly. 'Import and export.'

'Whatever,' his father said dismissively. 'Look, we have business to get on with.'

After the progress of various horses had been discussed, the meeting broke up with Lindsay saying she had to meet James at the station. Ross watched her go with regret, supposing that with her boyfriend on the scene she would be a less frequent visitor to Oakley Manor. She had already confided that her mother wasn't happy with the amount of time she had been spending with the horses.

Ross took advantage of a period of quiet to school Ginger. He was finding her increasingly difficult to understand. On this occasion she was willing, if not eager. Her flatwork was supple and obedient and she jumped with good style. Still Ross was not happy with her. She felt to him like an automaton, characterless and uninspiring.

Towards the end of the hour he had allotted the mare, he noticed Franklin Richmond leaning on the gate and he rode over.

'What did you make of this morning's demonstration?' he asked.

'He goes to a lot of trouble, doesn't he?' Richmond said. 'I'm awaiting the message that will undoubtedly follow. As I said before, it's as though he's playing with us. I think he felt the game was becoming a little too tame.'

Ross frowned. 'A dangerous sort of game.'

'I shan't pay him any more, you know,' Franklin said. 'I've had enough. I'm having the yard watched again, secretly. McKinnon will arrange it.'

'Do you think that'll work?'

'I don't know. I hope so. I've got to do something.'

'What do you know about Roland?'

Franklin laughed. 'Got your detective's hat on again? I've known Roland as long as I've known John. He hasn't spent much time here lately, but he went to school with my nephew Darcy. His relationship with his father is somewhat strained, but he's harmless. I'd describe him as a determined eccentric. Look, I've got to go. Work to do. Look out for yourself, OK?'

'Sure,' Ross said. 'You too.'

THE GLOUCESTER SHOW ran over the weekend. Although stabling was provided for competitors, Ross and Bill had decided to travel up on both days so they could enter the maximum number of horses.

The Oakley Manor contingent set out at six thirty in the morning.

Once on the showground, Leo and Danny unloaded the horses.

Franklin Richmond arrived at ten o'clock with Peter and a fair-haired, smartly dressed young man of about Ross's age whom he introduced as his nephew, Darcy. They were just in time to see Clown jump a clear round in his class, following it with an unlucky four faults in the jump-off. Peter was over the moon. Darcy confided in Ross that he didn't really understand the finer details of the game, but he knew his uncle thought Ross was doing a great job.

While Ross was walking Flowergirl round the collecting ring prior to her first class, Stephen Douglas passed by looking tense and unhappy. The reason, it transpired, was his ride in the class, an extremely powerful dark chestnut, whose sole ambition seemed to be to proceed as fast as possible in whatever direction he happened to be headed. Douglas had tried to combat the animal's natural inclination with a bewildering array of straps and curbs. The horse, far from being subdued, fought all the harder.

'That boy hasn't a hope of holding him,' Bill said, coming alongside Ross. 'He's just too much horse. Should have been gelded years ago but some pop star owns him and won't hear of it. I ask you, who'd want to breed a foal with that temperament? He's a failed racehorse, you know. Used to run away going down to the start and wouldn't go in the starting stalls when he got there.'

With his head tied down, the stallion could hardly see where he was going, and consequently made matchwood of three of the first five fences. Then the leather strap snapped, the stallion got his head up and was away. Douglas made a creditable attempt to control the horse for the next two jumps, which they took at racing speed, but thereafter the initiative belonged with the horse. They circled the ring three times before the chestnut slowed enough for his rider to jump off; the commentator announced that Stephen Douglas and Telamon had retired.

Douglas trudged past Ross just outside the collecting ring.

'Bad luck,' the American said.

'Piss off!' Douglas hissed venomously.

Ross shrugged philosophically.

Flo won her class, and went on to a third place later in the day. Simone was in sparkling form, narrowly beaten by Danielle Moreaux's gelding in her first class and turning the tables in the second.

Franklin Richmond and his family were waiting to congratulate Ross as he left the ring.

'I should say that has successfully laid the ghosts, hasn't it?' Franklin asked Ross quietly.

Ross nodded. 'I hope so.'

DAY TWO OF THE SHOW was a little less hectic. The lorry was full again, with Woodsmoke, Bishop and Ginger taking their turn. Also travelling with them was Gypsy, although Lindsay herself was making the journey in her boyfriend's car.

Ross was uncomfortably aware of Ginger's presence in the lorry. She had not misbehaved since her outburst of temperament in the school earlier that week, but the possibility was there. In the night the nightmare had struck again, and this morning he felt edgy and tired.

At the showground they parked and Ross leaned his head back and closed his eyes.

Voices outside. Lindsay had arrived.

'Hi, Ross. Good journey? Fit and raring to go?'

'Fine,' he lied. 'You?'

'Oh, it was lovely to be chauffeur-driven for a change,' she said. 'James, come and meet Ross Wakelin.'

The young man who stepped forward as Ross jumped down from the cab was tall, well built and good-looking.

Ross smiled and held out his hand. 'So you're the lucky guy. Pleased to meet you.'

'I've heard a lot about you,' James said. 'In fact, Lindsay talked of little else the whole way here.'

She protested: 'That's not true! We talked about a lot of things.'

He held his hands up, grinning good-naturedly. 'OK, OK! Keep your hair on, girl!'

'Well, I guess that sorted you out, fella,' Ross observed.

'Didn't it just?' James acknowledged, and departed to explore the showground with Lindsay on his arm.

The morning started fairly well. Ginger completed her first class efficiently but without flair. Bishop had an unlucky pole down in the same class, Lindsay was placed second in her first class of the day, and Woody won a top-score competition.

The Colonel arrived with Bill. They collected the latest news and results, and then took themselves off to the grandstand to meet Robbie Fergusson, who had come to see his horses jump.

Bishop was Ross's first ride after lunch and he mounted up in good time in order to give the horse a chance to settle. He rode round the outside of the main ring a couple of times, allowing his own thoughts to drift to Lindsay and James Roberts. The guy was pleasant enough, with no obvious inclination to flaunt what Ross knew to be his considerable wealth. But married to Lindsay . . . Ross couldn't see it. They didn't behave like lovers, more like old friends. Ross shrugged mentally. It was none of his business, after all.

'Mr Wakelin! Could I have a word?' A confident, well-spoken voice. The speaker was middle-aged, bespectacled and thin on top.

'Sure.' Ross reined in and dismounted.

'I'm a journalist.' The man flashed his press card. 'I write a column for the *Sportsman* and I'm doing a feature on the county showjumping scene. I'm interested in what *you*, as a newcomer to the English circuit, think of the standard at these shows.' He produced a tape recorder. 'Do you mind?' he asked, holding it up.

'No, I guess not. But I can't say I've thought much about it,' Ross said. 'I suppose there's a wider range of abilities represented than at similar events back home. You know, people who obviously keep one horse in their backyard and manage on a shoestring, whereas in the States you have to haul several hundred miles between shows and maybe spend the season on the road. You have to be pretty well-heeled to do that. I think it's good that everybody can have a go.'

'How do English horses compare with those in America, then?'

Ross laughed. 'What *is* an English horse these days?' he asked. 'Thoroughbreds are pretty much the same the world over and a lot of the horses in showjumping nowadays seem to be German or Dutch bred. There are good horses on both sides of the Atlantic.'

'You've come to England to take over the ride on Colonel Preston's horses. What makes you suppose you can improve on his previous rider's performance?'

Bishop was becoming fractious as riders gathered in the vicinity of the main ring for the start of the afternoon's bigger classes.

'Well, I can't guarantee that I will but I've had a fair bit of experience with young horses,' Ross said. 'Look, I really must get on. I'm sorry, you'll have to excuse me.'

'Of course,' the man said. 'Thank you for your time.' And without further ado, he melted into the crowd.

Ross vaulted into the saddle.

Lindsay rode alongside. 'I wondered where you'd got to,' she said. 'What did old Douglas want?'

'Not Harry Douglas?' Ross groaned. 'He said he was a journalist.'

'He *is* a journalist,' Lindsay said. 'He writes a column under a pseudonym. He's commentating here, too. What did you say to him?'

'Nothing important.' Ross frowned, trying to remember if he'd said anything that could be misconstrued. 'He seemed OK . . .'

Lindsay grimaced. 'The smile of the crocodile! He's torn several careers to shreds.'

'Thanks a lot! You've really put my mind at rest.' Feeling decidedly uneasy, Ross rode away to Bishop's next class.

In the timed jump-off, Ross had the advantage of going last and watched while the standard was set by King's Defender and his new jockey, Mick Colby. Half a dozen others tried and failed before Ross rode in on Bishop.

The horse didn't put a foot wrong. When Ross asked him to jump off an angle, he responded without fluster. Only when the final upright was landed perfectly and Ross steadied the horse after the dash for the timing beacons did he become aware of the roar of applause.

Several of the other riders slapped Ross on the back. He enjoyed the success philosophically. Another day it would no doubt be a different story. And he still had to ride Ginger in the last class.

Leo appeared to take charge of Bishop.

'Tell Danny to put the dropped noseband on Ginger,' Ross said, and went in search of a long, cool drink.

It was announced that competitors for the last class could now walk the course. This Ross did and then headed for the horsebox. He met Ginger coming in the opposite direction, but instead of being led by Danny, Lindsay was riding her.

'Hi, I thought you'd be about ready for her.' Lindsay smiled.

'Damn Danny!' Ross exclaimed. 'I particularly said I wanted her in a dropped noseband.'

'Shall I fetch it?' Lindsay offered. 'I don't think it was his fault. Leo was tacking her up.'

'No, never mind. I don't suppose it'll make much odds.'

Ginger was in a mood. He could sense it at once. Whereas that morning she had been obedient, now he felt open resentment radiating from her. She had never felt quite like this before. He was aware of a growing tension in his muscles. That wouldn't help. Horses are quick to sense the mood of their rider. He concentrated on relaxing.

Fourth to go in the class, Ross didn't have long to wait. He rode into the ring acutely aware of Robbie Fergusson's piercing, analytical eyes watching him from the grandstand.

Ross shortened his reins, and with seat and heels bullied the mare into an unwilling canter. As soon as the buzzer sounded he headed her for the first fence, intending to give her no time to think. It was an undemanding rustic pole over brushwood, but she barely slithered over it, clicking her toes on the top. The second fence followed quickly and Ross swung Ginger round to the third.

She slowed dramatically and Ross knew that he was fighting a losing battle. Her head came up, her stride grew shorter, and she stopped abruptly at the base of the third fence.

Ross knew from her demeanour that he hadn't a hope of changing her mind, but he also knew he had to give the appearance of trying. He turned the mare away to get a second run at it, and she bolted.

He put both hands on one rein and pulled her round. After three tight circles she stopped, head high and eyes showing white. She was just a hair's breadth away from berserking and the memory of those screams, those terrified faces, flashed across his inner eye.

It couldn't happen again. It must not.

Ross touched the brim of his crash hat, the signal for retiring from the competition, and turned Ginger back to the collecting ring. He hated giving in but feared the alternative.

The horses were loaded and ready to travel by the time the Colonel and Bill finally reached the lorry. The Colonel gave nothing away. Bill was looking rather less than ecstatic, though.

'You all right, Ross?' the Colonel asked. 'You could change places with Bill, if you wanted. He wouldn't mind taking the lorry home.'

Ross hesitated. He didn't particularly want to spend the journey hearing what Fergusson had had to say about his performance. The Colonel made the decision for him and within moments Ross was sinking into the passenger seat of Preston's Jaguar. The Colonel remarked that it had been an encouraging weekend. Relieved, Ross leaned back against the headrest, letting the waves of fatigue wash over him.

He woke with a start as the car turned into Oakley Manor yard. Sarah emerged from the tack room followed, Ross was surprised to see, by Darcy Richmond. As news of the day was exchanged, Ross noticed that the shy teenager was far more animated in Darcy's company than she had ever been in his. Presently Darcy excused himself, reminding Sarah that he would pick her up at half past eight. The girl positively glowed. Understanding dawned.

The Colonel departed and Ross went in search of a cup of coffee before the horsebox and its attendant workload arrived.

FOUR

U K NEWCOMER UNIMPRESSED WITH BRITISH TALENT.

Ross groaned aloud at the *Sportsman* headline. Bill had passed the paper over wordlessly as they sat down to breakfast on Monday. Ross read on. The article started with a misquote:

'I don't think much of the standard at county shows,' newcomer Ross Wakelin told me at the Gloucester Agricultural Show. Ross, who came to England after losing his job in America for reasons he was not prepared to discuss, now rides for Colonel Preston's yard at Oakley in Wiltshire.

Asked how he rated the English horses, he laughed and said, 'What is an English horse these days?' It seemed to be his opinion that British riders are less professional than their American cousins, and tend to keep their horses in their back gardens.

When asked how he intended to improve on the performance of the young rider he had replaced, Mr Wakelin, 27, implied that he had a great deal more experience—although yours truly has as yet failed to uncover any evidence of significant success in the States.

Ross smarted at the injustice of the piece.

Bill was watching him over a forkful of bacon. 'If you want to put people's backs up, you're going the right way about it.'

'I didn't say that,' Ross protested. 'Not the way he's reported it.'

'I think it's very unfair,' Maggie remarked. 'Just because Stephen wasn't up to the job.'

Leo sauntered in, yawning. He immediately spotted the paper and read it with ill-concealed relish. 'You won't be too popular if you say things like that,' he observed gleefully.

'Roger West rang earlier,' Bill announced. 'It *was* that hemlock plant that poisoned Sailor. And apparently the blood he took from Clown's stable was ox blood. I suppose it came from an abattoir.'

Ross frowned. 'Why would anyone want to do that? And what excuse would you give for wanting a bucket of ox blood?'

'And do you take your own bucket?' Leo put in, earning withering looks from the others.

ROSS AND BILL were just finishing evening stables when a silver Nissan sports car swept into the yard and Darcy Richmond eased himself smoothly out. 'Sarah still here?' he asked Ross.

'It's her day off. I think she's gone to London with her parents.'

Darcy looked briefly put out and then brightened. 'I was going to suggest going for a drink. I don't suppose you'd like to come?'

Ross's lips curved ironically. 'I'd make a poor substitute.'

Darcy laughed. 'Still, how about it?'

'Sure, why not?' The Colonel had called at lunchtime to postpone the usual Monday evening 'debriefing'.

Darcy drove them to a local pub. He was a pleasant companion. He looked pretty much as Franklin might have done twenty years ago, although whilst Franklin was dark, Darcy was fair, like Peter. Light hazel eyes looked out candidly from a face that was just beginning to thicken around the jaw line.

Ross learned that Franklin had provided for Darcy ever since Darcy's father—Franklin's brother—had died in a car accident when the boy was eleven.

'My father wasn't well off when he died,' Darcy explained. 'His business partner absconded with the contents of the bank account. He was a very unlucky man, one way and another.' Darcy smiled sadly. 'Uncle Frank's been great, though. He's treated me like a son. The best schools, university and a position in his company. My own father couldn't have done more.' Darcy paused, eyes glittering strangely in the half-light.

'And you get on well with Peter?' Ross remarked.

'Yes.' Darcy smiled warmly. 'He's a terrific kid. We're very close. He's gone out tonight. A school friend's birthday party. Local cinema and on to McDonald's, you know the sort of thing.'

Ross nodded.

'Uncle Frank married Marsha when I was fifteen,' Darcy continued, remembering. 'She was some lady. She was unfaithful, you know. She was like a butterfly, beautiful but flighty. She could never have settled for long.'

Ross digested this. Franklin hadn't admitted in so many words that his wife had been unfaithful, though Ross had guessed it.

They drank in silence for a moment, then Darcy looked at Ross. 'So, what's the story of *your* life then?'

'Just a crazy ambition and one long battle against the odds. I loved horses and, I guess, I loved the challenge, so I took it.'

'Well, it seems to have been the right move. I know Uncle Frank thinks you're a hot property.' Darcy smiled, reaching for Ross's glass. 'Another drink?'

Ross nodded and thanked him.

'I don't suppose he'll find another Bellboy in a hurry, more's the pity,' Darcy said, returning a few moments later with the drinks. 'In fact, he only got *him* after practically pinching him from under old Fergusson's nose. Who wasn't best pleased, I can tell you. "I've a mind tae take ye tae court over the matter."' Darcy did a fair, if exaggerated, imitation of Fergusson's Scottish tones. 'You've heard Bellboy was killed, of course?'

'Sure, Lindsay told me. Were you around when it happened?'

'No, I wasn't. I had a long weekend off work and went sailing. I wish I'd been here. My uncle was devastated.' Darcy shook his head, sadly. 'They never did catch the bastard responsible. Uncle Frank just says it was a one-off. He can't believe anyone would do that sort of thing to get at him. He's so good-natured, sees the best in everyone, but he's trodden on a few toes in his time, I can tell you. When you're in business you can't help it. And now, I hear, someone is threatening Peter's horse.' He looked disgusted. 'Honestly, how low can you go? Tell me, why do you suppose whoever it was used real blood? Surely red paint would have done? It's bizarre.'

'Horses hate the smell of blood,' Ross explained. 'To them it means death. As herd animals, they'd naturally run from it. Horses have very primitive instincts, you know.'

'I see. So Clown would have wanted to run from the smell, but not been able to. No wonder the poor creature was in a state.' He shook his head. 'There must be some sick, sadistic bastard out there.'

'You can say that again.'

On their way back to the yard, Darcy's phone chirruped from the dashboard. Darcy picked it up, glancing apologetically at Ross.

'What!' Darcy applied the Nissan's brakes as though a yawning void had opened up before them. The car slid to a halt. 'Oh, God! . . . Yes, I'll be there right away. Oh, God!'

He replaced the phone with a shaking hand and turned to look at Ross with wide, shocked eyes. 'Peter's been knocked down by a car,' he said. 'He's been rushed to hospital. They won't say how badly he's been hurt. Oh, God! It's all my fault . . .'

'Would you like me to drive?' Ross offered, after a moment.

'What? No. Yes, perhaps you'd better. Thanks.'

Ross got out of the car and went round to the driver's side. 'Move over,' he said briskly. 'You'll have to give me directions. Is it far?'

'No. Only about ten minutes. Odstock, near Salisbury.'

'OK.' Ross raced the silver car along the country lanes. 'How can you say it's *your* fault?' he asked.

'Uncle Frank wasn't keen on Peter going out tonight. He has to be so careful, because of kidnappers. I persuaded him. Peter desperately wanted to go and I took his side.'

'It was an accident,' Ross said. 'You can't keep people wrapped up in cotton wool. You mustn't blame yourself.'

FRANKLIN RICHMOND was pacing the hospital corridor like a caged lion when Darcy and Ross arrived. He and his nephew embraced, clinging to each other momentarily for comfort.

'How is he?' Darcy asked breathlessly. 'Is he going to be all right?'

Franklin shrugged. He had arrived, he explained, twenty minutes before, to be told that his son was in the operating theatre and he would have to wait to speak with the doctor. A nurse had assured him, however, that Peter was not on the critical list.

Ross, feeling surplus to requirements, wandered off and returned with two disposable cups of hot, sweet tea. Darcy accepted his gratefully but Franklin looked blankly at Ross.

'Drink this,' Ross urged. 'It'll do you good. Ease the shakes.'

Franklin took the cup obediently and began to sip. 'How did you come to be here?' he asked.

'I drove Darcy. We were out for a drink.'

The doctor, when he did come, explained that Peter had suffered two broken legs and extensive bruising and was presently being prepared for surgery. The fractures should heal without complication. There was no sign of internal injury and he was conscious. His father could see him briefly if he wished.

Franklin and Darcy followed the doctor and Ross kicked his heels until they returned a few minutes later.

Franklin, reassured that his son was in no immediate danger, had progressed beyond anxiety to all-consuming fury.

'I'll get the bastard who did this!' he promised.

Hearing the raw emotion in Franklin's voice, Ross remembered what he'd said about living with fear. It appeared now that he had an Achilles' heel in Peter. The thought that somebody else might also have recognised that made Ross's blood run cold.

333

NOT WANTING to be overheard, Ross made an excuse to drive into the village after breakfast the next morning and telephoned Franklin on his mobile from the side of a leafy lane. Peter, he was told, was progressing satisfactorily, though still very shocked and upset.

'*Both legs*, Ross,' Franklin said with anguish. '*Both legs* broken. He's only twelve and he's in so much pain.'

'Poor kid.' It wasn't enough, but what could he say? Ross hesitated to voice his suspicions. 'Do we know exactly what happened yet?'

'Yes, I spoke to the mother of the birthday boy last night. They were crossing the road on one of those automatic crossings . . . Apparently Peter dropped his pullover and stopped to pick it up. The lights were still red, but the car came from nowhere, accelerating, she said. The police think it was probably joy-riders.'

'Accelerating, you say?'

'Yes, I think that's what she said,' Richmond replied slowly. 'Yes, she did.' He paused, his voice trailing. 'Why do you ask? You're not thinking . . .?'

'I honestly don't know,' Ross said, unhappily. 'But I think you'll have to consider it. What if your Mr X is trying a change of tactics? It just seems too much of a coincidence, you making a stand over payments and this happening.'

'Oh, God, Ross! This is getting out of hand.' Franklin was clearly devastated. His voice deepened with defeat. 'I'll have to pay. I won't risk my son. Nothing's worth that.'

'Do the police have anything on the car?'

'Only that it was stolen. They found it half an hour or so after it hit Peter. It was in a field outside Salisbury, blazing merrily. They don't expect to catch the culprits.'

'Who knew that Peter was going on the trip? Darcy said it was a last-minute decision.'

'Poor Darcy. He's very cut up over this,' Richmond said. 'He's convinced he persuaded me to let Peter go, but I probably would've given in anyway.' He paused, thinking. 'I don't know who else could have known about the outing, except perhaps the parents of the other children.'

'I suppose McKinnon has checked your telephones?' Ross said.

'He does it every few weeks,' Franklin confirmed.

'See if he'll do it this morning,' Ross advised. 'I can't see how else anyone could have known about Peter's outing.'

Franklin sighed, reluctantly agreeing, and Ross rang off.

A COMBINATION of the sticky heat and Leo in one of his annoying moods had Ross feeling bad-tempered before the day was far advanced, and he was glad when Lindsay's MG turned into the yard. She hadn't come with the intention of riding but fell in quickly enough with Ross's idea of hacking the horses to the river and letting them splash around in the shallows.

She exchanged a flowery cotton skirt for Sarah's 'emergency' jeans, which were kept in the tack room in case of torrential rain or some other disaster. A string of pearls and matching earrings were taken off for safety.

She mounted Gypsy, and with Leo, Danny, Sarah and Ross on their mounts led a procession that wound its way through shady lanes to the copse that bounded the river.

Here they passed a pleasant half-hour letting the horses play in the water. Ross watched Lindsay laughing, the sun shining through her fair hair and thin cotton blouse, and found the knowledge that she was forbidden fruit increasingly difficult to accept.

'You look very serious,' she teased as they turned for home.

'I was thinking about Peter Richmond,' Ross said, half truthfully.

'I heard about that,' she said, frowning. 'What an awful thing to happen. Prison's too good for joy-riders. Like drink-drivers, they should be publicly flogged.'

'If they can catch them,' Ross agreed, glancing sideways at her fine-boned, determined face, and liking it just as much in anger as in laughter. He realised that he had loved the girl for quite a while.

When they arrived back in the yard, Roland ambled out of the stable office, a beer in his hand, and smiled up at the riders.

'Nice day,' he observed, looking infuriatingly cool himself, in a white linen suit. 'You're looking damned attractive as usual, cousin,' he said to Lindsay. 'You would appear to have lost a little weight, though,' he added thoughtfully, eyeing the jeans two sizes too big.

'Idiot,' she said affectionately. 'If you want to do something useful, you could always bring out a few more of those beers.'

'Is it the butler's day off?' Roland asked. 'Well, I suppose I could do it, just this once. Do you know, I shouldn't be surprised if I made a very good butler.'

As he wandered off into the stable office once more, Lindsay laughed. 'He's nuts,' she said. 'Anyone would think he hadn't two brain cells to rub together but he's really very bright. He only started acting the fool to annoy Uncle John, I think.'

AFTER THE EVENING MEAL, Ross was about to set off to visit Peter when Bill hailed him. He was wanted on the telephone.

'Hi, Ross, it's me,' Lindsay's cheerful tones greeted him. 'Look, I'm sorry to bother you, but I can't find my pearls.'

'*Your pearls?*'

'My necklace and my earrings. You remember, I took them off when I came out riding? I put them in my skirt pocket, and by the time I changed back I'd forgotten about them. I thought perhaps I'd dropped them in the office . . .'

'Well, I'll certainly have a look,' Ross assured her.

'Oh, what a nuisance! I'm sorry to be such a pain.'

'Nonsense.' But Ross was struck by an unwelcome thought. This wasn't the first time things had gone missing. 'Look, I'll go and have a look right now. I'll give you a ring if I find anything.'

He rang off with an idea forming in his mind, then gave the yard and tack room a sketchy search and climbed into the Jeep.

PETER RICHMOND was not alone when Ross was shown into his room at the hospital; his father and Darcy were at his bedside. With both legs raised in traction, Peter was looking pale and strained.

'Hiyah, soldier! How ya doin'?' Ross asked cheerfully.

Peter mustered an answering smile. 'Hello. I'm OK, thank you. But it does hurt. Dr Trent says I'll be up and about in no time.'

Ross pulled up a chair, admiring the young boy's courage.

'Sure you will,' he said. 'Look, your dad said he's fitted you up with a VCR, so I've brought a couple of our training videos. The first one's Clown, so you can see what kind of progress he's making. And you're not to laugh at the bit where I fall off!'

Ross saw instantly that he'd struck gold. Peter's eyes lit up eagerly and he thanked Ross profusely.

'I can see visitors will be just so much excess baggage from now on,' Franklin said.

Ross saw Darcy smiling at the invalid with shared enjoyment of the moment and thought that, though the boy might be lacking a mother's love, he certainly didn't miss out on family feeling.

He stayed a while, commentating at Peter's request on the first of the videos, before a nurse came to turn them all out.

Ross drove home steadily, his mind on his proposed plan of action. The yard was deserted. He had no excuse for backing out now. Leo rarely returned before closing time and Ross could usually hear his bike's powerful roar as it decelerated in the lane outside.

The dog padded up the stairs at his master's heels. Ross unlocked the door to his own room and let it in. Pausing only to collect a torch, he went out again, closing the door behind him.

Pulse rate accelerating, he stepped across the narrow landing and slotted his own door key into Leo's. It wouldn't turn. Then he tried the handle and the door opened smoothly. It hadn't been locked. Ross slipped into the room, closing the door behind him.

Discarded shoes and items of clothing littered the floor and hung from every chair back. The room resembled a jumble sale that had been hit by a tornado. It smelt faintly of tobacco smoke, which contravened yard rules. On the floor were a couple of bottles of spirits and, judging by the labels, Leo had expensive tastes.

Ross worked his way briskly through Leo's things. The wardrobe and the chest of drawers held a collection of designer garments and two or three leather jackets that would have cost the best part of two weeks' wages. Ross frowned. It began to look as though his suspicions concerning Leo's thievery were justified.

Hanging on a door hook was the denim jacket Leo often wore. Ross quickly went through the pockets. A pack of chewing gum and a tube of Polo mints, a few coins and two dogeared business cards. Ross casually turned them over: M. A. Kendall—Wholesale Butcher, and Simmonds-Fox & Son—Bespoke Tailors. With a sigh, he returned the objects to their respective pockets.

Suddenly a light came on in the yard, and Ross heard the door at the foot of the stairs open.

For an instant he froze. Then the cogs started turning again. There was nowhere to hide so he would have to bluff his way out.

He nipped across the room, grabbed and uncapped a half-full bottle of spirits and gulped a hasty mouthful, sloshing a little down his shirtfront for good measure.

Letting himself out onto the landing, he slammed the door behind him, then turned and gave a theatrical 'Shhh!'

Leo sprang up the last few steps, clearly furious.

'Whoops! Wrong door,' Ross said, slurring his speech. He patted Leo's arm and, with the extreme care of the somewhat less than sober, made his way past him across the landing. He almost made it.

Leo watched him for a moment or two, then with sudden fury lashed out and caught Ross's shoulder, spinning him round again.

'What were you doing in my room?' he demanded.

Ross forced himself to relax. 'Wrong door,' he repeated stupidly, looking at Leo through half-closed eyes. 'Not my room at all.'

Leo caught hold of the American's shirtfront with both hands and, bearing him backwards, slammed him into the doorpost. It caught Ross squarely between the shoulder blades, shocking the air from his lungs and cracking against the back of his head. He gasped involuntarily and through the momentary haze of pain heard the dog whine and growl on the other side of the door.

Leo's face was only inches from his own and as Ross's vision sorted itself out he saw the groom's fury relax into an unpleasant smirk.

'Been drinking, have you, Yank?' Leo said slowly, and then sniffed close to Ross. 'Maybe you have at that.' His grin widened.

Ross felt Leo's grip loosen slightly and seized his chance. Swinging his left hand sideways to find the door handle, he twisted it open.

With a rush the German shepherd filled the doorway, hackles up and lips bristling with a warning that was backed up by two rows of gleaming white teeth.

Leo's hands dropped away from Ross. 'OK, Yank. You win this time,' he conceded as he backed away. 'But if I were you I'd be careful. You may not always have your pooch around to look after you.' He retreated into his room and the door closed behind him.

Ross swung away from the doorpost with a painful sigh. His sleuthing had shown him how close beneath the surface violence lay.

ROSS ARRIVED at the Lea Farm evening show on Wednesday in a mood of increasing irritation. He was stuck with Leo, and was annoyed with himself for giving the groom a feeling of power over him. With his already shaky reputation, the rumour that he had hit the bottle could spell death to his career. It had been a spur-of-the-moment decision that, with hindsight, he regretted.

On the way to the show they had been followed for a stretch by a police car going about its duty and Leo took great delight in advising Ross to drive carefully. 'You wouldn't want to be breathalysed,' he remarked slyly. Ross ignored him.

Outside the exercise ring he discovered the Colonel, Lindsay and James. He went to greet them, his eyes on Lindsay's cotton-clad figure. She had twisted her hair into a knot on top of her head in a cool, sophisticated style. Ross experienced a sharp stab of jealousy seeing James standing with one arm casually circling her waist.

'No luck with the necklace, I'm afraid.'

Lindsay looked stricken. 'Oh, Ross, I should have rung you. James found it this morning, *and* the earrings. They'd fallen under the seat in the MG. I'm so sorry.'

'I'm just glad you found them,' Ross replied. 'So, did she drag you along again?' he commiserated with James.

Lindsay scowled at him. 'It was James's idea to come, not mine.'

'Well, I knew she wanted to come really and you know what women are,' James said, looking over her head at Ross. 'If they can't do what they want to, they sulk for days.'

'Oh! You're insufferable, both of you,' Lindsay gasped. 'Come on, Uncle John, take me away from these two chauvinistic louts!'

The Colonel obligingly tucked her hand through his arm and together they turned away. James grinned and followed.

Ross mounted Flowergirl and began to work at suppling the brown mare, thinking that he liked Lindsay's fiancé very much and yet at the same time wished him on the other side of the world.

ROSS LAY AWAKE for a while that night, once again regretting the episode of the night before. Leo had told Bill that the motorbike had a flat tyre, which explained the silence of his approach but not his early return. It would all have been more bearable if Ross's search had yielded something useful. He supposed he should be thankful he had not been caught going through the man's pockets.

Suddenly, as if someone had turned a light on in his mind, he remembered one of the business cards he had found. Its significance was blindingly obvious.

Clown had been soaked in ox blood. And where better to obtain a large quantity of blood than a slaughterhouse? It could surely be no coincidence that Leo was carrying the card of one 'M. A. Kendall— Wholesale Butcher' in his pocket.

Had Leo, then, been the prowler Ross had challenged that night in the yard? He didn't think so. *His* man had been tall and fairly broad, not of wiry build like the groom. Who then? And what of the other card? It would be hard to imagine anyone less likely to have used the services of a bespoke tailor than Leo.

THE NEXT DAY, Ross telephoned Edward McKinnon. He had ridden out on his own and made the call from a lonely hilltop.

McKinnon answered. 'Ross? What can I do for you?'

He told McKinnon of his suspicions about Leo's thieving and of his search of his room. He also mentioned the prowler he had encountered the night before Clown was daubed with blood.

McKinnon had heard about the prowler from Richmond. 'We checked on Leo Jackson to establish his whereabouts at the time of the Bellboy incident. At that time he was working in a racing stable in Ireland. So if he was responsible for this second incident, then it was probably on the instruction of another party.'

'From what you've told me about the extortionist,' Ross said thoughtfully, 'he doesn't sound the sort of character to get involved with a two-bit sneak thief like Leo. It seems more likely to me that Leo stole that business card along with something else—a wallet, perhaps. Besides, I would swear he was as surprised as the rest of us at finding Clown in that state.'

'Maybe. Anyway, I'll put somebody on to this Kendall—see if we can get some kind of a description from him.'

'Has anything more turned up on Peter's accident?' Ross asked.

'There was a message on Franklin's answerphone yesterday. The caller advised him to toe the line and said "It could have been worse."'

'So it *wasn't* an accident?'

'Well, possibly not.' McKinnon was cautious. 'The thing is, it was widely reported—the papers, local TV. Easy enough to claim responsibility after the event.'

'I suppose so. Look, I'd better go now. I'll call back tomorrow and see what you've come up with.'

His ride completed, Ross crossed the yard carrying saddle and bridle to hear raised voices from the tack room. In the doorway he all but collided with Darcy Richmond, who pushed past him with a muttered apology and made for his car.

Leo was inside, halfheartedly soaping a bridle and wearing a self-satisfied smirk.

'What have you said to upset Darcy?' Ross asked, heavily.

Leo curled his lip. 'Mind your own business, Yank.'

'Anything you have to say, in this yard, to one of the owners or their family, *is* my business,' Ross said forcefully.

Leo continued to sneer. 'He warned me to stay away from his girl,' he said. 'He needn't have bothered. I don't want the little mouse anyway. I prefer the other one—the classy blonde.'

'You wouldn't know class if it kicked your butt,' Ross said mildly, dumping his saddle down. 'When you've finished that, you can do this one,' he added, heading for the cottage and a cool drink.

Ross HAD TO GO into Salisbury the next morning and rang McKinnon from the Jeep when he got there. 'What news?' he asked.

'Well, we tracked down Kendall the butcher,' McKinnon reported. 'He was convinced we were from the Department of the Environment, Food and Rural Affairs and insisted that he would never sell ox blood to anyone. However, when we offered a little financial inducement he remembered that he *had* had an enquiry. It was a fairly young man, late twenties to early thirties, dressed like a countryman and wearing a flat cap and sunglasses. He said he was a member of a Civil War re-enactment group and that they wanted it to be as realistic as possible. Kendall thought he might have been Irish. Which tells us . . .?' McKinnon finished.

Ross thought for a moment. 'Which tells us the ox-blood man is almost certainly our original Mr X.' He paused. 'Any other news?'

'We debugged Richmond's house again. And we found a rather clumsy device, on the phone lines outside.'

'But, clumsy or not, that bug could have told Mr X where Peter was going to be last Monday, right?'

'It could,' McKinnon said. 'And another thing. We've been delving into Leo's murky past, and we discovered that in Ireland, about six weeks before he arrived here, a racing stable lad called Lewis Roach was involved in a pub brawl and half killed another lad with a broken bottle. He disappeared soon after. I faxed a picture to the stables and they identified our Leo as their Lewis Roach.'

'But what about his references? The Colonel said they were good.'

'It would seem there was indeed a Leo Jackson who left just before Lewis Roach. So when Colonel Preston requested references for Leo Jackson, the head lad was happy to tell him Jackson was a good worker and a fine upstanding citizen. Anyway, I just thought you should know. It's up to you what you do about him. Obviously you can't mention me, but watch yourself.'

'Thanks for the warning,' Ross said grimly. 'He's pretty much out-stayed his welcome anyway.'

THE OAKLEY MANOR horses attended two shows at the weekend and performed very well.

On a more personal level the weekend was not so harmonious. Leo was constantly rude to Ross, deliberately 'misunderstood' instructions and was found to be missing for large portions of the two days. Before the weekend was very far advanced, Ross had decided enough was enough; he would give Leo his marching orders at the end of the week if things didn't improve significantly.

Fortunately, he had Danny to help him in the meantime and on the second day Lindsay as well, although she spent much of the day with her parents and James, who also attended.

After Bishop won the Foxhunter class, she'd brought her family across to meet Ross as he left the ring after the prize-giving.

She ran forward and hugged him, eyes shining, as he dismounted. 'Ross! That was wonderful! I'm so *pleased* for you!'

Ross, unaware of her approaching family and caught up in the exhilaration of his win, swept her off her feet and swung her round. 'We did it, Princess! Wasn't he great?' he demanded. Then he kissed her soundly on the cheek and restored her to her feet.

'This, I take it, is Mr Wakelin,' observed Lady Cresswell coolly, appearing at Lindsay's shoulder. Lindsay flushed and Ross saw James come forward to put a proprietorial arm round her shoulders.

Ross removed his crash cap, and with his most charming smile said, 'A pleasure to meet you, ma'am.'

'Jolly well done!' Lindsay's father spoke from behind his wife.

James added his congratulations and gradually the gathering broke up, and Lindsay and her family drifted away.

As Ross loosened Bishop's girth he smiled inwardly. Lindsay's spontaneous display of affection could hardly have been more poorly timed, but as far as he was concerned she was welcome to repeat it whenever she liked.

FIVE

The following Monday was the hottest day of the summer so far. There had been no rain for weeks and the heat rolled across the countryside in heavy waves soon after dawn, settling in a smothering blanket on the dehydrated land. Ross had risen early and exercised the horses in most need of it before the first feeding. As the morning wore on he pottered round the semideserted yard doing odd jobs.

Shortly after noon, Leo strolled into the yard, helped himself to a beer from the office fridge and, for perhaps half an hour, followed Ross round the yard, propping himself in doorways, watching as the

American worked. Ross was careful not to let his irritation show.

Before the midday feeding, Ross remembered he had to change the dressing on a gash Flowergirl had sustained in the horsebox the previous day, low on the inside of her near hind. Ross tied the mare up and crouched in the straw beside her. He had removed the soiled dressing and was inspecting the wound when a shadow fell across him.

'Get out of my light,' he said irritably, looking up to see Leo silhouetted in the doorway, hand cupped round a cigarette he was in the act of lighting. 'And put that damned thing out!'

Leo said pleasantly, 'You put it out,' and tossed the lighted match into the dry straw directly behind Flo.

With an oath, Ross pounced on the spot where he'd seen it fall, ignoring the brown mare's indignant leap forward. The match was nowhere to be seen. He scrambled to his feet and stamped furiously on all the straw in the vicinity. He was rewarded by a tiny wisp of smoke curling upward to extinction.

Leo moved away, chuckling. Taking no chances, Ross scooped up the affected bedding and tossed it out onto the cobbles. Grabbing a water bucket, he doused the straw thoroughly.

He tracked Leo down to the hay barn, where he was lounging on the unopened bales, beer can in one hand and cigarette in the other. Without a word, Ross strode forward, plucked the glowing time bomb from his fingers and ground it out beneath his heel. 'Get the hell out of this yard,' he hissed, 'and don't ever come back!'

'Why, Yank, don't get so excited. It isn't good for you.' Leo laughed as he slid off the bales to stand in front of Ross.

'That's where you're wrong,' Ross said, accompanying the last word with a punch that had many weeks of frustration behind it. Leo staggered back and sat down abruptly. 'It's *you* it's not good for,' Ross finished with immense satisfaction. 'Now get out of my sight!'

Leo climbed to his feet, wiping blood from a split lip, and pushed past Ross out into the bright sunlight.

Ross followed him closely, intending to see him off the premises, but Leo shot through the doorway to the covered stables, and down the corridor. Ross darted after him. To leave Leo wandering around the stables in his present frame of mind was not an option.

Leo was in the tool store, an open-fronted recess between the central two stables in the row. Ross looked round for something with which to arm himself. For the first time he regretted the almost fanatical neatness of Bill Scott's regime. The corridor was clear from end to end. In desperation Ross lifted down the leather head collar that hung outside the nearest stable door. He stepped cautiously forward, stopping just short of the opening.

The tines of a pitchfork lanced out of the opening within inches of his face and buried themselves in the window frame opposite.

Ross swung his handful of leather, rope and metal as hard as he could round the brickwork at head height. He was rewarded by a grunt of pain, and ducked under the quivering pitchfork handle to follow up his advantage.

Leo had staggered back to the far wall. When he saw Ross approaching he snatched up a shovel. Aware of the inadequacy of his own weapon, Ross let go of the head collar and tried to grab the shovel instead, but Leo dodged and swung the shovel at Ross's head.

Ross took most of the force of the blow on his shoulder before it glanced off and grazed his cheekbone.

Leo hammered the back of the shovel, with sickening force, into Ross's bad knee. It gave way beneath him and he found himself with a worm's-eye view of the Victorian brick floor. He got no further than a half-crouch before collapsing again. He grasped his leg above the injured knee as if by pressure alone he could dim the searing pain.

He watched, powerless, as Leo selected another pitchfork from the back of the store. Slowly he came round in front of Ross, his back to the open corridor. He laughed, enjoying the moment.

Ross watched him come, wondering with a strange detachment if Leo actually meant to kill him. The situation seemed unreal.

'This time your effing dog isn't here to save you,' Leo sneered. 'I shut him in the office. It's just you and me, Yank.'

Leo stepped forward, brandishing the pitchfork menacingly, and then appeared to trip, his legs shooting from under him, and landed unceremoniously on the brickwork just feet from Ross, his head connecting with the floor with an audible crack.

Roland stood holding the pitchfork in his immaculately manicured hands.

'I don't know how you did that, but—thanks,' Ross said gratefully.

'This old brickwork is treacherous,' Roland observed. 'I always said someone would do themselves an injury on it one day.' He propped the fork up against the wall and regarded Ross with interest. 'I say, are you all right?'

'Oh, sure, I like it down here,' Ross said, pain and exasperation lending sharpness to his tone.

'Well, I should get up if I were you,' Roland advised. 'You'll get frightfully dirty.'

Ross held up a hand. As Roland hauled him to his feet, Ross caught at the cream-suited arm while he got his balance.

Roland watched his face. 'Is it your knee?' he asked.

Ross nodded and put his left foot experimentally to the floor. Pain lanced through his knee, up to his hip and down to his ankle. He paused, biting his lip, and then tried a little weight on it. It was pretty sore but it didn't give way, which was encouraging. Probably the damage was limited. He looked up.

'What are we going to do with . . .?' Ross gestured at Leo.

'Oh, I expect he'll be all right,' Roland said airily. 'He'll probably have a nasty headache, though. What did you do to upset him?'

'I hit him.' Ross told him briefly what had happened.

'Do you want to press charges?'

Ross shook his head wearily. 'I just want to see the back of him.'

Roland nodded. 'I'll see to that.Go and put some ice on that knee.'

In the doorway to the yard Ross met both Bill Scott and the dog.

'Leo,' Ross told Bill, 'has outstayed his welcome.'

Bill frowned. 'Well, I'm not surprised.'

Three-quarters of an hour, two ice packs, a bandage and a handful of painkillers later, Ross emerged from the cottage to see Leo strapping his possessions onto his motorbike. His saturnine features sported a rapidly purpling bruise. His hair and clothing looked suspiciously damp and it required little imagination to work out how Roland had restored him to consciousness.

Ross regarded him calmly, feeling no real animosity, rather a sort of bewilderment. As Leo strapped the last of his belongings into place, Roland and Bill came across the yard towards Ross.

Leo kicked the bike into life, swung it round in a sweeping curve and paused beside Bill. He had a triumphant gleam in his eye.

'I was going to leave anyway,' he stated, his sneer even more marked than usual. 'I've had enough of working with a cripple whose nerves are shot! Nobody can make it big when he hits the bottle. Didn't you wonder why he never went out? He's got his own cache of whisky in his room. Some nights he's so far gone he can't even find his way to the bathroom!'

Having delivered his parting shot, he roared out of the yard.

'Well?' Bill demanded. 'Is that true?'

'You're going to take his word for it?' Ross asked bitterly.

'You've never seen me drunk, have you?'

Bill snorted in disgust. 'I knew this would happen! I told the Colonel when he first mentioned you. You can't come back from something like that. It never works.' With a final scathing look at Ross, he stomped away.

'Never mind, old boy. Life goes on,' Roland observed brightly.

Ross regarded him wearily, considering this fatuous, even by Roland's idiotic standards.

ROSS AND DANNY travelled up to the Three Counties Showground at Malvern in the early hours of Wednesday morning. The schools had broken up and Bill had agreed that Danny could help at the shows, as a temporary measure.

The show itself was a big one and at nine o'clock, when they parked the lorry, the area was already abuzz with frenetic activity. Flustered mothers ran hither and thither, escorting pigtailed offspring on precocious ponies, while long-legged hunters and jumpers stalked through the throng bearing solemn-faced competitors. Grooms and helpers scurried among the forest of equine limbs, carrying tack and forgotten whips and gloves.

Somehow Ross managed to steer Clown unscathed through two rounds and finished with a trophy and a red rosette. Franklin Richmond, who had watched through the viewfinder of a video camera, met Ross with a warm handshake.

Only after lunch, when Ross was warming up Bishop for his first class, did a cloud appear on the horizon. In the distance, on the edge of the practice area, he spotted Leo talking to Stephen Douglas's groom. What on earth was *he* doing there?

He supposed he might be asking for work, although having obviously been dismissed from Oakley Manor wouldn't be the best of references. Uneasy, Ross nevertheless put Leo out of his mind and concentrated on the horse. Bishop performed with his customary flair, but lost the class to more experienced animals.

Having managed a creditable third in Bishop's second class, Ross rode him back to the box to transfer onto Woodsmoke for the final class of the day. When he rode past a neighbouring lorry the two grooms beside it nudged each other and all but pointed.

'Danny, is there something I should know?' he asked as he sat on the ramp and tried to ease the pain in his swollen knee, while Danny finished getting Woody ready. 'The way folks here are looking, I feel like the best-dressed man at a naturist convention.'

Danny didn't laugh. 'I think Leo's been talking,' he said unhappily. 'There's a rumour going round that your nerve has gone and you drink to keep going. They say Leo found out and you threw him out.'

Ross laughed harshly. 'I'd be pretty stupid to fire him if I wanted to keep him quiet, wouldn't I? Well, I guess it'll blow over.'

In the collecting ring again on Woody, Ross felt eyes boring into him from all directions. He tried to convince himself it was just his imagination, but to no avail. Several of the grooms and one or two of the riders were making no secret of their curiosity. It seemed the word was spreading like wildfire.

Whether his growing ill humour communicated itself to the usually sedate Woodsmoke, Ross couldn't tell, but the old horse went like a dream. In a hard-fought jump-off against the clock, Ross was astounded when the old campaigner managed second place.

Back at the box, Danny was over the moon. His joy was touching.

Ross relinquished Woody to the boy, climbed into the cab and collapsed onto the bench seat, heartily wishing the boy was old enough to drive the box. His leg had definitely had enough for one day. He closed his eyes.

'I say, old boy. The old horse did rather well, don't you think?'

Ross blinked into the evening sunlight, trying to focus on a coolly handsome face under a white Panama. He had had no idea Roland was even on the showground.

'Oh, hi! Where did you spring from?'

'Got a lift up with a friend,' Roland said, as though it was the most natural thing in the world for someone who professed little interest in horses to make the journey halfway across England to visit a show. 'Wondered if you'd consider giving me a lift home?'

''Fraid not, old boy,' Ross mimicked him, shaking his head regretfully. 'But you can drive, if you want.'

Roland smiled. 'Love to,' he said. 'If I can just remember how . . .'

'Just follow the white lines and stop at the red lights,' Ross said dryly. 'You'll soon get the hang of it.'

In due course, with horses loaded and Ross and Danny slumped in contented exhaustion beside him, Roland drove the heavy lorry home with offhand expertise.

After ten minutes or so of silence, Danny initiated Roland and Ross into a game that involved inventing fictitious institutions and societies using the letters on vehicle number plates. The game started with fairly sensible suggestions such as Retired Jockeys Home for RJH, but quickly degenerated. SSH, the Society for Schizophrenic Hamsters, rounded it off.

ON FRIDAY, ROSS had a call from Franklin Richmond, inviting him out for a meal that evening, ostensibly to celebrate the success of his rides at the Three Counties. They agreed a time and place.

Just after eight, scrubbed and presentably dressed, Ross climbed into the Jeep and set off for a country pub called the Dovecote, deep in the Wiltshire countryside.

Barely a mile up the road, he cursed and slammed on the brakes. He had forgotten the one thing Franklin had asked him to bring— Clown's trophy and rosette from the Three Counties, for Peter. He turned and headed at top speed back to the yard.

Leaving the engine running and the dog in the back, he raced through the door and took the stairs two at a time. His door was unlocked, and making a mental note to remember to lock it on the way out, Ross pushed it open and strode in.

A noise and a half-seen movement on the periphery of his vision caused him to turn his head but the action was never completed. Something hit him hard just above his left ear and he was out cold before he hit the floor.

Coming round, he became aware that he was lying on something soft and thought he must be in bed. He heard a movement and opened his eyes. Shades of colour swam about, making no sense at all. He blinked. Somebody was approaching. Memory returned and alarm bells rang. He struggled to focus, feeling desperately vulnerable. The figure, slightly clearer now, came closer.

'I should lie still if I were you, old boy,' an unmistakable voice advised him. 'You don't look at all the thing.'

Ross closed his eyes and opened them slowly. That was better. But with his vision came a crashing headache. He groaned. He was lying on the big settee in his bedsit. For some reason, Roland was there and he was holding the smug-faced mahogany Buddha.

'Found this on the floor at the top of the stairs,' Roland said. 'The archetypal blunt instrument.'

Ross's first thought on seeing Roland had been one of suspicion, but if Roland had just attacked him he'd hardly carry him to the sofa and wait around for him to recover consciousness, would he?

In spite of the violence of Leo's departure, Ross had not really considered the possibility that he would take his feud further.

'I don't suppose you saw anyone leaving?' Ross asked.

Roland shook his head. ''Fraid not, old chap. I came down to the yard—looking for you, as a matter of fact—and saw your Jeep outside with the engine running. I stopped for a chat with Darcy, who'd just come to pick Sarah up. When you didn't appear, I came on up.'

'And you didn't see anybody?'

'Not a soul. Turned the Jeep engine off, though,' Roland added.

'Thank you,' Ross said wearily. He looked round the room. 'Well, it would seem I disturbed a burglar. I can't imagine what they thought I had worth stealing. What was it you wanted me for?'

Roland looked momentarily lost. 'Oh, nothing that can't wait. Don't you think you ought to see a doctor?'

'Probably, but I guess I'll survive. I'm already late for a dinner date.' Cautiously, Ross stood up. He gingerly tidied his hair. His scalp was sore but the skin seemed unbroken.

'You'd better let me drive you,' Roland said.

Even though he was not sure he entirely believed Roland's version of events, he accepted his offer of a lift with gratitude.

Roland drove his white Aston Martin at speed and deposited Ross safely in the car park of the Dovecote barely ten minutes later than the appointed time. Ross thanked him and said he would call a taxi for the return journey.

Franklin took in Ross's slight pallor and instantly wanted to know what had happened. Ross told him the whole story, backtracking to Leo's departure.

'And you think it was Leo?' Franklin asked.

Ross nodded. 'I can't think who else,' he said.

Franklin shook his head in disbelief. 'He must be unhinged, Ross. He could have killed you.'

Ross was already uncomfortably aware of that. Had Roland in fact saved his life by coming up to find him when he had?

It was only a relatively short drop from the window at the back of his room into the sand of the schooling area. Very easy for somebody to leave that way. On the other hand, Roland had said he'd found the Buddha at the top of the stairs . . .

The waiter materialised, bearing their food. As they tackled an excellent game pie, Franklin sighed heavily. 'You know, I can't help feeling that it's a shame our friend Leo has such a cast-iron alibi for the time Bellboy was killed. From what you say, he's ruthless enough.'

'He's nowhere near smart enough, though,' Ross pointed out. 'His idea of subtlety is a smack in the face. Your guy is devious. He's not so hot-blooded; prepared to take his time.'

Franklin nodded. 'Nevertheless, I'm going to ask McKinnon to put a man on Leo. See if we can't catch him in the act.'

Ross stopped chewing in surprise. 'You don't have to do that,' he protested. 'You've got enough problems of your own.'

A smile hovered about Franklin's mouth. 'I don't intend to let a psychopathic ex-groom jeopardise my chances of seeing my horses jump at Olympia.'

THE TWO-DAY SHOW at the weekend passed off with reasonable performances from all the horses that attended, although none of them was quite good enough to carry off a prize. Ross was content. In all honesty, you had to expect days like that more often than not.

Several of Ross's acquaintances came up to him, expressing disbelief at his ex-groom's claims. Many more, unfortunately, turned their backs on him.

It became harder to remain philosophical when on Monday morning Bill Scott passed the *Sportsman* across the breakfast table. Scott said nothing but the look in his eyes warned Ross that something was amiss.

There on the equestrian pages was Harry Douglas's column. It bore the headline STRESS AND THE COMPETITION RIDER. The article began by citing the recent tragic case of a flat-racing jockey who had never quite regained the winning edge after suffering a fall. The article went on:

It is not always the extent of injuries that determines the severity of an accident, more the level of trauma or shock suffered. Some riders thrive on high risk; others ignore it; others find ways to deal with it. Most methods are harmless, such as yogic meditation and golf. Unfortunately, a few resort to artificial stimulants such as alcohol or drugs to help them through. Neither is a lasting solution, of course.

In my opinion it is up to each individual to recognise their limitations and withdraw from competition before they endanger themselves, their horses or, as in a case overseas last year, the spectators.

'Well?' Bill was obviously awaiting a reaction.

'Well, what?' Ross enquired coolly. Inside, he was seething.

'Well, that's you, isn't it?' the stable manager stated baldly. 'That bit about the case overseas . . . that's you.'

'I don't think it mentions my name,' Ross said.

Bill grunted. 'He doesn't need to.'

'Nobody will take any notice, Ross. You'll see.' Maggie smiled encouragingly at him. 'All the same, he shouldn't be allowed to write things like that.'

'Yeah, well, it's not worth worrying about,' Ross said.

Douglas's raking over the ashes of the incident was well below the belt. There *had* been casualties among the onlookers when his horse had somersaulted into the crowd that day. Most were minor, but one ten-year-old girl had suffered spine damage and was confined to a wheelchair. He had visited the child in hospital until her mother found out and screamed abuse at him. Many a time Ross thought of that little girl, and her thin, brave face regularly haunted his dreams, but to suggest he could in some way have prevented it . . .

Bitterness welled up and he got up and left the room, making for the cool of the tack room. Before he reached it, however, a Mercedes convertible swept into the yard bearing James and Lindsay.

'Ross!' Lindsay jumped out of the car as it stopped, looking totally adorable in floral print trousers and a cropped, lacy top.

'Hello, Princess,' he greeted her, smiling lazily.

'Ross! Have you read it?'

Ross sighed and nodded. 'I have.'

'It's not fair!' Lindsay protested.

'Life's *not* fair, Princess,' he said gently.

'Oh, don't be so bloody laid-back!' she said explosively. 'I know you're hopping mad, deep down. Nobody could blame you for what happened to that child. This article is libellous.'

'It's only libel if he mentions my name,' Ross pointed out.

'Lindsay,' James said, putting his arm round her, 'Ross is right. The best thing to do with this kind of spite is to ignore it.' He smiled at Ross. 'We really only called in to give you this.'

Ross looked down at the silver-edged envelope James was passing to him. His heart sank.

'It's our formal engagement party. Two weeks' time. I hope you can come,' James said earnestly, giving Lindsay's shoulder a squeeze.

Ross forced a smile. 'Congratulations! And thank you.'

When they had left, he stood staring despondently at the envelope, wondering what possible excuse he could find for not attending.

A BREAK IN THE WEATHER was long overdue. The atmosphere on Thursday afternoon was almost unbearably humid.

As Ross hosed Woody down after a long session in the school, Franklin Richmond drove into the yard.

'Leo is staying in the village,' he told Ross. 'At the Six Bells. McKinnon says he's not working, but spends a lot in the bar.'

Ross wondered if any of Leo's fellow guests were missing their valuables. Though, if that were his game, he couldn't hope to maintain it for long in one place.

'Anyway, McKinnon has a man camped practically on the doorstep, watching his every move, so Leo shouldn't bother you again. Or at least, if he does, we'll catch him at it.'

Ross thanked him and asked after Peter.

'He's much improved, thank you. The doctor thinks he'll be fit to come home in a week or so.' He paused. 'I've set up the payments again, Ross.'

'Sure, I understand.' Ross couldn't blame him.

'So we appear to have reached a stalemate with Mr X, don't we? Unless he makes a move, we haven't a hope of tracking him down. But he won't make one unless I provoke him by not paying, and after what happened to Peter, I can't bring myself to do that.' Franklin sighed, looking tired. 'Well, I'd better get on.'

Ross watched him drive away, wishing he could be of more help.

The yard was quiet. Danny and Sarah had ridden out on Simone and Gypsy, and Bill had gone out in the Land-Rover. Ross headed towards the tack room. He fancied a cold beer.

In the stable office, Roland sat with his feet up on the desk, a beer in one hand and the other gently pulling the dog's ears as it lay quietly beside him. He smiled pleasantly as Ross stopped short.

'Hi,' Ross said. 'Long time no see.'

'I was called away,' Roland said in reply. 'Business.'

'A Hepplewhite in distress?' Ross helped himself to a beer and opened it. 'Do you have crises in the antiques business?'

'You'd be surprised. A rare piece comes onto the market and it's an unholy scramble to get to it first.'

'You really love your work,' Ross observed with interest.

'Oh, I do,' Roland agreed with a gleam of sardonic amusement. 'It's a lot more exciting than you might imagine.'

They were interrupted by the sound of hooves in the yard and Ross went out to meet the returning riders. Roland followed him.

'I'm thinking of buying a horse myself,' Roland remarked conversationally, as they stood watching the youngsters unsaddle.

Ross turned, astounded. '*You* are?'

'Yes, why not? Thought you could ride it for me.'

Ross raised an eyebrow. 'Are you serious?'

Roland looked hurt. 'Oh, always, my boy. Always.'

LATER THAT EVENING the weather finally broke. Storm clouds gathered from late afternoon onwards, and at about ten o'clock the heavens opened. Half an hour later, as Ross and Bill finished their late rounds, the first rolls of thunder could be heard in the distance.

Back in his room, Ross lay on his bed, enjoying the sound of the long-awaited rain pounding the cobbles below and the wonderful drop in humidity that accompanied it. As the storm drew closer, the dog got up and padded to the window. He cocked his head on one side, listening, and whined. Then he turned and padded across the room to the door and whined once more.

'Oh, not now, you crazy mutt. You'll drown,' Ross told him.

The dog whined again, running to the window and back to the door.

Ross sighed and got to his feet. 'I guess a guy's gotta do what a guy's gotta do,' he said, and let the dog out onto the landing.

The dog ran down the stairs and, when the door at the bottom was opened, shot out into the rain-filled darkness. Ross settled on the bottom step to await his return.

He found himself going over Roland's surprising announcement. He couldn't really see Roland as a showjumping fan. But then, you couldn't really see Roland as anything, except perhaps an actor.

The dog hadn't come back yet. Ross opened the door wider and, squinting against the driving rain, whistled between crashes of thunder. There was no response.

He tried again. Nothing.

Ross cursed and ran back upstairs to fetch his waterproof stockman's coat and hat. If it hadn't been raining so hard he might have left the dog out there but it was just possible he could be barking at an intruder and Ross not hearing him through the storm.

The yard was awash. The low security lighting revealed sheets of rain being flung earthwards from the blackness above. Lightning split the sky with jagged streaks at frequent intervals.

Having satisfied himself that the dog was not in the yard or stables, Ross sprinted through the puddles to the schooling arena. The gate was shut and an accommodating lightning flash revealed it to be empty. He trotted to the opposite corner of the yard, where the path sloped down to the home field.

The hay-barn door stood open. It hadn't been at half past ten. Ross had checked it himself. So there *had* been somebody in the yard.

Ross wished he'd had the foresight to bring something with which to defend himself. He hadn't even brought a torch.

Heart rate rocketing, he stood to one side of the door and slid his left hand round and in to flick the light switch down.

The barn was empty.

Relieved, Ross closed the door, bolting it securely, and began to make his way along the outside of the hay barn. Feeling his way along the wooden wall, his foot met an obstruction and he paused, crouching to investigate. A flash illuminated the rain-sodden body at his feet just as his fingers identified the wet fur.

The sight of the apparently lifeless dog was imprinted on his mind in that one brilliant moment, and the deafening crash of thunder that immediately followed it drowned his cry of distress.

Shock numbing his senses, it was a moment or two before he realised that beneath his hands the dog's rib cage was moving slightly.

With urgency born of hope, Ross gathered the huge, limp form into his arms and slipped and slid his way back up to the yard, heading straight for the shed where the Land-Rover was housed. It was obvious the animal needed immediate veterinary attention.

Ross laid the dog in the back of the Land-Rover. He retrieved the ignition key from the ledge over the doorway and climbed into the front. A beam of light caught him directly in the face.

'What's going on?' a voice demanded. 'Ross?'

A flash of lightning illuminated the unmistakable features of the Colonel's son. He was hatless and, unsurprisingly, drenched.

'Out of the way!' Ross shouted. He gunned the engine.

'What's wrong?' Roland flashed his torch round the interior of the vehicle. 'Oh, hell! I'll ring Roger and let him know you're coming.'

Ross switched the lights on and accelerated out into the downpour. The windscreen wipers scraped frantically at the screen but made little impression. Water was cascading along the sides of the road and flooding across it in places. Branches littered the tarmac. The twelve miles to Roger West's animal surgery took an eternity.

The vet, alerted by Roland's call, was waiting for him, but it seemed a lifetime before Roger examined the animal on his operating table. The dog had regained consciousness but he had neither the inclination, nor perhaps the ability, to move. He gazed through pain-filled brown eyes at the two men.

Roger looked up, his expression sympathetic. 'His injuries suggest he's been hit more than once. There's one gash here, on his head, but he's also got several broken ribs and there are massive contusions. His spine may be affected.'

'Are you saying he'll be paralysed?'

Roger shrugged. 'It's a strong possibility. He could make a full recovery, though I'd have to say that that was doubtful.'

Ross nodded, digesting the information.

'What do you want me to do?' Roger asked gently.

Ross watched his dog for a moment longer, then looked away, unable to bear the unshaken trust in those beautiful eyes. 'You decide,' he said. 'Make a clinical decision. I can't think straight.'

'*Ross*, I can't do that!' Roger protested. 'I need your permission.'

'You have my permission to do what you think is best. I have to get back, check on the horses. Let me know what happens.'

Ross gently fondled the dog's ears. He bent and kissed the top of the sodden head, then left the surgery. Putting the Land-Rover in gear, he drove out onto the treacherous roads again.

The image of the helpless dog haunted him. *Who could do such a thing?* If he ever found out who was responsible . . .

He hit the steering wheel with a clenched fist as he drove.

By the time Ross returned the Land-Rover to the shed by the Scotts' cottage, the worst of the storm was over. He checked the horses, then climbed the stairs to his room feeling drained of emotion. Even the anger had abated a little.

In his bedsit, Roland lay sprawled on the sofa.

'How is he?' he asked, with what appeared to be genuine concern.

'Not good,' Ross said. 'I left him with Roger but I don't think there's much he can do. He'd probably be paralysed anyway.'

'Oh, I'm sorry. How did it happen?'

'I think somebody clubbed him,' Ross said bluntly, watching Roland closely for a reaction.

It was minimal. His eyes narrowed slightly and a muscle tightened in his jaw. 'Oh, hell,' he said, quietly but forcefully. 'Why would somebody do that? Not Leo again, surely?'

Ross shrugged, unable to say that Leo was being watched. How had life ever got so damned complicated? he wondered wearily.

There was one thing he had to know. 'What were you doing in the yard?'

'I was watching the storm from the house. I saw torchlight and came to investigate. I found you.'

After a period of brooding silence, Roland announced his intention of returning to his bed. 'Have to get my beauty sleep, don't you know?'

Roland was out of the door before it occurred to the American that that was the first time in the past hour or two that Roland had affected his upper-class-twit persona. So, it *was* just a front. Lindsay was right. Hot on the heels of this discovery came the realisation that he hadn't been carrying a flashlight when he'd searched the yard. Therefore, either Roland had seen the light carried by whoever had attacked the dog, or he was lying. And Ross must have been in the yard for a good ten minutes before he'd found the injured animal and *he* had seen no light.

Too depressed to think, he finished his coffee and fell into bed.

SIX

Nobody appeared to notice the absence of the dog the next morning. Ross was relieved. He didn't want to talk about it just yet. When the inevitable questions came, he had decided to let it be known that the dog had been hit by the barn door swinging in the wind.

Later in the day, he phoned Franklin on his mobile. He briefly related the events of the night before.

'God, Ross. I'm sorry!' the businessman exclaimed. 'If I could only get my hands on this bastard! You didn't see anything . . .'

'No, nothing. I suppose it's not possible Leo could have given McKinnon's men the slip?' Ross said.

Franklin sounded doubtful. 'It would certainly have been the night for it,' he allowed. 'But that's assuming Leo knew he was being watched, and unless McKinnon's men have been careless there's no way he could have known. Those men are professionals, Ross.'

'It does sound unlikely,' Ross agreed. 'The thing is, I had a phone call this morning. Somebody wanted me to know that what happened to the dog was no accident.'

'They called *you*?' Franklin was alarmed. 'Oh, God, Ross! I'm sorry! I feel responsible for all this. After all, I got you into it.'

'It's as much my fight as yours now.'

'No use asking if the voice rang any bells with you, I suppose?'

''Fraid not. It was kinda muffled.'

'And the dog?' Franklin asked. 'Have you heard from Roger yet?'

'I called him this morning but he still couldn't say one way or the other. He made it through the night but it's still touch and go.'

Ross said goodbye and switched off, sitting for a moment in thought. 'Be careful,' Franklin had said as he disconnected. Ross had to be, if he wanted to get through this with his career intact. Oakley Manor and the horses had become his life now. The trouble was that his life might be the price he had to pay. Somehow, somebody had found out that he was trying to help Franklin. 'Your dog is dead, Yank,' the harsh, indistinct voice had told him. 'And if you don't learn to mind your own business, you could be next!'

THE BIG SHOW of the weekend was on the Sunday, which dawned dry and bright. The sky was a clear blue, the sun warm and a light breeze began to evaporate the worst of the surface water, leaving the turf soft and springy.

As the Oakley Manor team parked their horsebox at the showground, Ross experienced the buzz that the start of a show always gave him. The Berkshire show was probably the most prestigious he had so far attended in England.

Danny and Bill had accompanied Ross in the horsebox. The Colonel himself was to arrive later in the morning, with Robbie Fergusson also promising to be there.

It was Ginger who produced the best result of the morning, winning her Grade-C class with a neat and obedient double clear round. Unfortunately, Fergusson had not arrived by that time and so missed his mare's finest hour.

Lindsay and James had travelled independently of the Oakley Manor team, bringing Gypsy to the show in a trailer. They seemed in high spirits and Gypsy obliged by winning a speed class.

The big chestnut, Telamon, appeared in the collecting ring for the first class of the afternoon, ridden by a heavy-handed young man, Jim Pullen. His relationship with the stallion appeared to be one of perpetual opposition. The horse looked full of fight and Ross wondered idly if he himself could ride the giant chestnut, and half wished he could try. As expected, the round was an unmitigated disaster, the chestnut taking three fences before bucking his rider off.

Lindsay rode alongside Ross. 'You really should try to disguise such unholy glee,' she admonished severely, with a twinkle in her eye.

'I didn't realise I was quite so easy to read. Do you often read my mind?' he asked jokingly.

'Oh, all the time,' Lindsay declared, laughing. 'You'd be surprised the things I know about you! So, can you come on Saturday?' she asked. 'Our party.'

'*This* Saturday?' he said, in the tone of one who had thought it at least a month away. 'Oh, hell! I'm sorry, Princess, I can't. I'm—that is, I've arranged to go out with Danielle.'

'Bring her along,' Lindsay said brightly. 'The more the merrier.'

'Well, I'll ask her, thank you,' Ross said, unable to think of a further excuse and making a mental note to advise Danielle of the plans he had inadvertently made on her behalf.

Bishop was in fine form, winning his first class and only missing a place in the next after slipping on a difficult turn in the jump-off. Ross put it down to his inexperience and was well satisfied.

As the afternoon wore on the prize money became more and more enticing. The Colonel had appeared just before lunch, chauffeured by Roland, and was soon joined by Robbie Fergusson. The Scotsman made no effort to come down and see his horses or their rider at close hand. Instead he sat in the members' stand and drank champagne while his horses performed below.

Both Ginger and Flowergirl were entered for the penultimate class of the day. The fences in this class were as big as anything Flo had ever tackled but she launched herself at them with enthusiasm and only came to grief at the very last obstacle, a formidable wall that she badly misjudged. Disappointed, Ross patted her shoulder and they left the ring.

Danny appeared out of the milling crowd leading Ginger and Ross passed Flo's reins to him in exchange for Ginger's. Settling into the saddle, he gathered up the reins. Ginger felt mulish. She had already worked up a sweat, just on her way from the horsebox.

'She's acting a bit weird, Ross,' Danny said, frowning. 'Back there, some idiot opened a can of lager practically under her nose. She nearly blew her top! I've never seen her like that before.'

I have, Ross thought grimly.

He rode the chestnut mare towards the main ring without mishap and joined the whirling mass of horses and riders warming up for the class. The practice area was far too small, and as other competitors rode past, occasionally brushing the mare with whips or swishing tails, Ross could feel the tension building within her again.

Somebody cut in front of Ginger, their whip flicking her face, and Ross felt the sudden, jerky signs of panic shudder through the mare. Her ears began to flick back and forth agitatedly and through the reins her mouth felt hard and unresponsive. She was on the verge of breaking but there was nowhere to go.

I've got to get her out of here, he thought urgently. I can't jump her like this. Afraid to touch her with his heels, Ross jumped off. Gripping her nostrils tightly with his left hand so that her breath whistled, he led her tentatively forward. She went in a series of short, jerky steps, alternately towing Ross along and pulling back. In this fashion he headed for the lorry park. Halfway there, she stopped shaking and started to walk more sensibly. Ross heaved a sigh of relief.

Bill said little as he took the chestnut from him, apparently accepting Ross's terse excuse that she was a little off-colour.

Ross wandered slowly back to the ringside.

'Ah, Ross, my boy.' Roland approached unseen. 'My esteemed papa sent me to find out if everything is all right. Our mutual friend Mr Fergusson is, to put it mildly, hopping mad. It seems he expected to be consulted before you . . . er . . . scratched his horse.'

'Consulted? There wasn't time for that! What was I supposed to do—use semaphore?' Ross exclaimed indignantly.

'Don't shoot me, old boy, I'm only the messenger! I'll tell him the animal got its fetlocks in a tangle or something.'

Ross smiled in spite of himself. 'Tell him the mare had done enough. That was a very big course, you know.'

Roland seemed disinclined to return to his father and Fergusson, and went with Ross to walk the course for the last class, then accompanied him back to the horsebox to collect Woodsmoke.

On the way they narrowly escaped being mown down by Telamon, who was proceeding crabwise through the crowd in spite of, or perhaps because of, Jim Pullen's best efforts to restrain him.

'Now that's a spirited creature!' Roland exclaimed. 'A real old-fashioned charger. Carry one into battle, don't you think?'

'I suppose. If one had a battle to go to,' Ross agreed, sardonically.

'Exactly so,' Roland said. 'Well, well. There's old Perry Wilson. Perry was my father's rider before Stephen Douglas. Nice to see you again, Perry old chap.'

Perry Wilson looked to be around forty, slight, with a thin face and wire-rimmed spectacles.

'Hi. Ross Wakelin.' Ross held out his hand in greeting.

'Hello. Well done, too.' Perry had a ready smile. 'You're doing a great job with those horses.'

On impulse, Ross asked, 'What did you think of Ginger when you used to ride her?'

Perry frowned. 'She seemed a nice mare. Very novice then, of course, but plenty of promise. Why? Are you having trouble?'

'I wondered if she'd ever been badly frightened in any way? She gets very uptight sometimes.'

'Not that I know of,' Perry said, shaking his head. 'She always seemed fairly placid. But then she was put in foal. There was some sort of upset . . . I can't remember the details, sorry. You could ask Annie Hayward. The mare was with her at the time.'

'Thanks. It never hurts to ask.'

'Too right,' Perry agreed. 'Well, I must get on. Nice to meet you, Ross. Roland.'

The last class of the day in the main ring had attracted a high-profile field. Woodsmoke was not daunted, however, and they swept out of the ring with a clear round, marred only by a momentary lack of concentration on Ross's part which almost resulted in Woody taking the wrong fence. Ross was furious with himself.

The public address system crackled. 'I should take more water with it, Ross,' Harry Douglas advised. 'But seriously, that was a nice round. At least the horse had his mind on the job! A clear for Ross Wakelin and Woodsmoke.'

The crowd laughed, unaware of the barbs hidden under the smooth tones.

Ross could see from a few of the sideways glances in the collecting ring that the implication hadn't gone unnoticed. He set his face in a mask of indifference. Changing onto Black Bishop, he concentrated on gaining Bishop's full attention and obedience.

For once, the horse seemed reluctant to respond, feeling awkward and unwilling, and Ross had to work really hard. He heard the hooter go for the start of Mick Colby's round on King's Defender and voices hush around the arena. Bishop still didn't seem himself.

Suddenly, from the arena came an appalling crash and splintering of timber, and the grunting thud of horseflesh hitting the ground. A gasp sounded around the ringside. Ross stood in his stirrups to see.

King was struggling to regain his feet among a tangle of red and white poles. Six feet or so away, lying ominously still, was his rider.

A stab of apprehension twisted through Ross. St John Ambulance workers bustled by, running across the ring. Ross hoped Mick was just winded. Nine times out of ten, that was all it was. A moment or two later an ambulance could be heard, threading its way through the crowds.

It seemed an age before the ambulance reappeared and made its way back across the showground. Shortly after this, King was led past by his girl groom. The horse seemed unhurt. Several people besieged the girl, asking for news of Colby, but she apparently knew nothing.

The loudspeakers apologised for the delay and expressed hope that Mr Colby would be all right. Next to jump, they said, would be Ross Wakelin on Mr Robert Fergusson's Black Bishop.

Ross was waved in by the stewards and, once the team of army cadets had finished rebuilding the shattered fence, the hooter sounded and he turned Bishop towards the first fence. It was a low, rustic pole and brush fence that would ordinarily have caused the black no problem at all, but he approached it at a choppy, unbalanced canter so unlike his usual fluent self that Ross was seriously worried that he might be lame. They cleared the obstacle, and Ross swung him towards the second, a formidable spread fence.

Bishop still wasn't happy. His ears were back and his head held high. As he saw what was expected of him he faltered, and when Ross tried to drive him forward he dug in his toes and refused.

For Ross this was more than enough to tell him all was not right. The horse had never before refused. With a young horse, nothing could be gained by forcing him on, and everything stood to be lost.

Glancing towards the judges' caravan, Ross touched the brim of his crash hat and nodded. With a sigh of disappointment he let the black walk from the arena on a long rein.

'I don't think we can blame Ross if nerves got the better of him there,' Harry Douglas said sympathetically from the commentary box. 'It isn't easy when you have just witnessed a nasty fall.'

Ross reached the collecting ring and dismounted, wearily wondering if Douglas Senior would ever tire of his sport.

'Ross!' Danielle was beside him, leading her grey mare. 'He has no right to say such things! He goes too far. Anyone with half a brain could see that Bishop was not right. It was no fault of yours.'

'Good thing I'm not sensitive,' he said with the ghost of a smile.

As he turned back to Bishop he came face to face with the Colonel and Robbie Fergusson. The Colonel was obviously concerned. 'Is there a problem, Ross?' he began, but Fergusson cut in abruptly.

'Yes, *he's* the problem! He flunked it! He's a spineless has-been who should never have been allowed back on a horse!'

Ross flinched inwardly but he held his temper. Only his desperate need to retain the ride on Bishop kept him from speaking his mind.

'Let's hear why a promising young horse was retired from his first major class after only one jump!' Fergusson sneered.

'Ross?' The Colonel spoke softly but there was no mistaking the underlying steel. *Don't let me down*, he was warning.

'The horse wasn't comfortable,' Ross stated with a studied calm. 'And I'm not about to ruin a potential Grand Prix horse for the sake of a single class.'

'Is the horse lame?' Fergusson snapped.

'No, I don't think so.'

'Then what?'

'I can't say, exactly. I just know he wasn't happy.' Ross didn't even begin to try to explain to Fergusson how a horse could communicate its discomfort to its jockey.

'More likely *you* didn't feel happy,' Fergusson suggested. 'I think you lost your bottle after seeing that other bloke stretchered off.'

'That's not so,' Ross asserted quietly. 'I don't like seeing anyone get hurt, but it had nothing to do with the way Bishop behaved.'

'Robbie . . .' The Colonel decided it was time to intercede. 'Couldn't this wait until we've all calmed down?'

'One minute. What about Red Queen?' Fergusson demanded of the American. 'Why was she withdrawn?'

Ross's heart sank. 'Ginger's different . . .' he began, and it sounded feeble even to his own ears.

'She won a class this morning!' Fergusson shouted. 'And this afternoon, for no reason at all, you pull her out of a class for which *I*—I'll have you remember—paid the entry fees. If you're not up to the job, Mr Wakelin, why can't you at least find the guts to say so?'

A number of possible replies occurred to Ross, none of which would tactfully defuse the situation. He remained silent.

'I think enough has been said for now. Let's get the horse back to his box,' the Colonel said.

Fergusson glared at him. 'I'll ring you in the morning to make arrangements about the horses,' he added as he turned away.

THE NIGHT FOLLOWING the Berkshire show, Ross was both mentally and physically fatigued; neither his mind nor his body would relax. He kept going over the row with Fergusson in his head, wondering if there had been anything else he could have said.

Damn Ginger! he thought for the thousandth time. *Should* he have taken her into the ring? He tossed and turned. His left knee ached with a grinding intensity that gradually developed into a throb. The bottle of whisky in the suitcase under the bed began to exercise a powerful attraction.

He ignored it successfully for four long hours, trying to force his restless mind to relax, to release the tension in his tired muscles.

It was hopeless.

In the still, dark hours of the early morning, despair began to creep in. His career was on the rocks again and it mattered even more this time than last. This time he had had a taste of the success he had been working for. The horses were just coming good, well on their way to qualifying for the top international shows. He had been given a second chance—and somehow he had blown it. People had been prepared to believe in him and he had let them down. No matter that he couldn't see how he could have played it any differently.

Bishop was the horse of a lifetime and without him, prospects for the yard, in Ross's present black mood, seemed bleak and unexciting.

He reached into the suitcase for the bottle. Without giving himself time to think, he removed the cap and tossed back three long pulls.

A comforting warmth began to spread through his body. He wiped his watering eyes and regarded the remaining liquid with a longing that dismayed him.

He was within a whisker of proving Leo right. Oblivion, albeit temporary, was a temptation, but it provided no answers.

At six o'clock he gave up the struggle to sleep, got out of bed and had a cold shower.

Sitting in the open window with a scalding cup of black coffee, he looked down at the yard. The horses in the outside boxes leaned over their doors, beginning to think of breakfast. Ross scanned the familiar faces with affection. Idly, he wondered where Bishop was. Usually the big black was one of the first to demand his feed.

Ross watched for several minutes longer, a sense of unease growing, then shoved his feet into his boots and hurried down to the yard.

Inside Bishop's box the big black was standing, resting one hind leg, his back slightly hunched. With a sinking heart Ross gave the animal a cursory examination before going in search of Bill.

He found the stable manager in the cottage, drinking coffee, and imparted the bad news.

'His back, you say? I'll ring Annie, then. And I'll let the Colonel know. Fergusson may ring this morning.' The little man grunted. 'Lets you off the hook, doesn't it?'

Ross blinked. The way Bill said it, you would think Ross had engineered the back problem himself. That Bishop's injury exonerated him from blame for their nonperformance the day before had not in fact occurred to Ross. His only concern had been for the horse.

ANNIE ARRIVED midmorning. 'Ross! Bill!' she boomed in greeting, marching up and opening Bishop's stable door. 'Did it at the show yesterday, did he?' she asked. 'Seems to have been a day for accidents. Chap in the pub said the lad who rides King had a broken collarbone and concussion. He'll be sore for a week or two.'

Annie began her inspection. After a few moments she looked up. 'Found the problem,' she announced. 'Like to come back here and hold his near hind up for me?'

Ross moved to the black's quarters. Annie placed one hand on the horse's back to relocate the problem. Then, with the heel of her palm and most of her not inconsiderable strength, she hit the animal.

Bishop staggered, nearly sending Ross flying.

'That seems to have done it,' Annie observed with satisfaction. 'Just a slight misalignment, pressing on a nerve. Probably the result of a slip. Rest him for a couple of days, then plenty of lunging to build the muscles up.'

'Beer?' Ross suggested, as they left the stable. Then, with a gleam in his eye, 'Or is it too early for you?'

'It's never too early, Ross, you know that.'

While they were quenching their thirst, Ross said, 'I wanted to ask you about Ginger. I believe you had her for a while?'

'Yes, two winters ago. Fergusson put her in foal when she was throwing up a couple of splints. She miscarried.'

'What exactly happened?'

'Some hooligans with a box of firecrackers,' Annie said, remembering with disgust. 'Got a kick out of seeing the horses run, I suppose. Poor old Ginger, she was in a terrible state. She wasn't lame by that time, so we abandoned the idea of breeding from her and Fergusson put her back in training.'

'Thanks, I think you've told me exactly what I wanted to know. She does seem to have a rather extreme reaction to loud noises, and I wondered why. And she's a little moody.'

Annie laughed. 'Mare's privilege,' she asserted. 'But I'm not surprised about the noises. She'll probably get over it, given time.'

IT BEING A MONDAY, the yard was deserted in the afternoon. Ross rode Ginger into the school with little optimism. The only way he could see of reducing the mare's fear of loud noises was by letting her grow used to them gradually. It would take weeks, possibly months, and he couldn't see Fergusson allowing him the time. He pushed the thought resolutely away. He *had* to keep the ride on Bishop.

He warmed the mare up and she behaved well, apparently in one of her better moods. Ross's spirits rose.

From his pocket, he took two small flat pieces of wood. Letting the mare walk round the school on a loose rein, he gently tapped the pieces together. The mare flicked her ears back enquiringly. He patted her, talking all the while, and then tapped them again.

Gradually he increased the volume of the taps. Ginger became more edgy, but didn't panic. Ross made much of her. After another ten minutes, he began to allow himself a glimmer of hope.

In the field beside the school, one of the Colonel's spaniels put up a brace of pheasant with a flurry of clucking and flapping wings.

Ginger's nerves, already stretched, snapped. She bolted blindly.

Ross was ready for her. With his legs clamped hard on her sides, he pulled her head round. With her eye almost at his knee she could do no more than stagger sideways for a few yards. She managed to retain her balance and halted, shuddering violently. Keeping the rein tight over her neck, he slid off and stood talking quietly to her. Slowly, she relaxed. He considered getting back on but couldn't raise much enthusiasm for the idea. He had just lost half an hour's progress in a split second and he hadn't the heart to start again.

Ross unsaddled the mare and turned her loose. He took off his crash hat and, tired and dispirited, limped back towards the yard with the saddle over his arm. He was almost at the gate before he lifted his head enough to see that someone was there and he'd been watched. His spirits fell another notch.

'Hi, Princess,' he said wearily.

'Hello.' Lindsay was gazing at the horse.

Ross balanced the saddle on top of the gate and leaned on it.

'Is it because she's a chestnut?' Lindsay asked abruptly.

It was a question he had asked himself a thousand times. Ginger . . . the horse in America . . . they were the same colour. Was it possible that his trouble with Ginger stemmed from a subconscious connection he'd made between them? Was he tense, and communicating his tension to the mare? Maybe a little, he admitted, but surely the basic problem was with her?

'Simone is a chestnut,' he reminded her defensively.

'*What* then, Ross? What's happened to you? You surely can't deny there's a problem? Just now I saw one of the toughest riders on the circuit let a novice horse get away with blatant disobedience. I saw him break the first rule of training that you should always end on a good note.' She was watching his face closely as she spoke. 'Oh, come on, Ross! Don't you know what they're saying about you?'

'People always talk,' he observed mildly. 'You don't have to listen.'

'Damn you!' Lindsay cried vehemently. 'Don't give me that "I don't care" routine. I know you better than that.'

He stared into the middle distance, eyes bleak, face shuttered.

'Don't shut me out, Ross. I just want to help.' Losing patience, she gripped his arm and pulled him to face her. 'Talk to me, damn you!'

She caught him off guard. For a moment he gazed down at her upturned, impatient face, and then his control slipped. With one finger he tilted her chin and, since she made no move to resist, bent to kiss her.

Lindsay froze for an instant, then her hand stole up into his hair and pulled him closer. For a moment nothing else mattered until, abruptly, Ross pulled away.

'That was stupid!' he said roughly. 'I'm sorry. Better forget it.'

Lindsay recoiled, hurt. 'Consider it forgotten,' she retorted roundly, and turned to open the gate.

Ross put out a hand to stop her. It seemed more important than ever that she should understand about Ginger.

'I'm not afraid for myself,' he said, trying to explain. 'It's just—the nightmares—that child, screaming. I can't let it happen again.'

Lindsay turned back, her eyes full of compassion. 'But it won't, Ross. It was a once-in-a-lifetime fluke. Vixen had a tumour. Ginger's a completely different horse.'

'Ginger is insane,' he stated bluntly. 'Last year she was frightened by some idiots with a firecracker and lost her foal. Now any sudden loud noise makes her freak out. If anyone got in her way . . .'

Lindsay glanced at Ginger, frowning. 'Are you sure, Ross? Is she really dangerous?'

He sighed. 'I don't know, Princess. I suppose time will tell. I just have a bad feeling about her and I don't want anyone else to be hurt. Least of all me,' he added with a self-deprecating grin.

Lindsay still looked troubled and Ross felt enough had been said. He smiled at her. 'Come on. Let's go in and have some coffee.'

Together they headed for the cottage, their easy relationship apparently restored. But Ross felt that it would never be quite the same again.

'I WANT YOU to be straight with me,' the Colonel said, opening the inquest that evening. They had both settled into leather armchairs with glasses of sherry to hand.

'Sure.' Ross nodded.

'I don't mean to imply that you haven't been in the past,' the Colonel added. 'It's just that sometimes I find you—shall we say, inscrutable? I find I have no idea what's going on in your head.'

Ross smiled faintly and said nothing. He felt strangely detached now that the crunch had come.

'Robbie Fergusson called this morning,' his boss said. 'He conceded that Bishop was obviously uncomfortable yesterday but doesn't accept that you were right to withdraw the mare.'

'So what now? Have I lost the ride?'

'I think that's up to you,' the Colonel said. 'Fergusson's not stupid. Even *he* realises that you get a sweet tune out of Bishop. The thing is, we obviously have a problem. He's not happy about the rumours he's been hearing concerning you.'

'Which one?' Ross asked, flippantly. 'The one that says I'm an alcoholic or the one that says I've lost my nerve? Or do you subscribe to the popular view that I drink to conquer my fear?'

'I take no notice of hearsay, myself.' The Colonel wasn't amused. 'But you must admit there's some kind of problem with Ginger?'

'I do. And I don't care if I never sit on her again,' Ross said bluntly. 'I don't believe she's safe. She's mentally unstable.'

'I see. Given that, what do you intend to do about her? She's entered in the New Forest Open next week,' the Colonel warned.

Ross sighed. 'If it's a choice between riding Ginger and losing them both, I'll ride the mare. But I'd like it to go on record that in my opinion she'd be far better retired to stud.'

'I respect your judgment,' the Colonel said. 'As far as I'm concerned, you don't have to prove a bloody thing. If you don't want to ride the mare it's not the end of the world. I'm sure we can withstand the loss of Fergusson's horses. No one here would blame you.'

Ross looked up, surprised and grateful for this gesture of support. 'It wouldn't do my reputation much good. Besides, Bishop is by far the best horse I've ever ridden, and I've no intention of watching somebody else ride him into the ring if I can possibly prevent it.'

'Another sherry?' The Colonel rose and poured two without waiting for an answer. He held one out to Ross.

'What about my reputation?' Ross asked, lifting one eyebrow ironically as he accepted the glass.

'Should I be worried?' the Colonel asked, his shrewd grey eyes on Ross's face.

'No.' Ross returned his gaze steadily.

The Colonel pursed his lips and nodded, apparently satisfied.

Not for the first time, Ross felt he was very fortunate in his boss.

'Were you aware that my son was intending to buy a horse?'

Ross blinked. 'Well, he did say something once, but no offence meant—you know how it is—I didn't pay much heed.'

'I know exactly how it is,' the Colonel said heavily. 'But apparently, this time Roland was quite serious. The horse is to arrive on Wednesday. God knows what sort of animal he'll have turned up.'

WHEN THE NEW HORSE arrived, Roland swung his immaculately shod feet off the office table where he'd been lounging and wandered out into the yard. Sarah and Danny emerged from stable doorways and Bill turned from his discussion with Ross to regard the horsebox with reluctant curiosity. As the box driver lowered the ramp and the partitions swung to one side, those waiting were treated to a dim view of a massive chestnut rump. The horse was led to the top of the ramp, where he stood with upflung head and eager eyes, surveying his new surroundings.

Bill Scott swore under his breath and Ross was inclined to agree with him. Telamon, the failed racehorse, marched purposefully down the ramp and shrieked a challenge to the world. From the stables, half a dozen excited voices answered him.

Bill swore again. 'Shit! That's all we need. A bloody stallion!'

Ross glanced at Roland and was amused to see a look of almost comical dismay cross his face. Could it be that for once the Colonel's son had failed fully to appreciate all the aspects of a situation?

'Well, can't it be muzzled or something?' Roland enquired.

'It's not a bloody dog,' Bill observed witheringly.

Roland looked hurt. 'Of course not. He's Ross's battle charger. I told my dear papa it was just what you needed to revive your tattered reputation,' he told Ross.

'Most likely break his neck!' Bill grunted, ever the pessimist.

'Ross'll manage him, won't you, Ross?' Danny stated confidently.

'Oh, sure,' Ross said lightly. 'No problem.'

Roland seemed anxious to see the horse ridden and reluctantly Ross agreed to try him that evening. Reluctantly because he guessed the event would attract interested onlookers and he would far rather have had a chance to become acquainted with the horse in private.

As he had feared, when Ross accepted a leg-up from Bill at half past seven, Roland reappeared with his father, Sarah, Darcy Richmond and Danny.

The stallion proceeded restlessly across the yard to the school on legs that punched the ground like steel pistons. Only in Bishop had Ross ever felt anything approaching this power, but whereas in the German horse it was controlled and smooth, in this animal it was raw and rebellious.

As soon as he heard the gate to the school click shut behind him he sent the chestnut on, sensing the bottled energy that would have to be released before he could even hope to communicate with the horse.

Telamon hesitated fractionally. A succession of riders who had strapped him down ever harder in an attempt to control his wildness had left him unprepared for this abrupt change of tactics.

Then, with a squeal of pure pleasure, he erupted into the centre of the school and proceeded to buck himself almost inside out. Ross stayed with him, gripping hard and letting his body follow through. Gradually the leaps levelled out and the chestnut began to run.

Ross let him go. This horse, though unruly, was not about to do itself any harm. Ross relaxed and began to enjoy himself.

After four or five circuits the stallion started to steady. Ross steered him towards one of the low schooling fences and he skipped over it. Encouraged, Ross inclined him towards the big parallel bars in the centre of the school. The jump was five foot square.

Telamon flicked his ears forward and forged fearlessly ahead. The red and white poles flashed by a good twelve inches below the stallion's hooves and the landing was smooth and effortless.

A cheer broke from the lips of those watching and Telamon shied violently and bucked again, almost catching Ross out. One more circuit of the school and the horse allowed Ross to slow him to a trot and finally to a halt by the fence.

Ross patted the arching chestnut neck and slid off the horse. Telamon turned to eye him, froth cascading from his chomping jaws. Ross had the distinct impression that the horse was very satisfied.

'I've never seen anything quite like it!' The Colonel was the first to find his voice. 'What do you use, Superglue?'

Ross grinned. 'I did a lot of horse-breaking in the States,' he said. 'It's just practice and a measure of luck.'

'Play it down if you like,' the Colonel said, 'but I don't know of many riders who could have stayed on that. I shall expect you to win at Brockenhurst—he's entered in the Open, you know.'

'Oh, boy!' Ross said with feeling.

SEVEN

On Saturday evening Ross cleaned tack with absent-minded thoroughness. The yard was quiet. Only muffled sounds of munching and snorting disturbed the warm stillness. He supposed the Colonel and Roland would be getting ready to go to Lindsay and James's party. The thought did nothing to improve his mood. He soaped and buffed the leather, lost in gloomy contemplation.

'Hello, Ross.'

Lindsay stood in the doorway. God only knew how long she had been standing there. She wore ski pants and a long, loose shirt.

Ross smiled. 'Hi, Princess. I hope you're not going to make a habit of sneaking up on me. It's not good for my blood pressure.'

'I'm sorry. Actually, I wasn't sure you'd still be here. I thought you were going out with Danielle,' Lindsay reminded him.

Ross could have kicked himself. 'And I thought *you* were having a party,' he countered. 'Shouldn't you be getting ready?'

'I came to check on Gypsy.'

'*This* time of night?' he asked, incredulously.

'Actually, I had to get out of the house,' she admitted, tracing the line of a scratch on the doorpost with her fingernail. 'Mother's getting on my nerves. She's so overpowering. She has to try and organise everybody.' She sighed. 'I suppose she means well, but . . .'

'Sure she does. She just wants everything to be right for you.'

'Not for *me*!' Lindsay burst out, looking all of a sudden very unhappy. 'She wants it for herself, so her toffee-nosed friends will be impressed. I'm even marrying the man *she* chose for me. The most eligible of eligible bachelors.' She stopped short, biting her lip. 'No, I didn't mean that. James is a great guy. I'm very fond of him.'

Ross supposed it was natural to get cold feet at the last minute. *Fond* was a strange choice of word, though.

'You'll be fine. You make a great pair,' he assured her. 'Look, can I get you something? A coffee? Beer?'

Lindsay shook her head. 'No. Thanks all the same. I'd better get back. I've got to change.' She made no move to leave, however, concentrating on the scratch on the doorpost once more.

Ross finished soaping the last bridle and started reassembling it. The silence was loud between them.

'Why don't you want to come tonight, Ross?' she asked abruptly.

'I . . . er . . . I don't have anything to wear,' he said lamely.

'It doesn't matter. There'll probably be all sorts there.'

Ross raised an eyebrow. 'Not jeans and cowboy boots,' he said. 'Your mother would crucify me!'

'Stuff Mother!' Lindsay countered forcefully. 'But it's not just that, is it, Ross? Is it Danielle?'

Ross felt cornered. 'No, it's not Danielle. I never did ask her to go out tonight. Sorry, Princess. It's just . . . I don't know. I guess I'm just not in the mood for partying.'

'Me neither,' Lindsay confided with a smile. 'Look, please say you'll come? It won't seem right otherwise. Roland will lend you something to wear. I asked him yesterday, just in case.'

'OK, I'll come. Now you'd better be on your way, hadn't you?'

Lindsay nodded. 'I knew you weren't going out with Danielle tonight. She's coming to the party with Roland.'

'You devious little . . .!' Ross threw his cleaning sponge at her and she ducked and ran out of the door.

ROSS TRAVELLED to the first day of the New Forest Show on the Tuesday with his mind all over the place. He'd spent less than an hour at Lindsay's party and he'd slipped away when the dancing began, unable to bear the sight of her, gorgeous in emerald silk, smiling up at James as they circled the floor.

Behind him in the lorry, four horses shifted and stamped on the straw-covered matting. The two mares, Ginger and Flo, occupied the foremost stalls, with the stallion, Telamon, at the very rear. In between was the solid figure of Woodsmoke, whose presence was supposed to quell any romantic notions the big chestnut might nurture.

Ross had a busy day. Ginger behaved herself, although she could not, by any stretch of the imagination, have been described as eager. Flo excelled herself, placing in both her morning classes.

The first of Ross's rides for the afternoon was Telamon.

When Danny boosted Ross into the saddle, the chestnut launched himself skywards. Ross had been ready and he let the animal have his head as much as possible, hoping that he would ease the kinks out of his system before he had to head for the ring.

That Telamon was wildly excited as he entered the ring was obvious. He crossed the turf in an extravagant trot, tail held high and nostrils cracking. To Ross he felt like a tightly coiled spring with a hair-trigger release. The crowd began to buzz with anticipation.

Ross concentrated on staying relaxed, hands gently playing on the reins to keep the horse's attention. As the hooter sounded, he let him spring forward into a canter. The horse negotiated the first fence with a kind of mini-explosion. Ross pushed him forward. Telamon took the next two fences without appearing to notice them and then allowed himself to be guided round the first turn towards the fourth.

A double of gates, a wall, parallel bars and a tricky upright were all traversed with scornful ease. Ross was leaving the horse to find his own stride as much as possible, knowing that interference only provoked conflict. Coming to the second last, however—parallel bars that you could comfortably have driven a small car between— he couldn't resist squeezing with his calves to ask for extra effort.

Telamon shot into the air, giving the poles at least eighteen inches' clearance, and landed running. Ross attempted valiantly to make the turn to the last fence but by now Telamon was convinced that running was the order of the day. They missed the jump by a good yard, still accelerating, and began to circumnavigate the ring.

Somehow Ross managed to thread the horse between the jumps to arrive on line with the last fence a second time. Obligingly, Telamon picked his feet up at the appropriate moment and they skimmed between the timing beacons to finish the course.

The stallion plainly thought it a huge joke, for as Ross sat back to try and ride him to a halt, he put in a buck of gargantuan proportions that sent the American over his head.

The crowd gasped collectively, then clapped and laughed as Ross picked himself up with a self-conscious grin and dusted himself down. It seemed that his supposed indiscretions were momentarily sidelined in the face of this new interest.

Outside, where Danny waited with a cotton sheet to throw over the chestnut's loins, Ross was greeted by Roland.

'I see what my revered father sees in the sport now. It really is quite exciting, isn't it? I'm looking forward to his next class,' Roland said with the enthusiasm of the newly converted.

All afternoon Ross was constantly changing horses and numbers and rings. Bill and Danny worked like termites, scurrying to and fro to make sure the right horse, wearing the right tack, reached the right collecting ring at the right time.

In the last class, Telamon entered the ring with the same high-stepping trot and screamed his excitement to the world in the way that only a stallion can. The jumps were considerably bigger than those in the earlier class but Telamon accorded them the same glorious lack of respect. Ross once again chose a policy of non-interference. It was only when they were passing the finishing markers that he realised they had, incredibly, jumped a clear round. The appreciative crowd cheered, enjoying the stallion's highly individual style.

Ross could not prevent an idiotic grin from spreading over his face as he returned to the collecting ring. This horse was one big, crazy son of a bitch but, hell, he could jump! And he, Ross, had the ride!

The Oakley Manor team couldn't have been more delighted. Their obvious pride lifted Ross as nothing else had done for a long time.

Half an hour later, he and Telamon were back in the collecting ring, waiting to be called for the jump-off. The course was tight and twisty, and didn't suit Telamon's wide, galloping turns, but the chestnut jumped clear again, and when two others faulted, Ross found himself lining up for a third-place rosette.

As he slid off the horse and loosened his girth, Ross heard a plummy, upper-class voice declare: 'They say he drinks, you know.'

'Well, if that's Dutch courage,' a second voice replied, 'I'm going to try some!'

ROSS WAS GREETED first thing the next morning, the final day of the show, by a note pushed under the door at the foot of the stairs. It read: *King Rat has bolted. The cat is in pursuit.*

Ross smiled to himself. McKinnon was obviously exercising his individual brand of humour at Leo Jackson's expense.

At the show he found another note awaiting him in the secretary's tent: *The rat has grown wings at Bournemouth and is going across the water. Cat now enjoying a saucer of milk. Good luck today.*

Ross experienced mild relief at the thought that Leo was out of the picture. Why, though, *had* he suddenly decided to leave? Had he realised he was being watched and was therefore unlikely to get away with any more mischief-making?

By midafternoon Ross had ridden in several classes, including the Foxhunter Qualifier on Ginger. Robbie Fergusson had appeared uncharacteristically in the vicinity of the collecting ring and watched, unsmiling, as Ross had coaxed the mare round the course to collect a total of eight faults for two fences down. Fergusson didn't speak to him when he came out, except to say that he hoped the American would wake her up a bit for the next class.

Ross refrained from saying what was on his mind. If the mare had looked as though she needed waking up, Ross knew it was entirely due to his own efforts to keep her calm. As soon as he'd sat on her, he'd sensed she was in one of her irrational moods.

There was no time to worry about her, though. Ross still had Simone to ride in the Foxhunter before he rode Ginger and Woodsmoke in the last class.

The indefatigable Simone achieved a faultless clear round, following it with a fast clear in the jump-off. The Colonel was delighted.

'Another step on the ladder to Birmingham, Yank,' he said, clapping Ross on the back. 'You made a bloody good job of that!'

The last class was the biggest of the day, in the size of both the jumps and the prize money. An impressive line-up of competitors was entered and the crowd stood five or six deep. The Colonel and Robbie Fergusson had seats in the grandstand.

Woody jumped a beautiful, polished clear. Ten minutes later Ross mounted Ginger and found her, if anything, several degrees more strung up than she had been earlier. All the danger signs were there: agitated ear movements, the whites of her eyes showing, and her stride short and jerky. She seemed totally spaced-out. He wondered how much would have to happen before Fergusson would consider him justified in retiring from the competition.

'She looks a bit wound up,' Lindsay commented from the rails as Ross paused for a moment. 'Is she OK?'

'No,' he said, matter-of-factly. 'She's crazy as a snake.'

'Perhaps it's nerves,' James said judiciously.

'Let's hope so, buddy,' Ross said heavily. 'Let's hope so!'

When his number was called, however, Ginger seemed to have shifted from spaced-out to mulish, in one of her typical mood swings. In this mode, Ross felt they were less likely to storm the grandstand than have two refusals and be disqualified at the first fence. Either way, his chances of keeping the ride on Bishop didn't look bright.

Ginger jumped the first two fences, albeit begrudgingly. Ross used all the strength he could muster to bully and coax her round the turn and towards the third fence, an imposing green and white parallel.

All the way he knew he was fighting a losing battle. Ginger had her mind firmly set against the jump. She dug in her toes a full stride away from the takeoff point and would go no further.

With little expectation of success, Ross swung the mare round, bullied a few more strides of canter out of her and turned her back towards the jump. Suddenly, in the crowd, not six feet from the mare's heels, a balloon burst with a sharp crack.

Nothing could have been calculated to upset her more. With a squeal, she ripped the reins through Ross's fingers and bolted.

The abrupt change from recalcitrant to hysterical caught him out and the mare was away before he could stop her. That her mind had ceased to function rationally was swiftly borne out by her flattening the floral centrepiece to the arena.

Urgently Ross calculated angles and distances but could see no hope of avoiding either a collision with the boundary railings and the fragile bodies beyond, or the double of white gates that formed fence ten, close to the side of the ring. Grimly, he chose the gates.

History was repeating itself.

Ross threw all his weight onto Ginger's left rein and stirrup in an attempt to throw her off balance and off-line. It worked. She stayed in the ring, hitting the first gate without making any effort to leave the ground and carrying it forward for a stride before it tangled in her front legs and her momentum sent her sprawling into the second.

Ross gripped instinctively, staying with her as she fell, and the whole eight-foot length of the gate collapsed on top of them.

For a moment Ginger seemed winded. Then she erupted into frantic action. With her body pinning his left leg to the turf, Ross tried in vain to protect himself from her scrabbling hooves. Her weight lifted from his leg twice, and twice fell back, before she finally made it to her feet.

A passing hoof thudded into his shoulder and another clouted the back of his crash cap. He felt a soft darkness overtake him.

VOICES FILLED his head. Voices asking if he could hear them. A voice suggesting he be rolled over. Another, sharper, saying to leave him be, the ambulance was coming. Ross lay still, feeling mostly numb.

'I have to see him!'

That sounded like Lindsay. Ross opened his eyes.

'How do you feel?' another voice enquired. 'Can you move?'

With an effort Ross used the arm he wasn't lying on to push himself over onto his back. Pain clamped his upper body in a vicelike grip but he'd been winded often enough to know that it would pass. Lindsay came into view, looking pale and distressed.

He smiled. 'Hi, Princess,' and was rewarded by a watery smile. Encouraged, he sat up just as an ambulance came alongside.

The voices protested. They really thought he should lie still.

Ross's vision swam and steadied. They were probably right, but once the medical fraternity got their hands on him he knew his leg would be examined and his fitness to ride would come under scrutiny . . .

'I'm OK, really,' he assured the faces round him. 'Just winded. Has someone caught my horse?'

The horse was being taken care of, he was told.

With the help of the doctor in charge, Ross climbed to his feet. A hot stab of pain burned through his ribs on the left side and he caught his breath. He could have cheered though. His bad leg, put cautiously to the ground, didn't buckle. It created its own kind of hell, which made him grit his teeth, but it held.

The doctor persuaded Ross to accept a lift out of the ring in the ambulance. Outside, he climbed out stiffly, thanked the medical crew, and was nearly bowled over by an enthusiastic embrace from Lindsay.

'Ross!' she cried. 'For a moment I thought . . . I was *so* scared! And you *were* right about Ginger, weren't you?'

He unwound her arms from about his neck, partly in deference to James, who was watching with an unreadable expression, and partly because her hug was making contact with a lot of sore places.

'I expect it looked worse than it was,' he said steadyingly.

He turned to where Danny was leading Ginger up for the vet to see. Her panic spent, she looked dejected, her chestnut coat dark with sweat and ears drooping unhappily. She was heavily lame. Ross wondered what Fergusson would have to say about the afternoon's events and felt suddenly tired and depressed. He accompanied Danny and Ginger back to the horsebox, limping.

The Colonel joined them *en route*, concerned for Ross's well-being and anxious for the horse. The American declared his intention to stick to his schedule and ride Woodsmoke in the jump-off and eventually the Colonel gave way.

'What did the vet have to say about Ginger?' Preston asked.

'He thinks she may have cracked a bone in her pastern. She'll have to be X-rayed.' Ross looked round. 'Where's the worried owner?'

The Colonel sighed. 'He said to forward the vet's report. He's gone home. Bloody man!'

By the time Ross had jumped Woodsmoke to second place in the jump-off, he was feeling like a football must feel after a gruelling Super Bowl. With steady, dependable Woody it was mostly a case of pointing him in the right direction and staying on. Had it been any other horse, he would probably have been forced to admit defeat.

Travelling back to the yard, Ross's head ached heavily, as did his ribs, and if he twisted or tried to bend too far, a sharp pain discouraged him in no uncertain manner. But time would heal, he knew. What worried him was the added damage that had undoubtedly been done to his knee. The mare had to pick *that* leg to roll on. At some point in this unsatisfactory train of thought, he drifted off to sleep.

IT SEEMED like any other morning until he shifted position and a thousand damaged nerve endings screamed in protest. As he waited for the sensation to pass, he realised he couldn't recall going to bed.

The stairs creaked and the door swung open.

Maggie Scott appeared. 'Oh, you're awake then,' she observed. 'How do you feel?'

'I've been better,' he admitted. 'What time is it?'

'Gone midday,' she said, drawing the curtains. 'You had us worried last night, you know. Fainting like that. The Colonel was proper cut up. Said he never should have let you ride Woody in that last class.'

'I've never fainted in my life,' Ross protested.

'Well, you did last night. We had a job to wake you at all when the horsebox got back. You were very groggy. Anyway, halfway across the yard you collapsed. It was touch and go whether we called the doctor or the ambulance. Bill had to half carry you upstairs. The Colonel was afraid you had delayed concussion, but I said I was sure they would have checked you for concussion in the ambulance at the show. I said all you needed was a good sleep, and the doctor agreed.'

'Thank you.' Ross was genuinely grateful. 'I'm sorry I caused such a fuss. Uh . . . did the doctor say anything else?' Somewhere along the line he had been changed from his riding gear into the shorts he wore in bed, and his heavily strapped knee would not have gone unnoticed.

'He said he thought you had some sore ribs and there would be a lot of bruising. Oh, and he asked about your knee but the Colonel said that was an old injury.'

Ross eased himself gingerly into a sitting position. 'Well, the sooner I'm up and about, the sooner the stiffness will wear off.'

When Ross finally made it to the yard, after taking a ridiculously long time to shower, shave and dress, he found Roger West talking to Bill and the Colonel outside the tack room.

'How's the mare?' he asked

'I'm afraid there's not much we can do for her, Ross,' Roger said unhappily. 'She's chipped her pastern.' He held up an X-ray and indicated the crescent-shaped bone within the hoof. 'And she's cracked her pedal bone. There's evidence of damage to the ligaments and tendons, too. She must be in a lot of pain. In addition to that, she seems mentally distressed. She'll not jump again, and from what I've been hearing it would be a bit of a risk to breed from her. Basically, we're just waiting to hear from Mr Fergusson.'

'I see.' Ross had expected it, deep down, but it didn't make the thought any the more palatable. The mare had run out of time.

He made his way over to the stables, where he spent quite a while with the mare. Trying to calm her. Apologising for not understanding soon enough and finally telling her she had nothing to fear; soon everything would be all right.

Ross was with the mare also, three hours later, when she was destroyed humanely in the home field, out of sight of the other horses, with her head in a bucket of oats and carrots.

They wouldn't let him work or ride, so Ross had a hot bath to try to ease his bruises and stiffening muscles, and then spent an hour or two stretched out on his bed, prey to self-pity and depression.

The only thing about the day that held any promise was the news from Roger West that, contrary to expectation, the dog had begun to rally. There were signs of movement in his back legs, although it was still too early to say whether he would regain full mobility. The vet suggested the dog go to Annie Hayward's to convalesce.

The evening found Ross making his way up to the main house in response to a request from the Colonel.

The Colonel was not alone in his study. Roland lounged non-chalantly in one of the worn leather armchairs.

'Hail the all-conquering hero, bloody but unbowed!' he declared.

Ross moved to one of the empty chairs, trying to minimise his limp. The Colonel handed him a glass of sherry. 'How do you feel, really?' he asked, regarding Ross keenly as he sat down. 'You had us worried last night, you know.'

'Sorry about that. I guess I was pretty tired, but I'm fine now.'

The Colonel raised an eyebrow.

'Well, a bit rough, maybe,' Ross admitted. 'But it'll wear off.'

'You were right about that mare,' the Colonel said. 'She seemed to go completely berserk. I've never seen anything like it.'

'I have,' Ross grimly.

'Of course, I was forgetting. You must feel the fates are against you. I mean, the chances of its happening twice to the same person must be millions to one.'

'That would depend,' Roland mused, 'on what triggered it.'

'And what the devil do you mean by that?' his father demanded.

'Keep your hair on, Father dear,' Roland advised, in his infuriatingly calm way. 'I was just thinking aloud.'

'Well, I appreciate you have to practise but try to do it quietly and in your own time.'

A respectful tap on the door put an end to the sparring. Masters took half a step inside. 'Phone call, sir. Lady Cresswell.'

'Thank you. I'll take it in the hall,' Colonel Preston said, rising.

As the door closed behind the Colonel, Ross leaned forward. 'What *did* you mean by it?' he asked Roland softly.

Roland shrugged. 'Oh, just that Leo was at the show yesterday.'

Ross stared. 'But, that's imposs—' Too late, he realised he was treading on dangerous ground.

'Impossible?' Roland hoisted a lazy eyebrow. 'Why should you say that, I wonder? Nevertheless, he *was* there.'

'How do you know? I didn't see you there.'

'Oh, but I was,' Roland replied smoothly. 'I went to see Danielle.'

'So, where did you see Leo?'

'The beer tent. Don't remember him having a balloon, though.'

Roland wore his habitually bland expression, as if they were just exchanging platitudes. What he was implying, however, put an entirely new complexion on the previous day's events.

So much for Leo being out of the country. The fact that he had gone to such elaborate lengths to make them think so made it obvious that he knew he was being watched. McKinnon's men were too practised, according to McKinnon, to have given the game away themselves. Therefore someone must have tipped Leo off. But who? Who could have known?

'Well,' Roland remarked lightly, getting up. 'Glad to see you on your feet again.'

Father and son met in the doorway. Roland bowed ironically. 'I bid you farewell,' he said grandly.

The Colonel collapsed into his chair. 'Where did I go wrong?' he asked with a sigh. 'He used to be such a nice boy. So normal!'

'Was that him?' Ross indicated a framed photograph that stood on a nearby trophy case. It showed two teenage boys holding aloft a large trophy between them.

'The one on the right.' The Colonel nodded. 'The other boy is Darcy Richmond. They went to the same school.'

'That would have been after Darcy's father was killed, I presume?'

'Yes, a couple of years. Though he wasn't exactly killed, you know. He committed suicide.' The Colonel shook his head sadly. 'A bad business. Took an overdose and drowned himself in his bath.'

'Thorough,' Ross commented. And somewhat different from the story Darcy had told, he thought.

'It was about the only thing he *did* do properly. He just couldn't see that Franklin had got where he was by plain hard work. Always trying to take short cuts, Elliot Richmond was. Franklin bailed his brother out until it became obvious that Elliot was never going to learn to be responsible. Franklin was a very good uncle to the boy. God knows what would have become of Darcy if he hadn't been.'

'What about Darcy's mother?'

'Long gone,' the Colonel said. 'An empty-headed bimbo who ran out when the money did.'

'Darcy told me his father was killed in a car accident,' Ross said.

Colonel Preston nodded. 'It was hard for him to come to terms with at his age. First his mother running out on him—as he saw it—then his father killing himself. I think the lad invented the accident story to comfort himself. I didn't realise he was still using it.'

He sipped his sherry thoughtfully. 'He's a nice enough boy really, though I think perhaps there were times when Frank showed tolerance when quite frankly a sound hiding would have answered better. The business with . . . er . . . women,' he said, apparently changing his mind midsentence. 'Still, he's turned out well enough. Darcy's been good to young Peter in his turn, you know. No true brother could have treated him better, and the kid worships him.'

'I've seen that,' Ross agreed. 'He seems to have a way with the boy. Doesn't share Peter's passion for horses, though.'

'No.' The Colonel turned his attention back to Ross. 'But what about you? Your knee, for example.'

'My knee is an old story,' Ross protested. 'It's getting better all the time.' And my nose is getting longer, he thought wryly.

The Colonel didn't look convinced. 'All right, but you take at least two clear days off or I'll march you off to the hospital myself!'

ROSS ROSE EARLY the next morning after an uncomfortable night and managed to shower and dress in a marginally quicker time than he had the day before. The bruises were developing colourfully and the swelling was beginning to subside.

In the yard he met Lindsay coming out of Flo's box with a mucksack. 'Oh, no, you don't!' she exclaimed. 'Uncle John's orders. Go and sit down, we've got it all under control.'

Ross was astounded. 'He called you?'

'No,' she said. 'I just came. Now do as you're told.'

He pottered aimlessly about the tack room for three-quarters of an hour while the mucking out was taken care of, remembering his very first morning at Oakley Manor when he had done just the same. So much had happened since then. What Ross didn't know was how much of his troubles could be ascribed to Franklin's extortionist, and how much to Leo. It was quite possible the extortionist could be using Leo's activities as a smoke screen.

It had also occurred to him that morning that Roland's tip about Leo's supposed presence at the show on Thursday might have been a smoke screen to hide his own involvement. But where was the motive? Ross could not imagine Roland had ever lacked for money. Besides, he had a good job in London in antiques.

Or did he? He was very vague about it and certainly didn't spend much time there. Ross made a mental note to ask McKinnon if Roland's finances had been scrutinised.

After breakfast, finding the prospect of a completely inactive day a drag, Ross decided to give Danny a jumping lesson on Flo.

After the session, Franklin's new Range Rover swept into the yard, bearing not only him but Darcy and Peter as well.

Ross was greeted with warmth and concern by Franklin.

'It's good to see you up and about, but are you sure you should be walking on that leg? It looks pretty painful.'

'Sure. It's OK, just a bit stiff,' he lied. 'Danny and I were just going in for a cup of coffee. Why don't you join us? Maggie's been baking.'

'Those are the magic words,' Franklin said. 'There is nothing we Richmonds like better than Maggie's homemade scones and gingerbread. Isn't that right, Peter?'

The boy smiled a little wanly from the back seat.

'He's feeling a bit under the weather. Just been for a physio session,' Franklin explained.

'Oh, bad luck, kid,' Ross said with real sympathy.

'Come on, young'un,' Darcy said, scooping Peter up. 'Let's go see what Maggie can find for you, shall we?'

Maggie poured coffee and produced quantities of fruit-cake and scones, and presently Lindsay, Bill and Sarah came in.

'Now tell me, Ross, how is it, really?' Franklin asked.

Before he could form a reply, Lindsay broke in. 'You're wasting your time, Frank. He could be at death's door and all he'd say would be, "Oh, I'm doin' fine."'

She mimicked Ross's accent perfectly and he joined in the general laughter, glad of the diversion.

Only Darcy seemed unamused. Strangely, he was scowling at Peter, who had cheered up no end and was laughing louder than anyone. After a moment, Darcy seemed to sense Ross's scrutiny, smiled at him and relaxed.

Maggie started to make more coffee, and James arrived.

'I didn't know you were here,' he said, settling next to Lindsay. 'I called at your parents' house. I thought we were going to Winchester for that exhibition.'

Lindsay put a hand to her mouth. 'Oh, James, I'm sorry! I totally forgot. The thing is, with Ross out of action they need help here.'

'Yeah, well, you could have let me know.'

It was the first time Ross had seen James even slightly impatient with her but he couldn't really blame him. For someone who didn't ride, Lindsay's preoccupation with the yard must be sorely trying.

She looked downcast. 'Can you forgive me?' she asked him.

James was human. He relented.

Moments later, Franklin stood up, announcing that he had some business with the Colonel, and Peter asked if he could watch the horses being fed. Bill offered to wheel him round the yard, so Darcy fetched his wheelchair.

When feeding was complete and Peter was wheeled back, Darcy was found to be engaged in what appeared to be a very heated discussion with Danny. They broke off immediately they saw the others and Danny marched off towards the cottage, scowling.

Coming back from the house, Franklin passed Danny and looked curiously at Darcy. 'What was that all about?' he asked.

Darcy shrugged, looking quite upset. 'Danny says he gave me a videotape to show to you and Peter, that he left it on the passenger seat of my car the other day. But I haven't seen it.'

Peter looked disappointed. 'Was that the one where Ross rode Telamon and he was like a bucking bronco?'

'I don't know. It could have been,' Darcy said dismissively, then smiled at his young nephew. 'Never mind. I expect it'll turn up. Come on, it's high time we were on our way.'

As Bill and Ross waved goodbye to the Richmonds and made their way back to the cottage, the stable manager wasn't happy.

'Danny's such a cloth-head, he's probably still got the tape somewhere himself,' he said. 'But he should know better than to argue with owners like that. I'll have to speak to him about it.'

Ross wasn't sure. Danny was invariably truthful. It was probably Darcy who had misplaced the videotape and didn't want to be the one to disappoint Peter.

After lunch, Ross drove to the saddler's to pick up a saddle that was in for repair. Sitting in the car park, he called McKinnon on his mobile. McKinnon's answerphone said he was out and please leave a message. Ross explained briefly about Roland's theory with regard to his fall at the show and his own vague suspicions about Roland.

As he switched off he saw a familiar figure filling the tank of a racy black hatchback at a petrol station on the far side of the road.

At the same moment, Roland looked up and saw Ross. He waved and the American waved back.

Ross wondered why Roland had forsaken his Aston Martin. Too conspicuous, perhaps? He started the Jeep, thinking that wherever he was these days, Roland never seemed to be far away.

EIGHT

Next morning Ross found another note under his door. He smiled as he read it. *Confirmed. The rat has doubled back, bolt hole as yet unknown. The antique has provenance. Hope you are recovering.*

Ross was glad that the Colonel's son seemed to be in the clear but much about him was still puzzling.

His return to the saddle the following day could not have been described as an unqualified success, but neither was it a total failure. From past experience, he knew he'd just have to grin and bear it. It was nothing like as bad as it had been after the original accident. At the end of the day, although his knee had protested vigorously, it hadn't let him down.

He spent a couple of hours with the Colonel, as usual, and was cheered by the news that Robbie Fergusson had agreed to leave Bishop at Oakley Manor for the time being.

'He wouldn't go so far as to admit that he was wrong about you,' the Colonel told Ross. 'So I should tread carefully for a bit.'

'I'll tug my forelock to him if it means I can keep the ride on Bishop,' Ross assured him. 'That horse is sensational.'

The Colonel nodded his agreement. 'And, according to Franklin, Fergusson's not the only one you're not flavour of the month with.'

'What d'you mean?'

'Well, apparently it's young Peter's birthday on Saturday and Darcy had planned a big day out for him, but it seems Peter would rather go to the Somerset and Avon Show to see you jump Clown.'

'Oh, dear. Darcy doesn't really see the attraction, does he?'

'No. And to be honest, I think he's a little bit jealous of you. You must know Peter thinks you're the bee's knees?'

'Well, yes. But surely Darcy doesn't take it seriously?'

'Oh, no,' the Colonel said. 'It just put his nose out of joint. He's taking Peter out on Sunday instead, so everybody's happy.'

ROSS SPENT A LONG NIGHT tossing and turning, kept awake by a disturbing train of thought as much as by his knee. He worked hard the next day, trying to shut out the unwelcome suspicions that were nagging at him, but by the time evening stables were finished, he knew he was fighting a losing battle. He telephoned Franklin Richmond from the stable office. Aware that there was a risk, ringing him at home, Ross said hurriedly, 'I can't talk now, but could we meet up later?'

'I could be free by half past eight or nine. Is it important?'

'It might be,' Ross said guardedly. 'Same place as last time?'

'OK. Make it nine then, to be on the safe side.'

A sound from the tack room sent Ross swiftly to the door. Roland stood there in the gloom, his pale-suited figure easily recognisable.

'Looking for me?' Ross asked pleasantly.

'As a matter of fact, yes,' Roland replied. 'Thing is, I've been stood up and wondered if you'd care to come out for a drink this evening?'

Ross was greatly impressed with this barefaced lie, as he was ninety-nine per cent certain that Roland had been eavesdropping.

'I'm afraid I can't,' he said. 'I already have a date.'

'And who is the lucky lady?'

Ross shook his head, grinning. 'Oh, no, you don't. I've already lost one of my girlfriends to you. I think I'll keep this one to myself.'

TWO HOURS LATER, Ross set out for the Dovecote under a sky that threatened rain. He supposed that he would soon have to think about trading in the Jeep for something more suited to the vagaries of the English climate. Something with a roof. Before he'd covered half a mile, however, all such mundane considerations had been driven from his mind by a discovery altogether more urgent.

He was being followed.

Preoccupied with wondering how Franklin was going to react to what he had to say, he'd missed his turning. As he back-tracked, a black hatchback passed him going in the other direction and a minute or two later, when he was held up by a tractor, the self-same car appeared behind him, two or three cars back.

Ross placed it. At the garage three days ago. Roland.

His old suspicions came flooding back. With a surge of annoyance, he determined to lose Roland.

His opportunity came soon. Coming to his missed turning, he swung into it only to be brought up short by a queue of traffic at a red light. When the lights changed, Ross dawdled, revving his engine until the signal changed to red once again. Then, leaving behind half a dozen hooting motorists, he accelerated down the single carriageway, swerved round an oncoming lorry at the far end, and sped away down the road.

In his mirror he could see the lorry still moving forward and beyond it two cars, one the black hatchback, who had tried to follow him and now met it head on. With any luck Roland would be held up for quite a while. All the same, Ross took a couple of diversionary turnings before resuming his journey.

Back *en route*, Ross checked his watch. *Damn Roland!* He was going to be late meeting Franklin. He put his foot down.

About two miles from the pub, he was held up by a Land-Rover that pulled out of a gateway into his path. He looked at his watch again. Five past nine. The Land-Rover was in no hurry. DRH, Damn Roland's Hide, Ross thought, reading the number plate out of habit.

Suddenly, the Land-Rover picked up speed and disappeared round a bend. Following, he found himself brought up short by a diversion sign. Ross shook his head in disbelief. The suggested route was a left fork that looked to be little more than a glorified farm track. Ross shifted gear and started down the lane. It was very rough.

Turning into the gloom of a stretch that was flanked by a copse, Ross swore. Skewed across the road, with its nose buried in a hedge, was the Land-Rover. Just to Ross's side of it was an open gateway leading into the wood. It almost looked as though the vehicle had tried to make the turn and missed.

Ross couldn't see whether anyone was still inside. He switched the Jeep's engine off and went to investigate. He approached the driver's window and looked in. Not a soul.

There was the slightest whisper of sound behind him and then a stunning blow to the base of his neck sent Ross sprawling against the side of the Land-Rover. His hands were pulled roughly behind his back, and he was pushed sideways until he was face-down on the bonnet with his nose pressed to the engine-warmed metal. What little he could see from that position was whirling crazily and he closed his eyes, feeling nauseous. Through the fog in his brain, he heard another engine approaching. A motorbike.

Any hopes of assistance that might have been forming in Ross's woolly consciousness were dashed as the man behind him commanded in broad Irish tones, 'Give me a hand before somebody comes.' The motorbike man came over and Ross's hands were tied behind his back. Then he was pulled upright, turned round and propelled through the open gateway into the wood.

After a few strides Ross stumbled, still muzzy. An arm came over his shoulder and a shiny, six-inch blade flashed in front of his face.

'Would you be knowing what this is, mister?' a soft voice enquired. Ross nodded. 'Well, you do as you're told. Now walk.'

As his head cleared, the significance of that Irish accent became all too depressingly clear.

The copse consisted of thickets of overgrown hazel coppice interspersed with larger beech trees. When they had gone perhaps a hundred yards, Irish grasped Ross's collar, swung him round, and dumped him unceremoniously at the foot of a tree.

Ross looked up for the first time at the mysterious Mr X.

He was of medium height and build, and wore jeans, a T-shirt and a black balaclava. For a moment, in spite of the gravity of the situation, Ross found it amusing. It seemed so melodramatic.

'What's so funny?' The other man had caught up. Unmistakably familiar tones. Lean, wiry form and again a balaclava.

'Hi, Leo,' Ross said conversationally.

'You fool!' the first balaclava said contemptuously. 'I told you to keep your bloody mouth shut!'

'I don't care. I want the Yank to know who's doing this to him.' Leo pulled his balaclava off and stepped closer.

'You certainly mix with the low life,' Ross observed to Irish.

There was a flurry of movement as Irish was shoved to one side, and Ross found himself looking down the barrel of a gun.

Suddenly the melodrama didn't seem so amusing. Everything inside him seemed to freeze. Ross closed his eyes, and clenched his fists and jaw to stop them from trembling.

Irish and Leo stood one on each side of Ross and hauled him to his feet. Leo then retied Ross's wrists firmly together in front of him.

A further rope was tied around the one that bound his hands and thrown over a sturdy branch about three feet above his head so that his wrists were pulled upwards. Leo tugged on it until Ross was on tiptoe and then tied it off. As the knot slipped tight, Ross found he could stand flat-footed again, for which he was grateful. His broken rib made its presence felt with every breath.

'Not such a wise guy now, are you, Yank?' Leo observed.

Ross watched while Irish rummaged in a haversack and drew out a full bottle of whisky.

'This shouldn't be too much of a hardship,' he said, standing up and coming towards Ross. 'I hear you have a liking for the stuff.'

Ross guessed what they intended and depression settled on him.

'I did warn you to keep your nose out of what didn't concern you,'

Irish said reasonably. 'You really should've listened.'

Irish removed the screw top and stepped to Ross's side. Leo shoved Ross roughly against the tree, put a hand under his chin and forced his head back. Something cold and metallic pushed its way between his teeth, and any intended resistance was effectively quelled.

The neck of the bottle slid between Ross's teeth next to the gun barrel and the strong, smoky-tasting liquid filled his mouth. He tried not to swallow, breathing through his nose, and a quantity of the spirit ran down his chin. His eyes began to water.

With a muffled exclamation, Irish used his free hand to pinch Ross's nostrils. It became either swallow or drown.

He swallowed huge gulps of the fiery liquid, then his throat and lungs constricted in panic. He tried to twist away.

Irish seemed to recognise his predicament, for the pressure on his nose released and he drew in a blessed lungful of air. The relief was short-lived, however. Moments later the process was repeated.

Some time later the gun barrel was removed. He was beyond resistance. The whisky flowed. Gagging and coughing, he swallowed.

Later he realised that the bottle had gone and he was sitting down. He tried to open his eyes but someone had attached lead weights to his eyelids. Later still, he found himself lying face down in the leaf mould. It seemed fairly comfortable so he stayed there.

LIGHTS. A rough blanket beneath him. Voices echoing off cream-painted walls. A kingsize headache.

'Is this the RTA? What have you brought him here for?'

'No other vehicles involved. Just drove quietly into the hedge. Got a tip-off and found him draped over the wheel of his car. Had an empty bottle on the seat beside him. Whisky.'

Somebody grunted. 'Has somebody gone for the doc?'

'He's on his way.'

A door banged. Ross groaned, opened his eyes and looked around him. Four walls, the bed and a john. With an effort, he sat up, his head hammering. His shoulders and arms were stiff and tender, and his ribs told of new damage. The way his stomach felt, he couldn't contemplate ever facing food again. He tried to recall the events of the previous evening but it was all a muddle of confused images.

The door opened. A fresh-faced young PC looked in. 'Cup of tea?'

'No, thanks,' Ross said with feeling.

A grey-haired police surgeon came in. 'Drink it. It'll help.'

He doubted whether anything short of chloroform would help but he took the cup obligingly and sipped. His mouth felt bruised.

'So. How are we this morning?'

'Well, I've had better mornings,' Ross said flippantly.

'I'm not surprised,' Grey-hair said. 'You'd polished off the best part of a bottle of Scotch, apparently.'

Ross frowned as a memory flickered on the edges of his consciousness. 'I didn't. I mean, I . . .' He shook his head. 'I don't drink—not like that.' An image almost settled in his mind's eye.

'Well, let's just have a little look.'

The doctor took a slim torch out of his bag and, asking Ross to look straight ahead, shone it into his eyes.

After he finished his examination, he said, 'You'll be right as rain just as soon as you get rid of that massive hangover.'

'I didn't drink by choice,' Ross persisted. 'There was someone else there. I was forced to drink.'

The doctor shook his head. 'We get dozens of cases like yours in here every week and most of them have some story to tell. Accept it, lad. I'm afraid they have all the evidence they need. Blood-alcohol levels probably three or four times the legal limit.'

Suddenly Ross began to feel shaky and a sweat broke out on his body. He sat down on the bed and was starting to roll up his sleeves when the doctor put out a hand and caught his wrist.

'What's this?'

Ross looked down. Both his wrists were red raw and slightly puffy. He frowned. 'I can't remember. I don't know what happened.'

'I think we should have a record of those,' the doctor suggested, producing a camera. 'In case your memory returns. They look like rope burns to me.'

Ross held his arms out to be photographed. 'When can I go home?'

'I expect you'll be able to leave as soon as you've been formally charged. You'll be bailed to appear in court at a later date.'

As the door closed behind the doctor, Ross lay back on the bed. Most of the previous evening remained a blank but one thing began to be depressingly clear. He'd been neatly set up.

AFTER BEING CHARGED, Ross found himself in the reception area, his belongings restored to him. His Jeep had apparently been left where the police had picked him up. The custody officer had offered to ring Oakley Manor and arrange for him to be collected but Ross declined. He decided a taxi would be infinitely preferable.

His mobile phone hadn't been among his belongings—presumably Leo had pocketed it—and while he wavered between finding the payphone and collapsing onto the nearest seat, an immaculately suited figure unfolded itself from behind a newspaper and stood up.

'Well, I must say it's about time,' Roland said peevishly. 'I've been sitting here for absolutely ages and the coffee is diabolical. I say, do you feel quite well? You don't look at all the thing.'

'Oh, I feel just tickety-boo,' Ross replied waspishly.

'That's all right then,' Roland said, happily. 'The car's outside, if you're ready to go.' He steered the American towards the door.

Outside Ross was assailed by four or five aggressive reporters bristling with microphones, tape recorders and cameras.

Beside him, Roland tensed and swore. 'Don't say a word!'

He guided Ross to his car, jostled all the way by the predatory newsgatherers. He opened the passenger door and propelled the American inside, then held up a hand to silence the persistent questions. 'I don't know what you've heard, but there's obviously been a mistake,' he announced, clearly and with authority. 'There is no story. Go and report a church fête or something.'

He slid smoothly into the car, started the engine and drove away.

Ross remembered abruptly that he was sitting in the very same car he had worked so hard to lose the evening before.

'Why were you following me last night?' he asked, with bluntness that a clearer head might have tempered.

Roland was not noticeably disconcerted. 'I wanted to see where you were going,' he said reasonably, throwing the car into a right-angled bend with no perceptible slackening of speed.

'I should have thought you already knew that,' Ross said.

Roland smiled unashamedly. 'Ah, call it incurable nosiness, if you will. I've always suffered from it. Lamentable, I know.'

Ross closed his eyes, feeling lousy.

'Just where did you abandon your Jeep, exactly?' Roland asked.

Ross stirred. 'The police said it was called Sandy Lane. How did you know where I was? And how the hell did the press know?'

'I don't know how the local press knew. I'm here on Father's orders. He was woken at half past seven this morning by an enthusiastic correspondent from the *Sportsman*, demanding to know if he was aware that his star employee was languishing in the local nick, faced with a drink-driving charge.'

Ross's heart sank. No chance then to plead his side of the story. There was no need to ask how the Colonel had received the news.

'You're very quiet,' Roland observed. 'Probably just not a morning person, I expect.'

Ross couldn't be bothered to summon another withering look.

The Jeep, when they came up with it, had no wheels, headlights or windscreen, and what was left was completely burnt out.

Ross was beyond feeling. With the news about the Colonel, he had touched rock bottom and there was nowhere lower to go.

'Drunks, I expect,' Roland said. 'There are a lot of them about.'

Ross had had enough. 'Why don't you just shut the hell up?' he demanded, rounding on him savagely.

Roland put his hands up in surrender. 'OK, OK.'

'So, which particular sorrows were you trying to drown?' he continued casually as they turned homewards.

Ross groaned from a combination of physical discomfort and mental frustration. 'For Chrissakes, I wasn't trying to drown anything! I didn't drink by choice. And if I *had* intended to, I would hardly have driven ten miles out into the country when I could have stayed in my room, would I?'

'Are you saying that somebody forced you? Who exactly?'

One of the few things Ross clearly remembered was Leo's gloating face but he couldn't expect anyone to believe that the ex-groom had done it on his own, and until he knew more he felt it would be wisest to pretend ignorance.

'I don't know,' he said. 'They kept their faces covered.'

'Well, did you tell the police?'

'I tried,' Ross said tiredly. 'I tried to get them to fingerprint the bottle too but they weren't interested. They've heard it all before.'

'But why should anybody want to set you up?'

'I don't know,' Ross replied guardedly. 'Someone with a grudge, perhaps. I'm not exactly Mr Popularity.'

'But there's a big difference between spreading rumours and doing something like this. I mean, it can't be easy to subdue someone and force a bottle of whisky down their throat,' Roland said.

Unless he had a six-inch blade and no compunction about using it, Ross thought, another chunk of memory slotting into place.

Roland suddenly swung the car into a lay-by and stopped. Leaving the engine running, he opened his door and got out.

'Won't be a moment,' he said airily. 'Got a call to make. Personal.'

He produced a mobile phone and walked away from the car.

Ross leaned back, closed his eyes and found himself wondering if Roland owned a knife. He remembered the ease with which Roland had handled Leo that day at the yard and it occurred to him that, for a man who appeared to spend most of his life masquerading behind a false personality, an Irish accent would hardly be a problem. But surely Roland couldn't have reached Sandy Lane before him when Ross had left him in that muddle at the traffic lights.

Or could he? Ross had wasted more time after leaving him behind, trying to cover his tracks, and he knew that Roland drove everywhere like a rally driver. If he had known Ross was intending to meet Franklin he could make an educated guess at the meeting place, having driven Ross there the evening he was knocked out. But if that was the case, why bother to follow him, and who had driven the Land-Rover? Nothing seemed to make much sense.

Roland reappeared, sliding back into his seat. 'So, how many ruffians were there?' he asked, as if the conversation hadn't lapsed.

'There were two. As to who they were, though, your guess is as good as mine. I'm afraid most of it is still a blank.'

'Post-traumatic amnesia,' Roland said matter-of-factly. 'The mind tends to blank out events too recently painful to remember.'

Roland swung into the long drive to the stable yard. 'My revered papa said he wished to see you the instant you got back, but I convinced him he would do better to wait until this evening.' He drew to a smooth halt in the yard and held out a packet of Alka-Seltzers. 'Take a couple of these and try and get some sleep.'

TEN MISERABLE HOURS crawled by. After a while the nausea began to subside. Sleep, however, had never been further from him.

From the yard below, the noise of business as usual floated up to taunt Ross. Nobody came up to see him. On the whole that was probably a good thing. He wondered if Lindsay was helping in the yard. He remembered her declaring vehemently that drink-drivers should be publicly flogged. It did nothing to improve his state of mind.

During those ten sleepless hours, Ross had had plenty of time to think. But his thoughts were largely unprofitable. If, as seemed probable, he had been waylaid to prevent him from passing on information to Franklin, then the strategy had succeeded. Whatever thoughts had prompted him to approach Franklin in the first place were staying stubbornly in the darkest recesses of his mind.

On the other hand, whoever had waylaid him could not have relied on Ross's memory loss, so he assumed their aim had been to scare him into minding his own business or to discredit him to such an extent that no one would be inclined to take him seriously anyway. Maybe they figured the charge would lose him his job, and maybe, he thought, they were right.

The Colonel didn't rise when Ross, having presented himself at the door of the main house, was shown in to the study. He was sitting at his desk and waved the American into the chair opposite.

Colonel Preston regarded Ross solemnly for a moment and then spoke quietly. 'Some weeks ago I asked you if I should be worried about the rumours of your drinking and you said no. Like a fool I believed you.'

Ross looked his employer straight in the eyes. 'It was the truth,' he asserted earnestly. 'It still is.'

'Then how do you explain this?' The Colonel reached into a desk drawer and produced a bottle of Scotch, two-thirds empty.

Ross didn't have to ask where it had come from. It was the one from his room. He felt a flash of anger at the intrusion but stifled it.

'I can't sleep sometimes. My knee gives me a bit of trouble. The whisky helps. Just a mouthful or two, never more.'

The Colonel raised his eyebrows.

Ross tried again. 'I've had that one bottle for weeks. I bought it at the airport. I might even have the receipt somewhere . . .'

The Colonel shrugged. 'That proves nothing. You could have bought any number since you've been here.'

Ross could see it all slipping away from him. His career, the respect of his new-found friends and this wonderful chance of a lifetime he'd been given. Even if he mentioned Leo he had no proof, and without the background information, which he had promised not to divulge, his story would test the gullibility of the average six-year-old. Sick at heart and unable to defend himself he was silent.

The Colonel looked up, directly into his eyes. 'I don't know what to do,' he said. 'I feel that to keep you on would be to betray the memory of my dear, sweet wife and daughter. And yet somehow . . . I couldn't understand how you could have done anything so stupid. You've always seemed so straight, so strong. Damn it, I liked you! *Why*, Ross?' the Colonel beseeched. 'Was it the pressure?'

'I *didn't* do it,' the American said, stung into self-defence by the disillusionment in the older man's face. 'I was set up. Framed.'

'Who then? Who did it?'

'I don't know. They wore balaclavas . . .' He tailed off, knowing it sounded ridiculous.

The Colonel was shaking his head slowly. 'I trusted you,' he said sadly. 'This whole business has turned sour on me. I haven't the heart for it any more. I think you'd better go now.'

Ross limped wearily out. The Colonel's disillusionment had been far worse than the anger he'd steeled himself to meet.

NINE

Ross awoke feeling stiff and bruised, but otherwise a lot better. He still hadn't reached the full fried breakfast stage but felt he might be able to manage coffee and toast. Much as he dreaded having to face the Scotts, he knew the moment had come, so he showered and dressed and made his way over to the cottage.

In the yard Sarah and Danny looked at him with awkward embarrassment, whereas Bill could barely bring himself to look at him at all. Hardly a word was spoken. The horses, at least, treated him the same as always.

After breakfast, eaten in strained silence, Ross asserted that he was fit and ready for business as usual, whereupon Bill favoured him with a doubtful look, and said he supposed they'd have to take his word for that. Ross was heartily glad when he was back outside with the horses.

Midafternoon, Roland appeared in the yard and joined Ross in the tack room. 'So how's the fallen hero?' Roland enquired.

'Beneath contempt,' Ross said ruefully. 'But otherwise much better, thanks. How's the Colonel?'

'Oh, he'll get over it. Franklin rang this morning and asked if you were all right. Said you were supposed to meet him but you didn't show up. He flatly refused to believe the official version of events. Seems he said you were stone cold sober at half past six and he couldn't see why you would drink yourself silly when you'd just made arrangements to meet him. He suggested that perhaps somebody else might have had a hand in it, so to speak. I believe he mentioned Leo . . .' He paused, watching Ross. 'Well, anyway, gave Father something to chew on.'

Ross was mildly surprised. 'The Colonel told you all that?'

'Well, no. Not exactly,' Roland said apologetically. 'I sort of happened to overhear it. You know how it is.'

Ross knew precisely how it was. With his talent for eavesdropping, Roland was wasted on the antiques trade; MI5 would welcome him.

Remembering what had happened to Roland's mother and sister, though, Ross wondered at his easy attitude now. Presumably *he* also believed Ross to be innocent. One thing was for sure: no one would know better than he just how damning such a conviction would be in the Colonel's eyes. *Could* he have been involved?

The two of them were just emerging into the sunlight when Lindsay's red MG turned into the yard. She sprang out and came over. She took in Ross's decidedly below-par appearance at a glance.

'So it's true,' she observed flatly. 'I was in London yesterday and when I got back the whole village was buzzing with it. I didn't believe it at first. Then I saw the papers and they were full of it.'

'It must be true, then,' he said whimsically. 'If it's in the papers.'

'Are you denying it?' Lindsay said. 'Looking like that?'

He was stung by her doubt. 'You seem to have made up your mind!'

'You forget, I've seen you hit the bottle before.'

'Once!' he countered angrily. 'What do you want? Perfection? You'd better go back to James for that.'

Lindsay stared at him, clearly hurt. 'You're right,' she said shakily. 'I expect too much. It's just—I thought I knew you. I guess I don't.'

'I guess not,' Ross agreed, his anger still running high.

She blinked at him, eyes bright with unshed tears. 'I don't know why I'm wasting my time. You obviously don't give a damn, so why should I? I just feel so sorry for Uncle John! And I wish I'd never told him about you.' She turned on her heel and walked back to her car.

Ross watched her go, his temper gradually ebbing and leaving him feeling tired and depressed. Why had he flown at her like that?

'You've done it now,' Roland remarked.

'Oh, shut up,' Ross said wearily.

JUST AFTER EVENING stables Franklin dropped in. He greeted Bill, and walked round the horses with Ross. 'I gather from the dirty looks that it's not the done thing to talk to you?' he said.

'No, I'm not exactly in favour,' Ross agreed lightly.

'That don't-give-a-damn front is all very well, Ross, but it won't do for me. You look awful. How are things, honestly?'

He looked away. 'Oh, pretty much like hell,' he said conversationally. 'Our Mr X certainly knows how and where to hit.'

'So it *was* a set-up! I *knew* it,' Franklin exclaimed triumphantly.

'Sure it was, a damn' good one,' Ross said with feeling. 'The Colonel is gutted. But thanks for the back-up.'

'I didn't know what to say, so this morning I told John I wondered whether Leo might have had a hand in it, just to give him something to think about. What *did* happen?'

'I set out to meet you but they knew I was coming and laid on a little diversion—just for me. As a matter of fact, Leo *was* there,' Ross confirmed. 'And I'm pretty sure our extortionist friend was too, but I still don't know who he is. He wore a balaclava throughout.'

'You're sure it was our Mr X and not just some thug Leo had found to help him get his own back on you?'

'If it was, he was Irish,' Ross remarked sceptically.

'Ah. I wonder how long Leo *has* been involved, then.'

'I've been thinking: what if Leo worked out who Mr X is and some of what he's up to? What if he faced Mr X with it and wanted to be cut in? We wondered how he managed to afford to stay at the Six Bells, and it was certainly no accident he got thrown out of here when he did. He was actively asking for it.'

'You might have something there,' Franklin said. 'But do you think it's Mr X's style to allow himself to be blackmailed?'

'Maybe not,' Ross admitted. 'But he might also think that Leo could be a useful tool, for a while at least. I mean, it really fogged things up, didn't it? Not knowing who was responsible for what.'

They wandered on in silence for a moment, both thinking hard.

'Can you tell me more about Tuesday evening?' Franklin asked after a moment.

Ross frowned. 'I still can't remember everything, just snatches. I remember being followed and trying to lose them.' He didn't think he'd mention Roland at this point. 'There was a Land-Rover and a diversion sign. When they forced the whisky down me I think I was in a wood. I remember being tied to a tree.' He paused. It was painful to remember. 'I . . . um . . . remember that Leo had a gun,' he said, and a cold sweat broke out on his body at the memory. 'But the rest . . .' His voice cracked and he shook his head.

Franklin perceived his distress and put a hand on his shoulder. 'I'm sorry,' he said. 'I had no right to get you involved in all this. I don't know how to thank you . . .'

'What for? I just seem to have muddied the waters.'

'The professionals have done no better,' Franklin observed. 'But I meant, thank you for caring enough to try. Anyway,' he glanced at his watch, 'I must be going. I called in on my way to the Chinese takeaway. It's Cook's night off and Peter has got it into his head he wants a Chinese.' He grimaced. 'Not my cup of tea, I'm afraid. I prefer good, traditional English cooking myself. It's the only thing I really miss about Peter's mother. When she could be bothered, Marsha was a dab hand in the kitchen.'

Ross hesitated, then gave voice to a suspicion he had long harboured. 'When did you find out about Marsha and Darcy?'

Franklin raised an eyebrow. 'You don't miss much, do you?'

Ross relaxed. It appeared he hadn't offended and, furthermore, had guessed right.

'I suspected,' Franklin said. 'But Darcy himself told me in the end. I couldn't blame him, exactly. He wasn't much more than a boy, after all. She was an attractive woman and always got what she wanted.'

'So you didn't fall out over it?'

'No, not really. The marriage was over by then, in all but name, and I couldn't see what good it would do to alienate the boy just when we needed to stick together as a family. He'd apologised, said it only happened once and the affair was over.' He opened the door of the Range Rover and paused. 'What made you think of that?'

Ross shrugged. 'Oh, I don't know, something he said once. More the way he said it, I suppose. I can't really remember.'

'He's always had an eye for the girls,' Franklin confessed. He started the engine. 'Look, Ross, take care of yourself, OK? Your first concern should be getting fit and winning classes.'

Ross grinned. 'OK, boss.'

THE COLONEL SENT a note to say that, if Ross felt up to it, the horses would compete as planned that weekend and he should prepare them accordingly. The note was brief and businesslike but Ross considered it a hopeful sign.

Although it was clear that his workmates still regarded him with disgust, the prospect of action gave the team a common aim. The atmosphere in the yard improved noticeably.

Saturday morning dawned fair but with a blustery wind, which had sprung up overnight. The preparations for the show ran smoothly, and when all the four-footed passengers were safely aboard, Ross made his way round to the driver's side of the cab.

'I think not,' Bill said firmly, coming up behind him. 'The Colonel would rather I drive.'

Ross felt quick anger rise in him but clenched his jaw against the retort. 'Suit yourself,' he said.

The show was a big one, which suited Ross. The smaller the concentration of people who knew him, the better.

The Richmond clan turned up to see Clown jump in two classes but, try as he might, Ross wasn't able to win a rosette for the birthday boy. Peter accepted the disappointment with his customary good manners but he was very quiet.

Before they left, Franklin told Ross that, in place of the written-off Jeep, he had an old Land-Rover that Ross was welcome to use for as long as he liked.

Or until they take my licence, Ross thought, thanking him.

'Well, actually, it was Darcy's idea,' Franklin admitted. 'It only sits around doing nothing. It's a bit rough, I'm afraid, but roadworthy.'

'You want to watch the clutch,' Darcy said, coming over. 'It's a bit of a sod, as I remember, but basically it's OK.'

Ross thanked him as well. Darcy waved a dismissive hand. 'Hey, forget it. It'll do it good to be used. We'll drop it by later.'

'That's great. I need to go over to Amesbury on Monday and I'm not quite sure whether I'm allowed to use ours at the moment.'

If Darcy had indeed been jealous of Ross's popularity with Peter, as the Colonel had suggested, then he appeared to have got over it now, Ross reflected. Perhaps he found it easier to contend with a tarnished idol. But Peter had certainly seemed subdued. Ross couldn't help wondering just what Darcy might have said to the youngster.

ON THE SECOND DAY of the show, when Telamon won one of the biggest classes of the afternoon, ahead of Stephen Douglas, Ross was over the moon. He felt a certain affinity with the rogue horse. After all, they were both badly in need of proving themselves.

'You did it, you crazy son-of-a-gun!' he said, slapping the arching red neck. Telamon tossed his head, sensing that he'd done well.

As they lined up to receive their rosettes, Stephen Douglas glanced across at Ross with what looked suspiciously like the beginnings of a friendly smile. 'Well done. You gave him a great ride,' he said.

Ross blinked. 'Thanks.'

It appeared to be a day for surprises and not all of them pleasant.

Ross rode Bishop into the ring feeling heartily glad it was his last ride of the day. The black had recovered from his injury and jumped with smooth precision. Ross was lifted by admiration for the horse.

As he walked him towards the exit, the loudspeaker announced, 'A lovely clear round there for Ross Wakelin and Black Bishop. Maybe one of the last times we shall see this partnership, as I believe the horse has been sold. A shame, that.'

Ross was stunned. How could it be that the show commentator knew before he did? His face stony, he rode through the collecting ring and onto the public thoroughfare before he dismounted.

'How do you feel about losing the ride, Mr Wakelin?' a voice enquired unctuously at Ross's shoulder, and he turned to find Harry Douglas smiling at him from behind a handheld tape recorder. 'Oh, you didn't know? Mr Fergusson phoned me this morning.'

'And you didn't waste any time spreading the glad tidings. I should've guessed it was you,' Ross added through clenched teeth. 'What have I ever done to you to make you hound me like this? Can't you see Stephen's better off where he is now?'

'Hound you? You're imagining things, Ross. I'm a reporter. I merely report what I see. People have a right to know.'

'Well I hope you're happy now you've dragged my reputation through the mud, because there's one advantage to being in my position. I've absolutely nothing to lose!' Then Ross hit Harry Douglas with all the weight of weeks of frustration powering his fist.

The reporter reeled back into the arms of the startled onlookers and slid down to sit on the trampled grass with an expression of amazement on his face.

'Put that in your bloody paper!' Ross said with satisfaction.

Stephen Douglas materialised at Ross's side as he plodded across the showground. 'I've been wanting to do that for years,' he said. 'He's been interfering in my life ever since I can remember. He tried to make me hate you because you took over my rides, but I lost that job before you ever came to England. I can see that now. And well,' he paused, awkwardly, 'I just wanted you to know I'm sorry.'

Ross waved a hand wearily. 'Forget it,' he advised. Then, mindful of the courage needed for such a speech, added, 'But thanks.'

Stephen drifted away to his next ride and Ross was joined first by Roland, then Lindsay and James.

'Is it true about Bishop?' Lindsay demanded immediately.

Ross hadn't seen her since she'd confronted him in the yard and

LYNDON STACEY

didn't know where he stood with her exactly. He hesitated.

'Who knows? Probably,' he said. 'Harry Douglas said so.'

'But how could Harry Douglas have found out first?' Lindsay persisted. 'Surely if it's true Uncle John would have been told?'

'Perhaps it was Fergusson's way of getting back at me,' Ross suggested. 'There's no love lost, you know.'

'But that's too much! It's *so* unfair!'

'Oh, Princess, not everyone has your sense of fair play, you know. You just have to roll with the punches.'

'There speaks a man of the world,' Roland observed dramatically, adding gently to his cousin, 'He's right, m'dear.'

Lindsay stopped in her tracks, glaring first at Roland, then at Ross. 'All right, make fun of me! But if you had a little more backbone, perhaps you wouldn't be in this mess!'

She turned away abruptly and, with a shrug, James followed her.

Soon after they had returned to the yard, the Colonel phoned Bill at the cottage to confirm that Fergusson had received, and was likely to accept, a substantial offer for Bishop from a wealthy farmer with a string of horses in Yorkshire. As Bill imparted this news to the team, his eyes rested on Ross with bitter accusation, and the unloading and settling of the horses was carried out in depressed silence. To Ross, the news seemed to signal the beginning of the end.

Alone in his room, after a late meal eaten halfheartedly, he sprawled on the sofa listening to the wind howling round the stables. The pain in his knee was many times worse than it had been when he first came to England and he knew he couldn't put off consulting a specialist for much longer. He was supposed to have had a check-up at the end of June but had known they would probably want to operate and surgery would put him out of action for several weeks. So what? It probably wouldn't matter now.

What caused such misery was the prospect of leaving Oakley Manor under a cloud. Franklin would speak up for him, he had no doubt, but the extortionist was still at large. What had he achieved?

Sighing, Ross levered himself off the sofa and limped to the kettle to make a cup of instant caffeine. A knock at the door halted him.

'Who is it?' he asked through the panel.

'Lindsay.'

Mystified, Ross opened the door. Lindsay was clad in a jade-green jersey dress that clung invitingly to her slim curves. Her blue-grey eyes met his for a moment and then fell. She looked unsure of herself.

'What's wrong?' he asked, concerned.

'I—er—' Lindsay hesitated, biting her bottom lip. 'I'm surprised you'd still want to talk to me,' she said with a rush. 'After some of the things I said to you.'

'I guess I can force myself,' he said nobly, mouth twitching with amusement. 'But, as I remember it, there was a fair bit of mud-slinging on both sides!'

'Well, I came to apologise,' Lindsay said, with the air of one determined to discharge her duty. 'I shouldn't have said what I did but it makes me mad when I see people I care for being treated like that!'

'Well, thank you,' Ross said, caught between frowning and laughing. 'But what made it so urgent that it couldn't wait till morning?'

Lindsay looked up at him. 'I *had* to come. I've been so miserable. I mean, you must have been feeling pretty awful anyway. You didn't need me making it worse. About Tuesday night—I never really thought you did that but you wouldn't defend yourself and it hurts Uncle John so. I wanted you to tell me that you hadn't. You see, it's just that it *matters*! Can I come in?'

Ross was somewhat taken aback by this final plea. His heart started to thump heavily. It was nearly eleven.

'Sure,' he said. 'But . . . um . . . Does James know you're here?'

'James told me to come,' Lindsay said. 'He said he knew when he was beaten, and . . .' She studied her feet, face reddening.

'And?' Ross had to be sure he was getting the right message.

'He said any fool could see that you loved me.' Her voice rose on the last words, turning them into a question.

'Oh, Princess!' Ross groaned, gathering her into his arms. 'What do you want with a crippled saddle tramp like me? James has everything: looks, wealth, charm. He's a great guy.'

Lindsay pulled away for a moment. 'Oh, don't be so bloody noble! I'm very fond of James but I've never loved him, I know that now.'

Ross put his arms round her and drew her into the room.

LINDSAY LEFT at first light the next morning, before anyone was about.

From the window, Ross watched her cross the yard, a slim figure incongruous in a jade evening dress, and smiled as she turned and waved before rounding the corner.

Ross's whole world had taken on a different complexion overnight. True, his problems hadn't miraculously disappeared, but neither did they seem so desperately overwhelming. Wherever he found himself in the future, he wouldn't be alone.

After breakfast, Ross announced his intention of going to pick up a new pair of riding boots. He wondered aloud if Danny would like to accompany him.

'Danny's got things to do here,' Bill said shortly.

'Young Peter is coming over for the day, Ross,' Maggie explained.

'Masters is taking us to Beaulieu motor museum,' Danny put in.

So Ross set off alone in the borrowed Land-Rover. Cutting across the hills to the northwest of Salisbury via the back roads, he saw the Wiltshire countryside spread out like a patchwork quilt below him. The road followed the ridge, curving round the head of a steep-sided valley. Here the rising wind buffeted the Land-Rover so heavily that Ross had to steer into it to stay on course.

Avoiding another car on the not over-wide road, he bumped into a pothole on the side and as he pulled back onto the tarmac had the uneasy feeling that the vehicle wasn't responding as it should. It seemed now to be pulling hard *into* the wind. As the incongruity of this dawned on him, the road rounded the valley head and the Land-Rover, without warning, lurched violently to the right, swerved wildly across the opposite carriageway, and hit the grass verge.

Immediately to the other side of the grassy verge the turf dropped away some 200 feet—a slope that must have been one in three. The Land-Rover tipped crazily towards the precipice, held up only by three rusty strands of a barbed-wire fence. The wire screeched and twanged and one strand gave way under the strain.

It seemed an age that the Land-Rover hung there, but it could only have been a matter of moments before the fence, having stretched to its limits, swung back with surprising elasticity, tipping the vehicle back onto three of its wheels. Ross lost no time in unfastening his seat belt and opening the door. His heart missed a beat as he saw the yawning emptiness beneath his offside front wheel, and he slid across the front seat and out of the passenger door, then sat down heavily on the verge with a hefty dose of the shakes. He rested his head on his knees and took slow, deep breaths to steady himself.

The low drone of an approaching car swelled and stopped as the driver pulled up alongside. A voice enquired, 'You all right, mate?'

Ross looked up. 'Yeah. Fine now, thanks. I don't suppose you know where I could find a garage with a tow truck, do you?'

The car driver nodded. There was a repair garage down in the valley. He knew the mechanic and would call in on his way..

In the next ten minutes, several more cars came by, all stopping or slowing to view the spectacle of the precariously perched vehicle.

'It's all under control,' Ross told them. 'I'm fine, thank you.'

'I'd say you were pretty lucky there,' a voice remarked.

'A tow truck's on the way . . .' Ross's voice tailed off. 'Oh, Jeez!' he groaned, recognising one of the officers from the week before.

'Well, well,' the policeman said. 'If it isn't our American friend. I must say, your parking hasn't improved. Just what exactly happened? Were you trying to get the cork out of a bottle?' He was clearly enjoying himself. 'Jim! Bring the breath box, will you?'

By the time the tow truck arrived five minutes later, Ross had had about enough of Police Sergeant Steve Deacon and his sidekick.

After the negative breath test, the two had requested vehicle documents. Franklin had left these in the glove compartment and they were all, to the disappointment of the sergeant, up to date.

'If I were you and I wanted to travel in the next couple of weeks, I'd take a bus. You'll have to get used to it sooner or later anyway. See you in court,' he said, as the Land-Rover was dragged back onto the road by the round-faced mechanic in the tow truck.

'Bloody charming!' the mechanic said, getting out of the truck and looking at the departing police car. Then, turning his attention to the Land-Rover, 'Not hard to see what's happened here.'

Ross followed his gaze. While its near-side front wheel pointed left, its offside companion was pointing in the opposite direction.

'Looks like the track rod's come off the joint, at a guess,' the mechanic said placidly, rubbing his bristly chin with a grimy paw.

Ross was thoughtful. 'Does that happen often?'

'Nah, not very. You'd spot it was loose on the MOT most likely.'

Ross had seen from the documents that the Land-Rover had been tested within the last month. 'Would it be possible for someone to arrange for it to happen?' he asked.

'Bloody hell! That's a bleeding question, that is!' the mechanic said, looking curiously at Ross. 'Yeah, I suppose it would. All you'd have to do would be slacken off the nut on the steering rack joint. You could even drive round with it like that. No telling when it would finally come apart. Could be one mile, could be ten.'

'Unless you hit a pothole . . .' Ross said absent-mindedly.

'That would probably shake it loose,' the mechanic agreed. 'But you don't seriously think someone did it on purpose, do you?'

Ross shook his head. 'Pay no attention to me, I'm paranoid,' he said with a slight smile. 'Can you fix it for me?'

Seated in the tow truck, heading for the workshop, Ross's mind was busy with several unpleasant but increasingly convincing suspicions. The police sergeant had unwittingly given his memory a prod when he'd checked the number plate with the registration papers. The first three letters were DRH. 'Damn Roland's Hide' Ross's subconscious had immediately quoted, and in an instant, memories of the previous Monday evening came flooding back. DRH had been the registration of the Land-Rover that he'd followed through the diversion, and that had set up the ambush.

'It was Darcy's idea,' Franklin had said when he had offered the Land-Rover to Ross at the show. Was Darcy Mr X?

At the garage, the mechanic showed Ross the tapered joint on which the steering track rod end sat. 'See here. It's been greased to help it slide. The other one hasn't been touched for donkey's years. Looks like you were right, mate. Bloody stupid sort of joke to play! If it was me, I'd half bloody kill whoever did this!'

'Mmm. I might just do that,' Ross agreed.

Having been assured that the Land-Rover was once more roadworthy, Ross settled his account, then resumed his journey.

Working on the premise that Darcy Richmond was indeed the extortionist and conveniently leaving aside the matter of motive for the moment, he tried to fit together the pieces of the puzzle.

Perhaps Leo had stumbled onto Darcy's trail by stealing his wallet and finding the business card. This would have led him to the connection with Clown, and given him enough leverage to threaten to expose Darcy if he wasn't cut in. Ross remembered the day at the yard when it appeared that Leo had upset Darcy. Perhaps Leo had faced him with what he had guessed.

If Darcy was indeed their Mr X, it would explain how he had managed to stay one step ahead of McKinnon's men. It had been a clever move to bug the telephone outside Franklin's house, thereby directing suspicion towards an outside listener, when all he would need to do would be pick up an extension or casually question his uncle. Although Darcy had his own pad, Ross knew he still had a room at his uncle's home.

Why had McKinnon eliminated Darcy from his enquiries? Ross supposed it was because of a lack of perceptible motive and the existence of an alibi for the night of the Bellboy incident. Darcy himself had told Ross he was away sailing that weekend. But what if he had moored and slipped back to Oakley Manor to slaughter the horse? Almost impossible to trace. And if Darcy *were* their man, it would account for Leo knowing that McKinnon's men were watching him.

Ross sighed. He hoped, for Franklin's sake, that he was wrong, but the more he thought about it the more probable it all seemed.

Ross had his own ideas as to the reason behind Darcy's campaign against his uncle but one fact refused to fit the overall picture. Darcy had apparently been prepared to risk Peter's life to gain his ends. Ross felt sure he had never faked his devotion to the boy. It was there for all to see, whenever they were together. He clearly resented anyone who threatened to replace him in the boy's affections.

Maybe that was why he had 'lost' Danny's videotape containing footage of Ross riding the bucking stallion. Peter already regarded the American with a certain amount of juvenile hero worship, as the Colonel had pointed out, and seeing him ride the rogue horse could have done nothing but enhance that image.

Ross recalled the evening they had gone for a drink. Perhaps, even then, Darcy had been sizing him up as possible trouble. Or perhaps Ross had been his alibi for the time of Peter's accident. Remembering how easily Darcy had mimicked Fergusson's Scottish accent, it was plain that assuming an Irish one would be no problem to him.

It wasn't possible to be sure exactly who had done what, and at whose instigation, but Ross was beginning to see that Darcy had harnessed Leo's hostility for his own ends. He was willing to bet that Leo had engineered most of the physical 'accidents'. Things like the attack on the dog bore the ex-groom's hallmark of spite.

It seemed likely that Sarah had been taken in. Now he thought about it Ross realised they were an ill-matched pair, but what better cover for Darcy making visits to the yard than to see her?

Using Leo as a willing tool, Darcy had tried again and again to weaken Ross's position in the yard. It was quite possible he had manipulated Harry Douglas in some way too. When, in spite of everything, the Colonel had stood by Ross, it was no wonder Darcy should have decided that the time had come to get rid of him.

Ross felt bitterly angry, for himself, for Franklin, who had shown his nephew nothing but kindness, for Peter, Ginger and the dog, all innocent victims, and for the Colonel and the other members of the Oakley Manor team who had suffered because of Ross's disgrace.

Ross began to plot Darcy Richmond's downfall.

BACK AT THE STABLES, the wind was rising. The oak trees behind the house tossed and strained, and the gravel was strewn with twigs and greenery. Anything that wasn't tied down was rolling around.

Ross put the Richmond Land-Rover in the shed in place of the other, which he parked in the yard. Bill appeared, and together they did the midday rounds: feeding, filling water buckets and tidying stables. All the while, Ross was engrossed with the problem of what had to be done and how to do it.

After lunch, Masters collected the eager youngsters to take them to the motor museum. They planned to go to the cinema after Beaulieu, so they wouldn't be back for several hours.

As the Jaguar swept out of sight, Ross made his way to the house. He needed to use a telephone and he dared not use the one in the stable office. To be overheard at this stage would foul everything up. The circumstances would never again be so ripe for exploitation. It *had* to be today. If, that was, McKinnon and Franklin agreed.

In the absence of Masters, the Colonel opened the door himself. His enquiring expression faded to one of resignation as he saw Ross. He stood back and waved the American past and into the study. Ross turned to face him.

The Colonel's eyes narrowed. 'Has something happened?'

'I . . . um . . . have something to tell you,' Ross said. 'But first, I need to use your phone.'

TEN

Two hours later, Ross sat back and watched his employer's face as he mentally digested what he'd heard. He had been a good listener, interrupting only occasionally with intelligent questions and he assimilated the information remarkably quickly. Ross supposed that was all part of his military training.

Finally the Colonel lifted his thoughtful gaze from the desktop and looked directly at Ross. 'All along I've struggled to reconcile what I was hearing of you with the impression I was forming of your character. The two just wouldn't mesh. It's a relief, in many ways, to know the truth.' He sighed. 'If only the whole thing wasn't such an infernal tangle. Poor Franklin!'

Ross nodded his agreement. It was good to be back on the level with this man for whom he felt a good deal of liking and respect.

'But is there no other way to resolve it all?' the Colonel said. 'If Darcy falls for this plan of yours, he'll be like a cornered bear, lashing out at whoever's closest, and that will be you.'

Ross shook his head. 'I wish there was another way, but it's important to catch him red-handed. It's the only way to be certain. McKinnon's men will be there to take over as soon as we've hooked our fish. I don't think there'll be any danger.'

The telephone on the desk rang, forestalling any further comment.

The Colonel answered it, listened and handed it wordlessly to Ross. It was McKinnon calling back.

'OK, it's on. You'll have all the back-up you need. One of my men will be with you about seven o'clock to fit the wire.'

As he replaced the receiver Ross's heart was thudding heavily.

'It's set,' he told the Colonel, calmly.

JUST BEFORE EIGHT o'clock, Ross was in Woodsmoke's stable, awaiting Darcy Richmond's arrival. He didn't doubt that Darcy would come, for a quarter of an hour earlier, knowing that Franklin would not be at home because he was with McKinnon, Ross had telephoned and asked to speak to him.

'Ross!' There was a pause while Ross imagined Darcy frantically speculating as to what might have gone wrong with his plan. 'Er, Uncle Frank's not here at the moment,' he went on, recovering his poise. 'Can I take a message?'

'Sure, thanks. Just tell him he needn't pick Peter up this evening because I've got to go out and can drop him off on the way. I've just got a phone call to make, then I'll run him home in the Land-Rover.'

He had put the receiver down smartly, pretending not to notice Darcy's urgent protests, and then lifted it again and left it lying on the table. The Scotts had been evacuated to the main house, and the Colonel would let his telephone ring unanswered, as instructed.

Suddenly, Woody pricked his ears. Ross heard the roar of a rapidly decelerating engine above the howl of the wind.

Darcy leapt from his car and immediately began shouting alternately for Peter and Ross. Receiving no answer, he ran to the door that led up to Ross's room. He banged briefly around before charging down again and out into the yard. Peering through the stable window, Ross saw him check the tack room and the stable office.

'Ross! Peter! Where the hell is everybody? Ross! Damn you! Where are you?' he yelled. 'Oh, God, please don't say they've gone!'

Ross stepped out of the stable. 'Looking for someone?' he called.

Darcy's eyes narrowed as he saw Ross. 'Where's Peter?' he hissed. 'And where did you come from?'

'I was hiding,' Ross said. 'I wanted to see what you'd do when you couldn't find us. Your reaction was pretty interesting.'

For a moment Darcy appeared to consider caution, but his hatred was stronger. He stepped closer. 'You sneaky bastard! You set this up, didn't you? How did you find out?'

'You damn near killed me this morning, you evil son-of-a-bitch!'

'I meant to!' Darcy had thrown caution to the winds. 'I wish I had, you bastard! You've ruined everything with your interfering nosiness. I should have hit you harder that night in your room. You sucked up to Franklin. You tried to turn Peter against me. I warned you twice and I thought, after the other night, you'd be finished! I thought the Colonel would throw you out. And Uncle Frank . . . I thought it would show him you're no better than the rest of them . . . But he stuck by you. Why?'

The last word sounded agonised and Ross got the impression that Darcy's hatred of him had now become even more prominent in his mind than the extortion plot.

'He stuck by you too, fella, even when you didn't deserve it.'

'He had a guilty conscience! He cheated my father and felt he had to make it up to me. So he played the Good Samaritan—sending his penniless nephew to expensive schools, giving him a job, forgiving all his sins. I screwed his wife, did you know?'

Ross nodded.

'And he forgave me!' Darcy gave a great shout of laughter. 'What a bloody saint! I told him it was just once but it was right from the start and he never guessed! It should have been half mine, you know, the company,' he added bitterly. 'My father owned half of it. Franklin tricked him and I'm going to make damned sure he doesn't do the same to Peter and me.'

'Is that why you tried to blackmail him?'

'I *did* blackmail him!' Darcy asserted proudly. 'I was going to bleed him dry and then take Peter from him. He was running scared until you came along and fouled it all up!'

Gotcha! Ross thought, triumphantly. That should be all that McKinnon needed to hear. Darcy had confirmed his guilt beyond doubt. The wind gusted mightily and somewhere in the distance a tree groaned and toppled with an impressive crash.

'What have you done with Peter?' Darcy asked.

'Nothing. He's at the cinema, as far as I know. He still has to rely on that wheelchair, though, doesn't he? Tell me, how do you live with yourself, knowing you did that to your own son?' He had no proof, but everything pointed to it: their physical similarity, Darcy's affair with Marsha and his jealousy over Peter's admiration for Ross.

Darcy's reaction removed any lingering doubt.

'No!' He almost screamed the word. 'I never meant that to happen! The driver was incompetent. He wasn't meant to hit any of the children, just scare them—to scare Franklin. It was just another threat.'

'You fool!' Ross said contemptuously. 'You had everything going for you but you just couldn't get rid of that chip on your shoulder. Well, you've had it now.'

'Says who?' Darcy sneered, stepping ever closer. 'Who's going to believe a drunken, nerve-shattered cripple with a grudge?'

Without taking his eyes off the American, he reached into an inner pocket and produced a flick knife with which Ross was uncomfortably familiar. The blade clicked open smoothly.

Where the hell was McKinnon?

Ross patted his torso. 'Maybe nobody *would* believe me,' he admitted. 'But I'd say you've been pretty convincing yourself.'

'You sneaky bastard!' Darcy hissed a second time. 'You're wired! Who's listening?' he demanded. 'Is it McKinnon?'

Ross stood his ground, keeping a wary eye on the knife.

'McKinnon. Your uncle. The Colonel. I'd say they've heard enough, wouldn't you? They'll be here any minute.'

Ross could only hope he could fend Darcy off for as long as it took them to get there. Where the hell were they? With a sudden, sickening sense of foreboding, he remembered hearing a falling tree. If it had been one of the limes at the end of the drive . . .

Darcy launched himself at Ross, his knife hand swinging for the American's belly. Ross blocked the thrust instinctively, and Darcy's foot lashed out, smashing into his knee. Ross fell back in agony, to land sitting against the stable wall.

As Darcy stepped forward to follow up his advantage, Ross could only watch. There was nothing within reach that could be used as a weapon. He was calculating the merits of pulling him onto a head butt when three burly men sprinted, shouting, into the yard.

Darcy decided to cut his losses. As two of the men ran forward, leaving one at the entrance to the Manor drive, he raced for the yard Land-Rover. Ross groaned inwardly. The keys were still in it.

Within moments Darcy had gunned the engine and he was accelerating across the yard, ignoring his pursuers' commands to stop. To Ross's surprise, Darcy drove hard at the five-bar gate into the home field. The gate hadn't been fashioned with the idea of withstanding an assault from an accelerating Land-Rover, and it didn't.

By this time, Ross had dragged himself up to a standing position. His left leg, when put gingerly to the ground, set up a protest that brought him out in a sweat.

The three burly individuals looked at the departing Land-Rover, then raced in unspoken agreement for Darcy's abandoned car.

'We'll take it from here,' one of them called to Ross.

Not in that, you won't, he thought sardonically, watching the silver beauty skid as it hit the wet grass of the field. He briefly considered the other Land-Rover, hidden away in the shed, but doubted if his knee would cooperate enough even to get it in gear.

With an ungainly action somewhere between hopping and skipping, he crossed the yard to Telamon's box. In front of his nose hung the stallion's halter and leading rein, left there in case of emergencies. This, he decided, definitely qualified as an emergency.

He grabbed the halter and within moments had caught the big chestnut. Ross had no time to fetch a saddle. He led the eager stallion outside and, with a flying leap, reached the sleek back and clung to it instinctively as the horse surged powerfully forward.

Four more men burst into the yard—two from the drive to the Manor and two from the lane. Ross shouted about the other Land-Rover as he guided his excited mount through the shattered remains of the gate to thunder in pursuit of the two vehicles.

Halfway across the field he passed the abandoned sports car. A few strides further on, he passed McKinnon's men running gamely in the wake of the Land-Rover, which had by now disappeared into the wood on the far side of the field.

Ross tried to guess where Darcy would make for. He decided that he would bear right inside the wood, heading for the track that led into a field beside Home Farm Lane. If Ross cut the corner, he estimated he could catch up with the Land-Rover before it reached the lane. It would mean jumping two sizeable hedges, but such was Ross's confidence in the stallion's ability that he didn't hesitate.

Telamon leapt with such power that Ross was hard put to keep his seat. He somehow managed to retain control, and after a moment caught sight of a figure hurrying towards the road.

The Land-Rover had presumably come up against an insurmountable obstacle, Ross thought, as he sent the horse in pursuit. Telamon entered into the spirit of the chase, and, as they drew level with the running man, Ross stuck out his foot and pushed. Darcy stumbled sideways and pitched headlong into the grass.

Attempting to stop and turn in one movement proved to be Ross's undoing. The stallion lost traction on the wet grass and almost fell. Sliding hopelessly, Ross half fell, half leapt to the ground.

Darcy was clambering to his feet not two yards from where Ross had landed, an action the American discouraged by throwing himself at him in a flying tackle. Darcy subsided into the grass again, moaning weakly. He appeared to be winded.

A quick search revealed the flick knife in an inside pocket. Ross transferred it to his own pocket. He removed his belt and used it to secure his captive's hands behind his back. Then he sat on him.

Ross looked round hopefully for Telamon but the horse had prudently taken himself off. He sighed, resigning himself to the fact that from here on in he would have to walk. Though he strained to see in the low light, Ross couldn't see any sign of McKinnon's men.

Darcy had begun to move beneath him now, and Ross decided to head for the lane in the hope that someone would have thought to try and head the fugitive off there. He rose painfully to his feet and hauled his protesting prisoner up after him.

'Shut up and walk,' he said unsympathetically.

Darcy walked, but he didn't shut up. He called Ross all the uncomplimentary names he could think of. Once they were through the gate in the lane, Ross's heart sank.

To his right, about twenty yards away, a sizeable tree lay squarely across the tarmac, effectively blocking any form of passage. To his left the way looked clear but to go that way would involve a walk of at least a mile and a half before he reached a road where there was any likelihood of flagging down a car.

'What now, smart arse?' Darcy enquired annoyingly.

'We wait. I'm still wired, don't forget. So I just have to say, "I've got Darcy. We're in Home Farm Lane", and someone will come.'

'You hope! What range does that transmitter have?'

Ross ignored him. He had no idea about range.

In the event, someone did come. Above the gusting wind he heard
the sound of an approaching vehicle and was almost immediately
blinded by powerful headlights sweeping round the bend. A figure
sprang from the vehicle and strode towards Ross and Darcy, silhouetted by the glare. Ross's relief was immense. 'Jeez, am I glad to see you!'

'Why, Yank, I'm touched!' an all-too-familiar voice sneered.

Leo! Ross froze in disbelief.

Darcy seemed to find the situation amusing. 'What now, *Yank?*'

Ross didn't answer, for the simple reason that he didn't know.

'I want you to meet an old friend of mine, Yank. Do you recognise
him?' He held one arm out sideways against the light. Leo was carrying his gun.

Ross pulled Darcy close in front of him, using him as a shield.

Leo laughed. 'A good idea, Yank! Always supposing I gave a shit
about him. But I don't. He was just a means to an end.' He lifted the
gun to shoulder-height.

Ross's pulse rate accelerated. Disappointed to have failed at this
late stage, his inclination was to goad Leo, to shake him out of that
irritating self-satisfaction and hope that anger made him careless.

'Yeah, I guess you must be pretty mad, if you've found out how
much Darcy's really been making from his little racket,' he said.

'What do you mean?' The gun dropped six inches or so.

'We're talking hundreds of thousands here,' Ross said, warming to
his task. 'What he offered you was mere chicken feed. If I were you,
I'd want fifty per cent, maybe sixty. After all, you've done most of
the hard work.' He had no idea how much Darcy had cost Franklin
but it certainly seemed to incense Leo.

'How much have you been holding back?' Leo demanded of Darcy.

'Nothing! I swear it!' Darcy was panicking. 'He's just trying to stir
you up. Can't you see? He's playing for time.'

Leo was silent for a moment. 'Maybe you're right at that,' he said
shrewdly. 'And then again, maybe there's some truth in it. I think I'd
like to find out, but not here. We'll take the car.'

This was not what Ross wanted at all. If he were to get in that car,
he would leave all chance of help from McKinnon's men far behind
him. He must play for more time. He slipped Darcy's flick knife from
his pocket and released the blade.

'How did you know where we were?' Ross asked Leo.

'I didn't. I was coming to see what had happened to the Land-
Rover. Darcy was expecting to hear that you'd had a nasty accident

and he wanted me to find out what had gone wrong. I should have told him to do his own dirty work,' Leo added sourly.

Ross tightened his grip on Darcy. 'Looks like a stalemate, doesn't it, Leo? You can't have the money without Darcy, and if you try to take him from me I'll stick this in him.' He raised the knife.

'Leo! Be careful! He'll bloody do it!' Darcy said in desperation.

Leo stepped closer. 'No, he won't,' he countered confidently. 'He hasn't got the guts. And besides, he knows he'll be dead if he does.'

Ross could see the faint gleam of Leo's teeth as, barely three feet away now, he smiled. Oh, hell! he thought.

He shoved Darcy towards Leo as hard as he could and dived towards the darkness of the hedge. He saw the two men stagger back and fall in an untidy heap against the car as he completed his roll and fetched up in the nettles and brambles beneath the hawthorn.

Ross lunged to his feet, hoping Leo had lost the gun when he fell. He hadn't. Two shots in quick succession whined over Ross's head as his knee gave way and reduced his intended sprint to an undignified scuttle. He reached the gate and scrambled over, landing on his backside in the wet grass of the field. He heard Leo curse and scurried, crabwise, into the shelter of the hedge once more.

The hedge ran for 100 yards or so in a straight line, all neatly cut and laid, and as impossible to penetrate as a stone wall. There was nowhere to run. Even supposing that running was an option.

Leo was climbing the gate now. A beam of light sprang from his right hand as he swung a torch, which blessedly failed to pick the American out. Then he turned away from Ross and began to search the far side of the gate first.

The wind had dropped but not enough, Ross hoped, for Leo to hear the swishing of his body snaking through the grass. In a vain attempt at a bluff, he moved in a commando-style slither, away from the hawthorn and out into the open grass. He kept his head low, resisting the temptation to look behind to see where Leo was, and, when he was perhaps fifty feet from the hedge, collapsed into the wet grass.

He felt horribly vulnerable. The grass was barely eight inches high. Ross could only hope that if Leo shone the torch his way, he would pass for one of the many molehills in the vicinity.

Leo had moved to the near side of the gate now, and was searching the area where Ross had until recently lain. Ross saw him swing the torch once more in a wide arc. Almost instantaneously, Ross heard a swishing in the grass behind him.

Darcy! he thought with a sick sense of failure. Somehow, while he was concentrating on Leo, Darcy must have got round behind him. Ross tensed himself to try to turn and come to his feet in one movement. This time he knew that he would use the knife if he had to. His situation was desperate. But just as he began his move he felt something brush his back and warm breath huffed in his ear.

Telamon, who had wandered over curiously to see why his master was full-length in the grass, threw up his head in alarm as Ross surged up suddenly, right under his nose.

His situation already betrayed, Ross grabbed at the lead rope, and flung himself, for the second time that day, at the horse's back.

The stallion plunged forward, and Ross clutched a handful of chestnut mane and hung on, sprawled across the horse's loins.

Something buzzed past his left ear as he struggled to pull himself to a more secure position and he realised with desperation that Leo was shooting at him again. Telamon was galloping blindly towards the gun, probably heading for the gate, and Ross was completely powerless to stop him.

Sick with fear, Ross dug his heels into the stallion's chestnut flanks and rode him hard at the man ahead. With any other horse, Ross knew it wouldn't have worked. Horses almost invariably avoid hitting human beings if it is within their power to do so.

Telamon perhaps sensed by his stance that Leo was aggressive, and he had developed an uncommon bond with Ross. Without hesitation, the horse galloped the last few strides towards Leo. He half leapt as he reached him, cannoning into the man's upper body and flinging him to the ground, and then plunged on.

Just as they reached the gate, both Ross and the stallion were blinded by the glare of a car's headlights as it turned into the field gateway. Telamon shied abruptly away, dumping Ross without ceremony onto the grass by the gatepost, which he used to pull himself painfully to his feet. Squinting, he tried to see beyond the light.

His one comfort was that, if it was Darcy, then at least he was unarmed. He was just wondering why, if it *was* Darcy, he didn't just turn the car round and go, when a metallic click sounded close to his left ear and something cold touched his temple. He froze.

'Hold very still,' a voice warned. 'You are just a millimetre away from the final mystery.'

Ross practically stopped breathing. Roland! Who was never far behind when there was trouble. Now where did he fit into all this?

A torch was flashed in Ross's face and the familiar, well-bred voice exclaimed: 'Good God, it's our American friend! Sorry, old boy. You should have said something.'

The gun barrel dropped and Ross almost fainted with relief. He managed a shaky grin. 'For a moment, I couldn't seem to think of anything appropriate.'

'Where's Leo?' Roland asked.

'Somewhere back there.' Ross waved a hand. 'Telamon knocked him down. I don't know how badly he's hurt.'

Another two vehicles drew up in the lane and disgorged their loads of passengers, and suddenly the night was full of noise and bustle.

'Ross!' Franklin hurried forward, deeply concerned. 'Are you all right? We just couldn't get to you. There are trees down all over the place. We were praying we wouldn't be too late.'

'Not half as much as I was,' Ross assured him. 'Yes, I'm fine.'

McKinnon approached. 'I incorporated a tracking device in that wire you're wearing,' he said to Ross. 'It's a good job I did, though I hadn't foreseen having to chase you half across the county.'

Ross grinned. 'I didn't foresee it myself but I couldn't face seeing him get away when we had him—confession and all.' Belatedly, he remembered Franklin's presence. 'I'm sorry,' he said, awkwardly. 'I was hoping we'd be proved wrong.'

Franklin shook his head, the courage that had sustained him for so long not deserting him now. 'No. I knew you must be right as soon as McKinnon put it to me. Looking back, I can see there have been pointers I should have spotted. I think I was wilfully blind.'

'Where's Darcy now?' Ross asked, looking round.

'Wearing a pair of particularly attractive matching bracelets,' Roland said, coming back from the field. 'Leo is dead. Broken neck, I should think.'

Ross turned and stared blindly at the figure lying beyond the gate. Heaven knew he had no reason to regret the man's passing, but to have been the direct cause of it . . . That was something else.

'We heard the shots, Ross,' McKinnon said. 'You had no choice.'

Ross forced his thoughts in another direction. 'Roland works for you, doesn't he? Did you recruit him like you did me?'

McKinnon smiled. 'Good gracious, no. He came to us straight from the army, five or six years ago now. He was looking for an interesting career without all the restrictions of army life. We suited him and he suited us. Very well, as a matter of fact.' He shook Ross's shoulder gently. 'Come on. We should be getting back. The Colonel will be wondering what has happened. Don't worry about this. My men will clear up here. One of them will phone the police when they're ready. A shocked passer-by, you know the sort of thing.'

Ross glanced at him. 'What about . . .?' He inclined his head towards the field. 'Won't there be trouble?'

McKinnon tutted. 'Nasty accident. Trying to catch a loose horse that's been frightened by the wind. Always a risky business . . .'

With a shock, Ross remembered Telamon. 'You'd better tell your men to keep that gate shut, there's several thousand pounds' worth of showjumper somewhere in this field.'

'Right.' McKinnon gave instructions to his men. 'Now, let's go.'

Darcy, McKinnon and one of his men travelled back to the Manor in one vehicle, while Franklin, Roland and Ross took another.

Franklin, who was understandably subdued, sat in the back to allow Ross to sit in the front where he could stretch out his leg.

'It was you, wasn't it, that night in the yard?' Ross said, looking across at the Colonel's son. 'You did some sort of judo on me, dumped me on the ground and lit out! Why didn't you tell me you were one of the good guys? You knew who *I* was.'

'I was under orders,' Roland said smugly. 'And I always do as I am told. There *was* an intruder that night, though. Darcy, I suppose. I think your dog chased him off.'

'But why shouldn't I have been told? I wasted a lot of time wondering what you were up to.'

'Because, old boy, to be blunt, we only had Lindsay's word for your character reference. Under stress you might have given us both away, for all we knew. Edward felt it was an unnecessary risk.'

Ross had to allow that that made sense, but it was ironic that on the night he was picked up for drink-driving he had worked so hard to lose Roland. If he had only known . . . He said as much.

Roland laughed and shrugged. 'I was supposed to be watching your back. McKinnon felt you were attracting rather a lot of attention from our friend. Sod's law you had to spot me that night. By the way, what *were* you in such a hurry to tell Franklin that night?'

'Something your father said set me thinking. He warned me that Darcy was pretty ticked off with me because of the way Peter was behaving, and the more I thought about it, the more I wondered about their relationship. God knows how I would have put it to you, Franklin!' he added, over his shoulder.

'You know, there have been times when I've wondered, seeing how Darcy is with Peter,' Franklin said soberly. 'But my comfort comes from the boy himself. He's a far stronger character than Darcy or my brother ever were. I think that's good enough for me.'

'Oh, and by the way,' Roland said. 'I think you'll find your drink-driving charge will be dropped. I persuaded our boys in blue to take a look at the bottle after all.'

'You phoned them on the way back,' Ross said, remembering. 'I wish I'd known. You let me suffer!'

'Suffering is good for the soul,' Roland said lightly. 'Besides, I didn't want you falling on me in gratitude. Ruins a decent suit, being fallen upon.'

WITHIN FIFTEEN MINUTES, both parties, minus Darcy, were ensconced in the Colonel's study.

The gathering was lit by paraffin lamps as the electricity supply had been a casualty of the storm. The gale largely seemed to have blown itself out now. The Colonel, his son, Franklin, McKinnon and Ross all gratefully accepted mugs of Irish coffee from Masters.

Peter and Danny were, they were informed, at the Scotts' cottage, under Maggie's indulgent eye, and Darcy was locked in an upstairs room, handcuffs still in place. Bill had been sent to recover Telamon.

Unable to hide his disability any longer, Ross lounged in one of the armchairs, his leg propped up on a footstool. A temporary layoff was obviously on the cards but the disappointment was tempered by the assurances of the three owners present that their horses would be saved for him. They would be kept fit but their competitive careers placed on hold. It was more than Ross had dared hope for.

'What about Darcy?' the Colonel asked McKinnon, carefully avoiding Franklin's eyes. 'I suppose he'll have to go to prison?'

'Well . . .' McKinnon hesitated. 'Franklin and I discussed that this afternoon and we agreed it would be better if we can keep this business out of the courts. The injured parties are all in this room—with the exception of Peter—and it isn't pleasant to have one's personal affairs dragged out under the public gaze. Of course, the decision rests partly with Ross, but if he agrees not to press charges, Darcy will be asked to sign a detailed statement witnessed by those present, and the family solicitor with whom it will then be lodged. In return, Darcy will return all the proceeds of his crime and leave the country on a one-way ticket. I think for the boy's sake he will do so.'

'Ross?' Franklin was watching him anxiously.

'That's fine by me. I don't think I want that kind of publicity any more than you do. To be honest, I've had a bellyful of publicity.'

Franklin's look held a wealth of gratitude. 'I don't know how to thank you,' he began earnestly.

'Please, don't. If I made any useful contribution it was as a catalyst. I think I charged round like a bull in a china shop. I mean, for a long time I had Roland down as the villain, for Chrissakes!'

'Roland?' the Colonel exclaimed through the general amusement. 'Good Lord! Why ever? He hasn't enough energy to be a criminal.'

Ross caught Roland's eye and he winked. Ross had asked him on the way home why he had never told his father what his real profession was. 'Oh, I don't know,' Roland had said. 'I expect I will one day. He's quite fond of me as I am, you know.'

After a few more minutes, McKinnon took his leave. As he left, Lindsay arrived, unaware of the preceding drama.

'I couldn't get through to the yard, there's a tree down, so I came round . . . Goodness, this is quite a crowd! What's been going on? Have I missed something?' she asked of no one in particular.

For some reason everyone looked at Roland.

'Why me?' he exclaimed in aggrieved tones.

Lindsay shrugged. 'Well, if it's some great secret . . . Ross will tell me later, won't you, Ross?' She moved across to sit on the arm of his chair, draping her arm round his neck.

Significant glances were exchanged around the room but Ross didn't care. His aches and pains felt more bearable by the moment.

'By the way,' Lindsay said, dismissing the mystery as of no importance. 'I've had an idea. I was wondering—do you think if we clubbed together we could buy Bishop for Ross to ride? I've got some money put by.'

Ross made a movement of protest, the Colonel and Roland looked thoughtful, and Franklin looked at his toes.

'I'm afraid,' he said in quiet apology, 'that this particular Yorkshire farmer has no wish to sell.'

LYNDON STACEY

Horse riding and writing are Lyndon Stacey's two great loves, so having the opportunity to combine them to produce *Cut Throat*, her first published novel, was a dream come true. She'd previously written a western and a medieval fantasy, but it wasn't until *Cut Throat* was finished that she felt confident enough to try to find a publisher for her work.

Her love of horses began in childhood, when she was seven years old and was lent a pony by a family friend. 'Since then I have almost always had a pony or a horse. I used to enter showjumping competitions when I was younger, and even now I love to watch it. I worked in a yard for a while after I'd left school, and a lot of the background for the book was inspired by the job I had at that time.' When it came to police procedures, however, she had to go out and do research, helped by a friend who works in the police force. 'He was very helpful whenever I needed to check up on details.'

Growing up the New Forest, where she still lives, she remembers making up stories from an early age, finding inspiration in books by Enid Blyton, who was her favourite author when she was a child. 'I used to love the way her characters were always eating the most wonderful meals, washed down with lashings of ginger beer, and so at the time I made sure that all my characters did that, too!'

Lyndon Stacey also works as an animal portrait artist, something she says she fell into by accident. 'I wasn't sure what I wanted to do when I left school and a careers advice officer suggested that I should try setting myself up as an artist. So, I did! I advertised at first, but soon began to get more and more work through word of mouth. I feel I'm very lucky to have ended up earning a living doing the things I enjoy most.'

Daddy's Little Girl

MARY HIGGINS CLARK

Little Ellie promised her sister she wouldn't tell. She kept the secret but paid the price: twenty-three years imprisoned by guilt.

Now it's time to set the record straight. So Ellie's going back. Back to where she lost her sister, her daddy and her home.

All because of one man.

One

When Ellie awoke that morning, it was with the sense that something terrible had happened.

Instinctively she reached for Bones, the soft and cuddly stuffed dog who had shared her pillow ever since she could remember. When she'd had her seventh birthday last month, Andrea, her fifteen-year-old sister, had teased her that it was time to toss Bones in the attic.

Then Ellie remembered what was wrong: Andrea hadn't come home last night. After dinner she had gone to her best friend Joan's house to study for a maths test. She had promised to be home by nine o'clock. At a quarter to nine Mommy went to Joan's house to walk Andrea home, but they said Andrea had left at eight o'clock.

Mommy had come back home worried just as Daddy got in from work. Daddy was a lieutenant in the New York State Police. Right away he and Mommy had started calling all of Andrea's friends, but no one had seen her. Then Daddy said he was going to drive to the bowling alley and to the ice-cream parlour, just in case she had gone there. 'If she lied about doing homework until nine o'clock, she won't set foot out of this house for six months,' he'd said to Mommy. 'If I said it once, I've said it a thousand times—I don't want her to go out after dark alone.'

'For heaven's sake, Ted, she went out at seven o'clock. She got to Joan's. She was planning to be home by nine, and I even walked over there to meet her.'

'Then where is she?'

They made Ellie go to bed, and eventually she fell asleep, waking only now. Maybe Andrea was home, she thought hopefully. She slipped out of bed and darted down the hall. Please be there, she begged. She opened the door. Andrea's bed had not been slept in.

Her bare feet silent on the steps, Ellie hurried downstairs. Their neighbour, Mrs Hilmer, was sitting with Mommy in the kitchen. Mommy was wearing the same clothes she had on last night, and she looked as if she'd been crying for a long time.

Ellie ran to her. 'Mommy.'

Mommy hugged her and began to sob. Ellie felt Mommy's hand clutching her shoulder so hard that she was almost hurting her.

'Mommy, where's Andrea?'

'We . . . don't know. Daddy and the police are looking for her.'

'Ellie, why don't you get dressed, and I'll fix you some breakfast,' Mrs Hilmer said.

No one was saying that she should hurry up because the school bus would be coming pretty soon. Without asking, Ellie knew she wouldn't be going to school today.

She dutifully washed her face and hands and brushed her teeth and her hair, then put on play clothes and went downstairs again. Daddy came through the kitchen door just as she sat at the table, where Mrs Hilmer had put out juice and cornflakes.

'No sign of her,' he said. 'We've looked everywhere.'

Ellie could tell that Daddy was almost crying. He hadn't seemed to notice her, but she didn't mind. Sometimes when Daddy came home he was upset because something sad had happened at work. He had that same look on his face now.

Andrea was hiding—Ellie was sure of it. She had probably left Joan's house early on purpose because she was meeting Rob Westerfield in the hide-out. Then maybe it got late, and she was afraid to come home. Daddy had said that if she ever lied again about where she'd been he'd make her quit the school band. He'd said that when he found out she'd gone for a ride with Rob Westerfield in his car when she was supposed to be at the library.

Andrea loved being in the band; last year she'd been the only fresh-man chosen for the flute section. But if she'd gone to the hide-out to meet Rob, and Daddy found out, that would mean she'd have to give it up. Mommy always said that Andrea could twist Daddy round her little finger, but she didn't say that last month when one of the state troopers told Daddy he'd given Rob Westerfield a ticket for speeding and that Andrea was with him at the time. Daddy had told Andrea, 'That guy is not only rich and spoilt, he's a bad apple through and through. When he kills himself speeding, you're not going to be in the car. You are forbidden to have anything to do with him.'

The hide-out was in the garage behind the great big house that old Mrs Westerfield, Rob's grandmother, lived in all summer. It was always unlocked, and sometimes Andrea and her friends sneaked in there and smoked cigarettes. Andrea had taken Ellie there a couple of times when she was baby-sitting her. Her friends had been mad at Andrea for bringing her along, but she had said, 'Ellie is a good kid. She's not a snitch.'

Ellie was sure that Andrea had left Joan's house to meet Rob. Ellie had heard her talk to him on the phone yesterday, and when Andrea was finished she was practically crying. 'I told Rob I was going to the dance with Paulie,' she said, 'and now he's really mad at me.'

Ellie thought about the conversation as she finished the cornflakes and juice. Daddy was standing at the stove, holding a cup of coffee.

Then, for the first time, he seemed to notice her. 'Ellie, I think you'd be better off at school. At lunchtime I'll take you over.'

'Is it all right if I go outside now?'

'Yes. But stay around the house.'

Ellie ran for her jacket and was quickly out of the door. It was the 14th of November, and the leaves felt sloshy underfoot. The sky was heavy with clouds, and she could tell it was going to rain again. Ellie wished they were back in Irvington. It was lonely here. Mrs Hilmer's house was the only other one on this road.

Daddy had liked living in Irvington, but they'd moved here, further up in Westchester, because Mommy wanted a bigger house and more property. When Daddy said he missed Irvington, where they'd lived until two years ago, Mommy would tell him how great the new house was. Then he'd say that in Irvington we had a million-dollar view of the Hudson River and the Tappan Zee Bridge, and he didn't have to drive five miles for a newspaper or a loaf of bread.

There were woods all round their property. Glancing back at the kitchen window to make sure no one had seen her, Ellie began to run through the trees. Five minutes later she reached a field. Feeling more and more alone, she ran across the field, then raced up a long driveway and darted round the Westerfield mansion—a small figure lost in the shadows of the approaching storm.

There was a side door to the garage, and that was the one that was unlocked. Even so, it was hard for Ellie to turn the handle. Finally she succeeded and stepped into the gloom. The garage was big enough to hold four cars, but the only one left after the summer was a van. Andrea and her friends had brought some old blankets, and they always sat at the back of the garage, behind the van, so that if anyone happened to look in the window they wouldn't see them. Ellie knew that was where Andrea would be hiding if she was here.

She didn't know why she felt suddenly afraid. She had to practically drag her feet to make them move. But then she saw it—the edge of the blanket peeking out from behind the van. Andrea *was* here! She and her friends would never have left the blankets out; when they left, they always hid them.

'Andrea . . .' Now she ran, calling softly so that Andrea wouldn't be scared. She was probably asleep, Ellie decided.

Yes, she was. Even though the garage was filled with shadows, Ellie could see Andrea's long hair trailing out from under the blanket. 'Andrea, it's me.' Ellie sank to her knees and pulled it back.

Andrea had a mask on, a terrible monster mask that looked all sticky and gummy. Ellie reached down to pull it off, and her fingers went into a broken space in Andrea's forehead. As she jerked back, she became aware of the pool of Andrea's blood, soaking through her slacks.

Then, from somewhere in the big room, she was sure she heard someone breathing—harsh, heavy, sucking-in breaths that broke off in a kind of giggle.

Terrified, she tried to get up, but her knees slid in the blood, and she fell across Andrea's chest. Her lips grazed something smooth and cold—Andrea's gold locket. Then she managed to scramble to her feet, and she turned and began to run.

She did not know she was shrieking until she was almost home, and Ted and Genine Cavanaugh ran into the back yard to see their younger daughter burst out of the woods, her arms outstretched, her little form covered in her sister's blood.

WITH THE EXCEPTION of when his team practised or had a game during the football season, sixteen-year-old Paulie Stroebel worked in Hillwood's service station after school and all day Saturday. Slow academically, but good with things mechanical, he loved to repair cars. With unruly blond hair, blue eyes, round cheeks and a stocky five-foot-eight frame, Paulie was considered a quiet, hard-working employee by his boss at the service station and something of a dopey nerd by his fellow students at Delano High. His one achievement in school was to be on the football team.

On Friday, when word of Andrea's murder reached the school, guidance counsellors were sent to all the classes to break the news. Paulie was in the middle of a study period when Emma Watkins, one of the counsellors, came in and informed the students that sophomore Andrea Cavanaugh had been killed, the victim of foul play.

The reaction was a chorus of shocked gasps and tearful protests. Then a shouted 'No!' silenced the others. Quiet, placid Paulie Stroebel, his face twisted in grief, had sprung to his feet. Fierce sobs racked his body, and as he ran from the room he said something in a muffled voice. The student nearest the door later swore that his words were 'I can't believe she's dead!'

Miss Watkins, who was fond of Paulie, was positive that his anguished words were 'I didn't think she was dead'.

That afternoon, Paulie did not show up at the service station, nor did he call his boss to explain his absence. When his parents got home that evening, they found him lying on the bed, staring at the ceiling, pictures of Andrea scattered beside him.

Both Hans and Anja Wagner Stroebel had been born in Germany, and they immigrated to the United States with their parents when they were children. They had met and married in their late thirties and used their combined savings to open a delicatessen on Main Street. By nature undemonstrative, they were fiercely protective of their only son.

Anja Stroebel acted instinctively when she saw the pictures on her son's bed. She swooped them up and put them in her handbag. At her husband's questioning glance she shook her head, indicating that he was to ask no questions. Then she sat down next to Paulie and put her arms round him. 'Andrea was such a pretty girl,' she said soothingly, her voice heavy with the accent that became stronger when she was upset. 'I remember how she congratulated you when you made that great catch and saved the game last spring. Like her other friends, you are very, very sad.'

It seemed to Paulie that she was talking from a distant place.

'The police will be looking for anyone who has been a particular friend to Andrea,' she said slowly.

'I invited her to a dance,' he said, the words coming haltingly. 'She said she would go with me.'

Anja was sure her son had never asked a girl for a date before. Last year he had refused to go to his sophomore dance.

'Then you liked her, Paulie?'

He began to cry. 'Mama, I loved her so much.'

'You *liked* her, Paulie,' Anja said. 'Try to remember that.'

On Saturday, quietly apologetic for not showing up on Friday afternoon, Paulie Stroebel reported for work at the gas station.

Early on Saturday afternoon, Hans Stroebel personally delivered a Virginia ham and salads to the Cavanaugh home and asked their neighbour Mrs Hilmer, who answered the door, to convey his deepest sympathy to the family.

'IT'S A SHAME Ted and Genine are both only children,' Ellie heard Mrs Hilmer say on Saturday. 'It makes it easier when there's a lot of family around at a time like this.'

Ellie didn't care about having more family. She just wanted Andrea back, and she wanted Mommy to stop crying, and she wanted Daddy to talk to her. He'd hardly said a word to her since she came running home and he grabbed her up in his arms and she managed to tell him where Andrea was and that she'd been hurt.

Later, after he'd gone to the hide-out and all the police came, he'd said, 'Ellie, you knew last night she might have gone to the garage. Why didn't you *tell* us then?'

'You didn't ask me, and you made me go to bed.'

'Yes, I did,' he admitted. But then later she heard him say to one of the cops, 'If only I had known Andrea was there. She might still have been alive at nine o'clock. I might have found her in time.'

Somebody from the police talked to Ellie and asked her about the hide-out. In her head she could hear Andrea saying, 'Ellie is a good kid. She's not a snitch.' Thinking about Andrea, and knowing that she'd never come home again, made Ellie cry so hard that the police stopped questioning her.

Then on Saturday a man who said he was Detective Marcus Longo came to the house. He took Ellie into the dining room and closed the door. She thought he had a nice face. He told her that he had a little boy her age and that they looked a lot alike. 'He has the same blue eyes,' he said. 'And his hair is just the colour of yours. I tell him it reminds me of sand when the sun is shining on it.'

Then he told her that four of Andrea's friends had admitted they went to the hide-out with her, but none of them had been there that night. He named the girls, then asked, 'Ellie, do you know any other girls who might have met your sister there?'

It wasn't like snitching if they had told on themselves. 'No,' she whispered. 'That was all of them.'

'Is there anyone else Andrea might have met at the hide-out?'

She hesitated. She couldn't tell him about Rob Westerfield. That would really be telling on Andrea.

Detective Longo said, 'Ellie, someone hurt Andrea so much that she isn't alive any more. Don't protect that person. Andrea would want you to tell us anything you know.'

Ellie looked down at her hands. In this big old farmhouse, this room was her favourite. It used to have ugly wallpaper, but now the walls were painted a soft yellow, and hanging over the table was a new chandelier that Mommy had found at a garage sale.

They always ate dinner in the dining room, even though Daddy thought it was silly to go to all the fuss. Mommy had a book that showed how to set the table for a formal dinner. It was Andrea's job to set the table that way every Sunday, even when it was just them. Ellie would help her, and they would have fun putting out the silver and china.

'Lord Malcolm Bigbottom is the guest of honour today,' Andrea would say. Then, reading from the book of etiquette, she'd place him at the seat to the right of where Mommy would sit. 'Oh, no, Gabrielle, the water glass must be placed slightly to the right of the dinner knife.'

Ellie's real name was Gabrielle, but no one called her that except Andrea when she was joking. She wondered if it would be her job now to set the table on Sunday from now on. She hoped not. Without Andrea it wouldn't be a game.

It felt funny to be thinking like that. On the one hand, she knew that Andrea was dead and would be buried in the cemetery in Tarrytown with Grandma and Grandpa Cavanaugh. On the other hand, she still expected Andrea to come into the house any minute, pull her close and tell her a secret.

A secret. But Ellie had crossed her heart and promised not to tell.

'Ellie, whoever hurt Andrea may hurt somebody else if he isn't stopped,' Detective Longo said.

'Do you think it's my fault Andrea is dead? Daddy thinks so.'

'No, he doesn't think that, Ellie,' Detective Longo said. 'But anything you can tell us about secrets you and Andrea shared may help us now.'

Maybe it wouldn't really be breaking a promise. If Rob had been the one who hurt Andrea, everybody should know. She looked down at her hands. 'Sometimes she would meet Rob Westerfield.'

Detective Longo leaned forward. 'Do you know if she was going to meet him there the other night?'

'I think she was. Paulie Stroebel had asked her to go to the Thanksgiving dance. She didn't *want* to go with him, but Paulie had told her he knew she was sneaking off to meet Rob Westerfield, and she was afraid he would tell Daddy if she didn't go with him. But then Rob was mad at her, and she wanted to explain to him.'

'How did Paulie know she was seeing Rob Westerfield?'

'Andrea said she thought he sometimes followed her to the hide-out. Paulie wanted her to be *his* girlfriend.'

WHEREVER ELLIE WENT, she felt in the way. After the nice detective left, she tried to find Mommy, but Mrs Hilmer said that the doctor had given her something to help her rest. Daddy spent almost all the time in his little den. He said he wanted to be left alone.

Grandma Reid, who lived in Florida, came up late on Saturday afternoon, but all she did was cry.

Mrs Hilmer and some of Mommy's friends sat in the kitchen. Ellie went outside and got on the swing. She pumped her legs until the swing went higher and higher. She wanted it to go over the top. She wanted to fall from the top and hit the ground and hurt herself. Then maybe she'd stop hurting inside.

It had stopped raining, but still there was no sun, and it was cold. After a while Ellie knew that it was no use; the swing wouldn't go over the top. She went back into the house, entering the vestibule off the kitchen. She heard the voice of Mrs Lashley, Joan's mother, and Ellie could tell she was crying. 'I was surprised that she left so early. It was dark, and it crossed my mind to drive her home. If only Ellie had told them that Andrea used to go to that garage the kids called the hide-out. Ted might have got there in time.'

Ellie went up the backstairs, walking softly so they wouldn't hear her. Grandma's suitcase was on her bed. That was funny. Wasn't Grandma going to sleep in Andrea's room? It was empty now.

The door to Andrea's room was closed. Ellie opened it as quietly as she always did on Saturday mornings, when she'd peek in to see if Andrea was still sleeping.

Daddy was standing at Andrea's desk. He was holding a picture in his hands. Ellie knew it was the baby picture of Andrea, the one in the silver frame that had *Daddy's Little Girl* engraved across the top.

As Ellie watched, he lifted the top of the music box he had bought for Andrea right after she was born. Daddy joked that Andrea never wanted to go to sleep when she was a baby, and so he'd wind up the music box and dance around the room with her and play the song from it, singing the words softly until she dozed off.

Ellie had asked if he did that with her, too, but Mommy said no, because she had been a good sleeper from the day she was born.

Some of the song's words ran through Ellie's head as the music drifted through the room. *You're daddy's little girl to have and to hold . . . You're the spirit of Christmas, my star on the tree . . . And you're daddy's little girl.*

As she watched, Daddy sat on the edge of Andrea's bed and began to sob. Ellie backed out of the room, closing the door as quietly as she had opened it.

Two
Twenty-three Years Later

My sister, Andrea, was murdered nearly twenty-three years ago, yet it always seems as though it was just yesterday.

Rob Westerfield was arrested two days after the funeral and charged with first-degree murder. Almost solely from the information I provided, the police were able to obtain a warrant to search the Westerfield home and Rob's car. They found the clothes he had worn the night he took her life, and though he had washed and bleached them, the police lab was able to identify bloodstains. The tyre jack that had been the murder weapon was found in the trunk of his car. He had washed that, too, but a tiny strand of Andrea's hair still clung to it.

Rob's defence was that he had gone to the movies the night Andrea was murdered. The cinema parking lot was full, and he left his car at the service station next door. He said that the pumps were closed, but he found Paulie Stroebel working in the garage and told Paulie he'd leave the car there and pick it up after the movies.

He claimed that Paulie Stroebel must have driven to the hide-out in his car, killed Andrea, then left the car back at the service station.

Rob said he'd left the car at the station at least half a dozen times to get dents fixed, and that on any of those occasions Paulie could have had a key made.

He tried to explain away the blood on his clothes and in the ridges of his sneakers by claiming that Andrea had begged him to meet her at the hide-out. He said she had phoned him at dinnertime the night she died. She told him that she was going to a dance with Paulie Stroebel and didn't want him to be mad at her.

'I didn't care who she went out with,' Rob explained at the trial. 'She was just a kid who had a crush on me. I'd caught her and her friends hanging out in my grandmother's garage, having a cigarette. I wanted to be nice, so I told her it was all right.'

He had an explanation for why he went to the garage hide-out. 'I got out of the movie and started to drive home. Then I got worried about her. Even though I told her I wasn't going to meet her, she said she'd wait there for me. I thought I'd better make sure she went home before her dad got angry. The light in the garage had burned out. I fumbled along and walked round behind the van. That's where Andrea and her friends used to sit on blankets and smoke cigarettes.

'I felt the blanket under my foot. I could just about make out that someone was lying there, and I figured Andrea must have been waiting for me and fallen asleep. Then I knelt down, and I could feel the blood on her face. I ran.'

He was asked why he ran. 'Because I was scared somebody might think I did it. But when I found out that the tyre jack in my trunk had blood on it, I knew it had to be Paulie who killed her.'

He was very slick, and his testimony was well rehearsed. But I was Rob Westerfield's nemesis. I remember being on the witness stand.

'Ellie,' the prosecutor asked, 'did Andrea call Rob Westerfield before she went to do homework with Joan?'

'Yes.'

'Did you hear the conversation?'

'Just a little of it. I went into her room. She was almost crying. She was telling Rob that she couldn't help it that she was going with Paulie to the dance. She didn't want Paulie to tell Daddy she met Rob in the hide-out.'

'Then what happened?'

'She hung up and said, "Rob wants me to leave Joanie's early and meet him in the hide-out. He's mad at me. He said I'm not supposed to go out with anyone else."'

'Then what happened?'

And then on the stand I gave away Andrea's last secret and broke the sacred promise I had made to her—the 'cross my heart and hope to die' promise that I would never tell anyone about the locket Rob had given her. It was gold and heart-shaped, and had little blue stones. Andrea had shown me that Rob had had their initials engraved on the back. I was crying by then because I missed my sister so much, and so, without being asked, I added, 'She put on her locket before she left, so I was pretty sure she would meet him.'

'A locket?'

'Rob gave her a locket. She wore it under her blouse so no one could see it. I could feel it when I found her in the garage.'

I remember trying not to look at Rob Westerfield. He kept staring at me. I could feel the hatred coming from him. And I swear I could read the thoughts of my mother and father: Ellie, you should have told us; you should have told us.

My testimony was pounced on by the defence attorneys. They brought out that Andrea often wore a locket that my father had given her, that it was on top of her dresser after her body was found, that I was making up stories or repeating the stories Andrea had made up about Rob.

'Andrea was wearing the locket,' I insisted. 'That's why I know it was Rob Westerfield who was in the hide-out when I found her. He came back for the locket.'

Rob's attorneys became furious, and that remark was ordered to be struck from the record. The judge turned to the jurors and told them not to consider it in any way.

Did anyone believe what I told them about the locket Rob gave Andrea? I don't know. The case went to the jury, and they were out for nearly a week. A few jurors leaned at first towards a manslaughter verdict, but the rest insisted on a murder conviction.

The two times Westerfield came up for parole, I wrote vehement letters protesting his release. But he has served twenty-two years in prison. This time the parole may be granted, and that is why I have come back to Oldham-on-the-Hudson.

I AM THIRTY YEARS OLD, live in Atlanta, and work as an investigative reporter with the *Atlanta News*. The editor in chief, Pete Lawlor, considers it a personal affront if anyone on the staff takes even a yearly vacation, so I expected him to hit the ceiling when I told him I needed a few days off immediately and might need more later.

'You getting married?'

I told him that was the last thing on my mind.

'Then what's up?'

I had not told anyone at the *News* anything about my personal life, but Pete Lawlor is one of those people who seems to know everything about everybody. Thirty-one years old, balding, and always fighting to lose those ten extra pounds, he was probably the smartest man I've ever met. After I covered the story of a murdered teenager, he said in an offhand manner, 'That must have been a tough one. I know about your sister.' He didn't expect a response, nor did I give him one, but his empathy did help.

'Andrea's killer is coming up for parole. I want to see if there's anything I can do to stop it.'

Pete leaned back in his chair. He always wore an open-necked shirt and a sweater. Sometimes I've wondered if he even *owns* a jacket. 'How long has he served?'

'Almost twenty-two years.'

'How many times has he come up for parole?'

'Twice.'

'Any problems while he was in prison?'

I felt like a schoolgirl being grilled. 'None that I know of.'

'Then he'll probably get out. So why bother?'

'Because I must.

Pete Lawlor doesn't believe in wasting either time or words. He just nodded. 'OK. Go ahead,' he said. But as I turned away, he added, 'Ellie, you're not as tough as you think you are.'

'Yes, I am.' I didn't bother to thank him for the time off.

That was on the Friday. The following day I flew from Atlanta to Westchester County Airport and rented a car.

I could have stayed at a motel in Ossining, near Sing Sing, the prison where Andrea's killer has been incarcerated. Instead I drove fifteen miles further to my old home town, Oldham-on-the-Hudson, and managed to find a quaint place that I vaguely remembered— the Parkinson Inn.

The inn was flourishing. On this chilly Saturday afternoon in October, the dining room was filled with family groups. I felt a moment of acute nostalgia. I remembered the four of us having lunch here on Saturdays, then sometimes Dad would drop Andrea and me at the movies.

The inn had only eight guest rooms, but one was still available. The sun that afternoon was uncertain, slipping in and out of clouds. I tossed my backpack onto the bed and almost smiled as I unpacked, realising that I had a nerve to criticise Pete Lawlor's wardrobe. I was wearing jeans and a turtleneck sweater. In the bag, besides a night-shirt and underwear, I was carrying only a long woollen skirt and two other sweaters. My favourite shoes are clogs, which is just as well because I'm five foot nine. My hair has kept its sandy shade. I wear it long and either twist it up or clip it at the back of my neck.

Pretty, feminine Andrea resembled Mother. I have my father's strong features, which work better on a man. No one would ever call me the star on the Christmas tree.

When I finished unpacking, I stood at the window staring out, and it seemed to me I was seven years old again and watching my father in Andrea's bedroom, holding the music box.

I REMEMBER that afternoon as the defining day of my life. I stood there, quiet as a mouse, watching the father I worshipped sobbing and hugging my dead sister's picture against his chest while the frag-ile sounds from that music box drifted around him.

I look back and wonder if it ever occurred to me to run to him, throw my arms round him, absorb his grief and let it mingle with mine. But even then I understood that his grief was unique.

Lieutenant Edward Cavanaugh, decorated officer of the New York State Police, hero of life-threatening situations, had not been able to prevent the murder of his beautiful, headstrong fifteen-year-old daughter, and his agony could not be shared with a fellow mourner, however close by blood.

Over the years I came to understand that, when grief is not shared, blame is passed round like a hot potato, thrust from one person to another, eventually sticking to the hands of the one least able to throw it away. In this case, that person was me.

Detective Longo lost no time following up on my violation of Andrea's trust. As her autopsy results were being studied, and preparations made for her interment in Gate of Heaven Cemetery, he was interrogating both Rob Westerfield and Paul Stroebel. Paulie protested that he had not seen Andrea on Thursday evening, and although the gas station closed at seven, he claimed he had stayed longer to complete some minor repairs. Rob swore that he had gone to the local cinema, and even produced a ticket stub as proof.

I remember standing at Andrea's grave, a single long-stemmed rose in my hand, and after the prayers had been offered, being told to place it on her casket. I remember, too, that I felt dead inside, as dead as Andrea had been when I knelt over her in the garage.

I wanted to tell her how sorry I was that I had told about her secret meetings with Rob, and with equal passion I wanted to tell her that I was sorry I hadn't told about them the minute we knew she had left Joan's but not reached home. But of course I said nothing. I dropped the flower, but it slid off the casket, and before I could retrieve it my grandmother stepped past me to place her flower on the casket, and her foot crushed my rose into the muddy earth.

After the funeral we went back to the house. The women in the neighbourhood had put together a spread, and a lot of people were there: our old neighbours from Irvington, my mother's new friends from our parish, her friends from her bridge club, and her fellow volunteers from the hospital. Many of my father's long-time friends and fellow officers were there as well, some of them in uniform. The four girls who were Andrea's particular pals, their eyes swollen with tears, were clustered in a corner.

I felt apart from all of them. My mother, looking very sad in a black suit, was sitting on the couch in the living room, friends on either side, holding her hands. She was composed, even though her eyes kept welling with tears, and several times I heard her say, 'I can't believe she's gone.'

She and my father had clung together at the graveside, but now they sat in different rooms—she in the living room, he on the enclosed back porch that was now his den. My grandmother was in the kitchen with some of her old friends from Irvington. I wandered among them, and though people spoke to me and told me what a brave little girl I was, I felt acutely alone. I wanted Andrea. I wanted to go up to my sister's room and find her there and curl up on the bed with her while she chatted endlessly on the phone with her friends or with Rob Westerfield.

Before she called him, she would say, 'Can I trust you, Ellie?'

Of course she could. He almost never called her at home, because she was forbidden to have anything to do with him, and there was always the worry that my mother or father might answer the phone.

My mother or father? Or was it just my father? Would my mother have been upset? After all, Rob was a Westerfield, and both Mrs Westerfields, senior and junior, occasionally attended meetings of the Women's Club, to which my mother belonged.

We got back to the house at noon. At two o'clock people started to say things like 'After all you've been through, you folks need a rest.' Having paid their respects, having sincerely grieved, they were ready to go home. Any reluctance in leaving was caused by the fact that they were also eager to be in our house the moment any developments in tracking down Andrea's killer were reported.

By then everyone had heard about Paulie Stroebel's outburst in school and knew that Andrea had been in Rob Westerfield's car when it was stopped for speeding last month.

Paulie Stroebel. Who would ever have guessed that a quiet, introverted kid like that would have a crush on a girl like Andrea, or that she would have agreed to go to the Thanksgiving dance with him?

Rob Westerfield. He had finished a year at college, and he certainly was no dope—anyone could see that. But the rumour was he'd been asked to leave. Apparently he'd wasted his whole freshman year. He was nineteen. What business did he have fooling around with a sophomore in high school?

'Wasn't there some story about his having been involved in what happened to his grandmother at her house?'

It was precisely as I overheard that particular remark that the doorbell rang, and Mrs Storey from the bridge club went to answer it. Standing on the porch was Mrs Dorothy Westerfield, Rob's grandmother and the owner of the estate where Andrea had died.

She was a handsome, impressive woman, broad-shouldered and full-bosomed. She stood very straight. Her iron-grey hair had a natural wave. She was wearing a beautifully cut, dark grey winter coat. She stepped inside, and her eyes swept the room as she looked for my mother, who by then was pulling her hands away from her friends and struggling to stand up.

Mrs Westerfield went directly to her. 'I was in California and could not get back until now, but I had to tell you, Genine, how heartbroken I am for you and your family. Many years ago I lost a teenage son in a skiing accident, so I do understand what you're going through.'

As my mother nodded gratefully, my father's voice rang through the room. 'But it wasn't an accident, Mrs Westerfield,' he said. 'My daughter was *murdered*. She was bludgeoned to death, and your grandson may have been the one who killed her. In fact, knowing his reputation, you must be aware that he is the prime suspect. So please get out of here. You're damn lucky that you're still alive yourself.

You still don't believe he was involved in that burglary when you were shot and left for dead, do you?'

'Ted, how can you *say* that?' my mother pleaded. 'Mrs Westerfield, I apologise. My husband . . .'

Except for the three of them, the crowded house might have been empty. Everyone was frozen in place. My father might have been a figure from the Old Testament. His face was as white as his shirt, and his blue eyes were almost black.

'Don't you *dare* apologise for me, Genine,' he shouted. 'There isn't a cop in this house who doesn't know that Rob Westerfield is rotten through and through. My daughter—*our* daughter—is dead! Now you'—he walked over to Mrs Westerfield—'get out of my house.'

Mrs Westerfield had turned as pale as my father. She gave my mother's hand a squeeze and walked hurriedly to the door.

My mother did not raise her voice, but her tone was a whiplash. 'You *want* Rob Westerfield to be the one who took Andrea's life, don't you, Ted? You know Andrea was crazy about him. You were jealous! If you had let her go out with him, or any other boy for that matter, she wouldn't have had to make secret dates.'

The skin over my father's cheekbones reddened. 'If she had obeyed me, she would still be alive today,' he said, his voice quiet but bitter. 'If you had not been kissing the hand of anyone named Westerfield—'

'It's a damn good thing you're not investigating this case,' my mother said, interrupting him. 'What about that Stroebel kid? What about that handyman, Will Nebels?'

'What about the tooth fairy?' Now my father's tone was contemptuous. He turned and went back into the den, where his friends were gathered, and closed the door behind him. Finally there was complete silence.

My grandmother had planned to stay with us that night, but sensing that it would be better if my father and mother were alone, she packed her bag and departed with a friend from Irvington. The reconciliation she hoped for between my mother and father after the bitter exchange of words was not to be.

My mother slept in Andrea's room that night and every night for the next year, until after the trial, when even the Westerfield money failed to save Rob from being found guilty of Andrea's murder.

Then the house was sold. My father moved back to Irvington, and my mother and I began a nomadic life, starting in Florida, near my grandmother. My mother, who had worked briefly as a secretary before marriage, got a job with a national hotel chain. Always very attractive, she was also smart and diligent, and worked her way up rapidly to being a kind of troubleshooter, which entailed moving every eighteen months or so to a different city.

Unfortunately, she applied that same diligence to concealing from everyone—except me—the fact that she had become an alcoholic, drinking steadily each day from the moment she arrived home from work. The drinking sometimes made her loquacious, and it was during those sessions that I realised how passionately in love she was with my father.

'Ellie, I was crazy about him from the time I first laid eyes on him. Did I ever tell you how we met?'

Over and over again, Mother.

'I was nineteen, working at my first secretarial job. I bought a car, an orange crate on wheels. I decided to see how fast I could go in it. All of a sudden I heard a siren and in the rearview mirror saw a flashing dome light. Your father gave me a ticket and a lecture that had me in tears. But when he showed up for my court date, he announced he was going to give me driving lessons.'

Other times she would lament, 'He was terrific in so many ways. He's a college graduate; he's got looks and brains. But he was only comfortable with his old friends and didn't like change. That's why he didn't want to move to Oldham. The problem wasn't where we lived. It was that he was too strict with Andrea. Even if we'd stayed in Irvington, she'd still have been making secret dates.'

Those recollections almost always ended with 'If only we'd known where to look when she didn't come home'. Meaning, if only I had told them about the hide-out.

I spent the third grade in Florida. The fourth and fifth in Louisiana. The sixth in Colorado. The seventh in California. The eighth in New Mexico. My father's cheque for my support arrived without fail, but I saw him only occasionally those first few years and then not at all. Andrea, his golden child, was gone. There was nothing left between him and my mother except bitter regret and frozen love, and whatever he felt for me was not enough to make him desire my presence. If only I had told about the hide-out.

As I grew up, my adoration for my father was replaced with resentment. What about asking himself, If only I had questioned Ellie instead of ordering her to bed? What about that, Daddy?

Fortunately, by the time I began college we had been in California long enough to establish residency, and I went to UCLA as a journalism major. My mother died of liver failure six months after I received my master's degree, and, wanting yet another fresh start, I applied for and got the job in Atlanta.

It proved to be a good move for me. At last I began to develop a sense of permanence. Fresh-out-of-college employees are not paid much at newspapers, but my mother's modest life-assurance policy gave me the freedom to furnish a small apartment. I shopped carefully, in secondhand furniture stores and at closing-down sales. When I had finished, I was almost dismayed to realise that I had unconsciously re-created the overall effect of our living room in Oldham—blues and reds in the carpet, a blue upholstered couch and club chair, even an ottoman.

It brought back so many memories: my father dozing in the club chair, his legs on the ottoman; Andrea pushing them over and plopping down; his eyes opening, his smile of welcome to his saucy, pretty child . . .

I always tiptoed around when he was napping. When Andrea and I were clearing the table after dinner, I would listen intently as he began to unwind over a second cup of coffee and tell my mother what had happened that day on the job. I was in awe of him. My father, I bragged to myself, saved people's lives.

Three years after the divorce he remarried. By then I had paid my second and final visit to him in Irvington. I did not go to his wedding, nor did I care when he wrote to tell me that I had a baby brother. Edward James Cavanaugh, Jr., is about seventeen now.

My last contact with my father was to write and inform him that my mother had died and that I would like to have her ashes interred in Andrea's grave. He wrote back, expressing sympathy for me and telling me he had made the arrangements I had requested. He also invited me to come and visit in Irvington.

I sent the ashes and declined the invitation.

THE MEMORIES made me restless. I decided to put on my jacket and drive around Oldham. I had already observed that the rural village I remembered had grown considerably. It now had the look of an upmarket Westchester town. As I was leaving my room, the phone rang.

It was Pete Lawlor. 'You seem to have a gift for being in the right place at the right time, Ellie,' he said. 'It's just coming over the wire services. The Westerfields are holding a press conference in fifteen minutes. Will Nebels, the handyman who was questioned in your sister's murder, has just made a statement claiming he saw Paul Stroebel in Rob Westerfield's car the night Andrea was killed. He claims he saw him go into the garage with something in his hand, then run out ten minutes later, get back in the car and drive away.'

'Why didn't Nebels tell that story years ago?' I snapped.

'He claims he was afraid someone would try to blame him for your sister's death.'

'How was it that he saw all this happen?'

'He was in the grandmother's house. He'd done some repairs there and knew the code for the alarm. He also knew that the grandmother had a habit of leaving loose cash in drawers round the house. He was broke and needed money. He was in the master bedroom, which has windows overlooking the garage, and when the car door opened, he got a good look at Stroebel's face.'

'He's lying,' I said flatly.

'Cover the press conference,' Pete told me. 'You're an investigative reporter.' He paused. 'Unless it's too close to home for you.'

'It's not,' I said. 'I'll talk to you later.'

Three

The news conference was held in the White Plains office of William Hamilton, Esq., a criminal attorney retained by the Westerfield family to prove Robson Parke Westerfield's innocence.

Hamilton opened the proceedings by introducing two men. One was Rob's father, Vincent Westerfield, in his mid-sixties, with silver hair and patrician features. The other, a visibly nervous, somewhat bleary-eyed fellow, who could have been anywhere between sixty and seventy, was Will Nebels.

'Will Nebels has worked in Oldham for years as a handyman,' Hamilton said. 'He often worked for Mrs Dorothy Westerfield at her country home, the one at which Andrea Cavanaugh's body was found in the garage. Along with many other people, Mr Nebels was questioned as to his whereabouts that Thursday evening when Andrea lost her life. Mr Nebels claimed at the time that he had dinner at the local diner and went directly home. He had been seen at the diner, and there was no reason to doubt his story.

'However, when best-selling true-crime writer Jake Bern, who is writing a book about Andrea Cavanaugh's death and Rob Westerfield's claim of innocence, spoke to Mr Nebels, new facts came to light.' Hamilton turned to Nebels. 'Will, may I ask you to tell the media exactly what you told Mr Bern.'

Nebels shifted nervously. He looked uncomfortable dressed as he was in a shirt and tie and suit that I was sure they'd put on him just for the occasion. 'I feel bad,' Nebels began, his voice hoarse. 'It's something I've been living with, and when the writer fellow started talking to me, I knew I had to get it off my chest.'

He then gave the same story that had come over the wires. He had seen Paul Stroebel drive up to the garage hide-out in Rob Westerfield's car and go into the garage carrying a heavy object. The insinuation, of course, was that the object was the tyre jack that had been used to bludgeon Andrea to death, the one that had been found in the trunk of Rob's car.

Then it was Vincent Westerfield's turn to speak. 'For twenty-two years my son has been locked in a prison cell amid hardened criminals. He has always protested his innocence in this terrible crime. He went to the movies that night. He parked at the service station where Paul Stroebel was working. Rob told him he was leaving his car. Paul has always denied this account of events, but now we have proof he was lying. While my son was watching that movie, Stroebel took his car to what they called the hide-out and killed that girl.'

He drew himself up. 'My son is coming up for parole. From what we are led to understand, he will be released from prison. That isn't good enough. With this new evidence we will seek a new trial, and we believe Rob will be acquitted. We can only hope that Paul Stroebel will be put on trial and placed behind bars for the rest of his life.'

I was watching the news conference on a television in the little sitting room on the main floor of the inn. I wanted to throw something at the screen. For Rob Westerfield it was a win-win situation. If he was found guilty again, he'd already served his sentence. If he was acquitted, the state would never put Paulie Stroebel on trial on the word of an unreliable witness. Nonetheless, in the eyes of the world he would be the murderer.

I guess other people had heard about the conference, because as soon as I turned it on they drifted in. The desk clerk was the first to make a comment. 'Paulie Stroebel. That guy wouldn't hurt a fly.'

'Well,' said a waitress, 'I wasn't here when it happened, but I've heard a lot of talk. You'd be surprised how many people think Rob Westerfield is innocent.'

At the conference, members of the media were hurling questions at Will Nebels. 'Do you realise you could go to prison for breaking and entering, and perjury?' I heard a reporter ask.

'Let me answer that,' Hamilton said. 'The statute of limitations has passed. Mr Nebels is in no danger of incarceration. He has come forward to right a wrong.'

'Were you promised any money in exchange for this testimony, Mr Nebels?' another reporter asked.

Exactly my question, I thought.

Again Hamilton took over. 'Absolutely not.'

'Has Mr Nebels made a statement to the district attorney?'

'Not yet. We wanted the public to be aware of his statement before there is any spin put on it by the prosecutor. The point is this—it is a terrible thing to say, but if Andrea Cavanaugh had been sexually molested, Rob Westerfield would have been out of prison long ago on DNA evidence. As it stands, it was his very concern that entrapped him. Andrea had begged him to meet her at the hide-out. The fact is, she was chasing him. She was a flirt, boy crazy, a "popular" girl.'

I cringed at the insinuation.

'Rob's only mistake was to panic when he found her body.'

The cameras switched to the news anchor. 'Observing this interview with us from his home in Oldham-on-the-Hudson is retired detective Marcus Longo. Mr Longo, what do you think of Mr Nebels's statement?'

'It is a total fabrication. Robson Westerfield was found guilty of murder because he *is* guilty of murder. I can understand the anguish of his family, but to try to shift the blame to an innocent, special-needs person is beneath contempt.'

Bravo, I thought. The memory of Detective Longo years ago sitting with me in the dining room replayed in my mind. Longo was about sixty now, his remaining hair a salt-and-pepper fringe round his head. But he had innate dignity.

The news conference was over, and people began to drift out of the room. The desk clerk, a studious-looking young man who looked as if he was fresh out of college, came over to me. 'Is everything OK with your room, Miss Cavanaugh?'

The waitress was passing the sofa where I was sitting. She turned and looked at me sharply, and I knew she wanted to ask if I was any relation to the young girl who was murdered in the Westerfield case.

It was the first indication that I would have to give up the personal anonymity I craved if I stayed in Oldham.

So be it, I thought. This is something I have to do.

MRS HILMER still lived in the same house down the street from ours. There were four other houses now separating them. It was obvious that the people who now owned ours had fulfilled Mother's dream for it. It had been expanded on both sides and at the back, and now it was a truly lovely dwelling, substantial yet graceful, with gleaming white clapboard and dark green shutters.

I slowed the car as I drove past, and then stopped. The trees had grown, of course. It had been a warm autumn, and even though it was now downright chilly there was still an abundance of gold and crimson leaves shimmering on the branches.

For an instant I was standing there in the dining room, holding in my arms the box of silver as Andrea carefully arranged the place settings. *Today Lord Malcolm Bigbottom will be our guest.*

Mrs Hilmer had been watching for me. The minute I got out of the car, the front door opened. A moment later I felt her fierce hug. She had always been a small woman, cosily plump, with vivacious brown eyes. Now her brown hair was completely silver. For years she sent Mother a Christmas card, and Mother would write back, putting a good face on our newest move. I had let Mrs Hilmer know when Mother died and had received a comforting note.

'Ellie, you're so tall,' she said now with something between a smile and a laugh. 'You were such a little thing.'

There was coffee on the stove and blueberry muffins fresh from the oven. At my insistence we stayed in the kitchen and sat at the banquette. For a few minutes she told me about her family. 'Eight grandchildren,' she said proudly. 'None of them live round here, but I still get to see them.' I knew she'd been widowed for many years.

I told her a little about my job, and then we began to talk about the reason I was back in Oldham.

'Ellie, since the day Rob was led out of the courtroom in handcuffs and shackles, the Westerfields have been insisting he's innocent. They've got a lot of people convinced of it, too.' Her expression became troubled. 'Having said that, I've got to admit I wonder if he wasn't convicted partly because of his reputation as a troublemaker.

Everybody was only too ready to believe the worst about him.'

She had seen the press conference. 'There's one thing I believe in that speech Will Nebels made,' she said flatly, 'and that's that he'd go into old Mrs Westerfield's house to look for money to steal. On the one hand, I wonder what they're giving him to tell that story, and on the other, I think how Paulie went to pieces in class when they announced that Andrea was dead. I watched that teacher testify in court. You never saw a more reluctant witness. You could tell how protective she was of Paulie, but she had to admit that she thought when he ran out of the classroom that he had said, "I didn't think she was dead."'

'How is Paulie Stroebel now?' I asked.

'Actually, he's been doing very well. For years after the trial he was terribly reticent. He started working in the deli with his mother and father and, from what I understand, kept very much to himself. But since his father died and he's had to take on more and more responsibility, he's really kind of blossomed. I hope this story of Will Nebels's doesn't unravel him now.'

'If Rob Westerfield gets a new trial and is acquitted, it will be as though Paulie has been found guilty,' I said.

Mrs Hilmer hesitated. 'Ellie, that fellow Bern who's writing a book about the case—he came to see me. I was careful of every word that passed my lips. But I'm telling you, he has a point of view. He asked if the reason your father was so strict with Andrea was that she would sneak off to meet a lot of different boys.'

'That's not true.'

'He's going to make it seem as if it was true.'

'Yes, she had a crush on Rob Westerfield, but at the end she was afraid of him.' It was something I hadn't expected to say, but when I did, I realised it was true. 'And I was afraid of him, too.'

'Ellie, I was there when you testified in court. You never said you or Andrea were afraid of Rob Westerfield. Be careful. That writer suggested to me that you were an emotionally unstable child.'

So that's the tack he's going to take, I thought. Andrea was a tramp, I was emotionally unstable, and Paulie Stroebel is a killer. If I hadn't been sure of it before, I knew now that I had my job cut out for me.

'Rob Westerfield may get out of prison, Mrs Hilmer,' I said, 'but by the time I finish investigating and writing about every dirty detail of his rotten life, no one will want to walk down the block with him. And if he gets a second trial, no jury will acquit him.'

ON MONDAY MORNING I had a meeting in Albany with Martin Brand, who was on the staff of the parole board. He was a tired-looking man of about sixty, with pouches under his eyes and a florid complexion. There was no doubt that he had heard many versions of my protest a thousand times over the years.

'Ms Cavanaugh, Westerfield has been turned down for parole twice. This time it's my guess the decision will be to let him out.'

'He's a recidivist.'

'You can't be sure of that.'

'You can't be sure that he's not.'

'He was offered parole two years ago if he'd admit to killing your sister, accept responsibility for the crime, and express remorse. He didn't take the offer.'

'Oh, come on, Mr Brand. He had too much to lose by being truthful. He knew you couldn't hold him much longer.'

He shrugged. 'I forgot that you're an investigative reporter.'

'I'm also the sister of the fifteen-year-old girl who didn't get a chance to have a sweet-sixteen party.'

The world-weary expression left his eyes for a moment. 'Ms Cavanaugh, I have little doubt that Rob Westerfield is guilty, but I think you have to resign yourself to the fact that he's served his time and that he's behaved himself. Even if he is guilty, incidents of recidivism almost vanish after the age of forty. Here's a piece of unwelcome advice: Go home to Atlanta and try to put this tragedy behind you.'

'That's good advice, Mr Brand,' I said. 'I'll probably take it someday, but not now.'

THREE YEARS AGO, after I'd written a series of articles about a serial killer in Atlanta, I received a call from Maggie Reynolds, a New York book editor. She offered me a contract to convert the articles into a book. The book did surprisingly well, even clinging for a few weeks to the bottom of *The New York Times* best-seller list. I called Maggie after I left Brand's office. She readily agreed to give me a contract for a book about Andrea's murder, a book that I promised would conclusively prove Rob Westerfield's guilt.

I figured the project would take about three months of intensive research and writing, and then, if Westerfield succeeded in getting a new trial, several months beyond that. The inn would be too confining and too expensive to stay in over the long haul, so I asked Mrs Hilmer if she knew of any rental apartments in the area.

She insisted that I stay in the guest apartment over her garage. 'Ellie, it's comfortable, it's quiet, and I'll be a good neighbour, not a nuisance who runs in and out.'

'You were always a good neighbour.' It was a great solution, and I assumed that repetition would dull the instant flash of pain that hit me now as I passed our old house.

I checked out of the inn, moved into Mrs Hilmer's guest apartment, and on Wednesday flew back to Atlanta, arriving in the office at a quarter to six in the evening. I knew there was no chance that Pete would have gone home. He was married to the job.

He looked up, saw me, grinned briefly, and said, 'Let's talk over a plate of spaghetti.'

'What about those ten pounds you're trying to lose?'

'I've decided not to think about them for the next couple of hours.'

Pete has an intensity that sends electric jolts into the people around him. He went with the *News*, a privately owned daily, right out of graduate school, and within two years he was managing editor. By the time he was twenty-eight, he was editor in chief and publisher, and the 'dying daily', as it had been labelled, had a new lease of life.

Hiring an investigative crime reporter was one of his ideas to rev up circulation, and getting the job six years ago was a stroke of luck for me. I had just been taken on as a cub reporter. When the guy Pete wanted for the position backed out at the last minute, I was told to fill in until a permanent replacement was found. Then one day Pete stopped looking for that replacement. I had the job.

We went to Napoli's. Pete ordered a bottle of Chianti and grabbed a chunk of the warm bread that had been deposited on our table. The wine came, was approved by Pete, and uncorked. I took a sip and plunged into what I had to say.

'I've been doing a lot of homework. The whitewash job on Westerfield has every possibility of succeeding. Jake Bern has already done an article on the case that will be coming out next month in *Vanity Fair*.'

Pete reached for another piece of bread. 'What can you do about it?'

'I'm writing a book that will come out in the spring, the same week Bern's is published.' I told him about my call to Maggie Reynolds. 'In the meantime I've got to counteract his articles and the Westfield family's press releases.'

Pete waited. That was another thing about him—he didn't rush to reassure. And he didn't fill in dead spots in the conversation.

'Pete, I'm aware that a series of articles about a crime committed twenty-three years ago in Westchester County, New York, might not be of great interest to a readership in Georgia, and anyhow, I don't think it's the right place to publish them.'

'Agreed. So what do you propose to do?'

'Take a leave of absence if you can give it to me. Or quit, write the book and take my chances after it's finished.'

The waiter came to the table. We both ordered cannelloni and a green salad. Pete hemmed and hawed for a minute, then decided on the Gorgonzola dressing.

'Ellie, I'll hold your job open for you as long as it's in my power, but I may not be around much longer myself.'

I was shocked. 'But the *News* is your baby.'

'We're getting too big for the competition. There's real talk of our being bought out for big bucks.'

'Where are you thinking of going?'

'The *Los Angeles Times* is probably going to make an offer. The other possibility is Houston.'

'Which would you prefer?'

He smiled. 'Until there's an offer on the plate, I'm not wasting my time making choices.'

Pete didn't wait for me to comment before he went on. 'Ellie, I've been doing a little research of my own on your case. The Westerfields have an impressive team of lawyers just waiting for a chance to earn a fortune. They have that Nebels guy, and, weasel that he is, some people are going to believe his story. Do what you have to, but please, if Westerfield goes to trial and gets acquitted, swear to yourself that you'll walk away from it.'

Pete meant his advice kindly, but that night, as I packed the things I needed for an extended stay in Oldham, I realised that even he had the feeling that, guilty or innocent, Rob Westerfield had served his time, that people would think whatever they wanted about the merits of the case, and that it was time for me to drop it.

Nothing wrong with righteous wrath, I thought. Except when it hangs around too long.

I drove back to Oldham, and the following week Rob Westerfield's parole hearing was held. As expected, the parole was granted, and it was announced that he would be released on October 31.

Halloween, I thought. How appropriate. The night that demons walk the earth.

Four

Paulie Stroebel was behind the counter when I opened the door of the delicatessen, setting the bell attached to it jingling.

My vague memory of him was centred at the old service station. He would pump gas into the tank of our car and then spray and polish the windshield until it gleamed. I remember my mother saying, 'What a nice boy Paulie is,' a sentiment that was never again uttered after he came under suspicion in Andrea's death.

I believe my memory of his physical appearance was partially–or perhaps even solely—based on pictures of him I saw in the newspapers my mother had kept—newspapers that reported every detail of Andrea's murder and the trial. Mother had never told me that she had this collection of newspapers, or the transcript of the trial. After her death I was shocked to learn that the bulky suitcase that accompanied our moves was actually a Pandora's box of misery.

I knew Paulie and Mrs Stroebel must have heard that I was in town. When he saw me, Paulie looked startled, but then his expression became guarded. His stocky body was more appropriate on a mature man than it had been on the teenager in the newspaper photographs. His pudgy cheeks had thinned out, and the expression in his eyes no longer had the bewildered look of twenty-three years ago. It was a few minutes before six o'clock—closing time.

'Paulie, I'm Ellie Cavanaugh.' I walked over to him and extended my hand across the counter.

He took it, his grasp firm, even uncomfortably strong. 'I heard you were back. Will Nebels is lying. I wasn't in the garage that night.' His voice was a hurt protest.

'I know you weren't.'

'It's not fair for him to say that.'

The door that separated the kitchen from the front of the store opened, and Mrs Stroebel came out. She walked with a slight limp.

'Ellie?' she said, hurrying round the counter.

After I testified in court, Mrs Stroebel had come up to me, close to tears, and thanked me. The defence attorney had tried to get me to say that Andrea was afraid of Paulie, and I guess on the stand I got pretty definite. 'I *didn't* say Andrea was afraid of Paulie 'cause she

449

wasn't. She was afraid Paulie would tell Daddy that she sometimes met Rob in the hideout.'

'It is so good to see you, Ellie. You're a young lady now, and I'm an old lady,' Mrs Stroebel told me as her lips brushed my cheek.

'No, you're not,' I protested. The warmth of her welcome, like the warmth of Mrs Hilmer's greeting, was a dart of light flashing through unshakable sadness.

'Put the "Closed" sign on the door, Paulie,' Mrs Stroebel said. 'Ellie, you will come home and have dinner with us, won't you?'

'I'd love to.'

I followed them in my car. They lived about a mile away, in one of the older sections of town. The houses were all late nineteenth century and relatively small. But they looked cosy and well kept.

The Stroebels' yellow labrador greeted our arrival enthusiastically, and Paulie immediately got his leash and took him for a walk.

Their home was just what I'd expected—immaculate and comfortable. I vetoed Mrs Stroebel's suggestion that I sit in one of the overstuffed chairs in the living room and watch the news on the television while she prepared dinner. Instead I sat on a stool at the kitchen counter, watching her work, offering to help, confident she'd decline.

'A simple meal,' she warned. 'I made a beef stew yesterday. I always serve it the second day. Much tastier.'

Her hands worked swiftly, rolling dough for biscuits, tearing greens for a salad. I sat quietly.

'Now,' she said, 'before Paulie gets back, you must tell me. Can the Westerfields do this? After twenty-two years, can they try again to make my son a killer?'

'They can try, but they won't succeed.'

Mrs Stroebel's shoulders slumped. 'Ellie, Paulie has come such a long way. You know, when he was a boy it was so hard. There is a kind of knowledge that is not for him. His father and I always worried so much. Paulie is such a sweet, good person. In school he was so lonely except when he played football.'

It was obviously hard for her to continue. 'Paulie was on the second team, so he didn't play much. But then one day they put him in the game, and the other team scored, and then Paulie at the last minute got the ball and made a touchdown that won the game. Your sister was in the band, the prettiest one of all. She grabbed a megaphone and rushed out onto the field. Paulie told me about it over and over—the cheer Andrea led for him.'

Her eyes glistened. 'Ellie, that was the most wonderful moment of Paulie's life. You can't know what it was like for him after Andrea died and the Westerfields tried to blame him. I believe he would have died to save her. Our doctor was worried that he might do something to himself. When you are a little different, a little slower, it is very easy to become depressed.

'He's been doing so well in the last few years. More and more he makes the decisions in the store. Like last year, he decided we should put in some tables and hire a girl to serve. Just a simple breakfast, then sandwiches in the afternoon. It's been very popular.'

'I noticed the tables.'

'Paulie will never have it easy. He will always have to work harder than anyone else. He will be OK unless—'

'Unless people start to point at him again and wonder if he's the one who should have been in prison for twenty-two years,' I said.

She nodded. 'Yes. That's what I mean.'

We heard the front door open. Paulie's footsteps and the labrador's short bark announced their arrival.

Paulie came into the kitchen. 'It's not fair of that man to say I hurt Andrea,' he said, then abruptly went upstairs.

'It is beginning to consume him again,' Mrs Stroebel said flatly.

THE DAY AFTER I SAW the Stroebels, I tried to reach Marcus Longo. The answering machine picked up, and I left a message and my cellphone number. For a few days I heard nothing.

I was terribly disappointed. After seeing how strongly Longo had expressed himself on television about Rob Westerfield's guilt, I'd thought he'd leap to the phone to get back to me. I'd just about given up on him, when on October 30 my cellphone rang. When I answered, a quiet voice asked, 'Ellie, is your hair still the colour of sand with sunbeams running through it?'

'Hello, Mr Longo.'

'I just got back from Colorado, which is why you haven't heard from me,' he said. 'Our first grandchild arrived on Tuesday. My wife is still out there. Can you have dinner with me tonight?'

'I'd love to.' I told him I was staying in Mrs Hilmer's guest apartment.

'I know where Mrs Hilmer lives.'

There was the slightest pause as we both thought that of course he did—it's just down the road from our old house.

'I'll pick you up at seven, Ellie.'

I was watching for his car and hurried downstairs when it pulled into Mrs Hilmer's long driveway. The driveway forks, and the garage with the guest apartment is at the end on the right. I didn't want him to take the wrong turn.

There are some people in this world with whom we feel immediately comfortable. That was the way it was with Marcus Longo as soon as I slid into the passenger seat.

'I've thought a lot about you over the years,' he said as he made a U-turn. 'Have you been to Cold Spring since you've been back?'

'I drove through it one afternoon. When I was a kid, my mother was always browsing around the antique shops.'

'It still has those, but now it also has some good restaurants.'

Oldham is the northernmost town bordering the Hudson River in Westchester County. Cold Spring is just over the line in Putnam County, directly across the Hudson from West Point. It is a particularly beautiful town with a Main Street that has the look and feel of the nineteenth century.

Longo had made a reservation at Cathryn's, an intimate Tuscan-style grill. There, at a corner table, we took each other's measure. Oddly, in person he looked older than he did on television. There were furrows round his eyes and mouth.

'I thought you'd be about five foot three,' he said. 'You were small for your age when you were young.'

'I grew quite a bit in high school.'

'You look like your father, you know. Have you seen him?'

The question surprised me. 'No. And I don't intend to.' I didn't want to ask, but I was too curious not to. 'Do you see him, Mr Longo?'

'Please call me Marcus. I haven't seen him in years, but his son, your half-brother, is a terrific all-round athlete. Gets lots of press in the local papers. And there were some nice write-ups when your father retired from the state troopers.'

'I assume Andrea's death was mentioned?'

'Yes, and there were quite a few pictures, both recent and from the files. That's how I can see how much you resemble him now.'

I didn't answer, and Longo raised his eyebrows. 'Obviously, that's a compliment. Anyhow, as my mother used to say, "You grew up nice."' Abruptly he changed the subject. 'Ellie, why are you here?'

'I had to protest against Rob Westerfield getting out on parole.'

'Even though you must have known you were wasting your frequent-flier miles,' he said quietly.

'I knew it was useless.'

'The doors will open tomorrow morning for Rob Westerfield, and he will walk out of prison. Listen to me carefully now, Ellie. There isn't the faintest doubt that he'll get a new trial. Nebels's testimony will probably be enough to cause reasonable doubt in the jurors' minds, and Westerfield will be acquitted.'

'That can't happen.'

'Ellie, you've got to understand something: the Westerfields need to *make* it happen. Robson Parke Westerfield is the last of the line of what used to be a fine and respected name. Behind that philanthropic façade, Vincent Westerfield is a greedy robber baron, but he craves respectability for his son. And *old* Mrs Westerfield demands it.'

'What does that mean?'

'It means that at the age of ninety-two she is still as sharp as a tack and in control of the family fortune. If Rob's name isn't cleared, she's leaving everything to charity.'

'Surely Vincent Westerfield has plenty of money.'

'Nothing compared to his mother's wealth. Mrs Dorothy Westerfield is a class act, and she no longer has blind faith in her grandson's innocence. Didn't your father throw her out of your house on the day of the funeral?'

'He did. My mother never got over being mortified about that.'

'Apparently neither did Mrs Westerfield. Your father publicly confronted her with the fact that the guy who robbed and shot her claimed to be in collusion with Rob.'

'Yes, I remember him shouting that.'

'And Mrs Westerfield has remembered it, too. Naturally she has wanted to believe that Rob was wrongly convicted, but the seeds of doubt have always been there and have only grown stronger. Now that she obviously is running out of time, she's put it to the father: if Rob is innocent, see that the stain is removed from the family name. Otherwise the Westerfield fortune will go to charity.'

'So the father has to prove Rob's innocence, and suddenly there's an eyewitness who saw Paulie Stroebel go into the hide-out. Is old Mrs Westerfield buying that story?'

'Ellie, what she wants is a new jury to review the case and render the verdict she wants.'

'And Vincent Westerfield is going to make sure what that verdict is.'

The menus came. I decided on one of the specials, rack of lamb. Marcus ordered salmon.

Over our salads I told him of my plans to write a book to refute Jake Bern's book. Then I asked him about the old story that Rob had been implicated in the break-in at his grandmother's home.

Marcus had a cop's memory for crimes. 'The grandmother was at her house in Oldham. In the middle of the night she heard some kind of noise and woke up. There was a live-in maid, but she was in a separate wing. When Mrs Westerfield opened the bedroom door, she was shot at point-blank range. She never saw her assailant, but he was arrested a couple of days later. He claimed Rob promised him ten thousand dollars if he finished her off. Needless to say, there was no proof. It was the word of a twenty-one-year-old high-school dropout with a long juvenile record against a Westerfield.'

'What would Rob's motive have been?'

'Money. His grandmother was leaving one hundred thousand dollars directly to him. She thought that sixteen wasn't too young to begin to handle and invest money intelligently. She didn't know that Rob had a drug problem.'

'She believed he wasn't involved in the shooting?'

'Yes. But she changed her will. That bequest disappeared.'

'So she may have had her doubts about him even then. What about Rob Westerfield's mother?'

'Another very nice lady. She spends almost all her time in Florida. She has a successful interior design business in Palm Beach. You can look her up on the Internet.'

'I've opened a website,' I said.

Longo's eyebrows raised.

'It's the fastest way to spread information. Every day I'm going to write about Andrea's murder and Rob Westerfield's guilt. I'm going to follow up every nasty rumour about him, interview his classmates from his prep schools and from Willow College. You don't get thrown out of schools without a reason. It's a long shot, but I'm going to see if I can trace the locket he gave Andrea.'

'How well do you remember it?'

'Now, it's blurry, of course. But at the trial I described it specifically. I have the trial transcript, so I know exactly what I said then. But you didn't ever believe that I actually touched it when I found Andrea's body, did you? Or that I heard someone breathing, or that the locket disappeared before the police came?'

'Ellie, you went from hysteria to shock. You testified that, when you knelt down, you slid and fell over Andrea's body. I don't think that in the dark, and with what must have been going on in your head, you could have identified feeling the locket.'

'She was wearing it that night. I'm certain of it. Why wasn't it on her when the police came?'

'A reasonable explanation is that he took it after he killed her. His defence was predicated on his claim that she was just a kid with a crush on him and that he had absolutely no interest in her.'

'Let's leave it at that for now,' I said, and he seemed as glad as I was to change the subject to his brand-new grandchild.

I HADN'T TURNED A LIGHT ON before I left, and when we got back to Mrs Hilmer's place the garage apartment looked dark and lonely. Marcus Longo insisted on walking me upstairs. He stood there while I fished for my key and inserted it into the lock. Then when I stepped inside, he said firmly, 'Double-lock the door.'

'Any special reason?' I asked.

'Ellie, I'm telling you to be careful.'

I was home just in time to catch the ten o'clock news. The big story was that Rob Westerfield was being released in the morning and that there would be an interview with the press from the family home in Oldham at noon.

I wouldn't miss it for the world, I thought.

THE NEXT MORNING I was in front of the television when the media covered Rob Westerfield's exit from Sing Sing in a limousine that had met him at the gate. The reporter of the channel I watched emphasised that Rob had always sworn he was innocent.

At noon I was back in front of the set for the unveiling of Rob Westerfield to the world. The interview took place in the library of the family home in Oldham. The sofa on which he sat was placed in front of a wall of leather-bound books. Rob was wearing a tan cashmere jacket, an open-necked sports shirt, dark trousers, and loafers. He had become even more handsome in his maturity. He had his father's fine features and had learned to conceal the condescending sneer of his early days. There was the faintest touch of grey in the roots of his dark hair. I could feel the bile rising in my throat.

His interviewer was Corinne Sommers, host of *The Real Story*, a popular syndicated Friday-night programme. She did a brief intro, then said, 'Rob Westerfield, it's an obvious question, but how does it feel to be a free man?'

His smile was warm. His dark eyes under well-shaped eyebrows seemed almost amused. 'Unbelievable, wonderful. I'm too big to cry, but that's what I feel like doing. I just go around the house, and it's so wonderful to be able to do normal things, like going into the kitchen and getting a cup of coffee.'

'Then you'll be staying here for a while?'

'Absolutely. My father has furnished a wonderful apartment for me near this house, and I want to work with our lawyers to get a speedy retrial. Corinne, I could have got parole two years ago if I'd been willing to say I killed Andrea Cavanaugh.'

'Weren't you tempted to do that?'

'Not for a minute. I have always maintained my innocence, and now, thanks to Will Nebels coming forward, I may at last have a chance to prove it.'

The rest of the interview might have been with a newly returned hostage. 'Besides clearing your name, what are you looking forward to doing?'

'Going to New York. Dining in restaurants that probably didn't exist twenty-two years ago. Getting a job.' Now a warm smile. 'Meeting a special someone. Getting married. Having kids.'

Getting married. Having kids. Things Andrea would never do.

'What are you having for dinner tonight, and who is going to be with you?'

'Just the four of us—my mother, my father and my grandmother. I asked for a pretty basic dinner: shrimp cocktail, prime rib, baked potato, broccoli, a salad.'

How about apple pie? I wondered.

'And apple pie,' he concluded.

'It seems as though you have pretty definite plans for the future, Rob. We wish you luck and hope that in a second trial you can prove your innocence.'

This is a journalist? I shut off the television and opened my laptop. I got online to my website and began to write: 'Robson Westerfield, the convicted murderer of fifteen-year-old Andrea Cavanaugh, has just been released from prison and is looking forward to prime rib and apple pie. The sanctification of this killer has begun, and it will be at the expense of his young victim and of Paulie Stroebel, a quiet, hard-working man who has had to overcome many difficulties.

'He shouldn't have to overcome this one.'

Not bad for a beginning, I thought.

EVERY DAY Sing Sing Correctional Facility discharges prisoners who have completed their sentences or have been paroled. They are given jeans, work boots, a jacket and forty dollars, and unless they are picked up by family or friends, they are issued with a train ticket. The train station is the equivalent distance of four blocks from the prison.

I reasoned that anyone getting out of Sing Sing at this time would almost certainly have known Rob Westerfield. That was why early the next morning I dressed warmly, parked at the train station and walked to the prison. There is constant activity at the gate. About 2,300 inmates were housed there, and jeans, work boots and a jacket are not particularly distinctive apparel. How would I be able to tell the difference between an employee getting off duty and a newly released inmate? The answer is, I couldn't.

Anticipating the problem, I had made a cardboard sign. I stood beside the gate and held it: JOURNALIST SEEKING INFORMATION ABOUT ROBSON WESTERFIELD. SUBSTANTIAL PAYMENT. At the last minute I had added the number of my cellphone—917-555-1261.

It was a cold, windy morning. The 1st of November. I stood for two hours holding the sign. Most people passing out of the gate stared at it, curiosity in their eyes. Some seemed to study it. A bulky man in his late forties, the earmuffs of his cap pulled down for warmth, snapped, 'Lady, haven't you got anything better to do with your time than investigate that creep?'

At ten o'clock, chilled to the bone, I gave up and walked back to the station parking lot. I was just at the door of my car when a man wearing jeans, a jacket and work boots came up close to me. He was about thirty, rawboned, with mean eyes and narrow lips. 'Why are you picking on Westerfield?' he asked. 'What's he ever done to you?'

'Are you a friend of his?' I asked, stepping back instinctively.

'What do you care?'

From the corner of my eye I was relieved to see a van pulling into the lot. At least if I needed help there was someone around. 'I want to get in my car, and you're in my way,' I said.

'Rob Westerfield was a model prisoner. We all looked up to him. He set a great example for the rest of us. Now, how much are you going to pay me for that information?'

'Let him pay you.' I turned and shouldered the guy away from me, pushed the remote, and yanked the door open.

He did not try to stop me, but before I could close the door, he said, 'Let me give you a little free advice. Burn your sign.'

Five

When I got back to the Hilmer apartment, I began to peruse the old newspapers Mother had kept. They were a godsend in my research on the life of Rob Westerfield. In several of them I found a mention of the two prep schools he had attended. The first one, Arbinger Preparatory School in Massachusetts, is one of the most exclusive in the country. He stayed there for only a year and a half before switching to Carrington Academy in Maine, which was described on its website as a school for 'students who haven't realised their academic or social potential', for 'students who may have difficulty adjusting to disciplined study'.

I decided to see both places for myself. I phoned the schools and explained that I was a journalist writing a book on Robson Westerfield, who had been a student there. At Arbinger I was referred to Craig Parshall in the media relations office. At Carrington I was passed through to Jane Bostrom, director of admissions. Both acknowledged that Jake Bern had been granted an interview at the request of the Westerfield family, and stated that without the family's permission they could not grant one to me.

I told Mrs Bostrom, 'I don't want to do a hatchet job on Carrington. I want to find out what Rob Westerfield was up to in his teenage years before he murdered my sister. If you gave a lot of information to Jake Bern, I want the same kind of access, and it might, in fact, serve your school much better to be cooperative.' I had told Mr Parshall essentially the same thing, and in the end, despite much protest, both agreed to meet me, and we scheduled appointments.

I hadn't run into Mrs Hilmer in a couple of days, but in the late afternoon she phoned. 'Ellie, this is a suggestion more than an invitation. I had one of my urges to cook today and ended up with a roast chicken in the oven. Would you like to come over for dinner? But please don't say yes if you'd rather just be quiet.'

I hadn't bothered to go to the grocery that morning and knew that my at-home choices were a cheese sandwich or a cheese sandwich. And I also remembered that Mrs Hilmer was a good cook.

'What time?' I asked.

'Oh, about seven.'

'I'll not only be there, I'll be early.'

As I hung up, I realised that Mrs Hilmer must think of me as something of a loner. She's partially right, of course. But despite my interior core of isolation, I am reasonably outgoing. When I worked late at the newspaper, I'd often end up having pasta or a hamburger with whoever was around. There were always two or three of us who weren't rushing home to a spouse or significant other.

As I washed my face, brushed my hair, and twisted it back up, I wondered when Pete would let me know which job he'd taken. I was sure that even if the paper wasn't sold immediately, he would move on. Where would he end up? Houston? Los Angeles? Our paths wouldn't cross much after the move. It was a disquieting thought.

The cosy apartment consisted of a large living room, with galley kitchen at one end and a medium-sized bedroom. The bathroom was off the short hallway between them. I had set up my computer and printer on the dining table, near the kitchen. I'm not a neat worker, and as I was about to put on my coat, I looked around as if with Mrs Hilmer's eyes.

The newspapers I'd been going through were scattered on the floor. The decorative fruit bowl and brass candlesticks that had been primly centred on the colonial table were shoved together on the sideboard. My appointment book and pen lay tossed on one side of the computer, next to the bulky trial transcript.

Suppose for some reason Mrs Hilmer walked back with me and saw this mess, I thought. How would she react? There was absolutely nothing out of place in her home.

I scooped the newspapers into something of an orderly pile. Then I dug out the big duffle bag in which I always carried them and dropped them into it. The trial transcript followed. I reasoned that the notebook and my pen weren't too aesthetically offensive. I moved the fruit bowl and candlesticks back to the table. I had started to put the duffle bag in the closet in the bedroom, then decided to take it with me. I don't know why. Call it a hunch—one of those feelings you just get, as my grandmother used to say.

It was a pretty long walk from the apartment to the house. Mrs Hilmer had told me that she'd had a garage built on to the house after her husband died, so that she didn't have to walk back and forth from the old one. Now the old garage beneath the apartment was empty except for gardening supplies. Walking in the dark silence, I could well understand why she hadn't wanted to make the trip at night alone.

'Don't think I'm moving in,' I told Mrs Hilmer when she opened the door and spotted the duffle bag. 'It's just become my constant companion.'

Over a glass of sherry I explained what was in it; then a thought occurred to me. Mrs Hilmer had lived in Oldham for nearly fifty years. She was active in the town—meaning she knew everyone. There were local people mentioned in those newspaper stories whose names meant nothing to me, but they'd surely be familiar to her.

'Would you consider going through these papers with me?' I asked. 'There are people quoted whom I'd love to talk to. For example, some friends of Andrea's from school, neighbours of Will Nebels, some of the guys Rob Westerfield hung around with. I wonder if it would upset you to read these old articles and maybe make a list of the people who are still around. I'm hoping, of course, that they may have known something that didn't come out at the time.'

'I can tell you about one of them off the top of my head,' Mrs Hilmer said. 'Joan Lashley. Her parents retired, but she married Leo St Martin. She lives in Garrison.'

Joan Lashley was the girl with whom Andrea had been doing homework that last night! Garrison was near Cold Spring, only a fifteen-minute drive from here. It was obvious that Mrs Hilmer was going to be a treasure trove of information.

I opened the duffle bag and put some of the papers on the table. I saw the look of pain that came over Mrs Hilmer's face when she picked up the first one. The headline read FIFTEEN-YEAR-OLD BLUDGEONED TO DEATH. Andrea's picture filled the page. She was wearing her school band uniform: a red jacket with brass buttons and a matching short skirt. Her hair was falling around her shoulders, and she looked happy and vibrant and young.

That picture had been taken at the first game of the season in late September. A few weeks later Rob Westerfield first met her at the bowling alley in town. It was the next week that she went for the drive in his car and he was stopped by the state trooper for speeding.

'Mrs Hilmer, I warn you,' I said. 'It's not easy going through this material, so if you think it would be too much—'

'No, Ellie. I want to do it.'

'OK.' I took out the rest of the newspapers. The trial transcript was still in the duffle bag. I took it out, too. 'This makes pretty unpleasant reading.'

'Leave it with me,' she said firmly.

MRS HILMER INSISTED on lending me a small flashlight for my return, and I must say I was glad to have it. I'd left on only a small night-light in the stairwell—my conscious effort to not run up her electricity bill. As I walked up the stairs, I was not sure if it was the best idea to be so frugal. The staircase was dark and shadowed, and it creaked under my steps. I suddenly became acutely aware that Andrea was murdered in a garage very similar to this one. They both originally had been barns. The old hayloft here was now the apartment, but the feeling of the structures was similar.

By the time I was at the head of the stairs, the key was in my hand, and with a quick turn of the lock I was inside and had bolted the door. I immediately stopped worrying about running up bills and began to turn on every light I could find: the lamps on either side of the couch, the chandelier over the dining table, the hallway light, the bedroom lights. At last I was able to heave a sigh of relief.

The table looked strangely neat, with the fruit bowl and candlesticks in the centre. Then I realised that something had changed. I had left my pen to the right of the appointment book, next to the computer. It was now on the left side. A chill shot through me. Someone had been here and must have moved it. But why? To go through the appointment book?

I turned on the computer and rushed to check the file where I kept my notes on Rob Westerfield. Just that afternoon I had jotted down a description of the man who had stopped me in the parking lot at the train station. It was still there, but now a sentence had been added: 'Considered dangerous, so approach with extreme caution.'

My knees felt weak. It was bad enough that someone had come in, but that he would flaunt his presence was frightening. I was certain that I had locked the door when I left. But the lock was inexpensive and wouldn't be much of a challenge for a burglar. Was anything missing? I ran into the bedroom and saw that the closet door, which I had left closed, was now slightly ajar. My clothes and shoes inside, however, seemed to be exactly as I'd left them. In the top drawer of the dresser I had a leather case of jewellery. It was all there, so it was clear that whoever came in was not a common thief. He had been after information, and I realised how blessed I was that I had not left the trial transcript and all the old newspapers there.

I checked the door again. It was bolted, but I wedged a heavy chair against it. Then I locked all the windows. Still, when I finally did fall asleep, I kept waking with a start. But the sounds I heard were simply the wind blowing the few remaining leaves from the trees.

It was only at dawn, when I woke for the fourth or fifth time, that I realised that whoever had gone through my appointment book knew I had a meeting that morning at Arbinger, north of Boston.

I planned to leave for Arbinger at seven o'clock. I knew Mrs Hilmer was an early bird, so at ten to seven I called her and asked if I could stop by for a moment. Over a cup of her excellent coffee I told her about the intruder and said that I would take the transcript and newspapers and get copies made of them.

'No, you won't,' she said. 'I have nothing else to do. I'm a volunteer at the library, and I'll use the copier in the office.' She hesitated. 'Ellie, I want you to move in with me. Whoever was in last night might come back, and, anyhow, I think we should call the police.'

'No to moving in with you,' I said. 'If anything, I should leave the apartment.' She began to shake her head, and I said, 'But I won't. I'm too comfortable being near you. And I've thought about notifying the police and decided it's a bad idea. There's no sign of breaking and entering. My jewellery is still there. If I tell a cop that the only disturbance was that someone moved a pen and added a couple of words to a computer file, I'd sound like one of those people who send threatening letters to themselves just to get attention.' I gulped the last of the coffee. 'There is something you can do, though. Call Joan Lashley and ask her if I can come and see her tomorrow.'

It was comforting to hear Mrs Hilmer say, 'Drive carefully,' and feel her quick kiss on my cheek.

ON MY WAY round Boston I got caught in some of the commuter traffic, so it was almost eleven o'clock when I drove through the carefully guarded gates of Arbinger Preparatory School. The handsome pink-brick buildings looked mellow and tranquil under the November sky. The long driveway through the campus was lined with mature trees that in season would form a lush canopy of leaves. It was easy to imagine why the kids who graduate from a place such as this received with their diplomas a sense of entitlement, a feeling of being a cut above the rest.

As I steered the car into the area designated for visitors, I recalled the list of high schools I had attended. Freshman year in Louisville. Second half of sophomore year in Los Angeles. Where was I next? Oh, yes, Portland, Oregon. And finally, back to Los Angeles.

I was admitted to the main building and directed to Craig

Parshall's office. The walls along the corridor were lined with grave-faced portraits of former school presidents.

Mr Parshall was a man in his late fifties who still wore his school ring. His thinning hair was perfectly combed, and he could not conceal the fact that he was nervous. His office was very handsome, with formal draperies, a Persian carpet just threadbare enough to guarantee its antiquity, and a mahogany desk, behind which he promptly retreated after greeting me. I settled in a comfortable leather chair.

'As I told you on the phone, Ms Cavanaugh—' he began.

'Mr Parshall, the Westerfield family has a goal in life to whitewash Robson Westerfield's reputation, have a new trial and get him acquitted. Success will have the de facto effect of having the world believe that another man is guilty of my sister's death. My goal is to see that that does not happen.'

'You must understand—' Parshall began.

'I understand that you can't be quoted on the record. But you can open some doors for me. By that I mean that I want the list of students who were in class with Rob Westerfield. I want to know if any were particular friends of his or, better yet, couldn't stand him. Who was his room-mate? And off the record—and I do mean off the record—why was he kicked out?'

We looked at each other in silence for a long minute, and neither one of us blinked.

'On my website I could easily refer to Robson Westerfield's exclusive prep school and not name it,' I said. 'Or I could put it this way: Arbinger Preparatory School, alma mater to His Royal Highness Prince Gregory of Belgium, His Serene Highness Prince—'

He interrupted me. 'Off the record?'

'Absolutely.'

'No naming of the school or of me?'

'Absolutely.'

He sighed, and I almost felt sorry for him. 'Off the record, the only reason Robson Westerfield was accepted here is that his father offered to rebuild the science building. And without a hint of publicity, I might add. Rob was presented to us as a troubled student who was never at home among his grade-school peers.'

'He went to Baldwin in Manhattan for eight years,' I said. 'Were there problems there?'

'None reported to us.' Parshall looked pained. 'Westerfield was from a fine family.'

'All right,' I said. 'Now let's get down to the nitty-gritty. What was it like having that guy on these hallowed grounds?'

'I had just begun teaching here, so I'm a first-hand witness. It was about as bad as it gets,' Parshall said. 'Robson Westerfield was a poster boy for the sociopathic personality. I am talking of the sociopath as someone born without a conscience, who has a disregard for and is in conflict with the social code as you and I understand it.'

'Then you had problems with him from the beginning?'

'Like so many of his ilk, he is blessed with looks and intelligence. He also is the last of a distinguished family line. His grandfather and father were students here. The grandfather, Pearson Westerfield, was a United States senator. We hoped that we would be able to bring out whatever good qualities there were in Rob.'

'Why did he leave in the middle of the year?'

'He viciously attacked another football player. The student was seriously injured. The family was persuaded not to sue, and the Westerfields paid all the bills. Maybe more. To that I can't swear.'

It dawned on me that Craig Parshall was being unusually frank. I told him so.

'I do not like to be threatened, Ms Cavanaugh.'

'Threatened?'

'This morning I received a call from a Mr Hamilton, an attorney who represents the Westerfield family. I was warned that I should give you no negative information.'

'May I ask what kind of information you gave Jake Bern about Westerfield?'

'His sports activities. Robson played on the squash team, the tennis team and the football team. He was also in the theatre group and was a genuinely talented actor. Bern managed to elicit some quotes from me that will sound very favourable in print.'

'How will Rob's leaving Arbinger be explained?'

'He took the second semester of his sophomore year abroad, in England, then decided to switch.'

'Could you give me a list of his former classmates?'

'You didn't get it from me, of course.'

When I left Arbinger an hour later, I had a list of freshmen and sophomores. Comparing them with the active alumni list, Parshall identified ten who were in the Massachusetts-to-Manhattan area. One of them was Christopher Cassidy, the football player Rob Westerfield had severely beaten.

IT WAS LATE AFTERNOON when I pulled into Mrs Hilmer's driveway and parked in front of the apartment. I'd stopped at the supermarket in Oldham and picked up some supplies. My plan was to make a simple dinner—steak, baked potato and salad—then watch television and get to bed reasonably early.

When I got into the apartment, I phoned Mrs Hilmer. She answered on the first ring, and her voice sounded troubled.

'Ellie, this may sound crazy, but I think someone followed me today when I went to the library.'

'Why do you think that?'

'You know how quiet this street is. But I was hardly out of the driveway, when I could see a car in the rearview mirror. It stayed a distance behind me, but it didn't turn off until after I'd turned into the library's parking area. Then the same car followed me home.'

'Can you describe it?'

'It was medium-sized, black or dark blue. It was far enough behind me that I couldn't see the driver, but I have the impression that it was a man. Ellie, do you think that whoever was in the apartment last night is hanging around here?'

'I don't know.'

'I'm going to call the police, and that means I'll have to tell them about last night.'

'Yes, of course.' I hated myself for the nervousness I heard in Mrs Hilmer's voice.

A squad car pulled up at the house ten minutes later, and after debating for a few minutes, I decided to walk over. The police officer obviously did not think much of Mrs Hilmer's suspicions. 'Whoever was in that car didn't try to contact you in any way?' he was asking her when I arrived.

'No.' She introduced us. 'Ellie, I've known Officer White for many years.'

He was a craggy-faced man who looked as though he'd spent a lot of time outdoors. 'What's this about an intruder, Ms Cavanaugh?'

When I told him, his scepticism was apparent. 'You mean your jewellery wasn't touched and the only evidence you have is that you think your pen had been moved and there are a couple of words in a computer file that you don't remember writing.'

'That I *didn't* write,' I corrected him.

'Mrs Hilmer,' he said, 'we'll keep an eye on the house for the next few days, but my guess is that you were a little nervous after hearing

Ms Cavanaugh's story and that's why you picked up on that car. Chances are it was nothing.'

My 'story', I thought. Thanks for nothing.

Officer White left in his squad car. We lingered for a moment outside and watched as the taillights disappeared onto the road.

'Ellie,' Mrs Hilmer said, 'I made copies of the newspapers and the trial transcript. Do you need the originals this evening? I'm meeting some friends for dinner and won't be back until ten o'clock.'

I hated the thought that I was afraid to have both the originals and the copies under one roof, but I was. 'I do need them,' I said. The sky was almost dark, but I could see the tension in her face. 'Did anything else happen?' I asked.

'Just a minute before Officer White came by, I got a phone call. I don't know who it was. The caller ID was blocked. But whoever it was said I should be careful keeping a psycho around me. He said that you'd been institutionalised for setting fire in a classroom.'

'That's absolutely untrue. My God, I've never spent a day in a hospital since I was born, never mind an institution.'

From the relief on her face I knew Mrs Hilmer believed me. But that meant, of course, that she had not instantly disbelieved the caller.

'But, Ellie, why would anyone say such a terrible thing about you?' she protested.

'Someone's trying to discredit me, of course. Mrs Hilmer, I think it's better if I move tomorrow. I'm safer at the inn, and certainly you'll have your peace back.'

'I think you *would* be safer, Ellie.' Mrs Hilmer paused, then added in all honesty, 'I guess I would feel safer, too.'

I collected the newspapers and transcript and walked back to the apartment, feeling almost bereft. I replaced my jacket with a loose sweater, kicked off my shoes, and stuffed my feet into ancient fleece-lined slippers. Then I poured myself a glass of wine and settled in the big club chair, with my feet on the hassock.

The sweater and slippers were my comfort clothes. For a fleeting moment I thought about my old comforter, Bones, the floppy stuffed animal who had shared my pillow when I was a child. He was on the top shelf of a closet in my apartment in Atlanta, sharing a box with other mementos my mother had kept: her wedding album, pictures of the four of us, baby clothes, and, most wrenching of all, Andrea's band uniform. For a moment I felt a childish resentment that Bones wasn't with me now.

AN HOUR LATER there was a subtle change in the weather. The faint rattle of a loose pane in the window over the sink was the first hint of a shift in the wind. I got up and pushed up the thermostat, then went back to the computer. Realising that I was in acute danger of feeling sorry for myself, I had begun to work on what would become the opening chapter of my book.

After some false starts, I knew that I should begin with my final memory of Andrea. And as I wrote, my memory seemed to sharpen. I could see her room with the white organdie bedspread and frilly curtains, the pictures of Andrea and her friends stuck in the frame of the mirror over the old-fashioned dresser that Mother had restored.

I could see Andrea almost in tears as she talked on the phone to Rob Westerfield, and then I saw her putting on the locket. As I wrote, I realised that there was something about the locket that still eluded me. Once again I was struck by the terrible risk Rob had taken in coming back to retrieve it the following morning, when I found her. Even as I thought of the harsh breathing and the nervous giggling sound he made as he hid on the other side of the van, my hands turned clammy on the keyboard.

On the witness stand, Rob claimed he was out jogging at that time. Suppose I had *not* slipped through the woods alone but had brought my father with me? Rob would have been caught in the garage.

At seven o'clock I turned on the oven and put in the lone potato to bake; then I went back to work. Shortly afterwards my cellphone rang. It was Pete Lawlor.

'Hi, Ellie.' Something in his voice that warned me to brace myself.

'What's the matter, Pete?'

'You don't waste time on chitchat, do you?'

'We never do. That's our agreement.'

'I guess it is. Ellie, the paper is being sold. It's definite now. The staff will be cut to the bone.'

'What about you?'

'They offered me a job. I turned them down. I asked about you, but they told me off the record that they don't plan to keep up the investigative reporter series.'

I'd been expecting that bit of news, but I realised how suddenly rootless it made me feel. 'Have you decided where you're going, Pete?'

'I'm not sure yet, but I may be seeing some people in New York before I decide. Maybe when that happens, I'll rent a car and drive up to see you, or you can meet me in the city.'

'I'd like that. I was kind of expecting that I'd get a postcard from Houston or LA.'

'I never send postcards. Ellie, I've been watching your website.'

'There isn't much on it yet. It's sort of like a sign you put on a shop you've rented: "Watch for the Grand Opening". But I am digging up stuff. If Jake Bern tries to portray Westerfield as an all-American kid, his book will have to be published as fiction.'

'Ellie, it is not in my nature to—'

'Ah, come on, Pete. You're not going to warn me to be careful, are you? Let's change the subject. Have you lost those pounds yet?'

'I did better than that. I decided I look good just the way I am. OK, I'll call you when I know I'm coming in. Or you can always call me, you know. Long-distance rates are pretty cheap at night.'

He disconnected before I could even say goodbye.

I pressed the END button on my cellphone and laid the phone down next to the computer. As I made a salad, the ramifications of losing my job began to sink in. The advance on signing the book contract would keep me going for a while, but what would I do when that was finished?

It was a question I pondered all through dinner, even as I tried to concentrate on the news magazine I'd picked up at the supermarket.

The cellphone rang again as I was clearing the table.

'You the lady who was standing outside the prison with a sign yesterday?' a husky male voice asked.

'Yes, I am.' Mentally I was crossing my fingers. The caller ID registered 'unavailable'.

'I might have something to tell you. How much you gonna pay?'

'I guess it depends on the information.'

'You pay first, then you hear. Five thousand dollars.'

'I haven't got that much money.'

'Then forget it. But what I can tell you would put Westerfield back in Sing Sing for the rest of his life.'

Was he bluffing? I wasn't sure, but I couldn't take a chance on losing the caller. I thought of my advance. 'I have some money coming in the next week or two. Give me some hint of what you know.'

'How's this? When he was whacked out on cocaine last year, Westerfield told me he killed a guy when he was eighteen. Is the name of that guy worth five thousand dollars? Think about it. I'll call back next week.'

I heard a click in my ear.

Suddenly it was a whole new ball game. I thought of the incident I heard about at Arbinger Preparatory School. It was possible Rob was guilty of other crimes before he murdered Andrea, and if the guy who had just called me was on the level and could give me the name of a murder victim I could verify, it would be easy enough to find out the facts of the case. I stood at the computer, looking down at my description of my sister in those last few moments that I was with her. I knew that to put Rob Westerfield back in prison was worth every cent I would ever earn in my life.

There was a glass of water beside the computer. I picked it up and lifted it in a kind of salute—a toast to Andrea and to the prospect of sending Westerfield back to prison.

I tidied up the kitchen and turned on the TV to watch the local news. The sports editor was showing clips of a basketball game. The winning basket had been made by Teddy Cavanaugh. The half-brother I'd never met was looking straight into the camera.

The cheerleaders began to chant his name.

Joan Lashley St Martin lived in a three-storey frame house in a lovely wooded area in Garrison. The white clapboard shingles glistened in the sunshine and were complemented by the hunter-green shutters framing the windows. I parked in the semicircular driveway, went up the porch steps and rang the bell.

Joan answered the door. She had always seemed tall to me, but I realised instantly that she hadn't grown an inch in these twenty-two years. Her long brown hair was now collar length, and her thin frame had filled out. I remembered her smile—she is one of those people whose smile makes the whole face seem beautiful. As we looked at each other, Joan's green eyes became moist.

'Little Ellie,' she said. 'Dear God, I thought you'd be shorter than I am. You were such a tiny kid.'

I laughed. 'It's the reaction I'm getting from everyone.'

She put her arm through mine. 'Come in. I have a pot of coffee going.' We walked through the living room that ran from the front to the back of the house. It was the kind of room I loved—deep couches, club chairs, a wall of books, a fireplace, wide windows that looked out at the surrounding hills.

We have similar taste, I thought. Then I realised that the similarity also extended to clothing. We were both dressed casually, in sweaters and jeans.

'My husband, Leo, is out with the boys,' she said. 'Between the four of them, life is one long basketball game.'

The table in the breakfast room was already set for the two of us. The percolator was plugged in on the sideboard. The picture window offered a stunning view of the Hudson River. 'I would never get tired of looking out of this window,' I said as I sat down.

'I never do. So many of the old crowd went down to the city, but a lot of them are coming back. The commute into Manhattan is only an hour, and they think it's worth it.' Joan poured the coffee as she spoke, then disappeared into the kitchen. She returned carrying a plate of corn muffins. We helped ourselves to them and began to talk.

She wanted to know about me, what I had been doing, and I briefly sketched in the years between the age of seven and the present. She had heard of Mother's death. 'Your father put a notice in the local papers,' she said. 'A very sweet one.'

I was sure Joan wanted to ask me if I had been in touch with him, but she must have sensed that I did not want to talk about him. Instead, as she sipped her coffee, she said, 'Ellie, like everybody else round here, I saw the Rob Westerfield interview. My cousin's a judge. He says there's so much pressure for a second trial that he's surprised they're not already into jury selection. You have no idea how manipulative the father is, and, of course, the grandmother has made huge donations to hospitals and libraries and schools round here.'

'You'll be called as a witness, I expect, Joan,' I said.

'I know it. I was the last person to see Andrea alive.' She hesitated, then added, 'Except for her murderer.'

We were both silent for a moment. Then I said, 'Joan, I need to know everything that you remember about that last night. I've read the trial transcript over and over. Your testimony was very brief.'

She put her elbows on the table and folded her hands together, resting her chin on them. 'It *was* brief. Neither the prosecutor nor the defence attorney asked me questions that, looking back, I think they should have asked.'

'What kind of questions?'

'About Will Nebels, for one,' she said. 'You remember how he worked for just about everyone in town at some point. He helped build your porch, didn't he?'

'Yes.'

'He fixed our garage door when my mother backed the car into it. My father used to say that when Will wasn't three sheets to the wind he was a good carpenter. But you could never count on him showing up.'

'I kind of remember that.'

'Something you wouldn't remember was that Andrea and I used to talk about the fact that he was a bit too friendly.'

'Too friendly?'

Joan shrugged. 'Today I'd say he was one step away from being a child molester. Any number of times when we bumped into him in the street, he'd give us each a big hug and call us his girls. Although never if an adult was around. We told each other how yucky it was.

'Now understand, he didn't molest us, but in retrospect he was a boozy sleaze who had a hell of a nerve. And there was no question in my mind that the one he really had his eye on was Andrea. I remember I joked to your mother and father that Andrea was going to invite Will Nebels to the Christmas dance. They never picked up that there was anything behind the joking.'

'My father missed that!'

'Andrea could do a great imitation of Will sneaking beer out of his toolbox and getting bombed while he worked. There was no reason for your father to look behind the joking.'

'Joan, I don't understand why you're telling me this. Are you saying that this story Will Nebels is telling now is anything but an outright lie that the Westerfields are paying him to tell?'

'Ellie, I'm wondering. I do know Will Nebels lost his driving licence at that time and was always wandering round town. I also know he had a thing for Andrea. Suppose she was hoping to meet Rob Westerfield in the garage hide-out and got there early. Suppose Will had followed her there and made a pass at her. Suppose there was a struggle, and she fell backwards. That was a cement floor. There was an injury on the back of her head that they blamed on the fact that she'd fallen after she was hit with the tyre jack. But isn't it possible she fell *before* she was hit?'

'The blow on the back of her head would only have stunned her,' I said. 'I know that from the records.'

'Hear me out. Let's assume for one single minute that—low-life that he is—Rob Westerfield's story is true. He parked his car at the service station, went into the movie, and, after it was over, drove to the hide-out, just in case Andrea was waiting for him.'

'And found her dead?'

'Yes, and panicked, just as he claimed.' She saw the protest forming on my lips. 'Hear me out, Ellie, please. It is possible that everyone has told parts of the truth. Suppose Nebels struggled with Andrea, and she fell and hit her head and was unconscious. Suppose he ran inside Mrs Dorothy Westerfield's house while trying to decide what to do. And then he saw Paulie drive up.'

'Why would Paulie have taken the tyre jack out of the car?'

'Maybe for protection, in case he ran into Westerfield. Remember that Miss Watkins, the guidance counsellor, swore Paulie had said, "I didn't think she was dead".'

'Joan, what are you telling me?'

'Try this scenario: Will Nebels followed Andrea to the garage and made a pass at her. There was a scuffle. She fell and was knocked unconscious. He let himself into the house, then saw Paulie drive up, get out the tyre jack, and take it into the garage. A minute later, Paulie is back in the car and speeding away. Nebels isn't sure if Paulie is going to get the police. He goes into the garage again. He sees the tyre jack that Paulie has dropped. Will Nebels knows he's facing prison if Andrea can tell them what happened. He kills her, takes the tyre jack, and gets out of there.'

'How did the jack get back in the trunk of Rob Westerfield's car?'

'Ellie, Andrea was murdered on Thursday night. Rob wasn't questioned until Saturday afternoon. It isn't in the trial transcript, but on Friday, Will Nebels was working at the Westerfields'. Rob always left the keys in his car. Will could easily have replaced the jack that day.'

'Where did you learn all this, Joan?'

'My cousin, Andrew, the judge, used to be in the district attorney's office. He was very familiar with the case. He's always felt that Rob Westerfield was a nasty, aggressive, worthless piece of humanity, but he also believed that he was innocent of Andrea's death.'

Mrs Hilmer was doubtful about Paulie's innocence. Now Joan was convinced that Will Nebels was the killer. Yet I knew with certainty that Rob Westerfield was the one who had taken my sister's life.

'As a hypothetical situation, it fits. But Rob Westerfield was in the garage when I was kneeling beside Andrea's body. I heard him breathing and I heard . . . It's hard to explain—a giggle, an odd gasping sound I'd heard before, one of the other times I was in his presence.'

'How often would you have been in his presence, Ellie?'

'A couple of times when Andrea and I walked downtown after school or on Saturday, he'd suddenly materialise. How much did Andrea tell you about him?'

'Not much at all. The first time I remember seeing him was in early October. Andrea was in the band, of course, and Westerfield came up to her after a game. I was standing with her. He made an outright play for her, saying how pretty she was, how he couldn't take his eyes off her. He was older and very good-looking, and she was flattered, of course. Plus, I guess your mother had talked a lot about how important the Westerfield family was.'

'Yes.'

'You do realise that she had been friends with him—if you can call it that—for only a month or so before she died.'

'Did you ever get the feeling that she'd become afraid of him?'

'I got the feeling that something was terribly wrong, but she wouldn't tell me what it was.'

'Do you know if Rob ever gave Andrea a locket?'

'She didn't mention it to me. If he did, then I never saw it. Your dad gave her a locket, though, and she wore that fairly often.'

Andrea had been wearing a V-neck sweater that night. That was why I was so clear about seeing her clasping the locket round her neck. It was on a fairly long chain and rested at the base of the neckline.

'Then to the best of your memory, she didn't have any jewellery on when she left your house.'

'I didn't say that. As I remember, she was wearing a thin gold chain. It was short, choker length.'

But that's *it*, I thought, suddenly remembering. Before she left the bedroom, Andrea had turned the locket round and let it fall down her back, between her shoulder blades. The effect was one of wearing a choker-length chain. I had carefully read the description of the clothing Andrea had been wearing when her body was found. There had been no mention of that chain.

I left Joan's house a few minutes later with the sincere promise that I would call her soon. I didn't tell her that unwittingly she had verified my memory of Andrea putting on the locket. Tomorrow I would describe the locket on the website.

It's another line to cast, I thought. Somebody out there might know why the locket was important enough for Westerfield to risk going back for it the next day.

FROM THE CLERK'S DESK at the Parkinson Inn, I could look into the restaurant and see that it was enjoying its usual weekend luncheon crowd. Today's group appeared to be particularly festive. I wondered if the sunny fall afternoon was having a cheering effect.

'I'm afraid that all eight rooms are booked, Ms Cavanaugh,' the clerk told me. 'It's been that way every weekend this fall, and will be till Christmas.'

Of course, that said it all. There was no use staying here during the week, then moving out for the weekend. I'd have to find another place. I decided to go back to the apartment and get out the phone book. But it was twenty to one, and all I'd had to eat was a corn muffin. I went into the restaurant, was promptly seated, and ordered New England clam chowder, with a green salad and a bottle of Perrier.

While I waited to be served, I nibbled crusty bread and began to analyse why I was feeling disquieted. It wasn't hard to figure out. The sobering truth was that people who I would have thought were as convinced as I was of Rob Westerfield's guilt were not taking my side.

They *knew* him. They knew what he was. And still they thought it was entirely possible he had spent his twenties and thirties in prison an innocent man. Sympathetic as they were to me, I was in their eyes the obsessed family member of the dead girl, unreasonable at best, manic and unbalanced at worst.

I know that in some ways I am arrogant. When I think I'm right, all the forces of heaven and hell won't budge me. Maybe that's why I'm a good investigative reporter. Now, sitting in this restaurant where long ago I sat as the smallest member of a happy family, I tried to be honest with myself. Was it possible, was it *remotely* possible, that the same drive that made me a good reporter was working against me now? Was I doing a disservice not only to Mrs Hilmer and Joan Lashley but to the man I despised, Rob Westerfield?

I was so intent on my own thoughts that I was startled when a hand came across my vision. It was the waitress with the clam chowder. 'Be careful,' she warned. 'It's really hot.'

I picked up the spoon, but before I could take the first sip, the party arrived for the reserved table next to me. I looked up, and my throat went dry—Rob Westerfield was standing beside my chair.

I laid down the spoon. He extended his hand, and I ignored it. He was a stunningly handsome man, even more so in person than he had been on television. There was a kind of animal magnetism about him, a suggestion of strength and confidence that is the trademark of many powerful men. His eyes were a startling cobalt blue.

'The hostess pointed you out, Ellie,' he said, his voice warm, as if we were acquaintances who happened on each other every so often.

'Did she, indeed?'

'She realised who you are and was quite upset. She has no other table for six and thought I might not want to be seated near you.'

From the corner of my eye I could see his companions. Two of them I recognised from the television interview—his father and his lawyer. They were looking at me, their expressions hostile.

'Did it occur to her that I might not want to be anywhere near *you*?' I asked.

'Ellie, you are mistaken about me. I want to find your sister's murderer and see him punished as much as you do. Can we get together and talk quietly?' He hesitated, then with a smile added, 'Please, Ellie.'

I realised that the entire dining room had suddenly become quiet. Since everyone seemed to want to be in on our exchange, I deliberately raised my voice. 'I'd love to get together with you, Rob,' I said. 'How about at the hide-out? That was a favourite place of yours, wasn't it? Or maybe the memory of bludgeoning a girl to death might be painful even for a consummate liar like you.' I threw a twenty-dollar bill on the table and pushed back my chair.

Without the slightest indication of being upset, Rob picked up the twenty and shoved it into the pocket of my jacket. 'We have a house account here, Ellie. Any time you come in, you're our guest. Bring your friends.' Again he paused, but this time his eyes narrowed. 'If you have any,' he added quietly.

I took the twenty-dollar bill out of my pocket, spotted the waitress, gave it to her, and left.

HALF AN HOUR LATER I was back in the apartment. The kettle was whistling, and I was putting together a cheese sandwich, complete with lettuce and tomato. By then the fit of trembling that overcame me in the car had passed, and only my hands, cold and clammy, reflected the shock of seeing Rob Westerfield face to face.

Over and over in that half-hour, a scene had been replaying itself in my mind. *I am on the witness stand. Flanked by his lawyers, Rob is sitting at the table reserved for the accused. He is staring at me, his eyes malevolent.*

The intensity of his concentration when he was inches away from me in the restaurant was just as absolute as it had been at the trial.

I took the sandwich and the tea to the table, got the Yellow Pages and opened my cellphone. Before I could begin to circle places where I could enquire about a monthly rental, Mrs Hilmer called.

'Ellie, I just got a call from my oldest granddaughter, Janey, who had her first baby last month. Well, Janey broke her wrist. I'm driving to Long Island and will stay a few days. After what's happened, I worry about your being out here alone.'

'I stopped at the Parkinson Inn, but they're all booked up for the weekend and for the next six or seven weekends as well. I'm just starting to call around to other inns and guesthouses now.'

'Ellie, my concern is only for you. Stay in the apartment until you find something suitable. I'm taking the copies of the trial transcript and the newspapers with me to Long Island. Take down Janey's phone number in case you want to reach me.'

I jotted it down and a few minutes later heard Mrs Hilmer's car headed down the driveway. I will confess that, after the shock of seeing Rob Westerfield, I was very sorry that she had left. I gave a mental shrug and returned to the Yellow Pages.

Then I started phoning local inns and guesthouses. It proved to be a dismaying task. The few that sounded possible were pretty expensive on a monthly basis, so I began looking through the newspaper at the Houses for Rent section.

Finally, after two hours, I was finished. I had six places lined up to see tomorrow. I was glad to be done because I wanted to get to the computer to write notes on my encounter with Rob Westerfield.

I opened the laptop and took a deep breath.

USUALLY I SHOWER in the morning, and if it's been a stressful day I shower again before I go to bed. Tonight I decided to go even further. I filled the tub with hot water and squirted in bath oil. It felt good just to lie there and soak. I stayed until the water began to cool.

I'm always amused when I see ads for seductive night attire. My own nightshirt was purchased from an L.L.Bean catalogue, and its companion piece is a flannel robe. Topping off that exquisite ensemble are the fleece-lined bedroom slippers.

The two-door dresser in the bedroom reminded me of the white antique-looking one in Andrea's room. As I brushed my hair in front of the mirror, I wondered idly what had become of that dresser.

You're daddy's little girl to have and to hold . . . You're the spirit of Christmas, my star on the tree . . . And you're daddy's little girl.

Unbidden, the words of that song ran through my head, and I once again envisioned Daddy in Andrea's room, holding the music box and sobbing. It was a memory I always tried to close off immediately. 'Finish brushing your hair, girl, and go to bed,' I said aloud.

With a critical eye I studied myself in the mirror. I usually wore my hair up, anchored with a comb, but now, taking a good look, I saw how long it had grown. Over the summer it became very blonde, and while most of the bleaching from the sun had faded, there were still bright streaks running through it. I recalled the remark Detective Longo had made the first time he questioned me after Andrea's body was found. He said that my hair, like his son's, reminded him of sand when the sun is shining on it. That was such a sweet description, and it felt good to think that it might be true again.

I watched the eleven o'clock news just long enough to be sure the world outside Oldham was still more or less functioning. Then, after checking the locks, I went to bed.

In my apartment in Atlanta I could always fall asleep easily. But it was different there, of course. I could hear faint street noises and sometimes music from the apartment next door. I would not mind a few metallic vibrations that signified the closeness of another friendly human being tonight, I thought as I readjusted the pillow.

I did eventually manage to fall into an uneasy sleep, the kind that makes you wish you could wake up. I was dreaming that there was somewhere I had to go. I had to find someone before it was too late. It was dark, and my flashlight wouldn't work.

Then I was in the woods, and I could smell a campfire. I needed to find a path through the woods. There was one, I was sure of it. I'd been on it before.

It was so hot, and I was beginning to cough.

It wasn't a dream! I opened my eyes. The dark room was filled with smoke. I was choking. I shoved back the covers and could feel the heat building around me. I'd burn to death if I didn't get out. Where was I? For a moment I simply couldn't orientate myself.

I forced myself to think. I was in Mrs Hilmer's apartment. The bedroom door was to the left of the bed. The apartment door was just past the hallway, on the left.

I gasped as my feet touched the hot floorboards. I heard a crackling overhead. The roof was catching fire. I knew I had only seconds before the whole building caved in.

I stumbled forward, groping for the door. Thank God I had left it open. I felt my way along the hallway and past the bathroom. The smoke was not as dense here, but then a wall of flame burst from the kitchen area of the living room. It illuminated the table, and I saw my laptop and my cellphone. The duffle bag was on the floor.

I didn't want to lose them. It took a second to pull back the bolt and unlock the apartment door. Then, biting my lips from the pain of the blisters forming on my feet, coughing and gasping, I ran to the table, scooped up the computer and cellphone in one hand and the duffle bag in the other, and fled back to the door.

Behind me the flames were leaping onto the furniture, and ahead the smoke in the stairwell was thick and black. Somehow I was able to stumble down the staircase. At first the handle of the outside door seemed to be jammed. I dropped everything and yanked and twisted with both hands. I'm trapped, I'm trapped, I thought as I felt my hair begin to singe. I gave a final desperate twist, and the handle turned.

I bent down for the laptop, phone and bag and stumbled out. A man was running down the driveway and rushed to grab me before I fell. 'Is anyone still in there?' he shouted.

Shivering and burning at the same time, I shook my head.

'My wife called the fire department,' he said as he pulled me away from the blazing structure. 'We live just down the road.'

Five minutes later, for the first time in over twenty years, I was sitting in the kitchen of my old house, wrapped in a blanket, a cup of tea in front of me. Through the French doors that led to the dining room I could see Mother's beloved chandelier, still in place.

I closed my eyes.

'It's OK to cry, you know,' Lynn Kelton, the lady who now lives in my old house said kindly. 'You've had a terrible ordeal.'

But I managed to blink back the tears. I felt that if I ever started shedding them, I'd never be able to stop.

Seven

The fire chief came to the Keltons' house and insisted on having an ambulance take me to the hospital. 'You must have inhaled a lot of smoke, Ms Cavanaugh,' he said. 'You need to be checked out.'

Oldham County Hospital kept me overnight, which was just as

well, since I had no place else to go. When I was finally in bed—after the soot and grime were removed from my face and body, and my blistered feet were bandaged—I gladly accepted a sleeping pill.

The room I was in was near the nurses' station, and I could hear the murmur of voices. As I fell asleep, I thought about how a few hours ago I'd been wishing for company. I never expected to have my wish granted this way.

When I was woken by a nurse's aide at seven in the morning, there wasn't a part of me that didn't ache. She checked my pulse and blood pressure and departed. I pushed back the blanket, swung my legs onto the floor and tried to stand up. Putting weight on my feet was terribly uncomfortable, but other than that I was in pretty good shape.

Was the fire an accident? I knew it wasn't. Although I never looked inside, Mrs Hilmer had told me that the garage under the apartment had very little in it except gardening tools. Gardening tools don't burst into flames. I had not the slightest doubt that that fire had been ordered by Rob Westerfield. Maybe he had given the assignment to a former lackey in Sing Sing.

I was sure that by now that Mrs Hilmer had been notified of the fire by Officer White—I had given him her granddaughter's phone number. I knew how distressing it would be for her to learn that her garage apartment was gone. Right now she must be thinking that no good deed goes unpunished, I thought unhappily. I would phone her, but not yet. How do you apologise for something like this?

Then I thought about the duffle bag and my laptop and cellphone. I remembered the nurse saying something about putting them away for me. I hobbled over to a locker-style closet, opened the door, and was delighted to see them piled neatly on the floor. I was equally delighted to see a chenille robe on a hanger. I was wearing one of those hospital gowns meant for someone the size of a Barbie doll.

The first thing I did was unzip the duffle bag and look inside. The crumbling first page of the *New York Post* with the headline GUILTY was still on top. I slid my hand down the bag and breathed a sigh of relief when I felt the leather case that I had been seeking.

Yesterday morning, just as I was getting into the car to go to Joan's house, it occurred to me that my next unauthorised visitor might rummage for valuables. I ran back upstairs, took the case from the drawer and put it in the duffle bag in the trunk.

Now I pulled out the case and opened it. Everything was there— Mother's engagement and wedding rings, her diamond earrings, my modest collection of jewellery. Gratefully I put the case back in the bag and carried the computer to the single chair by the window. I held my breath, exhaling only when the beep sounded, the screen lit up, and I knew I hadn't lost any of the material I had stored in it.

I know that I was in shock after the fire. Now, as my thinking cleared, I began to realise how very lucky I had been to escape, not only alive but not seriously burned. I knew also that I would have to be much more vigilant. One thing was certain: I had to be in a place where there was a desk clerk and other employees around.

Since I didn't have pen or paper, I used the computer to make a list of the things I had to do immediately. I had no money, no clothes, no credit cards, no driver's licence—all these had been lost in the fire. Who would be the lucky recipient of my pleading call?

I have friends in Atlanta, but I just didn't want to go into a long explanation. Pete was the only one in Atlanta who knew about Andrea and about why I was here. Pete? The thought of having to play the helpless female irritated me. I'm sure I could have called Joan Lashley St Martin, but her belief that Rob Westerfield was innocent of Andrea's murder made me reluctant.

A breakfast tray came and went, virtually untouched. The doctor arrived, checked my blistered feet, told me I was free to go home, and departed. I had a mental image of limping around Oldham in hospital gear, asking for a handout. At precisely that psychologically low moment, Officer White appeared with a sharp-featured man he introduced as Detective Charles Bannister of the Oldham Police Department. A hospital orderly was behind them carrying folding chairs, so I gathered that this was not going to be a quick bedside visit.

Bannister expressed concern for my well-being and the hope that after the ordeal I was feeling as well as possible. I immediately sensed that beneath the veneer of concern he had an agenda in mind, and it wasn't a friendly one. It didn't take me long to understand that he was determined to prove that I had made up the initial story about the intruder in the apartment, that I had set the fire to gain attention and sympathy for myself, while publicly accusing Rob Westerfield of trying to kill me.

'You were in danger of being burned to death, but according to the neighbour who saw you emerge from the building, you were carrying a laptop computer, a cellphone and a heavy duffle bag. Most people in an inferno don't stop to pack, Ms Cavanaugh.'

'Just as I reached the door to the stairs, a sheet of flames burst from the kitchen. It illuminated the table where I had left those things. They were very important to me, and I took that extra second to grab them.'

'Why were they so important, Ms Cavanaugh?'

'Let me tell you why, Detective Bannister.' I pointed to my lap. 'The first chapter of the book I am writing is in this computer. Pages and pages of notes that I have honed from the trial transcript of *The State* versus *Robson Westerfield* are also in it. I do not have back-up.'

His face remained impassive.

'I posted my cellphone number on a sign I was carrying outside Sing Sing prison. I've already received one very interesting phone call. That phone is my only chance to stay in contact. As for the duffle bag, it's in the closet. Would you care to see the contents?'

'Yes, I would,' Bannister said. 'I'll get it for you.'

I put the laptop on the floor. 'I prefer to keep it in my own hands.'

I tried not to limp as I rushed across the room. I yanked open the closet door, picked up the duffle bag, brought it back, sat down and unzipped it. 'I would prefer not to be showing these to you.' I spat out the words as I tossed newspaper after newspaper onto the floor. 'My mother kept these all her life. They are the news accounts— starting with the discovery of my sister's body and including the moment when Rob Westerfield was sentenced to prison. They don't make pleasant reading, but they do make *interesting* reading, and I don't want to lose them.'

I had to use both hands to pull out the trial transcript. 'Also interesting reading, Detective Bannister,' I said.

'I'm sure it is,' he agreed. 'Anything else in there, Ms Cavanaugh?'

'If you're hoping to find a can of gasoline and a box of matches, you're out of luck.' I took out the leather case and opened it. 'Go through this, please.'

He glanced at the contents. 'Do you always carry your jewellery with you in a duffle bag with newspapers or only when you suspect there might be a fire?' He stood up, and White jumped to his feet. 'You'll be hearing from us, Ms Cavanaugh.'

THIRTY MINUTES LATER I had another visitor, more surprising this time. My father.

The door was partially open. He tapped on it, then walked in without waiting for a response. We stared at each other, and my throat went dry.

His dark hair was now silvery white. He was a little thinner but held himself as erectly as ever. Glasses accentuated his keen blue eyes. He was still a good-looking man and hadn't lost that aura of inner strength.

'Hello, Ellie,' he said.

'Hello, Dad.'

I can only imagine what he was thinking as he looked at me garbed in a cheap hospital bathrobe, bandages on my feet. Certainly not the shining star of the song on the music box.

'How are you, Ellie?'

I'd forgotten the deep resonance in his voice. It was the sound of quiet authority that Andrea and I had respected as children. We had felt protected by it, and I, at least, was in awe of it.

'I'm very well, thank you.'

'I came here as soon as I heard about the fire at Mrs Hilmer's and learned that you'd been in that apartment.'

'You needn't have bothered.'

He'd been standing just inside the door. Now he pushed it shut and came over to me. He tried to take my hands. 'Ellie, for God's sake, you're my daughter. How do you think I felt when I heard that you barely got out alive?'

I pulled my hands away. 'Oh, that story will change. The cops think I set the fire as a grandstand gesture. According to them, I want attention and sympathy.'

He was shocked. 'That's ridiculous.'

He was so close that I caught the faint scent of his shaving cream. Was I wrong, or was it the same scent I remembered?

'I know you mean to be kind,' I said, 'but I really wish you'd leave.'

'Ellie, I've seen that website. Westerfield is dangerous. I'm desperately worried about you.'

'I can take care of myself. I've been doing it for a long time.'

'That's not my fault, Ellie. You refused to visit me. I've come to invite you, to *implore* you to stay with us. That way I can protect you. If you remember, I was a state trooper for thirty-five years.'

'I remember. You looked great in uniform. Oh, I did write and thank you for interring Mother's ashes in Andrea's grave, didn't I?'

'Yes, you did.'

'Her death certificate gave the cause of death as "cirrhosis of the liver", but I think "broken heart" would be more accurate. And my sister's death wasn't the only reason for that broken heart.'

'Ellie, your mother left me.'

'My mother adored you. You could have waited her out. You could have followed her to Florida and brought her home—brought *us* home. You didn't want to.'

My father took out his wallet, pulled out a card, and laid it on the bed. 'You can reach me any time, day or night.'

Then he was gone, but the faint scent of his shaving cream seemed to linger after him. I'd forgotten that sometimes I would sit on the edge of the tub and talk to him while he was shaving. I'd forgotten that sometimes he would spin round, pick me up and rub his face, thick with lather, against mine.

So vivid was the memory that I reached up and touched my cheek, almost expecting to feel the residue of damp suds. My cheek was wet, but it was with the tears that, for the moment at least, I could no longer deny.

I TRIED TO REACH Marcus Longo twice in the next hour. Then I remembered that he had said something about his wife still being in Colorado. I realised that there was a very good chance he had flown back there to have another adoring visit with his grandchild.

The nurse popped her head in and reminded me that checkout time was noon. By eleven thirty I was ready to ask if there was a social services office in the hospital, but then Joan called.

'Ellie, I just heard what happened. How are you? What can I do?'

Any pride that I had about refusing help because she didn't believe Rob Westerfield was a murdering animal evaporated. I needed her, and I knew darn well that she was as sincere in her conviction about his innocence as I was in mine about his guilt.

'Actually, you can do a lot,' I said. Relief at hearing a friendly voice made my own voice tremble. 'You can dig up some clothes for me. You can come and get me. You can help me find a place to stay. You can lend me some money.'

'You'll stay with us—' she began.

'Negative. No. You don't need your house to burst into flames because I'm around.'

'Ellie, you don't believe that someone set that fire!'

'Yes, I do.'

She considered that news a moment and I'm sure thought of her three children. 'Then where can you stay that you'll be safe?'

'An inn is my preference. I don't like the idea of a motel with separate doors to the outside. But the Parkinson Inn is booked.'

'I have a place in mind that I think will work,' Joan said. 'I also have a friend who's about your size. I'll call her to borrow some clothes. What's your shoe size?'

'Nine, but I don't think I can take the bandages off my feet yet.'

'Leo is a size ten. If you don't mind wearing his sneakers.'

I didn't mind.

JOAN ARRIVED WITHIN THE HOUR with a suitcase containing underwear, pyjamas, slacks, a turtleneck sweater, a warm jacket, gloves, the sneakers and some toiletries. I dressed, and the nurse brought in a walking stick I could use until my feet began to heal. On the way out, the billing clerk reluctantly agreed to wait for payment until I could have a copy of my medical insurance card faxed to her.

Finally we were in Joan's SUV. The borrowed clothes fitted quite well, and even though the sneakers looked wide and ungainly, they did a good job of protecting my painful feet.

'I made a reservation for you at the Hudson Valley Inn,' Joan told me. 'It's about a mile away.'

'If you don't mind, I'd like to drive to Mrs Hilmer's place. My car is still there, or at least I hope it's there. It was parked about two feet from the garage. I'm keeping my fingers crossed that a beam or some debris didn't fall on it.'

There wasn't a wall standing of the structure that had housed the cheery apartment Mrs Hilmer had so generously lent me. The area round it was cordoned off, and a policeman was standing guard.

Three men in heavy rubber boots were painstakingly examining the rubble and undoubtedly trying to pinpoint the source of the blaze. They looked up when they saw us, then went back to their probing.

I was relieved to see that my car had been moved about twenty feet towards Mrs Hilmer's house. We got out of the SUV to examine it. It's a previously owned BMW that I bought two years ago, the first decent car I've ever had. Of course, every inch of it was grimy with black smoke, and there were some blisters in the paint on the passenger side, but I considered myself lucky. I still had my wheels, even if I couldn't use them yet.

My shoulder bag had been in the bedroom. Along with everything else, my key ring was in it.

The cop on guard came over to us. He was very young and very polite. When I explained that I didn't have the key to the car and would contact BMW for a replacement, he assured me the car would be safe. 'One of us will be on the premises for the next few days.'

To see if you can pin the fire on me? I wondered as I thanked him.

Whatever lift in spirit I'd felt when I got dressed and left the hospital disappeared as Joan and I started to get back into her SUV. It was a beautiful, clear fall day, but round us the smell of smoke permeated the air. I fervently hoped that it would dissipate before Mrs Hilmer got back. That was another thing I had to do: phone and talk to her.

I could visualise the conversation. 'I'm really sorry I caused your guesthouse to burn down. I certainly won't let it happen again.'

'You're very quiet, Ellie,' Joan said as she turned on the ignition. 'How do you feel, really?'

'Much better than I dared hope,' I assured her. 'You're an angel. And with the money you are so kindly going to lend me, I am buying you lunch.'

THE HUDSON VALLEY INN was a perfect spot for me. It was a three-storey, wide-porched gingerbread kind of Victorian mansion, and the elderly desk clerk, Mrs Willis, went out of her way to give me a particularly nice room with a wonderful view of the river.

If there's anything I love, it's a river view. It's not hard to figure out why that is true. Our house in Irvington had overlooked the Hudson, and I lived there for the first five years of my life. When I was very little, I would pull a chair over to the window and stand on it so that I could glimpse the river shimmering below.

Joan and I walked slowly up the two flights to the room, agreed that it was exactly what I needed, and made our equally slow passage to the dining room. By then I felt as though all the blisters had given birth to septuplets.

A Bloody Mary and a club sandwich did wonders to restore a sense of normality to me.

Then, over coffee, Joan frowned and said, 'Ellie, I hate to bring this up. Leo and I went to a cocktail party last night. Everyone is talking about your website.'

'Go on.'

'Some people think it's outrageous,' she said frankly. 'I understand it was legal to register it in Rob Westerfield's name, but a lot of people think that was unfair.'

'Don't look so worried,' I said. 'I have no intention of shooting the messenger. And I *am* interested in getting reactions. What else are they saying?'

'That you should not have put those mugshots of him on the website. That the medical examiner's testimony describing Andrea's wounds make brutal reading.'

'It was a brutal crime.'

'Ellie, you asked me to tell you what people are saying.'

Joan looked so terribly unhappy that I was ashamed of myself. 'I'm sorry. I know how miserable this is for you.'

She shrugged. 'Ellie, I believe Will Nebels killed Andrea. Half this town thinks Paulie Stroebel is guilty. And a lot of people feel Rob Westerfield has served his sentence and been paroled, and that you ought to accept that.'

'Joan, if Rob Westerfield had admitted his guilt and expressed regret, I would still hate his guts, but there wouldn't be a website.'

She reached across the table, and we clasped hands. 'Ellie, there's another sympathy vote out there. It's for old Mrs Westerfield. Her housekeeper is telling everyone who'll listen how upset Mrs Westerfield is about the website and how she wishes you would at least shut it down until after a new jury has heard the evidence.'

I thought of Dorothy Westerfield, that elegant woman, offering condolences to my mother on the day of the funeral, and I remembered my father ordering her from the house. He couldn't tolerate her sympathy then, and I could not allow myself to be swayed by sympathy for her now.

'We'd better change the subject,' I said. 'We're not going to agree.' I hesitated about bringing up anything else controversial, but there was one more thing I had to ask her. 'Joan, I know you never saw the locket that I insist Andrea was wearing, but are you still in touch with some of the girls who were in school with you and Andrea?'

'Sure. And you can bet I'll be hearing from them, given all that's going on.'

'Would you ask if any of them ever saw Andrea wearing the locket I mentioned to you? Gold, heart-shaped, three small blue stones in the centre, and A and R—Andrea's and Rob's initials— engraved on the back.'

'Ellie—'

'Joan, the more I think about it, the more I believe that the only reason Rob went back to the garage was that he couldn't afford to have the locket found on Andrea's body. I need to know why.'

Joan didn't comment further after that. She promised she would make enquiries. Then she lent me $300, and we both managed a genuine smile as I paid for the lunch.

'Symbolic,' I said, 'but it makes me feel better.'

We said goodbye in the vestibule at the front door. Leaning heavily on the cane, I limped upstairs to the room, locked and bolted the door, carefully removed the sneakers and sank down on the bed.

The ringing of the telephone woke me up. I was startled to see that the room was in darkness. I fumbled for the light, and glanced at the clock as I picked up the phone on the bedside table. It was eight o'clock. I had been asleep for six hours.

'Hello.' I knew I sounded groggy.

'Ellie, it's Joan. Something terrible has happened. Old Mrs Westerfield's housekeeper went into Stroebel's delicatessen this afternoon and shouted at Paulie, telling him to admit he'd killed Andrea. She said it was his fault that the Westerfield family was being tortured. Paulie went into the bathroom and slit his wrists. He's in intensive care in the hospital. He's lost so much blood that they don't think he's going to live.'

I FOUND MRS STROEBEL in the waiting room outside the intensive-care unit. She was weeping quietly, the tears running down her cheeks. Her lips were clamped together tightly, as though she was afraid that parting them would release a tidal wave of grief. Her coat was round her shoulders, and even though her cardigan and skirt were dark blue, I could see dark stains that I was sure had been caused by Paulie's blood.

A large-framed woman of about fifty was sitting protectively close to her. She looked up at me, a hint of hostility on her face.

I wasn't sure what to expect from Mrs Stroebel. It was my website that had triggered the housekeeper's verbal attack. But Mrs Stroebel stood up and walked across the room to meet me. '*You* understand, Ellie, what they have done to my son,' she sobbed.

I put my arms round her. 'I do understand, Mrs Stroebel.' I looked over her head at the other woman.

She knew the question my eyes were silently asking and made a gesture with her hand, which I took to mean that it was too soon to tell if Paulie would make it. Then she introduced herself. 'I'm Greta Bergner. I work with Mrs Stroebel and Paulie in the delicatessen. I thought you might be a reporter.'

We sat together for the next twelve hours. From time to time we went in and stood at the entrance to the cubicle where Paulie was lying, an oxygen mask over his face, tubes in his arms, heavy bandages on his wrists. During that long night, as I observed the agony on Mrs Stroebel's face and watched her lips move in silent prayer, I found myself praying as well.

At nine fifteen a doctor came into the waiting room. 'Paulie is stabilised,' he said. 'He'll make it. Why don't you people go home and get some sleep?'

I TOOK A CAB back from the hospital. Along the way I had the driver stop so I could pick up the morning papers. I had only to glance at the front page of the *Westchester Post* to be grateful that in the intensive-care unit Paulie Stroebel did not have access to newspapers.

The headline was MURDER SUSPECT ATTEMPTS SUICIDE. The photo on the left was of Will Nebels. The one on the right was of a woman with severe features, in her mid-sixties. The centre photo was of Paulie behind the counter of the deli, a bread knife in his hand, and a surly expression on his face. The story was continued on page three, but I had to put off reading it—the cab was pulling up to the inn. Once in my room, I turned again to the newspaper.

The woman in the photo was Lillian Beckerson, Dorothy Westerfield's housekeeper of thirty-one years. 'Mrs Westerfield is one of the finest human beings who ever walked the face of the earth,' the newspaper quoted her as saying. 'Her husband was a United States senator, his grandfather was governor of New York. She's lived with this stain on her family name for over twenty years. Now, when her only grandchild is trying to prove his innocence, that woman who lied on the witness stand as a child is back trying to destroy him again.'

That's me, I thought.

'Mrs Westerfield was looking at that website and crying yesterday. I marched myself into that delicatessen and yelled at that man to admit what he had done. He kept saying, "I'm sorry. I'm sorry." Now, if you were innocent, would you have said that?'

You would if you were Paulie, I thought. I forced myself to keep reading. Colin Marsh, the guy who wrote this story, was one of those sensationalists who knows how to elicit and then manipulate provocative quotes.

He had looked up Emma Watkins, the guidance counsellor who

years ago swore on the stand that Paulie had sobbed, 'I didn't think she was dead,' when the class was told about Andrea. Miss Watkins told Marsh that she had always been troubled by Rob Westerfield's conviction. She said that Paulie was easily agitated, and that, if he had learned that Andrea had been joking about going with him to the dance, he might have been upset enough to lash out.

Lash out—what a delicate way to put it, I thought.

Will Nebels, that sleaze who used to like to hug teenage girls, was extensively quoted. With even more of a flourish than he had exhibited on television, he told Marsh about seeing Paulie go into the garage hide-out that night, carrying a heavy object.

I threw the paper onto the bed. I was both furious and worried. The case was being tried in the press, and I realised that, if I had read the story cold, even I might have been convinced that the wrong man had been convicted.

I opened the computer and got busy.

In a mistaken gesture of loyalty, Mrs Dorothy Westerfield's housekeeper stormed into Stroebel's delicatessen and verbally attacked Paulie Stroebel. A few hours later Paulie, already under great stress thanks to lies perpetrated by the Westerfield money machine, attempted suicide.

My sympathy goes out to Mrs Dorothy Westerfield—by all accounts a truly fine woman—for the pain she has suffered because of the crime committed by her grandson. I believe that she will find peace by accepting the fact that her proud family name may still be respected.

She needs to leave her vast fortune to charity. Leaving it to a killer compounds the tragedy that more than twenty years ago took my sister's life and that yesterday very nearly cost Paulie Stroebel his life.

As I transferred the text to the website, my cellphone rang.

'I been reading the papers.'

I immediately recognised the voice. It was the man who claimed to have been in prison with Rob Westerfield and said he heard him confess to another murder.

'I've been hoping to hear from you.' I tried to sound noncommittal.

'The way I see it, Westerfield's doing a good job of making that loony Stroebel look bad.'

'He's not a loony,' I snapped.

'Have it your way. Here's the deal. Five thousand bucks. I give you the first name of the guy Westerfield bragged about killing.'

'The *first* name!'

'It's all I know. Take it or leave it. I need the money by Friday.'

Today was Monday. I had about $3,000 in a savings account in Atlanta, and, much as I hated the thought, I could borrow the rest from Pete if the book advance didn't come through by Friday.

'Well?' His voice was impatient.

I knew there was a very good chance I was being conned, but it was a chance I decided to take.

'I'll have the money by Friday,' I promised.

Eight

By Wednesday evening I was reasonably back to normal. I had credit cards, a driver's licence and money. An advance on the book had been electronically transferred to a bank near the inn. The superintendent's wife in Atlanta had gone to my apartment, packed some clothes and shipped them to me overnight. My feet were healing. Most important, I had an appointment on Thursday in Boston with Christopher Cassidy, the student at Arbinger who had been severely beaten by Rob Westerfield.

On the other hand, Joan had been in touch with Andrea's high-school friends, and not one of them saw her wear any locket except the one my father had given her.

Every day I was running a description of the locket on the website, asking for any information anyone might be able to supply. So far there had been no results. My email was full of comments. Some praised what I was doing. Others vehemently objected to it. I had my share of weirdos writing as well. Two confessed to the murder. One said Andrea was still alive and wanted me to rescue her.

A couple of the letters threatened me. The one that I believed was genuine said he was very disappointed to see me escape from the fire. He added, 'Cute nightshirt. L.L.Bean, wasn't it?'

Had the writer been watching the fire from the woods, or could he be the intruder who had been in the apartment? Either prospect was intimidating and, if I wanted to admit it to myself, frightening.

I was in touch with Mrs Stroebel several times a day, and, as Paulie started to mend, the relief in her voice became more and more evident. However, so did the concern. 'Ellie, if there is a new trial and Paulie has to testify, I am afraid he will do this to himself again.' Then she added, 'My friends see your website. They say everyone should have a champion like you. I tell Paulie about it. He would like you to visit him.'

I promised I would go on Saturday.

Except for the errands I'd completed, I'd been staying in the room, working on the book and having my meals sent up by room service. But at seven o'clock on Wednesday evening I decided to go downstairs for dinner.

The dining room here was not unlike the one at the Parkinson Inn, but it had a more formal feeling. The table linen was white instead of chequerboard red and white, and the diners were vintage senior citizens, not the exuberant groups that frequented the Parkinson.

But the food was equally good, and after debating between rack of lamb and swordfish, I succumbed to what I really felt like having— the lamb.

I took from my bag a book I'd been wanting to read and for the next hour enjoyed the combination I love: a good dinner and a good book. I was deeply into the story when the waitress cleared the table and spoke to me.

'The gentleman at the next table would like to offer you an after-dinner drink.'

I think I knew it was Rob Westerfield even before I turned my head. He was sitting not more than six feet from me, a wineglass in his hand. He raised it and smiled.

'He asked if I knew your name, miss, and wrote this note.'

She handed me a card with Westerfield's full name embossed on the front: ROBSON PARKE WESTERFIELD. I flipped the card over. On the back he had written: *Andrea was cute, but you're beautiful.*

I got up, walked over to him, tore up the card and dropped the pieces in his wineglass. 'Maybe you want to give me the locket you took back after you killed her,' I suggested.

His pupils widened, and the teasing expression in his cobalt-blue eyes disappeared. For an instant I thought he would spring up and attack me.

I jerked my head at the waitress. 'Bring Mr Westerfield another glass of wine, please, and put it on my bill.'

SOMETIME DURING THE NIGHT the alarm was disabled on my car and the gas tank jemmied open. A very efficient way to destroy a car is to pour sugar into the gas tank.

The Oldham police in the form of Officer White responded to my call about my trashed BMW. While he didn't quite accuse me of pouring sugar into my own gas tank, he did mention that the fire in Mrs Hilmer's garage was definitely set, and that the remnants of the gasoline-soaked towels that had started the blaze were identical with the towels Mrs Hilmer had left in the linen closet of the apartment.

'Quite a coincidence, Ms Cavanaugh,' he said. 'Or is it?'

I DROVE A RENTED CAR to Boston for my appointment with Christopher Cassidy. I was furious that my own car had been trashed and concerned because I knew there was something else to be faced. I had thought that the intruder in the apartment had been looking for material that I might be using on the website. Now I wondered if his main reason for being there was to steal items to set the fire that almost took my life.

I knew, of course, that Rob Westerfield was behind it and that he had thugs like the one who came up to me in the parking lot at Sing Sing to do his dirty work for him.

The forecast had been for cloudy skies, but light snow began fifty miles outside Boston. The result was slippery roads and crawling traffic. I kept glancing at the clock on the dashboard, agonising at the traffic's slow pace. Christopher Cassidy's secretary had warned me that he was squeezing time for me into a very full day.

It was four minutes to two when I arrived breathlessly for the appointment, and Cassidy's secretary promptly escorted me to his private office. As I followed her in, I reviewed everything I had learned about Cassidy on the Internet: top of his class at Yale, a master's degree from the Harvard Business School, generous donor to many charities. He was forty-two years old, married, had a fifteen-year-old daughter and was an avid sportsman.

Obviously, quite a guy.

The minute I entered the room, he came out from behind his desk and extended his hand. 'I'm glad to see you, Ms Cavanaugh. Is it OK if I call you Ellie? I feel as though I know you. Why don't we sit here?' He indicated the sitting area near the window.

I chose the couch. He sat on the edge of the chair opposite me. 'Coffee or tea?' he asked.

'Coffee, please, black,' I said gratefully.

He picked up the phone from the table at his elbow. In the brief moment he spoke to his secretary, I had a chance to study him. His well-cut, dark blue business suit and white shirt were conservative, but the red tie with tiny golf clubs suggested a touch of the maverick. He had broad shoulders, a solid but trim body, a good head of sable hair, and deep-set hazel eyes.

He came directly to the point. 'Craig Parshall told me why you wanted to talk to me.'

'Then you know that Rob Westerfield is out of prison and probably will get a new trial.'

'And that he's trying to blame the death of your sister on someone else. Yes, I do know that. Blaming someone else for what he does is an old trick of his. He was pulling it when he was fourteen years old.'

'That's exactly the kind of information I want to put on the website. The Westerfields have found a so-called eyewitness to lie for them. In a second trial they have a good chance of getting an acquittal. Rob Westerfield becomes the martyr who spent over twenty years in prison for another man's crime. I can't let it happen.'

'What do you want me to tell you?'

'According to Craig Parshall, Westerfield beat you up pretty viciously when you both were at Arbinger.'

'We were both good athletes. There was one starting spot on the varsity for a running back. I got it. I guess he was brooding over it. A day or so later I was on my way back to the dorm from the library, a load of books in my arms. He came up behind me and punched me in the neck. Before I could react, he was all over me. I ended up with a broken nose and jaw.'

'And no one stopped him?'

'He had picked his time. There was no one around. Then he tried to say I started it. Fortunately, a senior happened to be looking out of the window and witnessed what happened. Of course, the school didn't want a scandal. The Westerfields have been big donors for generations. My father was ready to file charges but was offered a full scholarship for my younger brother if he'd reconsider. I'm sure that the Westerfields paid for that so-called scholarship.'

The coffee arrived. Cassidy looked reflective as he raised the cup to his lips. 'To the credit of the school, Rob was forced to withdraw at the end of the term.'

'May I tell this story on my website?'

'Absolutely. I remember when your sister died. I read every account of the trial because of Westerfield. At the time, I wished I could get on the stand and tell them what kind of animal he is. I have a daughter the age of your sister when she died. I can only imagine what your whole family went through.'

I nodded. 'It destroyed us as a family.'

'I'm not surprised.'

'Before he attacked you, did you have much contact with him in school?'

'I was the son of a short-order cook, on scholarship. He was a Westerfield. He didn't have time for me, and we pursued different activities. He joined the drama club and was in a couple of productions. I saw them, and I have to admit he was very good. He wasn't the lead in either play, but he was voted best actor for one of them, so I guess that kept him happy for a while.'

Cassidy stood up, and reluctantly I got up, too. 'You've been very kind—' I started to say, but he interrupted me.

'You know, I just remembered something. Westerfield obviously loved the limelight and didn't want to lose his moment of glory. He wore a dark blond wig in that play, and lest we forget how good he'd been, he used to put it on sometimes. Then he'd put on the mannerisms of the character, and I remember he even signed that character's name when he passed notes in class.'

I thought of Rob Westerfield showing up at the inn last evening and giving the waitress the impression he was flirting with me. 'He's still acting,' I said grimly.

I GRABBED A QUICK LUNCH and was back in the car at three thirty. The snow was continuing to fall, and the trip up to Boston began to seem like a picnic compared to the trek back. I kept the cellphone next to me on the front seat so I wouldn't miss the call from the guy who'd been in prison with Westerfield. He had insisted he needed the money by Friday.

It was ten thirty that night when I finally got back to the inn. I was just inside my room when the cellphone rang. It was the call I was expecting, but this time the voice I heard was agitated.

'Listen, I think I've been set up. I may not get out of here.'

'Where are you?'

'Listen to me. If I give you the name, can I trust you to pay me?'

'Yes, you can.'

'Westerfield must've figured I might be trouble for him. He's had a ton of money since he was born. I've had nothing. If I get out of here and you pay me, I'll at least have some. If I don't, then maybe you can get Westerfield for me on a murder charge.'

'I swear I'll pay you. I'll nail Westerfield for you.'

'Westerfield told me, "I beat Phil to death, and it felt good." Got that? Phil—that's the name.'

The line went dead.

ROB WESTERFIELD had been nineteen years old when he murdered Andrea. Within a year he had been arrested, indicted, tried, convicted, and sent to prison. Though he had been out on bail prior to his conviction, I could not believe that during those twelve months he would have risked killing someone else. That meant the crime had been committed earlier, between twenty-three and twenty-nine years ago. It was incredible to think that at thirteen or fourteen Rob might have committed a murder. Or was it? He'd been only fourteen when he assaulted Christopher Cassidy.

I reasoned that in those years he had been at Arbinger for a year and a half, then spent six months at a public school near Bath, in England, two years in Carrington Academy, and a term or so at Willow College, a nondescript school near Buffalo. The Westerfields have a house in Vail and another in Palm Beach. Rob must have visited those places. He also may have gone on class trips abroad.

That was a lot of territory to cover. I knew I needed help.

Marcus Longo had been a detective with the Westchester County District Attorney's Office for twenty-five years. If anyone could track down the homicide of a man with only a first name as a clue, my money would be on him.

Fortunately, when I phoned Marcus, I reached him instead of an answering machine. He was back from Colorado. 'I was going to tell you all about the baby,' he said, 'but that can hold. I understand a lot of things have happened since I've been gone.'

'I would have to agree with that, Marcus. May I buy you lunch? I need some advice.'

'The advice is free. I buy the lunch.'

We met at the Depot Restaurant in Cold Spring. There, over club sandwiches and coffee, I filled him in on my eventful week. He stopped me regularly with questions.

'Do you think the fire was set to scare you or actually to kill you?'

'I was more than scared. I wasn't sure I'd get out alive.'

'All right. And the Oldham police think you set it?'

'Detective Bannister has done everything but cuff me.'

'His cousin is a member of the same country club as Rob's father. That website is mighty provocative to anyone who's hand in glove with the Westerfields.'

'Then it's a success. Marcus—' I looked around to make sure that I could not be overheard.

'Ellie, do you realise your eyes keep darting around this place? Who or what are you looking for?'

I told him about Rob Westerfield showing up at the inn. 'He didn't get there until I'd almost finished dinner,' I said. 'Someone tipped him off. I'm sure of it.'

I knew that Marcus would warn me to stop putting inflammatory material on the website. I didn't give him the chance. 'Marcus, I received a call from someone who was in prison with Rob.' I told him about the deal I had made to buy information and then about the phone call last night.

He listened quietly, his eyes searching my face. He heard me out, then asked, 'You believe this guy?'

'Marcus, I knew I might be suckered into losing five thousand dollars. But this man was in fear of his life. He wanted me to know about Phil because he wanted revenge on Westerfield.'

'He referred to the sign you were holding up outside the prison?'

'Yes.'

'You're assuming he was a convict, so that means he probably was released that day.'

'That's right. I was hoping you could get a list of the prisoners discharged the day after Westerfield, then see if anything happened to any one of them.'

'I can do that. Ellie, you realise this also could be some nut playing games.'

'I know that, but I don't think so.' I opened my bag. 'I've made a list of the schools Rob Westerfield attended and the places where his family has homes. Does Westchester County have a database listing unsolved homicides that took place between twenty-three and twenty-nine years ago?'

'Yes.'

'Can you access it or get someone else to do it for you?'

'Yes, I can.'

'How about checking these areas, and looking for a victim whose name is Phil?'

He looked at the list. 'Massachusetts, Maine, Florida, Colorado, New York, England.' He whistled. 'That's a lot of territory. I'll see what I can do.'

'Tomorrow I'm going to put Christopher Cassidy's story on the website. No one would question his integrity. I haven't been up to Carrington yet, but I have an appointment on Monday.'

'Check the student roster there,' Marcus said as he signalled for the bill.

'I've thought of that. One of the schools might have had a student named Phil who tangled with Westerfield.'

'That opens the territory,' he warned. 'The students in prep school come from all over the country. Westerfield could have followed one of them home to settle a grudge.'

I beat Phil to death, and it felt good.

Who were the people who loved Phil? I wondered. Were they still grieving? Of course they were.

The waitress was placing the tab in front of Marcus. I waited until she had gone before I said, 'I can call my contact at Arbinger, and when I go to Carrington and Willow College I'll ask about students from Westerfield's time. Philip isn't that common a name.'

'Ellie, you told me you believe Rob Westerfield was tipped off that you were at dinner the other night?'

'Yes.'

'You told me your informant claimed to be in fear of his life?'

'Yes.'

'Ellie, Rob Westerfield is worried your website could influence his grandmother to leave her money to charity. Now he may be terrified that you could uncover another crime that might send him back to prison. Don't you realise how precarious your situation is?'

'I honestly do, but there's nothing I can do about it.'

'Yes, you can, Ellie! Your father's a retired state trooper. You could live in his house. He could be your bodyguard. Trust me, you need one. And something else: if that guy's story is on the level, helping to put Westerfield back in prison would help your father have closure, too. I don't think you understand how tough this has been on him.'

'He's been in touch with you?'

'Yes, he has.'

'Marcus, you mean well,' I said as we stood up, 'but I don't think you understand something. My father got his closure when he let us go and never lifted a finger to bring us back. Next time he calls, tell him to watch his son play basketball and leave me alone.'

Marcus gave me a hug as we separated in the parking lot. 'I'll call you as soon as I start getting answers,' he promised.

I drove back to the inn. Mrs Willis was at the desk. 'Your brother is waiting for you in the sunroom,' she said.

HE WAS STANDING in front of the window, looking out, his back to me. He was a good six foot three—taller than I'd realised when I saw him on television. He was wearing khaki trousers and sneakers and his school jacket. His hands were in his pockets, and he was jiggling his right foot. I had the impression that he was nervous.

He must have heard my footsteps, because he turned round. We looked at each other.

'Hello, Ellie. I'm your brother, Teddy.' He walked to me, holding out his hand.

I ignored it.

'Can't I just talk to you for five minutes?' His voice had not yet fully deepened, but it was well modulated. He looked determined.

I shook my head and turned to leave.

'You're my sister,' he said. 'You could at least give me five minutes. You might even like me if you knew me.'

I turned back to him. 'Teddy, you seem like a nice young man, but I'm sure you have better things to do than spend time with me. I know you've been sent by your father. He just doesn't seem to get the fact that I never want to see or hear from him again.'

'He's your father, too. Whether you believe it or not, he never stopped being your father. He didn't send me. He doesn't know I'm here. I came because I wanted to meet you. I've always wanted to meet you.' There was appeal in his voice. 'Why don't we have a soda or something?'

I shook my head.

'Please, Ellie.'

Maybe it was the way my name fell from his lips, or maybe I just have a hard time being downright rude. This kid hadn't done anything to me, anyway. I heard myself saying, 'There's a soda machine in the hall.' I started to dig in my bag.

'I've got it. What kind do you want?'

'Plain water.'

'Me too. I'll be right back.' His smile was both shy and relieved.

I sat on a brightly patterned wicker love seat, trying to figure out how to send him away. I didn't want to listen to a pitch about what a great father we had and how I should let bygones be bygones. Maybe he *was* a great father for Andrea and you, I thought, but I slipped between the cracks.

Teddy returned carrying two bottles of water. He sat in a chair. 'Ellie, would you come and see me play basketball sometime?'

It wasn't what I expected.

'I mean, couldn't we be friends at least? I always kept hoping you'd come and visit us. Maybe you and I can get together sometimes. I read your book last year, about the cases you've worked on.'

'Teddy, I'm awfully busy right now and—'

'I watch your website every day. The way you write about Westerfield must be driving him crazy. Ellie, you're my sister, and I don't want anything to happen to you.'

I wanted to say, 'Please don't call me your sister', but the words died on my lips. I settled for, 'Please don't worry about me. I can take care of myself.'

'Can't I help you? This morning I read in the paper about what happened to your car. Suppose somebody loosens a wheel or a brake in the one you're driving now? I'm good with cars. I could check yours out for you before you go anywhere, or I could even drive you round in mine.'

He was so earnest that I had to smile. 'Teddy, you have school and, I'm sure, plenty of basketball practice. Now I honestly have to work.'

He stood up with me. 'We look a lot alike,' he said.

'I know we do.'

'I'm glad. Ellie, I'm going now, but I'm coming back.'

Would to God your father had had the same persistence, I thought. Then I realised that, if he had, this boy would never have been born.

I WORKED FOR A COUPLE OF HOURS, refining the way I would present Christopher Cassidy's story for the website. When I thought I had it right, I emailed it to his office for his approval.

At four o'clock Marcus Longo called. 'Ellie, the Westerfields have taken a page out of your book. They have set up a website, too—comjusrob.com.'

'Let me guess what it stands for: "Committee for Justice for Rob".'

'You have it. I understand they've taken out ads for it in all the Westchester papers. Basically, the strategy is to present touching stories of people who were wrongly convicted of crimes.'

'Thereby linking them to Rob Westerfield, the most innocent of them all.'

'You've got it. Ellie, are you planning to put anything on your website about the other possible homicide?'

'I'm not sure. On the one hand, someone who sees it might come forward with information about a murder victim. On the other hand, it might tip off Rob Westerfield and in some way help him to cover his tracks.'

'Or to get rid of someone who could give damaging testimony against him.'

'That may already have happened.'

'Exactly. You must be very careful. Let me know what you decide.'

I WENT ONLINE and found the website of the Committee for Justice for Robson Westerfield.

It had been handsomely designed. There was a picture of a grave and contemplative Rob Westerfield, followed by stories of people who had been imprisoned for someone else's crime. The stories were well written and pulled on heartstrings. It didn't take a great leap to figure out that Jake Bern had been the author.

The personal section on the website made the Westerfields sound like American royalty. There were pictures of Rob as a baby with his grandfather, the United States senator, and at the age of nine or ten with his grandmother, helping her cut the ribbon on a new Westerfield children's centre. There were shots of him with his parents boarding the *Queen Elizabeth II* and dressed in tennis whites at the Everglades Club.

I guess the idea was to convey that it was beneath the dignity of this privileged young man to take a human life.

I clicked off. I sat for half an hour reviewing the pros and cons and trying to figure out how to handle publicising Westerfield's alleged confession of another murder.

Marcus Longo had talked about a territorial problem in trying to track down an unsolved homicide Rob Westerfield may have committed. The website was international. Would I be exposing anyone to risk by putting the name of the supposed victim out there?

But my unidentified caller was already at risk, and he knew it.

In the end I composed a simple entry:

> Sometime between twenty-three and twenty-nine years ago, it is alleged, Rob Westerfield committed another crime. He is quoted as saying, when he was high on drugs in prison, 'I beat Phil to death, and it felt good.' Anyone with information about this crime, please email me at ellie1234@mediaone.net. Confidentiality and reward.

I looked it over. Rob Westerfield will certainly read it, I thought. My unknown caller knows he's at risk, but suppose Rob knows someone else who has information that could hurt him?

There are two things an investigative reporter does not do: reveal sources and place innocent people in danger.

I put the entry on hold.

THAT EVENING I broke down and phoned Pete Lawlor.

'Your call is being forwarded to an answering service.'

'This is your former coworker who has enough interest in your well-being to enquire as to your state of mind, job opportunities, and health,' I said. 'A response will be appreciated.'

He called back half an hour later. 'You must be hard up for someone to talk to.'

'That's why you came to mind. May I ask where you are?'

'In Atlanta, packing up.'

'I gather a decision has been made?'

'Yes. A dream job. Based in New York, but with reporting from hot spots all over the globe.'

'Which newspaper?'

'Negative. I'm going to be a television star.'

'Did you have to lose ten pounds before they hired you?'

'I don't remember you as being cruel.'

I laughed. Talking to Pete had a way of bringing a dash of amusing everyday reality into my increasingly surreal life. 'Do you really have a job in television?'

'It's for real. It's with Packard Cable—one of the newer cable networks, but growing fast.'

'That's great. When do you start?'

'Wednesday. I'm in the process of subletting the apartment and putting stuff together to load in the car. I start driving up on Sunday afternoon. Dinner Tuesday?'

'Sure. It's good to hear your melodious voice.'

'Don't hang up. Ellie, I've been watching your website. If this guy is what you say he is, you're playing with fire.'

I already have, I thought. 'Promise you won't tell me to be careful.'

'I promise. Talk to you on Tuesday morning.'

It was nearly eight o'clock, and I'd been working steadily. I ordered room service, and while I was waiting I did a few stretches and a lot of thinking.

Talking to Pete had removed, at least for the moment, my tunnel vision. For the last couple of weeks I had existed in a world in which Rob Westerfield was the central figure. Now, for just a moment, I was looking past that time, past his second trial, past my ability to prove to the world the depth of his violent nature.

I could dig up and publicise every nasty, rotten thing he'd ever done. Perhaps I could track down an unsolved murder he had committed. I could tell his sorry, dirty story in the book. Then it would be time for me to begin the rest of my life.

Pete was already beginning his—a new base in New York, a new job in a different medium.

I locked my hands behind my head and began to twist from side to side. My neck muscles were tight, and it felt good to try to stretch them. What was not so good was the dismaying realisation that I missed Pete Lawlor terribly and would not want to return to Atlanta unless he was there.

I SPOKE TO MRS STROEBEL on Saturday morning. She told me that Paulie was no longer in intensive care and probably would be discharged after the weekend. I promised to drop by at three o'clock.

When I arrived, Mrs Stroebel was sitting by Paulie's bed. As soon as she looked up, I could see the concern on her face.

'He developed a high fever around lunchtime. There is an infection in one of his arms. The doctor tells me it will be all right, but I worry. Ellie, I worry so.'

I looked down at Paulie. His arms were still heavily bandaged, and he had several IVs dripping from overhead pulleys. He was very pale and kept turning his head from side to side.

'They are giving him an antibiotic and something to calm him down,' Mrs Stroebel said. 'The fever makes him restless.'

I pulled up a chair and sat beside her.

Paulie began to mumble. His eyes flickered open.

'I am here, Paulie,' Mrs Stroebel said soothingly. 'Ellie Cavanaugh is here with me. She came to visit.'

'Hi, Paulie.' I stood up and leaned over the bed.

His eyes were glazed with fever, but he tried to smile. 'Ellie, my friend.'

'You bet I am.'

His eyes closed again. A moment later he began to mutter incoherently. I heard him whisper Andrea's name.

Mrs Stroebel clasped and unclasped her hands. 'He is so afraid they will make him go back to court. No one understands how much they frightened him last time.'

Paulie whispered, 'But, Mama . . . suppose I forget . . .'

Mrs Stroebel seemed suddenly flustered. 'No more talk, Paulie,' she said abruptly. 'Go to sleep. You must get better.'

'Mama—'

'Paulie.' She laid a gentle but resolute hand on his lips.

I had the distinct feeling that Mrs Stroebel wanted me to leave, so I got up to go. She sprang up with me. 'Tell Paulie goodbye for me,' I said. 'I'll call tomorrow to see how he's doing.'

Paulie was beginning to talk again, tossing restlessly and mumbling incoherently.

'Thank you, Ellie. Goodbye.' Mrs Stroebel began propelling me to the door.

'Andrea,' Paulie shouted, 'don't go out with him!'

I spun round.

Paulie's voice was still clear, but now his tone was frightened and pleading. 'Mama, suppose I forget and tell them about the locket she was wearing? If I forget, you won't let them put me in prison, will you?'

Nine

'There is an explanation. You must believe me. It is not what you think,' Mrs Stroebel sobbed to me as we stood in the corridor outside Paulie's room.

'We have to talk, and you have to be absolutely honest with me,' I said. We couldn't do it then, though—Paulie's doctor was coming down the corridor.

'Ellie, I will call you tomorrow,' she promised, struggling to regain her composure.

I drove back to the inn on automatic pilot. Was it possible, was it *remotely* possible that all this time I had been wrong? Had Rob Westerfield—and indeed his whole family—been victimised by a terrible miscarriage of justice?

Paulie's response to a verbal attack had been to hurt himself, not someone else. I could not believe that Paulie had been Andrea's murderer. But I was sure that years ago Mrs Stroebel had kept him from telling something he knew.

The locket.

As I drove into the parking lot of the inn, I was overwhelmed with a crushing sense of the irony of what was happening. No one, absolutely no one believed that Rob Westerfield had given Andrea a locket and that she had been wearing it the night she died. But now the existence of the locket had been validated by the one person who would be terrified to publicly admit any knowledge of it.

I looked around as I got out of the car. It was a quarter past four, and the shadows were already long and slanting. A light wind was blowing the remaining leaves from the trees. They rustled along the driveway, and in my edgy frame of mind they sounded like footsteps.

The parking lot was almost full, and to find a space I had to drive to the furthest section, out of sight of the inn. I moved quickly as I made my way through the rows of cars. As I passed an old van, the door suddenly slid open, and a man jumped out.

I began to run, then tripped on one of the extra-large moccasins I'd bought to accommodate my bandaged feet. I frantically tried to regain my balance, but it was too late. My palms caught the worst of the fall, and every ounce of breath was knocked out of me.

The man was immediately down on one knee beside me. 'Don't scream,' he said. 'I'm not going to hurt you. Please don't scream!'

I couldn't have screamed. Nor could I have got away from him. My entire body was shaking from the impact.

'I was gonna email you, but I didn't know who might see it. I want to sell you information about Rob Westerfield.'

I looked up at him. His face was very close to mine. He was a man somewhere in his early forties, with thin, not particularly clean hair. He had a nervous way of sliding his eyes around, like someone who expects to have to make a run for it at any moment. He was wearing a worn lumber jacket and jeans.

I struggled to my feet.

'I'm not going to hurt you,' he repeated. 'It's risky for me to be seen with you. Hear me out. Are you willing to listen?'

If he had wanted to kill me, he'd had all the chance he needed. 'Go ahead,' I said.

'Would you sit in my van for a couple of minutes? The Westerfields' people are all over this town.'

'Say what you have to say out here.'

'I have something that maybe might stick Westerfield with a crime he committed years ago.'

'How much do you want?'

'A thousand bucks.'

'What have you got?'

'You know that Westerfield's grandmother was shot and left for dead about twenty-five years ago. My brother, Skip—he went to prison for that job. He died after he'd served half his time. Couldn't take it. He was always kind of sickly.'

'Your brother was the one who shot Mrs Westerfield and burgled her home?'

'Yeah, but Westerfield planned it, see, and hired us to do the job.'

'Why did he do it?'

'Westerfield was heavy into drugs. That's why he dropped out of college. He owed people big time. He'd seen his grandmother's will. The minute she croaked, a hundred thousand dollars would be in his pocket. He promised us ten thousand to do the job.'

'Was he with you that night?'

'Are you kidding? He was in New York at a dinner with his mother and father. He knew how to cover his back. My brother was picked up the next day. He had a record and was nervous about having to shoot the old lady. That was the reason he was there, but Westerfield wanted it to look like a burglary. Rob didn't give us the combination of the safe, because only the family knew it, and that would have given him away. He told Skip to bring a chisel and knife and scratch up the safe like he tried to force it open and couldn't. But Skip cut his hand and took off his glove to wipe it. He must have touched the safe, because they found his fingerprint on it.'

'Then he went upstairs and shot Mrs Westerfield.'

'Yeah. But nobody could prove I was there. I was the lookout and drove the car. Skip told me to keep my mouth shut. He took the rap, and Westerfield got off scot-free.'

'So did you.'

He shrugged. 'Yeah, I know.'

'How old were you?'

'Sixteen.'

'How old was Westerfield?'

'Seventeen.'

'Didn't your brother try to implicate Westerfield?'

'Sure. Nobody believed him.'

'I'm not certain about that. His grandmother changed her will. That hundred-thousand-dollar direct grant was taken out of it.'

'Good. They let Skip plead to attempted murder with a twenty-year sentence. He could have got thirty, but he was willing to plead to a max of twenty. The DA agreed to the deal so that the old lady wouldn't have to testify at a trial.'

'What's your name?' I asked.

'Alfie. Alfie Leeds.'

'Alfie, I don't know why you're telling me this. There's never been a shred of evidence that Rob Westerfield was in on that crime.'

'I have proof he was involved.'

Alfie reached into his pocket and pulled out a folded sheet of paper. 'This is a copy of the diagram Westerfield gave us so that my brother could get into the house.'

I recognised the Westerfield house and driveway. The garage hide-out was even depicted. Below the buildings there was a precise layout of the interior of the mansion.

'See, it shows where the alarm is and gives the code. Rob wasn't worried that disarming the alarm would draw attention to himself, because a lot of handymen and other employees knew the code, too. There's the library with the safe, the stairs to the old lady's bedroom, the section off the kitchen that was the maid's apartment.'

There was a name at the bottom of the page. 'Who's Jim?'

'The guy who drew this. Westerfield told Skip and me that he did some work on the house. We never met him.'

'Did your brother ever show this to the police?'

'He wanted to use it, but the lawyer they gave him said forget it. He said Skip had no proof Westerfield gave it to him, and the fact that he even had it just made Skip look bad.'

'Jim could have corroborated your brother's story. Did anyone try to find him?'

'I guess not. Have we got a deal? A thousand bucks for it?'

'How can I be sure that this isn't something you drew up?'

'You can't.'

'Alfie, if the lawyer had looked into this guy, Jim, and had told the DA about him and had shown the DA the sketch, they would have had to investigate the information seriously. Your brother might have got a better sentence in exchange for his cooperation, and Westerfield might have paid for his crime, too.'

'Yeah, but there was another problem. Westerfield hired both my brother and me to do the job. The lawyer told my brother that if the cops ended up arresting Westerfield, he could make his own deal and tell the DA that I was involved. Skip was five years older than me and felt guilty about getting me into it.'

'Well, the statute of limitations has run out for both you and Rob. But wait a minute. You say this is a copy of the original. Where is the original?'

'The lawyer tore it up. He said he didn't want it to fall in the wrong hands. He didn't know Skip had made a copy and given it to me.'

'I want this. I'll have the cash for you in the morning,' I said.

We shook hands. His skin felt somewhat grimy, but it was also callused, which said to me that Alfie did hard, heavy work.

As he carefully folded the paper into neat squares and put it in his inside pocket, I couldn't help saying, 'With this kind of evidence I just can't understand why your brother's lawyer didn't try to make a deal with the district attorney. It wouldn't have been hard to follow up on an employee named Jim who drew this diagram. The cops could have squeezed him to give up Rob, and you would have been tried in juvenile court. I wonder if your brother's lawyer sold out to the Westerfields.'

He smiled, baring stained teeth. 'He's working for them now. He's that Hamilton guy, the one who's all over television saying he's going to get a new trial and acquittal for Rob.'

WHEN I GOT BACK to the room, there was a message to call Mrs Hilmer. I'd spoken to her several times since the fire, and she'd been simply wonderful to me. Her whole concern was about my almost being trapped in the fire. You would have thought I'd done her a favour by being the reason the garage and apartment had been reduced to rubble. I agreed to have Sunday dinner with her.

I'd barely hung up, when Joan called. I'd also been speaking to her, but we hadn't seen each other during the week and I was anxious to return the money and clothes I'd borrowed. I'd had the slacks, sweater and jacket cleaned and the lingerie laundered, and I bought a bottle of champagne for Joan and Leo and another for the friend who was my size.

Of course that was not Joan's reason for calling. She and Leo and the kids were going out for dinner to Il Palazzo and wanted me to join them. 'Great pasta, great pizza, a fun place,' she promised. 'I really think you'd enjoy it.'

'You don't have to sell me. I'd love to go.'

In fact, after my parking lot encounter with Alfie I needed to get out. We agreed to meet at Il Palazzo at seven o'clock.

Joan and Leo and their three boys were seated at a corner table when I got there. I vaguely remembered Leo. He had been a senior at Oldham High when Joan and Andrea were sophomores.

It's inevitable that when people from those days see me for the first time, the first thing they think about is Andrea's death. They invariably comment on it or make an obvious effort to ignore it. I liked the way Leo handled his greeting to me. He said, 'I remember you, of course, Ellie. You were over at Joan's house with Andrea a couple of times when I stopped by. You were a solemn little kid.'

'And now I'm a solemn *big* kid,' I told him.

I liked him immediately. He was about six foot tall, solidly built, with intelligent dark eyes.

The boys' ages were ten, fourteen and seventeen. The oldest, Billy, was a senior in high school and almost immediately told me that his team had played basketball against Teddy's team. 'Teddy and I talked about the colleges we're applying to,' he said. 'He's a nice guy.'

'Yes, he is,' I agreed.

'You didn't tell me you'd met him,' Joan said to me. There was a satisfied look in her eyes.

'He stopped in to see me at the inn for a few minutes.'

The menus arrived, and Leo was smart enough to change the subject. My job in Atlanta certainly didn't expose me to many kids, but it was a treat to be with these three boys. Pretty soon, over mussels and pasta, they were talking away to me about their activities, and I promised Sean, the ten-year-old, that I'd play chess with him.

'I'm good,' I warned him.

'I'm better,' he assured me.

'We'll see about that.'

'How about tomorrow? It's Sunday. We'll be home.'

'Brunch about eleven thirty?' Joan said.

'Sounds great,' I told her.

The bar at Il Palazzo was a glass-panelled section of the dining room, directly off the entrance hall. When I arrived, I hadn't paid attention to anyone in there. But I noticed that during dinner Joan sometimes glanced past me, her expression troubled. We were sipping coffee when I learned the reason.

'Ellie, Will Nebels has been at the bar since before you got here. Someone must have pointed you out to him. He's on his way over, and from the look of him I'd say he's drunk.'

The warning wasn't fast enough. I felt arms round my neck, a sloppy kiss on my cheek. 'Little Ellie. My goodness, little Ellie Cavanaugh. Do you remember how I fixed your seesaw, honey? Your daddy was never any good at fixing stuff. Your mama used to call me all the time. "Will, this needs to be done. Will—"'

He was kissing my ear and the back of my neck.

'Get your hands off her,' Leo said.

I was literally pinned down. Nebels's arms were on my shoulders; his hands were sliding down my sweater.

'And pretty little Andrea. With my own eyes I seen that retard go in that garage carrying that tyre jack.'

A waiter was pulling at him from one side, Leo and Billy from the other. I kept trying to push his face away, but he was kissing my eyes. Then his moist, beery mouth was pressing against my lips.

Men from nearby tables came rushing over and forcibly dragged him away. I dropped my face into my hands. For the second time in six hours I was trembling violently. Concerned enquiries were coming from all sides of me. I could hear the manager sputtering apologies. You *ought* to apologise, I thought. You should have stopped serving that drunk hours ago.

I raised my head and smoothed back my hair. I glanced round the table at the concerned faces, and shrugged. 'I'm OK,' I told them.

I looked at Joan, and I knew what she was thinking. She might as well have been shouting it: Ellie, he was in Mrs Westerfield's house that night. He was probably drunk. What do you think he would have done if he saw Andrea go into that garage alone?

Half an hour later, after a fresh cup of coffee, I insisted on driving myself home. But on the way I wondered if I'd been foolish. I was sure I was being followed and wasn't about to risk being alone again in that parking lot. I drove past the inn and called the police on my cellphone.

'We'll send a car,' the cop at the desk told me. 'Circle back and turn into the driveway of the inn. We'll be right behind whoever is tailing you. Under no circumstances get out of the car.'

I drove slowly, and the car behind me slowed down as well. Now that I knew a squad car was coming, I was glad the car on my tail was still there. I wanted the police to find out who was in that car and why I was being followed.

I turned into the driveway, but the car kept going. A moment later I saw a dome light flashing and heard the wail of the police siren. I pulled over and stopped. Two minutes later the squad car drove up behind me. A cop got out and came up to the driver's door of my car. As I rolled down the window, I could see that he was smiling.

'You *were* being followed, Ms Cavanaugh. The kid says he's your brother and was making sure you got back here safely.'

'Oh, for goodness' sake, tell him to go home!' I said. Then I added, 'But thank him for me, please.'

I'D PLANNED to call Marcus Longo on Sunday morning, but he beat me to it. When the phone rang at nine o'clock, I was at the computer, with my second cup of coffee on the table beside it.

'Ellie,' he said, 'I've been in touch with the office at Sing Sing.'

'You've heard something?'

'Herb Coril, a convict who at one time was in the same cell block as Rob Westerfield, was discharged that morning you were outside Sing Sing. He was staying at a halfway house in lower Manhattan. He hasn't been seen since early Friday evening.'

'I got that last call on Thursday night at about ten thirty,' I said. 'Whoever called me was afraid for his life.'

'We can't be sure it's the same person or that Coril didn't just break the conditions of his release and take off. But I've never been strong on coincidences.'

I told Marcus about my meeting with Alfie.

'I only hope nothing happens to Alfie before you get that diagram,' Marcus said grimly. 'You do understand that, even with the diagram, you'll never get a conviction. Alfie was involved himself, and the diagram is signed by someone named Jim, whom nobody has ever met.'

'I know.'

'The statute of limitations on that crime has run out for all of them—Westerfield, Alfie and Jim, whoever that is.'

'Don't forget William Hamilton. If I could prove that he destroyed evidence that might have got his client a lighter sentence by implicating Westerfield, the ethics committee would be all over him.'

I promised to let Marcus see the diagram, then I said goodbye and tried to get back to work. It was slow, though, and after getting only a little more done, it was time to drive to Joan's for brunch.

JOAN AND I respectfully disagreed with each other about Will Nebels's performance the night before.

'Ellie, he was just plain drunk. How many people shoot off at the mouth when they've had too much to drink? My point is, that's not when they lie. It's when they're more likely to let slip the truth.'

I had to admit that Joan was right on that point. 'That's not the way I see it, though,' I explained to her and Leo. 'To me, Will Nebels is a spineless, gutless loser. Think of him as the stuff you pour into a jelly mould. You plan the shape you want, and then you have it.'

'I agree with Ellie,' Leo said. 'Nebels is more complex than he appears to be on the surface.' Then he added, 'That, of course, doesn't mean that Joan isn't right. If Nebels did see Paulie Stroebel go into that garage that night, he got smart enough to figure that the statute of limitations had run out and that it was safe for him to make a buck out of it.'

'Only he didn't figure this one out himself,' I said. 'They came to him. He agreed to tell the story they needed, and they paid him to tell it.' I pushed my chair back. 'Brunch was wonderful,' I said, 'and now I feel like winning a chess game from Sean.'

I WON THE FIRST CHESS GAME. Sean won the second. We agreed to a rematch 'really soon'.

Before I started home, I phoned the hospital. Paulie's fever had broken. 'He wants to talk to you,' Mrs Stroebel said.

Forty minutes later I was at his bedside. 'You look a lot better than you did yesterday,' I told him.

He was still very pale, but his eyes were clear, and he was propped up with an extra pillow. He smiled shyly. 'Ellie, Mama said you know that I saw the locket, too.'

'When did you see it, Paulie?'

'I worked at the service station. My first job there was to wash and clean the cars after they were fixed. When I cleaned Rob's car one day, I found the locket stuck in the front seat. The chain was broken.'

'You mean the day Andrea's body was found?' But that doesn't make sense, I thought. If Rob went back for the locket, he never would have left it in his car.

Paulie looked at his mother. 'Mama?' he appealed.

'It's all right, Paulie,' she said soothingly. 'It's hard to keep track of everything. You told me you saw the locket twice.'

I looked sharply at Mrs Stroebel, trying to decide if she was prompting him.

But Paulie nodded. 'That's right, Mama. I found it in the car. The chain was broken. I gave it to Rob, and he gave me a ten-dollar tip. I put it with the money I was saving for Mama's birthday present.'

'When was your birthday, Mrs Stroebel?' I asked.

'It was May 15th.'

'Six months before Andrea died!' I was absolutely shocked. 'So he didn't buy the locket for her,' I said. 'It was one that some girl may have lost in the car, and he had it initialled and gave it to Andrea.' I then asked, 'Paulie, do you remember the locket clearly?'

'Yes. It was nice. It was shaped like a heart, and it was gold, and it had little blue stones in it.'

'Paulie, did you ever see the locket again?' I asked.

'Yes. Andrea was so nice to me. She came up and told me how good I was at football and that I'd won the game for the team. That was when I decided to ask her to go to the dance. I walked over to your house, and I saw her going through the woods. I caught up with her outside Mrs Westerfield's house. She was wearing the locket, and I knew Rob must have given it to her. He's not nice. His car always had dents in it because he drove so fast.'

'Did you see him that day?'

'I asked Andrea if I could talk to her, but she said not then, that she was in a hurry. I went back into the woods and watched her go into the garage. A few minutes later Rob Westerfield went in.'

'Tell Ellie when that was, Paulie.'

'It was one week before Andrea died in that garage.'

One week before.

'And you never saw the locket again?'

'No, Ellie.'

'And you never went to the garage again?'

'No, Ellie.'

Paulie closed his eyes, and I could see he was becoming very tired. I covered his hand with mine.

'Paulie, I don't want you to worry any more. I promise you that it's going to be all right, and before I'm finished, everyone will know how kind and good you are.'

Paulie opened his eyes. 'I'm so sleepy. Did I tell you all about the locket?'

'Yes, you did.'

Mrs Stroebel walked me to the elevator. 'Ellie, even at the trial they were trying hard to blame Paulie for Andrea's death. I was so frightened. That was why I told him he must never talk about the locket.'

'I understand.'

'I hope you do. A special child will always need to be protected, even as a grown-up. You heard the Westerfield lawyer on television saying that in a new trial he would prove Paulie killed Andrea. Can you imagine Paulie on the witness stand with that man?'

That man. William Hamilton, Esquire.

'No, I can't.' I kissed her cheek. 'Paulie is lucky he has you, Mrs Stroebel.'

Her eyes lowered. 'He's lucky he has *you*, Ellie.'

AT SEVEN O'CLOCK I turned into Mrs Hilmer's driveway, which now had only one destination. My headlights picked up the charred remains of the garage apartment. For some incongruous reason I thought of the candlesticks and fruit bowl that had graced the dining-room table. Everything in the apartment had been chosen with care and required time and effort to replace.

I entered her home with apologies on my lips, but Mrs Hilmer would have none of it. 'Will you stop worrying about the garage?' She sighed as she pulled my face down for a kiss. 'Ellie, that fire was deliberately set.'

'You don't think I was responsible, do you?'

'Good Lord, no! Ellie, when I got back and Officer White came marching in here practically accusing you of being a pyromaniac, I gave him a real piece of my mind. But it's terrible to think that whoever got into the apartment when you were here for dinner that night actually stole towels to make it look as if you set the fire.'

'I took towels from the linen closet every day. I never noticed that any were missing.'

'How could you? The shelves were stacked with them. I went through a period of not being able to resist a bargain, and now I have enough towels to last me till kingdom come. Well, dinner is ready, and you must be hungry.'

Dinner consisted of shrimp creole, followed by salad. It was delicious. I asked about Mrs Hilmer's granddaughter and learned that her broken wrist was mending nicely.

'The new baby is adorable. But let me tell you, after a week I was ready to go home. The spirit is willing, but it's a long time since I had to get up at five o'clock in the morning.'

She said she had been watching my website, and I told her Christopher Cassidy's story.

'It just keeps getting worse. I was heartsick to hear about Paulie. How is he doing?'

'He's mending. I went to see him this afternoon.' I hesitated, not sure that I wanted to share with her Paulie's revelations about the locket. But then I decided to go ahead. Mrs Hilmer was absolutely trustworthy and a very good barometer of local opinion.

As she listened, her face became grave. 'Ellie, that locket is a double-edged sword, and in court Paulie could be the one hurt by it.'

I told Mrs Hilmer about Alfie and the diagram.

'We all felt the attack on Mrs Westerfield was an inside job,' she said. 'To think her only grandchild would plan her murder—it's beyond belief. I'd see her sometimes in town with Rob before he was arrested. Butter wouldn't melt in his mouth, he was so solicitous of her.'

Despite her protests, we cleared the table together and tidied up the kitchen. 'Are you going to rebuild the garage and replace the apartment?' I asked.

As she popped plates into the dishwasher, Mrs Hilmer smiled. 'Ellie, I wouldn't want the insurance company to hear me, but that fire turned out to be a good thing. I was well insured, and now I have an empty building lot. Janey would love to live up here. She thinks it's a wonderful place to raise her baby. They'll build a house, and I'll have my family right next door.'

I laughed. 'You've made me feel a lot better.' I folded the tea towel. 'And now I have to be on my way. I'm driving to Maine tomorrow, digging up more of Rob Westerfield's glorious past.'

'Janey and I read those papers and the transcript. It brings back how dreadful that time was for all of you.' Mrs Hilmer walked to the closet to retrieve my leather jacket. As I buttoned it, I realised I had not thought to ask if the name Phil meant anything to her.

'Mrs Hilmer, in prison, apparently while he was high on drugs, Rob Westerfield may have confessed to beating a man named Phil to death. Did you ever know or hear about anyone by that name from

514

around here who might have disappeared or been murdered?'

'Phil,' she repeated, looking past me and frowning in concentration. 'There was Phil Oliver, who had a terrible run-in with the Westerfields when they wouldn't renew his lease.'

'Do you know what became of him?'

'No. He moved away. But he had good friends here who are probably still in touch.'

'Will you check for me?'

'Of course.'

She opened the door, then hesitated. 'I know something or read something about a young person named Phil who died a while ago. I can't remember where I heard about it, but it was very sad.'

'Mrs Hilmer, think. This is so terribly important.'

'Phil . . . Phil . . . Oh, Ellie, it's just not coming to me.'

Of course I had to settle for that. But when I left Mrs Hilmer a few minutes later, I urged her to stop actively trying to remember the connection, and let her subconscious work on it.

The car that was following me tonight was much more subtle than the one Teddy had driven. He rode without lights. I only became aware of his presence when I had to stop to let traffic pass before I could turn into the driveway of the inn, and he stopped behind me.

I turned, trying to get a look at the driver. Another car was coming up the driveway from the inn, and its headlights illuminated his face.

Tonight it was my father who wanted to be sure that I got back safely. For a split second we looked at each other, then I turned, and he kept going down the road.

Ten

Alfie phoned me at seven o'clock on Monday morning. 'You still wanna buy it?'

'Yes, I do. My bank is Oldham-Hudson on Main Street. I'll be there at nine o'clock. Meet me in the parking lot at five past nine.'

'OK.'

As I was leaving the bank, he drove up and parked next to my car. From the street no one could have seen what was taking place.

He opened the window. 'Let's have the money.'

I handed it to him.

He counted it. 'OK, here's the diagram.'

I examined it carefully. 'Alfie, you know that the statute of limitations has expired. If the cops knew about this, you wouldn't get into any trouble. But if I show it on the website and write about what you told me, it might make the difference between Mrs Westerfield leaving her money to charities or to Rob.'

I was standing outside the van. He was sitting in it, his hands on the wheel. He looked like what he had become: a hard-working guy who never had much of a break.

'Listen, I'd rather take my chances on Westerfield coming after me than think of him rolling in big bucks.'

'You're sure?'

'Go for it. It kind of makes it up to Skip.'

I ALLOWED PLENTY of travel time for my drive to Carrington Academy in Maine. When I was escorted into the office of Jane Bostrom, director of admissions at the academy, her greeting was cordial but reserved. She was at her desk and offered me the seat facing it. She was younger than I had expected, about thirty-five, with dark hair and large grey eyes that seemed somewhat wary.

'Dr Bostrom,' I said, 'let me put my cards on the table. Rob Westerfield spent his junior and senior years in Carrington. He was kicked out of his former prep school because he assaulted another student. He was fourteen years old. At seventeen he planned the murder of his grandmother. She was shot three times and survived. At nineteen he bludgeoned my sister to death. I am at present tracking down the probability that he has taken at least one more life.'

Her expression became dismayed. She took a long moment before she spoke. 'Ms Cavanaugh, that information about Rob Westerfield is horrifying, but I have his file in front of me, and there is absolutely nothing that indicates a serious behaviour problem.'

'May I ask how long you have been employed at Carrington, Dr Bostrom?'

'Five years.'

'Then of course the only thing you have to go by is a record that may have been tidied up. May I ask if the Westerfields have made any significant contributions to Carrington Academy?'

'At the time Rob was a student, they helped to renovate and refurbish the athletics centre.'

'I see.'

'I don't know what you see, Ms Cavanaugh. Please understand that our students have had an emotionally rough time and need guidance and compassion. Sometimes they've been pawns in nasty divorces. Sometimes one or the other parent simply walked out of their lives. You'd be amazed at what that can do to a child's sense of worth.'

Oh, no, I wouldn't be amazed at all, I thought. In fact, I understand perfectly.

'Some of our young people can't seem to get along with their peer group or with adults or both. We run a tight ship here. Our students are expected to keep up their marks, take part in sports and other activities, and volunteer for community programmes'

'And Rob Westerfield achieved all these goals willingly and joyfully?'

I could have bitten my tongue. Jane Bostrom had given me the courtesy of an interview, and she was answering my questions. However, it was clear that if there had been any big problems at this school with Rob Westerfield, they had not been put on his record.

'Rob Westerfield apparently achieved those goals to our school's satisfaction,' she said stiffly.

'May I see a list of the student body while he was here?'

'For what purpose?'

'Dr Bostrom, when he was high on drugs in prison, Rob Westerfield made a statement to another convict. He said, "I beat Phil to death, and it felt good." Since he assaulted a fellow student at his previous prep school, it is not unlikely that while he was here, he had an encounter with a student named Phil or Philip.'

Her eyes darkened and became progressively more concerned. She stood up. 'Ms Cavanaugh, Dr Douglas Dittrick has been with Carrington for forty years. I'm going to invite him to join us. I think we'd better go into the conference room. It will be easier to spread out the roster lists on the table there.'

DR DITTRICK SENT WORD that he was in the middle of a lecture and would join us in fifteen minutes. Jane Bostrom seemed more comfortable with me by then and certainly willing to help.

'We want to watch for "Philip" as the middle name as well as the first,' she warned, as she opened the rosters. 'We have many students who are known by their middle names when they've been named after fathers and grandfathers.'

The student body totalled about 600 during Rob Westerfield's time at Carrington. I quickly realised that Philip was not a common name. The usuals—James and John and Mark and Michael—showed up regularly. And a host of others: William, Hugo, Charles, Richard, Henry, Walter, Lee, Peter, George, Paul, Donald.

And then a Philip. 'Here's one,' I said. 'He was a freshman when Westerfield was a sophomore.'

Jane Bostrom looked over my shoulder. 'He's on our board of trustees,' she said.

I kept looking.

Dr Dittrick joined us, still wearing his academic gown. 'What's so important, Jane?' he asked.

She explained and introduced me. Dittrick was about seventy, with a scholarly face and a firm handshake.

'I remember Westerfield, of course. He'd only been graduated two years before he killed that girl.'

'She was Ms Cavanaugh's sister,' Dr Bostrom interjected quickly.

'I'm very sorry, Ms Cavanaugh. That was a terrible tragedy.' He turned to Dr Bostrom. 'Jane, why don't you see if Corinne is free and ask her to come over. She wasn't the director of the theatre twenty-five years ago, but she was on staff then. Ask her to bring playbills from those performances Westerfield was in. I seem to remember that there was something funny about the way he was listed in the programme.'

Corinne Barsky arrived twenty minutes later. A slender woman of about sixty, with dark snapping eyes and a rich, warm voice, she was carrying several playbills.

By then we had isolated one more former student with the first name Philip and one with Philip as a middle name.

Dr Dittrick remembered that the student with the middle name Philip had attended his twentieth class reunion two years ago. Dr Bostrom's secretary ran the other student's name through the computer. He lived in Portland, Oregon, and made annual contributions to the alumni fund.

Corinne Barsky showed me the playbills. In each of them Rob Westerfield played the male lead. 'I remember him,' she told me. 'He was genuinely good. Very full of himself, very arrogant towards the other students, but a good actor.'

'Then you had no problems with him?' I asked.

'Oh, I remember him having a row with the director. He wanted to use what he called his stage name instead of his own name in the show. The director refused.'

'What was his stage name?'

'Give me a minute, I'll try to remember.'

'Corinne, wasn't there some kind of flap about Rob Westerfield and a wig?' Dr Dittrick asked. 'I'm sure I remember something.'

'He wanted to wear a wig he used in a performance at his previous school. The director wouldn't allow that, either. Rob wore his wig around campus as well, and got detentions because of it.'

Dr Bostrom looked at me. 'That wasn't in his file,' she said.

'Of course his file was sanitised,' Dr Dittrick said impatiently. 'How else do you think the athletics centre got a total renovation? All it took was President Egan's suggestion to Westerfield's father that Rob might be happier in school elsewhere.'

Dr Bostrom glanced at me, alarmed.

'Don't worry. I'm not going to print that,' I told her.

I fished out my cellphone from my shoulder bag. 'I'm going to get out of your way,' I promised them, 'but there's one call I'd like to make before I leave. I've been in contact with Christopher Cassidy, who was a student at Arbinger with Westerfield. He told me that Rob sometimes used the name of a character he played on stage.'

I looked up the number and dialled it. I was in luck and was put through to Cassidy immediately.

'What you wrote about me is great,' he said. 'Put it on your website.'

I asked if he remembered the character's name Rob had used in class.

'I checked around,' he said. 'It's from one of the plays he was in.'

'I remember the name,' Corinne Barsky was saying, excitement in her voice.

Cassidy was in Boston. Barsky was a few feet away from me in Maine. But they said it together. 'It's Jim Wilding.'

Jim! I thought. Rob had drawn the diagram himself.

'Ellie, I have to take another call,' Cassidy apologised.

'Go ahead. That's all I needed to know.'

He clicked off.

Corinne Barsky had opened one of the playbills. 'You may be interested in this, Ms Cavanaugh,' she said. 'The director used to have every member of the cast sign a playbill next to where they are listed.' She held it up and pointed. Rob Westerfield had signed not his own name but 'Jim Wilding' instead.

I stared at it for a long minute. 'I need a copy of this. And please take very good care of the original. In fact,' I said, 'I wish you'd lock it in a safe.'

TWENTY MINUTES LATER I was sitting in my car, comparing the signature on the diagram with the one on the playbill. I'm no handwriting expert, but when I compared the way the name Jim was signed on both documents, the signatures seemed identical.

I began the long drive back to Oldham, exulting in the prospect of exhibiting them on the Internet side by side.

Mrs Dorothy Westerfield would have to face the truth—her grandson had planned her death.

I must confess I thoroughly enjoyed the benevolent feeling that I was about to make a number of charities, medical facilities, libraries and universities very very happy.

I KEEP MY CELLPHONE on the other pillow. On Tuesday morning it began to ring and woke me up. As I gave a sleepy 'Hello' I glanced at my watch and was shocked to see that it was nine o'clock.

'Must have had a night on the town.'

It was Pete.

'Let's see,' I said. 'Driving from Maine to Massachusetts and across to New York State. It was the most exciting night of my life.'

'Maybe you're too tired to come down to Manhattan.'

'Maybe you're trying to wriggle out of the invitation,' I suggested, by now awake and on the verge of being disappointed and angry.

'My suggestion was going to be that I drive to Oldham, pick you up, and we find a place for us to have dinner.'

'That's different,' I said cheerfully. 'I have a great spot in mind, fifteen minutes from the inn.'

'Now you're talking. Give me directions.'

I did, and he congratulated me. 'Ellie, you're one of the few women I know who can give lucid directions. Is it something I taught you? Never mind answering. I can be there around seven.'

Click.

I sent for room service, showered, washed my hair and phoned a nearby nail salon to make an appointment. I even took time to study my limited wardrobe and decided on the leaf-brown trouser suit with the karakul collar and cuffs. The suit had been an impulse buy last year, and I had yet to wear it. Parading it out for Pete seemed like a good idea.

Actually, it was comforting to have something to anticipate at the end of the day. I knew it was not going to be easy writing Alfie's story and tying the incriminating diagram to Rob Westerfield. Not emotionally easy, because of the unbearable certainty that, if Rob Westerfield had been convicted of that break-in, Andrea would not have met him.

He'd have been in prison. She would have grown up and gone to college and, like Joan, probably got married and had children. Mother and Daddy would still be in that wonderful farmhouse. Daddy would have come to love it as much as she did and by now realised what a great buy it had been.

I would have grown up in a happy home and gone to college. Choosing to study journalism had nothing to do with Andrea's death, so I probably would be in the same kind of job. It's the career that held a natural attraction for me. I still wouldn't be married. I think I always wanted a career before a commitment.

If Rob had been convicted, I would not have spent my life grieving for my sister and yearning for what I had lost.

Now, even if I manage to convince Rob's grandmother and the entire world of his guilt, he still will get away with it. The statute of limitations has run out on that crime.

I beat Phil to death, and it felt good.

There is only one way I can get Rob Westerfield back behind bars and that is to track down Phil. Fortunately, there is no statute of limitations for murder.

By three thirty I was ready to transfer everything to the website: Christopher Cassidy's story and Rob's role in planning the attempt on his grandmother's life. I wrote that William Hamilton, Esq., had destroyed the original diagram implicating Westerfield in the crime. I ended the piece with the diagram and playbill displayed side by side. The 'Jim' signatures were startling in their similarity. I kissed my fingers in a salute to the story, pressed the appropriate keys on the computer, and an instant later it was out there on my website.

IT WAS A QUARTER TO FIVE when I got back to the inn. The multibillion-dollar cosmetic industry would go broke if it relied on people like me, but what little make-up I had was lost in the fire. It was time to replace items like mascara and blusher.

Tonight I was meeting someone I wanted to see and who wanted to see me. Whither do we wander? I didn't know and wasn't looking ahead that far. But for the first time in my life I was beginning to anticipate the future. It was a hopeful, satisfying feeling.

Then I walked through the door of the inn, and my half-brother,

Teddy, was waiting for me. This time he was not smiling. He looked uncomfortable yet determined, and his greeting was abrupt.

'Ellie, come inside. We have to talk.'

'I invited your brother to wait in the sunroom, but he was afraid he might miss you,' Mrs Willis said.

You're absolutely right, I thought. He *would* have missed me. I would have been upstairs like a shot.

I didn't want her to hear whatever he was going to say, so I walked ahead of him into the sunroom. This time he closed the door, and we stood facing each other.

'Teddy,' I began, 'you have to listen to me. I know you mean well. I know your father means well. But you can't be trailing after me. I can take care of myself.'

'No, you can't!' His eyes were flashing. 'Ellie, we saw what you put on the website this afternoon. Dad is beside himself with worry. He said that the Westerfields have to stop you now. You've become a terrible danger to them, and in the process you've put yourself in danger. Ellie, you can't do this to Dad or to yourself. Or to me.'

I put my hand on his arm. 'Teddy, I don't want to upset you or your father. I'm doing what I have to. Please, just leave me alone. You've got along without me all your life, and your father has got along without me since I was a small child. You don't *know* me. You have no reason to worry about me. You're a nice kid, but let's leave it at that.'

'I'm not just a nice kid. I'm your brother. Whether you like it or not. And stop saying "your father" to me. You think you know everything, but you don't, Ellie. Dad never stopped being your father. He's always talked about you. He told me what a great little kid you were. You don't even know it, but he went out to your college graduation and sat in the audience. He got a subscription to the *Atlanta News* when you started working there, and he's read every article you've ever written. So stop saying he's not your father.'

I kept shaking my head. 'Teddy, you don't understand. When my mother and I went to Florida, he let us go.'

'He told me you thought that, but it isn't true. He tried to get you back. The few times you visited him, you never said one word and wouldn't even eat. What was he supposed to do? Your mother told him there was too much grief to contain under one roof, that she wanted to go on to a new life.'

'How do you know all this?'

'Because I asked him. Because I thought he'd have a heart attack when he saw the last item you put on the website. He's sixty-seven, Ellie, and he has high blood pressure.'

'Does he know you're here?'

'I told him I was coming. I'm here to beg you to come home with me or, if you won't do that, at least to go some place where nobody except us knows where you are.'

He was so caring that I almost put my arms round him. 'Teddy, there are things you don't understand. I knew Andrea might have gone to meet Rob Westerfield that night, and I didn't tell on her. I've had to carry that blame all my life. I didn't save her, but when Westerfield gets his new trial, I have to try to save Paulie Stroebel.'

'Dad told me it was *his* fault that Andrea died. He was late getting home. He was starting to get suspicious that Andrea was still seeing Westerfield behind his back. He told me that he would never have allowed her to go to Joan's house that night.'

He believed what he was telling me. Was my memory so distorted? It wasn't that simple. But was my abiding sense of guilt only part of the picture? My mother let Andrea go out after dark alone. My father suspected Andrea was still seeing Rob but had not confronted her. And his attempts to protect her may have made her rebellious.

'Ellie, my mother was a widow when she met Dad. She knows what it is to lose someone. She wants to meet you.'

'I promise I will meet her someday. When I've seen this through.'

'You will talk to Dad? You will give him a break?'

'When this is over, we'll have lunch or something. I promise. And listen, I'm going out tonight with someone I worked with in Atlanta. I don't want either one of you following me around. He's picking me up here and will deposit me back safely, I promise.'

'Dad will be relieved to hear that.'

'Teddy, I have to get upstairs. There are a couple of calls I have to make before I go out.'

'I've said what I have to say. No, maybe I haven't. There's something else Dad told me that you should know. He said, "I've lost one little girl. I can't lose another."'

IF I HAD EXPECTED a hint of romance in our meeting, it was quickly dismissed. Pete's greeting to me was 'You look great,' accompanied by a quick kiss on the cheek.

'And you look as though you won a fifteen-minute shopping spree in Bloomingdale's,' I told him.

'Twenty minutes,' he corrected. 'I'm starving. Aren't you?'

I had made a reservation at Cathryn's, and while we were driving over, I said, 'Big request.'

'Let's have it.'

'Tonight I would like not to talk about what I've been doing these past weeks. You watch the website, so you know what's going on. I need to get away from it, so tonight is *your* night. Tell me every single place you've been since I saw you in Atlanta, every detail about the interviews you've had. Tell me why you're pleased about the job you're taking. You can even tell me if you had a hard time choosing between that very nice, and obviously new, red tie or another one.'

Pete has a way of raising one eyebrow. 'You're serious?'

'Absolutely.'

'The minute I saw this tie, I knew I had to have it.'

'Very good,' I encouraged. 'I want to hear more.'

At the restaurant, we looked at the menu, ordered smoked salmon and a seafood pasta, and agreed to share a bottle of Pinot Grigio.

'It's handy that we both like the same entrées,' Pete said. 'Makes it easier with the wine selection.'

'The last time I was here, I had the rack of lamb.'

He looked at me.

'I love to irritate you,' I admitted.

'It shows.'

Over dinner he did open up. 'Ellie, I knew the paper was on the way out. I was getting itchy anyway. In this business, unless you can see that you have a good reason to stay with a company, you've got to be aware of other opportunities.'

'Then why didn't you leave sooner?' I asked.

He looked at me. 'I'll take a pass on that one. But when it became inevitable, I knew for sure. I wanted either to get with a solid news-paper or to try something else altogether. That something else opened up, and I went for it.'

'A new cable news station.'

'I'm in on the ground floor. It has risks, of course, but substantial investors are committed to making it happen.'

'You said it involved a lot of travelling.'

'By a lot I mean the kind anchormen do when they're onto a big story.'

'You're not telling me you're an anchorman!'

'Perhaps that's too grandiose a word. I'm on the news desk. Short, clipped and hard-hitting is in these days. Maybe it will work. Maybe it won't.'

I thought about it. Pete was smart, intense, and got to the point quickly. 'I think you'll actually be good at it.'

'There's something so touching about the way you lavish praise on me, Ellie. Don't go overboard, please.'

I ignored that. 'Then you're going to be based in New York City and you're moving there?'

'I already have. I found an apartment. In SoHo. It's not great, but it's a start.'

'Won't that be kind of a big change for you? Your whole family is in Atlanta.'

'My grandparents were all New Yorkers. I used to visit them a lot when I was a kid.'

We waited silently while the table was cleared. Then when we'd ordered espresso, Pete said, 'All right, Ellie, we've played the game by your rules. Now I get my two cents in. I want to hear everything you've been up to, and I mean *everything*.'

By now I was ready to talk about it, so I told him all, including Teddy's visit. When I'd finished, Pete said, 'Your father's right. You've got to move in with him or at least not be visible around Oldham.'

'He may be right about that,' I admitted reluctantly.

'I have to go to Chicago in the morning for a meeting with the board of Packard Cable. I'll be gone until Saturday. Ellie, please go down to New York and stay in my apartment. You can be in touch with Marcus Longo and Mrs Hilmer and Mrs Stroebel from there, and keep up your website, but you'll be safe. Will you do that?'

I knew he was right. 'For a few days, until I can figure out where to go, yes, I will.'

When we got back to the inn, Pete left his car in the driveway and walked me inside. The night clerk was on duty.

'Has anyone been looking for Ms Cavanaugh?' Pete asked him.

'No, sir. Mr Longo and Mrs Hilmer called.'

At the foot of the stairs, he put his hands on my shoulders. 'Ellie, I know you've had to see this through, but you can't go it alone any more. You need us around you.'

'Us?'

'Your father, Teddy, me.'

'You've been in touch with my father, haven't you?'

He patted my cheek. 'Of course I have.'

Eleven

I dreamed a lot that night. It was an anxiety-ridden dream. Andrea was slipping through the woods. I was trying to call her back, but I couldn't make her hear me and watched in despair as she ran past old Mrs Westerfield's house and into the garage. I was trying to shout a warning, but then Rob Westerfield was there.

I woke to the faint sound of my own voice calling for help. Dawn was just breaking. It was going to be another of those grey, cloudy days we get in November.

Even as a child, I found the first two weeks of November unsettling. After the middle of the month the festive feeling of Thanksgiving was in the air, but those first two weeks seemed long and dreary. Then, after Andrea died, they became forever linked with the memories of the last days we spent together.

Those were my thoughts as I lay in bed wishing for an hour or two more of sleep. The dream wasn't hard to analyse. I knew that I needed to be very careful.

At seven o'clock I sent for room service; then I began to work on my book. At nine o'clock I showered, dressed, and phoned Mrs Hilmer.

'Ellie,' she said, 'I called you last night to tell you that I checked with one of my friends who's in contact with Phil Oliver. I told you about him. Phil Oliver is the man who lost his lease and had an ugly confrontation with Rob Westerfield's father. My friend told me that he's living down in Florida now.' She paused. 'Ellie, the one thing I'm sure of is that whatever I heard or read about "Phil"—it was only recently. And if this is any help, it made me sad.'

'Sad?'

'Ellie, I know I'm not making sense, but I'm working on it.'

'You've got my cellphone number, Mrs Hilmer. I'm going to be in and out so much. Will you call me on that number if you come up with the connection?'

'Of course.'

Marcus Longo was the next one on my list to call. I thought he sounded subdued, and I was right. 'Ellie, what you put on the website yesterday is inviting a massive lawsuit from both Westerfield and his lawyer, William Hamilton.'

'Good. Let them sue. I can't wait to depose them.'

'Being right isn't always a provable or successful legal defence. The drawing you claim is evidence of Rob Westerfield's part in the attempted murder of his grandmother was provided by the brother of the man who shot her. He's hardly a stellar witness. How much did you pay for that information?'

'One thousand dollars.'

'Do you know how that would look in court?'

'Let them sue. I hope they do.'

'It's your show, Ellie.'

'Two things, Marcus. I'm checking out today and going to a friend's apartment in Manhattan.'

'That is a great relief. Does your father know that?'

If not, I bet you'll tell him, I thought. 'I'm not sure,' I said. For all I knew, Pete had called him.

I was going to ask Marcus if he had had any success in following up on a homicide with someone named Phil as the victim, but he anticipated the question. 'So far, zero, blank, nothing to tie Wester-field to another crime,' he said. 'But I still have a lot of searching to do. We're also following up on the name Jim Wilding.'

We agreed to stay in close touch.

I called the hospital, hoping to hear that Paulie had been discharged, but he was still there.

Mrs Stroebel was with him. 'Ellie, he's much better. He wants to see you again. He is trying to remember something you said to him that he says was not correct. He wants to straighten it out.'

My heart sank. Something *I* said? Dear God, was Paulie confused again? 'I can come over and see him,' I offered.

'Why don't you come round at one o'clock? I will be here then, and I think that makes him more comfortable.'

More comfortable, I thought, or do you mean you want to be sure he won't say anything that will incriminate him? No, I didn't believe that. 'I'll be there, Mrs Stroebel,' I said. 'If I arrive before you, I'll wait for you to come before I visit Paulie.'

'Thank you, Ellie.'

I managed to get a few hours' work in, then I checked Rob Westerfield's website. More names had been added to the Committee for Justice, but nothing had been added to refute my story of his involvement in the attempted murder of his grandmother. I took that to be a sign of consternation in the ranks.

WHEN I GOT TO THE HOSPITAL, there was a buzz of activity in the lobby. I saw a group of reporters and cameramen clustered at the far end of the room. The woman next to me in the queue to get a visitor's pass told me Dorothy Westerfield had been rushed into the emergency room, suffering from a heart attack.

Her lawyer had issued a statement that last evening, as a memorial to her late husband, US Senator Pearson Westerfield, Mrs Westerfield had changed her will and would be leaving her estate to a charitable foundation charged with dispersing all of it within ten years. The only exceptions were small bequests to her son and some long-time employees.

'She was very smart, you know,' the woman confided to me. 'I heard some reporters talking. She had her pastor and a psychiatrist as witnesses that she was of sound mind.'

I'm sure that my gossipy informant did not realise that my website probably triggered both the will change and the heart attack. It was a hollow victory for me.

I was glad to escape into the elevator before a reporter could connect me with the breaking story.

Mrs Stroebel was already in the corridor waiting for me. Together we went in Paulie's room. His bandages were much smaller. His eyes were clearer, and his smile was warm and sweet.

'My friend, Ellie,' he said. 'I can count on you.'

'You bet you can.'

'I want to go home. I'm tired of being here.'

'That's a good sign, Paulie.'

'I want to get back to work. Were there many people in for lunch when you left, Mama?'

'Pretty good crowd,' she said soothingly, with a contented smile.

'You shouldn't be here so much, Mama.'

'I won't have to be, Paulie. You'll be home soon.' She looked at me. 'We have a little room off the kitchen at the store. Greta has put a couch and television in there. Paulie can be with us, do whatever he feels up to in the kitchen, and rest in between.'

'Sounds good to me,' I told them.

'Now, Paulie, explain what it is that worries you,' his mother encouraged.

'I found the locket and gave it to Rob,' Paulie said slowly. 'I told you that, Ellie.'

'Yes, you did.'

'Rob gave me a ten-dollar tip, and I put it with the money I'd saved for your birthday present, Mama.'

'That was in May, Paulie, six months before Andrea died.'

'Yes. And the locket was shaped like a heart, and it was gold and it had pretty blue stones in the centre.'

'Yes,' I said, hoping to encourage him.

'But something is wrong. *You* said something that was wrong.'

'Let me think.' I tried to reconstruct the conversation. 'The only thing I remember is that I said Rob didn't buy Andrea a new locket. He had the initials of their first names, Rob and Andrea, engraved on a locket some other girl had probably dropped in his car.'

Paulie smiled. 'That's what I needed to remember. Rob didn't have the initials engraved on the locket. They were already there.'

'Paulie, that's impossible. You found the locket in May.'

His expression became stubborn. 'Ellie, I remember. The initials were on the locket. It wasn't R and A. It was A and R. A.R.—in very pretty writing.'

I LEFT THE HOSPITAL with the sense that events were spinning out of control. The grey morning had evolved into an equally grey afternoon. I drove back to the inn, went upstairs, phoned room service, ordered a club sandwich and tea, and got out my suitcase. I wanted to pack right away. Then my cellphone rang.

It was Mrs Hilmer. 'Ellie, I don't know if this is helpful at all, but I remember where it was that I read a reference to someone named Phil.'

'Where, Mrs Hilmer? Where did you see it?'

'It was in one of the newspapers you gave me.'

'Are you sure?'

'I'm positive. I remember because I was reading it at my granddaughter's house. The baby was asleep, and I was going through those papers for names of people still here whom you might want to interview. And, Ellie, as I told you when we had dinner, reading about the trial brought everything back, and I was crying. Then I read something about Phil, and that was very sad, too.'

'But you're not sure what it said about him?'

'Ellie, that's why I think that even if I can find the item, I've probably got the wrong person in mind.'

'Why do you think that?'

'Because you're looking for a man named Phil. I read something about a young girl who died whose family called her Phil.'

I beat Phil to death, and it felt good.

Dear God, I thought, was he talking about a girl?

'Mrs Hilmer, I'm going to read every one of those papers.'

'That's what I'm doing. I'll call you if I come across it.'

I pushed the END button to terminate the call, grabbed the duffle bag, and dumped the yellowing, crumbling newspapers on the bed. I took the first one that came to my hand, sat down in the chair that faced the river and began to read.

The hours passed. Every so often I would get up and stretch. At four o'clock I sent for tea. I concentrated intensely, reading again line by line in horrifying detail the story of Andrea's death and Rob Westerfield's trial.

At six o'clock I took another break and turned on the news. Mrs Dorothy Westerfield had died at three thirty. Neither her son nor her grandson had been at her bedside.

I went back to reading the papers. At seven o'clock I found it, in the memorial section of the obituary page the day of Andrea's funeral. It read:

Rayburn, Amy P.
Remembering you today and every day.
Happy 18th birthday in heaven, our darling Phil.
Mom and Dad

A.R.—was she the girl who had owned the pretty locket? Did the initials stand for her name? Her middle initial had been P. Could it have been Phyllis or Philomena, shortened to Phil?

Paulie had found the locket in early May. Andrea was dead twenty-three years. If Amy Rayburn had owned the locket, had she died twenty-three and a half years ago? I called Marcus Longo, but there was no answer. I was frantic to have him check Amy Rayburn's name against homicide reports from that year.

I knew there was a Westchester phone book in the drawer of the bedside table. I pulled it out and turned to the R section. There were only two Rayburns.

I dialled the one in Larchmont. An older man answered.

'My name is Ellie Cavanaugh,' I said. 'It is necessary for me to speak to the family of Amy Rayburn.'

The voice suddenly became frosty. 'For what reason?'

'Please answer one question of mine, and I will answer all of yours. Was Amy the victim of a homicide?'

'If you do not know that already, you have no business calling our family.' The phone slammed down.

I called back, and the answering machine picked up. 'My name is Ellie Cavanaugh,' I said. 'Twenty-three years ago my fifteen-year-old sister was bludgeoned to death. I believe I have proof that the man who killed her is also responsible for Phil's death. Please call me back on—'

The phone was picked up. 'The man who murdered her served eighteen years in prison. What do you think you're talking about?'

THE MAN I HAD CALLED, David Rayburn, was the uncle of seventeen-year-old Amy Phyllis Rayburn, murdered six months before Andrea. I told him about Andrea, about Rob Westerfield's confession to a fellow inmate in prison, about Paulie finding the locket in Rob's car, and about its being taken from Andrea's body.

He listened, asked questions, then said, 'Let me call my brother now and give him your number.' Then he added, 'Phil was about to graduate from high school. She'd been accepted at Brown. Her boyfriend, Dan Mayotte, always swore he was innocent. Instead of going to Yale, he spent eighteen years in prison.'

Fifteen minutes later my phone rang. It was Michael Rayburn, Phil's father. 'My brother told me about your call,' he said. 'I won't try to describe my emotions or those of my wife at this moment. Dan Mayotte had been in and out of our home since he was in kindergarten. We trusted him like a son. We have had to make our peace with the death of our only child, but to think that Dan may have been wrongly convicted of her death is almost more than we can bear. I'm a lawyer, Ms Cavanaugh. What kind of proof do you have? My brother talked about a locket.'

'Mr Rayburn, did your daughter have a heart-shaped gold locket with blue stones or gems on the front and her initials on the back?'

'Let me put my wife on.'

I described the locket to Phil's mother. 'That has to be Phil's,' she said. 'It was one of those trinkets you pick up at a shopping mall. She loved that kind of jewellery and had a dozen chains with any number of pendants she'd slip on them. I don't know if she was wearing the locket the night she was murdered. I never missed it.'

'Do you have a picture of Phil wearing it?'

'She was fond of the locket. That's why she had it engraved. I'm sure I can find one.'

Her husband took the phone from her. 'Ellie, I understand you told my brother that the convict who heard Westerfield confess is missing. But as I understand it, there is no hard-and-fast proof to actually tie Westerfield to Phil's death.'

'No, there isn't. Not yet. Maybe it's too soon to go to the district attorney with what I know, but if you tell me the circumstances of your daughter's murder, I can put it on my website and see if it brings in information.'

'Ellie, we've been living that nightmare for over twenty-three years. I can tell you everything about it. It all began when Phil and her boyfriend were buying sodas before a movie and some guy by the counter started flirting with her. Dan was jealous and they quarrelled. She and Dan didn't speak for a while, but I guess they made it up. A week later they were at the pizza parlour, and the guy who'd been flirting with Phil the week before came in and started making Dan jealous all over again.'

'Did Dan describe him?'

'Yes. Good-looking, about twenty years old, dark blond hair. Dan said that his name was Jim.'

Jim! I thought. That had to be one of the times Rob Westerfield was wearing his dark blond wig.

'Dan accused Phil of planning to meet Jim there. She denied it and got up and stalked out. Everyone could see that she and Dan were angry with each other. Dan said he persuaded her to get in his car and talk things over, but she got sore at him again and got out of the car. She told him that she was going back to her friends and for him to get lost. According to him, she slammed the car door and started to walk from the parking lot, heading back to the restaurant. Dan admitted he was furious and said he gunned the engine and took off. Phil never made it to the restaurant. The next day her body was found.' Michael Rayburn's voice broke. 'She died of multiple fractures of the skull. Her face wasn't recognisable.'

I beat Phil to death, and it felt good.

I KNEW THAT I WAS already in jeopardy from the Westerfields and that now I was being downright reckless. I didn't care. I started Phil's story with the headline: WESTCHESTER DISTRICT ATTORNEY, TAKE NOTE!

My fingers flew over the keyboard. At nine o'clock it was finished. With grim satisfaction I sent it to the website. I closed the computer, packed my belongings, and went downstairs to check out.

I was paying my bill when my cellphone rang.

I thought it might be Marcus Longo, but it was a woman with a Hispanic accent. 'Ms Cavanaugh?'

'Yes.'

'I have been watching your website. My name is Rosita Juárez. I was housekeeper for Rob Westerfield's parents from the time he was ten years old until he went to prison. He is a very bad person.'

I gripped the phone. This woman sounded frightened. Don't let her hang up, I prayed. 'Yes, Rob is a very bad person, Rosita.'

'He looked down on me. He made fun of the way I talk. He was nasty and rude. That's why I want to help you.'

'How can you help me, Rosita?'

'You are right. Rob used to wear a blond wig. When he put it on, he would say to me, "My name is Jim, Rosita. That shouldn't be too hard even for you to remember."'

'You saw him put on the wig?'

'I have the wig.' There was sly triumph in the woman's voice. 'His mother used to get very upset when he wore it. She threw it in the garbage. I don't know why, but I took it out. I knew it was expensive, and I thought maybe I could sell it. But I put it in a box and forgot all about it until you wrote about it on your website.'

'I'd like to have that wig, Rosita. I'll buy it from you.'

'No, you don't have to buy it. Will it help to make people believe that he killed that girl—Phil?'

'I believe it would. Where do you live, Rosita?'

'In Phillipstown.'

Phillipstown was actually part of Cold Spring, not more than ten miles away. 'Rosita, may I come and get the wig from you now?'

'I'm not sure. My apartment is in a house, and my landlady sees everything. I don't want anyone to see you here. I am afraid of Rob Westerfield.'

For the moment all I cared about was getting my hands on the wig. Before I could try to convince her, she volunteered, 'I live a few minutes from the Phillipstown Hotel. If you want, I could meet you at the back entrance.'

'I can be there in half an hour,' I said.

'I will be there. Will the wig help to put Rob in jail?'

'I'm sure it will.'

'Good!'

I finished paying my bill and quickly put my bags in the car. Six minutes later I was on my way to acquire the tangible proof that Rob Westerfield had owned and worn a dark blond wig. I was hoping that samples of Rob's DNA would still be lingering within it. That would be definitive proof that the wig had belonged to him.

SOMETIME AFTER DARK the light mist had turned into a cold, battering rain. The windshield wipers of the car I had rented needed to be replaced, and before I had driven a mile I found myself straining to see the road.

The traffic became lighter the further north I drove on Route 9. The temperature was dropping, causing the rain to turn into sleet. It became harder and harder to see more than a few yards ahead, and I was forced to drive slowly.

As the minutes passed, I became frantic that I would miss Rosita. I was sure she would not wait around if I didn't show up on time.

I only gradually became aware that I was starting to go up a hill. It dawned on me that it had been a while since I'd seen any headlights coming from the opposite direction. I glanced at the dials. The Phillipstown Hotel was not more than ten miles from the Hudson Valley Inn, yet I had already driven twelve miles. Somewhere I had veered off Route 9. The road I was on now was clearly not the main highway and was getting narrower.

Furious at myself, I jammed on the brakes—a stupid thing to do, because I started to skid. I managed to straighten out the car and carefully began to make a U-turn. In that instant a red dome light went on behind me and blinding headlights flashed in my eyes. I stopped the car, and a police van pulled up beside me.

Thank God! I thought. I rolled down the window to ask the cop directions to the Phillipstown Hotel.

The window of the van rolled down as well, and the man in the passenger seat turned to face me.

I saw immediately that it was Rob Westerfield, and he was wearing a dark blond wig. With an unmistakable Hispanic accent and with his voice pitched to sound like a woman, he mockingly called, 'He made fun of the way I talk. He told me to call him Jim.'

My heart almost stopped. Past him I could just make out the face of the man who had threatened me in the parking lot of the railroad station near Sing Sing prison.

Frantically I looked round for a way out. I could not get round them. My only hope was to straighten out the car, floor the gas pedal, and keep driving blindly ahead. As I accelerated, I saw woods on both sides of me. The tyres were slipping, causing the back of the car to fishtail.

I knew I could not outrun them. I could only pray that this road might be taking me towards some kind of highway. They had turned off the dome light, but their bright headlights were still shining straight into my rearview mirror. Then they began to toy with me.

They accelerated until they were level with me, and the van slammed into the side of my car. The door behind me took the impact, and my head banged into the steering wheel.

They dropped back as I skidded from side to side. I was bleeding from a cut on my forehead, but I managed to hang on to the wheel and keep the car on the road.

Then suddenly they shot by me, angling in front of me and tearing the fender off my car. I could hear it scraping and dragging as I struggled to stay on the road, praying that soon I'd come upon an intersection or at least see another car.

But there were no other cars. As the road curved sharply, they slowed. I hesitated briefly, then accelerated, hoping to break ahead.

For a split second I glanced at them. The interior light was on in the van, and I could see that Rob was waving something at me. It was a tyre jack.

With a burst of speed, the van cut sharply to the right, directly into my path, forcing my car off the road. Helplessly I felt the tyres losing traction as the car went into a spin and then tumbled down the sloping embankment, heading towards a wall of trees.

I managed to hang on to the steering wheel as the car turned over several times. I covered my face with my hands as the car, right side up again, slammed into a tree and the windshield shattered. The sound of crashing metal and glass had been deafening, and the sudden silence that followed was ghostly.

My shoulder hurt. My hands were bleeding. My head was throbbing. But by some miracle I had not been seriously injured.

The final impact had caused my door to spring open, and sleet was pelting at me. Its cold sting kept me from losing consciousness. It was totally dark, and for a moment I felt extraordinary relief. I thought they were through with me.

But then I became aware that I was not alone. Nearby I heard harsh, laboured breathing, followed by the high choking sound that as a child I had described as a giggle.

Rob Westerfield was out there in the dark, waiting for me, just as he had waited for Andrea twenty-three years ago in the darkness of the garage hide-out.

The first blow of the tyre jack missed me and hit the headrest behind me. I clawed at the seat belt and released it. As I scrambled to the passenger side, I felt the second blow graze my hair.

Andrea, Andrea, this is the way it was for you. Oh God, please, please help me.

I think we both heard it at the same time—a car roaring round that last bend in the road. Its headlights must have caught the wreckage of my car, because it turned and came rushing down the slope.

Rob Westerfield was illuminated in the glare. But so was I, and now he could see exactly where I was.

Snarling, he turned back towards me. He leaned inside the car until his face was only inches from mine. I tried to push him away as he raised the tyre jack. I heard the scream of sirens as I shielded my head with my arms and waited for the blow to land.

I heard the thud before I saw the look of shock and pain on Westerfield's face. The tyre jack fell from his hand onto the seat beside me as he was thrust forward, then he disappeared. I stared out, unbelieving. The car that had driven down the slope was filling the space where he had stood. The driver had done the only thing possible to save my life: he had crashed his car into Rob Westerfield.

As the blazing lights of police cars turned the area into virtual daytime, I looked into the faces of my rescuers.

My father was driving the car that had hit Rob Westerfield. My brother was beside him. On Daddy's face I saw again the agonised expression that I remembered from when he knew he had lost his other little girl.

One Year Later

I often look back and realise how close I came that terrible night to sharing my sister's fate. From the time I left the inn, Dad and Teddy had been following me from a distance. They had seen a police van behind my car and assumed that I had finally requested protection.

They lost me, however, when I veered off the highway, so Dad called the Phillipstown police to be sure the van had stayed with me. That was when he learned that I had no official escort. The police told Dad where I probably had taken the wrong turn and promised immediate response.

Dad told me that when he came round the turn, the driver of Westerfield's van had started to pull away. He'd been about to follow him, but Teddy spotted the wreckage of my car. Teddy—the brother who never would have been born if Andrea had lived—saved my life. I often reflect on that irony.

Both of Rob Westerfield's legs were broken by Dad's car, but they mended in time for him to walk into court for his two trials. The district attorney for Westchester County immediately reopened the investigation into Phil's death. He obtained a search warrant for Rob's new apartment and found a cache of his trophies, mementos of his hideous crimes. God knows where he had them stashed while he was in prison.

Rob had kept an album of newspaper clippings about both Andrea and Phil, starting from the time their bodies were found. Next to them were pictures of Andrea, Phil and the other people caught up in the tragedies. On each page Rob had written cruel and sarcastic commentary. Phil's locket was pasted on the last page of the album. The caption under it read: 'Thanks, Phil. Andrea loved it.'

The district attorney requested the criminal court judge to overturn Dan Mayotte's conviction and to schedule a different trial: *The People* v. *Robson Westerfield.* The charge was murder.

I saw the locket exhibited at the trial, and my mind flew back to that last evening in Andrea's bedroom, when, close to tears, she had slipped it round her neck.

Dad was sitting next to me in court and closed his hand over mine. 'You were always right about the locket, Ellie,' he whispered.

Yes, I was, and at last I have made my peace with the fact that, because I saw her wearing it and believed she had gone to the hideout to meet Rob, I did not immediately tell my parents when she was missing. It may already have been too late to save her, but it is time to relinquish the possibility that it may *not* have been too late, and to stop letting it haunt me.

Robson Parke Westerfield was convicted of the murder of Amy Phyllis Rayburn.

In a second trial Rob and his driver were convicted of attempted murder for their attack on me.

Rob Westerfield's sentences are consecutive. If he lives another 113 years, he will be eligible for parole.

Will Nebels, when confronted with the evidence of Westerfield's guilt, admitted that he had been approached by Hamilton and offered a bribe to lie about seeing Paulie go into the garage that night. William Hamilton, disbarred attorney, is now serving his own prison term.

My book was rushed out for publication in the spring and did very well. The other book—the sanitised version of Rob Westerfield's sorry life—was withdrawn. Pete introduced me to the Packard Cable executives, and they offered me a job as an investigative reporter. It seemed like a good opportunity. Some things never change. I report to Pete.

But that's fine. We were married three months ago, and Dad gave the bride away.

Pete and I bought a house in Cold Spring overlooking the Hudson. We use it at weekends. I never tire of the view of that majestic river. My heart has finally found its home, the home I have been seeking all these years.

I see Dad regularly. We both feel the need to make up for lost time. Teddy's mother and I have become good friends. Sometimes we all go up to see Teddy at college. He's on the freshman basketball team at Dartmouth. I am so proud of him.

The circle has taken a long time to close. But it *has* closed, and for that I am deeply grateful.

MARY HIGGINS CLARK

When asked if she can explain the secrets of her popularity, Mary Higgins Clark says simply: 'Readers identify with my characters. I write about people going about their daily lives, not looking for trouble, who are suddenly plunged into menacing situations.' This approach has certainly made her latest best seller, *Daddy's Little Girl*, an absolutely gripping story. In it, Ellie, a journalist, returns to her roots twenty-two years after witnessing a murder scene as a seven-year-old, only to find herself the target of a killer as she strives to unearth the truth.

At the age of ten, while growing up in New York, Mary Higgins herself experienced a trauma, albeit one of a different kind. She arrived home from Mass one Sunday morning to find that her father had died. 'I had a terrible shock . . . The suddenness of his death jolted me into an awareness of the fragility of life.' From that moment on, her mother was faced with raising her three children alone; an achievement that left a lifelong impression on her daughter. 'My mother's example taught me resilience. And the characters in my books are resilient and resourceful. When calamity strikes, they carry on.'

The author feels that her Irish heritage was another important influence on her writing. 'The Irish are, by nature, storytellers,' Clark says. Indeed, she herself was only seven when she wrote her first poem. 'I also wrote diaries. I can read them now and look back at what I was like at different ages. I still keep diaries. They are a great help to my novels.'

Her first novel, *Where are the Children?*, written when she was a widow and mother of five young children, marked a turning point in Clark's life, setting her on the path to the success she enjoys today. Now, with twenty-four hugely acclaimed thrillers to her name, she is in the throes of writing her memoirs. She insists that it won't be a tell-it-all book of revelations, however. 'I'm blameless,' she says. 'I'm a nice Catholic girl from the Bronx.' And of course she has the diaries to prove it.

ACKNOWLEDGMENTS AND PICTURE CREDITS: *Chasing the Dime*: Pages 6–8 Eye Wire; Digital Vision; Page 145: © Jerry Bauer: *Under an English Heaven*: Pages 146–148: plane: Quadrant Picture Library; couple and landscape: Hulton Archive/Getty Images; pilot: Taxi/Getty Images; Page 199: extract from 'The Way You Look Tonight': Words by Dorothy Fields. Music by Jerome Kern. © T B Harms Inc., USA. Warner/Chappell Music Ltd, London W6 2BS (British Reversionary Territories only) and Universal Music Publishing Ltd, London W6 8JA (non-British Reversionary Territories). Lyrics reproduced by permission of IMP Ltd. All Rights Reserved. *Cut Throat*: Pages 286–287: The Image Bank; illustration by Claire Rankin; Page 419: © A.P. Turner; *Daddy's Little Girl*: Pages 420–421: man: Gettyone Stone; photomontage: Rick Lecoat @ Shark Attack; Page 539: © Bernard Vidal.

DUSTJACKET CREDITS: Spine from top: Eye Wire; Digital Vision; Quadrant Picture Library; Hulton Archive/Getty Images; Taxi/Getty Images; The Image Bank; Gettyone Stone.

Printed by Maury Imprimeur SA, Malesherbes, France
Bound by Reliures Brun SA, Malesherbes, France